THE DARK YORKSHIRE SERIES BOOKS 4-6

DARK YORKSHIRE COLLECTION VOLUME 2

J M DALGLIESH

First published by Hamilton Press in 2019

EXCLUSIVE OFFER

Look out for the link at the end of this book or visit my website at **www.jmdalgliesh.com** to sign up to my no-spam VIP Club and receive a FREE Hidden Norfolk novella plus news and previews of forthcoming works.

Never miss a new release.

No spam, ever, guaranteed. You can unsubscribe at any time.

A DARK YORKSHIRE CRIME THRILLER

BLOOD MONEY

J M Dalgliesh

“We know nothing in reality; for truth lies in an abyss.”

Democritus

CHAPTER ONE

THE AMERICANO WAS DRINKABLE NOW. Sitting in the café, having watched the world go by for the past thirty minutes, had given the liquid a chance to cool. Putting the last piece of his meatball panini into his mouth, he wiped his fingers, then his lips, with a paper napkin, before scrunching it into a ball and tossing it onto the empty plate. The mad rush of custom at this time of the day was easing off.

The establishment was still full. There were several families corralling their children in the narrow passages between tables. Presumably they were off school this week. Others, out for a dose of retail therapy, compared their purchases and discussed their next port-of-call. The general noise level meant voices were often raised to be heard above the sound of the coffee grinder and steam wands. He didn't care. His mind was a picture of calm, weeding out the unnecessary and focussing on the task at hand.

The day was overcast, the lack of direct sunlight meant the room was darker than usual. The entrance door opened as three people came in. The first held the door for the others, allowing an unwelcome blast of cold air. Some glanced in the direction of the newcomers, conveying unspoken displeasure at the draught. The street beyond the full-height window he was sitting next to was remarkably busy for a week day.

The sound of a beating drum turned his head. A throng of people were approaching from the east .

They stood out as they navigated York's pedestrianised zone. Whistles blew and those seated around him also looked out. Men and women of all ages and colours marched past. Those at the head of the column were clutching a banner. The ones who followed, brandished placards or blew into whistles with fervour.

His phone on the table vibrated. Glancing down as the text message flashed up, he shot a brief look across the street beyond the demonstrators and towards the figure directly opposite him, standing in the recess of a shop entrance. They made eye contact and he nodded, almost imperceptibly. The movement was acknowledged and the man casually set off. The attention span of those within the café was limited. The notion came to him that these people cared little for the demonstration passing by outside. They had better things to be doing: shopping, eating and chatting. *If only they knew,* he thought to himself, standing. Their lives were so simple, so superficial… so boring.

Leaving the half-cup of coffee on the table, he slipped his phone into his pocket and picked his way through the people seated around him. Wrapping his scarf around his neck, he buttoned up his overcoat in preparation for the temperature drop as he went outside. Brushing against one woman, he uttered an apology but she didn't hear it nor did she flinch, too engrossed in her conversation.

Stepping out into the street, he thrust his hands into his coat pockets. The weather had taken a turn for the worse. The brief spell of clement weather, the incredibly delayed Indian summer, someone he'd overheard call it, was now a distant memory. More rain threatened. This reminded him of home, although it was still warmer. At least *that* was his recollection.

Two police officers strolled past, accompanying the stragglers waving their placards in the air, their breath sending clouds of vapour around them as they walked. No doubt, the higher concentration of resources would be found at the counter protest, that engineered by the nationalists across the city. He admired the provocative nature of launching an anti-immigrant rally in a city with few migrants along with a high concentration of students. It was sure to draw attention which, of course, was the intention.

Setting off in the opposite direction, he felt his phone vibrate again. Taking it out of his pocket he registered the text and increased his pace. The last time he had walked the route it took him twelve minutes but today he had some ground to make up so would be quicker. Central York had an abundance of cut-throughs and passages that could assist in traversing the city, if you knew where they led and how to find them. Another message came through. This one brought a smile to his face. They had stopped briefly, either distracted or their presence had been noted. No matter. Everything was well in hand.

Leaving the hub of the merchant's quarter behind, he had to step from the narrow pavement into oncoming traffic to navigate a gaggle of window shoppers. Eyeing a break, he sprinted across the road, raising a hand in thanks to the nearest driver.

Taking a right onto Fossgate, he headed further out of the centre. The crowds rapidly thinned, as popular shops were replaced with niche establishments once he crossed the river. Fossgate became Walmgate and business premises intermingled with small, modern residential blocks.

Upon reaching his destination, he stopped, eyeing the communal entrances to each block. No one was coming or going, so the opportunity to slip through was unavailable. Knowing the security doors were not fit for purpose for someone of his skill set, he acknowledged they were merely time consuming. Of an evening, it would certainly be workable to enter that way but in broad daylight, a little too brazen even for him.

Further along were the gated entrances, giving access to the gardens at the rear. He found them to be locked. They were of metal construction, six feet high, and cast with spikes at the top. Decorative but not effective against anything but an opportunist. A quick glance around to ensure he would pass unnoticed, and within seconds he had scaled the railings, hoisted himself over the top and dropped unobserved to the other side. Casually walking to the rear, he cut to his left and found himself in a grassed courtyard area overlooked only by the residential flats of the block. Nothing stirred. The uniform small, square windows of every flat had net curtains or dropped blinds. People here valued their privacy, even if it came at the cost of natural light. Moving with purpose, he walked to the fourth window along on the ground floor.

One last look around and he withdrew a metal strip, concealed within his coat. An inch wide, smooth and incredibly slim, he slipped it between window and frame, jockeying it into position. Once happy, he thrust it upwards and felt the reassuring sensation of the latch moving away. The window cracked open and he eased it out towards him. Putting his tool away, he brushed aside the curtain and clambered in, pulling the window closed behind him. The process had taken only the briefest of moments.

The room was as he had found previously, spartanly furnished and stale, desperately in need of some fresh air. Inspecting the dining table, he scanned a magazine that had been left open upon it, this month's *National Geographic*. Alongside that was a book on the fundamentals of economics.

A clock ticked on the wall in the narrow kitchen. A cat stretched out on the sofa, eyeing him suspiciously. He ignored it and walked towards the hallway.

Off to the left was the bathroom and another door to the one and only bedroom. To the right, three metres away, was the front door, accessed from the communal entrance. Glancing at his watch, he knew there wouldn't be long to wait.

As if on cue, a key was inserted into the lock, apparently in somewhat of a rush as the bearer struggled to get it into place. A vision of a flustered man came to mind as the latch disengaged and the door flew open. Taking a step back from view, he held his breath so as not to make his presence known, becoming one with the wall. He was a picture of measured calm, despite the adrenalin rush. The sound of someone entering and swiftly closing the door behind, dropping the latch and hastily attaching the security chain assured him that their quarry was aware of his presence.

Reaching into his coat, he withdrew the weapon, no more than six inches in length and easy to conceal. Depressing the power button, he allowed it a moment to activate. Stepping back into the hall, the resident was startled to find a man standing before him, gun raised. The red laser, levelled a dot directly to the centre of his midriff. He raised a hand in supplication.

"No, wait—"

The request was never completed. The barbed probes were deployed, punching through his heavy winter clothing and delivering their burst of energy. Both sensory and motor nervous systems were overwhelmed and the target dropped to his knees with a barely audible grunt, wide-eyed and straining every visible muscle. Covering the distance between them with speed, he pressed the Taser against the bare skin of the man's neck. Deploying the second charge incapacitated him yet further. The target slumped sideways to the floor, losing consciousness.

With a large stride, he stepped across the fallen man and over to the door. Activating the button to override the security lock to the communal entrance, he heard the outer door click open via the intercom. Next came the sound of the others moving through. Leaving the door to the flat ajar, he returned his focus to the man lying prostrate at his feet. Grasping him unceremoniously by the collar at the back of the neck, he dragged him down the hallway and into the living room.

The door to the flat was pushed open. A group passed, their footsteps echoing from the polished floor of the communal passageway. He closed the door to the flat behind them. It was time to get to work.

CHAPTER TWO

THE DOOR to the courtroom closed behind him and Caslin breathed a sigh of relief. Confident he'd conveyed his evidence in as an efficient and devastating manner as he could, he allowed himself the slightest of smiles, eyeing those standing a little way off along the corridor. For their part, they shot daggers in his direction. The three of them stood watching him as he made his way towards the washrooms. Caslin's throat was dry. Two hours on the stand had taken its toll but the end result would be worth it. Up next was their star witness. The clerk of the court called the name, as Caslin sidled past the three goons who, he was certain, would love nothing more than to wade in on him. Caslin chanced a wink in their direction. One bristled, only for another to place a calm, restraining hand on his forearm.

"Not here," he said softly.

"As you were, gentlemen," Caslin said, with a grin, turning his attention away from them. His feet suddenly felt that bit lighter. People stood in small groups, others sat alone waiting to be called in to give their evidence.

Courts were strange places, alien to most. The mix of fussy tradition, staid protocols and anxiety-inducing waiting periods all contributed to an air of suspense and trepidation. To Caslin, this week was a culmination of hard graft, months of stress and hopefully, a successful conclusion.

Pushing open the door into the gents, he held it for a young man leaving. He was barely eighteen years of age and ashen-faced, sporting a flattened hair-style and an ill-fitting off-the-peg suit. Either he had delivered his testimony or was about to. Caslin felt for him. Years in the job gave him trust in his instincts to spot a scumbag and that lad wasn't one.

No one else was present and Caslin took in his own appearance in the mirror. Despite the sunken eyes, having not slept particularly well, as was usual when due in court the following morning, he felt he looked in rude health. Having made a real effort in recent months with both his diet and exercise regime, his physical shape was improving. Running the warm tap, he cupped his hands underneath and gently placed his face into his palms, ensuring he didn't dampen his clothes. Daily, he wore a suit he wouldn't be too bothered if a drunk happened to spew on, but in court credibility was everything and appearance counted.

The entrance door flew open and Caslin jumped, instantly alert to the threat. DC Terry Holt burst in, a look of panic in his eyes.

"Sir. You better get back in there," Holt stated unequivocally. Caslin felt water running down his face and brushed it away with the back of his hand as it threatened to drip down onto his pristine, pressed shirt.

"What's up, Terry? What's going on?"

"Your man, Marquis. He's blown it!" Holt said.

"What do you mean, *blown it*?"

"Recanted his entire statement on the stand."

"What?"

"The confession, implicating the others... his entire bloody testimony... he's thrown us under the bus!"

Caslin pushed past Holt, who was too slow to get out of the way but resisted the urge to break into a run as he made his way back to Court Number Two. The men he had casually provoked, watched his approach only this time they bore the smug expressions. Caslin held his demeanour in check. They already knew. They knew in advance this was going to happen. Caslin felt sick as he took the stairs up to the viewing gallery, Holt only a step behind.

Easing the door open, they slipped back into the courtroom. The atmosphere was heavy. The assembled journalists, voyeurs and associated parties watched on intently as the judge intervened, asking direct questions of the witness.

"I wish the record of this court to be very clear. Are you indicating, Mr

Marquis, that there has been police collusion in your appearance here today?"

"I am, Your Honour, yes," was the reply. Caslin stared down at the woman standing in the dock. Her expression was one of profound confidence, in stark contrast to the cold, stern look she had aimed at him whilst he was on the stand. Whatever had been said already, she knew she was walking out of court this morning. Caslin felt a knot of anger tighten in his chest. Turning his focus to the witness stand, he took in Anthony Marquis. It had taken Caslin months to turn him from an integral administrator into a mine of information. Only when he was sure the Crown Prosecution Service would have enough to convict, had he acted. Now, the case was unravelling right before his eyes.

"And to clarify, you are accusing officers of encouraging you to fabricate incriminating documentation against the defendant. Along with willfully coercing your testimony here today?" Judge Barker-Riley said.

"One officer in particular, My Lord," Marquis said.

"That officer would be?" the judge asked. Caslin knew what was coming, he muttered under his breath.

"You little shit." The words were heard by those near to him, causing several to glance in his direction but didn't carry to the chamber below.

"Detective Inspector Caslin, My Lord," Marquis said. There was a muted intake of breath from many within the courtroom, sparking conversations between those seated in the gallery. The judge called for calm.

"This is a very serious allegation, Mr Marquis. Do you stand by it?" Marquis glanced towards the dock before looking the judge square in the eye.

"Absolutely. DI Caslin has manipulated me, threatened both myself and members of my family with arrest and incarceration, unless I helped him bring evidence against the accused. I admit, I should have been stronger and not gone along with it but… Mr Caslin is an imposing figure with a lot of power in this city. His reputation speaks for itself."

"My Lord," the prosecution QC stood, his intonation showing how rattled he was, "hearsay regarding a serving police officer's reputation, one whom I am obliged to convey has an impeccable record of service—"

"You are correct," the judge said, cutting him off with a raised hand. "However, despite this not being the first occasion where a defendant uses police coercion as a defence, it is not often that the primary witness alleges the same with equal passion. I find this illuminating and... startling, to say the least."

"I also... see the issues with progressing in this case, My Lord—"

"As do I," the defence barrister cut in. "I must state that to see a successful conclusion to this case in favour of the Crown, based on the testimony we've heard today, will be challenging."

"I am inclined to agree," the judge replied.

Caslin looked to the prosecution QC who was preparing to respond, more in vain hope rather than expectation.

"Perhaps, we might seek an adjournment in order to assess what we have heard..." he stammered. He was attempting to buy them breathing space to try and regroup. Caslin found himself repeating the words *come on, come on,* over and over in his head.

"I might suggest that this trial cannot continue without sufficient evidence against the defendant, My Lord," the defence barrister offered.

Judge Baker-Riley sat back, mulling over his next course of action. The courtroom fell entirely silent. All eyes were on the judge and many, including Caslin, held their breath.

"I am inclined to agree with the defence counsel," he said, following a period of silence that seemed to hang for an eternity. "Unless I can be met with an argument to countermand that conclusion." All eyes fell on the Queens Counsel, representing the Crown Prosecution Service. He looked crestfallen at best, mortified at worst. He could find no words in response. Caslin let out his breath. It was over.

"They can't throw it out, can they?" Holt asked, unable to take his eyes from proceedings.

"He's about to," Caslin muttered in reply, glancing across at Danika Durakovic's associates, seated at the other end of the gallery. Several were looking at him, a few with broad smiles, others with menace. "She's going to walk."

"No way," Holt said, meeting Caslin's eye. As if on cue, the judge's voice carried over them.

"I see no alternative but to dismiss the jury in this case. I will also confer my wish that this case is reviewed with an immediate and far-reaching investigation," he said, with authority. There were audible gasps within the courtroom. "How we managed to reach this point in a High-Court Trial without this situation coming to light, I will never understand. I shall be writing to the Chief Constable of North Yorkshire Constabulary and initiating an investigation into policing standards under her command."

"And it gets worse," Caslin said quietly, to himself.

"What's that, sir?" Holt said.

"A storm's coming, Terry," Caslin replied, as if that answered everything. "Come on. We've seen enough."

Holt turned to head out of the viewing gallery. Caslin glanced down to the dock, only to see the accused looking directly at him. It was unusual for him to see Danika Durakovic without her trademark, large sunglasses. Her complexion was as pale as usual, even in the height of summer, she maintained the same look. Only now, he could read her gaze. The half-smile set upon her face belied the malevolence that her eyes cast towards him. He was back in her sights and he knew it. They remained locked together for a further few moments as neither wanted to be first to break off.

"Sir?" Holt called to him. Regrettably, Caslin broke eye contact and turned towards Holt, holding the door open for him.

"Yes, Terry. What is it?"

"It's the DCI, sir."

"Is she on the phone, already?" he asked, making his way up the steps to the door.

"No, sir. She's waiting in the QC's chambers downstairs."

Caslin shook his head. This day had started positively but was now rapidly descending into his worst in recent memory, and he had many recollections to choose from.

Caslin allowed Holt to lead the way and upon reaching the end of the passageway, he recognised a court assistant standing by the access to the barristers' chambers. As they approached, he opened the door ushering them through. Entering the room, Caslin found it furnished similar to a gentleman's club lounge with leather Chesterfield seating. A polished-hardwood desk was positioned to his right and matching panelling lined the walls. He caught sight of DCI Angela Matheson across the room, standing with her back to him. She was looking out of one of several windows overlooking the court entrance but at what, he didn't know.

"Ma'am," he said in greeting, one that Terry Holt repeated as she turned to face them. From the expression on her face, she was seething.

"Care to explain, Inspector?" she said with no attempt to mask her aggression, not that she ever did.

"They got to him," Caslin said. "They got to him and we didn't see it. It's the only explanation."

"Well, not the only explanation – from what Marquis has just said on the stand," Matheson said.

"Oh, come on. You're not buying into his conspiracy bullshit, surely?"

"No. Of course I don't, Nathaniel," she replied, tempering the outburst that was brewing. "But I told you, when you first brought this to me a year ago that you had to be absolutely bang on if you were going up against her organisation. No one has been able to get near her operation until now and this experience will probably ensure no one else gets to her any time soon."

Caslin looked away. Danika Durakovic had managed to inherit her late husband's contacts, allowing her to sidestep prosecutions as easily as he had managed to. Caslin knew why.

Their organisation was in bed with the intelligence services. A fact he had found out at great personal cost, not that he could voice the knowledge. Bringing Danika down was a challenge, one he'd relished and thought he was about to fulfil.

"I'm not done yet," Caslin said with steel resolve. The door to the chamber flew open and the prosecuting counsel marched in. Without greeting, he hurled his folders onto the desk before him. They scattered, some of the contents falling to the floor but he didn't care, such was his fury. Pulling off his wig, that also joined the paperwork. He turned on Caslin.

"You assured me that he was sound, Inspector," he said accusingly.

"He is… was," Caslin replied, "we can have him on perjury charges."

"I don't doubt that, Inspector, but please, do advise me of when he was lying, then or now?"

"You're out of line!" Caslin said. "They got to him. We can go again."

"A retrial?" the QC said. Caslin nodded. "Our star witness has just testified that he fabricated all the paperwork that we are using to gain a conviction. Not only that, if we get him to recant what he has just said, how on earth is he going to be credible to a jury in any future trial? Explain that to me, would you?"

Caslin drew a deep breath, "We can't just drop it. Danika will never allow such weakness again. Her guard will be up. We'll not get an opportunity such as this—"

"It is over, Inspector. I know you want this one but please accept it, this case is done. You're going to have enough on your plate in the coming months as it is."

"What do you mean by that?" Caslin asked, knowing exactly what he was insinuating.

"People will want answers as to how we spent what we have over the last six months, only to have it burn down, before our very eyes?"

"Setbacks happen—"

"Setbacks!" the QC cut in. "You'll need more than that when you're called in, Nathaniel."

"My conscience is clear," Caslin said.

"As is mine but where the public purse is concerned someone has to shoulder the responsibility and I assure you, it will not be me."

"Charming," Caslin muttered, drawing a stifled laugh from Terry Holt.

"You won't be laughing when you're back in uniform, walking the city centre in the early hours of a Friday night, Terry," Matheson said, putting Holt back in his place. The latter nodded an apology and remained tight-lipped. "Really, Nathaniel, what with the Neo-Nazis being in town just itching for a fight with the counter protestors, we also have journalists from across Yorkshire camped within the city to cover it. They'll be all over this like a rash. You pick your moments, you really do."

"Me? How is all that my responsibility?" Caslin said.

The conversation was interrupted by Matheson's phone ringing. She stepped away from the others to the far side of the room to take the call. The conversation was largely one-sided, therefore Caslin assumed it wasn't a subordinate she was conversing with. Seldom did Matheson allow anyone else to dominate the conversation.

Caslin turned his thoughts to today's events. He could understand the reaction. Six months of diligent case preparation and resources had just been thrown to the wind. Beyond that, the level of personal and professional humiliation before the media and your peers would be galling. Caslin understood that. His humiliation was yet to come.

"Right. Nathaniel, you get a reprieve," Matheson said, hanging up on her caller and walking back over to where they waited.

"Ma'am?" Caslin asked.

"DS Hunter's at the scene of a suicide but I want you to get yourself over there and check it out."

"Why? What's going on?"

"She can fill you in on the details. It'll get you out of the way while I try and contain the fallout from all of this," she said, waving her hands in the air in a circular motion. "I'm already getting enquiries from the chief superintendent which has probably spread from further up the chain. The press will be all over this… and you."

Caslin put the flat of his hand against his chest in a mocking fashion, silently mouthing the word "Me?"

Matheson ignored the gesture, "I want you out of the way. That means no comments to the media or anyone else for that matter. You'd better be the grey man for the next few days until we can figure this out."

"So, you won't let me go and nick Marquis for lying his arse off then?"

"No, I bloody won't," Matheson said forcefully. "Stay away from him and stay away from Durakovic. Is that clear?"

Caslin nodded although he was none-too-pleased with the agreement. He excused himself. The CPS counsel didn't acknowledge his farewell and the cynic inside Caslin assumed he was already being prepped as the one for the slaughter.

Leaving the chamber, he took a deep breath and let it out loudly as he walked. People were milling about him as he went, and taking out his phone, he looked up Hunter's mobile number and went to press call. Paying no attention to what was in front of him, he became aware of a physical presence and stopped abruptly. Glancing up, he found himself face to face with Danika Durakovic. Lowering his phone to his side, Caslin forced a smile as convincing as he could make it.

"Danika," he said.

"Inspector Caslin." Her expression stoic.

"What can I do for you?" he asked, glancing behind her at the half-dozen bodies who appeared to accompany her everywhere.

"I wanted to offer you my commiserations."

"Oh, I doubt that very much."

"Sadly, I fear we won't be seeing much of each other in the coming days."

"Why are you so sure? This is just the first round."

"Come now, Inspector. I fully intend to launch litigation proceedings against you and your colleagues for harassment, perjury, pretty much anything my legal team can come up with and, trust me, I pay them enough to be creative."

"I look forward to it. Perhaps they'll be able to keep you up to speed on visiting days but I doubt it."

"I won't see any jail time, Inspector. Your case has fallen apart and your witness is no longer cooperating—"

"Yes, however did you manage that?" Caslin asked, through a forced grin.

"Good people allow their moral compass to guide them. He followed his."

"I wouldn't bet on him sticking to his story. I can vouch for that."

"He's of no further use to you, Inspector," Danika said as a matter of fact. "He is, how does the saying go… a busted flush?"

"I'll be seeing you, Danika. Never doubt it," Caslin said, fixing her with a stare as he stepped to the side and made to move past her.

"Don't leave it too long, Inspector Caslin," she called after him.

Caslin ignored the group of her associates having lost the stomach for responding to their arrogance. *Their arrogance.* He couldn't help but see his own hubris in this day's events. Cursing himself under his breath, he scanned for Hunter's telephone number once again and left the courthouse.

CHAPTER THREE

ONCE CASLIN HAD RETRIEVED his car from Fulford Road, he took the A64 out of the city for the journey north towards Hildenley.

Set within the conservation area that made up the sprawling beauty of the Howardian Hills, his destination was nestled between Castle Howard to the west and the nearby town of Malton, off to the east. Before reaching the latter, Caslin took the turn onto Braygate Street and slowed, keeping his eyes open for his target. He had spoken to Hunter and knew to keep a look out for recessed gates leading to a private driveway.

He needn't have worried. Parked up before the gated entrance was a liveried police car. Pulling up, he acknowledged the officer standing alongside the vehicle. Lowering his window, he brandished his warrant card for he wasn't familiar with the constable who took several moments to confirm Caslin's identity.

"If you head up the driveway to the house, sir, keep to the left as you approach. The CSI team are setting up and you might get boxed in. You'll find DS Hunter down at the boathouse on the south side of the lake," he said, indicating to his right with a gloved hand.

Caslin thanked the constable and resumed his journey up the gravelled drive. On both sides were a line of trees, planted in a uniform manner. Despite their current, barren appearance it was clear they were immaculately maintained. As were the grounds, set further back from the road. Manicured hedgerows, dedicated beds that were already primed to offer colour from the onset of spring. A glance at the temperature gauge on his dashboard, reading only two degrees, reminded him that spring was still some way off. The recent dive in temperatures following on from an unusually mild December was winter's latest grab for attention.

The driveway curved up on an incline around to the left and the building honed into view, through the trees. A mansion was an apt description, stone-built with an imposing style and grandeur that didn't fail to impress. Caslin knew it to be a building that was centuries old. He guessed it was of late-Tudor or early Jacobean construction. The façade was broad with two imposing bay windows either side of the huge entrance doors. One was easily three metres in height. The stone mullions in that bay alone would have been sufficient for a structural support in most forms of modern buildings. Caslin caught sight of Iain Robertson, the head of North Yorkshire's forensic investigators. He greeted Caslin with a wave as he parked up.

"I was under the impression this was a suicide?" Caslin said, referring to the number of vehicles nearby. Apparently, Robertson had most of his team present.

"Jumping to conclusions without assessing the scene?" Robertson chided him playfully.

"Fair comment," Caslin replied.

"Anyway, I thought you were in court all day today?"

Caslin shook his head, his expression spoke volumes, "Don't go there, I beg of you."

"That bad?"

"Worse," Caslin said, offering little. He caught sight of DS Hunter appearing at the crest of an exterior staircase on the east side of the mansion.

"Hello, sir," she called down to him. Caslin nodded to Robertson leaving him to assemble his equipment and hand out assignments to his team members. Heading in her direction, Caslin met Hunter at the halfway point between them.

"What do we have?" he asked.

"A deceased male, in his late fifties. We believe it's the owner, sir. He was found hanged, by members of his security this morning around half-past eight. They called the paramedics who then called us upon arrival."

"Suspicious?"

Hunter shrugged, "At first glance, am I ever not?"

"Good point."

"He went out for his usual morning run. When he failed to return, shortly after eight, they went looking for him. He was found in the boatshed. I'll lead you down," Hunter said. They turned and made their way back to the steps, Hunter had come from. A whistle came from behind, grabbing their attention. Caslin stopped and glanced back over his shoulder.

"Don't make a mess of my crime scene!" Robertson barked at him.

"Now who's jumping to conclusions," Caslin said with a half-smile, turning and trotting to catch up with Hunter. He scoped the number of security cameras mounted on the exterior, eyeing the grounds as well as himself. They descended the steps, framed on either side by crafted balustrades of stone, and onto a lawned area stretching some distance in front of them down to the lakeside. Circumventing the house, Caslin eyed more cameras. He was intrigued for it seemed over and above what he would expect.

"How come you're out of court so early?" Hunter asked him as they walked.

"Later, Sarah. Much... later," he replied, killing her inquiry dead. Hunter knew not to push it.

There was a breeze carrying across the lake drawing the cold of the water straight at them. Caslin shivered. Approaching the water's edge, Hunter guided them off to the right along a path leading to the boathouse. Clearly a later addition to the estate of the main house, it was a narrow, two-storey building, also of stone construction. Set back and nestling into the trees in what was a natural cove by the side of the lake, it blended well with the surroundings. There was a pitched slate-roof, covered in moss and a small balcony to the front accessed from the upper floor. A pier ran out into the water on one side, while on the other was a ramp to aid extracting boats from the water. A set of arched double doors opening straight onto the lake were currently closed.

Hunter took them to the rear of the building where they located the pedestrian entrance. They both donned boot covers and latex gloves in order to preserve the integrity of the scene. Until they determined otherwise, they'd consider it to be a crime scene. Stepping into the gloomy interior, Caslin immediately spotted the deceased. He was laid out flat off to the left. In front of them, tied up, was a small speedboat. There would easily be room for at least two more mid-size crafts but presently, that was the only one present. A brief inspection showed it to be covered and Caslin touched the casing of the outboard motor finding it cold.

Joining Hunter alongside the dead man, he briefly assessed the body. He was in his fifties with greying hair that would once have been of the darkest black. He was dressed in a red tracksuit and sported running shoes which, by the assembled detritus in the treads, indicated he had recently been moving through the grounds and most likely, the surrounding woodland. Nearby, Caslin noted a noose, fashioned from a thick rope the likes of which were commonly used by traditional fisherman. He'd seen similar attached to lobster pots in the coastal villages frequented during his childhood holidays. Casting his eyes around, Hunter noticed and appeared to read his thoughts.

"The emergency responders untied him from there," she said, pointing to one of the roof trusses above them spanning the width of the building. Caslin turned his focus to where the rope could have been secured once looped over the beam. He found several rusting, metal cleats attached to the outer wall. Any of them, he deemed, would've been sufficient for the cause. "He used the difference in height between the jetty and the water for the required drop."

"His staff didn't bring him down?" Caslin asked, surprised. Hunter shook her head.

"Apparently not, no."

"Was he alive when the paramedics got here?" Caslin asked.

"No, they were on scene eight minutes after the call."

"That was fast."

"They were attending an RTA not far from here but weren't required. They received the call on their way back to the ambulance station. When they brought him down there was no sign of a pulse but they attempted a resuscitation anyway. He remained unresponsive."

"Right," Caslin said aloud, processing what he was seeing before him. Turning his attention back to the body, he noted the man looked familiar. "I know him, don't I?"

"You'd have to have been living under a rock for the past few years not to, I reckon," Hunter said. "Nestor Kuz—"

"Kuznetsov," Caslin finished for her, "of course. Wasn't he in court for something last week?"

"Yeah, contesting a business arrangement. Suing one of his former partners as I understand it," Hunter confirmed.

"It wasn't going well, I recall," Caslin said, scanning the man's heavily-lined features. He knew of the Russian Oligarch's reputation, both as a ferocious businessman and a vocal critic of the regime back in his homeland. He was a controversial figure, popular in the columns of the print media but not one that Caslin often paid particular attention to. "I see why Matheson isn't taking any chances with this one."

"Sir?"

"Any suicide note?"

"Not that we've found so far. The door was apparently locked from the inside." Caslin stood and looked back towards the door. Scanning for other potential entry and exit points, he eyed several. There were windows set into the opposing walls. Each were single-glazed and opened onto land, running adjacent to the building. There were the double doors, used to take the boats out onto the lake and, turning his eye to the stairs in the far corner, there was also the access to the balcony he'd noted on their approach.

"I wouldn't put a lot of stock in that," Caslin said aloud, returning to the body. "Strange."

"What's that?" Hunter asked.

"In my experience, suicidal people aren't usually focussed on their personal fitness prior to killing themselves. Not beyond the realm of possibility I guess," he mused. "Also, his face is a little too purple under the circumstances. Do you know what I mean?"

Hunter nodded her agreement, "First responders said similar. They expected the face to be paler in a self-induced hanging. Much of the colour has already drained since they brought him down."

"Make sure Robertson is aware, would you?"

"I will."

"Terry Holt should be back at Fulford Road by now. Get him to do a work-up on this guy. We'll go through it later when we get back."

Caslin knelt down again, leaning over to enable a closer inspection of the deceased's neck, attempting to assess the markings left by the ligature. Without wishing to disturb the body further, Caslin viewed as best he could what looked like a V-shape, imprinted in the folds of skin where the rope had wrapped around the throat. Beneath the inch-wide groove were scratch marks, superficial and random. Hunter saw him checking them out.

"I'd imagine he was clawing at the rope as he was dying. An indication of foul play?" she asked.

"Or that he had a change of heart," Caslin countered. Hunter nodded briefly. Flicking his eyes around, Caslin looked for any indication of a struggle. Nothing was apparently disturbed. Although he conceded there was very little present in the boathouse that could have been. In one corner, a number of containers were visible, probably with fuel or oil for the boats.

Similarly, to the rear, were built-in shelving that housed spare parts, buoyancy aids and associated equipment. None of which appeared to have been moved in quite some time. Probably not since the previous summer judging by the levels of dust.

Returning to the deceased, Caslin checked the back of his hands looking for damage to his knuckles, abrasions, cuts, or even evidence of soil to indicate he had been knocked to the ground in an altercation or dragged to his place of death. He found nothing. Caslin was hopeful that the pathologist, Dr Alison Taylor, would be able to find something if they'd missed it.

Rising, he crossed to the windows. Noting the simple latch and no further security, he also found one that had a corner of the pane missing. A cursory examination of the floor saw no signs of broken glass. Studying the glass further, he assessed the damage to be historic and therefore unlikely to be linked. The frames of both windows were wooden and in dire need of maintenance. In one case the entire frame was movable, with the minimum of pressure from his bare hand, away from the main fabric of the boathouse such was its degradation. Opening the window closest to him, he carefully extended his arm. The window opened outwards in a vertical arc. Without someone else to hold it clear, a single adult would struggle to climb out without catching themselves on the rotten wood of the frame or the brass latch that secured it closed. It would not be an optimum exit route in order to flee the scene. Spying the beam, at least six inches thick, securing the arched access to the lake proper, Caslin knew that no one left via those doors.

Walking to the front of the building, he looked out across the lake through several gaps in the aging planks that made up the doors. The house and its associated estate were substantial with sprawling wilderness in every direction. There wasn't a boundary in sight. There was every possibility that someone could have accessed this location by boat, using the lake as an escape route and departed the scene under cover of the surrounding woodland. Someone would need to walk the perimeter of the lake to check for any sign of recent activity.

"Who did you say found him?" Caslin asked, glancing back to Hunter.

"A member of his security team."

That aroused Caslin's interest, "How strong is the detail?"

"Five," Hunter confirmed, "at least, those present today."

"And where are they now?"

"Back in the main house. I have them downstairs in the library. There are officers with them. So far, no one's saying much. They are Russian nationals, though. I'm giving them the benefit of the doubt in that, perhaps, their English isn't very good."

"Get a hold of Fulford Road and tell them to have an interpreter on standby just in case. Would it be harsh to imply they're not very proficient at their job?"

"Depends on whether or not you see this as suspicious?" Hunter said playfully.

"Like you, I see everything as suspicious," Caslin replied, coming alongside her, "it comes with the warrant card. Any family members?"

"He was divorced. His wife remained in Russia as far as I've managed to ascertain from the staff. The housekeeper appears to know the most or at least, she's more talkative than anyone else. She's visibly upset."

"His protection detail?"

"Not so as you'd notice but then again..." Hunter allowed the thought to tail off.

"What?" Caslin asked, making eye contact with genuine curiosity.

"I get the impression they aren't too keen on women. Not those in authority in any case. Unless, I'm just too sensitive?" she said with mock indignation.

"I got you. Next of kin?" Caslin asked.

"He only has one daughter. She studies at university, in London. Someone is on their way to speak with her as of now. Presumably, she'll head up but I'm not sure if she'll do so under her own steam."

Noise from outside carried to them signifying the arrival of Iain Robertson and his team of technicians. Caslin stepped out to greet him as they set about their individual assignments.

"Ruined all my trace evidence?" Robertson said, with a grin, his blue coveralls rustling as he moved.

"There wasn't much for me to damage, if I'm honest," Caslin replied.

"Is that so?" Robertson replied in his characteristic, strong Glaswegian failing to mask his sarcasm. Not that he was trying, mind you. "I'll be the judge of that, if you don't mind? Don't tell me, DI Caslin has actually come across a crime scene where he believes there wasn't a crime committed?"

"Perhaps," Caslin agreed. "Although, it's a little too clean, for me. If you follow me?"

"Aye, I know you well enough. Don't fret. If there's something to find, I'll find it."

Caslin knew it to be the case. Iain Robertson was the most thorough crime-scene analyst he had ever worked with and he'd worked with the best.

"Sarah," Caslin said to Hunter, "I'm going to have a word with the security team. You coming?"

She shook her head, "I reckon you'll do better without me, judging from the reception they gave me earlier. I'll recap what we discussed with Iain and you can fill me in later."

"Fair enough. Library, wasn't it?" he asked. Hunter nodded.

Leaving them to crack on, Caslin headed back to the house. It certainly wasn't unusual for wealthy people to have an entourage. In many cases, they were as much a symbol of status as a Bentley or a holiday home in the Caymans. That in itself meant little but why a businessman required a personal protection detail of that number gave rise to many questions. Least not, who was he afraid of and why would that be?

Ascending another beautifully carved staircase to the rear of the house, Caslin approached a uniformed officer. He pointed out the entrance to the building as well as to the library, just inside and to the right.

Pleased to be indoors, away from the bitter breeze sweeping across the lake, Caslin undid his coat and entered the library. It was an impressive sight. A double-height room with a gallery that wrapped around three walls above him in a U-shape.

Natural light poured in through a bay window, also double height, with a superb view of the lake and the woodland beyond stretching into the distance. The collection on display was equal to those preserved in the many stately homes, Caslin had visited over the years. There must have been thousands of tomes, many of which were leather-bound in traditional style and Caslin couldn't help but scan a few of the titles as he passed by.

Unsurprisingly, many of those he eyed were written in the owner's native Russian and so meant little to him. Although, he was pleasantly surprised to recognise the odd name.

At the centre of the library, Caslin found the men he sought, seated upon casual sofas, set out before a grand fireplace. The warmth radiating from the logs, burning in the grate, was welcome. One of the men stood off to the left, sipping at a mug which Caslin assumed contained tea or coffee, judging from the rising steam. He was immediately envious. The remaining four were spread over the seating, under the watchful eye of another uniformed constable. The latter acknowledged Caslin as he approached.

Caslin scanned the men, without saying a word. Clearly, they were all of a strong physique. Not necessarily heavy-set or full of muscle but evidently athletic in build. Those seated were all dressed in suits, quality materials, nothing off the rack. Caslin could tell the difference. The other wore suit trousers but with only a tight-fitting, white V-necked T-shirt above.

Caslin noted the jackets of the four men seated, appeared to be oversized or badly cut in stark contrast to the quality of the fabric and associated tailoring. He also knew that to be merely the response of the ill-informed. These men were professionals and their suits were tailored to factor in shoulder holsters for their personal weaponry. However, Caslin would put money on it that they wouldn't find a single firearm that wasn't currently licensed or under lock and key, as per their legal obligation.

Those four men paid Caslin little heed. They didn't flinch at his arrival nor did they appear remotely interested in addressing his requirements. The solitary figure, standing beside the fireplace, was a different case altogether. His eyes had not left Caslin from the moment he entered. For his part, Caslin had pretended not to notice, preferring to carry out his own examination. Now he turned his attention towards him. The man radiated gravitas. He was the leader of this group that was certain. Caslin took note of his heavily tattooed upper torso and forearms. A brief look at the others showed that they too, were adorned in a similar fashion. Their clothing however, masked any close inspection.

"You are the senior investigating officer here?" the standing man asked, in heavily-accented but otherwise perfect English.

"I am. Detective Inspector Caslin," he offered, "and you are?"

"Grigory Vitsin," he replied but offered nothing more.

"Which of you found Mr Kuznetsov?" Caslin asked.

"That was me," Vitsin stated.

Caslin nodded, "You have worked for Mr Kuznetsov for a long time?"

"Many years, yes."

"Can you think of any reason for Mr Kuznetsov to have taken his own life?" Caslin asked, scanning the faces of all those assembled as he spoke. No one appeared to be remotely considering the question, let alone listening to him, much to his irritation. Caslin chose to conceal the feeling for now.

"You must forgive them, Inspector Caslin. They speak very little of your language," Vitsin stated, almost apologetically.

"They might find it easier going about their day in this country, if they did."

Vitsin smiled, "Within Mr Kuznetsov's world there was little need. With our native language there are more than enough Russian speakers living here, within the UK."

"Can you tell me why your employer might take his own life?" Caslin asked again.

Vitsin shrugged, "He was a strong man. A proud man. Sometimes, men like this cannot live without both."

"Meaning?"

"I know little of these things but it is clear to see that his life was spiralling beyond his control," Vitsin shrugged. "A man can only fall so far." Caslin thought on that for a moment, pacing slowly around the room before coming to stand alongside Vitsin. He cast his eyes over the man's body art. The patterns across his chest weren't clear to see but Caslin could make out the image of a dagger, passing through the neck. The hilt was depicted on one side and the point appeared out of the other. In passing, he counted at least four drops of blood dripping from the tip of the blade onto what looked like a flaming star.

"Interesting work," Caslin said, inclining his head towards Vitsin's chest.

"You admire body art?" he asked.

"Not my thing, if I'm honest." Caslin casually cast an eye over the Russian's forearms. The right arm had what looked like a woman sitting with a fishing line seemingly caught on her dress. It struck him as an odd motif for such an evidently alpha-male to bear. "But I'm aware the detail is often symbolic of a deeper story. Is that fair?"

Vitsin inclined his own head, in response, "Sometimes."

Caslin returned to the subject of Kuznetsov, "Have you any knowledge of threats to Mr Kuznetsov? Anyone who would wish him harm?"

"Why do you ask? He killed himself."

"Did he?" Caslin asked. The four men seated appeared to understand that comment as a couple of them, almost imperceptibly, glanced furtively at each other.

"Of course, he did," Vitsin said flatly, unfazed by the question. "No one could have got to him without us seeing." Caslin turned to look out of the window towards the lake and the boathouse, although, the boathouse wasn't visible from here.

"He runs alone, your boss?" Caslin asked, locking eyes and trying to read the man standing before him. Caslin assessed this guy must be one hell of a poker player for he could determine nothing from his lack of a reaction. Vitsin merely went back to drinking his coffee. The smell of which carried to Caslin, only making him want it more.

"Every day," he confirmed. "Thirty minutes. The same route, around the estate."

Caslin did a quick bit of mental arithmetic, "That's probably around three miles?"

Vitsin shrugged, "Give or take?"

"That's quite a period of time to be out of your sight and away from your protection," Caslin said, casting a sideways glance towards the bay window.

"It was his choice."

"Did you object?" Caslin asked. Vitsin shrugged. "Humour me. Anyone you know that may have wished him harm?" Caslin repeated.

Vitsin shook his head, "Like I said. He was a tough man. In business. In life. Many people did not like him."

"So, he has enemies?"

"Quite probably, yes."

"And you? What is your role, here?"

The Russian didn't respond, breaking eye contact and moving to a single armchair and seating himself. "Grigory?"

"I have nothing more to say. You should get on with your job."

Caslin smiled, "Thank you for your time. I'm sure I will have further questions for you. I trust you'll make yourself available."

Vitsin nodded.

Caslin eyed the others one last time. Three of them refused to make any eye contact at all but the fourth met his gaze. His eyes were cold, unforgiving. Caslin had the impression all of these men were no strangers to the law either in this country or another. As for Vitsin, Caslin could take his rebuttal one of two ways. As head of security his pride was dented due to dereliction of duty or, the more interesting and darker possibility, he knew far more about Kuznetsov's death than he was prepared to share. Either way, Caslin intended to get more acquainted with him.

CHAPTER FOUR

TAKING the turn off of Fulford Road into the police station, Caslin couldn't fail to see the media scrum waiting on the steps up to the front doors. Picking his way through, he circumvented the outside-broadcast trucks arranged in a haphazard manner along the length of the road and on into the parking area. It was early afternoon and by now the opportunity to find space inside the secure yard to the rear, would no longer be possible. That degree of anonymity wouldn't be afforded to him. Finding one of the last available parking spaces, he reversed the car in and turned off the engine whilst considering his options. Getting through the waiting journalists was unappealing. Entering through the rear gates would be more agreeable and indeed preferable. He opted for that.

Getting out of the car, he locked it and headed for the eight-foot high security gates. He'd only covered half the distance before he caught sight of movement in his peripheral vision. Someone had seen him and he was high profile enough to be recognised. The death of Kuznetsov would already be trending, leading the news headlines and most likely the lead story on the next edition's front pages. His untimely death had lit the touch paper. Caslin increased his pace, pretending to be unaware of those moving towards him. Barely seconds later, the mass of assembled press also saw him, assuming the others knew something they didn't and the chase was on. Within moments, Caslin was where he hadn't wanted to be, besieged by journalists and nowhere near the solitude of the station.

"Inspector, are you investigating?" someone shouted, thrusting a microphone before him. Caslin pressed on as politely as he could. He had to keep moving.

"Was he murdered? Any suspects?"

"There will be a statement issued in due course," Caslin offered, the swarm seeming to increase with every step that he took.

"Does that mean it's suspicious?" another asked. Caslin ignored him as well as any further questions, his frustration beginning to mount. After what seemed like an age, he reached the relative sanctuary of the security entrance. Respectfully, the crowds parted allowing him to swipe his key card and pass through the outer door. Once inside, he found the custody suite to be a sea of calm in stark contrast to the barely organised chaos he'd left behind.

Acknowledging the custody sergeant as he passed by, Caslin made it to the stairs and headed for CID. The fact that he was now at the centre of the two biggest cases to break in recent months in York, failed to escape him. In reality, he was silently hopeful that Kuznetsov did indeed take his own life. Otherwise, the coming storm he'd predicted earlier was likely to be more intense than he'd initially envisaged. Entering the CID squad room, Caslin saw Holt deep in conversation with DC Kim Hardy. As he approached, both constables greeted him.

"Terry, tell me about Nestor Kuznetsov," Caslin said, continuing past and heading directly for his office. Holt fell into step behind him. Caslin took a seat behind his desk and Holt pulled up a chair. DS Hunter joined them having been momentarily behind Caslin on their return to the station. She closed the door and remained standing.

"Iain Robertson will give us a preliminary report on his findings by close of play," she said.

Caslin nodded his approval, "Terry?"

"Nestor Kuznetsov, sir," Holt began. "A Russian national. He's been resident in the UK since 2003. Owner of multiple businesses. He made his fortune in the post-Soviet era investing in former state-owned utilities and mining interests. He set up a television station and a mobile phone network. Both of which proved successful.

In recent years, his firms have fallen foul of multiple corruption scandals relating to the flouting of regulations, tax evasion and several investigations centering on accusations of embezzlement. Many of his assets, valued in excess of $17 billion dollars, have been frozen or seized over the past decade in Russia and other European countries with executives facing trial back home. Add to that the winding-up order brought by HMRC that is currently going through the courts at the same time, he owed a lot of money.

The estate where you've just come from, his apartment in the city centre and several properties in Kensington, were all about to be seized. He was in real trouble, financially speaking."

"That was my understanding too. Hence why he was attempting to claw back funds from one of his former business partners," Caslin said. "The case ended last week. I read about it in the *Financial Times*. Kuznetsov lost."

"That's right, sir," Holt agreed, looking at his notes. "He was trying to obtain £2.5 billion in damages. Money that he believes he was owed from another UK resident, Russian Oligarch. However, the judge said, in his summing up that he was an uninspiring witness and I quote, *a man who treats the truth as a transitory, flexible concept... that he is willing to mould in order to suit whatever story he desires to concoct*."

"Ouch," Hunter said. "That's pretty damning."

"Yeah. The British judicial system must come as something of a shock when you've been used to theirs back home," Caslin said.

"How so, sir?"

"I worked a few cases involving Russian mafia gangs during my time at the Yard. Territorial expansion sparked some tit-for-tat shootings. It was an eye-opening crash course in Russian Organised Crime to say the least. The Russian judicial system has over a ninety-eight percent conviction rate once a case comes to trial."

"Seriously?" Hunter asked.

"Absolutely. The rich and shameless may well get their own way and never reach a court but the problems arise when they come up against someone with a far greater reach. Then, they're screwed. Not that I'm passing comment on Mr Kuznetsov directly. I'm certain most of these Russian billionaires are good value for hard work and ethics," he said with sarcasm. "What brought him to the UK?" Caslin asked, indicating for Holt to continue his summation.

"Necessity," Holt stated. "Although, he officially moved here in the spring of 2003, when he was granted political asylum. He actually arrived in 2000. In the nineties, he was a wealthy businessman and philanthropist. He co-founded a political party, *New Democracy*. With this as a platform, backed by a media boost from his own television station, he was elected to the Russian Duma in '98."

"If he came to us in 2000, it couldn't have been a very successful stint for him," Caslin mused.

Holt shook his head, "Quite right. I'm not up to speed with all the details yet. That period of Russian politics didn't lend itself well to detail and scrutiny. It was a bit like the wild west, no rules, no boundaries. A smash and grab for whatever you could get and then hold. Fortunes were made and then some lost, in the years following the collapse of the Soviet Empire."

"Yes, except the Russian Empire remained largely intact with a lot of ruthless bastards set on exploiting the situation," Caslin added.

"I'd put Kuznetsov as one of those, sir," Holt stated. "He came from relative obscurity to be closely allied with established politicians and rubbing shoulders with the richest men in the country."

"So, he had powerful friends?"

"And powerful enemies," Holt continued. "We have three reports, filed by Kuznetsov, alleging that his life was under threat. The most recent being in October of last year."

"And where did he allege the threats originated?" Hunter asked.

"Each report had its own name attached to it. The latest one implied it was the Russian State apparatus who were targeting him."

"Nice and easy, then. We'll stop by the Kremlin for a chat," Caslin said with mock authority, drawing smiles from his colleagues. "Any credibility given to the allegations?"

Holt shook his head, "It doesn't appear so, sir. As with his recent court action, Kuznetsov appears to be light on detail, or indeed, evidence."

Caslin sat back in his chair, digesting Holt's analysis of the deceased. As always, he resisted the temptation to form an early judgement. Too often, he had been presented with overwhelming evidence at breakfast which was devastatingly rebuked by mid-afternoon. No matter what this looked like, there was still much work to do.

"What do you want us to do, sir?" Hunter asked. Caslin sat forward, resting his elbows onto his desk and forming a tent with his fingers.

"On the face of it we have a slam-dunk suicide. A wealthy, powerful man, set to lose everything ends it all to avoid the humiliation. Nice and neat. That may prove to be the case but let's humour my curiosity for a little while. At least until we get the Scenes of Crime report and Dr Taylor's had a chance to carry out an autopsy. Terry," he pointed a finger at him, "get a hold of everything that you can on these threats to his life. I want to know if there are any legs in them. I know they've already been looked at but the man is dead now and that changes our angle of focus. Who did he point the finger at, where were they and is there any substance to it that you can find? Judging by him being granted political asylum, I presume it's safe to say his list of enemies far outstrips that of his friends. So, get me a list of those as well. They might be able to shed some light on his life."

"Do you think they'll be willing to?" Hunter asked. "As you found with his staff, people in his circle tend not to hold a high tolerance for scrutiny."

"Not being forthcoming could be equally telling."

"What about me, sir?" Hunter said, as Holt scribbled down Caslin's instructions.

"Speaking of his employees. That security detail. I want you to find out everything you can on them. They may well have been his bodyguards but the leader has definitely done time. Those tattoos he's sporting are badges of honour for the Russian mafia. I've seen the type before with Eastern Bloc, ex-cons. Maybe none of them have been imprisoned here but I'll bet they've done real time back home. I want to know what for, their backgrounds, everything?"

"If it turns out not to be a suicide, you think they're involved?"

"I wouldn't rule it out. As much as the Russian mafia have their own codes of conduct, I doubt these guys wouldn't turn on their own mother if the price was right. Start with Grigory Vitsin. He seems like an odd choice for a paranoid billionaire, more used to the finer things in life."

"Sir?"

"If you could afford Spetnaz, why would you hire gangsters? They're a lower level of expertise. Tough, ruthless, certainly but far from predictable or, for that matter, stable. Unless of course—"

"They're more your kind of people?" Hunter finished for him.

"Exactly. Get to work."

Both detectives made to leave but Caslin indicated for Hunter to remain behind for a moment. Holt closed the door on his way out while Hunter took the seat that he'd vacated.

"What's up, sir?" she asked. Caslin met her eye before looking off to his left at nothing in particular.

"I just thought we could have a chat."

"Regarding?" she replied, flatly.

"What with the impending culmination of the case against Durakovic, I haven't had a chance to sit down with you. I figured I'd give it a few days and once things quietened down but, as it stands, I don't see it slowing down around here—"

"There's really no need," Hunter said.

"Sarah, please," Caslin said softly. He returned his gaze to her but she looked down. No matter what she said, he knew her confidence was at a low ebb. "I know you've really been through it, what with the time off and not taking the promotion. I'm trying to—"

"I know what you're trying to do, Nate," she looked up and met his eye. "But what do you want me to say? That I struggle to sleep at night. That Steve is sick to the back teeth of being married to a moody bitch? That I'm pissed off that I had to pass up the move to Thames Valley? Well, all of those," she snapped, "and then some!"

Caslin felt he'd picked his time wrong, not that there was a good one, "This might not be the easiest of cases to break you in on."

"It's hardly my first case, is it? I'll manage."

"Look, if you need some time to settle in, I can take the weight off of you."

"No, you can't," she said defiantly. "I'm your detective sergeant and I'll bloody well manage. The same as everyone else. Okay?" The last was said accusatorily. Caslin merely nodded. Hunter got up and made to leave.

"Sarah," he called after her. Having reached the doorway, she turned back to face him. "You're a damn fine police officer and when you're ready, you'll be a damn good, inspector." She smiled and departed. He felt some of the weight lift from his conscience. Whether she was ready to be back or not, he wasn't sure but Hunter had passed her evaluations and it was out of his hands. Not that he would ever voice the concern but he suspected something had changed within her. Only time would tell how that change might manifest itself. Besides, Caslin knew he was the last person in the world who could claim that traumatic experiences hindered your ability to do the job, at the required level. Were that definitive, he would've been out of work, years ago.

Even so, Caslin felt a degree of responsibility for her suffering. Her trauma was caused in part by decisions he'd taken in that case. Hunter could have been killed. The resulting trauma had seen her walk a long road back.

Opening up his laptop, Caslin fired it into life. Moments later, he brought up a search page and tapped away at the keys. Within a few minutes his request for information on Russian mafia tattoos proved fruitful. Such was the level of folklore surrounding the practice of decorating themselves, he found a wealth of resource with ease. Scrolling through photographs, the majority taken of prison inmates over the course of the previous fifty years or so, Caslin searched for those he had seen on Vitsin.

It didn't take long for him to come across a variation of the flaming star alongside a substantial array of religious iconography, crosses, angels and demons among them. The significance of the star was such that it denoted authority within the mafia. Vitsin was high up the food chain or had been at one time. The dagger through his neck advertised he'd committed murders in prison with each drop of blood signifying a kill. The tattoo was borne as a mark to indicate the killer was available to take on contracts.

Caslin passed over detailed shots of inmates identifying as homosexual or marking their criminal heritage as well as others sporting inked versions of pre-Soviet medals. The latter, highlighting their proud status as enemies of the state. Eventually, he came across the image depicted on Vitsin's forearm. It wasn't an exact match but undeniably similar. A woman catching her dress on a fishing line. The image related to rape and marked the man who bore it, in this case Vitsin, as a serial rapist. Sitting back in his chair, Caslin figured it wasn't too much of a stretch to imagine Kuznetsov's entire security apparatus was recruited from the ranks of the Russian mafia.

A knock at the door brought him back from the immersive darkness of Russian Organised Criminals. DC Kim Hardy was waiting patiently for him to notice her. He didn't know how long she'd been standing there. He beckoned her in.

"Sorry to interrupt, sir," she said.

"That's okay, Kim. What can I do for you?"

"DCI Matheson wants to see you."

"Tell her I'll see her in her office in about five minutes."

"She wants you upstairs with the chief superintendent."

Caslin exhaled heavily, blowing out his cheeks, "I guess I should've anticipated that."

"There's more. I've just seen ACC Sinclair heading up as well," Hardy said, almost apologetically. Caslin sank back further in his chair, raising his gaze to the ceiling.

"Okay. I definitely didn't see that coming. Thanks, Kim." She smiled weakly and with a bob of the head, turned and left. It didn't matter what explanation he could come up with, regarding that morning's debacle in court, Caslin knew he wasn't going to come out of it without something of a kicking. The presence of the assistant chief constable told him that in all likelihood, he'd be getting a real pasting. Reaching out, he closed down the lid of the computer. Taking a deep breath, he stood up and braced himself before heading upstairs.

CHAPTER FIVE

CASLIN MADE his way up to the next floor. The events surrounding the apparent collapse of the Durakovic trial turning over in his mind. Should he have seen the manipulation of their chief witness coming? Undoubtedly. Since the death of her husband, Danika had proven more than adept at running his affairs. Having seen off a challenge to her authority from the organisation's head of security, she now commanded a fearsome reputation of her own. Caslin cursed himself for failing to get this one over the line.

Approaching the office of Detective Chief Superintendent Mark Sutherland, Caslin paused, acknowledging the welcome of his secretary. She reached for the phone but Caslin indicated for her to hold off on notifying the occupants of his arrival. She appeared slightly perplexed but smiled warmly as he took a deep breath, composing himself. With a brief nod, he returned her smile and she made the call. Moments later, he opened the door and passed through. Sutherland rose from behind his desk and greeted him.

"Nathaniel," he said stiffly, "thank you for joining us."

"Not at all, sir," Caslin replied, taking a measure of those present. Angela Matheson nodded in his direction and even ACC Sinclair cracked the briefest of smiles in his direction.

Another man sat alongside the assistant chief constable but Caslin hadn't come across him before. He was in his late fifties, immaculately attired and, evidently, not interested in conversing. He barely looked up from the paperwork he held before him in his lap. The notion that the latter represented the Crown Prosecution Service came to mind.

"We need to have the conversation about this morning," Sutherland said.

"I have my thoughts, sir," Caslin began. "I would argue that it's a little early to form any conclusions. Once I've been—"

"Forgive me, for interrupting, Nathaniel," DCI Matheson cut in. "I think we're at cross purposes. We've called you in to speak about Nestor Kuznetsov."

"Oh… I see," Caslin said, glancing around. ACC Sinclair was paying him no attention, scanning through some documentation. The man he didn't know, now sat, watching him intently, casually chewing on the arm of his spectacles. Caslin found his curiosity piqued. He splayed his hands wide before him. "To what end, sir?" Sutherland stood from behind his desk and crossed to the window. From here, he could view the front entrance to the building, besieged with journalists who showed little sign of leaving.

"You see that lot, down there?" he asked, rhetorically. "They came to our city because they can smell blood. There's a curious situation arising in our society at present. The desire to suppress the voices of certain groups of people and then scream loudly at their lack of a platform. Thereby, creating a problem where there shouldn't be one."

"I'm sorry, sir," Caslin said, "but I don't follow."

"What your superintendent is saying, Inspector," ACC Sinclair said, looking up from whatever he was reading, "is that our illustrious university, in what I believe to be a well-meaning policy of not allowing a voice for extremists, has sparked something of a backlash. The media have fuelled it and come here in their droves. After all, this isn't Bradford or Oldham. Race relations here have always been somewhat harmonious."

"We're not known for our large immigrant population, sir," Caslin attested. "Largely because we don't have any."

"And so, for this little enterprise, they've been shipping them in," Sinclair added.

Caslin was definitely confused, "Immigrants?"

"No, Inspector. The extremists," Sinclair stated.

"The far-right campaigners," Matheson offered. "Martin James, who I'm sure you'll remember was due to be speaking at an event at the university this week has come anyway despite having his invitation withdrawn.

It would appear, he has brought as many of his membership as he could muster along with him. They've descended on the city, several hundred strong and we're led to understand that more are coming. James has tapped into the mood of the day, rebranding himself as something of a free-speech advocate. People are flocking to him as if he's some kind of saviour to our democratic freedoms.

Intelligence anticipates an increase in the arrival of counter protestors which will coincide over the course of the weekend, with them expected to number in their thousands. They've picked York as their battle ground and we're stretched."

"Nothing that we can't handle, sir," Caslin said confidently.

"I don't doubt that for a second, Nathaniel," Sutherland said. "We've cancelled all uniform rest days for the remainder of the week and South Yorkshire and Humberside have offered us support, should we require it. No, the problem is the number of journalists present. They've stoked what was a decision made by the ruling body of the Students' Union and turned it into a national conversation on free speech. As usual, they're looking to amplify the story."

"Sir?" Caslin inquired, still none the wiser as to why he was standing there. "What's this got to do with Kuznetsov?"

"Nestor Kuznetsov was a champion of free speech," Sutherland said.

"He was?" Caslin was genuinely trying to refrain from laughing. To his mind, Kuznetsov was better described as a victim of the game of thrones that Russian oligarchs appeared to revel in.

"At least, a self-proclaimed one," Sinclair chimed in. "I understand your thinly veiled scepticism, Inspector. He was vocal about the state apparatus attempting to silence him both before, when he was in politics and since he came over to us. His death segues nicely into the media consciousness of the day."

"Are you aware of something that I'm not?" Caslin asked.

Sutherland shook his head, "His suicide is far from welcome, particularly today."

"If indeed, it was a suicide, sir?" Caslin said.

"And that is what you are being tasked to find out, Inspector," Sinclair said.

"Do what you do, Nathaniel. Only do it fast," Sutherland added. Caslin attempted to read the expression of his chief superintendent. New to his current role, Caslin was yet to figure him out. His predecessor had been difficult, often self-serving and led to them having something of a strained relationship but Caslin knew where he stood most of the time. DCS Sutherland, on the other hand, was an entirely different character. One whom, Caslin hadn't warmed to as of yet. Although nothing was ever said, the feeling appeared mutual. The present affability therefore, was unsettling. "We don't want the speculation surrounding this case to gather pace. Once it's rolling, an avalanche is unstoppable. Do you understand?"

"It's very clear, sir," Caslin said.

"Thank you, Inspector. DCI Matheson will require daily briefings which she will then bring to me," Sutherland said before dismissing him. Caslin bid him farewell, doing the same to Sinclair and the other man who hadn't made a sound throughout the entire meeting and made no attempt to rectify that.

Leaving the office, Matheson fell into step alongside him. She didn't speak until they were through the fire doors and into the stairwell, heading down towards CID.

"Don't let the pleasantries fool you, Nate," she said, in a hushed tone, placing a restraining hand on his forearm. Caslin stopped on the stairs. Matheson glanced down, seeing they were alone. "They want this squared away, as soon as possible."

Caslin smiled but without genuine humour, "This isn't my first rodeo."

"Take it seriously, Nate. They'll be watching and this better not go the way—"

"The way of what?" Caslin said, with more edge to his tone than he'd intended.

Matheson took a deep breath, casting another eye around them to ensure they wouldn't be overheard, "On another day, they'd be tearing strips off of you for what happened this morning in court."

"Meaning?"

"Meaning?" she repeated, "Meaning something else has come over the horizon to eclipse your debacle in court this morning."

"Difference of opinion," Caslin countered.

"And the weight of opinion is determined by your rank," she replied, curtly. "Make no mistake, they'll happily hang it around your neck and let you hang yourself should the need arise."

"There's a thought," Caslin replied. "Makes you wonder why they didn't?"

"Unwittingly or not, you trade on your past successes, Nathaniel. At the end of the day, they won't protect you. Not without someone in your corner," she lowered her voice further, taking on a calmer tone. "It doesn't matter how good you are or what results you get."

"Who's in my corner? You?" Caslin asked.

Matheson locked eyes with him, "Yes. Until such time as I can't be."

Caslin flicked his eyebrows. At least, she was being honest. Any other answer would've been a lie, "What's with the hurry?"

"Like it or not," Matheson said, glancing over her shoulder to double check she wouldn't be overheard, "some cases come with a higher profile than we would like or than they might deserve. Just do your job efficiently and with minimal fuss."

"I won't compromise the investigation."

"I know that. Nor am I asking you to."

"Then what are you asking of me?"

"Just watch where you tread, Nathaniel. Ice can break, sometimes when you least expect it."

Footfalls on the polished stairs came to their ears and Caslin noted the approach of DS Hunter from below. They both fell silent as she made the final turn on the staircase, surprised to find her senior officers standing before her.

"Sorry, Ma'am," Hunter said, appearing awkward. "I didn't mean to interrupt."

"Don't worry, Sergeant. We're done here," she said, making to head back through the doors, towards her own office.

Caslin took a couple of steps back up to the landing, calling after her, "Who was that, in the super's office? You know, silent Stan, sitting on his own?"

Matheson stopped, holding the door open with one hand and looking over her shoulder at him, inclining her head slightly, "Watch your footing, Inspector."

He nodded, "I always do." With that, Matheson walked through, allowing the door to swing closed behind her. Caslin sucked air through his teeth, eyeing the departing figure of his DCI through the glass window of the door. Further down the corridor, he saw her meet up with the senior officers as they left Sutherland's office. Caslin took out his phone. Holding it up to the glass, he used his camera to zoom in and snap a shot of the group whilst they said their farewells in the narrow corridor.

"What was all that about?" Hunter asked.

"Not sure," he replied, not wishing to elaborate further and putting his phone away. Turning to face her, he asked, "What did you want me for?"

"Raisa Kuznetsova is downstairs, sir."

"The daughter?"

"Yes, sir. She's driven up from London."

"Has Iain Robertson removed her father's body, from the scene?"

Hunter nodded, "We just need the identification to take place and then Dr Taylor can begin the autopsy."

"You've spoken to Alison?"

"She called me, sir, to see if I knew when the next of kin would arrive. From what I can gather, she's been asked to fast-track it."

"That's becoming a recurring theme, today."

"Sir?" Hunter asked. He shook his head, indicating for them to head downstairs.

THIS WAS one of his least favourite aspects of the job. Caslin took a step back as Dr Taylor pulled the sheet back to reveal the face of Nestor Kuznetsov to his daughter, Raisa. In one movement, she expertly folded the sheet back beneath the chin, thereby masking the marks left by the ligature, on his throat.

Raisa gasped almost inaudibly. That was the first time where she had offered any reaction to the events of the day, having barely spoken a word since they met back at Fulford Road. Up to this point, Raisa Kuznetsova had maintained an impassive stance. This left Caslin to consider whether she was either in shock or managing her composure with a personal strength far in excess of most bereaved relatives, in his experience.

Raisa nodded almost imperceptibly, unable to take her eyes away from her father. At that moment, her eyes welled up and a solitary tear escaped to run the length of her cheek. Her face cracking, she stepped forward and reached out to touch her father's face only for Caslin to step forward and place a reassuring hand on hers.

"I am sorry, Miss," Caslin said softly, as she turned her anguished expression towards him. "I'm sorry."

She understood, or at least drew back her hand, accepting she wasn't able to make contact. Until certain there had been no foul play, they couldn't allow any potential contamination of the evidence. It was cold but necessary. Guiding her away from the mortuary table, Alison Taylor recovered the body while Caslin led Raisa back out of the room. No matter who had died, even when the deceased was someone Caslin figured society could do without, he always felt for the relatives. Everyone was someone's parent, child or loved one.

Hunter closed the door behind them once they reached the corridor. Caslin offered Raisa one of the chairs off to their left. She declined. Withdrawing a tissue from her handbag, she wiped away the tears gathered in her eyes and attempted to correct the run of mascara she figured had now smudged. Despite her best efforts, she failed. Caslin was impressed. He judged her to be in her early twenties but carried herself as he would expect someone of greater years. Nor did she dress as he expected, being clothed in high-quality garments more befitting of an executive rather than a student. She met his eye and Caslin had the notion that she was assessing him just as much as he was her.

"Who did this to my father?" she asked, in only slightly accented but otherwise perfect English. Caslin was momentarily taken aback.

"We are keeping an open mind," he replied, "but… we have to concede the possibility that he took his own life."

"No," she retorted. "Not my father."

"You seem certain," Hunter said.

"I am," she replied, glancing at Hunter. "If you knew my father, you would also understand that what you suggest is not possible."

"Were you close? With your father, I mean," Caslin asked. She inclined her head in his direction.

"Not particularly," she said. "He was… a difficult man. Driven, opinionated and decidedly arrogant. These characteristics made him a hard man to spend time with but I loved him, all the same."

"And yet, you're certain he wouldn't have taken his own life?" In most cases, he would give relatives space with which to find their feet following the death of a loved one. However, this time, Raisa seemed willing to talk.

"Not him."

"When did you speak with him, last?" Hunter asked, taking out her pocketbook.

She thought on it for a moment before answering, "Perhaps, three days ago."

"Was he concerned about anything?" Caslin asked, "Did he seem himself or depressed, anxious maybe?"

"No!" she snapped. "I told you. This is not a path he would ever have chosen."

"He had a recent court case. Were you aware of that?" Caslin asked.

Raisa nodded, "Yes, against that..." She left the thought unfinished. Locking eyes with Caslin, her expression changed to one of calm menace. He was startled but hid it well. "He was far from a perfect man, or father, and in business... well, he could play games as well as the next but he valued two things ahead of all else. His family and his country."

"Does he have any other family members?"

She shook her head, "Not here but back home in Russia, we have many."

"He must have missed them, judging by what you say," Hunter offered.

"I know what you are suggesting but you are wrong," Raisa countered. "My father has recently professed to a willingness for him to return home."

Caslin was surprised, "Was that even possible under the circumstances?"

"He has been conversing with the Kremlin through intermediaries for some months now. My father knew it would be difficult but spoke positively about it with me. As much as your country welcomed him, it is not Russia. It is not home."

"How advanced were these discussions?" Caslin asked.

"There are many who would rather he never returned or at least, only returned to be imprisoned," Raisa said with venom. "Perhaps, some of those got their wish."

"Can you give us any names, who you might con—" Hunter began but Raisa's attention was drawn away, looking over her shoulder as the doors at the end of the corridor opened. Two men came through. All present recognised them as they approached. Grigory Vitsin smiled as he came to stand before them, acknowledging Caslin. Both officers returned a polite greeting but Raisa merely fixed him with a gaze that Caslin found hard to read.

"Raisa," Vitsin began, speaking to her in their native tongue.

"You should speak English, Grigory," she instructed him. Vitsin's smile faded but his eyes didn't leave her.

"You should have called," he began again. "We would have met you and brought you here. There was no need for you to go through this alone."

"I wasn't alone," she countered, flatly, indicating Caslin.

"All the same," Vitsin said, "you should have called. We will escort you now. Make sure you are safe."

"Like you did my father?" she asked with a measured belligerence. Vitsin seemed unfazed by her tone. The smile returned. Caslin didn't like it.

"We would be happy to take you wherever you wish to go, Miss Kuznetsova," Caslin said, flicking his eyes towards Vitsin. She turned to him.

"There's no need, Inspector, but thank you for the offer," she said politely, glancing in his direction. Caslin took one of his contact cards, from his wallet.

"We have your details but, in the meantime, should you have the need, you can reach me on this number at any time," he said. She took the offered card. "If you ever want to talk." Taking the card and placing it in her pocket, she smiled in appreciation.

"Come, Grigory," she said, pointing towards a large suitcase resting against the wall. "My bag is over there." Before he could respond, she set off along the corridor. Caslin stifled a grin as Vitsin appeared to bristle. The latter turned to the other man he'd arrived with, gesturing towards the case. He scurried over and collected it. For his part, Vitsin was away, attempting to catch up with the departing Raisa without another word. They watched the three Russians leave in silence. Caslin exhaled a deep breath.

"Now that's a dysfunctional relationship if ever I saw one," Hunter said.

"Not a lot of love lost there," Caslin agreed. "I wonder why?"

"Let's find out," Hunter replied.

CHAPTER SIX

CASLIN ENTERED the pathology lab finding Dr Alison Taylor leant over her desk reading through some paperwork by artificial light.

"Things must be important to have you working over the weekend?" he said, playfully.

"Good morning, Nate. You're right. There does seem to be a little tension surrounding this one doesn't there?" she replied, standing and removing her glasses. Indicating to the body, lying on the mortuary slab, she crossed the short distance to it with Caslin coming alongside. "The cause of death was a combination of asphyxia and venous congestion. The deceased's body was more than adequate to apply the fifteen-kilo weight required to act as the constricting force. The ligature compressed the laryngeal and tracheal lumina which in turn pressed the root of the tongue against the posterior wall of the pharynx. Ultimately, this led to a blockage of the airway. The rapid rise in venous pressure within the head was caused by the tension exerted onto the jugular veins. Only two-kilos of weight would be sufficient."

Caslin leaned forward inspecting Kuznetsov's still form, "Well, I'll take your word for it, Alison. The marks around the neck are distinctive?" Caslin asked, indicating a wide, yellowish area a little over an inch wide.

"A few hours after death, the area of tissue affected by the ligature can assume the discolouration along with a texture of aging parchment," Dr

Taylor explained. "The depression in the skin is narrower than the ligature itself, encircling the entirety of the neck apart from where the knot was located. You'll note the thin line of congestion, the haemorrhage, above and below the groove at various points on the neck?"

Caslin observed where she was indicating, "That tells us what?"

"Whether there's a suggestion of post-mortem hanging or not."

He cast her a sideways glance, seeking clarification, "Is that a possibility here?"

"I'll get to that," she inclined her head. "First off, let me tell you what I can say with certainty."

"Go ahead," Caslin said.

"The paramedics brought him down when they arrived, removing the noose. Therefore, I've had to make some assumptions regarding how the knot was tied, the rope attached and so on. I have had a conversation with Iain, at the scene, to limit the number of those assumptions. Now, the course of the groove, defined by the noose, tells me the knot was tight to the skin of the neck on the left side of the head. The impression left by the rope is at its deepest and nearly horizontal, on the side of the neck opposite to the knot. As the ligature approaches the knot the mark turns upwards towards it. This produces an inverted 'V'. The apex of which corresponds with the site of the knot. The ecchymosis... the bleeding under the skin, coupled with the abrasions on the surrounding tissue, are suggestive of suspension taking place while he was alive. I've sent a sample of the underlying tissue to the lab for a microscopic analysis, in order to test for any reaction within the tissue," she explained.

"That will confirm it, either way?" Caslin said.

"Patience, Nathaniel."

He smiled, mouthing a silent apology. "I have an issue surrounding a lack of rope fibres present on the victim's hands. I would expect to find them in the case of a suicidal hanging, although never in a post-mortem hanging. You should press Ian Robertson for an analysis of the rope and its relationship to the beam."

"Relationship?"

"The beam will show evidence of whether the rope was moved up, as in when the body was elevated after death as opposed to the rope moving downwards from above, as the body drops. The latter is obviously what you'd expect to see in the event of a suicide."

"What about defensive wounds or signs of a struggle?"

"There are scratches around the neck, indicative of clawing at the ligature as one might expect to find. There's no indication these were injuries more conducive to having resulted from an assailant perpetrating the act, than from a suicidal person having a change of heart. I did, however, find significant levels of saliva at the angle of the mouth. This pairs well with death by hanging. The glands would have been stimulated by the ligature, leading to increased salivation. I've found no other significant injuries that might extend to defensive wounds."

"How about insignificant ones?" Caslin asked.

Dr Taylor smiled, "I found grazes on his right elbow and the corresponding shoulder blade. They were recent. Soil samples, taken from the outer layer of his running kit, imply he took a tumble at some point earlier in the day. Even with the frozen ground, if the area was shrouded by trees or vegetation it would still have been soft enough to mark."

"Apparently, he was out for his morning run around the estate."

"He may well have slipped. They are not severe injuries but worth investigation in my view."

"We'll walk the route and see if there's a tie in," Caslin said, thinking aloud. "Anything else?"

"Nothing to suggest foul play, no," she replied.

"So, where are you taking this if suicide is the likeliest outcome?" Caslin asked.

"I never said that," Dr Taylor smiled, crossing back over to her desk and returning with a file. Opening it, she moved to her wall-mounted light box. She pressed the power switch and Caslin came alongside as the neon-tubes flickered into life. Arranging three X-ray scans next to one another, Dr Taylor pointed to the first. "I take these routinely, looking for any obvious signs of violence. In a case of hanging, victims over the age of forty are prone to the fracturing of the larynx. Less so, if they're younger."

"So, if you're over forty, you're past it?" Caslin joked. "Terrific."

"Only in matters of being hanged, until dead," Dr Taylor replied, with a grin of her own. Caslin smiled. It had been some time since they had been able to share anything but a professional conversation. Internally, Caslin hoped she had forgiven him for his pathetic attempts at maintaining their now defunct relationship.

"Silver linings."

"The X-rays," she said, indicating them with her index finger. Caslin refocussed his attention. "I found no fractures, either to the larynx or any other part of the body to suggest a violent strangulation and let's face it, who willingly allows themselves to be asphyxiated?"

"Unless of course, they are unconscious," Caslin said.

"True," Dr Taylor agreed. "Although, a deadweight is far harder to suspend in an atypical hanging, where the body is fully elevated. Particularly, if disguising a homicide as a suicide." Caslin cast his eyes over the remaining two images. Both were X-rays of the upper body.

"Now, having led me all this way, you're going to tell me you found something that blows all of this ambiguity out of the water, aren't you?"

Dr Taylor laughed, "Take a look at the next two. This one," she pointed to the third image along, "is a close-up of the second." Caslin looked and although he could see they didn't appear correct, he couldn't say why. Dr Taylor interpreted his expression and elaborated. "Look at the vertebrae, at the top of the spine but the base of the neck."

To Caslin, the area looked like a mass of white and he couldn't make out any breaks or artificial objects present, "Help me out. What am I looking for?"

"Ankylosing Spondylitis," she confirmed. Caslin looked to her, raising an eyebrow in an unspoken query.

"I think I've heard of that," he said, narrowing his eyes. "It's something to do with inflammation of the joints, isn't it?"

Dr Taylor nodded, "Very good, Nathaniel. Yes. It causes the vertebrae and lumbosacral joint to ossify due to inflammation. As the disease progresses, it can lead to the vertebra fusing together. It's often painful, particularly as it develops and can affect seemingly unrelated areas of the body. The legs, hips, and in forty percent of cases, the anterior chamber of the eye. Mr Kuznetsov had quite an advanced condition, judging by the medication I found in his toxicity-screen along with what Iain Robertson confirmed was back at the house."

"His medication?" Caslin questioned, for clarity.

She nodded a confirmation, "The main symptom for us to consider in this scenario is the restriction of his movement."

"It was significant?" Caslin asked.

"Iain confirmed the knot used was a reef. For him to tighten that knot so close to the skin, at the rear of his neck, would be something of a challenge. Not least because he is right-handed and the knot was tightened—"

"On the left side," Caslin finished for her.

"Exactly. There is the possibility that the knot moved as the slack of the rope was taken up but I see no evidence to confirm that."

"Are you saying he couldn't have done it?"

Dr Taylor held up a hand, "I'm afraid I can't be so definitive, Nate. However, I'm confident enough to say that in my opinion, he would have found it very difficult and to envisage him doing so is problematic at best."

Caslin considered everything Dr Taylor had told him, churning the key points over in is head. Her findings caused concern.

"You throw up something of a dilemma for me, Alison," he said. "You're not doubting the cause of death but whether he was capable of actually carrying it out. Could his medication have given him enough respite from the pain in order for him to manage it?"

"Absence of pain doesn't negate the fusing of the vertebrae though," she said, shaking her head. "I'm not convinced he would be able to raise his hands across and behind him, to sufficiently tighten the knot. It isn't a case of pain. It's more a physical impossibility."

"Which brings us back to why someone would not fight to survive. Basic human instinct dictates you'd react, wouldn't you?"

Dr Taylor nodded emphatically, "One of the first symptoms would have been a loss of power and subjective sensations such as flashes of light and ringing or hissing in the ears. At that point the survival instinct would override everything else and a conscious person would react. If the pressure continues however, intense mental confusion soon follows and all power of logical thought disappears. By then, he would've been unable to help himself even if the notion occurred. There follows a loss of consciousness."

"Any sign of a sedative in the tox-screen?"

She shook her head, "I found nothing that leads me to believe he wasn't conscious during the asphyxiation."

"How long would it have taken?" Caslin asked, walking back over to the body and looking intently at the ligature markings as if hoping to see something they'd missed.

"Had we found a fracture in the cervical vertebrae death would have been instantaneous but even in this case, it still would have been rapid. Perhaps three to five minutes."

Caslin thought on it, "That's a long time for a conscious man to be subdued without a struggle, especially without leaving an indication of having done so. Could we be looking at a professional?"

"If it's a murder, then I would expect nothing less," she said, thinking aloud. "They barely left a sign they were ever there. In this scenario, I would add that circumstantial evidence becomes of paramount importance."

"Sadly, that doesn't bring a case to trial," Caslin said despondently, "and rarely a suspect to the interview room."

"Unfortunately, you're not going to be able to prosecute anyone off the back of my report. With that said, I would doubt very much if a coroner would rule anything but an open verdict, on this one. Of course, we must consider the possibility that he didn't fight because he chose not to."

Caslin glanced at her, "That this was an assisted suicide?"

Alison nodded, "If he couldn't do it himself but wanted to. It's possible. He wouldn't be the first."

"Thanks, Alison," Caslin said. "You've given me a headache that I don't see an easy cure for."

"You're welcome, Nate," she replied. "It's good to see you. It's been a while." Caslin smiled. She was right. He had been keeping his distance to avoid any chance of an awkward meeting. Alison, on the other hand, hadn't exhibited any similar concerns and now he felt foolish. That wasn't a sensation he either cared for or wanted to experience.

"I know," he began, "I guess… you know how it is, right?"

Alison smiled warmly, "Don't worry, Nate. Besides, sometimes things happen for the best. There's no need for you to avoid me."

He nodded in a relaxed manner as if he was surprised she felt the need to bring it up. He wasn't convincing. Having mumbled a brief request about her sending him a copy of her finalised report, Caslin left pathology and headed out to his car.

There was something about Alison's demeanour that struck him as odd. Not out of character as such but not in keeping with how she usually came across with him. Resolving to give it more thought later, should the opportunity arise, he pushed it from his mind. Reaching the steps to the building, Caslin trotted down them and into the car park. The wind had dropped, ensuring the morning was far warmer than it had been in recent weeks.

Turning his thoughts to the demonstration of the previous day, he realised it was merely a warm-up to the main event of the coming weekend. The next march was scheduled for that very afternoon, with the anti-fascists lining up at midday in the shadow of York Minster. The emotionally charged warriors representing either side had to wait until they'd finished the working week before they could make their feelings known.

The plans of the far-right, those expected to cause any potential unrest were not yet known. Since arriving in the city, they had broken up into smaller groups, presumably to confuse the police and make tracking them more difficult. So far, they were being proved right. Taking out his phone, he called Hunter. She picked up within three rings.

"Sarah, where are we with Kuznetsov's security?"

"Not very far, sir," Hunter replied. "I've been onto the Russian Ministry of Internal Affairs but they've not been forthcoming. I was passed around several departments before I got through to anyone even remotely interested."

"And what did they give us?"

"Still waiting on a call back, sir."

Caslin sighed, "I suppose that was to be expected. All right, get onto Europol and see if any of the names are tagged."

"Way ahead of you, sir," she said triumphantly. "We got a hit on three of them. Two are low-level *Brodyag* or—"

"Foot soldiers," Caslin interrupted, "each with a speciality that they bring to the team."

"You've come across these types before then?"

"Yes. Go on."

"Those two have records detailing their arrest in an alleged protection racket in the south of France. Although no charges were brought against them. They were subsequently deported, three years ago."

"And the other?" Caslin asked.

"Your friend, Vitsin."

"Tell me about him."

"He's also popped up on the radar of the Gendarmerie. He was an *Avtotitet*, a captain or brigade commander, aligned with the *Mikhailov Bratva*, based in Rostov-on-Don, Southern Russia. Intelligence had him at a more senior level running a *Sovietnik* or support group. There was some kind of investigation surrounding bribery of state officials and he went to ground."

"I would've thought that was par for the course when it comes to Russia," Caslin said, reaching his car and unlocking it.

"Most likely the bribe was not enough or there was some kind of internal power struggle with Vitsin coming off worse. Either way, he reappears six months later in Montpellier, France. The French came across him and he was visible enough for them to document his comings and goings for a while at least, before he again, disappears from view."

"Until now," Caslin said, putting his key in the ignition and firing the engine into life. "Keep digging, Sarah. I'm on my way back to Fulford Road. I reckon this isn't going to be as cut and dried as some people might have hoped."

"I will, sir, but before you go there are a couple of things."

"Okay, go on," Caslin said, sitting back in his seat and leaving the car ticking over in neutral.

"Firstly, we're a bit thin on the ground today. The DCI has had to allocate a lot of the team to today's protests. Management are worried it's all going to kick off."

"Might do," Caslin said. "What's the second thing?" Hunter didn't speak. Caslin checked his phone to make sure the call was still connected. It was. "Sarah?" he asked again, hearing her breathing at the other end of the line.

"There's no easy way to tell you this, sir."

Caslin eyes were drawn to a young family passing by. Focussing his attention squarely on the call, he asked, "What is it, Sarah?"

"It's Sean, sir. Your son."

"What about him?"

"He's in detention. Here, at Fulford Road."

"Don't be daft."

"Sorry, sir. He was picked up in a raid last night, carried out by the Drug Squad."

"Last night?"

"Yeah. Apparently, he didn't have any ID on him and lied about his name, age, everything. Understandable I guess, seeing as who his father is. They've only just found out downstairs."

Caslin's head dropped and he rubbed fiercely at his forehead with his one free hand. "Oh, for fu—"

"I'm sorry, sir. Should I let Karen know?" Hunter asked carefully, referring to Caslin's ex-wife. Caslin took a deep breath and took a moment in an attempt to gather his thoughts, exhaling heavily before answering.

"No, don't do that. I'm heading back now. I'll take care of it," he said, hanging up. A momentary pulse of irritation passed over him. Karen hadn't let him know that Sean had failed to come home. Although, the boy was fifteen and as such had some leeway regarding what he did with his time. Maybe he had permission. Even so, he was still only fifteen. Pressing the mobile to his lips, he thought on what he should do, but all that dominated his mind was a growing sense of frustration. With a resigned shake of the head, he tossed his phone onto the passenger seat. Fastening his seatbelt, he engaged the car in gear and set off out of the car park, pulling onto the ring road and heading for Fulford.

CHAPTER SEVEN

TAKING the turn into the car park of the police station, Caslin was relieved to see the assembled journalists had decamped for the day. Most likely they were in the town centre covering the protest marches; to witness the anticipated confrontation. Getting out and locking the car, he made his way to the rear entrance and the custody suite. Even as he entered his pass code into the security pad, he was still unsure of how he would respond to his son's arrest. The initial anger had subsided. Neither of the children had given him much of a headache over the years. Certainly, Sean had felt the brunt of the negativity since the break-up of the family. Shifting schools, looking out for his mother and being a stable influence on his younger sister had taken their toll. Then there was last year. Caslin felt immensely guilty for that, regardless of whether he could've prevented it or not didn't matter.

The door buzzed as he opened it and walked through into the reception area. The custody sergeant glanced up from behind his desk.

"Hello, sir," he said, trying to be casual. Caslin approached. Two constables were nearby and both acknowledged him but quickly made themselves scarce. Perhaps they were on the move anyway but to him it felt like they were getting out of his way. No doubt, the news would be across the station by now.

"Hello, Mike," Caslin said as he greeted Mike Edwards, the custody sergeant, an ascetic-looking man with a narrow, well-lined face. "Where do you have him?"

The sergeant indicated towards the interview rooms, "He's in number five. Once he told us who he was and his age we got him out of the cell."

Caslin raised a hand, in supplication, "Don't worry. I know how it is. What's the story?" he asked, with an air of resignation.

"He was present at an address on the south side of the city, when it was raided last night. It was a planned op, shaking down a number of low-level dealers."

"Yeah. I know they've been getting a bit cocky of late," Caslin said. He glanced around. No one was within earshot. "What did they find him with?"

"A bag of weed. Nothing too serious."

"Thank God for that," Caslin said, relieved.

"Well, that's the good news."

"What's the bad?"

"He was also carrying a little over four-hundred in cash." Caslin was open-mouthed.

"Where the hell did he get that kind of money from?" he said, before formulating his own answer. Edwards met his eye. Clearly, the sergeant was thinking the same thing. Caslin felt fatigued all of a sudden. He shook his head in disbelief. "What was it, five?" he asked, pointing towards the double doors. Edwards nodded and Caslin set off to find his son.

Coming before Interview Room Five, Caslin paused, closing his eyes. He took a deep breath and let it out slowly. The doors adjoining the custody suite opened and an officer came through. She hesitated upon seeing him, slowing her walk ever so slightly. Caslin glanced to his right.

"Sir," she said, rigidly, nodding in his direction as she passed by. Caslin returned the greeting with a bob of the head but he didn't speak. Muttering quietly under his breath, he knocked on the door and entered without waiting for a response.

Sean was sitting on a chair, opposite him and behind a table. His head was down, face resting in the palms of his hands. Upon hearing someone enter, he glanced up. Seeing his father standing before him all colour appeared to drain from his face. Not wanting to meet his eye, Sean returned his gaze to the table before him.

Caslin didn't speak, merely chewing on his lower lip as he turned his attention to the constable standing off to the left. With a flick of the head, Caslin indicated for the officer to leave and he did so. The two of them were alone. Caslin closed the door behind the departing chaperone. The latch clicked and he remained with a steadfast hold on the handle, not wanting to turn to face his son. Another flash of anger bubbled beneath the surface and the urge to tear strips off Sean was tempting.

"Dad, I'm sorry," Sean said, before Caslin had a chance to speak.

"What are you sorry for exactly?" Caslin asked in a far more accusatory manner than he'd intended, turning around and leaning his back against the door. Sean visibly appeared to crumble. His head dropped and within moments, he was shaking as tears came unbidden to his eyes. Caslin felt his anger subside almost immediately. The guilt returning with a vengeance. He gritted his teeth. Somehow, they'd reached this point. He didn't know how but Caslin felt like he was to blame. Less than twelve months ago, he had almost lost his son at the hands of a professional mercenary. A teenager, swept up in something totally beyond his control or understanding. That day, Caslin saw the face of evil, up close and personal and nearly lost something precious to him.

Crossing the room, he perched himself on the edge of the table, placing a reassuring hand on his son's shoulder. Sean lifted his head. His eyes were brimming with tears, red and swollen.

"I'm so... sorry, Dad. I never meant to..." Sean stammered. Caslin pulled him in close and hugged him with both arms, as tight as he dared, looking to the ceiling as he did so.

"We'll sort it out, son," he said. "We'll sort it, don't worry. Wait here. I'll be back."

Caslin disengaged from his son, stood up and made his way out of the room. In the corridor outside, he found the constable waiting for him. They exchanged places in the room and Caslin headed back to the custody suite. When he arrived, he found two officers booking in a man who had failed to appear at court the previous day and had been picked up as a result.

"I'd have thought you'd have to leave that sort of thing, today?" Caslin said as the man was frog-marched down to the detention cells. Sergeant Edwards grinned.

"The magistrates wait for no man," he said. "But you're right. We'll have to put him up over the weekend and drag him back to court first thing Monday."

"Fair enough," Caslin replied. "So, what am I looking at with Sean?"

Edwards glanced around, lowering his voice. "The arresting officer is probably looking at a caution for possession. The quantity he was holding was minimal. Personal use only. After all, the dealer was the target. But," he paused, selecting his words carefully, "there is a sticking point. This guy deals more in heroin and spice than anything else. He's a proper low-life and Sean was carrying a lot of cash. If our team had gone through the door ten minutes later..."

"I know what it looks like," Caslin said. Edwards relaxed a little. He didn't want to spell it out and with Caslin, he didn't need to. "Where do we go from here?"

"Sean's currently the little fish in a big pond. For now, he's free to go but he'll need to be interviewed with an appropriate adult present in a day or so. Whether that's you or not, I'd advise—"

"Yeah, don't worry. I'm sure his mum will come in," Caslin said, already dreading the conversation he was going to have with Karen. He thanked the sergeant and returned to fetch Sean. Minutes later, they were back in custody collecting Sean's possessions. Just as they were signing off the paperwork, DCI Matheson appeared. She caught Caslin's reluctant eye, beckoning him over. He directed Sean to take a seat on a bench to wait for him and crossed the short distance to where she stood.

"Ma'am," he said, meeting her stern expression with one of her own.

"Nathaniel. I suspect I don't need to tell you how bad this looks?"

"Not really," he replied, casting an eye back to his son.

"There won't be any special favours regarding this," she said flatly. Caslin was annoyed by that.

"I wouldn't expect any."

"Good. I trust this won't become a distraction?"

"Not at all, Ma'am," Caslin said. "I'll run him home, speak to his mother and be right back. Provided, that is, that's all right with you?"

Matheson turned to face him, "This is not a good look for you and reflects on the team."

"I don't see that," he countered. "He's a kid. They have lapses in judgement, do stupid things. It happens all the time. It has sod all to do with the team or my ability to do my job."

"We can agree on one thing. He is a child," she said, fixing her attention on the waiting teenager, looking very much the lost little-boy. "And I'm a firm believer that the behaviour of the child reflects their parenting. I suggest you sort your family out, Inspector. I think you've taken enough hits to your reputation already this week."

Caslin made no further comment as Matheson made to leave. He indicated in the direction of the exit and beckoned for Sean to join him.

"Who was that?" Sean asked, approaching.

"My boss," Caslin replied.

"She didn't look very happy with you."

"Very astute, Sean," Caslin said, pressing the door release to the outer chamber, unlocking it. They stepped out into the caged air lock which in turn, gave them access to the car park.

"Is that my fault?" Sean asked, as they walked. Caslin put an arm around his shoulder.

"No. She always looks like that," Caslin said, faking a warm smile. It didn't fool anyone. They were barely ten yards from the building before a shout came, from behind.

"Sir!"

Caslin turned to see Terry Holt coming across from the direction of the main entrance. He was red-faced and out of breath, by the time he came before them.

"What's up, Terry?" Caslin asked. Holt glanced at Sean, not wishing to speak. Caslin passed his son the car keys and pointed to where he was parked. Sean said nothing but walked over, unlocked the car and got into the passenger seat.

"Uniform were asked to carry out a welfare check on a guy in town. They think it's something we should definitely take a look at." Caslin glanced towards the car. Sean was already busy, tapping away on his mobile phone. "I could check it out with Hunter if… well, you're busy or something?"

"No, it's all right, Terry. Give me the address," he said, turning back to face Holt. "You head over and I'll meet you there in a bit. I'll have to drop him off first," he said, indicating Sean, "but I won't be long."

"Right, sir," Holt said. "I'll text you the address."

Caslin walked over to the car and got in. Sean passed him the key fob and he inserted it into the slot before pressing the start button. Firing the engine into life, Caslin fastened his seatbelt. Sean did the same. The windscreen of the car was misting over even in the short time, Sean had been waiting. Caslin pressed the button to initiate the heated windscreen and set the blowers to maximum. The two sat without conversation, accompanied by the noise of the fans until Caslin judged his visibility was good enough. They left the car park and Caslin turned out onto Fulford Road and accelerated, leaving the city behind them. Karen's house was only a fifteen-minute drive away, into the suburbs. They drove in silence for a while but as their destination neared, Sean became more agitated.

"What did she say?" he asked, staring out of the window at the passing trees.

"Who? Your mum?" Sean nodded. Caslin noticed in the corner of his eye. "I've not spoken to her, yet."

"Right," Sean replied, turning to him. "What *are* you going to say?"

Caslin shook his head, "I've no idea. I'm a bit pis..." he stopped himself, "a bit annoyed with her to be honest. She didn't call to say you hadn't come home. I'd have expected her to."

"She was out," Sean said, "and I can take care of myself."

"Maybe you can but what of your sister?"

"Lizzie spent the night at a friend's," Sean offered, returning his attention to the passing landscape.

"And your mum went out?" Caslin asked. Sean nodded.

"It's a regular thing."

They arrived at the house soon after. Karen's car wasn't in the driveway. Checking the time on the dashboard clock, it was lunchtime. He wondered whether she had come home and gone out again or hadn't come home at all. Quite frankly, it was none of his business.

"What time does your mum usually get home? If she's out, I mean?"

Sean shrugged, "It depends on what time she has to pick Lizzie up, I guess."

"Well, she's with me almost every other weekend. Does she go out a lot?" Caslin replied, drawing another shrug of the shoulders. Caslin thought about it. He should have called her from the station but it was too late now. "All right, look, you need to take a shower and get your head down, for a bit. I'll call your mum later."

"All right," Sean said, pulling on the door handle. Caslin reached across and stopped him from getting out. Sean met his eye.

"We still have a lot to talk about," he said sternly. "Not least what you were doing there."

Sean sighed, "Dad, I was scoring some weed."

"And where did you get four-hundred quid from?" Sean slumped back in his seat but offered nothing in explanation. "You'll need to say something, Son. It's not going away. You were carrying money to buy enough that'd qualify you as a dealer. If you'd already made the buy..."

"Dad..."

"Don't palm it off." Caslin turned his attention to a far-off point somewhere in the distance. He adopted a more conciliatory tone, "I know how it works. Everyone knows someone and whoever's in stock determines who makes the purchase. You were scoring for your mates as well, weren't you?" Sean remained silent, staring straight ahead. "You've put me in one hell of a position, you know that?"

"Yeah, that's right, Dad. It's all about *you*. It's *always about you*!"

Sean got out of the car at speed, slamming the door shut before Caslin had a chance to respond. He stalked off up the driveway. Caslin watched as he dug out his house keys from his pocket and unlocked the front door, stepping inside. The door closed without him casting even a cursory glance in his direction. Not that Caslin expected him to.

That feeling of guilt returned. Sean spent months in counselling the previous year. Sleeping pills helped to subvert the night terrors but there was always the sense that they were only battling the symptoms and never getting to grips with the cause. Caslin had hoped they were making headway. Sean's need for the medication had dipped and his school reports were improving. He sighed. Maybe this was little more than the usual teenage response to life. Another stage in the transition from adolescence to adult-life that needed to be experienced. With a heavy heart, he pushed it from his mind, resolving to give Karen a call before she would return home, not that he knew when that would be. In the meantime, he looked up the address, Terry Holt had sent through. Slipping the car into reverse, he turned around and set off back into the city.

Leaving Heslington behind, the build-up of traffic was steadily increasing on the approaches to the centre. Caslin skirted the university campus, bringing him into York from the south-east. Even this route started to slow as he reached the Old St. Lawrence Church, just short of the ring road. Here the cars were inching forward at a frustrating pace and it took a further ten minutes before Caslin was able to take the turn onto Walmgate and pass through the ancient, fortress walls of the city.

The police cordon was easy to spot and an officer directed him to park up on the pavement, such was the limited space available. Traffic was still moving out of the city, this being one of the main thoroughfares but passage was cut to one lane due to the police presence and tempers were fraying on a Saturday afternoon.

The communal entrance was taped off and a uniformed constable stood guard with others marshalling the bystanders. One officer lifted the cordon to allow him to duck beneath it. A number of locals were gathering behind the tape, peering through the open door and trying to make out what was going on beyond. Their curiosity was similar to those passing an accident on the motorway, a ghoulish voyeurism. Caslin was met by DC Holt at the open door to a ground-floor flat.

"Hello, sir," Holt said with a pale, grim expression. That piqued Caslin's curiosity because it took a lot to unsettle the experienced detective constable.

"What do we have, Terry?"

"Uniform understated it, sir," he offered. "I've never seen anything like it… it's… bloody awful in there."

CHAPTER EIGHT

HOLT STEPPED ASIDE ALLOWING Caslin to take the lead. When he entered the smell hit him first. The best he could figure it to be was a mixture of cigarette smoke, sweat and faeces. The air was stale and the atmosphere oppressive. The hall was nondescript with four doors leading off it. Glancing over his shoulder, Holt indicated for him to walk to the end. The first door, set to his right, was closed.

"Bedroom," Holt told him. The next two doors were almost opposite each other, staggered on either side. This time, he needed no guidance. The door to the left was open and Caslin could tell that this was the focal point of what was undoubtedly a crime scene.

Caslin held his breath as he stepped into the room, exercising great caution not to disturb any evidence as he went. Little more than four feet away, a man was kneeling on the floor with his back to Caslin. The curtains were drawn restricting natural light to a bare minimum that crept through the narrow crack between them. Further light came via the arched access to the kitchen but even this was subtle and did little to illuminate the room. Artificial light was provided by two lamps, one wall hung to Caslin's right and a further reading lamp, set upon a table in the far corner. The gentle hum of the passing traffic in the background was accompanied by the ticking of a wall-mounted clock.

Walking forward, Caslin was joined by Terry Holt.

"I've requested CSI," he said quietly. "They'll be here within the hour."

Caslin nodded slowly, his eyes scanning the room. "They'll be busy," he said, without looking at Holt. Approaching the kneeling figure to within a couple of steps, mindful not to threaten the integrity of the forensic evidence, he dropped to his haunches to assess the victim. The man was perhaps in his early fifties although in this light it was difficult to tell. He appeared to be of Asian or of middle-eastern origin, stripped naked and kneeling on what Caslin guessed to be a prayer mat, judging by the size and pattern. His hands were clasped into his lap before him and his head was bowed as he was slumped slightly forward. Evidently, someone had worked him over. The man's body, his back in particular, exhibited early signs of bruising and multiple lacerations. The wounds stretched from one shoulder across the full width of the body to the other. Matching injuries were visible to the ribcage at the front and sides.

The face was swollen, consistent with a severe beating. Crouching further, Caslin positioned himself to see the man's face from below. He recoiled.

"What is it?" Holt asked. Caslin flicked his eyes up for a second before returning to inspect the dead man.

"His eyes have been removed," he said softly.

"Why would someone do that?" Holt asked, fear edging into his tone. Caslin didn't answer. The cheeks were swollen and split in places. As were the victim's lips although they were set apart due to something being wedged into the mouth. Caslin couldn't make out what it was. Blood had now ceased flowing. Most of the injuries, Caslin could see were superficial and not life threatening. Painful, certainly but wouldn't have led him to bleed out. However, in contrast, it was clear his throat had been cut. A wound four inches long, as well as substantially deep, stretched across the neck just below the larynx. As a result, the torso, waist and legs were all soaked in blood. The blood on the body was dry. Much of it had flowed down seeping into the prayer mat and carpet, pooling into a deep shade of crimson. This had saturated the floor and still appeared sodden such was the volume. The smell of excrement was intense. Caslin figured the deceased's bowels must have relaxed upon death.

"Take a look around for the eyes, would you?" Caslin said.

"Where?" Holt asked.

Caslin shot him a look of consternation, "I don't know. Just use yours, yeah?" Holt nodded and set off.

Turning his attention away from the body, Caslin surveyed the remainder of the scene. There was blood spatter across three of the walls as well as areas of the ceiling. In several places, they took the form of curves or arcs. No doubt, Robertson would confirm but having attended enough violent homicides in the past, Caslin knew this to be cast-offs. The blood was thrown from a weapon as it decelerated before and after each swing or blow. Looking around, Caslin noted a small dining table and two chairs. One of the chairs had been pulled out and it too, was covered in blood. Gaffer tape was visible on the arms and at the base of the legs. Apparently, it had been sliced through with a sharp blade. Checking the victim's wrist, hair was missing. Standing up, Caslin crossed to the chair and took a closer look at the remnants of the tape. Hair was visible, embedded in the adhesive. The victim had been forcibly removed at speed. Turning, he glanced at the wall directly in front of the kneeling man. Caslin held his breath. Roughly five-feet high and three wide a white cross had been crudely spray-painted onto it with the words *vermin out* scrawled alongside. Caslin let his breath out slowly.

The silence was interrupted by a stifled scream. Caslin jumped momentarily before running into the hall, calling out, "Terry?" He found Holt in the bedroom.

"Sorry, sir," Holt said, looking sheepish. "It startled me."

"What did?" Caslin asked, glancing in the direction of the bed where Holt was pointing. Caslin dropped to one knee and lifted the overhanging duvet so he could see under the bed. A pair of eyes were staring at him, narrow and frightened. "Terry, it's a bloody cat."

Holt nodded, "I know. Sorry. I didn't see it and it hissed at—"

"All right," Caslin said, interrupting him. Spotting a carrier atop the wardrobe, Caslin crossed the room and brought it down.

Indicating for Holt to block one side of the bed to deter the animal from escaping that way. Caslin went to the other. Reluctant to be clawed, he put the carrier close to where the cat waited before attempting to flush it out. He needn't have worried. The safe haven of the carrier was appealing and the animal darted in. Caslin swiftly closed the door and dropped the latch.

Holt shook his head. "I don't like cats, sir. Horrible creatures."

"We can leave it here, for now," Caslin said, standing and heading back into the living room. Holt went with him.

"I've checked the bathroom and the kitchen. I couldn't find the eyes unless they've been well-stashed. Do you think he took them?"

"Who?"

"The killer?" Holt asked.

"Or killers," Caslin mused, scanning the room. "You know what, Terry? This took a lot of time and patience. Despite what we see we're not looking at an act of uncontrolled fury here." Caslin swirled his hand in the air and indicated the scene before them. "There was method applied to this. The eyes were probably cut out for a reason."

"What reason?"

"A message, perhaps? I don't know. That's what we're going to have to figure out," Caslin replied. He walked across the room and casually inspected the spartan contents of a bookcase. There were two books on philosophy, several on economics and another on the history of finance. He couldn't see any items of sentiment. There were no picture frames, family photographs or belongings to signify a personal association. Looking around, Caslin noted there was no television nor a place set aside for one. Nothing appeared to have been disturbed or ransacked, putting a doubt in his mind as to robbery being a motive. "What's his name?"

Holt consulted his notebook, "According to the neighbours this flat is rented to a Farzaad Amin."

"Who called in the request for a welfare check? The same neighbours?"

Holt shook his head, "No, sir. By all accounts, the neighbours only found out when uniform tried to gain entry this morning."

"They didn't hear anything?" Caslin asked, surprised.

"Apparently not, no," Holt said. "But I'll follow up on what uniform heard when I go door-to-door, once CSI get to work."

"Good," Caslin said. "This would have made quite a bit of a commotion. Someone had to have heard something. What do we know about Mr Amin?"

"Not known to us, sir. No priors, nothing."

"All right. Find out what you can from the neighbours and we'll see where we go from there."

"Do you think he was killed during prayer time, sir?"

Caslin glanced across at the deceased and then towards the window as if looking at something in the distance, "I doubt it. I'm pretty sure this is staged."

Holt seemed perplexed. Looking around, he tried to assess what Caslin saw in order to reach that conclusion, "You seem confident. Why do you think so?"

Caslin fixed him with a stare, "He's facing north."

Holt raised a questioning eyebrow, "So?"

"You've not spent a lot of time around Muslims, have you?" Caslin replied. "If he was praying, he'd be facing east."

Hunter's voice carried to them, from the front door. By the accompanying noise level, she was not alone. Caslin judged CSI had arrived at the same time. He called back in response. Moments later, DS Hunter appeared from around the corner. Her first reaction was arguably the same as theirs. One of abject horror.

"Good Lord," she said quietly, furtively looking around. Iain Robertson came to stand behind her. He also took a sharp intake of breath.

"Right. Everybody out of my crime scene, if you don't mind?" he said, in his gruff Glaswegian. Caslin knew not to argue and the team had a lot to process. They would be there for some time.

"Terry, you and Sarah start by canvassing the neighbours," he instructed. Holt nodded but Hunter appeared lost in thought. "Sarah!" Caslin said, forcefully getting her attention.

"Yes, sir. Sorry, what did you say?"

"Go with Terry. Find out what you can about this guy. If he had many friends, how did he live, what he got up to?"

"Will do," she said, seeming glad to be leaving the room. She turned and Terry Holt followed her out. Caslin stepped across to speak with Robertson.

"There's a cat in the bedroom," he said. "I've got it crated. Presumably, you'll be quite happy for me to shift it?"

"Is it a suspect?" Robertson asked, jovially. Caslin cast an eye around the room. Robertson wasn't deterred, "You have to laugh at death as much as life, Nate. Without it, you're as good as lost."

Caslin nodded, "The cat?"

"Aye. As long as it doesn't have any blood on it. Does it?"

"Not as far as I could tell."

"In that case," Robertson said, "be my guest. I don't want it running around contaminating the forensics. What'll you do with it?"

Caslin shrugged, "Get one of the neighbours to take it or something."

Leaving Robertson to get himself set up, Caslin went to the bedroom and retrieved the carrier. Making his way out of the flat, he could hear conversations already happening as his officers canvassed the neighbours.

Emerging into the bright sunshine, Caslin blinked and shielded his eyes with his one free hand. The sun was sitting low in a crystal-clear, blue sky. A larger crowd was gathering now. Word must have spread. Unlocking his car, he put the carrier on the back seat before relocking it and heading back towards the building.

Parked on the other side of the street, he noted a black limousine. The metallic paint sparkled into the afternoon sunshine. Unsure of the model, Caslin thought it could be a Maybach. It wasn't every day that you saw one of those kicking about. A uniformed chauffeur sat in the driver's seat, bearing a cap and gloves. Shielding his eyes against the sun, Caslin tried to make out the figure sitting in the rear but couldn't. Clearly, they were drawing a higher status of voyeur these days.

A few voices carried from the crowd seeking answers to questions about what was going on. Caslin turned his attention to them and scanned the assembled. The thought occurred as to their motivations. Many were merely curious, others, so bored that this was the most excitement they'd experienced in years. Family or friends could arrive seeking knowledge about their loved ones. Occasionally though, there were the others. Those who took pleasure in seeing the response to their efforts. A killer might return to observe the goings on, revelling in the chaos they had created.

Caslin stood and watched them for a few moments trying to spot anyone who stood out. A lone figure, standing in silence. Someone taking photographs or filming the incident on a mobile phone. Anyone who looked like they didn't belong. Satisfied that no one fitted his criteria, he returned inside.

Farzaad Amin's flat was one of two on the ground floor. Caslin saw Hunter at the top of the stairwell. He trotted up the polished stairs, his shoes echoing as he went. She waited for him. When he reached her, he noted her odd expression.

"Are you okay?" Looking beyond her, over her shoulder, he registered Holt casting a sideways glance in their direction.

"Yes. Of course," Hunter replied, almost defensive in her tone. "Why wouldn't I be?"

Caslin shrugged, "No matter. What have you got?"

Hunter consulted her notes, "There was no answer when we called at the other flat on the ground floor. The neighbours say it's currently vacant. The inhabitant went into a care home and the housing association haven't reallocated it yet. We've had more luck up here. Neither of the incumbents on this floor knew him very well. They say he's quiet, keeps himself to himself. They've never seen him receive any visitors. Although, he was always amiable whenever they crossed paths."

"What do they know about him?"

"They believe he's from Afghanistan. Whether he has refugee status or is an asylum seeker, neither were sure."

"How long has he lived here?" Caslin asked, watching Holt say goodbye to an elderly gentleman and come across the landing to join them.

"Several years by all accounts."

"When you get back to Fulford Road, give the Home Office a call and try and to ascertain his status. It might be relevant."

"We've got something of a hate-crime, sir," Holt said, coming alongside. He glanced at Hunter, "You all right?"

"Yes, Terry. I'm fine," she snapped.

"The thought had occurred, Terry but why? What do you have?" Caslin asked him.

"The above neighbours," he paused to check his notes. "The Sahni family reckon Amin's been getting some serious grief from the locals. As have they, on occasion."

"Which locals?" Caslin said, glancing out of the window overlooking the street beyond. The crowd appeared to be increasing by the minute.

"Kids, mainly," Holt said.

"Come off it, Terry," Caslin said. "That, downstairs, wasn't done by kids picking on the neighbourhood brown guy."

Holt shook his head, "No, no, but there's been talk about him interfering with them. The kids, I mean. Some are alleging he's a nonce."

"Well if he is, it's the first we are hearing of it," Caslin said. "Try to get some more details, would you? We'll have to consider every possibility but let's face it, this wouldn't be the first time a bit of a loner has that accusation thrown at him. Particularly, if he's a foreigner."

"Yes, sir," Holt said, turning and heading off up to the next floor.

"Any weight in that, do you reckon?" Hunter asked.

Caslin thought about it, "Kiddie-fiddlers are usually on our radar in some capacity or another and he wasn't. I guess that's not conclusive, though. What was done to him looked personal to me. Not kids, not a burglar. Much more than that."

"A relative?" she suggested. "A father of a victim?"

Caslin thought on it, "It'd take a special kind of someone to have the stomach to do what was done downstairs."

"True. That's not to say we don't have them here in York. What do you make of the religious overtones?" Hunter asked.

"Best to keep that quiet for as long as possible," Caslin said, lowering his voice. "That's the last thing we need this weekend. You crack on with Terry. I'm going to head back to Fulford and see if there is anything in the database similar to this. I have the feeling this wasn't the first time our guy did something like this."

CHAPTER NINE

DESCENDING THE STAIRS, Caslin sensed the situation outside was escalating. Raised voices carried into the foyer of the communal entrance, punctuated by the occasional shout. Picking up the pace, he took the last few steps at a canter, emerging into the daylight and a fractious scene. The crowd of onlookers appeared to have swollen within the past few minutes and the number of placards visible above the throng indicated trouble was brewing. A situation of interest to the local residents was now turning into something deeper.

The four officers, tasked with maintaining the security of the cordon were currently standing between two distinct groups, numbering approximately thirty in total. The crowd were spreading out into the road and blocking the remaining lane. No traffic was flowing. Beyond, more people appeared to be heading their way. One man had taken to a dwarf wall, elevating himself above the others in order to address those assembled. He was in his forties, sporting closely-cropped hair and smartly dressed in a suit and tie. Reaching down, someone handed him something and he raised it to his mouth. It was a microphone, attached to a portable megaphone held by another.

"Who wants to be free?" he called into the microphone. Immediately, a raucous cheer went up alongside several denouncements from others. "Mass migration is eroding Europe's Christian culture to the point that we, the indigenous population, no longer have a place to call home."

The crowd began to chant, "Yes! Yes!" Sensing the situation was about to deteriorate further, Caslin took out his mobile and dialled the station. With officers spread out across the city, he knew that they needed to be here.

"Open immigration has brought them to us, with no affinity or allegiance to the country they've ended up in. This is *our fault* because we don't demand it changes!" the speaker shouted.

"England for the English!" someone shouted, only for others to begin repeating it along with accompanying applause. The opposing sides were advancing on each other, jostling for position. More officers arrived having escorted protestors from the town centre. Caslin was incensed at how the policing plan had apparently fallen apart in such a spectacular fashion. The sides were never supposed to meet.

Tempers frayed as accusations were traded. So far, bravado was all that was on display but it wouldn't take much for that to change. Caslin's call was answered and he requested immediate support as he assessed the developing melee. DC Holt came alongside, appearing flustered.

"What's all this?" he said. Caslin didn't have time to answer.

"Family. Church. Nation," the speaker stated to rapturous applause. "We need to rebuild our country based on our traditions, our culture and our beliefs. Our sense of self is ebbing away because of a cancer gnawing away at the heart of our democracy. Our system, the police," he said, pointing towards the thin line of high-vis jackets, struggling to keep the conflicting groups apart, "defend rapists, criminals and paedophiles."

The volume of opposing chants escalated, "Racists out! Racists out!"

A missile was thrown towards the speaker, narrowly missing him as he flinched, ducking to avoid it. Both Caslin and Holt stepped forward, vainly trying to support their fellow officers in pushing the sides apart. A man screamed for Caslin to step aside, he was flushed with rage and cut a physically imposing figure. Caslin bellowed at him to step back. An arm brushed past his face from behind, striking out at the man, Caslin was trying to control. Instinctively, Caslin turned, reaching out to grip the jacket of the man throwing the punch. Something struck the back of his head, he didn't know what. Almost all perception of the big picture was lost as the small contingent of police threatened to lose what little control they'd had up until now.

Glancing up, Caslin saw one of the placards launched over their heads, coming down into the nationalist ranks. A roar of anger followed and the crowd surged forward. Pushed off balance, he stumbled backwards losing his grip on his charge as well as his footing. A gap opened up between himself and the uniformed constable alongside, as the group pressed onto them. A fearful shout went up nearby but from whom, he didn't know. Feeling a kick to his back, Caslin grimaced. That was followed by something striking the side of his face. Whatever it was, fist or missile, it stung and brought tears to his eye. Trying to re-establish contact with his colleagues and maintain the line, Caslin reached out. The nearest officer attempted to link arms. Another surge came. This time from the rear and the link was broken. Caslin tripped on an unseen kerb and fell forward. He hit the ground harder than anticipated, the force of the swell pushing him down at speed. The instinctive reaction was to panic, fear flashing through his mind but he fought against it.

Caslin tried to stand, only for the movement of those around him to knock him back. Someone took a firm grip of his jacket and he was hauled back onto his feet. Relieved to see Terry Holt pulling him upright, he conveyed his gratitude with a nod. Sirens greeted them, arriving from beyond the city gates. The blue lights of two vans and several patrol cars approaching were a welcome sight. Managing to regain their composure, the two officers returned to the fray. Scuffles were breaking out as the illusion of control was given over to unfolding chaos. The crowd became a blur of angry faces. Some were masked with only their visible fury highlighted in their eyes.

The newly-arrived reinforcements formed up and drove forward into the crowd. The spearhead moved to draw Caslin and the other isolated colleagues back into the relative security of the ranks. Almost as swiftly as the situation had deteriorated, a semblance of order was restored with the scuffles breaking up.

Caslin retreated from the line, spotting the duty commander arriving to take charge and marshalling the increasing uniformed presence. He was relieved to be clear. Looking around, the speaker who'd incited the crowd was nowhere to be seen. The anger and aggression from each side was still vocal but further violence was deterred by the volume of the police presence. Several key antagonists from both sides were targeted and pulled away from their associates. Most were dragged kicking and screaming into custody.

"Are you okay, sir?" Holt asked, pointing to the side of Caslin's face. He reached up and felt something wet. Inspecting his fingers, he found blood but figured it to be superficial. Holt passed him a tissue and Caslin pressed it against the side of his head, near to the temple. His ears were ringing and he felt a little dizzy. "Pity some of us didn't care to get involved," Holt added with an edge to his tone.

Caslin looked back in the direction of the building. DS Hunter stood in the doorway. Seeing both of them watching her, she turned away and dropped out of sight. Caslin removed the tissue. It was saturated with blood, failing to stem the flow.

"Well, we're all a bit out of practice when it comes to crowd control," Caslin replied, brushing away the comment. Looking around, he was confident that everything was back under control. Across the street, the Maybach was still there. That piqued his curiosity and Caslin walked towards it. Reaching for his pocketbook, he was intent on noting the vehicle's registration. The action proved difficult with only one hand. The engine started and before he could get into position to view it, the car moved off. Not at speed but with gradual acceleration. Coming past where he stood, Caslin eyed the passenger seated in the rear who remained impassive, focussed on the road ahead with not even a glance in his direction.

"Anything interesting?" Holt said, coming to stand alongside and reading Caslin's expression.

Caslin shrugged, making a mental note of the licence plate. "It's been an interesting day, Terry."

"Too right," Holt replied. "You ought to get your face looked at."

"I will, later. Why don't you finish up inside," Caslin replied, pointing back towards the flats and putting his pocketbook away. A wave of dizziness washed over him and he felt unsteady on his feet.

"I think I'll run you to the hospital first. Just in case," Holt said. Caslin was about to object but feeling a trickle of blood run down the side of his face, dripping off onto his arm, encouraged him to change his mind.

"All right," he agreed.

It was already pushing 9 pm by the time he pulled the door to his apartment, in Kleiser's Court, closed behind him. Flicking the light switch with his elbow, illuminated the hallway. His face felt tender and he tentatively lowered himself to his haunches and emptied his arms of everything he was carrying. Walking to the bathroom, he pulled the cord and went to inspect himself in the mirror.

Turning sideways to get a better look, he was dismayed. What he'd initially thought to be a minor wound now sported seven stitches and a deepening colour that would soon be a mixture of black, purple and yellow, as the bruising manifested. The cut ran forward, for an inch, across from the base of his temple and narrowly missed the corner of his eye. Being a Saturday afternoon and considered a low priority by the triage nurse, Caslin spent four hours waiting to be seen at the hospital. There followed a trip to the X-ray department, an inordinate wait for the results and the application of the sutures themselves.

At least the wound was sealed and provided he kept it clean, no infection should follow. Opening the cabinet in front of him, he took out a blister-strip of paracetamol.

Leaving the bathroom, he went into the kitchen and rooted through the cupboards. Not finding anything suitable, he opened the fridge, locating a half-used pack of raw beef-mince at the rear. Taking it out, he tipped the contents into a bowl.

Returning to the hall, he knelt down and unhooked the latch to the front of the pet carrier. Opening the door, he coaxed out the cat with the promise of food. It gradually emerged. Having spent a lot of time in the safety of the confines of the crate and indeed, Caslin's car, the traumatised creature was now far calmer. He wasn't really a cat lover nor a fan of any pet if he was honest but it proved a bit late in the day to arrange any alternative. Holt flatly refused to take it, claiming allergies as an excuse, so what other choice did he have so late on a Saturday evening?

Picking up the pack of dressings and alcohol solution, the staff at the hospital had furnished him with, Caslin went into the living room. Tossing the package onto the sideboard, he threw his keys alongside it. Reaching for a glass, he took the stopper from a bottle of Macallan and poured a healthy measure. Crossing to his chair, he sank down. Popping a couple of tablets from the strip, he put them in his mouth and swallowed hard. Washing them down with some whisky, he closed his eyes.

The thudding pain behind his eyes was irritating but nothing he wasn't used to. He heard movement alongside him and opening his eyes was surprised as the cat leapt up onto his lap. His first thought was to brush it aside but as he reached forward, it nuzzled against his hand, purring in an almost hypnotic, repetitive chant. He smiled and instead began stroking it.

"If you insist," he said quietly.

The intercom buzzed. Caslin glanced at the clock. It was late for a personal call but not late enough for the weekend drunks to be messing with him. The cat was reluctant to move and so, Caslin slid it off to one side, depositing it onto the chair as he stood. Finishing his scotch, he placed the empty glass on the coffee table and headed to the front door. The movement caused the banging in his head to intensify once again.

"Hello," he said, activating the intercom.

"Hi Nate, it's me."

Caslin was momentarily thrown, hearing the voice of his ex-wife, "Erm… Karen. Yes, of course. Come on up." He released the exterior door and heard her pass through it before he disconnected the speaker. Chiding himself for not having called her earlier, as he'd planned to, he took a deep breath. Unlocking the front door, he quickly stepped back into the living room. Scanning the interior, he judged the standard acceptable for a visitor, even one as particular as Karen. Returning to the hall, he pulled the door open to see her out on the landing. She stood with her hands before her, nervously rubbing her palms together.

"Hi," she said quietly. Caslin looked at her, smiling. She returned the smile with one of her own, accompanied by an inquisitive flick of the eyebrows. "Can I come in? Or should we talk out here?"

Caslin snapped out of it, shaking his head, "Of course, please." He gestured for her to enter, stepping back to make room. She came past him and he ushered her into the living room. "I'm sorry. I meant to call you but…"

Closing the front door, he followed her in. She turned to face him, taking in his appearance. "My god, your face. Are you okay?" She reached towards his face with her hand. Caslin flinched.

"Oh, this," he replied, touching a hand to his cheek, "It's nothing, really. Looks worse than it is but that's why I didn't call. Who's got Lizzie?"

"She's staying over at a friend's this weekend," Karen replied, her eyes drawn to Caslin's left. She inclined her head slightly, indicating towards the armchair. "Since when have you had a cat?"

Caslin looked. The cat was sitting up, eyeing them expectantly. "That's… a long story."

"What's its name?" she asked.

"I… just call it… Cat," Caslin said.

"You have to give it a proper name. Is it male or female?"

"No idea," Caslin said.

"You haven't looked?"

"I respect its privacy," Caslin said with a smile. "Do you want a drink?"

Karen nodded, taking off her coat and placing it across the arm of the sofa, "I could do with a glass of wine. Red, if you have it?" Caslin walked through to the kitchen, returning with a half-decent Bordeaux he hadn't finished from a previous night. "Sean filled me in on what happened. How much trouble is he in?"

"With us? A hell of a lot," Caslin said, passing her a freshly poured glass. He should let it breathe but he knew his ex well enough to know she wasn't bothered. "With the police? I'll have to speak to the lead investigator tomorrow or Monday. We can take it from there."

"You can fix it?" Karen asked hopefully.

Caslin smiled, "Anything can be fixed." He tried to sound upbeat and positive. If the truth be known, on this occasion, his influence might not be enough.

"I read him the riot act. But, to be honest, my heart wasn't in it."

"I know. He's had a rough year," Caslin agreed, the guilt returning. "It feels pretty harsh to go in too hard on him but, at the same time, maybe laying off him has brought us here. Listen, I haven't eaten. Would you like to stay for dinner? I'm planning one of my specials."

"Indian or Chinese?"

"I figured Indian. They're closer," Caslin said with a smile.

"I'd like that," Karen said. "It's good to see you looking well, Nate. This is the best I've seen you in ages. Apart from your face being all smashed up. Mind you, most people would say it's an improvement." Caslin laughed. "I mean it, though. You look in good shape. You've stuck to your twelve steps… and you've even got a cat," she said, sipping at her wine and sitting down on the sofa. Caslin crossed to the sideboard and took out a leaflet for his preferred takeaway restaurant.

"It is a return to the good old days in many respects," Caslin offered, passing her the menu. She declined.

"Whatever you fancy is fine," she said. "I'm not fussy."

"You can't have been. You married me," Caslin joked. They both laughed.

"You see," she said. "That's more like the old Nathaniel. Whatever happened to him?"

"He married you for a start," Caslin countered. Karen nearly blew wine from her nostrils as she laughed. He turned away from her, crossing to the front window and looking down on the cobbled streets of York's Shambles.

The weekend festivities were getting underway as the onset of spring tentatively threatened to come upon them. Just for the moment at least, Caslin was able to put the horrific nature of his day to one side. Scrolling through his contacts, he dialled the restaurant, a smile on his face.

CHAPTER TEN

THE WHIR of the machine pumping boiling water through the filter head was a comforting sound, first thing in the morning. Sunlight streamed through the kitchen window giving the false impression of warmth outside. Once the cup was full, Caslin picked it up and placed it on the warming plate above. Removing the head, he knocked out the contents and refilled it from the grinder. Setting that back into position ready to make another, he was interrupted by the buzzer of the intercom. Leaving the kitchen, he walked down the narrow hall to the front door and lifted the receiver.

"Morning, sir," DS Hunter said. He buzzed her through the communal entrance into the lobby. Unlocking the front door, he left it ajar and returned to the kitchen. By the time she had ascended the stairs and entered the apartment, he was already filling the second cup of coffee. Hearing the machine, she came through to where he stood offering him a brown paper bag. Taking it from her, he glanced inside.

"Nice. Thanks," he said, admiring the selection of pastries. Taking a plate down from one of the cupboards, he tore open the bag and tipped them out. The cat appeared from nowhere, leaping onto the table and making a beeline for the plate. Hunter laughed and Caslin scooped it up, placing it back down on the floor. "Remind me to get some cat food later, would you?"

"I'd also suggest a litter tray," Karen added, stepping over to the kitchen window where the cat now waited expectantly. She opened it allowing the creature access to the fire escape.

"Good call," Caslin replied.

"I figured you'd want—" Hunter started before stopping as Karen appeared in the living room. Hunter was open-mouthed. "I'm sorry," she said, casting a sideways look towards Caslin. "I didn't realise you had company."

"That's okay," Karen replied. "How are you, Sarah?"

"Very well... Karen. Thanks," Hunter replied, looking and feeling a little awkward. "You?"

"Me, too," she replied, glancing down.

Caslin picked up one of the coffees and crossed the kitchen. Confident he was the only one not experiencing a level of discomfort, he made to pass the cup to Karen but noticed she had her coat across her forearm.

"I'd better be off, Nate. I know it's early but I've things I need to do."

"You don't have to," he said warmly.

"It's okay," she said. "Besides, you've clearly got work to do anyway."

He put the cup down on the kitchen table. "No problem. I'll see you out."

Karen held up a hand, "There's no need really. I know the way." He smiled, leaned in and kissed her on the cheek. "Thank you for last night," she said, with a nervous smile. Looking to Hunter, she offered a broader smile, "Nice to see you again, Sarah."

"You, too," Hunter replied, returning the smile and bobbing her head before looking away. Karen left via the living room. Caslin picked up the coffee he was intending to present to his ex and instead, passed it to Hunter.

"Coffee?" he said.

"Thank you. So..." Hunter said, holding the cup with both hands to warm her fingers, "you and Karen, eh?"

"Stop it," Caslin said, turning his back and reaching for his own cup. Internally, he was grinning. "So, what brings you to my door, this early, on a Sunday morning?" Hunter sipped at her drink but found it far too hot for her liking. Putting it down on the table, she fished out her notebook from an internal pocket of her coat.

"When I got back to the station yesterday, I ran the background on our victim, Farzaad Amin. The initial checks proved accurate. He has no priors, no convictions. According to the national database, he's not come up on the radar of any constabulary."

"No legs in the rumour of child abuse, then?"

Hunter shook her head, "I've also been to the National Crime Agency and they've no record in Child Exploitation and Online Protection either. If he's up to anything, we've nothing to substantiate it. I've asked Terry Holt to follow up and see if anyone can verify the allegations. Some of the neighbours have documented complaints about the locals, though. Anti-social behaviour in the main. Although, there were two incidences of bottles being thrown, along with racist abuse aimed at the ethnic minority residents of Amin's block."

"Kids?"

"It would appear so. Nothing came of it."

"Good work," Caslin said, leaning against the kitchen counter and blowing the steam from the top of his brew. "What did he do for a living, Farzaad Amin?"

Hunter returned to her notes, "That's where I'm struggling. The neighbours implied he arrived here from Afghanistan as an asylum seeker at the end of the mission. Or at least that's what they believed. If so, until his status was confirmed, he wouldn't be able to work."

"And?" Caslin asked, not seeing an issue.

"UK forces pulled out of combat operations back in 2014. Most of those who assisted our troops applied around then or before the withdrawal. Interpreters and the like – others who worked overtly with the occupying forces – were concerned about retaliation."

"From our former enemies, once our protection was removed. Yes, I know," Caslin said. "Did Amin work for ISAF?"

"That's just it, sir," Hunter continued. "I can find no record of him in the Home Office database. I can't tell you when he arrived in the country or what the details surrounding his asylum application were. Likewise, there's no confirmation of his status. No tax registration or national insurance number has been issued in his name."

"Have you been on to the department?"

"Yes but, what with it being a Saturday afternoon I was brushed off. Apparently, I'll need to speak to a case handler on Monday."

"Bank account or credit card?" Caslin queried, thinking hard. "He'll have to be paying his way somehow."

"I spoke to Iain Robertson this morning. He's finished cataloguing the contents of Amin's flat and is shipping everything back to Fulford Road as we speak. We'll be able to go through the paperwork there." Caslin picked up a cinnamon swirl to go with his coffee and took a bite.

Speaking through a mouthful, he waved the pastry in Hunter's direction.

"While I think about it," he said, wiping his mouth with the back of the same hand, "get some names for those at the demo yesterday. Particularly that one stirring it with the megaphone. Add those nearest him to the top of the list as well. If it is a racially-motivated attack, then we have plenty of new faces floating about town to shake down."

"Will do, sir," Hunter said, making a note.

Caslin picked up his coffee and walked towards the living room, "I'll take a shower and then we can head in. Make yourself comfortable."

CASLIN SURVEYED THE BOXES, now stacked upon the desks in the CID squad room. Scanning through the nine-page inventory, he called out two box numbers. Indicating the first was for Terry Holt.

"Yours contains the financials, Terry. We're still none the wiser as to how this guy funds his existence," he said, re-reading the list. "I know, by all accounts, he led a simple life but where did he get his income from? If he has a job where is it? Who did he work for and with? Once you know that, I want you following up on his colleagues, clients, delivery personnel, everything. Has he fallen out with anyone? Is there a grudge being brought to bear? Likewise, is there anyone in his circle who has form for violence, racially motivated or otherwise?"

"What if he isn't working, sir?" Holt took the lid off of his assigned archive-box and removed several large, sealed, plastic bags, placing them on the desk in front of him.

"The man still had to eat, Terry. Find me who was picking up the tab," Caslin said, returning his attention to the inventory. Scanning down, through the subsections detailing the contents he paused, hovering his finger over the description of a charger for a mobile phone. Resuming his search, he flipped through the following pages until he came across a list of the deceased's reading matter. "No phone."

"What's that, sir?"

"No mobile phone."

"Not that was found at the scene, no," Hunter said.

"And yet, he had a charger stuck in the wall," Caslin said. "This guy liked reading. His books were focussed on economics, science and the like."

Hunter nodded, "That'd be fair to say. So?"

"That's pretty heavy reading matter. I didn't see anything else that he may have occupied his time with. No computer, stereo... he didn't even have a television."

"And yet, he had a mobile phone?" Caslin nodded. "Who doesn't these days? You can barely get by without one."

"True," Caslin said. "Still seems odd, mind you. At the very least, it's missing so let's find out as much as we can. Start chasing the providers and with a bit of luck it was a contract and we could get some joy with his call history. Something tells me this wasn't a burglary gone wrong."

"The racial motive is pretty strong, sir," Hunter said. "Judging by what we found at the scene."

Caslin nodded, "Undeniable. Particularly, bearing in mind the unrest we have in the city at the moment. Anybody else find it curious how the black shirts turned up when they did?"

"You mean, Martin James and his Free Templars?"

Caslin nodded, "Is that who it was?"

"Yes. Along with the Seventh Brigade of the Free Templars," Holt added. "Or at least, the five of them holding their flags with that printed in the corner."

"What is it with these fascists and their suits and uniforms?" Caslin asked.

"If you want to preach hate, you've got to do it in decent threads," Holt said with a cutting smile, "apparently."

"What do we know about them?"

Hunter flicked through her notes, "A substantial amount. Martin James, as he likes to be known these days, has also gone under the names Simon Brown and Gary Wilson. His real name is Peter James Osgood-Bellamy. Presumably, his birth name doesn't fit the *man of the people* persona that he wants to put across. Book sales to think about and all that."

"Strewth, he can write?" Caslin asked.

"Several books, sir. Although, you won't find them on the high street. I'm also certain they won't mention his two convictions for assault, one being a domestic attack on a former partner or his nine-month sentence for fraud, three years ago. He served six months in Pentonville for the last one."

"And the assaults?"

"He was given a year-long suspended for the first and spent another, tagged on licence, for the second. No subsequent arrests."

Caslin thought about it, "Motivations?"

Hunter shook her head, "Nothing racial if that's where you're going?" Caslin frowned, indicating for her to continue. "As for his lieutenants, they're a nasty bunch. Several of those present at the demo are well known to their local police. We've convictions ranging from ABH, possession of offensive weapons to burglary and incitement to commit racial violence. They're definitely worth a thorough look at in this case."

"Okay. Get a dossier together and we'll go one by one. See if we have intel on their movements prior to Saturday's altercation. If any of them were in the vicinity of Amin's place let's get them in. Seems odd, though…" he said, the thought tailing off.

"Sir?" Hunter asked.

"That they were so vocal under the circumstances."

"They were on the scene quickly, weren't they?" Hunter said. "Although, the word was out right enough and local gossip was rife about what was going on."

"Surprised you noticed," Holt said to Hunter, without making eye contact.

"Meaning?" Holt shook his head.

"Well, you know. What with beings indoors."

"And just what do you mean by that?"

"Enough. The pair of you. The thing about word spreading, though…" Caslin said, raising an eyebrow as he coaxed out the thought from his mind, "is that James and his nationalist idiots aren't local. Someone said we had a call about Amin's welfare."

"That's right," Holt said, glancing up from a loose collection of utility statements.

"Who called it in? Do we know yet?"

Holt shook his head, "It was anonymous, sir. I've got the recording from the log but they used a payphone."

"I'm amazed he found one that still worked. So, for all we know, it could've been the killer tipping us off?"

"I guess that's possible, but why do that? It just puts us onto him sooner."

"Or distracts us, pointing the investigation away from him and towards the demonstrators."

"I'll see if I can locate any CCTV from the area around the phone box," Holt said. "Maybe we'll get lucky."

"Good idea, Terry. In the meantime, Sarah," he indicated Hunter, "is there anyone local who might fit this particular bill? I'm thinking of anyone with a record of racially aggravated violence, affiliations to neo-Nazi groups or such? In the absence of anything direct, let's cover the obvious and take it from there." Caslin stood and picked up his coat.

"Where are you headed, sir?" Hunter asked.

"I'm off to see Dr Taylor to get the preliminaries from her. The detail will follow tomorrow but I'm hoping she can give us a steer. Robertson's promised his initial assessment of the crime scene in a couple of hours. I'll be back for that. What's the time in Kabul?"

"I've no idea, sir," Hunter said, sounding bemused. "Why?"

"They can't be much more than four or five hours ahead," Caslin offered. "If the Home Office is rubbish on a Sunday, perhaps their Interior Ministry may be more useful?"

Hunter smiled, "Can't hurt to ask."

Caslin left CID, turned to the right and headed for the stairs. The skeleton team staffing the station on a Sunday meant he didn't cross paths with anyone. Despite all scheduled rest days being cancelled, the majority of officers were out on patrol or beating the streets trying to ensure the demonstrators were kept apart from one another. His footfalls echoed in the corridor as he made his way to the front entrance. Passing out through the security door to the lobby, he noted the civilian staffer on the front desk. He didn't recognise her, assuming she was new. Casting a sideways glance, he smiled, one that she returned. Reaching the front door, the sound of voices came to his ear in far greater numbers than he'd anticipated.

Stepping out into the brilliant sunshine, Caslin shielded his eyes whilst they adjusted. At the bottom of the steps, barely six feet wide, he faced a bank of people perhaps twenty strong. They blocked his path. It didn't take him long to realise who they represented. On either side of the front line stood two men. Both were dressed in black with matching military-style berets, sporting white gloves that covered much of their forearms. They held Union Flags aloft embroidered at the edges with gold thread. Behind them were others, hoisting black flags, each with their own golden trim.

At the head of the group stood a man who Caslin recognised from the protests of the previous day. Martin James, self-styled advocate for free speech with his neatly-trimmed hair and pin-striped suit, was standing front and centre. Observing Caslin exiting the police station, he stepped forward.

"And here is one of those covering up for the paedophiles that our government insists on bringing into our country!" he called in as dramatic a fashion as he could.

Several of the group backed up the comment with muted appreciation. Caslin took a deep breath. The urge to return inside and slip out via the back was tempting. Only then, did he notice the assembled journalists off to his right-hand side. Looking beyond the crowd, Caslin judged his car was a minimum of fifty yards away. Steeling himself, he walked forward descending the steps.

"Anything to say in response to that accusation?" a voice came at him from the journalists. Caslin ignored it, pressing on. The crowd allowed him some space although not much.

"Defenders of paedos and rapists," James continued his verbal barrage as Caslin walked past him. "It makes me sick!" Caslin couldn't check himself in time. He turned to face his accuser, finding himself up close and far too confrontational in his stance.

"There is no cover up," he countered. Turning to the journalist who asked the question, he sneered, "What's being discussed is a blatant lie. No doubt fuelled by this idiot!"

"It's Rochdale all over again," James argued, referring to a high-profile case of sexual-grooming of vulnerable children that'd occurred in the city.

"There's no evidence for that, *none!* You and your lot are the problem here. We've got no issues with immigrants in this city," Caslin snapped, pointing an accusatory finger. Martin James smiled in return. "Any issue that's raised, any suggestion of impropriety and people like you descend on it with your dog-whistle rhetoric. We're investigating a murder. Nothing more."

"Free speech," James countered to much applause and cheering from those around him. "And you've all heard it. They're turning a blind eye... again!"

Caslin turned away, with a shake of the head and resumed his walk to the car. A microphone was pushed in front of him and he brushed it aside scowling at the man holding it.

"You lot aren't much better," Caslin stated, increasing his pace.

Photographers were taking pictures of him and Caslin regretted his part in the entire altercation. With hindsight, he should never have engaged at all. He knew better than to do so.

No one followed him to his car and he was relieved to reach the sanctity of the interior. Pulling the door closed, he started the engine and pulled away as quickly as he dared. Once out of the car park, he turned right onto Fulford Road and travelled barely a hundred yards before pulling into the kerb. Putting his hazard lights on, he sank back in his seat and tilted his face skywards. Pressing into his eyes with the heel of his palms, he sought to calm down. Martin James was one hell of a self-publicist who knew how to keep himself relevant. Of that, Caslin had no doubt. Something told him, he hadn't seen the last of him and his so-called Templars.

Glancing over his shoulder, he eyed a break in the traffic. Pulling out, he resumed his drive across the city to Alison Taylor's pathology lab.

CHAPTER ELEVEN

If the station was considerably quieter on the weekend, then pathology was a ghost town in comparison. Caslin waited at the entrance for what seemed like twenty minutes but in reality, was less than ten, for Alison to come up from her laboratory and let him through.

"If you could see your way clear to not delivering me a body for a couple of days, I'd appreciate it," she said, with a warm smile, pulling the door open. "A weekend off would be nice."

Caslin grinned, "I'm sorry. Death waits for no one." Dr Taylor returned the smile and they set off back into the building. Despite being indoors, Caslin drew his coat about him. "I know you have to keep it cool for the bodies but any chance the rest of the place can be a bit warmer?"

"The heating's on a timer," she explained. "It's Sunday. No one is supposed to be here. I pulled an all-nighter with your man. So, once we're through I won't be here either."

At that point, Caslin noticed the dark rings under her eyes. He should've picked up on that earlier. Within a couple of minutes, they arrived in the mortuary. Dr Taylor crossed to her workstation in order to retrieve her notes. Caslin looked around for the body.

"He's in D4, if you want to pull him out," she said, realising what he was thinking. Caslin scanned the numbering of the storage refrigerators where she indicated and located the unit. Pulling the handle, he swung the door open and pulled on the shelf. The metal tray slid out effortlessly on its runners. Farzaad Amin was enclosed in a black mortuary bag. Dr Taylor came alongside, passing him a small tub of nasal decongestant. Unscrewing the lid, he dabbed a little of the gel under his nostrils. The burning sensation began almost immediately, intensifying within seconds and bringing tears to his eyes. This was, however, far more agreeable than the smell of a decomposing body.

Caslin unzipped the bag, running it down to Amin's waistline. Paradoxically, the body seemed in a far better condition than when he had last seen it at the crime scene. Despite the extra incisions, caused during the autopsy process and subsequent stitching, the wounds appeared less violent now what with the excess blood having been cleaned away.

"You'll need to unzip it further," Alison said without looking up, familiarising herself with her notes.

"Really?"

"Yes. You'll see," she replied. Caslin did as instructed, running the zipper down. No further explanation was necessary as Caslin noted Amin's penis had been removed approximately halfway up the shaft. Even to his untrained eye, the process was executed somewhat roughly. Caslin winced at the barbarity of the action.

"Cause of death?" he asked.

"A massive haemorrhage following a single cut to a carotid artery, in the throat," Dr Taylor confirmed. Caslin moved to the victim's head and inclined his own in order to get a better view. He could see several wounds whereas previously, he'd only noted the one. "I would suggest that the victim didn't remain still to allow his throat to be cut. The wound itself, that caused the arterial rupture, is not large. As you can see, there are several other, shallow incisions above and below. That suggests the head was not sufficiently immobilised and there was a brief struggle."

"Why do you think it was brief?"

"The number of other cuts tell me there was resistance but they are not random enough to indicate he was moving significantly."

"Someone was holding him?"

"Probably," she confirmed.

"Two killers?" Caslin asked, casting a glance up to her.

"Possibly. However, the other injuries he sustained prior to that would've left him weakened and so, that would require speculation on my part. Interestingly though, most homicides of this nature, where a throat is cut, produce similar results.

The wound is usually located from just below the ear and then runs obliquely downward and medially across the throat, towards the other side. If the killer is right-handed, the cut is deeper on the victim's left side and tails off as the blade comes across to the right, ending slightly lower than the starting point. The opposite being true with a left-handed individual.

This is the norm if the killer is standing behind the victim and pulling back on the scalp in order to open up the target area. However, in this case, the killer was standing in front and towering over the victim."

Caslin assessed the wound. It was far less significant than what she was describing, as were the other, more superficial cuts, nearby.

"These are shorter and more angular," Caslin said, looking to her for reassurance of his assessment. She nodded.

"Indicative of the killer standing before him," she confirmed. "They are more like swipes or slashes, rather than a methodical cut."

"Frenzied?" Caslin asked.

She shook her head, "I would say not. They were still delivered with an element of precision."

"What of the other injuries?" Caslin asked, scanning the bruising to the face and abdomen.

"He was severely beaten. Probably with a blunt implement although I cannot tell you what it was. They could have been caused by a cosh or just as likely by a rounded chair leg. I didn't find any wood fibres present in any of the wounds so, I'd speculate that something specific was brought for the task.

Makeshift weapons, such as chair legs or ornaments will splinter or fracture upon impact, leaving forensic evidence in the wound. I've found none of that in this case. He has multiple fractures of the ribcage, both front and back. His fingers are all broken. Several in more than one place and I'm sure you've not failed to notice the number of cuts elsewhere to the body?"

"You can't miss them," Caslin said flatly, his eyes running the length of the deceased's body. There were too many to count.

"Fifty-six individual knife wounds. None of which were severe enough to kill or incapacitate but accumulatively, very damaging. It looks more like torture to me. They appear random but, if you are a student of anatomy, as I am, you would be aware that in the most part these wounds are located in areas that would be extremely painful for the victim."

"Anything left forensically that could help identify who the killer is, skin samples, that kind of thing?"

"I'm sorry. As much as I'd love to make your life easier, I've been unable to locate any forensics that will assist you. There's no skin under the fingernails. No defensive wounds that might offer up indicators that the attacker could be injured. Perhaps Iain Robertson and his team may have something but sadly, I don't."

"To take that much of a beating in silence would be impressive," Caslin said, thinking aloud. "The neighbours reported hearing nothing untoward and this must've gone on for quite some time."

"Unsurprising," Dr Taylor said. "He had his tongue cut out." Caslin raised his eyebrows in shock.

"Then what's the point of the torture? If he can't speak, he can't tell you anything."

"It strikes me that you have a particular kind of sadist, on your hands," she replied. Caslin rolled his eyes heavenward.

"I noted something was wedged in his mouth."

"That would be the end of his penis," Dr Taylor confirmed. Caslin exhaled deeply. "I believe it was removed post-mortem, judging by the blood flow from the area. I trust that Iain Robertson will find the tongue because I have no sign of it here."

"What would be the point of that?"

She shook her head, "Symbolism, maybe? Perhaps he wanted to emasculate him for some reason, either driven by hatred or religious ideology. An attempt at humiliation or simply to send a message."

"To whom?"

"That escapes me," she shrugged, "but there will be a reason. There always is. Likewise, the removal of his eyes. They were gouged out with a smooth implement. Although, the trauma to the surrounding tissue is obviously severe, it was done with skill."

"See no evil, speak no evil…" Caslin mumbled under his breath. "Do you think the killer had experience of doing similar previously?"

"Quite likely, yes. Whether or not in a professional capacity, I couldn't say but this wasn't the first time."

"Anything else?" Caslin asked in a forlorn tone, thinking over what he had been told.

"There are two marks to the chest," she said, leaning over and indicating two small puncture marks on Amin's chest, barely an inch apart. "I nearly missed them at first what with the level of trauma to the upper body, in particular. But I got to thinking about the lack of defensive wounds, bearing in mind I couldn't see any injury that may have accounted for him being incapacitated. For example, a massive blow to the head."

Caslin eyed them, "A Taser?"

Dr Taylor nodded, "I believe so, yes. If you look at his wrists and ankles, you can make out skin abrasions where he was restrained. Probably to a chair. If he was resistant to that process, there would be some indication, a greater depth to the abrasions of the skin perhaps, but there isn't. The only deduction I can make is he either went willingly into a torturous death or he had no opportunity to resist." Caslin thought on that for a moment before passing comment.

"I felt the scene was staged, his kneeling as if in prayer. The cross painted on the wall in front of him. Would he have been dead before the staging took place, do you think?"

Dr Taylor looked down at her notes and cast a sideways glance over the body. With a shake of the head, she met his eye, "Impossible to say. If he expired prior to setting the scene, it becomes difficult to manhandle the deadweight into position."

"If you are doing so alone, yes," Caslin offered.

"Agreed. Judging from what Iain told me from the scene, the amount of blood loss would most likely suggest he bled out in situ, where you found him. That would mean he either died afterwards or shortly before because, as you know, the blood will flow for a time post-mortem."

"How long do you think it took him to bleed out from this type of injury?"

"It's quite possible his heart was still pumping for up to ten minutes, maybe more, but I'd doubt it."

"He would have been aware of what was happening?"

"Absolutely. Whether or not he had the strength or will to try and do anything about it, is another matter entirely."

Caslin zipped up the bag, pausing as he reached the neckline of the deceased. The speculative image of Amin's last moments in this life flashed through his mind. An image of abject horror. Whoever did this, someone so depraved they could stomach such an intense level of violence, he was sure it wasn't their first. It couldn't possibly be. Closing the bag, he took a step back and Alison pushed the tray back into the fridge, closing the metal door. The latch snapping into place echoed through the lab. Once again, he felt cold.

"Nate..." she said, trying to get his attention. "Did you hear me?"

He glanced across and met her eye, "Sorry. What did you say?"

"I was saying I'll write the report up tonight and get it over to you first thing. If that's okay?"

"Yes, yes. Of course," Caslin replied, rubbing at his face.

"Are you okay? I mean, we've not seen an awful lot of each other, aside from the last couple of days anyway."

He smiled, weakly, "I've just got a lot on my mind. And, I had a late one, last night."

"At A and E?" she asked, indicating the stitches on the side of his face whilst brazenly inspecting the handiwork. "I didn't want to mention it. Are you all right?"

Caslin shrugged off the question. He also had no intention of sharing with his ex-girlfriend the reason for his lack of sleep: spending the night with his ex-wife. Memories of which flooded his mind, pushing aside the last moments of the victim. They raised his spirits and he smiled to himself.

"I'm fine, it's just a scratch," he said. "You know what the emergency room is like on a Saturday. All drunks and sports injuries. It takes an age to get seen."

Alison Taylor agreed, "So, you're all right, generally speaking?"

"Yes, I'm fine," he replied. "Thanks for pulling this off, so quickly. You'll probably want to get your head down. I'll let you get off."

He turned and headed out of the lab. Dr Taylor returned to her workstation and he was aware of the sound of her notes landing on the desk. Caslin grasped the door handle and pulled it when she called after him.

"Yes, I'm fine too, Nathaniel. Thanks for asking." He paused in the doorway but didn't look back, somewhat aware of both the rhetorical nature of her comment as well as his personal failings. The realisation of the latter in itself demonstrated an improvement in his character but was, sadly, nowhere near enough to make up for the flaws in his social skills. Silently cursing himself, he left the lab allowing the door to swing closed behind him.

Passing out through the main entrance lobby, Caslin ensured the door locked back into place as he left the building. The wind was picking up and the chill that it brought, cut through his overcoat, causing him to shiver. Pulling his coat tightly about him, he picked up the pace and headed for his car. Once inside, he fired up the engine and set the demisters to maximum. The windscreen was already fogging over. Taking out his phone, he called Hunter.

"Sarah, is Iain ready for the briefing?"

"Yes. We're all set here, just waiting on you."

"I'll be back in about fifteen minutes," he said, glancing at the clock on his dashboard.

Hanging up, he put the phone back into his pocket and wiped the window next to him. Eyeing the skies, they threatened rain. The sun wasn't due to set for another couple of hours but with the dark, brooding clouds rolling in from the west it was hard to tell where the sun was. At least the rain would cancel out the frost. Judging the screen to be sufficiently clear, Caslin engaged first gear. As he did so, he caught sight of Alison Taylor leaving via the front door as he had only minutes earlier. She walked with a mobile clasped to her ear, laughing as she chatted, unaware of him watching her.

A pang of regret struck within, catching him off guard. He could honestly say he hadn't given her much thought since their relationship had run its course, so why now? She reached her Audi and the lights flashed as she unlocked it. He shook his head, telling himself it was probably due to revisiting the feelings he had for Karen, thereby stirring the emotions within that'd unsettled him. Regardless, he decided to not think about it anymore. Although, Alison's perceived happiness troubled him but he didn't know why.

"Stop living in the past, Nate," he told himself, looking away and moving off, attempting to cast aside any lingering thoughts about their chequered past.

CHAPTER TWELVE

Despite the increase in traffic due to people hitting the post-Christmas sales, the drive back to Fulford Road was uneventful. The demonstrators were still present at the front of the station and so he took a circuitous route around to the rear. At least now, they were being supervised by a uniformed presence. The security gates parted and he drove through. Finding a narrow space alongside a liveried van, he reversed the car in.

Entering through the custody suite, he acknowledged the duty sergeant and made his way to the stairs. Taking them two at a time, he entered CID moments later. The team were assembled and ready for the briefing. Offering an apology for keeping them waiting, Caslin pulled up a chair. Casting an eye across the two wipe boards, set up alongside the desks, Caslin scanned the new information. Iain Robertson had spent the morning updating the one relating to Farzaad Amin's death.

The crime-scene photographs brought back the stark memories that he'd managed to push aside, in the previous twenty-four hours. The brutality was equally shocking the second time around. Robertson cleared his throat, garnering the attention of the assembled detectives. Conversation ceased as people focussed on him.

Robertson's eyes flicked to the entrance doors and he nodded towards a latecomer. Caslin glanced over his shoulder, seeing DCI Matheson entering. She perched herself on the end of a desk towards the rear of the room, folding her arms.

"Okay, folks," Robertson began, "I've got an abbreviated copy here for all of you. Please take one and pass them on."

Hunter picked up half of the stack, piled on the nearest desk and handed it to Terry Holt who took the top one and moved them along. Hunter sent the remainder in the other direction. Caslin took a copy and began leafing through the pages.

"I'll give you the headlines," Robertson continued. "There were no clear indications of a forced entry but the security of the flat was insufficient. Slight abrasions on this window latch," he pointed to a photo up on the board, alongside another documenting a black mark, "and a boot scuff, on the corresponding window sill, indicate this is the point of entry. It took some finding. The window was closed, latch set in place. It's fair to assume the killer, or killers, left via the front door."

"Killers?" Caslin said.

"Two partial footprints, left in the victim's blood, have been identified. They have tread patterns on the soles that don't match any other footwear present in the flat. One was alongside the chair that the victim was strapped to. More on that later. The other was found alongside the prayer mat, Mr Amin was found kneeling on. They are both incomplete and neither measures up to more than a sixth of the available coverage. It does however, give us enough to confirm two other people were at the scene either at the time of Amin's death or very shortly after."

"Any fingerprints?" Hunter asked.

Robertson shook his head, "We swept the property twice and found only those belonging to Amin himself. I would go so far as to say the residence had been thoroughly cleaned. The prints we found were in the kitchen on cupboard doors, handles and utensils. No prints were found in the living room, the bathroom or the access hallway including the front door. We're not talking about a quick wipe down either. Whoever was there did a good job of masking their presence."

"Dr Taylor says the victim was tortured over a period of time," Caslin said, lifting his eyes from the paperwork he was reading through. "How long do you think they were on the scene?"

"That depends on how many were involved in the clean-up," Robertson said. "The victim sustained a prolonged assault. I've also discussed the injuries with Alison and we are agreed, in that we cannot ascertain what weapon, or weapons, were used.

Despite an extensive search, nothing was left at the scene that fits the bill. Likewise, none of the victim's knives were used. The knife block, in the kitchen, is full and no trace evidence was found on any of the blades. We can only presume that the weapons were taken away and therefore, it is reasonable to assume, were also brought with them to the scene."

"What about the paint on the wall?" Caslin said, eyeing the photograph on the board depicting the white cross alongside one of the graffiti.

"Acrylic based, deployed from an aerosol. The standard formula you will find for sale in auto-factors or DIY shops. For use on rigid metals, glass fibre or plastics. It's too common to narrow down to a purchase point. The choice of wording was interesting, though. The use of the word 'vermin' has connotations," Robertson said, talking to Caslin.

"Vermin is commonly used within far-right propaganda. Often in reference to those of Jewish descent but also ethnic minorities," Caslin said for the uninitiated.

"Are you approaching this as a racial hate-crime?" DCI Matheson asked, from the back of the room. Caslin stood, so she could see him better.

"Not at this stage, Ma'am," he replied. "With everything that's going on at the moment we'll keep it in the mix, but it's just as likely to be misdirection at this point."

"And you're basing that conclusion on what?"

"I prefer to follow the direction of travel the evidence sends us rather than the route set out by the perpetrators," he countered. She acknowledged his answer and didn't comment further. Caslin indicated for Robertson to continue.

"We have failed to locate the victim's eyes or tongue," Robertson said gravely. A few people exchanged concerned glances. "We've explored the building's drainage in case of disposal there, but found nothing. It is possible that they were flushed and any evidence sanitised before our arrival.

Alternatively, the more macabre conclusion is they could have been taken as trophies. The remaining details that I can offer relate to the blood spatter," he continued. "You'll find detailed illustrations within your individual reports. The victim was strapped to one of his dining chairs, secured at the wrists and ankles with duct tape.

There, he received the bulk of his ordeal. He was stripped naked and tortured. The arcs of blood on the surrounding walls and ceiling tell us this. The victim defecated in the chair before he was cut free and dragged the short distance to the prayer mat, where we believe he was positioned in the manner in which he was found."

A few brief questions were traded but nothing beyond clarification issues. Caslin stood as the briefing ended and the team returned to their assigned tasks. Taking Robertson by the forearm, Caslin led him aside.

"Nestor Kuznetsov," Caslin said. "Have you found any evidence to indicate anyone else was present in the boathouse?"

Robertson shook his head, "No, nothing to place anyone else at the scene."

"That's what I thought."

"Doesn't mean I think it was a suicide, mind you."

"No?" Caslin asked. "Can you tell me why?"

"Not really," he replied. Caslin was momentarily puzzled. Robertson noticed, elaborating, "Everything points to death by his own hand. The boathouse was apparently locked from the inside. There's no sign of a struggle nor any damage to the interior or contents of the building. Psychologically speaking, his life had taken such a battering it is easy to conclude why he'd have taken the decision to check out."

"Got to say it, Iain. You're not selling suspicious very well," Caslin said with a smile.

"Well, that's just it, isn't it," Robertson said. "It all points to suicide and yet, according to his medical records, there's a possibility that he couldn't have managed it."

"Exactly, Iain. A possibility. That's not evidence."

"I know that," he countered forcefully. "But sometimes… you just have a feeling about something, right? It's like you with your man, Farzaad. It's too clean. Too obvious."

Caslin nodded, thoughtfully, "Sometimes things are obvious, though. Maybe we're guilty of overcomplicating by looking too deeply."

"That's the job," Robertson replied quietly with a stern expression. "Ma'am," he said to the approaching DCI Matheson.

"Nathaniel. Can I have a word in your office?"

"Of course," Caslin replied, before saying goodbye to Robertson and thanking him for the speed of his report.

Following her into the office, he closed the door behind them. Something in her demeanour was a little off. They may not have the greatest working relationship over the course of her tenure as DCI but he could read her well enough.

"Where are you with the Kuznetsov suicide?" she asked, pulling out a chair.

"I'm still not convinced it was a suicide," Caslin replied, walking behind his desk. Matheson rolled her eyes and he sought to head off the direction the conversation was likely to take. "His daughter is adamant."

"His daughter, who he barely appears to spend any time with—"

"Who is still the closest person to him, barring his gangster security detail anyway," Caslin said.

"He was bankrupt, going from billionaire status to nothing," Matheson argued. "Men like him don't take failure well."

"Men like him never accept failure. They get what they want one way or another."

"And if all his options expired?" Caslin took a deep breath breaking the eye contact Matheson appeared to cherish during a confrontation.

He sighed, "Raisa, his daughter, claims he was negotiating a return to Russia. That he was homesick and looking to find a way back."

"Perhaps his request fell on deaf ears?" Matheson said. "Either way, I don't see an awful lot left for you to investigate. There are a few minor anomalies contained within the pathologist's report but aside from that, I fail to see why you're not deferring this one to the coroner and moving on."

"This is too high profile to pass off so quickly. We'll only fuel the conspiracy theories if we don't do a thorough investigation," Caslin said, pulling out his chair and sitting down.

"And if we spend too long on it, the end result will be the same. They'll claim we're hiding something."

"I'm not ready to tie it off just yet but," he added swiftly, "I do take on board your concerns."

"Don't patronise me, Nathaniel," Matheson chided him. "I'm not a junior detective. I'd also like to know why the chief constable has received a complaint about you?"

"Me?" Caslin asked, incredulous. "What have I done?"

"Accusing the press of fuelling racial hatred," Matheson said, stony-faced.

Caslin frowned, "When did I do that?"

"This morning. Outside the station during your verbal confrontation with the demonstrators," Matheson informed him.

Caslin sank back in his seat, pressing a thumb and forefinger to his eyes, "Oh, yeah. I remember." Matheson stood up and made to leave the office. She stopped as she reached the door, gripping the handle, poised to open it and looked back at him. She spoke in a softer tone.

"The chief constable was asked for an interview for this evening's television news," she said. Caslin's heart sank. "She declined, obviously. However, they will be running footage of the confrontation, so you ought to brace yourself."

"Local or national?"

"National," Matheson said.

"Great."

"You need a quick win, Nathaniel," Matheson said. "We both do."

With that, the DCI departed leaving the door to his office open. Caslin turned his attention to the window and his view of the infantry barracks in the nearby compound running adjacent to the grounds of the station. The light was fading and it was raining. He didn't hear Hunter enter.

"Sir?" she said, gaining his attention.

"Yes, Sarah. What do you have?"

"I contacted the Interior Ministry in Kabul."

"How did you get on?"

"Very well. They were extremely helpful, which was a pleasant surprise."

"What could they tell us about our victim?"

"Absolutely nothing, sir," Hunter said, enthusiastically. Acknowledging Caslin's disappointment, she continued, "But that's where it gets interesting. They have no record of a Farzaad Amin emigrating to the UK. The only mention they found of that name recorded in their files was of a civil servant working in a low-level administration role."

"Same guy?" Caslin asked. Hunter shook her head.

"No. He retired last year, shortly after his sixtieth birthday. Oh, and he still lives in Kabul." Caslin sat forward, resting his elbows on the desk in front of him, interlocking his fingers. Hunter met his eye. She found this as intriguing as he did, he could tell. Pushing his chair back, he stood and walked around the desk and out into the squad room. Hunter followed.

"Terry," he called. Holt scurried over from the other side of the room. "Where did you get to with Amin's financials?"

"No employer, as far as I could see from his bank statements, sir. There is a possibility he worked cash-in-hand but I don't see it. There's no evidence of him being the manual-labouring type. He does, however, have a payment going into his account twice a month. Equal amounts on the same days of each month. Regular as clockwork."

"How much?"

"A thousand pounds, sir," Holt stated. "But it doesn't say where the money comes from."

"Two grand a month. How is it paid?"

"Via BACS, sir," Holt said. "I've asked the bank for clarification of where the payments originate but they're unwilling to say. Not without a warrant anyway."

"They know this is a murder inquiry, right?"

"Yes, sir. I explained that."

"Get a hold of a magistrate. Obtain a warrant," Caslin said.

"It's Sunday afternoon, sir," Holt replied. Caslin fixed him with a stare. Holt didn't protest any further, merely nodded and returned to his desk. He'd already picked up his phone before Caslin turned back to Hunter.

"I want to know who Farzaad Amin is and I want to know now," he instructed her, heading back into his office and pushing the door closed.

"Yes, sir," Hunter said to herself. "Me, too."

Caslin cut a frustrated figure pacing his office. Up until now, all the available evidence indicated that Amin was the victim of a vicious, racially aggravated assault. That was, however, Caslin's biggest issue. So much of the evidence had been laid out for them and the real detail, the forensics they would expect to find, had been sanitised. To Caslin, this signified an understanding of police procedure or at the least, a knowledge of forensic methodology. A knock on the door snapped him out of his thought process. Holt entered with a smile on his face.

"I've got a magistrate who is willing to see me. It'll mean heading out to his golf club but we'll have the warrant for Amin's bank account by the close of play," Holt said with enthusiasm. "That means I can be on to the bank first thing."

"Good work," Caslin told him. The detective constable appeared to hover in the office doorway, almost as if considering whether or not to say what was on his mind. "What is it, Terry?" Holt stepped in, closing the door behind him. He appeared nervous but buoyed by Caslin's willingness to hear him out.

"I wanted to have a word, sir," he said, glancing over his shoulder in the direction of the squad room beyond. Caslin followed his line of sight, catching Hunter's eye for a fleeting moment.

"And?"

Holt cleared his throat. "I've been in the job for ten years now. CID for the last four," Holt said. "I know my performance hasn't always been...

the most prolific in terms of results but… I've improved. I mean, I've made a real effort…"

"You want a leg-up?" Caslin said in conclusion.

Holt nodded, "I think I've earned it."

"Earned it?" Caslin said, furrowing his brow.

"Yeah," Holt stated. "With Hunter moving to Thames Valley, I thought I'd have a good shot at making DS but now, what with her staying put, I don't see it happening." Caslin sat back in his chair, putting his hands behind his head and interlocking his fingers. "I mean, she's a decent officer and all but do you think she's still up for it?"

"Are you saying she isn't?"

Holt shrugged, "Not exactly."

"Then what, *exactly*?"

"Well, you saw it yourself the other day. When it goes down, do you honestly think she'll have your back, or mine, when it comes down to it?" Caslin sat forward, placing his palms on the desk before him and drumming his fingers. In the corner of his eye, he saw Hunter watching them, doing her best to appear casual. He wondered whether she knew what they were discussing. Turning his gaze back to Holt, he fixed his gaze on the younger man.

"Let me make something very clear to you, Terry," Caslin said, his tone taking on a level of menace that most seldom witnessed. "DS Hunter is a far superior detective to you, in ways that you will never comprehend. Even working sub-par, she puts you in the shade and if I hear you questioning her competence or attitude in this way again, you and I will be having words. Bottom line, Terry, you go before she does. Is that clear enough for you?"

Holt visibly shrank before him. However he'd envisioned the conversation playing out, this wasn't it. Ashen-faced, he was at a loss for words, merely murmuring, "Yes, sir."

"As for your performance," Caslin went on, "when I first came to Fulford Road, you were underperforming in all aspects, other than studying the form at the bookies. It did not go unnoticed." Holt looked down, averting his eyes from Caslin's gaze. "With that said, you're right. You've improved. You'll walk through the exams but whether you'll make a decent sergeant remains to be seen. If you want me to back you, then really *earn it*, Terry. Prove to me you're capable but don't do it by stepping on your colleagues. One day, you might need them and we've all got long memories."

Holt raised his head and met the stare of his senior officer. He nodded an acknowledgement and stood up, leaving the office without another word. Caslin watched him go, annoyed by his comments but at the same time, admiring the renewed ambition that had always appeared to be so sorely lacking in the DC.

Glancing across to Hunter, Caslin noticed her gaze was tracking Terry Holt all the way back to his desk. He would never share the thought with Holt nor anyone else for that matter, but he'd be lying if he said he hadn't contemplated similar concerns about his detective sergeant. Hunter was different since she'd returned. A brush with death was traumatic and hers had severely impacted her personal life, not only her career. Time would tell whether or not she could find her way back.

In his mind at least, she deserved the shot. Scooping up his phone from the desk, Caslin scrolled down through his contacts until he found his target and dialled it. The call connected and was swiftly answered.

"Just the man," a voice said from the other end of the line. "I was hoping to pick your brains over something."

"Great minds think alike," Caslin replied. "The usual?"

"The usual," the voice responded and both men hung up.

Caslin stood up, crossed the room and pulled on his coat. Slipping the mobile into a pocket, he left his office. Passing Hunter in the squad room, he drew her attention.

"I'll be on the mobile if anyone needs me," he said without breaking step. Hunter fell into step alongside him. Once out of the squad room and the earshot of others, she stopped him.

"Can I ask what that was about before, with Terry? It looked pretty heated and he's been quiet ever since."

Caslin met her eye, "Nothing to be concerned about. Okay?" Hunter didn't break the eye contact, almost as if she was trying to read inference into Caslin's expression but failing to do so.

"Okay," she replied. Caslin set off, leaving her alone in the corridor. He sensed her watching him as he made his way to the stairs. No good would come from him enlightening her as to what Holt had said. If she was curious as to where he was heading, she didn't voice it.

CHAPTER THIRTEEN

THE PUB WAS DOING a brisk trade for early on a Sunday evening. It would appear that the darkening of the skies leant itself to being in an establishment found largely underground. The Cellars were equal to the needs of its patrons throughout the year. In the summer, they were blessed with a large walled beer-garden that could comfortably accommodate a hundred people or more. Whereas in the depths of winter, the vaulted brick ceilings and atmospheric lighting of the old cellars themselves proved to be quite a draw.

Caslin found Jimmy Sullivan in a booth in the lower tier. The next table had a small group of diners seated at it, enjoying an early meal. Caslin slid into his seat opposite his friend. A pint was pushed across the table which he gratefully accepted. Acknowledging Sullivan by way of taking a mouthful of beer, he wiped the froth from his mouth with the back of his hand.

"How's life treating you, Jimmy?"

"Better than if I was a billionaire," Sullivan replied with a cheeky wink.

"There is that," Caslin replied with a smile. "What can you tell me about him?"

"Kuznetsov?" Sullivan replied, Caslin nodded. "Atypical of his kind. A real rags-to-riches story. If I wrote it as fiction, my editor would toss it aside as too far-fetched."

"He came from obscurity, didn't he?"

"Son of a coal miner from a provincial town. He made some acquaintances that served him well. As the Soviet Bloc collapsed, he found he was well placed to benefit. He had a knack for media, a natural talent you might say. The technological revolution that we all got swept up in back in the nineties, changed things."

"Some of us are still trying to catch up," Caslin stated, seeing off half his pint.

"As I understand it, he just understood the way things were changing and turned it to his advantage," Sullivan continued. "What with those old party allegiances that he'd fostered, he found himself in the unlikely position as something of a kingmaker when it came to politics."

"Sounds like you know him pretty well?"

Sullivan smiled, "It's my job to know."

"So, what went wrong?"

"Ahh..." Sullivan said, drinking from his glass. "Arrogance, greed, alongside the old adage of becoming a victim of his own success."

"How so?"

"He rapidly made himself the *go to* man of the moment. You know what politics is like. The rewards are fantastic, whichever country you're running in. With that comes a lot of competition. Once you pick a side, you make enemies. And let's also not forget we're talking about a man who seemed to revel in poking the bear."

"With a landscape such as the one in Russia, even those on your side will come to fear you," Caslin added. Sullivan nodded, draining his glass. He pushed the empty across the table, in front of Caslin, who finished his own at the same time.

"Your round."

Caslin stood and made his way up to the next level, picking his way through the throng towards the bar. Putting the glasses on the counter, he thought about Sullivan's words. Had Kuznetsov overreached? If his enemies were powerful political figures, there may well be some mileage in the threats made against his life. That would place his investigation against formidable opponents. The barman took his order, two more pints and a couple of chasers to go along with them. Receiving the change from a twenty, he pocketed the money and picked up the tray bearing their drinks. Returning to the booth, Caslin negotiated the steps down and Sullivan picked his drinks up before he'd managed to set the tray down on the table.

"Cheers," he said, downing the scotch in one. Caslin followed.

"If you had to guess," Caslin asked, "hypothetically speaking, were he to have been killed, where would you target your focus? The politics or the business?"

Sullivan laughed but lowered his voice before answering, "He was a Russian billionaire. Do you really think you can separate the two?"

"Humour me." Sullivan sat back, pursing his lips as he considered the question. After a few moments he leant forward, placing one hand on the table and the other on his fresh pint.

"Much of his business interests have been seized in the past few years."

"Either in the east or, more recently, by European governments. I know."

"Those that they are aware of anyway," Sullivan said, his eyes flitting about the bar. Caslin sat forward in his chair.

"I understood he was facing a winding-up order and was practically broke?"

"So, they say," Sullivan said. "Personally, I don't buy it. Not that I doubt the competence of the HMRC, mind you. When it comes to money, they are surprisingly efficient if they choose to be."

"Meaning?"

Sullivan took a large swig from his drink, looking around to make sure those nearby weren't paying them any attention before continuing, "Guys like Nestor Kuznetsov, who made it big very quickly, came onto the international radar in quick succession. Some of them were *apparatchiks* – politicians who survived from the old communist regimes – others arose out of the ruins of the KGB. They were lesser-known faces. Some, such as Kuznetsov, were tied to these people and made fortunes off the back of them. Whoever they were, they didn't want their money staying in the Motherland but to move it was, and still is, not easy."

"Why did they need to move it?" Caslin asked.

"Not least because they'd acquired it in an underhand, if not illegal fashion. If they'd stolen it, either through purchasing state-owned assets at knockdown prices, bribery or a mixture of both, what was to stop others from stealing from them?"

"They had to get it out of the country where it would be safe," Caslin concluded.

"Exactly. Once into the international markets, the state apparatus was nullified," Sullivan said emphatically. "The problem is, state controls on the levels of financial movement restricted how much they could transfer. The regime didn't want an exodus of wealth so they sought to control it through ever tighter means. Factor in European money-laundering regulations and you have quite a problem with which to overcome."

"They can get around these problems, though?"

"Of course. You just need to be creative that's all."

"Sounds easy," Caslin mused with a hint of sarcasm.

"Far from it," Sullivan continued, "but once you have a network of foreign assets to call upon it is eminently doable."

"Assets?"

"Willing locals. A network of people with vested interests to help you. We're getting into offshore accounts, shell companies, trusts that administer philanthropic funds. All of which will be used to funnel money in and out of countries to fund investment projects, property deals, business acquisitions and the like."

"They still need to transfer money, though. Right?"

Sullivan rocked his head from side to side, scrunching up his nose as if to imply Caslin was on the right track, "Sort of," he said. "Look at it this way, for example. You have a deal that needs financing back in Moscow. Your asset, a UK national, agrees to buy a property you own in Belgravia," Sullivan referenced one of the most prestigious property locations in London, "to fund the purchase, he takes out a mortgage but instead of transferring the money to you, he invests it in your Moscow scheme. When the deal comes off, the profits from the development come in and only then does he pay you the purchase price."

Caslin thought on it, "So, what happens next?" Sullivan chuckled at his lack of comprehension, irritating him.

"What do you mean? That's it. It's done. You've raised money to pay for your investment without having to transfer anything out of Russia. The profits come back, paying you for the house in Belgravia, paying back the mortgage and none of it is in your name. The trail becomes hard to follow, particularly if your involvement is kept a secret."

"But you don't have the money."

Sullivan shook his head, "No but your trusted lieutenant does and it's untraceable to you. What's more, it's clean as a whistle."

"What happens to the money then?"

"Your associates will buy cars, property, whatever you like. You purchase them at stupid prices, sell them on, draw your money that way. Of course, often you never see or touch any of these assets. They are bought and sold in seconds, laundering millions in a few strokes."

"Sounds crooked," Caslin said, sipping at his pint.

"Oh, absolutely but, and this is the kicker, it washes the money to the point of being untraceable."

"And that was important for the likes of Kuznetsov?"

"With Kuznetsov, he is hardly popular in some parts of eastern Europe these days. As soon as his money is tagged somewhere, someone will go after it. It was in his interests to be as opaque as possible."

"Are you suggesting Kuznetsov had money that we are not aware of?"

"Without doubt."

"Where?"

Sullivan shook his head, grinning as he raised his pint to his lips.

"Now, if I knew that, so would the HMRC, wouldn't it? Besides, I'm a journalist. You're the detective!"

Caslin sank back in his chair, cursing himself for hoping that Sullivan was about to give him a massive heads-up. If he was right, however, analysing Kuznetsov's associates could provide a strong lead.

"Not a suicide then?" Sullivan asked.

"I never said that."

"You didn't have to. It's written all over your face."

"Is it that obvious?" Caslin asked. Sullivan grinned.

"What about the other one? The murder of the paedo?"

Caslin shook his head, "He's not a paedophile as far as I'm aware. Not having a great deal of joy with that one, though, if I'm honest. It's early days."

"Doesn't help to have Osgood-Bellamy in town either, does it?" Sullivan said. Caslin shook his head. "Nasty piece of work, he is," Sullivan added.

"Tapped into the mood of the public, though. Somehow, he's being touted as some kind of hero. Not too long ago, the likes of him wouldn't have gained any traction at all," Caslin said bitterly.

"Sign of the changing times."

"Hopefully, it's more of a blip than a sea change."

"Amen to that," Sullivan replied, standing. Indicating towards Caslin's drink with his own empty glass, he asked, "Same again?" Caslin checked the time, knowing that he probably shouldn't but nodded an affirmative anyway.

THE SOUND of the clapper striking *Great Peter*, York Minster's largest bell, carried from the North-West Tower across the city to signify the time had reached eleven o'clock.

Caslin stumbled on the uneven slabs beneath his feet. At least, that was his excuse. Although, he sought to mitigate the outcome of the impromptu drinking session by acknowledging it had been a while since he'd spent an entire evening with a friend, at his favourite haunt. Jimmy Sullivan was good company. Quick witted and, almost always, relaxed company.

The evening had passed swiftly. The journalist's knowledge of the darker elements of society never ceased to amaze Caslin. His own world was forever populated by shady individuals who most members of society only ever came across in works of fiction. They were both paid to wade through the cesspool, albeit for different reasons.

One day, Caslin thought he might find out what motivated his friend to do what he did. For himself, Caslin was driven to make a difference. As the years passed, the tiers of success became harder to measure. Feeling a little nauseous, Caslin reckoned it probably hadn't been the best idea to head back to Sullivan's apartment after leaving the Cellars. Hopefully, the walk back into the centre to his home in Kleiser's Court would revive him a little.

A shriek cut through the still air of the freezing night, startling him. Stopping in his tracks, Caslin looked around in an attempt to determine where it originated from. At this time on a Sunday night, most of the city was deserted without even the hum of traffic to break the silence. The clouds parted, revealing a bright, full moon in the sky above. The surrounding area was bathed in silver light, eerie and foreboding. Another scream. Caslin took off along the street, making a right turn at the next intersection. Within fifty feet of the turn, he saw a figure slumped on the steps at the entrance to a building.

Breaking into a sprint, he approached the woman, dropping to his haunches alongside her and reaching out he touched her shoulder. She looked up at him, fear and borderline panic in her eyes. Tears wet her face and she was shaking.

"What is it? What's happened?" Caslin asked. She couldn't speak, such was her emotional state but raising her right hand, she pointed into the building. Caslin looked at the entrance doors, now realising where he was. He was outside the Islamic Centre, the largest mosque in the city.

One of the double doors was open and Caslin could see a flickering light further inside. At first, he thought it was the electrics but within moments the light grew in size and intensity. The building was on fire.

"Is anyone inside?" he asked. The woman nodded. Rising, he rummaged through his coat pocket searching for his phone as he took the steps, two at a time. He was inside before he made the emergency call for assistance, requesting the attendance of all three emergency services.

The entrance lobby was empty, spartanly furnished with a noticeboard detailing upcoming events, prayer times and the like. A wide staircase was set off to his right, providing access to the upper floors and a corridor in front of him led further into the building, now lit by an orange glow. Caslin hesitated but only for the briefest of moments. He knew where he had to go, towards the flames.

Moving forward, the fire appeared to be confined to an interior room, he deduced to be roughly halfway into the bowels of the building and on the eastern side. Slowing as he approached the doorway, Caslin steeled himself.

Peering around into the room, he saw the fire was taking hold. The far side of the room was ablaze where the flames were at their most intense. They were climbing the curtains and the walls, running at pace across the ceiling, spreading throughout the room. Black smoke billowed out into the corridor where Caslin stood, fanned by the breeze of a broken window at the heart of the fire.

At that moment, the lights went out as the electrics shorted. He ducked low, covering his mouth and nose to limit his intake of the acrid smoke. Beside a table, frighteningly close to the advancing flames, a man lay apparently unconscious. Keeping low, Caslin made his way towards him. The intensity of the blaze was such that he had to use his coat as a shield.

Coming alongside the stricken man, Caslin knelt. He was elderly, probably well into his seventies and dressed in a cream thobe that stretched from shoulder to foot. Seeing no sign of visible injury, Caslin knew he had to get them out and fast. He could feel the intensity of the heat against his skin and it was alarming. He unceremoniously took a hold of the older man, grasping him by the clothing of his chest and hauling him upright. Glancing back towards the door, their only exit, Caslin was dismayed to see the flames rolling down from the ceiling above and licking at the doorframe. He assessed they had but seconds to escape.

Finding the strength from within, Caslin hoisted the man up and across his shoulders. Despite his age, he was far from frail and his frame was significant. Caslin suddenly felt a surge of fear, borne from a realisation that he might not be able to manage. Brushing the feeling aside, he made for the door, almost stumbling at two points under the weight of his load. The polystyrene roof tiles of the suspended ceiling were falling all around them, some on fire, others raining down droplets of molten plastic. The flames were in the cavity and spreading with frightening speed. Caslin staggered towards the door, knowing they would have to pass through the fire itself. He did so at pace.

Reaching the sanctuary of the corridor beyond, he found it too was now filled with black smoke. Above him, the heat from the ceiling told him they were in serious trouble. Breathing heavily, he set off for the entrance but he could no longer see the streetlights beyond, such was the ferocity of the flame and the smoke. Every breath stung within his lungs and seemed to offer less air. Every step became more laboured and Caslin felt his panic rising. Trying to keep low, away from the smoke, proved to be impossible with his charge across his shoulders and Caslin stumbled. Both men crashed to the floor.

Knowing that to remain where they were, even for a few seconds, could be the difference between life and death, Caslin rolled back onto his front and pulled himself up onto his knees. Visibility was now such that he couldn't see his hand in front of his face. Scrabbling around in the dark, he located the unconscious man's upper body and looped his own arms under the armpits, interlocking his hands across the chest. Having completely lost his bearings, Caslin felt the heat from the fire was more intense before him. Therefore, he set off down the corridor in the opposite direction, confident that was the way out.

His eyes were stinging and water was running from them along with the sweat. Trying to hold his breath, fearful of the toxic cloud surrounding him, Caslin found the going tough. He knew the distance to safety, once in the corridor, was less than forty feet from the source of the fire but it seemed an interminable distance now. Why weren't they safe already? The thought flashed through his mind that he'd taken the wrong decision and was now leading them into the building and not out of it. Panic threatened to consume him but he kept going.

With each step his charge felt heavier as did his own body. Each movement was slower. From nowhere, he felt a surge of pressure come at them. Before he knew it, Caslin found himself flat on his back with a rush of colour passing over him in stark contrast to the black that'd encompassed them thus far. Darkness followed and Caslin lay there. The polished concrete floor was solid beneath him, unforgiving and yet comfortable. The will to move was lost on him as was any sense of urgency. Caslin closed his eyes only to sense movement alongside, bringing him back to reality. A small, dancing, white light flashed before him. Suddenly, he felt something take a firm hold of him and he was moving again. This time, he was being dragged along the corridor only at a far greater speed. Caslin could see movement around him but no detail, just a vague notion that he was no longer alone.

Within moments they were outside. Caslin coughed. A violent, hacking cough that racked his entire body. A hand placed a mask over his mouth and nose, the oxygen that flowed into his lungs from it was a relief. Rolling his head to the side, against the protestations of his medic, Caslin scanned the scene for the man he'd left behind only to see him being lifted onto a gurney with paramedics and firefighting personnel in attendance. Only then, could Caslin relax. As his senses stabilised, Caslin took note of the two appliances dispatched to tackle the blaze along with several ambulances. Police were also in attendance, cordoning off the area and assisting the firefighters in doing their job.

"Sir, is there anybody else left in the building?" a voice asked. Caslin looked over to see the station officer standing alongside, identifiable by his white helmet.

"I'm sorry. I've no idea," he replied honestly, removing his mask. The man left without another word and Caslin could hear him handing out instructions to his assembled team. There was no sign of the woman he had encountered outside the mosque when he'd first arrived. He assumed she was being taken care of. Now feeling no ill effects from the alcohol he'd consumed, the surge of adrenalin having successfully countered it, Caslin considered the fire. Tapping the forearm of the paramedic who was in the process of wrapping a blanket around him, to fend off the cold and any potential advance of shock, he sought the attention of the station officer. The paramedic brought the officer back. Caslin, feeling in better control of his faculties, sat up but kept the oxygen mask close to him. He spoke between deep draws.

"I'm not sure what happened but from the look of the room, where the fire started, I'd say there was an accelerant in play."

"How are you so sure?"

"The intensity of the blaze where it originated. It was too fast. There were no appliances, open fires or anything like that that would justify such a fire to start there," Caslin explained. "The window to the adjacent street was also smashed."

"Thanks, I'll tell the investigator as soon as he arrives," the officer said.

"The man. The one I tried to pull out."

"The Imam? It looks like he suffered a heart attack," the officer told him. "His wife was with him and claims something was thrown through the window at them. It all started from there. Probably the window you were talking about. By the sounds of it, the police will have another investigation on their hands."

"Like I'm not busy enough," Caslin said. Then it must've dawned on the officer that Caslin was a policeman. "Something knocked me over, before your team pulled me out."

"We think there was a flashover. It's a bit early to say but possibly that was caused by the fire reaching the kitchens."

"Right," Caslin said quietly. The officer nodded to him and excused himself. Caslin took another draw on the oxygen.

"We're going to take you to hospital and assess how much smoke you've inhaled, okay?" the paramedic told him. Caslin acknowledged him but offered no further comment as he watched the hoses of the brigade appliances being trained on the building. The fire had spread rapidly. If anyone else was inside, chances are it was already too late for them.

CHAPTER FOURTEEN

Caslin climbed out of the passenger seat onto the pavement on High Petergate, a stone's throw from York Minster. Handing the taxi-driver a ten pound note, he didn't wait for the change and set off for home. His apartment, located in the historic Shambles, was a mere two-minute walk away nestled amongst the artisan shops and cobbled streets.

During the day, the ability to negotiate the crowds at any time of the year was essential. However, nothing moved at this hour. Satisfied he'd suffered no major damage from his earlier exploits that evening, the medical staff discharged him. A chest that tightened each time he drew breath along with the occasionally hacking up of phlegm, the colour of coal dust, was considered normal under the circumstances. Discomforting, certainly but unworthy of an extended stay. A conclusion Caslin was more than happy with. He'd had enough of stays in hospital to last him for quite some time.

Rounding the corner onto Stonegate, he was a few steps from home. Glancing at his watch, it was a little before three in the morning and it felt like it. He unlocked the communal access door, entered the passageway and trotted up the steps to his apartment. The exertion brought on yet another coughing fit and he had to brace himself against the wall of the stairwell. Entering his apartment, he didn't bother to flick on the lights. Instead, he walked into his living room, illuminated with an orange glow by the lights hanging from the buildings in the street outside. He chose not to draw the curtains and ignored the fleeting notion to pour himself a scotch, instead, sinking into his armchair and resting his head. Any feeling that he'd had a drink earlier in the day had long since left him. The only urge he had left to fulfil was that of sleep. Closing his eyes, Caslin sought to clear his mind of the jumbled thoughts gnawing away at him.

The Kuznetsov case had more to it, his instinct told him so. More pressing though, was the spark of racial hatred threatening to set light to the city. His fear was such that the attack on the mosque was but the beginning and although on this occasion, no one had died, any further escalation could well change matters. Fortunately, it transpired no one else was in the building when the fire was lit and the Imam was now in a stable condition, at least, when Caslin had left the hospital. Had he not been passing, Caslin was well aware they'd have another murder case on their hands rather than an arsonist to chase down.

Caslin awoke with a start. It took a moment to get his bearings. Still dark outside, he glanced at the clock on the wall. It was nearly four in the morning. He must've dozed off in the chair. There was a forceful knock on the door to his apartment. Figuring that was what had woken him, he dragged himself upright, ignoring the pain that screamed at him as a result of stiffened muscles. Crossing to the front windows overlooking the street, he cast a wary eye down onto Stonegate. Everything was still, without any movement in sight. There was another knock. Whoever was seeking his attention had already bypassed the security door to the communal entrance or had he left it open? He couldn't remember. Whoever was so keen to see him would, in all likelihood, wake his landlady in the next apartment if they didn't rein it in.

Making his way into the hallway, he approached the door and peered through the spy hole. Two men stood on the landing, one in front of the door while the other waited a few steps to the rear, facing down the stairwell. He didn't know them, of that he was sure but the first appeared somewhat familiar. Unhooking the latch, Caslin opened the door. The man standing before him was probably in his late fifties, smartly dressed in a well-tailored overcoat. His facial appearance was well manicured, clean-shaven and bearing frameless glasses. He smiled warmly, in greeting.

"Inspector Caslin, I believe?" he said in a tone matching his smile. Caslin bobbed his head in acknowledgement.

"You do know what time it is, don't you?"

"I apologise, Inspector. I'm still on Washington time," he said sincerely. Caslin did a quick calculation in his head.

"Still makes it late," he said, wondering whether he was right.

"Indeed, but some things just cannot wait," he agreed. "My name is Walsh, Cory Walsh. May I come inside?" he asked, removing his gloves and offering Caslin his hand. Caslin took it and inclined his head to invite him inside.

Caslin glanced beyond him as he stepped aside, allowing his visitor room to enter, towards the other man standing patiently in the background. As if aware of the attention, he glanced in Caslin's direction but only for a fleeting moment. He was younger, focussed. Caslin had seen the likes of him before, most likely ex-military, now working in the private sector. Walsh turned to see Caslin checking out his associate.

"My friend will wait outside, Inspector Caslin. We are quite sure I am safe with you."

"Any reason you wouldn't be safe anywhere else?" Caslin asked, pushing the door to and directing his guest into the living room.

"One can never be too careful," Walsh replied, eyeing the surroundings as he entered the room. Caslin followed, flicking on the nearest light. The lamp caused him to blink with it being far brighter than the light permeating the apartment from the street outside. Caslin offered a seat with an open hand, leaning his back against the wall and folding his arms before him.

"What brings you to my door in the middle of the night, Mr Walsh?"

"Forgive the clandestine approach, Mr Caslin. I know it appears a little cloak and dagger but I do have my reasons," Walsh said, putting his gloves together and placing them neatly on the dining table alongside him. "I saw you the other day at the demonstration on Walmgate. The one that got out of hand. You saw me too, didn't you?"

"I did," Caslin recalled. Walsh had been the passenger in the Maybach. He hadn't gotten around to following up on the licence plate. Presumably now, he no longer had the need. "Why were you there, Mr Walsh?"

"Please, you can call me Cory," Walsh replied.

Caslin shrugged. "If you like."

"I was in the city for a meeting. A rallying call so to speak. That's what I do these days, since I retired from my business activities."

"What kind of business did you do, Mr Walsh?"

"Investments, brokerage. I ran my own firm, quite successfully I should add, for several decades."

"Financial securities?"

Walsh nodded.

"And now?"

"I'm a lobbyist, you could say," Walsh said, with a smile. To Caslin, he carried the confidence and assuredness of a successful man but also managed a quiet affability that made him come across as an instantly likeable figure. Which Caslin felt was odd, for he rarely liked anyone on their first meeting. "My work takes me all over the developed world. Sometimes I lose track of exactly where I am."

"And ensures you keep odd hours."

"Quite true, Nathaniel," Walsh said grinning. "Do you mind if I call you, Nathaniel?"

Caslin shrugged to indicate he didn't mind, "What is it I can do for you?"

"Am I to understand you are leading an investigation into the murder that occurred the other day. The one at the flat, Farzaad… I'm sorry, his name escapes me."

"Farzaad Amin," Caslin offered. It wasn't being withheld and had been splashed across the media over the previous few days. "What of it? Did you know him?"

Walsh shook his head, "No, I'd never met the man. However," he said, shaking an index finger pointedly, "I am led to believe that you are following this up as a racially-motivated crime. Would this be correct?"

Caslin grimaced, exaggerating his expression, "I'm sorry. There's no way I can discuss an ongoing case with a civilian. I'm sure you understand. A couple of questions of my own spring to mind, though. How do you know that, hypothetically speaking and… why do you care enough to come to my door in the middle of the night? I have to tell you, *pretty creepy*, if you weren't such a well-mannered guy."

Walsh smiled, "Let me just say, I move in influential circles. Sometimes, I come across information that's not widely disseminated."

"That doesn't make me feel any more comfortable, I have to say," Caslin offered. "So, why are you here?"

"I think you're approaching this from the wrong angle," Walsh said, fixing his gaze on Caslin.

"Is that so? Tell me why?" Caslin asked, intrigued. Walsh smiled. Reaching into an inner pocket of his overcoat, he retrieved a small notebook and pen. Placing the book on the table, he opened it up to a blank page and scribbled something. Tearing the page out and folding it in half, he returned both notebook and pen to the confines of his coat and stood up. Picking the paper up from the dining table, he crossed the room to stand before Caslin. Holding out the slip of paper, Caslin reached over and took a hold but Walsh didn't release his own grip. Caslin met his eye.

"If I were to tell you what I think I know, Inspector. You would probably have me sectioned," he said, releasing his hold on the paper. Caslin took it but kept his gaze on the man standing over him. "I often find it better for someone to choose their own path with which to reach their destination. That way, the journey is far more rewarding. Perhaps then, we can speak again. Please don't get up. I'll see myself out."

Caslin broke eye contact as Walsh left the living room, turning his attention to the piece of paper. He casually opened it as the sound of the latch to his front door, clicking into place, came to his ear.

There was a name written upon the paper, alongside a mobile phone number. The name was Alexander Nairn. Placing the paper on the side table next to him, Caslin stood and crossed the room. Coming to stand before one of the windows overlooking the street, he glanced down as Walsh and his minder exited Kleiser's Court and set off along Stonegate. He watched them until they disappeared from view a few seconds later.

There was something about that name that chimed in Caslin's memory but for the life of him, he couldn't remember why. Absolutely certain that he had never met the man nor come across him in an inquiry, Caslin left the window and returning to his seat, scooping up his phone. Accessing the internet, he typed in the name and hit return. Within moments a list of web links came up and then he realised. Alexander Nairn had been killed the previous year in York.

Caslin vaguely remembered the incident but knew it was covered by colleagues based out of the Acomb Road Station. Refreshing his memory with detail from a local newspaper, Caslin read how the property financier had committed suicide by throwing himself in front of a train. It had been broad daylight on a hot summer's day, witnessed by dozens of commuters. Nairn had died instantly. Scanning through several entries on the returned list, Caslin was none the wiser as to how the unequivocal suicide fitted into this case. Blowing out his cheeks, he brought his palms up to his face and rubbed at his eyes with the heel of his palms. Suddenly, he felt tired.

Scrolling through his contacts on his phone, Caslin reached the CID telephone number for the Acomb Road Police Station. He waited patiently for the call to be answered. It wasn't long.

"CID," an abrupt voice answered.

"DI Caslin, Fulford Road," he said.

"Hello, sir. It's Mark Sampson. Trouble sleeping? What can I do for you?"

"Hi Mark. I know it's going back a bit but do you recollect the Nairn suicide from last year? The guy threw himself—"

"In front of a train," Detective Sergeant Sampson finished for him. "Aye, I do. What of it?"

"Who was the investigating officer?"

"Oh… you've got me there. I'd have to look it up. Why do you ask… at four-thirty in the morning?"

Caslin laughed, "You know me, Mark. I couldn't sleep. Any chance you could fish out the file for me? I'll be over to yours first thing to have a look."

"Yes, of course. It's been a quiet one tonight. Only the little matter of the fire-bombing over your way that's put everyone on edge. It's mental. Did you hear about that?"

"Yeah, yeah, I heard something about it," Caslin said.

"Leave it with me and I'll dig out what I can. I'm not sure how much there will be, though. It was a pretty clean suicide, investigation wise anyway."

"Thanks, Mark. I'll see you," Caslin said, hanging up.

Rising from his seat, Caslin tossed his phone aside and headed into the bedroom. Not bothering to get undressed, he sank onto the bed and closed his eyes. However, sleep would not come.

THE SOUND of the car horn caught his attention. Checking for a break in the traffic, Caslin trotted between two cars and crossed to the other side of the road. Hunter leant across and opened the passenger door for him. Caslin levered it further open with his foot and slid into the seat. Passing Hunter, one of the coffees he had just purchased while waiting for her, he placed his own precariously onto the dashboard as he attached his seatbelt.

"How are you, after last night?" Hunter said.

"I'll be grand, don't worry," he replied, retrieving his coffee cup before Hunter pulled back out into the commuter traffic. The car behind flashed their lights, Caslin caught a glimpse in the side mirror unsure of whether it was an act of aggression or not. Hunter didn't comment so nor did he. Hunter negotiated the traffic of the ring road like a professional. A professional racing driver anyway. She never used to drive in such a manner, always being measured and methodical. Much like her approach to life in general.

"So, are you going to tell me why we're heading to Acomb Road?" she asked, tapping her steering wheel and sounding the horn to encourage a car in front to edge forward and allow her to take the next left turn. The car did so and she accelerated through the gap, the nearside front tyre sliding along the kerb.

"The station isn't going anywhere you know?" Caslin said. Hunter flicked a glance in his direction but said nothing. "Do you remember a suicide from last year? A guy killed himself by jumping in front of a train?"

"Vaguely," Hunter said. "What of it?"

"That's exactly what I intend for us to find out," Caslin replied, looking over at her. He considered taking the lid off his coffee cup, preferring not to drink through the slot but, as Hunter took another turn and he braced one arm against the door to steady himself, he thought better of it.

They pulled into the car park of the station ten minutes later. Far smaller than Fulford Road, largely due to the size of the area they policed, the officers based at Acomb Road were responsible for covering the western side of the city. Getting out of the car, Caslin finished what remained of his coffee while Hunter brought hers inside with them. They signed in at the front desk and were buzzed through into the back offices. They had both been here many times, Hunter in particular was greeted warmly by every face they came across. Having been stationed there in her first role within CID, as a detective constable, six years previously, she was a popular member of the team and most hadn't seen her since her enforced absence from the job.

On the way up the stairs they came across DS Sampson on the half-landing, presumably on his way home following the night shift.

"Sir," he said, shaking Caslin's hand. Hunter got a quick embrace bringing a big smile to her face. "It was DC Watkins who investigated your man, Nairn. He's upstairs," Sampson said, indicating over his shoulder, "I told him you were coming."

"Thanks, Mark," Caslin said. "Did you take a look yourself?"

"I did, aye," he replied. "I didn't see anything odd about it, though. Why, what's your interest?"

"Only a passing one," Caslin replied. Sampson acknowledged him, offered Hunter a wink and set off downstairs.

They resumed their course up to CID, entering the compact squad room moments later. DC Watkins noted their arrival and came over to greet them. He shook their hands in turn. Caslin hadn't come across the young man before. He guessed he was new to the team seeing as Hunter appeared to have no connection with him either.

"Tell me about Alexander Nairn," Caslin asked, as he was passed the case file and opened it to examine the contents.

"Relatively straightforward, sir," Watkins began. "A property financier, cum-developer. Left his office one afternoon and made his way to the railway line, clambered over a security fence and stepped in front of the next passing train."

"Witnesses?" Caslin asked, without looking up from the file.

"At least seven, sir," Watkins said. "Two people reported seeing him standing behind the fence before scaling it to gain access to the line. The others watched as he casually walked onto the line as the train approached."

"Was there anyone nearby that he was communicating with or perhaps talking to on the phone?" Hunter asked.

Watkins shook his head, "No. He was alone on the track. Witnesses reported he appeared very calm. He was a well-dressed businessman who looked out of place there but no one saw a cause for alarm until the approach of the train."

"Were you able to ascertain his state of mind? Any history of mental illness, anxiety?" Caslin said, glancing up.

Again, Watkins shrugged in the negative, "Not at all. His colleagues stated he appeared quite normal. He had a stressful job but nothing that appeared to overburden him. I must say, his wife was shocked but, speaking with her later, she seemed to piece past behaviours together. Ultimately, she wasn't surprised by what he did."

"The coroner ruled it as a suicide," Caslin said, scanning the transcript of the coroner's summation.

"Yes. We couldn't see it any other way."

"And there was nothing unusual. Nothing that struck you as odd or out of place?" Caslin asked.

Watkins shook his head, "Not at all. It was my first case but, even refreshing it in my mind this morning I don't see I would have done anything differently. It was a slam dunk."

"Appears so," Caslin replied.

"Sir?" Watkins enquired. Caslin looked to him, raising his eyebrows. "Can I ask why you want to know? Did I miss something?" he asked, looking and sounding nervous. Caslin shook his head.

"Not as far as I'm aware. It looks pretty concrete," he reassured him and watched as a weight appeared to lift from the young man's shoulders.

"So, why are you looking into it?"

"I'm not. Not really," Caslin replied with a half-smile. "Nairn's name has come up in an unrelated matter and we have to follow it up. That's all. Can we borrow this?" he asked, indicating the file he held in his hands.

"You'll have to sign for it," Watkins replied before realising he was stating the obvious.

"Of course," Caslin replied. Watkins turned to find a pen and Caslin passed the file to Hunter. She looked him in the eye with an inquisitive gaze. She knew there was something here but had no idea what Caslin was looking for. She leafed through the paperwork while Caslin signed the appropriate documentation. "There you go," Caslin said, handing the sheet back to the detective constable.

"You'll let me know if I can help, won't you?" Watkins asked. Caslin nodded. "Or, if you come across anything… you know, that…?"

"We will, son. We will," Caslin said, clapping him on the upper arm. With that said, they bid farewell and left CID. Hunter tucked the file under her arm as they descended the stairs back to the ground floor.

"What's going on, sir?" she asked quietly, once she was confident they'd not be overheard.

"There's one thing missing from that file," Caslin said, lowering his own voice as they made their way along the corridor towards the front desk.

"What's that?"

"A reason."

"C'mon, sir. There isn't always a reason someone does this."

"True," he agreed. "But young Watkins up there didn't have much cause to look for one."

"And we do?" Hunter pressed, as they walked through the security door into the lobby and out into the car park.

"Oh, yes," Caslin replied in an upbeat tone. "We most certainly do."

"What are we going to do with it?"

"Let's start with his colleagues."

CHAPTER FIFTEEN

Caslin felt his phone vibrating within his coat pocket. Closing Nairn's case file in his lap, he took out the phone and briefly looked at the screen before putting it away without answering. Hunter glanced at him, her expression conveying an unasked question.

"Matheson," Caslin said.

"Do I take it she has no idea where we are?" Hunter asked, turning off the engine and withdrawing the key. Caslin shook his head.

"She'd only worry," he replied, smiling. Opening his door, he got out. Hunter did likewise. Caslin glanced around. Their destination was a modest two-storey office building, nestled in between several similar, making up a small commercial development just beyond the city limits. Caslin judged they were close enough to take advantage of the public transport system but equally well positioned to exploit the road links in and out of York. The site was modern and not short of tenants for the office space.

They made their way to the entrance, Caslin noting the names attached to the allocated parking spaces set out in front. Two regular discolourations in the brickwork indicated plaques had been removed fairly recently, from spaces adjacent to one another. Hunter reached the door first, opening it and indicating for Caslin to go ahead. Walking through, Caslin observed the interior. There were four desks. Two were clearly unoccupied, judging by their level of tidiness, with a third that had several piles of paperwork strewn across it in an apparently haphazard manner. They were welcomed with a warm smile from the only person present, a lady, seated behind the remaining desk. She rose and came around to greet them.

"Good morning," she said. "My name is Lisa. How can I help you?"

"Good morning. We're looking to speak with Thomas Grey," Caslin said, eyeing her. She was in her forties, power dressed and approached with a confidence that Caslin found momentarily unsettling. He didn't know why, seeing as he had never held any issue with women as authority figures. Grey was Alexander Nairn's business partner, named in the file that Caslin had been reading through on their journey back into the city from Acomb Road.

"I'm afraid Mr Grey's schedule is already full today. Would you like to make an appointment?"

Caslin brandished his warrant card, "We don't need one." Lisa eyed his credentials, glancing in Hunter's direction who smiled in return.

"Oh, I see. May I ask what it is regarding?"

"Certainly. It's regarding the death of one of your colleagues, Alexander Nairn." She tensed at the mention of the name, almost imperceptibly, but her professional persona slipped for the briefest of moments. Caslin picked it up nonetheless.

"Please bear with me, if you wouldn't mind?" she said, taking a step back before turning and walking the short distance to her desk. Picking up the phone, she dialled an extension. The call was answered quickly and she turned her back on them, speaking at an almost inaudible level. Hanging up, Lisa turned to face them. The mask of business-like demeanour had returned. "He'll be with you shortly. Please take a seat, if you wish," she said, indicating an L-shape sofa arrangement in the corner behind them. Both of them chose to remain standing. Lisa returned to sit behind her desk while Caslin scanned the walls of the office.

There was a list of companies framed on the wall. Seemingly, this office housed the business activities of several others who were also registered at the same address. Elsewhere, there were copies of articles from professional publications citing awards attained by the company as well as photographs taken of successful developments, both at home and abroad. Caslin found his attention drawn to a commercial high-rise building in a skyline, he thought looked vaguely familiar.

"Where is this?" he asked Lisa who in turn, glanced up from her desk and looked over at the picture.

"Singapore."

"Oh," Caslin said, realising he was mistaken. "Do a lot of business there?"

"Not as much as we used to."

"Any particular reason for that?" No answer was forthcoming, though, as a door opened further along the only corridor into the building and a figure emerged. He almost glided down the corridor towards them. Caslin could tell he was eyeing them up as he approached. Acknowledging them with a nod, Caslin spotted an earpiece.

"Mr Grey will see you now," Lisa said.

The man sent to accompany them stepped aside, allowing Hunter and Caslin to go ahead with the gesture of an open palm. He fell into step behind them, keeping a respectful distance until they reached Grey's office. Their escort came past and opened it, indicating for them to enter. They were greeted by a suited man, in his fifties, who eagerly came across the office to shake their hands. He was stocky in frame, balding, with a well-lined face and tanned complexion. Evidently, he wintered in sunnier climes.

"Thomas Grey," he said, taking Caslin's hand.

"DI Caslin and DS Hunter, from Fulford Road CID," Caslin said.

"This is about Alex's suicide, I understand?"

"Of sorts."

"Please, sit down," Grey said, offering them a chair as he went to sit down behind his desk. "Would you like a coffee or something?"

"No, thank you," Caslin said, pulling out a chair and sitting down, Hunter alongside him. Glancing over his shoulder, Caslin saw Grey's minder, for he had no doubt that was what he was, take a position behind them to his left. He stood with his back to the wall, arms crossed behind his back but remained attentive.

"How then, may I help? I understood the inquest was closed last year," Grey asked, sitting forward, elbows on his desk.

"It was," Caslin began. "We're following up on another angle that has subsequently come to the fore. What can you tell us about Mr Nairn's state of mind at the time of his death? Why would he have taken the decision that he did that day?"

Grey blew out his cheeks, sitting back in his chair, "Hard to say, if I'm honest. I wasn't around much at the time as I'd been working away, on site."

"You deal in property?" Caslin asked.

Grey nodded. "It's a little more complicated than that. Acquisitions, developments, off-plan trading and the like."

"I see. Where is your largest market, would you say?"

"We are global, as are our investors," Grey announced, "and it's a globalised economy, no matter what some people may seem to think these days."

"So, were you aware of any difficulties that Mr Nairn was experiencing, financial, domestic or otherwise?"

"I thought this had all been covered?" Grey replied.

"Humour me," Caslin countered.

"Nothing specific." Grey shrugged. "But he was always someone who felt the pressure. They say divorce and buying a house are the most stressful things you can ever experience and he did the former. The latter, well, that's what we do, magnified by a factor of a hundred."

"Seems an odd profession to take up, in that case," Caslin said.

"I don't think either of us ever planned it, back in the day but we worked hard and you get out what you put in, don't you?"

"You knew him well?" Hunter asked. "I mean, you go back a long way?"

"Absolutely. We met in our twenties, got on well and it snowballed from there."

"Mr Nairn didn't have any business worries other than the general stress you mentioned?" Caslin asked.

Again, Grey shook his head, "No. Business has never been better. Susan, his ex, wasn't surprised about his suicide, though. She said he'd been struggling for a while but I didn't have a clue. I was just too busy to notice, I guess. To be honest, I really miss him both as a friend and as a business partner. It's been a tough six months. Why are you investigating Alex again?" Grey asked, sitting forward once more.

"We're not," Caslin said. "His name came up in an unrelated matter and we're following up."

"What matter?" Grey pressed, meeting Caslin's eye.

"We'll leave it there for now, Mr Grey," Caslin said, standing.

"Oh, really," Grey said, sounding surprised which piqued Caslin's interest.

"We're not sure how Mr Nairn fits into it but don't worry, we'll get to the bottom of it soon enough," Caslin said, smiling and trying to convey a determined attitude. Hunter cast him a fleeting glance but said nothing.

Grey took a deep breath, "Right you are. Well, if there is anything else you need, please get in touch and I'll see what I can do."

"Thank you for your time," Caslin said, offering his hand. Grey took it, shaking vigorously. Hunter smiled and inclined her head as she stood and the two of them made for the door. The minder opened it and they passed through, into the corridor. They were left to make their own way out.

Reaching the reception, Caslin stopped at Lisa's desk. She was just finishing a call and hung up as Caslin spoke.

"Lisa, can I ask you a couple of questions?" he asked. She nodded. "Did you know Mr Nairn well?"

"Yes, he was a wonderful man and a great boss. It was such a shame what happened."

"Were you here that day?" Hunter asked.

"Oh, yes. The office was full. We were much busier back then."

"Busier than now?" Hunter asked.

"Very much so," Lisa said, lowering her voice and nervously glancing behind her, back down the corridor. "There used to be four of us out here but now it's only me."

"They keep you busy?"

"Not recently," she replied.

"What can you tell us about that day, when Mr Nairn took his life?" Caslin asked.

"It started much as any other," Lisa began, "with a scheduled progress meeting between Mr Nairn and Mr Grey but it went a little sour."

"Mr Grey was also here that day? I mean, he wasn't away?"

"Yes, of course he was here. They only ever went away together. We used to call them the Krays. You know, after Ronnie and Reggie? They were like inseparable twins. Not that they are gangsters or anything," Lisa quickly stated. Caslin indicated for her to continue. "Part way through the meeting some men arrived, wanting to speak with both Mr Grey and Mr Nairn. It got a little nasty."

"Who were they?" Hunter asked.

She shook her head. "I don't know. Mr Grey said they were investors but I'd never met them before, but… they weren't the usual type of clients that we see here in the office."

"How so?" Caslin asked, intrigued.

"They were… I don't know how to put it. A little bit on the rough side. I mean, don't get me wrong, they had money, that was clear but they were… intimidating. I've never seen Mr Grey as animated as he was that day."

"What can you tell us about them?" Hunter asked.

"Not much, really. Foreign."

"Foreign?" Caslin noted. "Where from?"

"I don't know but they spoke English with an accent. Eastern Europeans, I would say."

"What was the issue?"

"They wanted payment. Apparently, they felt they were owed money and it was late in coming. There was a lot of shouting before they eventually left. I never found out the full details. I've no idea which development they were involved in, mind you. Mr Grey dealt with it personally. It was all very strange, though."

"What was?" Hunter asked.

Again, Lisa looked over her shoulder as if fearful of being overheard before leaning closer towards them, "Mr Nairn had expensive tastes. To be fair, they both share a love of material things but Mr Nairn kept an antique watch collection here, in the safe, in his office. He handed it over to those men before they left."

Caslin glanced at Hunter who met his eye and flicked her eyebrows as if to signal she was equally intrigued, "Tell me, what did Mr Grey's security do while all this was going down?"

"He didn't have them then. They appeared shortly after this incident. He always has one with him in the office and never goes anywhere without the others."

"Shortly after Mr Nairn committed suicide?"

"Yes," Lisa said, her brow furrowing as she spoke. "He'd never mentioned the need for any security up until that day."

"What happened after they left, the investors?" Caslin said.

"Mr Nairn came out of his office. He was pale… visibly shaken up. Frightened, even."

"And then?" Caslin asked.

Lisa shrugged, "He left the office without another word. That was the last time I saw him. Mr Grey told us the next day that he had been found on the railway line."

"Had you noticed any change in Mr Nairn in the period running up to his suicide?" Hunter asked.

"He was worried… preoccupied," Lisa replied. "Particularly, so soon after his friend's passing."

"His friend?"

"Martin Pocock," Lisa said. "He was a lawyer friend of both Mr Grey and Mr Nairn but I believe he was closer to Mr Nairn. He was a lovely man."

"And he died?"

"Yes, it shook them both up. The week before Mr Nairn's death, his helicopter crashed on its approach to Burleigh Park, on the weekend of the Horse Trials."

"How awful," Hunter said. "What did Mr Nairn say about it?"

"Nothing directly. He was clearly upset and had me cancel an order for his own helicopter the following day."

"He was buying one?"

Lisa nodded, "Yes. The exact same model."

"Did you give a statement about any of this to the police?" Caslin asked.

"No, I wasn't asked to," she replied. "Why, should I have? Is something wrong?"

Caslin shook his head, "No, no. We're just following up on a separate matter, don't worry. Here, take this," he said, passing her one of his contact cards from within his wallet, "and if you think of anything else, please give me a call. No matter how insignificant you think it might be. Okay?"

They excused themselves and left the building. Neither spoke until they were in the confines of Hunter's car. She started the engine.

"What do you make of all that?" she asked, looking over to him. Caslin thought about it for a moment before responding.

"I reckon there's far more to Mr Grey than he is willing to share with us. If business is booming why has he shed employees? Plus, how many property developers have you ever come across who feel the need for a personal protection team?"

"None. Makes you wonder where his investors come from?" Hunter said. "And the others, Nairn and Pocock? The former was a definite suicide."

"Without a doubt," Caslin agreed. "Too many witnesses. What drove him to it, though, is still very much open for debate. When we get back to Fulford Road get a run down on Pocock and try to find out what brought the helicopter down. It could just be an unfortunate coincidence but you know how I feel about them. Likewise, let's take a closer look at Thomas Grey. Do me a favour," he said, glancing over his shoulder behind them, "and pull up around the corner, would you?"

"Sure. Why?" Hunter asked, engaging the car in gear and reversing out of their parking space.

"Just a hunch," he replied. Hunter set off as if they were leaving the car park only to turn in and pull up outside the building across from Grey's office. They were close enough to keep the entrance in view but far enough away to be confident they wouldn't be noticed. Caslin sat back in his seat and sought to get comfortable.

"Where are we going with all of this?" Hunter asked, putting her head against the rest behind her. Caslin sighed. He knew he didn't have a proper answer, not yet anyway.

"We've been steered in this direction for a reason," he said. "Although at this point, the reasoning escapes me."

"Who's pointing the finger?" Hunter asked but Caslin didn't reply, choosing to keep it to himself. At least for the time being.

They didn't have long to wait. The door to Grey's business opened and out stepped the man himself, mobile phone pressed to his ear with his bodyguard one step behind. He was clearly agitated and saying something that Caslin couldn't make out from such a distance. He was certainly unhappy.

Grey reached his vehicle, a black Land Rover Discovery and unlocked it. Turning to his minder, with his back to Caslin and Hunter, he gesticulated with a raised hand, appearing dismissive. Whatever was said, he ended the call, tossed the phone into the car and climbed into the driver's seat slamming the door shut behind him. The bodyguard stood on the path alongside the car and watched as the Discovery was fired into life. The reversing lights came on and the vehicle moved.

"Right. This is us," Caslin said and Hunter sat upright, turning the key in the ignition. The car started and Hunter waited until Grey had reached the main road and was making the turn out, heading west. Only then did she engage first gear and set off to follow.

"Where do you think he's going?" Hunter asked.

"I don't know but he's rattled," Caslin said as Hunter slid into the line of traffic. They were four car lengths behind and heading towards the city centre.

Approaching the medieval walls, traffic slowed to such an extent that they would have no problem keeping up with him unless they got stuck at one of the traffic lights. Grey remained on the circular road, navigating around the city rather than entering the centre itself. "Oh, how much would I give to know what he's thinking right now?" Caslin said aloud.

Following the road, they crossed the Ouse, via Skeldergate Bridge, in sight of Clifford's Tower and watched as Grey took the next right followed by an immediate left onto Cromwell Road. Here, he pulled the car into a row of empty parking bays in the shadow of an established line of Beech trees. Hunter continued on up the hill and only pulled in herself once they were a relatively safe distance ahead, so as not to be observed. Caslin shifted in his seat, looking back down the road at the Discovery. Grey remained inside and Caslin thought he was making another phone call.

"Keep it running," Caslin said quietly. Hunter was watching proceedings in the rear-view mirror.

"Do you think he's waiting for someone?" she asked. Caslin didn't respond. He was curious and couldn't help but think they were onto something. His only wish was to know what. A few minutes passed and Grey put his phone away, resting both hands on the steering wheel. Staring straight ahead, he couldn't seem to keep his hands still for more than a few moments.

Soon after, another car came down the hill, passing them and slowing as it approached Grey's, before pulling in, in front of it. It was a silver Mercedes with tinted privacy-glass so they were unable to ascertain who or how many people were inside. Hunter noted down the registration number and picked up her radio, requesting the control room carry out a check on the vehicle with the national database. Having read out the index plate, she put the radio down and waited.

The daytime running lights switched off as Grey stepped out from his car and approached the Mercedes. A man opened the door to the front passenger seat and climbed out. He was heavily built, with a shaved head. He glanced around, surveying the immediate area before opening the rear door. Grey waited on the path, looking nervous, shifting his weight from one foot to the other and looking around furtively. A woman got out of the Mercedes. She cut a stylish figure, white-blonde hair, cut in a bob and sporting a cashmere overcoat, carrying past the knee.

Caslin knew her. The trademark oversized, cat-eye sunglasses were present, as was the pale, ivory skin of her complexion. Hunter's radio crackled as the results of the PNC check came back on the Mercedes. She picked up the unit only to pause as she registered what she was seeing.

"Well, I'll be damned," Caslin muttered, under his breath.

"What the hell is she doing here?" Hunter added, equally surprised.

"I have no idea but I'm going to enjoy finding out," Caslin replied as he watched Thomas Grey shake hands with Danika Durakovic.

CHAPTER SIXTEEN

THEY WATCHED as the conversation between Durakovic and Thomas Grey continued for several minutes. Grey became increasingly flustered as he drove home whatever point he was making. For her part, Danika remained calm with an impassive expression that Caslin knew only too well. From experience, he found it virtually impossible to interpret. Danika shook her head at several of the points Grey was conveying. This only seemed to further agitate him. Then it was Grey's turn to listen and despite several attempts to interrupt her, he did so with a pained expression on his face.

By now, Hunter had taken her camera from its case, tucked behind the driver's seat and was busy taking shots of the impromptu exchange.

"What do you think they're talking about?" she asked, just as Grey raised his hands, dramatically emphasising his point.

"When we get back to Fulford let's run a search through the Companies House Portal and see if any of Grey's business interests tie in with Danika's. I very much doubt these two were old school friends."

"Grey's name has never come up in relation to Durakovic before?" Hunter asked.

Caslin shook his head. "Not that I recall. The only property interests I remember she's involved in were multiple small to medium-sized enterprises that she uses to wash her money," he said, thinking about it while Hunter snapped away. Grey stood, crestfallen, as Danika turned away from him, sliding into the backseat of the Mercedes and the door was closed for her. He shook his head slowly, turning his face skywards.

"Sounds like he didn't get the response he was looking for," Hunter offered, taking a last photo of the encounter.

"It doesn't, does it?" Caslin replied. Grey watched the car pull out and set off in the direction that they themselves had come from. Rubbing his face with a palm, Grey's appearance was drained of the brash confidence that he'd exuded back in his office. The moment passed and anger flared within the businessman. Stalking back to the Discovery, he got in and slammed the door shut. Sparking the engine into life, the wheels squealed as he set off at speed. Pulling a U-turn in the road despite an oncoming vehicle, whose driver sounded his displeasure, Grey accelerated away in the direction of his office. Caslin and Hunter were left to consider what they'd witnessed.

"Shall we go?" Hunter asked.

"Aye," Caslin agreed. "Let's keep Durakovic's involvement to ourselves for the time being. Yes?"

Hunter looked over to him, attempting to read his expression, "Why?"

"Our recent brush with her has ruffled a few feathers upstairs," Caslin explained. "I don't want any suggestion the result of that case is clouding my approach to this one. At least, let's keep it under wraps until we know how this comes together."

"Forgive me, sir," Hunter said, Caslin met her eye, "but how does Nairn fit into our current case load? I mean, have we not got enough on already?" Caslin blew out his cheeks, weighing up a response. "After all, if you're asking me to keep quiet, I deserve to know what's going on. Right?"

Caslin nodded, "Someone, who I believe is close to Farzaad Amin has indicated we should look closer at Nairn's suicide."

"How is this person connected to Amin and what's their motivation?" Hunter said. Caslin turned his gaze forward and away from her.

"I don't know."

"Might he be... don't take this the wrong way... but, might he be playing you?"

Caslin let out a deep sigh, "There's always that possibility but I don't see it."

"How can you know?"

"You're right. I can't," Caslin conceded. "But it's fair to say that there is something going on here we're not aware of and I expect to find out exactly what it is. If I happen to get another crack at Danika along the way, then that's an unexpected windfall I'll happily accept. Can you go along with that?"

Hunter met his gaze and smiled, "Of course, I can."

THE SHORT JOURNEY back to Fulford Road was made in silence. Caslin kept replaying everything he knew about Danika's business operations in his head, trying to link her with Thomas Grey but none were forthcoming from memory. Furthermore, any connection to Farzaad Amin eluded him completely. Entering the station, they were buzzed through the outer security door. Making their way along the corridor, they took the left onto the stairs and up towards CID. A call came from below as they reached the landing of the first floor.

"Mr Caslin!"

Caslin glanced over the balustrade, down to the ground floor. It was one of the civilian desk clerks calling him, but ashamedly, he didn't know his name. Leaning back, out of view, he silently mouthed the question to Hunter who rolled her eyes.

"Simon," she whispered. "Don't worry, he's only worked here for a year or so."

"I've been busy," Caslin said, leaning over and calling down. "What is it, Simon?" he asked, shooting a wink in Hunter's direction.

"There's someone waiting to see you," he called. Caslin thought about asking more questions but instead, turned to head back down, lingering on the first step.

"You crack on with pulling the details on Pocock and the helicopter crash. Also, have Terry Holt gather any available intel on Thomas Grey. I'll see you in CID in a minute," he said, resuming his course down to the waiting clerk.

"Leave it with me."

"What do you have for me?" Caslin said as he reached the ground floor.

"I have a Mr Mitchell, Geoffrey Mitchell, waiting to see you in the visitor's room," Simon offered, guiding Caslin in the right direction. Now, Caslin remembered who Simon was. A former engineer, retired from his career and now having taken up residence on the front desk at Fulford Road as part of the civilian administration team. A new job to keep him busy. A slightly pompous man who believed no one knew the station better than he did. Not that his approach was borne out of arrogance, merely a lack of self-awareness regarding his impact on those around him. Harmless enough and probably a very decent man but not one that many wanted to find themselves alone with during the working day.

"What does he want, do you know?" Caslin asked, immediately regretting doing so.

Simon shook his head, "No. He would only speak with you. Reminds me of a cartoon I saw in the paper a few days ago. There was this man, sitting in an office and—"

"Another time, Simon," Caslin said as they reached the security door to the station lobby. Caslin opened it, passed through and turned immediately left to access the visitor's room. Never had he been so relieved to be walking blindly into a room as he was at that very moment. Entering, he swiftly closed the door behind him. If Simon took offence it wasn't evident. The man waiting for him rose from his seat before Caslin had a chance to introduce himself.

"Nathaniel Caslin?" the man asked. Caslin nodded, taking in his measure as he offered his hand. Geoffrey Mitchell took it. The grasp was far from firm and rapidly dropped. Caslin guessed he was in his early fifties, of slim build and smartly dressed in a high-end suit. He appeared to be nervous, his eyes flitting to Caslin and then quickly away.

"How can I help you, Mr Mitchell?" Caslin asked, indicating for them to take a seat. Mitchell shook his head.

"No, thank you," he declined. "This won't take long."

"Okay," Caslin replied. "What can I do for you?"

"I'm here to ask you to stay away from Karen," he said flatly. Caslin was thrown.

"I'm sorry. What?"

"Karen, your *ex-wife,*" Mitchell reiterated. "I want you to leave her alone."

Caslin felt a pulse of anger course through him, *"Leave her alone?"*

"Yes," Mitchell said, fixing him with a hard stare. "Look… I know the two of you have a long history and… the bonds between husband and wife are strong, particularly when there are children involved but… it's time that you moved on."

"Who the hell do you think—"

"I'm Karen's future," Mitchell cut in. "You are very much her past."

"Well, maybe that's for her to decide?"

Mitchell walked around from behind the table where initially he'd been seated, coming alongside Caslin and looking at him sideways. His demeanour was not threatening nor intimidating but calm and measured.

"Karen told me… she told me what happened between the two of you the other night," he said, his voice cracking momentarily as Caslin cast his eyes to the floor, inclining his head slightly. "It's understandable under the circumstances but you should be aware that it will not be happening again." Mitchell continued on and only stopped when he grasped the door handle. He waited there, both men with their backs to each other. "Please ensure I don't have to come here again, Nathaniel. It's embarrassing for me and I have no doubt that it's humiliating for you."

Caslin heard the creaking of the door hinges, coupled with the draught of air drawn in from the lobby beyond, as Mitchell left the room. The flash of anger subsided to be replaced by a curious mixture of guilt and sadness, akin to the realisation that a worst fear was now a brutal reality.

He took a deep breath and held it, attempting to overcome the swirling emotions within that were trying to assert themselves. Reaching up, he probed his temples in a circular motion with his fingertips before pressing them firmly against fiercely shut eyes. Standing in silence, he heard his phone beep inside his pocket. Taking it out, he saw he'd received a text message. It was from Karen and simply read – *I'm sorry*.

There was a knock and Caslin turned, replacing his phone in his pocket as he did so. Simon was standing there. His expression was one of concern.

"Are you okay, Mr Caslin?" he said. Knowing he wasn't standing before the most observant or intuitive member of the team, Caslin felt the need to gather himself.

"I'm fine, Simon. Thank you for your concern," he replied, forcing a smile. This seemed to satisfy him.

"They're looking for you upstairs," Simon offered.

"Thanks." Caslin stepped out from the room and increased his pace to ensure he walked alone.

ENTERING CID, Hunter clocked Caslin and made a beeline in his direction. She held a wedge of paper in her hands as she approached him. Reading the expression on his face, her own changed.

"Are you all right, sir?"

"Yes, why?"

She shook her head to indicate it was irrelevant, "Anything interesting going on downstairs?"

"No," Caslin replied bluntly, probably with a sharper edge to his tone than intended. Hunter appeared not to notice. "What did you find out?"

"The Air Accidents Investigation Branch sent me over a copy of their report. I'm just going through it."

"And?"

"The helicopter came down in good weather on its approach to Burleigh House. The ensuing fireball that followed upon impact killed both the pilot and passenger, Martin Pocock. The AAIB carried out an exhaustive inquiry that only finished last month. They found the machine had a well-documented maintenance record with no history of material failures or breakdowns."

"And the cause of the accident itself?" Caslin asked, mulling it over.

"They couldn't determine a compelling reason for it to come down in the manner that it did. Ultimately, they concluded it was *most likely* due to pilot error," Hunter stated, glancing at the document in hand.

"The traditional get-out clauses are still favoured then?" Caslin asked with no attempt to hide the sarcasm. "What of the pilot? What do we know about him?"

"Sam Abrahams," Hunter said, flicking back a page. "A former captain in the Army Air Corps. Served tours in both Gulf conflicts and the Balkans. Spotless record. He was cited as an above average pilot with three decades of experience and also worked, for a time, as an instructor. He had no known medical condition to indicate he was unfit to fly."

"And what of the machine itself? Any history of design flaws or similar accidents affecting that particular model of aircraft?" Caslin asked.

Hunter shook her head in the negative, "Not at all. It has one of the best performing safety averages in the industry."

"Pocock?" Caslin asked, just as Terry Holt joined them.

"I've got that here, sir," Holt said, brandishing his notes. "He was a successful lawyer having had a career that saw him work for several of the more prestigious city firms. He developed a reputation for being a specialist in contract negotiations, specifically surrounding the structuring of property investment finance. Having left his last appointment, he set up a company of his own that proved successful and catapulted him even further up the food chain. Not a rags-to-riches story but certainly upwardly mobile. No priors. Not even a parking ticket."

"Tell me, was his current situation investigated at the time of his death? Anything that was considered suspicious?"

Hunter shook her head, "No. The AAIB carried out their investigation and the jury at the inquest concluded it was a case of accidental death."

"His firm. Who's running it now?" Caslin asked.

"It collapsed shortly following his death," Holt stated. "Companies House records show it was racked with debt and from what I could find out there was no one to take the helm after the accident. A winding-up order was served by Revenue and Customs three months ago."

Caslin caught Hunter casting him an advisory flick of the eyebrows and he turned to see DCI Matheson entering CID. He acknowledged her approach and indicated for the junior officers to leave. Holt swiftly departed whereas Hunter managed to greet their superior before returning to her own desk. For his part, Caslin fell into step alongside Matheson and they headed for his office.

"I missed the morning briefing today," she said, as he closed the door behind them. Caslin offered her a seat but she remained standing.

"That's okay, I can bring you up to speed," Caslin said.

"That would be nice but first," Matheson said, "perhaps you could tell me why *you* missed the morning briefing?" Caslin sank into the chair behind his desk, casting a glance through the window into the squad room. He caught Terry Holt's eye; who was attempting to observe the goings on without appearing to be doing so. Caslin rolled his tongue across the inside of his lower lip. Matheson followed his gaze. "Don't blame Terry. You put him in that position."

Caslin shook his head slightly, "I had to follow up on a lead. It was important and the team here know their tasks."

"What took you to Acomb Road?" Matheson said, folding her arms before her. Word certainly spread fast.

"The suicide of Alexander Nairn last year, could well be related to the Amin killing," Caslin offered, judging Matheson knew more than she was letting on. He had to assume his leg was already in the bear trap and sought not to make the situation worse.

"How so?" Matheson replied without skipping a beat, confirming Caslin's suspicions.

"That's exactly what I'm trying to find out, Ma'am."

"And how have you come by this information?"

"A tip off," Caslin lied. "Anonymous."

The DCI unfolded her arms, softening her stance, "Do you think you can trust it?"

Caslin nodded solemnly, "There are legs in it for sure. How exactly it comes together, I'll be honest, I don't know... yet. But, I will."

Matheson stood in silence, almost as if she was assessing him. Most likely, he figured she was weighing up how forthcoming he was currently being. In truth, that was only as far as he felt he had to be whilst appearing convincing.

"What intelligence have you turned up regarding who was in town on the day of the murder?" Matheson asked, switching tack. Caslin figured he'd passed the test, at least for now.

"Those names on the alt-right?"

She nodded.

Caslin shook his head, "Despite their best efforts to throw us off by splitting into smaller groups, most of those with form were tracked by our intelligence teams. At this time, we can't be certain of their whereabouts at the time of the murder, so there is still the possibility that one or more of them were involved."

"And how are you following up that line of inquiry?"

"We've gathered up as much of the CCTV, available across the weekend, as we could and we're running it through facial recognition software to track them and their whereabouts but—"

"But?"

"It's a painstakingly slow process with the available resources," Caslin said.

"Then perhaps... and please feel free to take this suggestion on board, you might want to focus on the more likely scenario rather than chasing the ghosts of last year?" she said with a cutting edge to her tone.

"It's worth following up, I assure you and until it's clearly to the contrary, I'll keep all available lines of inquiry open," Caslin countered, sitting forward in his seat and resting his elbows on the desk.

Matheson fixed him with a stare, "I want an update before the close of play, Nathaniel. I'm expecting to speak with the chief superintendent this evening before he delivers his press conference and it would be good for me to have something useful to say."

"I'll do my best, Ma'am," Caslin said respectfully. With that said, his senior officer turned and left his office.

Sitting back in his chair, he watched as she crossed the squad room, pausing as she came alongside Hunter's desk. Words were exchanged but as to what was said by either of them, he had no clue. Shortly after, Matheson made to leave CID and Hunter shot him a concerned look in passing. The DCI was certainly trying to keep him on a short leash and he was well aware that she'd still be both willing and able to hang him with it should the need arise.

Taking out his mobile, Caslin fished a slip of paper out of his wallet and unfolded it. Tapping the number into his phone, he spun his chair to the left enabling him to look out of the window. The sun was shining through the branches of the barren trees, belying the bitterness of the wind. The call connected and he waited patiently as the phone rang at the other end. Just when he was expecting the voicemail to cut in, the call was answered.

"Inspector Caslin, I wasn't expecting to hear from you so soon," Cory Walsh said, in greeting.

"Well, what can I say, you make a compelling argument," Caslin replied, turning back to observe his CID team, hard at work. "I think we need to talk."

"I'll message you when I get a moment," Walsh said and the line went dead. Caslin was surprised, removing the handset from his ear and checking the screen to see if the call really had been disconnected. It had. Standing up, he put the phone down and walked to the window, putting his hands in his pockets. His phone vibrated, followed by the accompanying sound of the beep to signify he'd received an SMS. Reaching back, he picked up the phone. Opening the message, he found it to be brief – *King's Staith, 10pm.*

Caslin deleted the text and put the phone in his pocket. He knew the street well. It was at the edge of the city centre on the quayside of the River Ouse and opposite the warehouses of the old merchant's quarter. The latter were now mostly luxury apartments with a historic view. Hunter appeared in the doorway to his office. He beckoned her in.

"What do you want me to do regarding Thomas Grey, sir?"

"Turn over his business affairs. Try to find any link to Danika Durakovic. If nothing shows there, search for anything that stands out as odd, particularly in relation to financing. These guys are wealthy but they're not funding their projects with their own capital. See if you can find out whose money they have access to? Make sure you do it quietly, though," he said, casting a sideways glance at Terry Holt.

Hunter followed the direction of his gaze and nodded, before turning to leave, "Will do, sir."

"Sarah?" Caslin called after her. She looked back at him, over her shoulder. "What did Matheson want?"

Hunter glanced away before answering, "Nothing much. She just said…"

"Said what?" Caslin asked, sensing reticence.

"She said to be careful."

Caslin nodded, chewing his bottom lip and raising his eyebrows.

"Sage advice," he said, waving her away. Hunter was only too pleased to.

CHAPTER SEVENTEEN

CASLIN DREW his coat about him, increasing his pace in an effort to shake the cold from his body. The bitter wind, channelled by the buildings cut through the narrow city streets in a fierce reminder that winter was far from over. The crisp sunshine of earlier in the day was now replaced by a dark, brooding expanse of cloud cover, threatening to burst into freezing rain at any given moment. Departing Spurrier Gate, Caslin took the right turn onto Bridge Street in the direction of the River Ouse. Upon reaching the bridge instead of crossing, he accessed the steep steps down towards King's Staith and left the hum of the traffic to pass above him.

Descending to the quayside, the sound of music and laughter carried to him from the nearby pub. For most of the year this area was well served by patrons sitting at tables along the riverside, making it one of the popular places to enjoy an evening out. However, for the next few months at least the cobbles would be accompanied by silence with only the water, lapping against the quay, one of the few sounds to be heard when the traffic died down.

Looking around, Caslin was alone. Thrusting his hands into his pockets, he chastised himself for forgetting to bring his gloves. In the lee of the bridge, he'd felt the benefit of shelter from the wind but once clear of it the icy breeze struck him. Turning his back, he sought to give his face some respite. Walking forward a few yards, he was able to get a clearer view along the river. In the distance, with the aid of the street lighting, he could see a man walking his dog on the edge of the Tower Gardens but he was heading in the opposite direction of him. Checking the time, it was a little after ten and Caslin shifted his feet. They were numb.

The sound of footfalls behind caused Caslin to turn as another descended the stone steps from above. The man was in his thirties, well dressed for the conditions in a blue all-weather coat and a woollen hat. He bore Caslin no heed as he walked past, taking the second turn onto Cumberland Street and heading up towards the city centre. Caslin eyed him for a brief moment before checking his watch again.

Without knowing where the meeting would take place, Caslin decided to get some circulation through his body and set off in the direction of the Tower Gardens. Passing Lower Friargate, he glanced up the street to see if a car was parked up, potentially waiting for him. A man stood a little way off with a mobile phone pressed to his ear, laughing and joking in conversation with someone but he was paying no attention to his surroundings. Caslin walked on.

A line of terraced, Georgian Townhouses ran to his left for the next hundred yards. Where he walked, at the quayside level, were the arched accesses to the basements. Now being used as garages or general storage areas, they were prone to flooding as and when the river burst its banks which it was liable to do with more regularity than Caslin remembered from his youth. Glancing up at the terrace, lights were on but curtains were drawn. The end of King's Staith brought him to the Boat Dock, where tourist trips along the river began and ended with the architecturally stunning, Skeldergate Bridge in the background.

Exhaling heavily, Caslin turned and looked back from where he'd come. The street was deserted. Reaching into his pocket, he took out his mobile phone and scrolled through the contacts until he found Walsh's phone number. Leaning against one of the many bollards lining the quay, Caslin waited patiently for the call to connect. It did so but failed to be answered. The call rang out after thirty seconds without cutting to voicemail. Checking the screen, he saw the connection had been terminated. He redialled, only to be diverted to voicemail as soon as a connection was made.

Putting the phone away, he looked around. A sense of irritation came to him. No doubt, Walsh would have a reason for being late or unreachable. Caslin didn't feel as if he was being played for a fool. After all, Walsh had approached him and not the other way around. With it now pushing half-past ten, Caslin figured he'd call it a day. Walking back the way he'd come, he reached the steps but on the spur of the moment, rather than head up, he ducked into the King's Arms for a swift nightcap. A wall of heat struck him as he opened the outer door. Business was far from brisk with only the regulars apparently in situ and Caslin was able to approach the bar with ease.

Ordering a pint of beer and a whisky chaser, he handed over a twenty and waited for his change, acknowledging the barman with a nod when he returned. A fire crackled in the hearth, comforting on a dark winter night. Caslin took a table at the front of the building with a window overlooking the river. Tossing his coat and scarf onto a free chair, he sank down. It'd been a long day. Rubbing at his face with his palms, he took a deep breath and then reached for the scotch, downing it in one fluid motion. The sting barely registered as he put the empty glass down and picked up his beer.

Running the events through his head, Caslin sought to make sense of the investigation. Without Walsh's intervention, he'd be far deeper into the workings of the neo-Nazi groups currently flooding the city rather than toying with Thomas Grey and the demise of his two associates. Keeping that information from DCI Matheson, among others, was both necessary and telling. He had nothing concrete with which to base these inquiries on and they wouldn't stand up to any form of scrutiny.

The door behind him opened as more latecomers entered. Caslin sipped at his pint. The two arrivals walked to the bar and signalled the barman for his attention. Caslin's thoughts drifted to Kuznetsov's apparent suicide.

He was still bothered by that case, not so much because of any evidence of foul play because there wasn't much of that, more his own reaction to the death. Had the fallen billionaire been an unemployed bricklayer found hanged in his garage, would Caslin be as sceptical about the suicide? He hoped he would approach them equally but the nagging voice in his head wondered whether he was guilty of somewhat overplaying the significance of one man's breakdown. *Why was that?* Self-analysis was useful, up to a point but beyond that merely caused analytical paralysis. Caslin cast his doubts aside and returned to his drink. A handful of patrons made to leave, clearly having had a cracking evening, and stumbled out of the door, behind him.

Caslin smiled and cast an eye around the pub. The two latecomers were propped up at the bar, one seated on a stool, the other standing alongside. Something caught his attention. The two weren't talking although the one standing had his back to him. Caslin stifled a yawn and then flexed the muscles in his shoulders, rolling them backwards in a circular motion to try and release the tension. Glancing at the clock on the wall, he knew he should head back rather than order another drink.

Standing up, he drained the remaining half of his pint and picked up his coat and scarf. Returning the empty glasses to the bar, the staff were out of sight when he looked to acknowledge the service and so, left without a word. Stepping out into the cold night air saw him shudder, such was the contrast from within the pub. Pulling his elbows tight to his sides, he rubbed his hands together before putting them in his coat pockets.

Heading to the right, Caslin mounted the steps up to Bridge Street and the most direct route home across the city centre to his flat, in Kleiser's Court.

A bus passed by on the road above, the rumbling sound replaced by the sound of the pub doors opening behind him. A brief glance over his shoulder saw a figure leave the King's Arms. The man braced against the cold, pulling a hat over his head and he too, began the steep climb to the street above. Caslin continued on. Cresting the top of the stairs, he angled right and eyeing a break in the late-night traffic, trotted across the road to the other side.

Reaching the old church on the corner, Caslin passed the entrance to Feasegate and crossed onto High Ousegate. The street narrowed and with its mix of three and four-storey shop units, it felt more enclosed. For some reason he felt on edge as if the hairs on the back of neck were upright.

Very few people were around at this time of night and Caslin became aware of someone walking a short distance behind him but on the other side of the road, over his right shoulder. Pausing at a shop window, Caslin made as if he was checking out one of the interior product displays, lingering over the detail whilst keeping half an eye on the reflection in the glass. As the figure honed into view, it was indeed the man who had left the pub at the same time. He paid no attention to Caslin and walked on, head down and earphones in.

Caslin shifted his eyes and watched as the figure disappeared from view in the reflection from the shop window. Stepping back, he looked to his right as the man reached the end of the street and took a left. Shaking his head, Caslin smiled at his own paranoia and set off.

Part way along High Ousegate was Peter's Lane, a narrow cut-through between the buildings – used largely by employees of the various businesses. The lane, little more than an alley, eventually opened out onto

Market Street. Caslin passed down it. Only one source lit the route, an overhanging lamp near to a kink further up the passage. Barely a shoulder's width at its narrowest, the lane would be almost unnavigable if not for the seeping light pollution from the streets at each end. His footsteps echoed on the stone flags beneath his feet, reverberating off of the brick walls to either side of him.

Approaching the turn, where he expected the passage to widen to a more comfortable norm, allowing vehicular access, Caslin sensed someone else had entered behind him. Following the path to the left, Caslin chanced a glance back the way he'd come before disappearing from view. With scant seconds to make a judgement in the dark, he couldn't make out any details of who was coming towards him. A few metres ahead and the path turned once again, this time sharply to the right. Increasing his pace, Caslin made it around the corner and scanned the scene. There were multiple doorways, recessed rear-entrances to shops and their associated flats above as well as various gated routes into other buildings.

There were multiple options for where he could choose to conceal himself. A wooden door that offered access to a small yard was ajar and Caslin brushed aside some collapsed cardboard packaging with his foot in order to open it further and allow him in. He then pulled the door closed just enough to shroud his presence but still leaving him a view of the passage. He retreated into the shadows and waited.

Moments later, a man came into view, walking briskly. The same man Caslin had eyed in the reflection of the shop window. No longer was he the casual stranger making his way home from the pub. Now, he gave the impression of a focussed individual, alert and determined. Caslin recognised him. Not only had he been drinking with the other man back at the pub, but he had also appeared on King's Staith earlier, passing by Caslin and heading into town. Caslin waited, absolutely certain that he was being followed.

From his own experience, Caslin knew that surveillance teams seldom worked alone and this man certainly had at least one colleague. Confident he'd allowed enough time for his pursuer to round the next bend before he came out from his hiding place, Caslin edged forward. Reaching the next bend, he risked a glance around the corner. Having reached the junction with Market Street, the man was pacing with a phone clamped to his ear. Such was the emptiness of the city at this time of night, Caslin could make out every word.

"No. I think I've lost him... yeah, Market Street... probably heading home," he said, responding to questioning from the other end of the line. "I don't know... I didn't see anyone… okay, I will."

The man put the phone in his pocket and looked in both directions, unsure of which way to go. Caslin followed, a dozen paces behind. Quickening his own pace, he sought to make up the ground between them with the brighter lights and noise of the busier street to mask and detract from his approach. Setting himself, Caslin was buoyed at how his makeshift plan had played out. Confident he could comfortably challenge the man in a more public area, he stepped it up.

Late-night revellers passed by, granting further cover and Caslin increased the speed of his approach. Barely two steps behind, he braced to take down his target only to see him turn at the final moment with impossibly quick speed, dropping his shoulder as Caslin reached out. An iron grip took a hold of Caslin's forearm and without the time to process what happened, he found himself upended, seeing the streetlights above pass by in a whirlwind of blurred, orange light.

Striking the flag stones at an alarming rate, Caslin felt the air burst from his lungs. He rolled and came upright, lunging at his opponent who, in turn, advanced on him. Throwing himself forward into the man's midriff, Caslin clasped his arms around him and drove his head into his stomach. His opponent groaned as he was forced back and against a shop window, flexing under the pressure. The advantage was short-lived as Caslin felt a knee rise into his stomach, striking him forcefully. The pain shot up through his chest and again, the wind was knocked from him.

Losing his grip, Caslin slumped to his knees and was thrown backwards as the man pushed off. Trying to stand, a fist struck him across the left cheek and he was sent sprawling to the ground, arms flailing.

Panic flared within as he made to stand. Having lost both the element of surprise and the upper hand, Caslin knew he was in trouble. A crushing blow struck his ribs and he doubled over. The kick saw him collapse into a heap. Some excited shouts came from distance and Caslin sensed hesitation in his opponent because no further blows were forthcoming. Rolling onto his side, fearing the next onslaught, he was surprised to see a figure sprinting away along Market Street. Looking around, he was alone, once again.

Stumbling to his feet, clutching his side and using a wall to brace himself, Caslin winced as he stood. The shouts had come from intoxicated passers-by, eyeing the combat and seeking yet more entertainment. They slowed their approach as the realisation dawned on them that it was all over. Still, they mocked and jeered at the man who'd come off second best.

For his part, Caslin mouthed an expletive in their direction, which only encouraged them more and set off for home. Little more than a two-minute walk, the remainder of the journey back to his flat felt like it took far longer. Being no stranger to taking a kicking it had, however, been a while since his last and every step saw him wince with pain.

Reaching the entrance to Kleiser's Court, Caslin ensured he was alone when he unlocked the door to the communal passage and passed through. Locking it behind him, he leant against the wall and took a moment to catch his breath, appreciating the feeling of security. Thoughts rushed through his mind. Questions he had no answers to. There was no doubt that someone was taking a keen interest in his investigation but who and to what end, he had no clue.

Taking a deep breath caused him to grimace, such was the pain in his side. The stairs were taken slowly, each step sending a shot of pain throughout his body. Entering his flat, he pushed the door closed with the back of his heel, hearing the reassuring click of the latch as he walked into the living room. Letting out a groan as he dropped his shoulder and slipped off his coat.

Caslin passed over to the sideboard and overturned a glass. He took the stopper out of a bottle of Macallan with his teeth and poured himself a large scotch. Picking up the glass, he turned and went back to the hall and on into the bathroom, one hand supporting his left side at all times. First taking a mouthful of scotch, he put the glass down alongside the basin and, flicking on the vanity light, assessed himself in the mirror.

Turning his face sideways, the area around his left eye was reddening and already closing as a result of the swelling. It stung as he reached up, probing gently with his fingertips. Another mouthful of scotch followed before he felt prepared enough to remove both his jumper and shirt. Inspecting his ribcage, he found it was incredibly tender to the touch and he knew the bruising would be substantial. There was also a strong likelihood that he'd cracked several ribs but he hoped not. The notion that he should go to the hospital to get checked out came and went in an instant. If he had indeed cracked any ribs, they'd do little with them. He'd spend most of the night waiting to be seen and then be sent home and told to take it easy.

Running the cold-water tap, Caslin cupped his hands beneath the stream. With difficulty, he bent over and doused his face. The sensation was refreshing although punctuated by intense shots of pain. Picking up a flannel, he soaked it in the cold water and gently touched it to the side of his face before doing the same to his abdomen. It caused him to wince once again and he let out a deep sigh.

Finishing his scotch, he turned off the tap and left the bathroom with every intention of revisiting the bottle of Macallan. Something caught his attention. Standing in the hallway, he reached up and flicked on the light.

On the mat, in front of the entrance door, lay a brown C4 envelope. Not absolutely certain that it wasn't there when he'd arrived, Caslin crossed over to it. With difficulty, he crouched down and picked it up. The weight was significant. There was no addressee on the front, stamp or identifying mark to indicate where it had come from. Caslin tucked it under his arm and listened intently for any movement beyond the door. There wasn't any. Unlocking the door, he eased it open and glanced out onto the landing. Nothing moved and the security light, running off a two-minute timer, was no longer lit. Whoever left the envelope had long since departed.

Closing the door, Caslin locked it and made his way back through to the living room. Tearing open the envelope, he tipped the contents, a wedge of paper documents, out onto the coffee table and then retrieved the bottle of Macallan. Gently lowering himself into his chair, he placed the glass on the table next to the paperwork and poured himself another drink. Reaching up, he clicked on the lamp, bathing him in a soft light.

"Let me have a look at you," Caslin said to himself, picking up the first clutch of paper.

CHAPTER EIGHTEEN

THE ENVELOPE CONTAINED photocopies of official government documentation. Putting aside his immediate scepticism, a brief scan through the batch of papers revealed letters, reports and memos, all written on headed paper from their respective arm of the civil service. Caslin found himself looking at communiques from the Foreign and Commonwealth Office, the UK Treasury and the Home Office to name but a few. In every piece, he saw redacted sections, often heavily, concealing names, addresses or in many cases entire paragraphs. All of which, Caslin found to be frustrating as understanding what was being discussed would be tiresomely difficult.

A casual inspection revealed a lack of commonality to bring them all together. Sifting through, he put aside those that were heavy on figures and short on detail, turning his attention to a transparent sleeve holding papers stamped 'Eyes Only'. Sipping at his scotch, Caslin unhooked the string that bound the folder shut and opened it, withdrawing the contents. The first he laid eyes on was a one-page summary of a man, by the name of Valery Fedorin. Casting an eye over the photograph at the top of the page, he noted a serious-looking man, angular of face with a dark complexion, particularly around his eyes. Across the image was an official stamp to signify Fedorin was deceased.

Flicking through the remaining pages, Caslin counted six in total and all were similar dossiers on individuals with each recorded as having passed away. A sense of unease swept over him. The papers appeared authentic but never trusting what was fed to him was one of the first things he'd ever learnt in this job.

Returning to the first of the six, Caslin read through Valery Fedorin's recorded history. He had been a local official in *Troitsk* when he died as a result of a heart attack. It was a place Caslin had never heard of, so he looked it up, finding it to be a small district roughly forty kilometres south-west of Moscow. Fedorin's demise struck him as untimely and a little surprising bearing in mind he was only thirty-six at the time of his death. He was married and had two children, a son and a daughter. His birthplace, Rostov-on-Don, was listed as was his entire educational and employment history. The latter appeared largely related to local government, albeit at a low level. Nothing stood out to signify he should be of interest to UK law enforcement, let alone the Secret Service.

Turning to the next, Caslin found this one to be closer to home. He was a UK national, fifty-four years old, by the name of Dean Strauss. Strauss worked as a planning consultant, specialising in commercial infrastructure according to his summary. Having been born and raised in Chorley, Lancashire, he grew up and attended Balliol College, Oxford. No mean feat in itself, let alone for a working-class boy from the north of England.

Scanning to the bottom, Caslin sought out his cause of death. Strauss had died in what was recorded as a botched mugging in Berlin, four years previously. No one was listed as having been arrested, let alone convicted of the assault. Cross referencing Fedorin's details, Caslin sought to link the two but nothing obvious was forthcoming. Putting them aside, he moved quickly to the next with an expectation that clarity would come about soon enough.

The third detailed the life of a French solicitor who died in a car accident in Marseille barely six months ago. By all accounts, it was a hit-and-run in an unpopulated area on a rural road. No witnesses were recorded as having been present at the scene. Moving to the next, Caslin found a suicide of an Israeli financier who had thrown himself to his death from the roof of an apartment block in Tel Aviv.

The next dossier had apparently been forwarded to the UK agencies from the FBI. Another businessman, a naturalised UK citizen of Ukrainian descent, who had been found dead in his Floridian holiday home. The cause of death was recorded as an overdose of barbiturates. Immediately, Caslin found that interesting. He hadn't seen a death from barbiturates in a long time and this incident had been recent, only two years prior.

No stranger to sedatives, anti-depressants and illegal highs, Caslin knew the market for these synthetic drugs, used to slow the central nervous system, had been more or less eradicated. Their prescription use was almost entirely superseded by benzodiazepines, with far fewer side effects and a much lower risk of accidental overdose. There were no details as to why or who had passed the file on to UK intelligence.

The remaining summary was that of a German man who had succumbed to complications following a stroke. He was listed as an employee of the BMF, the German Federal Ministry of Finance, although on secondment to the EU's Fiscalis 2020 programme at the time of his death. Caslin took out his phone and did an internet search as he had no idea what it was. Within minutes, he found it to be a six-year programme facilitating the exchange of expertise and information between European Tax administrations. Returning to the dossier, there were seemingly no suspicions raised regarding the death either at the time nor subsequently at home in Germany.

Re-examining each death, he double-checked for any links that might tie all, or any, of them together. Drawing air through clenched teeth in frustration, Caslin tossed the summaries aside. On the face of it there were no geographical, professional or causes of death that suggested the cases were related. Somehow though, they were closely associated enough to draw the attention of the Intelligence Agencies of both the UK and the United States. If these files were genuine, they'd also found their way into the public domain. That did not happen without significant effort on someone's part.

Turning his attention to the other paperwork, Caslin first poured himself another scotch. His attention was drawn to an export licence, issued from the DTI, the Department for Trade and Industry. The licence was granted late August, the year before last and issued to a company by the name of *Henderson Holdings Limited.* The terms and conditions along with what the licence sought to facilitate the export of, as well as the associated values, were redacted as was the name of the person receiving the warrant. The reference at the top of the letter however, was not. The licence referred to *Project Obmen.*

Caslin sat back, sipping at his drink and wondered what the title referred to. Picking up his phone, he reconnected to the internet and typed the name into the search box. Initially, the search engine queried whether he had typed the name in error but below that were multiple hits against websites.

The first two related to German-Russian exchanges of academic expertise within the fields of culture and education. The next, highlighted regional educational-exchange programmes between Norway and Bulgaria. Beyond that, the hits proved to be ever more unlikely, linking to a low budget made-for-television film of a similar name.

Caslin closed down the search, acknowledging the decreasing relevance the further down the page he read. Following the brief inquiry, he was left none the wiser as to what Project Obmen could be referring to.

Finding a clutch of email transcripts, Caslin began to read through them. Many of the names, both senders and recipients, were redacted but their sources were not. They were internal emails sent across the UK government's servers. He found threads originating in the Foreign Office passing through the House of Commons and even the occasional link to the governing party's central headquarters. Frustratingly, almost the entire content of each thread had been redacted. Often, the surviving text were merely the conjunctions or transitional words. There was no way Caslin could even begin to understand the context or subject matter being discussed, only that they had been passed back and forth over a period of weeks and, in some cases, months.

Many of the threads originated from the Foreign and Commonwealth Office. It was one of the emails from this department where Caslin found a name, *F. Michaelson*. Scanning through the remaining emails, he found only one more reference to Michaelson. Within the thread, he appeared to be querying an inconsistency regarding a *register*. Although, any ability to further scrutinise the matter was severely hampered by an overuse of thick, black lines.

Caslin drew breath. The only register he knew of that might be of interest to a civil servant would be the Register of Members' Interests. This related to the personal affairs of parliamentarians in their wider lives. Every sitting member of the Commons had to respect a code of conduct with declarations of any financial interests that could potentially influence them. This ranged from financial reimbursements to company directorships, investments or familial connections.

Exhaling deeply, Caslin pondered whether Michaelson's query was significant or not.

Glancing at the time, it was well into the early hours. Sitting forward in his seat, Caslin placed his glass down and drummed his index and forefinger against the table, piecing it together. Picking up his phone, he scrolled down the contacts list, hovering over the name when he found it.

Hesitation was not something he was ever accused of and he dialled the number, closing his eyes as the call connected. It rang for an inordinately long time before a male voice answered. It was a gruff acknowledgement. Caslin had certainly woken him.

"You do know what time it is, don't you, Nathaniel?"

"I'm sorry, sir. I didn't feel it could wait."

"What do you need?" Kyle Broadfoot asked. Caslin's former boss, now Assistant Chief Constable and head of the North Yorkshire Crime Directorate, didn't seem fazed by the lateness of the call. He knew his former charge only too well.

"Your connections, sir," Caslin replied, sweeping his eyes across the papers in front of him, "your connections."

LEANING against one of the four giant Doric columns of the Neo-Classical Yorkshire Museum, Caslin waited. Sipping at the coffee he'd purchased on the short walk from his flat in Kleiser's Court, his other hand was firmly planted in his coat pocket. With very little wind, the clear skies overnight had left a silver sheen across the manicured grounds sweeping out in front of him. The tree line, a little over a hundred yards away, masked his proximity to the city centre. In the distance to his left was the Minster, towering above the old town. Beyond the trees, the museum gardens continued on down to the banks of the River Ouse with York's central train station on the far side. The hum of the traffic, as commuters set about their day, carried to him on the breeze.

His thoughts drifted to Karen. Having not spoken to her since being warned off by her partner, Caslin felt a pang of guilt. Undoubtedly, he was certain she would want him to keep his distance. After all, she chose to share what happened between them and must have been aware of the potential consequences in doing so. It would have been easy to keep it concealed. At least, as easy as it ever is to keep a dark secret from those with the closest emotional ties. A matter of conscience perhaps?

His guilt arose from the situation with Sean. As parents, they needed to come together to support him and ease the boy through the damaged place he'd wandered into. As things stood, Caslin couldn't see how they'd be able to achieve that under the circumstances. Movement to his left caught his eye and Caslin turned to see the approach of Kyle Broadfoot.

His face was pale and he bore a pained expression as he took Caslin's offered hand.

"Good morning, sir," Caslin said. Broadfoot nodded, in a return greeting inclining his head slightly.

"What on earth have you been up to?" Broadfoot asked, pointing at the side of Caslin's face.

"Oh… that… I fell down the stairs."

"They can be slippery, can't they?" he replied, obviously unconvinced. "Shall we?" he said, with an open palm, indicating for them to take a walk. "I don't fancy standing still for too long. Not on a morning like this."

Caslin agreed and they took the path that wound alongside the ruins of the medieval St Mary's Abbey and headed deeper into the gardens. Glancing over his shoulder, Caslin noted someone hovering in the colonnade at the entrance to the museum. He was unashamedly watching them.

Broadfoot noticed, "My driver. He'll wait there." Caslin thought no more about it.

"What did you find out?" Caslin asked, cutting to the chase.

"Direct as always, Nathaniel," Broadfoot said, with a smile.

"Well, you know me, sir. I'm not one for the formalities."

"True enough. I'm surprised you came to me with this. Tell me first why you're not using your own resources? I know you have them and, in the past, they've often proved far more useful than mine."

Caslin thought on that for a moment. It was true, he had connections of his own but they were strained these days.

"It's difficult to explain," Caslin said truthfully. "To do so would be a little… I don't know… rude? For want of a better word."

Broadfoot laughed, shaking his head, "Nate Caslin is worried about causing offence? I'd better make a note in my diary. A day to remember for the memoirs." Caslin smiled, glancing away and squinting in the bright morning sunshine. "Anyway. You served me quite a task to be delivered in such a short time."

"I have the feeling time is of the essence with this case," Caslin countered. "Besides, you have access to significant resources. Enough to get me a result, anyway."

"You seem very confident of that."

"You're here, aren't you?" Caslin said with an almost imperceptible shrug of the shoulders, finishing the last of his coffee and depositing the cup in a waste bin as they passed.

"The name you are after is *Finlay Michaelson*. He was a member of the civil service working in the Foreign and Commonwealth Office," Broadfoot offered.

"You said *was*. Where is he now?"

"He no longer works for the FCO, having left his post earlier this year," Broadfoot replied. "In fact, he left the government entirely."

"Where is he now?"

Broadfoot shook his head, "I don't know. Do bear in mind you only tossed this in my direction a little over seven hours ago."

"What did he do? At the FCO, I mean," Caslin asked, ignoring the senior officer's mild dig at him.

"Michaelson was a Grade 2 Senior, working in investment and business relations with UK trade and industry. He took the lead in supporting relationships between UK business and foreign enterprise."

"Do we know why he left?" Caslin asked. Having taken the left fork in the path they now arrived at the York Observatory. It was a small hexagonal structure, crafted from stone and encircled by well-established trees. Broadfoot stopped, turning to face Caslin.

"Now that's where it got a little interesting. In short, no. I haven't got the reason he left the civil service nor any specifics on what he was working on when he did so. Not through lack of asking, I might add but I'm waiting on people coming back to me. Nathaniel," he said pointedly, "I never have to wait for people to get back to me. Not when requesting such basic information and, let us not forget, Michaelson was a senior official but not a permanent undersecretary nor sitting at director level."

"What does that tell you?" Caslin asked as Broadfoot resumed walking, Caslin falling into step alongside.

"That inquiries relating to Michaelson or his portfolio are flagged somehow."

"Flagged? By who?"

Broadfoot shrugged, "Could be any number of departments. I don't know but… it's certainly intriguing."

"What about *Project Obmen*? Anything?"

"No. Sorry. I've nothing on that. Had Michaelson made any direct references to it?" Broadfoot queried.

This time Caslin shook his head, "No, he didn't but with everything I received, it seemed significant. What with Michaelson being concerned with business affairs, I hoped he was linked to it and that would fill in some of the blanks."

"Can't help you there," Broadfoot said. "Speaking of sources. You asked after Cory Walsh?"

"I did. What can you tell me?"

"As much as you have probably found out under your own steam, I imagine," Broadfoot said. "A successful businessman. A billionaire, largely self-made. He's been making waves in recent years. Not only here in the UK but it's fair to say in much of the developed world."

"Why? What's he up to?"

"Lobbying anyone who will listen."

"To what end?"

"Tightening of financial controls in global markets," Broadfoot stated. "He's been trying to toughen up the regulation put upon foreign investments and money flows. It's almost a one-man crusade against financial corruption."

Caslin blew out his cheeks, "Good luck with that."

Broadfoot agreed, "If anyone ever wanted to move a mountain, it's him. Walsh hasn't been without success, mind you. He's been instrumental in legislative changes in over a dozen jurisdictions in the last five years. Some powerful names have had assets frozen or been blacklisted in the financial markets as a direct result of his campaigning."

"So, he wasn't lying when he suggested he has enemies?" Caslin said rhetorically.

"It's a stance that's won him as many enemies as it has friends. There have been repeated attempts to have him extradited on international arrest warrants. They've become almost an annual event for him. Not that any government has sought to enforce them."

"Who filed the warrants?"

"Russia. All of them," Broadfoot replied. Caslin didn't respond but he felt Broadfoot's gaze fall upon him. "Are you tying Walsh's crusade to the Kuznetsov suicide?"

Caslin looked away, his eyes drawn to the cenotaph in the memorial gardens on the opposing riverbank, directly opposite them. "No. To be honest, Kuznetsov has never been mentioned in this context. Unless, you know something I don't?" he said, stopping and meeting Broadfoot's eye.

Broadfoot chewed on his lower lip momentarily prior to answering.

"There has been some chatter," he replied.

"Regarding Kuznetsov's death?" Caslin clarified. Broadfoot nodded.

"GCHQ has reported a noticeable rise in high-level communication in the run up to, as well as the aftermath of, last week's events. Following on from Kuznetsov's death things dropped back."

"Do you think they're related?" Caslin asked.

Broadfoot locked eyes with him for a brief moment before breaking it off. His shoulders dropped at the same time. "It's your case, Nathaniel."

"One that I'm being pushed to sign off, sooner rather than later."

Broadfoot sighed, "Unsurprising. Under the circumstances."

"What circumstances?"

"Big picture, Nathaniel," Broadfoot said, setting off once more and gazing at some unidentifiable point in the distance. "The UK government has only recently come out of a decade of frosty relations with the Kremlin. The strength of that relationship has been tested again recently. Whether Kuznetsov's death was a suicide or something more sinister doesn't really matter."

"I think it matters to his family," Caslin stated, cutting a sharp edge to his tone.

"Not when it comes down to international relations. When the interests of the Crown are threatened everything else becomes secondary," Broadfoot replied. "Even an unfounded hint of impropriety could do untold damage."

"That's not my problem," Caslin said.

"Make sure it doesn't become so," Broadfoot replied. "I understand things haven't been great for you recently back at Fulford Road." Caslin flicked his eyes at Broadfoot and away again. The grape vine was evidently still intact.

"Really? I get on all right with Matheson. She's a decent enough DCI," he said as convincingly as possible.

"And Sutherland?" Broadfoot asked, referring to his successor as Caslin's detective chief superintendent.

He shrugged, "I've had worse."

Broadfoot grinned, "As an aside, I was disappointed you didn't take up my offer."

"I know," Caslin replied, not wishing to discuss the subject any further. "It wasn't the right time" was all he was willing to say. Wishing to change the subject, Caslin took out his phone. "Can you have a look at something, for me?" he asked, opening up his gallery folder and flicking through the photographs. Scrolling to the bottom, he found what he was looking for and passed the handset across. Broadfoot took it, holding it at arm's length to try and make out the detail.

"I don't have my glasses," he said, apologetically.

"Zoom in," Caslin suggested. "I just want to know who that is beyond Matheson, standing with Sutherland and ACC Sinclair?" Broadfoot used his thumb and forefinger to enlarge the image. The picture was the one Caslin had taken through the glass from his vantage point at the top of the stairwell, following the meeting he had been summoned to where he'd been practically ordered to tie off the Kuznetsov case. Broadfoot handed the phone back. His expression was impassive. "Well?"

"Commander Niall Montgomerie," Broadfoot said flatly. "He heads up SO15."

"SO15? That's the Counter Terrorism Unit."

"Yes. I work with them regularly," Broadfoot said. "I should imagine, he was present in York because of the tensions surrounding the protests."

"You imagine?" Caslin said, raising an eyebrow. "In your position, shouldn't you know?" Broadfoot nodded, his expression hadn't changed, remaining unreadable but Caslin knew him well enough to know that Montgomerie's presence was news to him. "Speaking of that intelligence chatter, you mentioned."

"Go on," Broadfoot said.

"Any increase relating to activities among the far-right groups? A suggestion that they had something special planned, a new campaign maybe?"

Broadfoot shook his head, "Nothing of note that would necessarily raise a threat level. We knew they were coming to York but that's been common knowledge for some time. As to carrying out a statement of intent, violent or otherwise, no, I'm not aware. That's not to say it's inconceivable, mind you."

"They're getting more organised, aren't they?"

Broadfoot agreed with regret in his tone, "Gone are the days where you find a bunch of skin-heads getting smashed and trashing a few Asian-owned newsagents. Your modern fascists, the skilled manipulators, are educated, well-financed, dress like Hipsters and are well aware of what we do to curtail their activities. Three-quarters of referrals to the government's deradicalization scheme are for those indoctrinated in right-wing ideology."

"Three-quarters…" Caslin replied, dumbstruck.

"I fear there's an ideological war coming, Nathaniel," Broadfoot said solemnly, offering Caslin his hand by way of saying goodbye. Caslin took it. "Just not the one most people in this country expected to see. Should anything else come my way I think you'll be interested to hear, I'll be in touch. In the meantime, should you need me you know where I am."

"Thank you for your time, sir."

Broadfoot set off, leaving Caslin standing alone in the grounds of the museum. He watched the senior officer depart, his driver coming to meet him and the two headed for the car park. Caslin remained where he was, mulling over what he had learned. Perhaps, the key point he found most enlightening was the unintentional offering. With everything Broadfoot said, the leap from Walsh to Kuznetsov was the most telling. Farzaad Amin's name never came up, not even in passing. To Caslin's knowledge, Nestor Kuznetsov had no bearing on Cory Walsh nor Amin's death and yet, Broadfoot drew the link. Intentional or otherwise it set Caslin's mind racing. Taking out his phone, he called DS Hunter.

"Sarah, it's Caslin. Drop everything you're doing and find Finlay Michaelson."

"Finlay Michaelson. Got it," Hunter said. "Who is he?"

"The key," Caslin replied and hung up.

CHAPTER NINETEEN

HUNTER NEGOTIATED the overtaking manoeuvre with ease. For once, Caslin felt certain she'd demonstrated enough caution. Leaving the tractor and its trailer behind, the car accelerated. Making the next turn in the road, Caslin reached up and tilted the sun visor. They were heading west, away from York towards Long Marston, a small village barely seven miles from the city. Slowing as they approached the outer limits of the village, leaving the open farmland behind them, Caslin focusing his attention on the road ahead.

"There should be a left turn coming up, signposted for the Village Hall," he said peering into the distance. As expected, they came to the intersection and Hunter took the turn onto Angram Road. There were houses to either side of them. A mixture of modern homes designed to blend seamlessly in although failing to do so, nestled in between aging brick buildings constructed over the past few centuries. Many were easily identifiable as converted agricultural buildings, juxtaposed alongside traditional farmhouses, often striking an odd-looking contrast with one another.

The houses to their left were replaced by a perimeter wall, running adjacent to the road and stretching forward for several hundred yards. Caslin knew this wall, with its mature trees beyond, shrouded their destination from the roadside. Ahead, the village church could be seen towering over an upcoming line of three or four houses at the edge of the settlement boundary.

"This one?" Hunter asked, slowing further and annoying the vehicle that had sped up behind them.

"Yes, the entrance should be just up here on the left," he replied, pointing with his forefinger. No sooner had he spoken, the turn onto the driveway came into view as the wall curved in and away from the highway. Hunter flicked on the indicator. The brickwork of the boundary wall must have been set prior to the advent of modern vehicles, such was the limited space on either side of them. The car following them accelerated aggressively once they were clear. Evidently, the driver was in a hurry.

The driveway was gravel lined and cut immediately back in the direction they had come before winding off to the right and up towards a large, detached Georgian farmhouse. Caslin cast an eye over it as they pulled up, coming to a stop. The brick building, with its stone detailing, clay pantile roof and elegant twelve-pane, sash and case windows struck an imposing figure in the mature gardens that surrounded it. Many of the curtains were still drawn, despite the setting sun now being at the rear of the house. Hunter glanced around. A detached, double garage lay ahead of them. It was closed with the fallen leaves of the established garden banked up against the doors, driven there by the wind.

"No car outside. It doesn't look like anyone's home," she said.

Caslin unclipped his seatbelt and opened his door. "We're expected. She'll be home," he replied, getting out. Hunter followed suit.

They approached the entrance. The door was oversized and original, judging by the thickness along with the detailing. Modern reproductions were easy to spot. There was no need to knock as the door opened before they reached it. The woman who stood before them cracked a weak smile. She was in her sixties, Caslin guessed, of slim build with a heavily-lined face. Her eyes were sunken and the welcoming expression appeared forced. Caslin recognised only too well the physical manifestations that coincided with mental torment.

"Mrs Michaelson?" he asked, already sure of the answer.

She nodded. "Inspector Caslin?"

He took out his wallet, showing her his warrant card. She barely glanced at it, merely stepping aside and beckoning them to enter. "Please, come in."

"This is Detective Sergeant Sarah Hunter," Caslin offered, as he stepped forward. Hunter smiled, in greeting, with another returned in her direction by their host. Mrs Michaelson led them along the hallway into the interior of the house, ushering them into what Caslin figured to be the drawing room.

An open fire crackled in the hearth. The room was traditionally decorated with wood-panelling to waist height on all four walls. Two large sofas were set facing each other to either side of the fireplace. It was here that they were guided to and offered a seat. A wall clock ticked and wood crackled in the hearth.

"Would you care for some tea or perhaps coffee?" they were asked graciously. Both Caslin and Hunter declined. Mrs Michaelson sat down opposite them, looking uncomfortable. Judging by her demeanour since their arrival, Caslin figured she wasn't a sedentary person and sitting still was not in her general make-up.

"Thank you for agreeing to meet with us, Mrs Michaelson," Caslin began, she smiled.

"Please, do call me Miranda."

"Once again, I am very sorry for your loss."

"Thank you, Inspector," she replied. Miranda Michaelson bore the stark pain of losing her husband. "Please, how can I help you?"

"As I said on the telephone, we're investigating a case in which your late husband's name has come up. Within his role in the civil service, he may well have been aware of details we're yet to uncover or may have come across some names of those who are involved," Caslin said softly. "I certainly don't wish to cause you any undue distress. Did he ever mention his work to you?"

Miranda shook her head, "I am terribly sorry, Inspector. Finlay didn't speak to me about his work. He rarely ever did. Perhaps earlier in his career, when he was confident he was in line for a promotion but even then, never in any great detail. Regarding anything within the last few years I'm afraid I can be of little help to you."

"Could we ask about why he retired when he did?" Hunter asked.

"Of course, yes," Miranda said, turning to her. "Everything was getting rather fraught domestically. I returned to nurse my mother… oh, it must be… four years ago now. She was finding the house to be far too much for her to cope with. Finlay remained in London, obviously, but he would travel up as and when he could manage to."

"And this caused…" Caslin struggled to find the correct word, "friction, between the two of you?"

"After a while living apart begins to cause problems. The pressure was certainly mounting," Miranda replied, her voice tailed off as she glanced out of the nearest window at nothing in particular.

"So, your husband took early retirement?" Hunter asked.

"Mother was ailing and I needed the support."

"And he moved here to help you," Caslin said.

"To be closer to me, yes," Miranda confirmed. "Or, at least, that was what he *said*."

Caslin sat forward, interested, "You have your doubts?" Miranda stiffened slightly. Had he not been looking directly at her, Caslin may have missed it.

"He would still spend hours in his study," she said, an edge to her tone. "Even though he was supposedly retired. I never got the impression that he ever really wanted to give it up. To be fair, he'd worked hard to get where he had and if the truth be known, I think he found it galling to step away because of the needs of my family."

"The relationship was difficult?" Hunter pressed but took care to be gentle.

Miranda chuckled, "Finlay referred to my mother as an *Ogre*. They never took kindly to each other. My father, on the other hand, was altogether different. Finlay was like the son he'd never had. They got on famously."

"Can you tell us about your husband's state of mind around the time of his death?" Caslin asked. "Did he convey any feelings to you or appear stressed, agitated, about anything?" She thought on it for a moment before answering.

"He was certainly withdrawn," she said. "More so than I'd ever experienced with him prior to that. However, he found our separation equally challenging and after four years of virtually living apart, I'm not entirely sure how recent that change in his manner may have been. I had no idea that he was… having the thoughts that he was."

"I am sorry you are having to revisit all of this," Caslin said.

"That's quite all right, Inspector. I think on it every day." The statement only led him to feel even worse.

"How is your mother?" Hunter asked. Miranda met her eye.

"She also passed away, two months ago," she said. "I have laid her to rest alongside my father just as she would have wanted."

"I am sorry," Hunter said, wishing she'd never asked. To lose her husband through suicide along with her remaining parent in such quick succession must have been extremely difficult to process.

"Don't worry, Dear. You weren't to know," Miranda said, warmly.

"Your husband's study, may we see it?" Caslin asked.

Miranda nodded. "Certainly," she said, rising. Caslin and Hunter also stood. "Please, come this way."

They were led from the drawing room, back into the hallway. Heading down the hall and to the left, Miranda showed them to a room at the rear of the building. Coming to stand before the door, she stepped to the side and turned to face them. "I must admit, I haven't been in there since... since I found, Finlay," she said, in halting speech.

"That's okay. There's no need for you to come in," Caslin said, placing a reassuring hand on her forearm. Miranda appeared grateful. "Tell me, has much been touched or moved from in there?"

She shook her head, "No. No one's been in there. Just the paramedics... oh, and the constable who came along after. I haven't felt ready to tackle it, not yet. You see, it was my father's study before Finlay took it over and, well... he passed away from a heart attack in the same room. They were so alike, those two. It is somewhat fitting, I suppose."

"Thank you," Caslin said, grasping the handle. Miranda excused herself.

"I will wait for you in the drawing room," she said before leaving them alone. Caslin cast Hunter a sideways glance and opened the door.

Caslin led the way. The room was almost a perfect square, with dual-aspect windows. The southern-facing pane allowed the room to flood with light as the winter-sun dropped low on the horizon. A traditional, hardwood desk was on one side of the room, set in from the wall, with the east-facing window behind the chair. Caslin indicated for Hunter to inspect the shelving units, stacked to shoulder height with lever-arch folders, while he approached the desk.

Coming around to the other side, Caslin pulled out the chair and sat down. There was a banker's desk-lamp in situ, antique brass fitting with an emerald-green shade. He pulled the switch and it bathed the surface of the desk in artificial light. Nothing much adorned the desk apart from a solitary wedding photograph, its dark brown hue giving away its age, and a little stationery so Caslin turned his focus to the drawers.

Glancing down, he noted the two pedestals, one to either side of him. Both had four drawers with one large double-width drawer interconnecting both units. He opened this one first and inspected the contents. Aside from some blank sheets of headed paper, a letter opener and some assorted envelopes of various sizes, he found nothing to pique his interest. As he was pushing it closed, he spied a ring of keys. Picking them up, he counted three, guessing they were for the locks to the desk. They were small, brass, with intricately cast patterns on the bow. Closing the drawer, he inserted one of the keys into the lock. It slid in effortlessly and the mechanism turned with ease.

Switching his attention back to the pedestals, he tried the drawers one by one. Checking all eight, Caslin found none of them to be locked. Then he set about going through them again although this time he spent more time on each as he analysed the contents. More than half of the drawers were empty and of the remaining ones, Caslin found nothing of note. There were old utility bills, some correspondence relating to a function being arranged in the local village and a scattering of receipts but nothing relevant. Having optimistically expected to find a diary, some handwritten notes or copied files that might generate a new lead, Caslin was left disappointed. Sitting back in the chair, he exhaled deeply. Hunter looked over from where she was scanning through a folder.

"Nothing?"

Caslin shook his head.

"No. If Michaelson brought his work home with him on the weekend, he didn't leave it here," Caslin said, dejected. "What about you?"

"Same here," she replied. "Most of this stuff relates to the farm and its holdings. Maybe he didn't keep anything after he retired or his files were down in London. He would've had his own digs down there after all."

Caslin blew out his cheeks, "Then what was he doing holed up in his study?" A thought struck him. Picking up the keys once more, he tried one in the lock of the first drawer in the pedestal to his right. The key turned smoothly. Pulling out the drawer, he then pushed it closed and then did the same again, only slower. Repeating the process with each drawer, Caslin found none of the locks to be stiff and the drawers were smooth in transition from closed to open. Pursing his lips, he sank back in the chair. Hunter crossed the room to join him, giving up on her search.

"A penny for them?"

"The drawers," he said, indicating them with a general sweep of his hand before scooping up the keys. She looked at them and then back at him.

"What of them?"

"They all work," he replied, as if that answered everything.

"I don't understand."

"This is an old desk. An antique, not a reproduction."

"So?"

"If you don't use them, things like these locks..." he pointed to the first drawer, down to his right, "the mechanisms are liable to seize up or at the very least, the wood swells, warps, stiffens, whatever, making keys harder to turn. Not here. Every lock works like a charm. The same with pulling out the drawers. There are no runners, no bearings to make it smooth. If you don't open them regularly, they'll get stiff or screech."

"So, the desk was well used?" Hunter asked, not quite following his line of thought.

"Very much so," Caslin confirmed. "And yet, half the drawers are empty and none of them were locked."

"And... if they were frequently locked..." Hunter followed the logic.

"That's right," Caslin said. "There must have been something to secure more valuable than headed paper and a few old electricity bills."

"But there's nothing," Hunter stated, glancing around the office. Caslin followed her lead and scanned the room for anything that might catch his attention. There were two canvas paintings, hanging on the walls. One to the left of the south-facing window, depicting a landscape, along with another above the fireplace. The latter was an inset, cast-iron Victorian addition with intricate detailing. A work of art in itself.

Coming out from behind the desk, Caslin crossed to the fireplace and examined the canvas hanging above. It was a portrait, seemingly of one of Miranda's ancestors. A portly man, with an angular jaw and red-faced complexion. Judging from the clothing he wore, Caslin assumed he may have been the first to own the family residence at some point in the eighteenth century.

"Look at these," Hunter said, over her shoulder. Caslin came to stand alongside her. She was casting an eye over some photographs, framed and hanging on the wall behind the desk. "This must be Finlay and Miranda, fairly recently," she said, pointing to a photograph apparently taken on a warm, sunny day. Miranda appeared much as she did now albeit with a far more relaxed demeanour and brighter eyes. The man next to her, with an arm around her shoulder was smiling and Caslin knew it to be Finlay Michaelson having come across his picture in the coroner's case file prior to making the drive out to Long Marston.

They were either photographs of family holidays from over the years or what looked to be special occasions, perhaps in far-flung locations but in many cases it was impossible to tell. Caslin hovered over one of the couple sitting astride horses with mountains in the background.

"I'd say that was Argentina, if I had to guess," Hunter offered, seeing Caslin focusing on it.

"Really? You sound sure."

"Stephen and I travelled to Patagonia shortly after we got engaged. The light and the landscape are memorable. Those mountains behind them look like the Austral Andes," Hunter said. There was something in her tone that struck a chord with him. A note of melancholy perhaps? He wasn't sure and chose not to mention it.

"I've never been," Caslin said, moving along and scanning the next picture. Taking a step back, he focused on the arrangement. There was something odd about it but he couldn't quite put his finger on what had sharpened his focus. Hunter noticed.

"What's up?" she asked.

Caslin shook his head, "I'm not sure. Can you put the main light on please?"

The sun had dropped below the horizon and the gloom of a winter afternoon was now sapping the light from around them. Hunter crossed the room and flicked the switch. The five-way, wrought-iron chandelier counteracted the growing darkness. At first glance, the arrangement of the framed pictures looked haphazard at best. They were not all of a uniform size, some were set in landscape while others were in traditional portrait style. Even so, something didn't look right to his eye.

Coming to stand before the desk, Caslin sought to tease out the thought currently lodged in the back of his mind. From this vantage point, he could see a slight discolouration in the wall between two pictures. Hunter caught sight of his lingering gaze and followed his eye.

"What is it?"

Caslin didn't answer but walked around the desk and approached the point he was focusing on. Reaching up with his right hand, he ran his fingers lightly across the wall. They stopped at a point and he tapped it with his index finger.

"The paper," he said, turning his body side-on and moving closer. "The paper has been bleached by the sun and here," he tapped the wall again, for emphasis, "there's a hole."

"There was another picture hanging there?" Hunter asked, scanning the remaining images. "What about over there?" she said, pointing to another anomalous gap between two frames and bearing a similar contrast. Caslin crossed to it and located a nail-hole for a picture hook.

"Good spot," he said, confirming the find. "We need to know when they were taken down."

"And why?" Hunter said quietly.

Caslin nodded his agreement. "I think Miranda is going to have to come in here after all. I'll go and get her."

"TAKE YOUR TIME," Caslin said. Miranda Michaelson stood in the centre of her late husband's study, staring at the desk in front of her. Clearly, she was struggling to maintain her composure. The last time she was in that position was when she'd found her husband of forty-two years slumped at his desk, having ingested an overdose of painkillers.

"I don't know what I'm looking for," she said, her voice threatening to crack at any moment.

"Anything unusual or out of place, no matter how small or insignificant you might think it," Hunter offered by way of encouragement. Miranda closed her eyes, looking to the floor and took a deep breath. Lifting her head, she reopened her eyes appearing focused on what she had to do. Both Caslin and Hunter waited patiently. Miranda started with the desk, drawing her gaze across the surface before shifting her attention away.

"What about the contents?" Caslin suggested, indicating the drawers.

She shook her head, "I never went into them. Finlay was quite insistent that I should stay out of his work affairs and besides, he always kept them locked. The Official Secrets Act and all of that." Caslin nodded, briefly flicking his eyes to Hunter who indicated she'd noted the significance of the comment. Miranda turned and looked around the room, pausing at the portrait over the fireplace.

"A relative?" Caslin asked. Her eyes lit up momentarily and a brief smile crossed her lips.

"My great-great-grandfather, yes," she confirmed, with pride. "He bought this house with proceeds from investments made overseas." Miranda continued on, concentrating hard on the task set for her. Caslin did a little calculation in his head, giving a fleeting consideration to whether the profits needed to purchase a house such as this would have been garnered through means considered, these days at least, to be of an amoral origin. His thoughts were punctuated by an exclamation. "There!"

"What is it?" Caslin asked.

"A photograph is missing right there," Miranda said, pointing. "And another," she added, crossing to where Hunter had noted the second space.

"Do you know when they came down?" Caslin asked, endeavouring to contain his enthusiasm. It was soon dashed.

"No, I'm sorry," Miranda said. "I don't come in here very often."

"Do you remember what the pictures were of?" Hunter asked. Miranda thought on it for a while, her expression a mask of concentration.

"One was of a fishing trip, I think. Finlay went on it a few years ago. It was in the Mediterranean with some colleagues. He was quite excited as I recall. The photo was taken on board the yacht. Finlay appeared terribly dashing in that one."

"Who was he with?"

She shook her head, "It was some freebie excursion sponsored by companies through the DTI, I believe."

"Was it an official Department of Trade and Industry junket?" Caslin asked.

"I've no idea," Miranda scoffed. "It was several years ago and like I said, Finlay didn't discuss his work."

"And the other one?" Hunter asked but Miranda was noncommittal.

"I don't recall. I'm sorry."

"Did your husband have a computer here, at home?" Caslin asked.

Miranda nodded. "Yes, he had a laptop. He kept it there, in his desk." Caslin glanced over to Hunter, whose impassive expression belied the same feeling he was suppressing. They were on the right path. He knew it.

"WHAT DO YOU THINK?" Hunter asked. "Someone else has been in there, haven't they?" Caslin looked back at the house as she turned the car around and set off along the driveway. The tyres crunched on the gravel and Hunter remembered to turn on her headlights before they reached the highway.

"Miranda swears blind only herself, the ambulance crew and the police officer who attended, entered the study. Then it was the undertaker and a detective constable who we know signed it off as a suicide on the same day. Other than that, no one has been in there."

Hunter shot him a sideways glance, "So, that's that?"

"Is it hell," Caslin retorted. "You're right. Someone's been in there and cleaned it out."

"Do you think she knows who?"

"Some people are natural actors but not her," Caslin said, shaking his head. "I'll bet they did it under her nose and without her knowledge or consent. I want to know who and why? Michaelson was neck deep into, or up to, something. I'm absolutely certain of it. What I would give to know who was with him in those photographs."

"Someone made an effort to ensure no one would," Hunter replied.

"Or what he was involved in."

"Whatever it was it drove him to take his own life," Hunter said.

"That's what they say."

"Where do we go from here?"

"I want you to set up surveillance on Thomas Grey. For one, he's stressing about something and, more importantly…" he let the thought tail off.

"More importantly?"

"Well, first and foremost, he's still alive."

CHAPTER TWENTY

NURSING HIS PINT, Caslin's gaze drifted beyond the vaulted, brick ceiling and up into the next tier of Lendal Cellars. A man was propped up, one elbow resting against the bar, complaining about his day to anyone who'd listen. By all accounts, his friends were just as tired of listening to it as he was. The pub was quiet tonight. On any given day, the clamour of the crowd would merge into a general hubbub, replacing an overheard conversation with anonymity. This evening though, the freezing temperatures and driving rain were keeping people away.

For Caslin, the short walk across the centre to his favourite haunt was neither a distraction nor an escape. He did his best thinking alone and over the years had realised he could be alone even in a crowd. It was a state of mind. From his seat in a booth, situated in the lower section, Caslin could see right across the pub. Immediately clocking the figures as they entered from above, he watched them descend the steps. The first casually scanned the few people present whereas the other two, only a step behind, moved with the grace and agility of predators, furtively glancing around, assessing patrons as a hunter would their targets. Caslin had wondered how long it would be before he'd see them again.

One of the accompanying men dropped off, remaining in the upper bar, near to the main entrance and set himself with his back to the wall and a clear line of sight in Caslin's direction. The other continued on, with

Cory Walsh, towards him. The latter offering a partial wave as they approached. Caslin flicked him a greeting with a bob of his head.

"I figured you'd be stopping by at some point," Caslin said.

Walsh smiled warmly, splaying his hands wide, "Please accept my apologies for missing our appointment the other night. I was called away at short notice." Walsh removed his coat, followed by a scarf, and carefully folded the coat before laying both across the back of the padded seat to the booth. Sliding in opposite Caslin, he nodded another greeting before glancing towards his associate. "I'll have a scotch," he said, looking to Caslin who nodded. "Make that two," Walsh instructed and the man departed.

"Did you go anywhere nice?" Caslin asked.

Walsh exhaled heavily, "Copenhagen."

"Beautiful."

"It is," Walsh agreed, "but I flew in and out. I was only there for a couple of hours."

"Your phone didn't work?" Caslin said, mildly hostile. Despite accepting there could be justifiable reasons for his failure to show, Caslin still didn't appreciate being stood up. Walsh grinned. Caslin figured it was forced.

"I am genuinely sorry," Walsh said. He eyed the side of Caslin's face, taking in the bruising that was now a deeper shade of purple. "It would appear your time, since we last met, has been… eventful?"

Caslin finished his pint, placing the empty glass on the table. "Someone followed me the other night. When we were supposed to meet," he said, seeing no reason to keep it a secret, figuring Walsh knew more than he was letting on. He always seemed to be at least one step ahead. "But that's not news to you is it?"

"I'm not surprised to hear that, Nathaniel. If you weren't already under some form of surveillance, covert or otherwise, I'm certain you would've been soon enough," Walsh stated, with a brief shake of the head.

"Were they following me or looking for you?"

Walsh inclined his head slightly, appreciating the logic, "That, I couldn't say."

"Is that why you bailed on our meeting?" Caslin challenged. Walsh met his eye.

"I was in Copenhagen. Like I said," he replied, adopting a defensive posture. Walsh's associate arrived with two scotches, placing them on the table. He then stepped aside to Caslin's left, keeping his back to the wall and facing the open bar. His eyes never ceased scanning the room.

"Who is following me?" Caslin asked.

"It could be any number of people or agencies…" Walsh said with a brief shrug of his shoulders, picking up his glass. "Good health," he said, before sipping at the contents.

"Even yours?" Caslin asked, leaving his own drink where it had been placed. Walsh laughed. Caslin was sure it was genuine on this occasion.

"You think I would have you followed to our own meeting and then fail to show?" he said with a smile, shaking his head in a dismissive gesture. "And people accuse *me* of being paranoid." Caslin flicked his eyebrows at the absurdity of his own suggestion, sweeping up his glass and tilting it in Walsh's direction.

"Cheers," he said, tasting the scotch. "If someone is following me in order to get to you, you're taking a risk in coming here tonight."

"I take precautions, Nathaniel. It has become something of a habit… a very necessary one, in fact. I trust you received my little package?"

Caslin nodded, "Yes, thank you. I guessed it came from you. Well, you've certainly got my attention. Care to fill in the blanks?"

"What would you like to know?"

"Your connection to Farzaad Amin. How about starting there and we'll see how we go," Caslin said, sitting back and stretching one arm out, resting it on the back of the seat. "You said you didn't know him but that's not true."

"We go back a way," Walsh said, sucking air through his teeth, "and that's not an easy question to answer."

"I have time," Caslin said, revisiting his scotch.

"I'm sure you've done your homework on me by now?" Walsh asked, peering over the rim of his glass as he raised it. Caslin inclined his head.

"Naturally."

"And what did you find out?"

"You're a businessman. A very successful one by anyone's measure," Caslin added, "who's turned his hand to political lobbying."

"Is that what they say now? For a time, I was considered more of a revolutionary… an activist. Then I was downgraded to the more vanilla term of a *campaigner*. It loses some of its edge, don't you think?"

"I've also heard of *a one-man crusade*. How about that?"

"I do like that. It has a certain ring to it," Walsh said, grinning. He finished his scotch. Turning to his minder, he requested a refill. Caslin followed suit, finishing his scotch in one fluid motion. Walsh indicated another for him as well.

"Amin?" Caslin pressed.

"Amin was one of you," Walsh said, but before Caslin could respond, he continued, "in law enforcement, at least. Do you know how I made my fortune, the first time around?"

"No, I didn't get that far."

"You remember the Cold War and how we know now what life was like behind the Iron Curtain?" Caslin indicated he did. "Well, when that period came to an abrupt, undignified end and the former Soviet States began to open up politically, for a time at least, so did the world of commerce. Out of the ruins of a failed system new markets arose like a phoenix from the flames. Prime opportunities for those who had the capital, along with the courage, to embrace them. The likes of me were welcomed with open arms. We had the expertise. We had the knowledge."

"A lot of people got rich," Caslin said.

"Very," Walsh agreed, "almost overnight in many cases. I was one of those who started wealthy and enriched myself even further. Celebrated in Forbes, lauded by investment analysts the world over. I must admit, I thought I was a king."

"It didn't last?"

"On the contrary, the returns lasted for well over a decade… and then things began to change. A little at first, incremental changes below the surface that slipped by largely unnoticed."

"What kind of changes? What are we talking about here?" Caslin asked, interested.

"The wealth began to coalesce around the few, perhaps two to three hundred individuals, give or take. I mean personal wealth on a scale that most people just can't comprehend. Obviously, there were many others sitting below at different levels of the food chain and still are. But these few, in particular, began to soak up not only most of the money but all of the power. So much so that they began looking beyond the confines of their relatively young business empires and seeking out new challenges. New ways to exert their influence on the world. Money, in of itself, just wasn't enough anymore."

"For some people there will never be enough."

"True."

"Are you talking about politics?"

"Very astute, Nathaniel. These men knew how they'd come across their fortunes. They were often former members of the Politburo, high-ranking officers of the KGB or its successor, the FSB. They had the contacts, the training, as well as the skills to manipulate and succeed, particularly with a weakened government operating largely in chaos. It's no great secret that after the fall of the Communist system organised crime within Russia and her satellite states exploded into life with rapid expansion into the same areas I've been talking about."

"Russian gangs have operated for years, some for centuries."

"Of course, you are right. But now, they were doing so with the aid of those who once sought to stunt them. The foxes were taking charge of the hen house, so to speak. They were awash with cash."

"Are you saying all of the money was dirty?"

"After a fashion. Assets were open to access like never before. Infrastructure, gas and oil reserves – state assets owned and operated by a failing system. Without a strong government, businessmen could purchase these assets at knockdown prices, as little as a few dollars in some cases. Overnight, their true value was listed on the markets and you have billionaires made from absolutely nothing!" He snapped his fingers as if to dramatise the point.

"How was that even legal?" Caslin asked, incredulous.

"Technically, it wasn't but it was a new world for these guys. Greasing the right wheels allowed these deals to go through with precious little oversight."

"They paid off the authorities?"

"Absolutely. You have to remember the state of these places at the time. The governments were largely bankrupt. Many of these officials hadn't been paid in months. An approach, offering what equated to several years' worth of pay for what, signing over something that meant nothing to you personally? That was a no brainer."

"And this is how you were making your money?" Caslin said, as their second round of drinks arrived. Walsh sat back, the enthusiasm for his story visually draining from him, momentarily.

"There were no losers," he argued, although Caslin sensed he said so with little conviction. "At least, for a while."

"Go on," Caslin said.

"As I said, the power began to centre on a few and they, in turn, were jockeying for position. Whoever held the strongest list of contacts in their phonebook tended to win out. On occasion, the same people were being paid off by competing groups. Anyway, I digress," he waved his hands in a circular motion, "as the governments reorganised and reasserted some control, so the questions began to be asked. That is where Amin comes into it. Although, that's not his real name."

"What is his real name?"

"Kadyrov. Marat Kadyrov is how I knew him," Walsh said, his tone shifting from one of confident explanation to sadness, remembering a lost friend. "He was ideological. Perhaps naïve in his views of how things should be, but a very decent man. When I came across him we were on opposing sides. He was tasked with investigating organised crime and ascertaining how far their operations had penetrated the state apparatus.

Substantially, I would say but that's another story. Well before I ever met him, he'd been deployed by the intelligence services to infiltrate a Muscovite criminal organisation with links to other gangs throughout the Caucasus. His ethnic Kazakh background gave him the credibility that many of the other agencies just didn't possess. That experience made him an outstanding candidate for this new role."

"Hence why he could be passed off as an Afghan asylum seeker here in the UK?"

"It would appear so."

Caslin raised his glass, "Did he investigate you?"

Walsh inclined his head, "In a way, yes. He was following the money trail and I chanced across his radar."

"How did Kay… Kad…?"

"Kadyrov," Walsh confirmed.

"How did he wind up here in the UK, living under a false name?" Caslin asked, leaving out the more obvious question of *why he couldn't find any record of it?*

"He was a tenacious investigator, Nathaniel. You would have liked him. The two of you have much in common. To my knowledge, he'd uncovered a scandal involving the sale of construction contracts across several Moscow Oblasts."

"Oblasts?"

"I'm sorry. They are administrative centres or zones," Walsh explained. Caslin bid him to continue. "Marat's belief was that these contracts were granted off the back of multiple bribes, paid to various levels of government officials. The last I spoke with him, he was due to take his findings to his superiors with an expectation they would sanction more funds to enable him to widen his investigation."

"I guess it didn't go down that way?"

"I'm afraid that what followed I am not a party to," Walsh said. "However, suffice it to say, I didn't hear from Marat again. It was as if he disappeared. Apparently, it looks very much like he did so with the aid of your intelligence services."

"He turned to us?"

"My belief is that he offered up everything he had on his investigation to your agencies in exchange for safe passage to the UK."

"But you don't know?" Caslin asked, leaning forward.

Walsh shook his head. "When Marat vanished, he was helping me."

"How?"

"There's a way of doing things in Russia, Nathaniel. What you have you may not necessarily get to keep. Do you understand? Why do you think your country is awash with wealthy oligarchs, buying up houses, football clubs, expensive cars and any other material goods that catch their eye? Here, they can keep what they have."

"Someone explained that to me once. They came after you, didn't they? Or at least, your money."

"As I said, you are very astute, Nathaniel." Walsh's tone tinged with regret. For the first time, Caslin noted a real change in demeanour of the man sitting opposite him. Up until now, his confidence appeared unshakeable. A self-belief, no doubt garnered from his success in the business world appeared to be creaking under the weight of reality. "I found money was missing from my investments in Russia. Somewhere along the line funds were being syphoned off at an alarming rate. I couldn't trust my internal staff to recover it. I had no idea where the seals had been breached."

"So, you approached Kadyrov?"

Walsh nodded, "I figured that he was already moving in the right circles. He was different to others I'd come across over there – honest, perhaps? A man of integrity, certainly."

"And?"

"Shortly after was when he vanished," Walsh said, deflated. "I tried to contact him but he didn't return my calls. A little time passed and I approached members of his circle only to find that they too had been lifted from the street. I went to his family and it was only then that it dawned on me."

"What happened?"

"They were detained. I never found out why."

"What did you do?"

"I took the only sensible course of action. I left, as quickly as possible," Walsh said, picking up his glass and seeing off the contents.

"The country?"

"My home, the country, my business. Everything," Walsh stated evenly. "Once I was clear I set about liquidating my holdings. I did so as quickly and as quietly as I could. I figured that if they knew what Marat knew, all that I had told him, then they'd be coming for me and everything that I had. My fears proved to be extremely accurate as it turned out."

"How much did you lose?"

"Initially, a little over $200 million was unaccounted for," Walsh said, without skipping a beat. "I transferred out the remaining funds in the course of the following weeks and months. That isn't easy by the way. There are tight controls on moving that kind of money. Shifting it without triggering any alarms was no mean feat."

"And Kadyrov, how did you find him in the UK?"

"I didn't," Walsh said. "He contacted me several days before his death. He caught me completely off guard."

"Why?"

"I thought he was dead," Walsh stated, "or rotting in a Siberian labour camp."

"What did he want?"

"To meet," Walsh said, glancing around nervously. No one was within earshot apart from his minder.

"And?"

Walsh shook his head, "I was abroad with commitments I couldn't shake. By the time I was able to get back to the UK – it was the day he died, Nathaniel. The meeting never took place."

Caslin thought about it for a moment, "And his murder… who are you putting that down to?"

Walsh looked him square in the eye, "I'm a numbers man, Nathaniel. An analyst. I approach everything through the prism of the percentages. If I had to judge I would suggest someone is covering their tracks. Everyone knows what I am about these days. Marat certainly did. Why else would he contact me? Find out who had the most to lose from Marat's voice being heard and you will have your answer. I wouldn't rule out an agenda closer to home, though."

"Rather than one Russian-based?"

"It must be considered," Walsh said with a shrug. "If he was here at the convenience of your authorities, they might not appreciate my presence either."

"You have a high opinion of yourself," Caslin said, only partly in jest.

"If you have a strong belief in coincidence you may discount the suggestion, by all means."

"You steered me towards Alexander Nairn and his suicide," Caslin said, shifting the subject. "What do you know of him?"

"I know he racked up significant frequent-flyer miles between the UK and Moscow. Marat had him down as aiding the flow of money in and out of the city."

"Whose money?"

"Only a dead man could tell you that, Nathaniel. Not me."

"Thomas Grey. Nairn's business partner. What do you know about him?"

Walsh shrugged, "Not a name I'm familiar with. I'm sorry."

"Have you heard of a civil servant by the name of Finlay Michaelson or Project Obmen? Those names also appear in the files you sent me."

"If I had all the answers, Nathaniel, I wouldn't need you, would I?" Walsh said as he stood up. He picked up his scarf and wrapped it loosely around his neck before pulling on his overcoat.

"Is there somewhere you need to be?" Caslin asked, silently considering what had provoked the all-to-sudden departure.

"We're both searching for answers to the same questions."

"But is it for the same reasons?" Caslin fixed Walsh with a stern gaze.

"Only time will tell," he replied, with a smile. Glancing to his minder who signalled they were good to go, he set off towards the upper bar and the exit. Pausing as he placed his foot on the first step, he turned to Caslin, looking over his shoulder. "Thank you for your company, Nathaniel. I'm sure you'll be in touch."

Caslin replied with a brief nod of the head, raising his glass and tilting it in Walsh's direction. Digesting the new information, Caslin couldn't help but wonder if the developing case was a little above the level of a detective inspector from North Yorkshire Police. He felt his phone vibrate. Reaching for it, he found the call had disconnected before he could answer. The signal had been lost. Being underground in a brick cellar, he was impressed he'd managed to obtain a signal at all.

Sliding out from his seat in the booth, he picked up his coat and climbed the steps. Casually acknowledging the bar staff with a wave, he crossed the lower bar and mounted the next flight of stairs whilst reading the missed call alert. No sooner had he reacquired service upon reaching the street outside, the phone rang. It was Hunter.

"Sir, I put that surveillance detail on Thomas Grey but it's not good news," she said, sounding crestfallen.

"Why, what's going on?"

"We tried to pick him up at his office, then at home but he wasn't at either."

"Okay, keep looking—"

"No, sir, you don't understand, Uniform found his Discovery abandoned on an industrial estate out towards Clifton Moor. I'm on my way over there now."

"And Grey?"

"No idea, sir. I've put out his description but nothing yet."

"Send me the address and I'll meet you there."

CHAPTER TWENTY-ONE

THE KEYLESS FOB was resting on the central console and the lights of the dashboard display were on. The gearstick was set to the drive position and the logical assumption was the engine had either stalled or switched itself into an idle-mode. Caslin stepped back from the driver's door, open wide, with the corner wedged into the damp mud of the verge running to the side of the road. Arguably, the door had been opened in a hurry.

Scanning the road, he saw no rubber residue on the tarmac. Although the falling rain would have ensured there would have been none. Eyeing the length of the car from wing to rear, the paintwork was immaculate without scuff or scrape. In fact, there was no evidence nearby to suggest the car had left the highway involuntarily. Turning his attention back to the Discovery's interior, Caslin turned his collar up against the elements. The rain was now coming down in a steady drizzle with the light breeze making it feel even colder than earlier in the day.

"Was the door open when you got here?" Caslin asked over his shoulder, seeing the approaching Hunter.

"Yes. The traffic officers found it exactly as you see it," she confirmed, coming to stand behind him.

Caslin donned a pair of latex gloves and leant inside, casting an eye around the cabin. He looked for the obvious, blood stains or tears to the upholstery, anything that could imply a confrontation violent or otherwise. There were none. The leather, stitched into both the seats and doors, was as pristine as you might expect from such a prestigious marque of vehicle appearing as if it was fresh off the forecourt. A jacket lay casually across the rear seats but aside from a couple of fuel receipts, dated earlier in the week, and a fountain pen left in the pocket of the door, Caslin could see nothing of note.

"Did you find anything?" he asked Hunter, retreating from the car.

"A mobile phone. A set of keys, presumably for home and office," Hunter said. "That's it."

"Anything in the boot?"

"Nothing. It's empty."

"Any sign of Grey's security detail?"

Hunter shook her head, "No. I had the same thought, so I contacted Lisa. You remember, from his office?"

"Yes, of course. And?"

"She said Grey turned up to work alone this morning. She didn't know why and he went straight through to his office without a word."

"Interesting," Caslin said, considering the possibilities.

"She also told me he remained there alone, all day, flatly refusing to take calls and left unexpectedly around two o'clock this afternoon."

"Did she know where he was heading?"

"No. He didn't say."

"Anything happen of note, today?"

"Apparently not, no."

"And when did Uniform locate the car?"

"Shortly after nine, sir. A member of the public was finishing a back shift and called it in on their way home after finding it apparently abandoned. They thought it odd."

"Did they report seeing Thomas Grey or anyone else hanging around? Another car perhaps?"

Hunter shook her head, "There's not a lot of through-traffic around here this late in the day." Caslin surveyed the area. They were standing on the outskirts of an industrial estate with warehouse units in one direction and open farmland in the other. Within a half mile were large out-of-town retail units set alongside a bowling alley and chain restaurants, whereas here, once the businesses shut down for the day, there was nothing. Whatever motivated Thomas Grey to come to this location of an evening totally escaped him.

"Did you take anything useful off the phone?" Caslin asked hopefully.

"It was locked," Hunter said, confirming what Caslin already figured to be the case. "Although forensics have green lighted me bagging it and I've sent a runner over to Iain Robertson to see what he can do. He's pretty confident."

Caslin nodded approvingly, "Get a warrant for the records. Disturb someone's evening or wake them up if it comes to it. We need to know who he was talking to and where he's been in those seven hours. People don't drop off the face of the earth unless they want to or—"

"Someone forces them," Hunter finished for him. There was movement behind them as members of the CSI team arrived to run the forensic rule over the car.

Caslin addressed the lead officer, "Be thorough. I need help to fill in the blanks and I'll take whatever you can give me."

"Yes, sir," the lead figure said.

Caslin turned to see a uniformed constable standing a short distance away trying to get his attention. He looked to Hunter and inclined his head to indicate she should join him. They made their way across the road bracing against the increasing intensity of both the wind and the rain.

"What do you have?" Caslin asked as they approached her.

"I've found a briefcase up against the perimeter fence over there," the constable said, indicating behind her towards the edge of an industrial compound.

She led the way and they stepped up onto the verge which, due to the combination of rain and uncut grass, was rapidly becoming treacherous under foot. Illuminated by the constable's torch, Caslin and Hunter spied the briefcase. It was open with what appeared to be the contents strewn nearby. Loose sheets of paper, trapped in the sprawling vegetation, were wet-through and proved largely illegible whilst others were being carried on the wind, distributed to a far wider area.

Kneeling, Caslin inspected the briefcase itself. Without touching it, he eyed the locking mechanism and found neither of the catches had been forced. Whoever had opened it did so with knowledge of the code or the owner hadn't shifted the numbers in order to secure it. Still wearing his gloves, Caslin lightly checked the remaining contents. The internal sleeves contained several folders and Caslin partially pulled one out, casually thumbing through the papers and clocking the letterheads for Grey's company. Reluctant to risk their ruin, he quickly put them back where he'd found them. Glancing at Hunter, he said, "Make sure forensics detail this and then get it back to Fulford Road and go through it."

"Will do," Hunter replied.

"Good spot, Constable," Caslin said, standing.

"Thank you, sir."

Caslin pointed at the briefcase, "It's a pain in the backside but I want you to walk this stretch of road and retrieve everything that looks remotely like it may have come from that briefcase and pass it to DS Hunter."

"Yes, sir."

"What do you think?" Hunter asked him, falling into step alongside as Caslin reached the highway. He contemplated his answer before speaking. Stopping, he glanced back towards the uniformed constable before looking in the direction of the Discovery, with three CSI officers crawling all over it.

"Despite his best attempt to appear calm to us, Thomas Grey is hiding something. His behaviour seems somewhat erratic at best since we paid him a visit."

"Because of us do you reckon?"

Caslin flicked his eyebrows up accompanied by a slight shake of the head, "He didn't surround himself with private security because of us but we rattled him. Of that I'm certain. It's just that I can't quite figure out why."

"And why did he ditch the bodyguards?"

"Perhaps he came out here to meet someone."

"Without his protection?"

"He met Danika Durakovic without them," Caslin said, meeting Hunter's eye.

"You think she has a hand in this?"

He shrugged, "And therein lies one of the mysteries here. We were all over Danika's operation for what, the better part of eight months?"

"At least."

"And Grey didn't pop up on our radar once," Caslin said. "Considering how well they seemed to know each other, don't you find that a little odd?"

Hunter nodded, "We need access to Grey's phone to see who he spends time talking to."

"That's where I'm headed," Caslin said. "You get the scene squared away and I'll meet you back at the station."

"The warrant could take a while," Hunter said, "particularly at this time of night."

"I have faith in you, Sarah," Caslin said with a wink and a smile. He turned and headed back to his car. Increasing his pace, Caslin reached the car and clambered in, happy for the respite from the rain. Such was the volume of water in his hair the moment he leant forward to put his key in the ignition, water ran down his forehead. Shaking his head, he wiped his brow with the palm of his hand before starting the car. The windscreen was already steaming up and he set the blowers to maximum. Reaching for his mobile, he found Iain Robertson's number and dialled it.

"I know what you're going to ask and no, I haven't accessed the phone yet," Robertson replied from his laboratory, without the courtesy of even a basic greeting.

"Please tell me you're not waiting for a warrant?" Caslin replied, also happy to dispense with the pleasantries. Robertson laughed.

"The last time the authorities tried to get the encryption of one of these handsets cracked by the manufacturer they fought it tooth and nail. It took months… and they won, too."

"Yeah, I could do without that," Caslin said, turning on the wipers to clear the screen in front of him.

"I figured you wouldn't have the time for that—"

"Nor the patience," Caslin cut in.

"Indeed. So, I've been designing an ingenious hack. Off the record, obviously," Robertson said with a reassurance that came involuntarily with his Scottish accent.

"You can crack it yourself?" Caslin asked without meaning to sound sceptical but the tone did so involuntarily.

"You don't keep me around for my charming demeanour," Robertson replied.

"Your brilliance never ceases to amaze me. I'm on my way. I'll see you in fifteen to twenty minutes," Caslin said, hanging up.

Caslin put his mobile down and engaged first gear but as he did so the handset beeped. Taking the car out of gear, he glanced at the screen and saw he'd received a text. The number was unfamiliar to him. Opening it, there was only one sentence. It read: *Your new friend is in danger.* Caslin sat back, touching the handset to his lips. The message wasn't signed. Intrigued, he typed out a short response – *Which friend… and who are you?* – there was a pause that lasted long enough for Caslin to figure he wasn't going to get a response but just as he was about to set off again, the mobile beeped. He read the reply – *Trust me.*

No stranger to the occasional threat over the years, Caslin had to admit this struck him as a little different for he had never received a warning via his mobile before. There was one obvious candidate, the mysterious texter could be referring to but if it was him, Cory Walsh, then this wasn't new information. After all, the man was a walking advert for paranoia. Caslin pushed for some clarity – *And you are…?* – he waited for a reply but none was forthcoming. Having let a few minutes pass, he put the mobile down and allowed his mind to wander as to who might be offering him the heads-up as well as why.

CASLIN FOUND Iain Robertson hunched over a table in his lab paying close attention to something in front of him. He'd expected to find him peering into a computer screen in an attempt to hack the passcode to Thomas Grey's mobile using some kind of self-designed algorithm.

Instead, Robertson glanced up and met his arrival with a scalpel blade in hand with slivers of what looked like jelly on the table before him, alongside Grey's handset and pieces of rolled out Plasticine. Robertson met Caslin's quizzical look with a broad smile.

"It's more twenty-first century than you probably think."

"It'd have to be," Caslin replied, approaching the table. "Any joy?"

"You timed it about right. I'm not far off finding out," he replied, turning back to what he was doing. Caslin watched as Robertson peeled out a thumb-sized blob of what looked under closer inspection to be a transparent silicon from a knob of the Plasticine. Laying it before him, he then took the scalpel and began slicing a thin portion across the domed lump, taking great care not to break the surface. For some reason, Caslin held his breath, reluctant to speak and risk breaking the obvious concentration. Once Robertson was through, he sat up, the sliver of gelatinous material on the edge of his forefinger and exhaled deeply. "That ought to do it."

"Do what? What is that anyway?"

"That, young man," Robertson began, despite him being only three years senior to Caslin, "is how I'm going to get you into this mobile."

"Okay, I'll bite," Caslin said. "How?"

"First, one of my techs lifted a decent fingerprint from Grey's Discovery. The engine start button provided a rather detailed one. Once I had that, I applied a little magic dust to the print…" Caslin eyed him suspiciously. "Okay, I scanned it into my computer at a 300dpi resolution. Then, I mirrored it, shrank it back to normal size and printed it out onto a glossy, transparent slide. Using silver conductive ink alongside standard black, I could produce a fingerprint to fool the sensor."

"Ahh... right. That's more of what I was expecting," Caslin said with approval. "So, what's with all the play dough, jelly and stuff? Although, I see you're missing the glitter glue and farmyard shapes."

Robertson laughed, "Problem was, it didn't work. I've seen it done with some brands but this is top of the range and I think the software recognised the fact it was a copy."

"How so?"

"Your biometric sensors pretty much work the same way across the manufacturers. You record your print and it registers your pattern. The handset need only recognise three points of your pattern to unlock the phone, sometimes more but the premise is always the same."

"But that didn't work?"

Robertson shook his head. "The poorer systems can be fooled by a photocopy, believe it or not. Whereas the more secure ones are a little smarter. They might require ridge definition on the pad, a raised print for example. However, this model," he said, indicating Grey's handset, "goes a step further."

"Go on," Caslin said, genuinely interested whilst suddenly concerned about the security of his own mobile.

"I'll show you," Robertson said, smiling and turning back to his handiwork. He lifted the sliver of jelly and, reversing the handset on the table before him, laid it carefully over the fingerprint sensor. "This system was developed a couple of years ago but is still being applied to the manufacturer's ridiculously expensive current model as if it's new tech. The software not only detects the presence of the ridges but also whether there is any heat behind the print."

"So, the owner has to be alive?"

Robertson frowned, "Do you ever think you've worked too many murders, Nate? I was going for 'present' and not necessarily still alive. The idea is this will bypass anyone faking a print. I suppose, to follow your train of thought, the actual finger must be used and in theory, would still need to be attached to the owner. Or then again, still warm as a minimum."

"Now who's worked too many crime scenes?" Caslin said playfully.

"Possibly," Robertson agreed. "To get around this problem, I took the print and spayed it with a fine mist of glue. Then, I pressed it into a mould fashioned from the Plasticine, ridges and all. I mixed a fast-setting epoxy-resin or crazy-glue, if that helps you to understand," Robertson said in a condescending, paternalistic tone which caused Caslin to crack a smile, "and poured it in. I've allowed it to set, then sliced out the print and here we are."

"Is it going to work?" Caslin asked, turning his gaze to the mobile.

"Let's find out," Robertson stated. Reaching forward, he lightly placed a forefinger onto the print he'd so carefully created and pressed down. A split-second later, the phone vibrated and lifting the handset revealed an unlocked screen. Robertson's face split a broad grin. "Never trust the advertising," he said with a nod, passing the handset to Caslin.

"You truly are a magician, Iain."

"I know," Robertson replied. "Just not fully appreciated within my lifetime."

Caslin took the offered handset and set off for CID, already tapping through to the stored text messages and recently dialled lists. In both, he found multiple entries dated for that very day. Already the excitement was building. Reaching the door out of the lab, Caslin paused and turned back to Robertson, already beginning to clear up the mess he'd made.

"Iain, out of interest. How do I secure my phone?" he asked. Robertson looked skyward for a moment, considering the question.

"I would argue that if someone is duplicating your fingerprint using 3D printers, epoxy-resin or latex copies… then you have bigger problems in your life than securing your mobile phone."

Caslin nodded, "Good point."

CHAPTER TWENTY-TWO

HUNTER ENTERED CID just as Terry Holt connected the mobile to his laptop. Now, what was visible on the handset was displayed on a projector screen. Caslin acknowledged her arrival and filled her in as she took off her overcoat, shaking off the excess water before hanging it up.

"We're in," Caslin explained. "Grey had a text conversation during the day."

"Who with?" Hunter asked, pulling up a chair and rubbing her cheeks to freshen her face. The clock ticked past midnight but there was no sign of anyone looking to go home.

"It's an unknown number," Holt said, "but they know each other. That much is clear."

"Put it up," Caslin said, pointing to the large screen. Holt did so, bringing up the conversation with a couple of clicks. "The first one was received by Grey before eight this morning." Hunter turned her attention to the thread.

07:52

We need to talk.

07:57

I know… it's been a while. Things been manic.

08:00

Arriving today. I expect to see you.

08:20

York? When?

08:22

Will call. I want an answer.

08:43

Not easy. Working on it.

"The number's unknown but where does it originate?" Hunter asked. Meeting Holt's questioning glance, she continued, "The international code?"

Holt looked at the number, "It's +7. Where's that?"

"Russia," Caslin stated, even further intrigued by the revelation. "Run the number through the system and see if we can track where it's been and where it is now. If the carrier's passed through an airport today, it might help us pin down a name to go with it or at least, narrow the list.

"Interesting that Grey knew who it was despite not having the number saved," Hunter added. "When do they communicate further?"

Holt scrolled down, "Around lunchtime."

13:30

Checking in. You'd better be worth my time. They're pushing.

13:34

I'm on my way. I'm trying.

13:36

No excuses. No time.

"Is there any more?" Caslin asked.

Holt shook his head, "Not in this thread. They haven't communicated before either."

"Not on this number," Hunter said. Holt shot her a dark look. She ignored him.

"What would we give to have been a fly-on-the-wall in that meeting? What are they talking about do you think?" Caslin said aloud.

"Money," Holt said. "Got to be. Grey's into property and that's all about money at the end of the day."

"Go through the emails and other text threads to see if you can grant us a steer," Caslin said to Holt. Turning to Hunter, he continued, "Track the number. Find out where it is and where it's been."

"You think this person has a hand in Grey's disappearance?"

"I think it's related but too early to say in what way. He left his office shortly after two, I recall. It's reasonable to suggest he was on his way to that meeting. Track Grey's phone at the same time and see if the two intersect. Then we'll have a location. You never know, we may find Grey himself."

"I'll get on it," Hunter said, rising from her seat. Caslin returned his gaze to the text thread up on the screen. Whoever the newcomer was, reading between the lines, Thomas Grey was giving them the run-around to such an extent that they'd travelled to York to confront him. Whether Grey had an appropriate answer could well determine the condition in which they would him. That is, *if* they could find him.

"Sir," Hunter called from across the squad room. Caslin turned to see her with a phone pressed to her ear and an excited expression upon her face. "We've got him." Caslin jumped up, grabbed his coat and hurried across the room, shouting over his shoulder to Holt.

"Terry, take over from Sarah and map their paths. I'll give you a call later."

"Will do, sir," Holt replied. If he was annoyed at being passed Hunter's tasks as well as his own, he didn't show it. A reaction that didn't go unnoticed by his senior officer. Such was the team's determination to get a result.

"Where is he?" Caslin asked as Hunter left the room alongside him.

"Here, in York. He's at Bootham Park."

Caslin stopped and turned to her. "The psychiatric hospital?" he asked, looking puzzled. "I thought that'd been declared unfit and closed down."

"It was. Then they realised there was nowhere else to take people and reopened it."

"Bootham borders Clifton. Grey's car was abandoned… what… a quarter of a mile away?"

"If that."

"Come on. Let's get over there."

BOOTHAM PARK HOSPITAL was sited adjacent to York's main hospital on the northern edge of the city centre. In order to reach it, Caslin had to cross the River Ouse twice when navigating the city centre but fortunately, in the early hours, their journey took less than fifteen minutes.

Turning off Clarence Street they took another couple of left turns in quick succession before pulling into the car park of the imposing three-storey Victorian building. The car park was nigh on deserted and Caslin was grateful the rain had ceased. The breeze was ever present and he braced against the cold. The clouds had momentarily cleared revealing a crisp night, bathing the open grounds in front of them in a silver light.

Hunter got out of the passenger side and closed the door. Caslin locked the car and they headed down the path towards the entrance. Off to the right was the hospital's chapel, cutting an eerie figure set within the surroundings of the barren trees. They reached the front door, a double door of heavy wooden construction set front and centre in the neo-classical frontage. Pressing the buzzer, they waited, illuminated only by the moonlight as the sound carried through the interior of the building.

The intercom crackled into life and they were greeted by a female voice.

"Hello, how can I help?"

"DI Caslin and DS Hunter from Fulford CID. We called ahead," Caslin said, glancing up at the camera above and to the right of the door.

"Please come in," the voice said and the accompanying click indicated the door was open. Hunter pushed the door inwards and they stepped through. Barely had they closed the door behind them, they were met in the lobby. Caslin watched her approach. She was in her forties, dressed in black trousers, a blouse and a pink cardigan. The photo, clipped to the cardigan, was the only indication that she was staff. "Hello, I'm Grace Anderson."

"DI Caslin," he said once again, showing her his warrant card. Grace eyed it briefly and then acknowledged Hunter, beckoning them to follow her. The lights in the communal area appeared to be on a timer with minimal illumination.

"You're here to see Mr Grey, I understand?" Grace asked. "I'm sorry, I didn't take your call."

"That's right," Caslin replied. "What is his condition?"

"I'll leave the discussion of diagnosis to the attending specialist, if you don't mind," she said, leading them up a staircase and onto the first floor.

"You're not a doctor?" Hunter asked.

Grace shook her head, "No. I'm a facilitator. Dr Ashman will meet with you."

"Thomas Grey was admitted earlier tonight," Caslin said.

"Yes. Shortly after 8 p.m." They reached a half-landing between floors and she led them to the rear and into a two-storey wing tacked on at some point in the past. "He was admitted to our acute inpatient ward for assessment."

"Is that complete?" Hunter said.

"I believe so, yes," Grace replied, approaching a locked door. She swiped a pass key and the lock disengaged. Stepping aside, she allowed them to enter first. The corridor was brightly lit in stark contrast to where they'd been. It was clear they were standing in the lobby of a secure unit. A small nurse's station was set in front of them with three doors beyond, each with the same locking system as the one behind them. From behind the desk a young man rose to greet them. Caslin was mildly surprised to find this was Dr Ashman and he was at least ten years Caslin's junior. Although, that seemed to happen more frequently than it used to.

"Dr Ashman?" Caslin asked, offering his hand. The young man took it.

"Inspector Caslin. Pleased to meet you," Ashman said, smiling. He then shook hands with Hunter. "Please, come through to the office."

He led them into what was a shared office, little more than a four-metre square rectangle with a solitary desk, multiple filing cabinets and shelves. Almost everywhere they looked was stuffed full of loose paperwork, files and folders. Dr Ashman seemed to notice.

"You'll have to forgive our apparent untidiness. We were closing, then reopened for emergency cases and now we take on outpatients as well."

"It takes time to ramp everything back up?" Hunter asked.

Ashman shook his head, "Most of the hospital is still mothballed and the latest swing of the pendulum will see us shut down pretty soon. A new unit has been given the go ahead by the planners."

"Couldn't make up their mind?" Caslin asked casually.

"I think we were a knee-jerk response to the lack of mental-health provision currently available in the system," Ashman stated, offering them both a seat. Caslin declined. For his part, Ashman leaned against the desk, folding his arms before him.

"Thomas Grey?" Caslin asked.

"Admitted last night," Dr Ashman confirmed, reaching for a folder on the desk. Opening it, he scanned the first page. "You'll understand I must respect patient confidentiality?"

"Of course," Caslin said. "However, this is a murder investigation and Mr Grey is a figure in our investigation."

"He came to us exhibiting both physical and mental trauma."

"To what extent, physical?" Hunter said.

"He has superficial cuts to both wrists. Early toxicological tests have returned evidence of amphetamine ingestion," the doctor said. "Accident and Emergency performed a gastric lavage to remove the contents of his stomach, just in case, and then shipped him over here after their initial assessment."

"How do you view the cuts? Are they defensive wounds?" Caslin asked. The doctor shook his head.

"Not in my opinion, no. They are more likely to be self-inflicted."

"Is Grey suicidal?"

"That shifts me into an uncomfortable position of supposition," Ashman said.

"Uncomfortable… how?" Caslin pressed. Ashman sucked air through his teeth before setting his expression in a frown.

"I wouldn't suggest his heart was in it."

"He's faking?" Hunter asked.

"The levels of amphetamine in his blood stream would suggest otherwise," Ashman said, "and without doubt he has been expressing levels of mania that are entirely consistent with a paranoid complex."

"Driven by what? Recreational drugs?"

Ashman shook his head whilst scanning the file before him, "This is his third stay with us and he's exhibited the same behaviour on each previous occasion but this is the only time drugs have come back positive in his samples."

"Can we speak with him?" Caslin asked.

"Certainly, but you might find him somewhat erratic. I'm reluctant to prescribe any anti-psychotic medicine until I'm sure of what is currently in his system. That won't be until mid-morning at the earliest."

A piercing alarm sounded throughout the ward, everyone in the room jumped in shock. Dr Ashman was first to react and hotfooted it out of the office, Caslin and Hunter only a step behind. Grace Anderson met them in the lobby and responded to the doctor's unanswered question.

"One of the patients has attacked a nurse," she said. Caslin found her matter-of-fact tone slightly alarming. He figured it was a reasonably common occurrence.

"Which patient?" Ashman asked.

"Mr Grey," she replied. Caslin and Hunter exchanged glances. A male nurse joined them and together they passed through the furthermost door into the ward. The small party broke into a run and the noise level increased as they approached the scene of the disturbance.

The corridor opened out into what Caslin assumed to be a patient's activity room. Chairs and tables were upended in every direction. Two nurses were attempting to restrain Thomas Grey on the far side of the room. For his part, Grey was resisting to such an extent that his face was a shade of deep crimson as he hurled abuse at both men. The three staggered slightly to the left and Grey managed to free an arm, striking the man to his right a downward blow with the point of his elbow.

Caslin was shocked to see such a change in the businessman. A third nurse crossed the room under instruction from Dr Ashman to try and subdue Grey. Caslin tried to follow but felt the doctor's arm come across his chest to deter him.

"Please allow my team to do its job, Inspector," Ashman said firmly. Regrettably, Caslin did as requested. At that moment, Grey broke free and grabbed hold of the first person he could, sinking his teeth into the man's ear. The nurse screamed. Grey released him, spitting out a mixture of blood and saliva, gleefully screaming at the injured man.

"You bastards won't take me!" he shouted, blood staining his teeth and lips as he was forced backwards, staring wild-eyed at those trying to subdue him. "I'll fucking die first!" Losing his footing, or having his stability forcibly taken away, saw Grey fall to the floor. All three nurses, now with the upper hand attempted to pin Grey to the ground. Caslin's thoughts passed to the multiple occasions where he and his colleagues had come across drunks who needed to be arrested. On some occasions, such was the ferocity and determination of their quarry, it could take six grown men to manage the situation and take the man down.

Almost as quickly as the drama had arisen it subsided. Grey was placed into restraints, including the deployment of a spit-hood and despite his best efforts, he could no longer wreak damage on the staff. He was unceremoniously carted away, presumably to a secure private room. An eerie silence descended. Caslin felt his heart race. A quick glance at Hunter saw her confirm similar. Grace excused herself, leaving the three of them alone.

"I'm sorry, Inspector Caslin. Your conversation with Mr Grey will have to wait," Ashman said, tension in his voice. Caslin nodded his understanding.

"Tell me. Has Grey behaved like this on the other occasions that he's been here?"

Ashman shook his head, "Never violently, no. He has been known to kiss other patients and there were a couple of incidents where he… how should I put it… he has wandering hands, with certain members of staff."

"Charming," Hunter said, raising her eyebrows.

"Not only with the women," Ashman offered, "and I don't see that as overtly sexual behaviour. Speaking from a purely clinical standpoint anyway."

"Do the women see it that way?" Hunter asked.

"Not always," Ashman replied, with a brief shake of the head, before adding, "nor do the men, by the way." Hunter exhaled heavily, smiling, as much from the release of tension as from the doctor's light-hearted additional comment.

"When will you let us speak with him?" Caslin asked.

"First thing in the morning. You won't get a lot of sense from him now.

"When he was admitted, did he have anything on him at all?" Caslin asked.

Dr Ashman shrugged, "Nothing, apart from the clothes he was wearing."

"Any of these drugs you were talking about?"

"No, sorry. What is all this about?"

"That's just what we're trying to find out, Doctor," Caslin said, his eyes drifting away in the direction where they had taken Grey.

Caslin's mobile rang and he excused himself from the conversation, stepping away to the other side of the room. It was Holt, back at Fulford Road.

"Sir, I've had some joy with the mobile networks," he said excitedly.

"Go on."

"I tried to find out who the mystery number is registered to but what with it being a Russian company and it being the middle of the night, I've had no luck. However, I tracked the signals back to see which of the local transmitters the two have connected with and looked for a link. They cross paths in only one place."

"Give me some good news, Terry," Caslin asked, drawing Hunter's attention to the conversation. He beckoned her over.

"South-west of York, sir," Holt said with enthusiasm. "And seeing as our mystery caller was travelling in to the area, I thought it likely he would be staying at a hotel. There are only two that are within range of that particular repeater station."

"Good work, Terry," Caslin said. "Have you called them yet?"

"No, sir," Holt replied. "I figured it'd be better to turn up unannounced."

"Agreed. Which hotels?"

"The Windsor Garden Lodge and The Centennial. If it were me, I'd start at the latter."

"Why?"

"Judging by the circles these guys tend to move in I'd expect five-star all the way. The Windsor would be slumming it at only four."

"Text me the address and we'll meet you there," Caslin replied. Hanging up, he turned to the waiting Hunter. "Looks like it's going to be a long night, Sarah."

CHAPTER TWENTY-THREE

THE LOBBY of The Centennial Hotel was of a noticeably higher standard than most others Caslin had frequented. His initial perception of the double-height atrium was that five stars didn't do the building justice. The lobby opened up to reveal marble panelling to the walls, ornately decorated archways to the interior and stunning frescos that drew the eye upwards.

An open fire crackled away to his left, despite the lateness of the hour, with leather seating of the finest craftsmanship set out before it. The ambient lighting was calming and soft music played. Caslin recognised the artist, a modern classical piece by Elskavon but he couldn't recollect the title. The concierge appeared at reception from a back room, Terry Holt a step behind. He saw Caslin and Hunter, acknowledging them with a brief wave. He came from behind the desk as they approached.

"What do we have, Terry?" Caslin asked.

"Only one man fitting the bill checked in earlier today, sir," Holt said, barely concealing his excitement. "A Russian national by the name of Alexander Koliokov. The system tells us his key card hasn't been active since lunchtime."

"So, he's here?" Hunter asked. Holt nodded.

"Room number?" Caslin asked.

"311. This way," Holt stated, setting off and indicating the direction of the lifts. "Third floor."

The concierge followed on, appearing rather interested. Caslin guessed this wasn't his usual night shift. The interior of the lift matched the plush surroundings, polished steel walls that shone with a golden tint. The doors slid open and they stepped out onto the third floor. They all looked for the numbering to guide them but a voice spoke from behind.

"To the right," Caslin glanced back and thanked the young man who was accompanying them. The small party made their way along the corridor until they reached Room 311. A 'do not disturb' sign hung on the door handle. Holt met Caslin's eye and he nodded. The constable rapped his knuckles on the door three times. They waited but there was no sign of movement within. That was unsurprising bearing in mind they were approaching one o'clock in the morning. Holt tried again only this time with more force. Still, there was no reply. Caslin turned to the concierge standing a few steps behind them, watching expectantly.

"Open it," he said flatly. The young man didn't hesitate and came forward producing his master card. He placed it into the slot and the LED changed from red to green. Caslin indicated for him to step away to a respectable distance. Taking a firm grip of the handle, he eased it down and cracked the door open. Collectively, the three took a deep breath. Terry Holt was first through with Caslin and Hunter a half-step behind.

"Police!" Holt barked in an authoritarian tone. It wasn't a raid but they wanted to be sure the resident knew who was coming. No one responded as they entered. The lights were out, the suite in darkness. Hunter located the nearest light switch and illuminated the entrance hall. Koliokov had booked into a suite consisting of two bedrooms, a lounge, the bathroom as well as access to a private roof terrace. The group spread out and searched for the Russian, flicking on lights as they went.

"Nothing in either bedroom apart from a suitcase," Hunter called out.

"Bathroom's clear," Holt shouted. Caslin stood in the lounge hands on hips.

The room was dressed to perfection. It barely looked as if anyone had been present since the hotel staff had last serviced it. A gust of cold wind drifted over him and Caslin turned to see the curtains swaying gently. He was joined by the other two. He indicated towards the doors where the breeze originated. The access to the roof terrace.

The three moved over and Hunter threw back the curtains. Outside, despite the darkness, they could make out the figure of a man sitting alone in a recliner. Caslin saw a switch to his right and assumed it was for the outside. He pressed it and the figure was bathed in a pool of off-white light, strung out around the terrace. The mix of soft light amid the now falling rain cast an eerie picture particularly as the water had aided the spreading pool of red beneath him.

"Explains why he didn't answer," Hunter said under her breath. Caslin gently pushed the door open with his elbow ensuring he didn't touch the handle and potentially damage any forensic evidence. Drawing his coat about him, he turned to Holt.

"Go back downstairs with the concierge and take a look at their CCTV. I want to know if this is Koliokov and whether anyone else turned up who cannot be accounted for today. Was he alone, did Grey show up and if so, who was he with? And while you're at it, give Iain Robertson a call and get his team out here."

"I'm on it," Holt said, turning to leave.

Caslin followed Hunter out onto the terrace. Both were careful where they put their feet. The falling rain was pooling on the stone tiles of the terrace, washing the man's lifeblood out from beneath him. They got as close as they dared. He was obviously dead and had been for some time, his pale features drained of all colour. He wore suit trousers and a pink and white striped shirt, unbuttoned at both collar and cuff. A cursory examination revealed his wrists had been cut but vertically rather than horizontally as the majority of suicide victims tended to do. Doing so ensures a faster rate of bleeding and in turn brings on an expedient death.

Further to those wounds, Caslin counted at least four, but possibly five, slashes to the throat three to four inches long. Two of which appeared relatively shallow but others were evidently deeper.

"I don't see any defensive injuries," Hunter said, raising her voice above the howl of the wind and the driving rain. "And I can't see any weapon," she added, casting an eye around them.

Caslin shook his head, "Nor me."

"Looks like an elaborate suicide," Hunter said but sounded less than convinced. "With a vanishing blade, too."

"Travel all the way to York from Russia to top yourself on the roof of a poncey hotel," Caslin said appearing dismissive.

"It doesn't make any sense," Hunter agreed. "Maybe he didn't like what Grey had to say?"

"Or maybe Grey didn't appreciate the visit?" Caslin said before glancing skyward. The rain was increasing in intensity. He looked around, noting the terrace wasn't overlooked by any other hotel window. Surrounding them was open land. A small estate with a well-designed and cultivated landscape of trees and foliage. The nearest building adjacent to this one was well over three hundred metres away, without a clear sightline. "Let's go and see what this guy brought with him and then catch up with Terry and the hotel cameras."

The two of them returned to the lounge grateful to be out of the rain. This time they were more thorough but the detailed search provided nothing fruitful. Koliokov had unpacked upon his arrival but all he brought with him was an overnight bag containing two changes of clothing and essential toiletries. Inside the bag, Caslin found the man's passport and opening it to the photograph page, he was quite certain this was the man sitting outside in the rain. He brandished the passport towards Hunter who leaned over and nodded her agreement. Hunter opened a drawer beside the bed and took out a black, leather wallet. Opening it, she thumbed through the contents.

"Anything interesting?" Caslin asked.

"A few thousand Roubles. A couple of hundred in Sterling. Credit cards and…"

"What is it?"

"… a picture of a girl young enough to be his daughter by the look of it."

"Maybe it is his daughter?" Caslin said. Hunter exaggerated her expression turning the corners of her mouth down.

"Not dressed like this," she said, removing the picture, turning it and presenting it to him. Caslin scanned the image of the young woman, barely eighteen in his opinion and scantily clad in erotic lingerie in a provocative pose. He blew out his cheeks.

"Well, you'd bloody well hope not," he concluded. Hunter replaced the photograph back into the wallet.

"Any sign of his phone?" she asked.

"No," Caslin replied, heading back into the lounge. Hunter followed. Crossing the room to the bar, Caslin spied an open bottle of scotch. Approaching, he found there were two glasses on the counter and he sniffed at them. Both had contained scotch but were now empty. There was an ice box open alongside them. Koliokov had either drunk two glasses himself or shared a drink with another. Caslin hazarded a guess it was Grey. He pointed them out to Hunter, "Make sure CSI lift the prints off of these. I'd put money on it one of these has Grey's prints all over it."

"You think he's at the centre of all of this don't you?"

"Perhaps not the centre but he's involved and could be the key to unlocking what's going on."

"You sound quite sure of that."

"There are a lot of people moving in and around his circle who are turning up dead at the moment and there's one thing for certain," Caslin said, leaving the thought hanging in the air.

"What's that?"

"He's the one who is still alive," Caslin said flatly.

"For now."

"Sure, he's probably in the safest place right now."

A uniformed officer arrived at the entrance to the suite and Caslin told him to secure the scene until forensics arrived. Together, Caslin and Hunter made their way back downstairs to the lobby and found Holt sitting in the concierge's office analysing the security footage.

"What do you have for us, Terry?" Caslin asked. Holt sat back in the office chair and spun it around to face them.

"We have Thomas Grey arriving shortly before two thirty this afternoon," Holt said, indicating to the monitor beside him. The concierge hit play and they rolled the camera footage on. They watched as Grey entered the hotel lobby and purposefully made his way to the reception desk. A short conversation followed and the clerk made a telephone call whilst Grey waited. He stood before the counter one hand in his pocket.

"Looks pretty relaxed, I'd say," Hunter said.

"He does but it's shielding his anxiety. Look how he's drumming the fingers of his free hand on the counter and shifting his feet. He's trying hard to appear casual but I'd say he's anything but."

"Good shout," Holt said. "I'd missed that."

"Is he alone?" Caslin said.

"Yes," Holt said. They watched as the clerk replaced the receiver and the two shared a few more words before Grey set off in the direction of the lifts. "Presumably he's just been given Koliokov's room number. No one follows him. There's another angle showing Grey enter and exit the lift alone on the third floor. We don't have him entering Room 311 but he reappears in the lobby barely fifteen minutes later."

"That's quick," Hunter said, surprised.

"Doesn't give him much time for that scotch," Caslin said, Holt looked up quizzically but didn't pursue the question. "Can you bring it up?"

"Of course," Holt said and moments later they were watching Grey re-entering the reception from the lifts. However, on this occasion, he appeared agitated. Every movement was in haste as he glanced about the reception changing direction several times before heading for the entrance doors and out into the car park.

"Was he looking for something or someone?" Hunter asked.

"Almost as if he was expecting someone," Caslin said. "Terry, can you roll that back so we can see it again please?" Holt did so and they watched the footage again. "Can you see any indication he's been in a confrontation? Damage to his suit, dark patches that could be blood perhaps?"

They all viewed the footage intently seeking the telltale sign that Grey had a hand in Koliokov's death. Holt slowed the footage down in places and replayed it in others but the images were just too small to give that level of detail.

"Do you think he *is* looking for someone or not?" Holt asked.

"What are you thinking, Terry?"

"I was just wondering if he might have been trying to avoid being seen. Look here," Holt pointed to the screen with the pen in his hand, "he changes direction twice and both times are when either a member of staff or another guest comes close. What's he hiding?"

"Blood?" Hunter asked. "Although that's pure conjecture at this point."

"Terry's right, though," Caslin agreed. "Maybe he doesn't want to be tied to the scene."

"Didn't notice the cameras," Holt added sarcastically.

"Maybe not thinking straight?" Hunter said.

"All right," Caslin said, "let's walk through it. Grey arrives for an impromptu meeting with someone he's been avoiding. What that's about we can only guess at but most likely it's to do with—"

"Money," Holt interrupted. "Most likely big money at that."

"Yep," Caslin agreed. "I would suggest Grey either owes Koliokov or they have a joint commitment and Grey hasn't come through with his end of the deal. Koliokov wants answers because he's feeling the pressure at his end."

"And Grey doesn't have them or, at least, not the answers he wants to hear," Hunter said.

"Which leaves us with the question – was Koliokov dead or alive when Grey arrived?" Caslin asked.

"Or when he left?" Holt added.

"To follow it through," Hunter continued, "Grey leaves having instigated, or come across, a suicide or committed a murder and staged it as a suicide. Does he then have a mental collapse due to the pressure of the situation and winds up at Bootham Park?"

"What are you suggesting?" Caslin asked.

"It's convenient is all I'm saying. What if Grey could have had himself committed for his own safety? As you said earlier, he's in the safest place possible right now."

"That would suggest he walked in on something and he's... what... hiding in Bootham Park?" Caslin asked. "And people say I'm cynical," he mused openly.

"No," Hunter countered, "real cynicism would be to suggest that if he had a hand in Koliokov's death, being detained under the Mental Health Act gives him an out if it ever comes to trial? After all, what did Dr Ashman say regarding his apparent suicide attempt – his heart wasn't in it?"

Caslin sighed. Hunter was right in both scenarios. They needed to talk to Thomas Grey and get his view of the day's events but that wasn't going to happen until the morning. He rubbed at his temples with the tips of his fingers, suddenly feeling the fatigue wash over him.

"All right, let's call it a day now and go home, get some rest. Grey isn't going anywhere and let's face it nor is Koliokov. Tomorrow morning, we should be able to get Iain's initial thoughts on what went on here tonight. Likewise, we'll be able to get some sense out of Grey and figure out just what is going on. Terry, first thing tomorrow I want you to run a check on this number," Caslin said, passing a slip of paper with the mobile number where the mysterious texts were being sent from.

"Okay. Who does it belong to?"

"That's what I'm hoping you can tell me. If not, tell me where it's been would you?"

"Yes, sir," Holt said, taking the paper and reading the number as if trying to glean some information to get ahead of the game.

"Shall I pick you up in the morning and we can head straight over to Bootham Park?" Hunter asked.

"I'll meet you there. I've got an errand to run first."

"Sounds intriguing."

"I figured I'd stop by and have a word with Danika."

Hunter exchanged a worried glance with Terry Holt before looking back to Caslin, "Durakovic? Do you think that's wise, under the circumstances?"

"Why? Because I've been warned to stay away from her?"

"The thought occurred, yes," Hunter replied. Caslin grinned.

"Sometimes you take all the fun out of this job, Sarah, you really do," he said with a wink. Hunter raised her eyes to the ceiling accompanied by an almost imperceptible shake of the head. Holt looked to the floor masking a nervous smile.

CHAPTER TWENTY-FOUR

Caslin pressed the intercom button. There was a brief delay until a gruff voice answered.

"I'm here to see Miss Durakovic," he said.

"Do you have an appointment?" the male voice responded, in heavily-accented English. Caslin cocked his head slightly and sighed looking up at the camera to his right.

"You know who I am. Just open the bloody door."

A few seconds passed and Caslin heard the locking mechanism retract before the oversized entrance door opened. He was met by two men, nondescript henchman of Danika's retinue. He recognised neither. The first beckoned him inside with the second closing the door behind them and falling into step as they made their way through the house.

Caslin was surprised to find once the door closed the outside noise of central York dissipated quickly, despite their proximity to the train station and the press of the daily commute. Danika Durakovic lived in a Georgian townhouse, part of a redevelopment in the city centre only attainable for the rich or shameless. Danika fitted comfortably into both categories. Approaching a set of full-height double doors, Caslin was told to wait as his escort passed through them and into the room beyond. He looked to the other chaperone.

"Nice place you have here. Immoral earnings paying well this year?" he asked with a casual flick of the eyebrows. The man said nothing but he smirked. Caslin found it smug and unsurprising. The wait was momentary as the doors before him parted and he was ushered in.

Danika sat behind a large ornate desk crafted from hardwood and traditionally adorned with a green leather finish, watching his approach intently. Immaculately presented as always, in her white suit, blonde bob and fastidiously applied make up. Her hands were set out before her forming a tent with her fingers, elbows to the desk. The tips of her fingers touched her lower lip and Caslin assessed her as curious, if not amused, by his presence.

"To what do I owe this honour, Mr Caslin?" she asked, her lyrical tone purring as it came to him.

"Are you sure you don't want to pat me down?" Caslin asked with a hint of sarcasm, eyeing the two extra bodyguards present to his left and right, with both his former escorts standing behind him. Danika laughed. It was genuine.

"Really, there is no need," she said, casting a glance at the associate closest to her right. "I have it from highly-placed sources that you have been instructed to steer clear of me."

"Is that right?" Caslin said, inclining his head slightly. She was correct.

"And yet, here you are."

"In the flesh," Caslin stated, smiling.

"I'll spare you some time, Inspector but please be brief. I have a business to run."

"Yes, running an empire of prostitution, drugs and general racketeering can be time consuming can't it?"

The smile faded, "My solicitors have your chief constable's office on speed dial, Inspector. What do you want?"

"Information."

"From me? The last person you drew information from within my organisation proved far from reliable."

"I can make it worth your while."

"How so?" Danika replied, sitting back in her chair. The curiosity piqued once again.

"You and I both know I've been warned to stay away from you," Caslin began. Danika nodded her affirmation. "And you and I both know that's unlikely to happen."

"You are persistent, I'll give you that," she said. "What is it you are offering?"

"How about a period of grace?" Caslin said.

"Temporary?" Caslin nodded. "So appealing, Inspector but not much of an offer. If I'm to be honest."

"Anything more than that would be a lie," Caslin stated. "You know I think you're a low life. One day I'll take you down and anyone standing alongside," he said, casting a glance to her right and meeting the gaze of who he perceived was her most trusted lieutenant. They stood, locked in a steely gaze until Danika broke it.

"You offer little by way of favour, Inspector. I trust what you want is worth similar?"

"Very astute," Caslin said. "I want to know your connection with Thomas Grey?"

"Ahh… I see, Thomas," Danika stated, her face splitting a broad grin. "It is a fleeting one. He worked with my late husband on occasion rather than with me." Caslin figured that to be truthful bearing in mind Grey had failed to materialise in his previous investigation of her affairs.

"So why did he come to you?"

Danika's grin remained in place although the corners of her lips gave away the slightest tell that he had caught her off guard, if only a little. "Thomas always had the capacity to be sloppy. Most of the time he is prudent but when the pressure comes about, he has the capacity to make rash moves and that leaves him vulnerable."

"Likewise, anyone who he does business with?"

"Quite so, Inspector. Hence why I do not."

"He is in trouble?"

"Is that a question or a statement?"

"That's what I want you to tell me. What did he want when he came to you?"

Danika took a deep breath looking sideways to her associate who met her eye with an unreadable gaze. Caslin waited. She returned her focus to him.

"Thomas wanted to know if I could help him."

"With what?"

"I have connections. I know people," she said as if that answered his question. Caslin indicated he wanted more. "It would appear, Thomas has fallen foul of those who you really want to stay on the right side of."

"Which people?"

"The scary kind," Danika said flatly. "The type you never want to meet."

"Even you?"

"For some it's an occupational hazard," Danika said. "Thomas wanted my help to head them off."

"He wanted your protection?"

Danika laughed, "You have a very high opinion of my levels of influence, Inspector. As it happens, so did Thomas. No, he sought my intervention on his behalf."

"And what did you tell him?"

"That... unfortunately... plans were already in motion," she replied coldly. "There was nothing I could do for him."

"What plans?"

"Of that, I cannot say."

"Or won't?"

Danika didn't respond but Caslin had his answer. "Grey's business has been struggling for a while now. Do you know why?"

"I'm afraid you have exhausted my knowledge of Thomas Grey's affairs, Inspector," Danika said, "as well as my patience. No doubt we shall speak again but I trust it won't be in the near future?"

Caslin met her stare and held it. He was not going to get any more information than he already had, despite a cast-iron certainty she knew far more than she was letting on. Without doubt, Grey was in trouble. If Danika was frightened for him, and bearing in mind what was happening to his associates, then he was on borrowed time.

The meeting was over and Caslin was escorted from the office without a farewell and back out to the street. The door closed behind him and Caslin set off to his car. The thought occurred that perhaps the mysterious texts he was receiving were unrelated to Cory Walsh and directed towards Grey. His relationship with Walsh was low profile and he had kept it largely to himself.

Despite the relationship Caslin endured with Kyle Broadfoot being somewhat fractious on occasion, his superior held his confidence and he had no reason to doubt him. Maybe he was reading more into the messages than he should have. Thomas Grey was in real jeopardy and his money troubles were the logical root cause. But who did he owe and where was the money? Caslin was looking forward to putting these questions to the man himself.

Turning away from the main traffic route, the background noise level dropped and Caslin took out his mobile. He called Terry Holt at Fulford Road.

"How are you getting on with that phone number I gave you last night?"

"I have as much as I can for now," Holt said apologetically. "It's an unregistered burn phone purchased here in the UK."

Caslin wasn't shocked, "What else can you tell me?"

"With the help of the manufacturer and network provider I was able to track it through the supply chain back to where it was distributed and sold. It was purchased in London. Incidentally, that is where much of the network activity takes place. Other than that, it's frequently used here in York. Sometimes both locations in the same week," Holt explained.

"Any particular location, here in York, I mean?"

"It's weird."

"How so?"

"The only records I have place it in the city centre where there are multiple hits but nowhere else."

"What does that tell us?"

Holt thought about it, "Either the owner lives in the city and never ventures out, always arriving by train…"

"Plausible," Caslin agreed. "Or?"

"Or they switch the phone off whenever they leave the centre," Holt concluded, "which is weird, if you ask me?"

Caslin reflected for a moment, "Tell me, where is it now?"

"It's not currently active on the network, sir. But I've flagged it and should it be turned on, I'll get a notification."

"Good work, Terry."

"Hunter's here and wants a word," Holt said as Caslin was about to hang up.

"We've had a package delivered, sir," she said, excitement edging into her tone.

"What is it?"

"Miranda Michaelson. You remember Finlay's widow?"

"Yes of course. What about her?"

"She turned up a copy of one of the photographs that were missing from the wall of her husband's office. You remember? She really liked one of them and Finlay got her a copy but she'd forgotten all about it. We jogged her memory," Hunter said. "I've scanned it and I'm emailing you a copy. You should get it any second." Caslin flipped through to his email account on his phone.

"Yes, I have it," he said before downloading the attached file. "What about the other one that was missing?"

"No such luck but she added that she thought it was a shot taken in the inner sanctum of Westminster but she still couldn't recollect who Finlay was with."

Slowly, the picture revealed itself to him. It was as Miranda had originally described. A shot taken on a fishing trip somewhere in the Mediterranean.

Five men, appearing as close friends, huddled together at the stern of the yacht brandishing their catches and grinning to the camera. On the right was Michaelson and next to him was a face Caslin didn't recognise who had an arm around the shoulder of none other than Thomas Grey. The two remaining men, Caslin knew very well. On the far left stood the larger-than-life figure of Nestor Kuznetsov, grinning broadly. Alongside him was the familiar face of Cory Walsh.

"Son of a bitch," Caslin muttered.

"What's that, sir?" he heard Hunter say almost inaudibly. He brought the handset back to his ear, feeling a wave of embarrassment wash over him. Not through his choice of language but more because he felt like an idiot. The realisation that he may have been played somewhere along the line.

"Nothing. Don't worry," he replied, multiple scenarios cascading through his mind as he tried to bring everything together. He exhaled deeply. What the hell was going on?

"We have some leads to follow up on. I'm going to try and find out who these guys are," Hunter said, "along with where Grey, Michaelson and Kuznetsov tie in."

"Okay, great," Caslin said, reluctant to offer his own take until he had something coherent to say. "Actually, I want you to pass that on to Terry Holt so you can meet me at Bootham Park. I'm on my way over there now. Tell him to focus on the old guy with his arm around Grey, would you?"

"Why him, in particular?" Hunter asked.

"Because I know who the other one is already," Caslin said before hanging up.

As he walked, Caslin pieced together a timeline of events as he saw them. Michaelson, in his role at the Foreign Office, worked within business and trade relations. This brought him into contact with the likes of Walsh and Kuznetsov. Grey's presence suggested investments in property deals. The logical follow through would be to assume they were possibly shady in origin or at least financed unconventionally. Michaelson, however, from Caslin's understanding, had made some inroads into something that he considered potentially unethical. What Caslin figured to be a reference to the Register of Members' Interests. Furthermore, Walsh had been a vocal campaigner for transparency and good conduct in international business in recent years.

The two scenarios were poles apart and yet somehow, they were enmeshed together. One thing was for certain, Kuznetsov had severe financial woes, being declared bankrupt and subsequently those within his sphere were finding similar events befalling them. Not least, several winding up dead in questionable circumstances. Apparently, while Kuznetsov was riding high, so were those around him and similarly when he fell, the others went down like a domino effect. Caslin's phone vibrated in his pocket.

Taking it out, he saw a text message alert. It was from his unknown advisor. The message read – *They know where he is. Protect him.* Moments later, Holt was calling. Caslin answered.

"Where is it, Terry?" Caslin asked. Holt was immediately thrown at the psychic abilities of his DI but gathered himself quickly.

"Central London, sir," Holt confirmed.

"Can you be more specific?"

"No, it's already been switched off. The handset was active for less than a minute and sent a text—"

"To me," Caslin cut in. "It's a warning. I think someone knows where Grey is and they're looking to put him down… permanently. I think we need to take Thomas Grey into protective custody. Speak to Matheson and get some bodies over to Bootham Park and we can take it from there."

Caslin hung up and then scrolled through his contacts picking out a number and dialling it. He increased his pace. The phone rang at the other end and just as he was about to give up the call was answered.

"I'm a little busy, Nathaniel. Can this wait?"

"You lied to me!" Caslin said, his tone one of controlled anger. "More than once."

"I guess it can't," Cory Walsh replied.

CHAPTER TWENTY-FIVE

"YOU TOLD me you had no connection with Nestor Kuznetsov," Caslin said, "and yet here I am, looking at a shot of the two of you holidaying together. You look pretty tight from where I'm standing."

"I was protecting myself... and you, for that matter," Walsh countered.

"Is that so?" Caslin said. "How does this fly for you? A business associate of yours, heavily into illegal money laundering and bribery turns up dead in suspicious circumstances. That doesn't look good for the poster boy of international financial ethics does it?"

"You're getting carried away, Nathaniel," Walsh said calmly.

"Convince me. Give me a good reason not to have you arrested on suspicion of Kuznetsov's murder."

"To my knowledge, Nestor's death was a suicide."

"There are far too many Russian-backed money-men killing themselves at the moment and all of them tied either to you or Nestor Kuznetsov," Caslin said.

"You're quite right, Nathaniel. There are. I've tried my level best to keep my contacts safe and preferably out of sight until it was time to blow it wide open."

"Blow what wide open?"

"Listen, this goes beyond simple money laundering, although that's a major part of it. We're talking billions of dollars in cash and assets. That's what Nestor was. He enabled money to be funnelled out of Russia.

Moscow imposed strict procedures to restrict the flow of capital out of the country. An exodus of money leaves the system vulnerable. People need to get creative in order to do that."

"Why do they have to?" Caslin asked.

"Modern Russia doesn't work like the United Kingdom, Nathaniel. Just because you have possession of money or assets it doesn't mean you get to keep it. The rule of law is dictated by whoever holds the power. No, the only way you can keep what you have is hold it where they can't touch it."

"You mean abroad?"

"Exactly. Particularly in a country such as yours where the judicial system is *almost* incorruptible," Walsh explained. Caslin reached his car, unlocked it and got in.

"And Kuznetsov facilitated this?"

"Yes. He was one of many who made a fortune off the back of state assets and used that to his benefit."

"So, you're saying the Russian State are trying to get their money back?" Caslin asked, eliciting a chuckle from the other end of the line. That annoyed him.

"It's not their money. It's the citizen's money. The taxpayers. Look, see the Russian Oligarchy as something of a game of thrones. The power shifts and coalesces behind different figures who each have a stake in the game. They are all after the same outcome: to obtain as much wealth and power as they can. To do so, they need to be on the right upward curve to do well. If you make a mistake, then your world can collapse around you."

"Like it did for Kuznetsov?"

"Correct. He cultivated his own network but overplayed his hand. The upshot was he had to leave the country but he didn't stop."

"He lost out politically but his location in the UK meant he was in a perfect position to help others funnel money out of the country," Caslin said. The clouds were clearing if only a little.

"That's right."

"His enemies want what he and his circle have and also to cut off his route for others."

"Yes."

"So why not just take out Kuznetsov? Why are they going after the others?" Caslin asked, feeling stupid.

"Because Kuznetsov is one of many. How many wealthy Russians do you know who live in London, let alone elsewhere in the world? They all need access to those with the skills to shift money around using a variety of methods. They take advantage of multiple shell companies, trust funds, hedge funds and the like. Not to mention investing heavily in real estate and infrastructure projects.

You need a small army of people to pull this off. They have the skills. If you cut down the top man another will step in and utilise the network. No, they need to kill it dead and send a message to anyone else who thinks they might like a piece of that action. If you have the right skill set then you can join in. You may well draw fantastic wealth to you but it's a high-stakes business and ultimately the reciprocity for all that money is your blood… and maybe that of your family."

"Who are these enemies you speak of back in Russia?" Caslin asked. There was a pause at the other end and Caslin had to check that the line hadn't been disconnected. It hadn't. "Cory?"

"In Russia, when you break it down there is ultimately only one man who wields that much power."

"You're talking about the president?" Caslin said softly, not quite believing the words coming out of his mouth.

"The richest man in the world bar none," Walsh confirmed. "With his own worldwide network of people laundering money in plain sight.

"Get out," Caslin said, wanting to disbelieve him but knowing in his heart it was true.

"Aided and abetted by non-Russian nationals the world over," Walsh said. "They don't just use their fellow citizens to do this but also utilise those more sympathetic to their goals."

"How do you mean?"

"How much Russian money is there invested in the banking system or in the London property market? What do you think would happen if that was withdrawn? This isn't hidden, Nathaniel. This is in plain sight as I keep telling you. That is why I kept you in the dark. It was as much for your protection as for that of me and my sources."

Caslin drew breath, "What of Thomas Grey?"

Walsh sighed, "He's a fixer. A damn good one."

"A fixer?"

"Adept at moving money without setting off alarm bells. He is very skilled when it comes to property investments."

"Tell me about Project Obmen? I believe it got Finlay Michaelson killed."

"You're not wrong," Walsh said. "*Obmen* means interchange in Russian. It's a large infrastructure project south of Moscow, part of the city's expansion. Effectively building new districts projected to house upwards of two million people over the course of the next fifteen to twenty years.

You're talking all utilities, public roads and railways, subway trains, leisure facilities. It's one of the largest and most ambitious construction projects going on right now anywhere in the world."

"How did this get Michaelson killed?"

"The details... I don't know... and that's the god's honest truth, Nathaniel. Nestor was heavily invested against my advice. There was certainly a lot of money to be made but pulling it off in the Kremlin's backyard was a big ask. Had they managed it, then that would have been one in the eye for the powerful and one hell of an embarrassment for the president. Nestor always had to push it that extra yard, you know? He overexposed himself and those around him."

"And now they're paying the price," Caslin said.

"I wasn't trying to fob you off, Nathaniel. I really am busy. I'm on my way to a meeting but we can talk more later if you want."

"Okay. I'll give you a call if I have time later today," Caslin said. "Where are you anyway?"

"I'm giving a deposition around lunchtime. I'm travelling there now," Walsh said. "Part of that whole *blowing it open* thing, I was telling you about."

"Okay, take care of yourself and I'll speak to you later."

"I always do, Nathaniel. You know that." Walsh hung up.

Caslin put his mobile in his pocket and started the car. The scale of the investigation threatened to overwhelm him and now he understood why the case had been allocated for a swift closure.

Frosty international relations would take a turn decidedly for the worse if it became public knowledge that effectively, the Russian State was executing their enemies on British soil. From a political point of view, the loss of life to a few low-level criminals paled into insignificance in comparison to an international incident with a global power.

However, it wasn't only criminals who were paying the price. Marat Kadyrov was a diligent investigator examining the theft of public assets and in his mind, until he found out otherwise. Finlay Michaelson was a civil servant doing his job. It didn't matter how high the pyramid went, Caslin was damn sure no one would get a free pass if he had anything to do with it. Maybe those at the very top were out of his reach but there would be plenty in between who were not.

TAKING the turn into Bootham Park, Caslin pulled up alongside Hunter's car. It was empty, so he figured she was inside. Stepping out, he braced against the cold. The rain of the night before had passed to be replaced by an overcast day with a light wind. The temperature was low but at least the weather had lost some of its bite. He set off towards the entrance only to see Hunter emerge and walk in his direction with an expression like thunder.

"What's going on?" Caslin asked as she got within hearing distance.

"They've only gone and bloody discharged him."

"Since when?"

"Eight, this morning," Hunter said barely concealing her anger.

"Can they do that?"

"Apparently, he wasn't sectioned. He self-presented and was therefore a voluntary inpatient. They carried out an assessment this morning and judged him not to be a danger to himself or others and let him out."

"You have got to be bloody kidding me?" Caslin said. "He looked pretty dangerous last night when he took apart those nurses."

"No one has filed a complaint and until they do, Grey is free to go," Hunter said.

"Who picked him up?"

"He got a taxi," Hunter said. "I don't know where to but I've got the company name and I've given them a call to find out where he was dropped off. I'm waiting on them coming back to me. There was a shift change and the day staff don't know."

"I'll bet it's one of two places, either his apartment or the office. Put a call into ops and get Grey's description out there. He is to be detained on sight for his own safety."

"Sir?"

"I think his life is under threat. You head over to the office and I'll go to his place. If the taxi firm get back to you let me know or meet me there, yeah?"

"Got it," Hunter said and both of them got into their respective vehicles and set off.

Caslin remembered that Thomas Grey had a penthouse apartment in the city. He managed to keep it in the settlement following an acrimonious divorce from his wife during which he had spent three months in prison for failing to grant the court access to his finances. Knowing what he now knew, Caslin figured the reason for Grey's refusal was obvious. The apartment was in the shadow of York Minster, in the heart of the city's old town, not far from where Caslin lived in Kleiser's Court.

Leaving his car in a side street, the remainder of the journey was spent negotiating the narrow streets impassable by car. Even in the grip of winter, tourists were beginning to congregate around the Minster for guided tours. Caslin brushed past them without apology, such was his haste to get where he was going.

Grey's residence was located in a converted brewery building, now a bespoke refurbishment of luxury apartments. Turning the corner, Caslin heard a muffled shout and looked up to see a body falling from above, arms flailing as he came down. Within seconds he hit the railings on the edge of the street with barely a sound.

Caslin broke into a sprint, covering the ground in a matter of seconds. Thomas Grey was stretched out before him, impaled with the points of three metal railings protruding from his abdomen. One passed through his right shoulder. The second pierced his left lung, back and front, with the third having punched through the thigh of his left leg. Caslin stepped forward, putting his arms under Grey's body in a vain attempt to take the weight of the body and ease the draw of gravity. Grey convulsed, his body in spasm as he involuntarily spat blood from his mouth.

Realising the impossibility of his chosen course of action, Caslin tried his best to support him with one hand and call for help on his phone with the other. Blood was pouring from multiple wounds and seeping into Caslin's clothes as well as onto his hands. The latter were slippery and he swore as his handset slipped out of his grasp.

"Hang in there, Thomas," Caslin said under his breath.

"Bloody hell!" Hunter's voice came from behind him. He was pleased to see her. The taxi firm must have confirmed the drop off to her and her arrival couldn't have been better timed. "What can I do?"

"Get us some back-up and call an ambulance," Caslin barked, "and the Fire Brigade. They'll need to cut him off these bloody spikes!" The weight of the businessman was not insignificant and supporting him was not a task Caslin was finding easy. A few passers-by came to see what the commotion was about and without being instructed ran over to assist Caslin. Between the three of them, they took Grey's weight but what Grey knew of it was debatable. His body was going into shock.

Casting his eyes upwards, Caslin spied an open window on the top floor. That was where Grey had fallen from. Jumped or pushed, Caslin was unsure? He was itching to get upstairs and find out. Hunter got off the phone.

"They're on their way. ETA five minutes," she said before following Caslin's gaze. "Did you see anyone?"

"Nope," Caslin replied, his voice straining due to the physical exertion. Grey's breathing was ragged and coming in gasps which in turn, were spacing further and further apart. Caslin already knew their efforts would be in vain. He looked up at the window again. "We need to get in there."

"We need to wait for back-up," Hunter said, meeting his eye. Caslin knew that was what the rulebook said but hesitation only gave a would-be assailant those extra, precious seconds to make good their escape.

"I know. I would go…" he said, imploring her with his eyes. It was an order he couldn't give. Hunter took a couple of steps towards the entrance only to stall a moment later. Looking back at him, he could see the fear in her face. She couldn't hide it even if she wanted to.

"I… I'm sorry… I can't," she stammered. Caslin cursed under his breath and looked away. Sirens could be heard approaching from the south and a patrol car arrived alongside an appliance from the nearby Kent Street Fire Station. Caslin instructed the two police officers to assist the members of the public in supporting Grey and once he was sure the appliance crew were aware of their responsibilities, he detached himself and ran towards the entrance. Hunter followed.

Residents had come from within their apartments once they heard the sirens, giving Caslin and Hunter access to the communal parts of the building. They located the stairwell and took the stairs two at a time. Caslin outpaced his detective sergeant and reached the threshold of the top floor nearly a full minute ahead of Hunter.

He approached the door to Grey's flat and found it secure. Hunter arrived behind him and Caslin pointed to the locked door. She moved aside and he stepped back. A short two-step run up and Caslin drove the base of his foot at the lock. The first attempt was unsuccessful but with a second, the door began to give but wouldn't break. A third attempt saw Caslin give in. It was a fire door and was unlikely to give way.

"I'll be back," Hunter said and took off down the stairs. Caslin tried to catch his breath. The exertion of the run and the efforts to break down the door were catching up with him. A few minutes later, Hunter reappeared with one of the firemen in tow. He carried with him a hydraulic ram. Hunter directed him to the door and he applied the cylinder to the lock. The pneumatic system was deployed and seconds later the door burst open as the locking mechanism gave way. Caslin pushed open the door and ran in, Hunter only a step behind.

Inside, the lounge area was a scene of devastation. The coffee table was overturned, whatever had been on it was now scattered across the floor. Two chairs were upended and there was broken glass sprayed out in a radius of roughly a metre. Hunter looked at Caslin.

"Fight?"

He shrugged, "Possibly. Careful what you touch." He made his way over to the open window and looked out. The paramedics had arrived and were clearly trying to stabilise Grey while the appliance crew set up their cutting gear. It looked as if Grey was still alive. At least, for now. Caslin found his attention drawn to the exterior window ledge. It was crafted from stone and was original to the building, garnering the build-up of debris one might expect. There were eight distinct lines that he could make out, almost as if they were gouged out of the natural accumulation on the stone.

"What do you see?" Hunter asked, coming to join him. He pointed out the marks. "What do you make of that?"

"I heard a shout or a muffled scream, I'm not sure which just as I rounded the corner to see Grey falling."

"My god, that's awful. Do you think he may have jumped?" Hunter asked. Caslin pointed to the marks again.

"I don't know of many suicides where the victim shouts or screams before the fall and fewer still who cling onto the window ledge to preserve their life that bit longer. Do you?"

"No," Hunter said. "And you didn't see anyone?"

"No." Pressing his fingers against his eyes, Caslin cursed.

"Where do we go from here?" Hunter asked. Caslin shook his head. His phone beeped and he saw another text. Feeling thoroughly deflated, he opened it – *You must protect hm. Why aren't you acting?* Caslin shook his head and typed out a reply – *It's too late. They've already got to Grey.* The response came back immediately and it was angry – *They were always going to get to Grey. He was dead months ago, he just didn't know it. Why aren't you in London??? I told you they know where he will be…*

Caslin looked out of the window at the scene below. The frenetic activity had ceased. Grey was still impaled on the railings and it was clear that he had passed away. Caslin was crestfallen. Turning his thoughts back to the spate of texts, he called Terry Holt back at Fulford Road.

"Yes, sir. What can I do for you?"

"You tracked this mobile for me. You said it was in York and London but never left the city centre?"

"Right."

"Where does it report most frequently in London?"

"Wait one and I'll check," Holt said. Caslin cast Hunter a glance and she was curious as to where he was going with the inquiry. "The area the phone connects to the network towers is triangulated in central London, between the Embankment, Leicester Square and… Holborn. I'm sorry, sir, my knowledge of London's geography is sketchy. I don't know where that is."

"That's where you spend your time if you have a bit of money," Caslin offered. "Tourist central at the weekends but…"

"What are you thinking?" Hunter asked.

"Where does Raisa study?" Caslin asked.

"Kuznetsova?" Hunter clarified. Caslin nodded. "At the London School of Economics, I think. Why?"

"That's on the edge of Covent Garden."

"So?"

"If you were studying at the LSE, and you had a bit of money behind you, you might choose to live in Covent Garden which is slap bang in the middle of the area Terry just gave me. I would live there if it were me and I had Raisa's background."

"You think she's what… the source?"

"The other guy in the photograph, Cory Walsh," Caslin explained, "campaigns against financial fraud. He was a friend of Nestor Kuznetsov's and I believe he was feeding him information as was Marat Kadyrov and possibly, Finlay Michaelson. It may be what got them killed."

"And this Walsh… they're taking out his sources? He must have some powerful enemies."

"Trust me, you wouldn't believe me if I told you the half of it but yes, it's a distinct possibility. Terry," Caslin turned his attention back to his phone, "are you still there?"

"I'm still here."

"Is the handset active?"

"Erm… yes. It is," Holt confirmed. "Heading south along the Victoria Embankment."

"Terry, get me a helicopter."

"I beg your pardon?" Holt said with obvious surprise.

"Get onto the National Police Air Service and get me a chopper, now.

And tell them to make sure it's fuelled. Don't take no for an answer. Then I want you to route me a call through to Niall Montgomerie. He's the commander of the MET's Counter Terrorism Unit."

"Leave it with me," Holt said and hung up. He didn't know what was going on but he knew better than to question him once a course of action was set.

Turning to Hunter, Caslin said, "Come on. They can pick us up from Dean's Park. That's the closest place they can safely land a helicopter."

"Where the hell are we going?" Hunter asked.

"We're off to London…" Caslin said before adding, "to see the queen." He said it with such a straight face, so Hunter would no idea whether he was serious or not but she fell into step, regardless.

CHAPTER TWENTY-SIX

CASLIN'S PHONE rang as the distinctive sound of rotor blades could be heard approaching from the west.

"Caslin," he said. It was Terry Holt.

"I have Commander Montgomerie for you, sir. I'll patch you through." The line beeped and Caslin knew they were connected.

"Commander, I don't have a lot of time so I'll need to keep this brief," he began.

"Go ahead, Inspector."

"I have a real and present threat against the life of Cory Walsh, obtained from a credible source," Caslin explained. "Walsh is due in Parliament today to deliver a deposition. I understand from my source that an attack is highly likely."

"That's one of the most protected complexes in the country. How will they manage that?"

"I don't have the details, sir, but my guess is that Walsh's campaign relies upon a degree of media coverage to keep it in the mainstream. He is unlikely to enter Parliament by way of the back door. This is one occasion where he will want to be high profile and visible," Caslin said, raising his voice to counter the incredible noise coming from the twin engines of the descending helicopter.

"Who is your source?" Montgomerie asked.

"I would prefer not to say at this stage, sir. I believe she is under duress and with what she knows I imagine the hit team are keeping her very close by. That's why my contact with her has been sporadic and limited. She is already in the area and if she is, then so are they. DC Holt can provide you with jackets on the suspects and DS Hunter and I are en route to London. Walsh is due to appear at lunchtime."

"Perhaps we should contact him and postpone his appearance?"

"I'll guarantee he won't go for that, sir," Caslin practically shouted as he made his way to the waiting helicopter, stooping to avoid the downdraft of the spinning blades. "Besides, if we postpone, so will they. At least on this occasion we'll have the drop on them."

"Call me when you land," Montgomerie stated. Caslin cancelled the call and made up the short distance remaining to the helicopter. The officer seated in the rear opened the door looking first to Hunter and then Caslin.

"No one's told us where we're going," he said, looking confused.

"Well, you and your co-pilot friend are staying here," Caslin stated, pointing to the front and indicating one of the pilots to disembark.

"You can't leave us here," the man said.

"Yes, I think you'll find I can... out," he said firmly. Hunter glanced at him.

"I've never been in a helicopter," she said with a half-smile.

"Don't worry," he said, offering her a hand as she climbed up into the rear, "it's just like taking a ride in your Giulietta."

Minutes later, the rotors were at maximum speed and they were lifting off. With only space for three passengers, the two crew members who remained behind watched with a degree of bemusement as their ride ascended into the sky without them.

"What's the flight time to London?" Caslin asked once he'd figured out the internal communication system.

"I'd say it's around two hundred miles and usually we would be looking at around ninety-minutes' flight time," the pilot advised. "Although with a favourable wind I can probably shave ten to fifteen off that. Are we heading for the London Helipad at Battersea?" Caslin shook his head, a movement unnoticed by the pilot, concentrating on gaining them elevation out of the city.

"No, I want you to set down on the roof of Scotland Yard," Caslin stated. In the rear, Hunter grinned but no one saw.

"I'll need clearance for that," the pilot said.

"You'll have it," Caslin said with confidence whilst secretly hoping he could deliver on the promise.

THE PILOT PROVED to be incredibly accurate with his estimation as they found themselves entering London airspace within an hour. In order to accommodate their approach without a scheduled flight plan, Air Traffic Control directed them to approach via the east and come into London along the path of the Thames at a height of five hundred feet. They were given clearance to descend once they had passed Blackfriars Bridge and then Waterloo Bridge, bringing them into visual sight of Scotland Yard.

"Are you feeling like you're coming home?" Hunter asked from the rear.

Caslin smiled, "Hardly. They moved from Broadway a couple of years ago and put it here. They brought the name with them but I've never set foot in this building."

"Shame," Hunter said. "Still, maybe you'll get to see some of your old friends." Caslin didn't respond. He hadn't considered that possibility and the thought filled him with anxiety. He buried it.

They touched down on the roof-top helipad and both Hunter and Caslin clambered out. Caslin threw the pilot a brief wave in appreciation and they were stepped away from the chopper. Both of them felt unsteady on their feet and Caslin's hearing was affected by the changes in noise and pressure they'd been subjected to. They were met as they reached the steps down from the pad. A young officer, shielded his eyes from the dust disturbed from the rotating blades.

"I'm DS Collins. Commander Montgomerie has asked me to assist you, sir," Collins shouted in order to be heard above the roar of the engines.

"Get us to the House of Commons as quickly as you can," Caslin shouted, leaning in.

"That's a three-minute walk, sir. Once we're out of the building. This way," Collins said, guiding them along a walkway and towards the roof-top access door. Passing through, Caslin was momentarily thrown. A grinning face greeted him as the bearer came striding towards them. It took a moment for him to recognise her. She had grown her hair and altered the colour, at least he thought so but was often the last to notice such things.

"Nate Caslin," she said approaching and throwing her arms around him. He tensed but was warmed by the gesture. Hunter raised an eyebrow but said nothing as the woman ended the embrace. "Someone told me you were coming but I couldn't quite believe it."

"It's great to see you," Caslin said, his own face splitting a broad and genuine grin. "You're looking well. I'd like to catch up but it'll have to wait."

"I know. I'll catch you later," she said as the group moved on.

"What's the state of play with Walsh's protection?" Hunter asked, casting a curious glance in the direction of the woman as they went.

"Under orders from Commander Montgomerie we've not communicated with Mr Walsh. However, we've deployed spotters on the adjacent buildings and we have roaming plain-clothes teams outside. The pictures of the suspects provided by your DC Holt have been circulated to every member but as yet they haven't been seen. We are looking to intercept before they can make a move on the target."

"Excellent," Caslin said, glancing across at Hunter and reassured that SO15 were at the top of their game. They took the lift straight down to the lobby with no stops at any other floor. They left the building, stepping out onto the embankment and Caslin took an immediate right heading for the Houses of Parliament.

"Do you really think they'll try and carry out a hit outside such a high-profile location?" DS Collins asked, almost as if he thought it a near impossibility.

"Walsh rarely stays in the same place for any length of time. I think he spends his life travelling the globe and keeps his inner circle incredibly small. That way, his organisation is tight and trustworthy. They might not get a better shot at him than they will today."

Midday in central London, around the Houses of Parliament was never a quiet occasion. People were milling, grabbing an early lunch or dashing to the next meeting. Parliament was sitting following the Christmas break which brought out the journalists, commentators and lobbyists who routinely filled the Commons.

Caslin eyed the surrounding buildings on both sides of the Thames but he couldn't make out the spotters that Collins assured him were present. He felt his apprehension rising. There was something of a media scrum threatening to develop as print journalists jockeyed for position with television crews aiming to get the best shot. Cory Walsh was today's draw. Caslin felt he had played down his deposition appearance today.

DS Collins advised him Walsh was scheduled to present evidence to the Treasury Select Committee regarding the role played by money laundering in the UK banking system. His appearance was expected to be the lead story on all major news networks in the country with Walsh promising an explosive revelation. This scenario only managed to heighten the trepidation that Caslin fostered. In Walsh's own words, this was a high-stakes business and Caslin wanted to ensure that at least one man didn't forfeit his life in pursuit of a code of decency like so many others already had.

Caslin's phone rang and he answered it without looking at the screen such was the attention he was paying to the gathering crowd.

"Sir, it's Terry Holt. I thought you'd want to know the phone is active. Are you on site?"

"We're outside Parliament, Terry. Where is she?"

"I have her just crossing at Lambeth Bridge and taking a right through the Victoria—"

"Tower Gardens," Caslin finished for him. He drew the attention of DS Collins, "Tower Gardens. Heading this way."

Collins took up his radio and relayed the information to the undercover team as well as the spotters. Everyone responded they had no eyes on the target. They were close and Walsh was due at any moment. Caslin looked to his left, down Abingdon Street and Millbank beyond. To the right was Parliament Street with the Square in the foreground. From a close personal protection point of view this was a nightmare scenario despite the high level of police presence. There were any number of buildings where a sniper could operate without fear of discovery and the volume of people made spotting individuals a nightmare. They waited. Holt was still on the line and Caslin asked him, "Where are they now?"

"The signal's dropped. I don't know. When is Walsh due?"

"Any moment," Caslin confirmed hearing the tension in his own voice. He looked to Collins who shook his head. The crowd appeared to surge towards the road and Caslin figured the star of the show had arrived. Flash bulbs went off at an astonishing rate as Cory Walsh stepped out onto the pavement. His ever-present bodyguards were by his side and uniformed police officers sought to keep the crowd at bay but it was nigh on impossible. Caslin scanned the crowd.

"Talk to me, Terry," he asked, stress creeping into his tone.

"I don't know. It's probably down to the surrounding buildings disrupting the signal," Holt stated, staring at his screen. Caslin searched the crowd before him for recognisable faces. And then there was one if not two.

"There!" he said, pointing them out to Hunter and before anyone else could react, he set off. Caslin was certain one of them was Grigory Vitsin and the other, one of Kuznetsov's security team.

They were within two metres of each other and closing in on Cory Walsh's entourage. Caslin tried to shout to Walsh's bodyguards or the officers accompanying him to the entrance of Parliament but with the media barrage of shouted questions and calls for photographs there was little chance of him being heard. The targets were on the other side of the crowd and Caslin burst into the melee pushing and shoving without recourse to try and get to intercept Vitsin or to reach Walsh's side.

Protests were thrown in his direction but he ignored them as he unceremoniously battled his way through. All of a sudden, the crowd parted before him and Caslin saw the second target and hurled himself forward. His approach was noted at the last moment and he took a blow to the side of his head for good measure but Caslin pressed on taking as firm a hold as he could.

Using his momentum, he put the man off balance, placing his own leg behind the target's and flipping him backwards. They both ended up striking the pavement with Caslin atop his quarry. The advantage of surprise was quickly lost however and despite having the initial upper hand, Caslin found himself heaved sideways and away. His opponent was younger, stronger and clearly more adept at street fighting. Caslin rolled and came to his feet just in time to block an incoming strike. He failed to block the second or the third and felt a swift kick to his stomach and he crumpled.

Looking up through the corner of his eye, he expected the knockout blow only to see a blur pass before him, swiftly followed by his opponent hitting the ground face first. The fog in his mind cleared and he saw Hunter standing before him, extendable baton in hand.

Rising, Caslin had no time to convey his gratitude as Vitsin came into view, barely steps from Walsh. Caslin screamed and charged forward. Walsh's security reacted at the same time and advanced to intercept the Russian. The first took a glancing blow from a cosh as Vitsin wielded it from side to side. His expression, one of maniacal fury.

The second grasped Vitsin's wrist and they became locked together in a battle of wills as much as one of physical combat. Caslin raced forward and dived head first into Vitsin's midriff, knocking the wind out of him. The Russian staggered but managed to maintain his position until DS Collins arrived in the fray and between the three of them, they managed to overpower and wrestle him to the ground. Despite their superiority, Vitsin continued to fight like a man possessed of an inner strength that Caslin couldn't comprehend.

"You've failed, Grigory," Caslin barked as they disarmed him. "It's over."

A scream went up from behind and Caslin felt the crowd surge once again, only this time away from them. Vitsin was on the floor with both Walsh's security and DS Collins pinning him to the ground. Caslin knelt and turned to see Cory Walsh staring at him, a look of astonishment upon his face. He took a step forward, then staggered for two more before collapsing to the ground. Caslin looked around and then he saw her. Her hair was cropped short and recently dyed. She cut a figure in stark contrast to the one he remembered but it was undeniably her.

"Nyet, Raisa!" Vitsin shouted from his position on the floor before letting out a guttural, primal scream that carried despite the commotion encompassing them. Caslin saw the blade in her hand. It was four inches long and glistened with fresh blood. Cory Walsh's blood.

Hunter stepped forward striking Raisa's wrist with her baton and the blade dropped to the floor, as did the young woman with a corresponding yelp of pain. Hunter was on to her in a flash, pinning her down and securing her with handcuffs. Caslin scrambled over to where Walsh lay, immediately seeing the darkness spreading beneath his neatly pressed white shirt.

"Call for an ambulance!" Caslin shouted to no one in particular as he reached forward, tearing open the shirt and looking for the entry wound. He found it in the chest and he applied pressure with both hands to try and stem the flow of blood. There was only the one wound but the blood was reddish-brown.

Caslin knew that was serious. The darker the shade of blood, the more vital the organ was that had been punctured. He was in no doubt that Walsh's heart had ruptured. Caslin sought to comfort him as Walsh reached out, gripping his hand. Their eyes met and Walsh appeared to be pleading with him, fear etched into his face but no words were forthcoming. Caslin watched as the light faded from his eyes and within moments, Cory Walsh was dead.

Caslin tore his eyes away from the man lying before him, fighting back the tears. He looked to Hunter who stood a few feet away appearing somewhat shell-shocked. Raisa Kuznetsova hung her head refusing to meet anyone's gaze. Grigory Vitsin wept unashamedly. Caslin scanned the crowd, watching on intently in a stony silence. An eerie calm descended before The Palace of Westminster, the likes of which was unseen with the possible exception of Remembrance Sunday. Caslin's gaze fell on one figure in particular. He seemed to notice the scrutiny and turned to walk away. Caslin stood. His hands as well as his forearms were covered in Walsh's blood but he didn't care.

Stepping away, he saw Hunter looking at him, her mouth moving but he didn't register the words. Walking past her, Caslin followed the retreating figure towards the main entrance picking up his pace as the man glanced back over his shoulder and noted the interest. He in turn, increased his own speed passing through the security gate having revealed his identification to the officer on duty. Caslin approached but the uniformed constable held up his hand.

"I'm sorry, sir, but the Palace is in lockdown," he said. Caslin took out his warrant card and raised it whilst identifying himself.

"I'm DI Caslin from North Yorkshire Police."

"I'm sorry, sir, but you're not cleared," the officer stated.

"Then tell me who that was." Caslin indicated towards the man who had been allowed through only moments earlier. "You can do that, surely?"

"That was Lord Payne, sir." Caslin looked beyond the officer and stared towards the entrance as if willing the man back into view.

"Should I know him?"

"I wouldn't know, sir."

"He looks familiar but I can't place him," Caslin muttered, flicking a dismissive gesture towards the constable signifying it didn't matter and turning away. Hunter came to join him.

"Are you okay?" she asked. Caslin cast one furtive glance towards the building behind them and gave a casual shake of the head.

"Ah... forget it. It's probably nothing."

CHAPTER TWENTY-SEVEN

ENTERING THE CUSTODY SUITE, Caslin and Hunter were guided towards the cells. DS Collins led the way. The booking-in area was rammed. There was hardly ever a quiet day for the MET. A whistle drew his attention and Caslin turned and to his surprise it was aimed at him. Hunter clearly recognised the woman they'd briefly encountered earlier as they came down from the helipad. Caslin warmly welcomed her approach.

"Isabel," he said in greeting. There was no embrace on this occasion. "You're looking great."

"I can't say the same for you," she replied, "but the black suits you… and it's flattering." Caslin glanced down at his shirt and laughed nervously. Someone had been kind enough to raid the stores and find him some clean clothes. He now wore the jet-black undershirt of the MET's standard issue uniform. Hunter exaggerated the clearing of her throat. Caslin glanced across.

"Oh, sorry. DS Hunter meet DI Isabel Covey."

"Sarah," Hunter added. "Pleased to meet you."

"Likewise," Covey said taking Hunter's offered hand.

"Isabel was my DI when I was based here," Caslin added, remembering their time fondly.

"DCI now, Nate," Covey added, with a wink.

Caslin inclined his head, "Congratulations. Thoroughly deserved, I expect."

"Yes, it was," she said smiling. "Listen, I have to go but check in with me before you shoot off, will you?"

"I promise," Caslin said.

"You promised three years ago, too," Covey said, moving away before looking over her shoulder and adding, "but you broke that one." Caslin waved with a mock grimace.

"Shall we?" DS Collins asked, inclining his head towards the cell block. "I don't know how much time we will have." Caslin agreed.

A uniformed constable came with them, holding a set of keys. He led them into the block and took the second left turn. The corridor was short with doors to eight cells, four on each wall, facing one another. Approaching the second one on Caslin's left, the constable slid in a key and unlocked it pulling the metal door wide. He stepped aside.

"Give him five minutes," DS Collins told the officer who nodded. Caslin entered but the others remained outside and the door was closed. Raisa Kuznetsova sat with her legs brought up before her, hugging her knees on the vinyl-coated mattress, the only source of comfort in the eight-by-four-foot room. Her head was pressed forward and she rocked gently to and fro. She didn't acknowledge his arrival.

"Raisa." Caslin sought her attention. After a few moments she took a deep breath, sniffed, drew her wrist across the base of her nose and raised her head. Her eyes were puffy, bloodshot and lined red. She had been crying. Her right hand and wrist were bandaged, no doubt down to the force of Hunter's strike with her baton.

"What do you want, Mr Caslin?" she asked softly, her voice almost cracking with emotion. She was clearly trying to process the enormity of what she had done this day. It wasn't going well.

"I just want to know why?" Raisa snorted a laugh in response but it wasn't genuine humour, then the tears fell once more.

"You couldn't possibly understand," she said dismissing him.

"Probably not," Caslin said. "He was a friend of your father's."

"Who got him killed," Raisa bit back.

"And your father walked a dangerous road. One largely of his own choosing. Cory Walsh didn't deserve for his life to end like that." Raisa looked up and met his eye, quietly replying with a slight shake of the head.

"No, he didn't."

"Then why?"

Raisa remained silent for a few moments. Caslin waited patiently. She stared at a nondescript place on the wall appearing thoughtful as she wiped the tear streaks from her face.

"Have you ever heard of *Maskirovka*?" she asked, her gaze returning to him.

"No," Caslin replied, shaking his head.

"My father explained it to me when I was a little girl," she said with a warm smile. "*Maskirovka.* The age-old Russian art of deception. It is ingrained in our culture or at least, within the military. They still teach it to the officers – have done for centuries."

"Go on," Caslin encouraged, moving closer and asking if he could sit. She nodded and he sat down alongside her.

"It is quite simple really," she explained, her expression taking on another faraway look. "*Deny, frustrate and obfuscate* was how my father used to put it. Apply those terms to any act of Russian foreign policy and you will see Maskirovka in action – Crimea, Ukraine… assassinations…" she said the last, rolling her head in Caslin's direction and meeting his eye with a fleeting look. "Just when you think you know what is going on… everything changes… and by the time you catch up it is usually too late." Caslin sat back, resting his shoulders and the back of his head against the tiled wall of the cell.

"What are you telling me, Raisa?"

"That it's too late for you, Inspector Caslin," she said with regret edging her tone. "You want to understand?"

"I do, yes."

"My mother still lives in Moscow," Raisa said, before adding almost inaudibly, "and I have a half-sister, Roxanna. She is only seven. So much confidence. Roxanna can light up a room just by entering it. She's adorable and I would do anything for her, Inspector. Anything." Caslin realised he'd been holding his breath and exhaled deeply.

"They could have come here, to the UK. There is always a way. We could have protected them," he said, thinking aloud.

"And tell me who is going to protect them from you?" Caslin found that to be an odd question and his expression conveyed the feeling. Raisa turned to face him, sitting cross-legged and raised her chin, taking in a deep breath. Caslin met her gaze. "Oh… Mr Caslin. I think you are a decent man but…" she said softly, reaching across and gently placing the palm of her hand on the back of his and pressing down ever-so-lightly, "you still don't understand these things and I'm not sure you ever will."

There was a double knock on the door. Caslin held their eye contact for a few seconds longer. He figured there was more that Raisa could say to enlighten him but at the same time, he had the sense that she would say nothing further.

"It is time," he said. Raisa turned away, dropping her feet to the floor and stood up. As did Caslin.

"What happens now?" she asked fearfully.

"Did they not say?"

"I don't think I took it all in."

"You've been charged with Cory's murder. You'll be taken from here to a magistrates' court where, no doubt, they will refer you to Crown Court for trial. In the meantime, the magistrate will give their permission for you to be held on remand in prison until the date of your trial is set."

Raisa smiled nervously, "Piece of cake, right?" Caslin nodded, reaching across and gripping her upper arm in a gesture of support. Despite what she had done, he still felt protective over her. The cell door opened and Caslin felt her physically beginning to shake as two officers stepped through to collect her. He was unsure whether this was a result of an adrenalin surge or the dawning realisation of the magnitude of her predicament. She was handcuffed and led from the cell, casting a last glance back at him over her shoulder. He stared forward, expressionless. DS Collins appeared once the three were out of the cell.

"Next one?" he asked. Caslin nodded.

GRIGORY VITSIN WAS SITTING on the floor at the far end of his cell. He glanced up as Caslin entered but said nothing. He cut the look of a broken man, far from the brash arrogance that Caslin had attributed to him in the past. The cell door was closed behind him and Caslin leant against the wall, his hands in his pockets. Neither man spoke for a full minute before Caslin broke the ice.

"All of this could have been avoided if you had just come to me rather than sending those cryptic texts."

Vitsin snorted a derisory response, "And you would have believed me?"

"I may have." Vitsin laughed.

"You..." he said, much more like the man Caslin expected to see, "would have trusted... me? I don't think so." Caslin often kept an open mind but on this occasion, the Russian had a valid point.

"Probably not," he said, with a shrug.

"Honesty," Vitsin said, nodding. "For that, I salute you."

"How long have you and Raisa been an item?" Caslin asked. Vitsin shot him a dark look. "It's pretty obvious. Remember I am a detective."

"For almost a year now," he replied, confirming Caslin's suspicions. That was why Holt's tracking of the mobile records showed it so frequently in both London and York. "How did you know?"

"I didn't. Not until this afternoon anyway. I presume her father didn't know?" Caslin asked. Vitsin shook his head in reply. "I guessed not. That's why you always switched the phone off when you got back to York, so you never ran the risk of her calling you once you were back by Kuznetsov's side on his estate."

"He would have gone mad. His daughter taking up with scum like me," Vitsin said. "And he would have been right. She deserves better than me. What will happen to her: Raisa? She will be going to prison for a long time, yes?"

Caslin nodded, "Yes. A long time."

"How long?"

Caslin thought about it, "It's premeditated murder. If she pleads guilty, then she'll get a reduced sentence but we're still looking at life with a minimum term of eighteen to twenty years. If she has a decent legal team around her, they may be able to successfully argue some mitigating factors and bring that down a bit."

"That is a very long time," Vitsin said, looking up at Caslin with a forlorn expression.

"Yes, I'm afraid there's no way around it."

"And me?"

"The bodyguard you thumped has no interest in pressing charges but they're looking to have you deported for causing a public disturbance and affray," Caslin said flatly. "The decision hasn't been rubber-stamped yet but it's looking likely."

"It gets me out of the way, doesn't it," Vitsin said with a smile.

"You could be home by midnight."

"You know that deportation order may as well be my death warrant?" Vitsin said, his expression one of resignation. "I won't even make it out of the airport before they pick me up."

"You could help me to help you," Caslin suggested.

"How so?"

"You could tell me why you killed Nestor Kuznetsov?" Caslin asked casually. The question brought another laugh from the Russian, this one boomed out as he shook his head in disbelief. "There's no need to deny it. I know Kuznetsov was unable to set his own noose in the way it was secured. The pathologist believes it's nigh on a medical impossibility. Did he ask you… or beg you to help him?" Vitsin looked up and met Caslin's eye and at that point, he knew his theory was correct irrespective of whatever response was forthcoming.

"I underestimated you, Inspector," Vitsin said. "Back home many of the detectives are either incompetent or corrupt. Some are both… that, I assure you is a tragic combination."

"He wanted your help to die and you agreed."

"Yes. He was about to lose everything. His business, his money… property… along with his reputation."

"His reputation?" Caslin scoffed. "You say that as if he had a decent one!"

"He knew what he was," Vitsin argued, his eyes narrowing at Caslin's sneering response. "But he still had his dignity. They were about to strip him of even that. Nestor couldn't face the humiliation. He asked, pleaded… and then he begged me to help him."

"He could have gone out a different way. Gone solo with some pills and a bottle of vodka."

Vitsin chuckled, "You don't know him. Despite all his bluster and arrogance, he needed someone by his side that he could trust. He wanted it clean and yes, I helped him. I do not regret it."

"Go on the record," Caslin said. Vitsin shook his head. "If you go on the record you'll be arrested and face a manslaughter charge. At worst, you'll do seven to ten years and then you'll be out."

"And what then? I will still be deported."

Caslin had to concede the point, "Yes, in all likelihood."

"Then what is the point?"

"Things may have changed back home. It is a long time." Vitsin processed the idea. Caslin could see the thoughts churning through his mind.

"And what of Raisa? She will still be in prison."

"She will get out eventually."

"I will be an old man by then, Inspector whereas Raisa will still have time for a proper life. Perhaps, even a family," he said with regret, "but it will not be with me."

"You could give her the choice. She may surprise you."

Vitsin smiled but it was without genuine humour, "And you think she will still love the man who confesses to killing her father? She blamed Walsh. It didn't matter what I said. Had I told her, she would have blamed me. I didn't want to lose her, Inspector."

There was a knock at the door and it opened outwards. DS Collins stepped forward clutching some paperwork.

"This has come through from the Home Office, sir," he said. "Mr Vitsin is set to be deported today."

Caslin turned to Vitsin, "You have the legal right to challenge the—"

"I won't be challenging anything," Vitsin said, interrupting him and standing up. "It is time for me to go home," he said, offering his hand. Caslin took it and they made eye contact in a show of mutual respect. Both men set out to achieve one goal that day… and both failed.

CHAPTER TWENTY-EIGHT

CASLIN LEFT the cell without another word acknowledging DS Collins with a brief nod as he passed. Hunter was waiting for him in the corridor.

"What do we do now?" she asked.

"Head home, I guess. There's nothing for us here."

"For a moment I thought you were home," Hunter said playfully. Caslin laughed.

"I don't suppose the helicopter is still on the roof is it?" Caslin asked. Hunter shook her head.

"I can arrange a lift over to King's Cross for you," a voice said from behind. They turned to see DCI Covey approaching. She stepped aside, allowing free passage for Vitsin to be escorted from the cell block. He walked with his head high and Caslin noted him silently mouth the words 'I love you' to Raisa as they crossed paths in the custody suite.

"Much appreciated," Hunter replied.

"You'll be in time to catch the last train," Covey said. "Unless you fancy a night in the city. It'd be like old times."

Caslin smiled, "Another time, I promise."

"There's that word again," Covey said, grinning.

"Are you looking for us?" Caslin asked.

"Commander Montgomerie asked that I convey his gratitude to the two of you. He was impressed with how you carried yourselves today."

"I'm not," Caslin grunted. "We had one goal and completely screwed it up. I don't suppose he mentioned anything about Walsh's deposition?"

"The dossier he was due to present was brought in, if that's what you mean?"

Caslin nodded, "And what is to be done with it?"

"It will be assessed and passed on to the relevant authorities."

"Assessed by who? Which authorities?"

Covey shrugged, "I don't know, sorry. Come on, let's get you guys squared away. We'll have time to grab a bite to eat if you fancy it?"

"Not for me," Caslin said, heading back towards the custody suite. "I've lost my appetite."

Covey passed Hunter a questioning look, "I guess some things never change. Any idea what's got into him this time?"

"None," Hunter replied, setting off after Caslin, "but I guess we're passing on the meal."

She caught up with Caslin as he was leaving the custody suite, the double doors nearly catching her in the face as he released them, such was his turn of pace.

"Nate!" she called, trying to get his attention. He slowed and looked back at her.

"Sorry, I didn't know you were there."

"What's gotten into you?" she asked. Caslin shook his head and set off again, purposefully striding along the corridor. "Where are you even going?" He stopped. She had a point. He had no idea where he was going.

"There's something wrong. I can feel it."

"You and your instincts again," Hunter said, smiling. Caslin didn't return her good nature. Taking out his mobile, he called Terry Holt back at Fulford Road.

"Terry, do you have any news for me?"

"Nothing major," he said. "Oh, hang on, I did have some joy with that photograph the old widow brought in… Miranda Richardson."

"Michaelson," Caslin corrected.

"Yeah, her. Anyway, I've identified the other guy in the photo. It came up on Google image, can you believe that? You'll never guess who it is, though. He's a member of the House of Lords."

"Payne," Caslin said firmly. Holt was surprised.

"Yeah! Lord Payne. How the hell did you know that?"

"Did you check him out?"

"Only the headlines of his bio. I mean, what with Walsh being killed today, I figured there wasn't a great rush to go into detail."

"What did you find out?" Caslin asked, guiding Hunter into an empty room off the corridor. She flicked on the lights and he switched the call onto loudspeaker as she closed the door. Holt's voice sounded disembodied and there was an echo on the line. They ignored it.

"Lord Payne of Whittingdale," Holt began. "Seventy-four years of age, he was made a life-peer in 1996 by the then Conservative Prime Minister. Attended Eton before going on to Oxbridge—"

"Anything more recent?"

"Erm… let me see," Holt said, clearly scanning through his notes. "Has had a successful business career on the boards of several multi-nationals and still sits on the board of one or two. He's currently Deputy-Chair on the Treasury Select Committee… should I go on? I mean, I pulled his associations from the Register of Lords' Interests."

"Michaelson wrote about the register. What businesses is he still actively involved in?" Caslin asked. Hunter's interest was piqued. She leaned in closer.

"ITF… where he's a non-executive director, they are tied to big pharma… YP Global Holdings… again non-exec…" Holt sucked air through his teeth as he scanned his notes. "Henderson Holdings Ltd."

"That one!" Caslin said. "What's the interest there?"

"He's the current chairman of the board," Holt stated. "Why?" Caslin hung up. Hunter stared at him. Caslin closed his eyes.

"What's going on?" Hunter asked him. "Who are Henderson Holdings?"

"They were involved in Project Obmen. Michaelson was querying export licences granted to them a couple of years ago."

"And Michaelson knew Payne," Hunter said.

"And Michaelson is very much dead having raised concerns about a conflict of interest."

"You don't think…" Hunter began but didn't finish the question. Caslin furiously rubbed at his temples with the palms of his hands releasing a controlled howl as realisation dawned.

"Cory Walsh said he was going to blow it wide open today. They were his exact words when he spoke to me earlier," Caslin said, locking eyes with her. "Lord Payne is the deputy-chair of the committee that Walsh was scheduled to come before."

"You do know what you're saying don't you?" Hunter said, lowering her voice as if fearful someone would overhear. Caslin didn't have an opportunity to respond as DCI Covey appeared at the doorway.

"There you are!" she said. "I'll give you that lift to the King's Cross now if you like?"

"I'd like to speak with Commander Montgomerie beforehand, if you could see to that?" Caslin asked. Covey shook her head.

"He anticipated you would. He told me he would be in meetings for the remainder of the day so he'd be unavailable. But, if you wanted to leave your details with his office, then he'll set up a telephone call later in the week." Caslin looked at Hunter. She was thinking the same as him.

"Later in the week?" Covey nodded. "Bastard. We'll see about that." Caslin brushed past her and stalked into the corridor beyond. "Which way is his office?"

"Is there a problem?" Covey asked, following.

"I want a word."

"You're wasting your time," Covey said, catching up to him. Caslin turned to face her.

"It's my time to waste."

"He won't see you," Covey hissed, lowering her voice.

Caslin shook his head. "What do you know about this?"

"About *what*?" Covey countered. "I know Montgomerie. I've worked for him for the last couple of years. If he sets a position then it takes an awful lot to shift him. He's like an oil tanker. Forget it, Nathaniel. You're not going to get anywhere with this and..."

"And what?"

Covey shook her head. It was a telling gesture.

"For your own sake... just let it go," she implored him. Caslin knew then without another word being said, Covey was looking out for him.

"I'll not need the lift. I'd prefer the walk," he said, meeting her eye. "It was good to see you, Isabel. Congratulations on the promotion but forgive me, I need some air."

"Nate... I'm sorry," Covey said as he departed. Hunter came alongside, appearing awkward. "Some people don't change. He's still bloody impossible." Hunter gently chewed her lower lip before tilting her head slightly to one side.

"You'll get no argument from me," she said, offering a weak smile before following her DI.

"Something I said?" Covey asked.

"Don't worry. I'll see you," Hunter said over her shoulder and took a right turn, roughly in the direction Caslin had gone and also where she remembered the main entrance to Scotland Yard would be found.

HUNTER WALKED out into the late afternoon sunshine. The wind was up bringing a much-needed change in the weather. The long shadows cast by the trees lining the road stretched across to the edge of the River Thames. Hunter walked for ten minutes along the Victoria Embankment before she found Caslin. He was seated on a bench adjacent to the stone wall, separating the path from the water below. She hesitated about approaching him. He appeared lost in thought, staring across the river in the direction of Westminster Bridge with the London Eye in the background.

Summoning some courage, Hunter walked up to him and sat down alongside but said nothing. After a few seconds, he glanced towards her and away again.

"Beautiful scene," she said. Caslin looked around, nodding his agreement.

"Yes, it is," he said. Hunter noted he was toying with the black leather wallet she knew contained his warrant card, turning it over and over in his hands.

"What are you thinking?"

He blew air out of his nose and smiled, "Whether it's all worth it." He added no further detail.

"Walsh's evidence will never see the light of day, will it?"

Caslin shook his head, "I very much doubt it. All this time we were looking to the east when the demon was in our own back yard."

"Payne?" Hunter asked. Caslin shrugged.

"Or someone else with a vested interest. We'll never know, will we? Walsh told me these shady characters have established networks spanning both countries and nationalities. Where there's money you'll find plenty willing to sacrifice their morality in exchange for a few quid."

"You think it stretches to the likes of Montgomerie?"

Caslin shrugged, "Kyle Broadfoot once suggested that when it came to the greater interest of the Crown any others may well become subordinate. Is the commander involved? Probably not but we all have our paymasters, don't we?"

"I don't doubt you. Do you think we've had two teams operating at the same time and working to keep the secrets? One international and another domestic?"

"That would be my guess," Caslin said with a sigh. "Independent of one another and answering to different masters but each with similar goals. Michaelson made waves, asked questions... made himself a threat."

"Farzaad Amin, Kadyrov, whichever – a domestic hit?"

"He made enemies in the one place he thought he was safe," Caslin concluded. "Is it beyond Russian intelligence to find a defector in the UK? Probably not – but when have the Russians ever cared enough about what we think to try and misdirect us?"

"The race angle, you mean?"

Caslin nodded, "Kadyrov was an inside job. I'm certain."

"How can you be so sure?"

"Too much theatre. They wanted to have us chasing the hard-right extremists. The Russians wouldn't bother their arse with all that."

"Their approach is subtler. They go for the extravagant only when they want to make a statement," Hunter said. Caslin agreed.

"You know, Raisa told me at length how her father described the Russian art of deception. She called it *Maskirovka*."

"Right."

"I think we have a few of our own quite skilled in that department. Far better skilled than you and me anyway," he said quietly. "No offence," he added, glancing over to her.

"None taken," Hunter said. Caslin fell silent, slipping back into himself. They sat in silence, staring across the Thames for a few minutes.

"Can I tell you something my father once told me?" Hunter asked.

"Sure. Go ahead."

"It's one of the fondest memories I have from my childhood. It might even be how I ended up joining the police force," Hunter said, remembering the day many years previously. "He told me about a famous quote, I can't remember it exactly, so forgive me for paraphrasing. He said that all it takes for evil to flourish is for a good man to do nothing. Have you heard that before?"

"Yes," Caslin said, smiling. "I think it was Edmund Burke who said it... or something very similar. What's your point?" he asked, looking at her. She met his eye and placed a reassuring hand on his forearm.

"Don't do nothing, Nathaniel. Please," she replied, glancing at the wallet in his hand. They locked eyes and Hunter held his gaze for a moment longer. She shuddered against the cold. The sun was deceptive and sitting still only made the cold penetrate that much deeper. She stood up. "I'm going to make my way over to Kings Cross. I'll get us the tickets and you can meet me there. I'll be grabbing a coffee and something to eat nearby. Okay?"

Caslin nodded, "Okay."

"Call me when you're ready," Hunter said, walking away.

Caslin was left alone. He watched as two small vessels passed by on the river, considering what Hunter had said. He glanced in the direction she had walked but she'd already disappeared from view. Opening his wallet, he eyed both his warrant card and the adjacent constabulary crest. Closing it, he stood up and crossed the pavement to the wall, turning his gaze to the water. Sunlight glinted off of the surface leaving a silver sheen flickering in the ebb and flow. Taking a deep breath, he reached into his pocket and withdrew his mobile. Scrolling down through the contacts, he found what he was looking for and dialled the number. The call was quickly answered.

"Nathaniel, this is unexpected. What can I do for you?"

"The vacancy we discussed. Is it still open?"

Kyle Broadfoot drew breath, "It can be. Do you want it?"

"One condition."

"And that is?"

"I get to choose my own team."

"That… might not be possible."

"I'm afraid it's non-negotiable," Caslin said firmly. There followed a period of silence as Broadfoot mulled it over.

"I'm sure we can work something out," he replied finally.

"Done," Caslin said and he hung up. Touching the top of the handset to his lips, he stared back across the water at a couple walking along the opposing riverbank. "I will do something," he told himself quietly.

A
DARK YORKSHIRE
CRIME THRILLER

FEAR
THE
PAST

J M Dalgliesh

CHAPTER ONE

THE OTHERS LOOKED like they were settling in for the night so he stood, turned and lifted his coat from the back of the chair. Slipping his right arm into the sleeve amid howls of protest alongside the laughter accompanying the anecdote being loudly recounted, he shook his head.

"It's getting late and you guys aren't going anywhere."

"It's not late," came the joint response from several around the table.

"I'm driving and I've had too much already," he countered.

"Aww… Jody, just get a cab. The evening's only just getting started."

"I've got a lot on tomorrow."

"That's the joy of being the boss. You get to make your own hours."

"And I still need to pay the bills," Jody replied, shaking his head and zipping up his jacket. Glancing through the window to the car park beyond, he tried to assess whether or not the rain had stopped. The darkness enveloped almost everything in view and what little he could see was masked by the condensation on the panes. "I'll see you guys in the morning," he said, heading off. Glancing back at the small group revelling in their impromptu gathering, he blew out his cheeks and muttered under his breath, "Those of you who make it in any way."

The pub was popular, even midweek, and he had to pick his way through the bar avoiding elbows, chairs and stools as he went before reaching the side door leading to the car park. The toilets were adjacent to the exit and he hesitated. Did he need to go? No. He'd be home in less than ten minutes and he could wait. The sooner he was out of here the better. Pushing open the door, it swung away from him. The wooden door had seen better days. A length of gaffer tape secured a large crack in the pane alongside chipped paint and multiple dents and scrapes - most likely down to the enthusiasm of the patrons coming and going over the years. The nights here were often rowdy. He had to admit to being involved upon occasion.

Stepping outside the stark contrast to the interior struck him and he shuddered against the cold. Descending the steps to the car park on unsteady feet, he walked towards where he'd parked the car. Calling a cab to get home would be sensible but he dismissed the thought. It wasn't far. Light rain was falling and he looked up at the nearby streetlight to better judge the intensity. It was much the same as when he'd arrived two hours earlier. Had he known the plan, if indeed it was the plan to have a session at the pub, he would've declined the offer. However, it was sold to him as a catch-up meeting. To be fair that wasn't unusual and often took place in a pub. More often than not it was also this establishment. It had been a while since he had been into the office and his absence was leading to friction, he could feel it even if nothing was being said. He couldn't afford to allow that to continue and feared it was already too late but, in any event, he'd made the effort.

Jody looked back over his shoulder towards the pub as he approached his car. He could make out the team - his business partner along with their small entourage of administrators - still inside, their movements showing the party was in full swing. Turning back, he eyed his BMW and crossed towards it fishing out the fob. He smiled to himself but it was tinged with elements of relief and regret. The relief came from the knowledge he'd managed the evening without having to be too vocal. Expecting a grilling for not pulling his weight in recent weeks, he found the absence of business talk to be refreshing. The regret was born out of keeping secrets. Necessary secrets. After all, that was the nature of the beast but somehow, on this occasion at least, it felt disloyal. *Who was he to talk about loyalty?* Loyalty, a virtue which was by all accounts diminishing in importance within the circle he moved in. Once it had been one of the primary requirements but apparently not anymore. The sense someone had his back was a distant memory and paranoia was now, his closest friend.

Perhaps it had always been this way and what he hankered for was a vision of a nostalgic past that never truly existed. His father always told him people lived in the memories of days gone by and, as a result, missed what was unfolding before their very eyes. Having never understood what that statement meant, it was easy to dismiss but now, many years too late, his father's words made perfect sense to him.

Shrugging off the melancholy that threatened to take root, he opened the door. Not wishing to get rainwater running onto the driver's seat, he took off his coat and threw it into the rear. A sound nearby made him look in the direction he thought it came from. There were two recycling points at the edge of the pub's boundary, large metal deposit bins for clothes by the look of them. Taking two steps forward, he waited for his eyes to adjust to the surroundings. Illuminated only by the streetlights, the surrounding trees and bushes were shrouded in darkness and their gentle sway in the breeze was barely visible. Jody stood still, the hairs on his neck raised as he stared into the gloom. What had he heard? The rain was forgotten and he ignored the fact his hair was now soaked through. Water began to run down his face and yet still, he peered into the shadows.

"Is anyone there?" he called, narrowing his gaze. No reply. A car passed by on the road, the familiar sound of displaced water breaking his train of thought. Realising he had been holding his breath, Jody retreated towards the car. Noting the rain driving in through the open door and onto the leather interior, he cursed himself. Irritated at allowing his imagination to run riot, he reached the car and took hold of the frame of the door. With one last look back towards the trees he shook his head, smiling and feeling foolish. "Get a grip, man," he said, under his breath.

Jody didn't hear the movement behind him nor did he see the reflection of the amber streetlights glinting off the hammer head as it came down on the back of his skull. He fell, unconscious before striking the ground. Several more blows followed with the only accompaniment being the sound of his assailant's exertions whilst wielding the weapon. There was no resistance.

Soon, all that could be heard was the sound of the intensifying rain coming down in sheets and striking the tarmac all around him.

CHAPTER TWO

The locals were gathering. The persistent rainfall that carried throughout the night was easing and the curiosity along the length of the police cordon was clear despite the hour. DI Caslin sipped at his coffee. It was still hot and he needed it. The sounds of normality came on the wind from the adjoining streets as the residents of York awoke and set about their day with the school run and daily commutes going on as normal. By now this street would usually be bustling with like-minded people heading out to work or arriving to open their businesses for the day but, for now at least, the immediate scene was more reminiscent of an apocalyptic war film than central York. A figure appeared and Caslin recognised the brigade's station officer stepping out from the building, roughly sixty yards away and looking in his direction. He beckoned them forward with a wave of the hand. The structural surveyor had given the all clear and the investigation could begin.

"That's us, sir," DS Hunter said. Caslin nodded, putting his coffee cup down onto the bonnet of the car alongside Hunter's and they set off. The building was a charred wreck, a ruin set in the middle of a terrace of shop fronts. The adjacent properties were undamaged by the ravages of the fire but unsure of their structural integrity, Caslin and his team were held back until the scene was assessed and deemed safe for them to enter.

"Let forensics know they have access, would you?" Caslin said. Hunter bobbed her head in acknowledgement.

"Any statement, Inspector?" someone called from a distance. Caslin looked over his shoulder and beyond the cordon, spying an approaching journalist. The cameraman walking alongside her was desperately trying to get the footage up and running, giving away her profession. Caslin wasn't surprised. In the current age such events were massive news with the media anticipating headline grabbing acts of terrorism until proven otherwise.

"I'm sure there will be something issued later on this morning but we have nothing to add from the earlier release," Caslin said, continuing his walk towards the building.

Approaching the entrance, the scale of the devastation became clearer. At least it used to be the entrance but now the entire frontage was blown out with rubble, timber and glass strewn across the road. The windows of the surrounding properties in every direction were smashed, their residents evacuated to a safe area at a local community hall. The local supermarket had initially been set up as a makeshift triage centre. The staff working the night shift stepped up to assist the emergency services until the required resources could be marshalled. Caslin eyed the scene, grateful the explosion happened when it did and not during the forthcoming rush hour when a far higher number of people would have been present or passing by. The carnage would have been significantly magnified had the explosion occurred even a short time later.

"DI Caslin?" a voice came to him from inside the building, drawing his attention. From within the blackened interior, Caslin saw the approaching figure of the brigade's fire investigator.

"This is Mark Francis. He's our senior investigator on the scene," Station Officer Wardell said, introducing them.

"Good morning," Francis said, offering his hand to Caslin. "Pleased to meet you."

"DI Caslin and DS Hunter. Is it okay for us to explore?" Caslin asked, taking the offered hand.

"Of course. Just watch your footing, would you? There's a lot of water and the building is precarious in places."

Caslin turned his collar up and indicated for Hunter to join him. The volume of water put down by the three appliances in dealing with the flames, stopping the spread of fire to the adjoining buildings, was such that it now ran from the interior walls and what was left of the ceilings. Many upper floor joists survived the initial force of the explosion only to collapse subsequently due to the intensity of the fire along with the water used to douse it.

"What are we looking at?" Caslin asked. The investigator glanced about them.

"The explosion centred just behind me," he said, gesturing towards the rear of the room they were standing in, roughly at the centre of the building. "Which rules out a gas leak."

"You're certain?" Hunter asked, taking notes.

"Absolutely. The supply comes into the building at the rear due to the proximity of the gas main running along the street parallel to this one," he confirmed. "This row of buildings is somewhat unusual in that respect. The seat of the fire is such that I'm quite happy to rule out a gas leak as the source."

"In that case, do you have any idea as to what was the source?" Hunter asked.

"Well, this is only an initial assessment but I'm happy to give you a rundown of where the evidence is taking me."

"Please do," Caslin said, looking the immediate area up and down. He considered it a miracle that anyone survived the blast let alone the accompanying fire.

"Basic fire science indicates there has to be fuel, oxygen and an ignition source to spark the fire that led to the explosion," Francis explained. "Ruling out the most common, that being the gas supply, I'm looking for electrical faults either in the building's wiring or appliances. The seat of the fire, here behind me, doesn't appear to be caused by any dodgy cabling. If anything, I'd say the place was rewired fairly recently. Within the last decade based on the condition of the consumer unit and the installation sticker. It is housed in the kitchen to the rear so was shielded from the blast by an interior load-bearing wall."

"Appliances?" Hunter asked.

"None present in the vicinity of the fire," Francis replied, with a brief shake of the head.

"That pushes us towards arson?" Caslin suggested.

"We still have a lot of work to do but that'll be my working hypothesis, yes," Francis concurred. "Two casualties were found over there," he said, pointing to the edge of the room they were currently standing in. "I believe they were pronounced dead at the scene," he said, looking to Wardell for confirmation.

"Yes, they were pulled from the building by the first responders and pronounced once clear."

"They were in the same room as the explosion?" Caslin asked. The station officer nodded.

"And the other victims?" Hunter asked, looking around.

"I believe they were in the outer reception, closest to the street," Wardell confirmed.

"And they'd be separated from the other two by what...?" Hunter asked, trying to visualise the interior before the force of the blast had ripped it apart.

"A false wall, basic timber studwork faced with plasterboard," Francis said. "Pretty common in a minicab booking office such as this, I'd imagine."

Caslin pictured the building as it had once been. An outer reception or waiting area for customers and drivers to hang around in with a hatch to the interior where the booking clerk would sit, taking calls and dispatching the cars.

"Any sign of an accelerant?" Caslin asked.

"Not that we can see. We will often find a concentration of flame in an area where petrol has been poured, such as when your average pyro empties a can of petrol through a letter box."

"Or when someone is trying to conceal the evidence of a crime by burning the building down," Caslin said, looking around.

"That's right. Those are the two main reasons leading to arson on this scale. We have none of the corresponding evidence here," Francis explained. "Your explosion is what set light to the building."

"What are we looking at?" Caslin asked, sensing this wasn't the result of a tragic accident as he had secretly hoped it would be. This was far more sinister.

"I don't think we're looking at anything particularly sophisticated," Francis stated. "It's an improvised device, fairly small, judging from the lack of structural damage but certainly packing enough of a punch to knock out the frontage as well as all the glass in the general vicinity and set the building ablaze."

"Are you confident this must have been placed here?" Hunter queried. Francis looked at her.

"Rather than anything in situ that may have gone off accidentally?"

Hunter nodded, "Exactly."

Francis thought on it for a moment, "I can't see any scenario where this could be accidental. Unless they wanted to place a firebomb somewhere else and it went off here by mistake. I'm afraid you will have to wait for a more detailed conclusion but I'll liaise with your forensics team once they get on site."

"Let's keep this to ourselves for the time being, if you don't mind?" Caslin said. "I don't want to create a panic. Otherwise people will jump to conclusions and assume it's an act of terrorism and we can do without unjustified reprisals." They all agreed. The initial statement offered to the press implied that a gas leak may have led to the explosion and Caslin saw no reason to change that yet. "Thanks, Mark. May we go further?" he asked.

"Certainly. But don't head upstairs. The floors above aren't likely to come down but they're far from safe to walk on. The cellar is intact and the fire spread upwards so the ground floor and basement are structurally sound although the cellar is flooded for obvious reasons."

Caslin thanked him and left him to get on with the remainder of the inspection. Turning to Hunter, he indicated they should look around. They both took out torches and progressed into the building proper, picking their way through the debris. The going was slow as they were careful not to contaminate any potential forensic evidence.

"Made a hell of a mess," Hunter said, sidestepping a pool of water and shielding her head from the water trickling down from above.

"What did he say the casualty count was?"

"Two dead and three injured. Two of the latter are critical requiring emergency surgery and the other is stable but unconscious. Add that to the residents evacuated during the night and the numbers increase."

"Injuries?"

"A few cuts from flying glass. Shock and a reaction to the cold mainly. The fear of a secondary explosion or building collapse meant they were unceremoniously dragged out, many in their bedclothes and a number of them are elderly."

"Staff or clients inside the cab office?" Caslin asked.

Hunter shook her head. "No IDs yet. Terry Holt is at the hospital trying to get the names and we're working on the assumption that at least two were manning the office and the remainder could be a mix of customers and drivers. There was one car immediately parked outside and that is registered to the business but we don't know who was driving it last night."

"Could have been much worse," Caslin said quietly, angling the beam of his torch towards the floors above. "And this is definitely one of Fuller's, yes?"

Hunter nodded, "I double checked."

Caslin took in a sharp breath, "Pete's going to be pissed off."

"Who would be stupid enough?" Hunter countered. Caslin inclined his head. She had a point. Pete Fuller was a name to be fearful of, not only in York but across all four counties making up the greater Yorkshire area.

"He's been gone some time though."

"Who's running the organisation now? Is it still the boys?" Hunter queried.

"Last I heard. Ashton was taking the lead with Carl backing him up and running the muscle."

"Looks like he doesn't have the iron grip that his father did."

"I'm not aware of anyone chancing their arm but maybe someone's taken a view that now's the time," Caslin floated the theory. He hoped that wasn't the case. The three largest crime syndicates operating in the city stuck to their own patches. There was the occasional skirmish as the lower levels tried to make names for themselves at the expense of their rivals but, on the whole, they kept their distance. That approach was good for business and all of them were very much focussed on money above all else.

"Or the Fuller boys are spreading their wings," Hunter added.

"Stepping out from Pete's shadow?" Caslin clarified.

"And someone wants to put them back in their box."

"We need to speak to them and gauge what their response will be. Nip it in the bud before things get out of hand. Also get onto the National Crime Agency and see if there is any intelligence we're unaware of regarding Fuller and his crew. It wouldn't be the first time they'd neglected to keep us in the loop."

Further conversation was interrupted by the ringing of Caslin's mobile. Glancing at the screen, he saw it was DC Terry Holt.

"Terry," Caslin greeted him.

"Sir, I'm at the hospital," Holt began, his tone conveyed he wouldn't be delivering good news. "Another one has died in theatre. Her injuries were too severe."

"That's three. What of the others?" Caslin asked.

"One stable but is currently in a medically induced coma and the other is still in surgery. I've nothing further on the latter."

"Any idea who they were?"

"I've identified one, a Matt Jarvis. Looks like he was trying to get a cab home."

"If he was in the front office, he'd have been furthest from the explosion so that'd make sense," Caslin explained.

"Got off lightly… so to speak," Holt said before correcting himself.

"I know what you mean. Keep me posted," Caslin said before hanging up. He looked to Hunter, "We had better go and see Ashton."

"I doubt we'll get a warm welcome."

Caslin smiled, "Ashton is level-headed… at least, as level-headed as you can get when you're a narcissistic sociopath."

"And he's widely considered to be the sensible one," Hunter added with a wry grin.

They stepped out of the building. Looking back, Caslin scanned the mix of damp, charred timber and brickwork still smouldering in the early morning light. The thought came to him that if they didn't solve this case quickly, they might see an escalation in similar acts being committed. The death toll would only increase and the chances of more innocents being caught in the crossfire amplified.

Heading in the direction of the cordon, in place at both ends of the street, Caslin noted their approach was being watched by the journalist who had spoken with him earlier. With a flick of his head, he ensured Hunter had registered her presence to ensure she also remained tight-lipped. Caslin was adamant they needed to keep a lid on this situation for as long as possible. They were prepared for the questions this time and Caslin took a deep breath as they reached her location. A uniformed constable, there to maintain the barrier between the public and crime scene, lifted the tape allowing them to pass under.

"Inspector, any news on the number of casualties?" she harangued him as soon as he was beyond the safety of the cordon.

"A statement will be released later. I'm afraid I have no news for you," he said politely but firmly, leaving no doubt as to his desire to not enter into conversation.

"Any word from Peter Fuller?" the journalist asked. Caslin stopped. This wasn't the office junior sent out to cover a story in the early hours. She clearly knew the lay of the land and had done some homework. He very much wished he hadn't. Stopping, he indicated for Hunter to get the car and turned towards the journalist. The camera was filming across her shoulder and directly at him, including the backdrop of the destroyed building. Caslin shuffled sideways knowing the dramatic scene would now be out of shot.

"We are yet to speak with the owners of the premises in question," he began. "Our thoughts are very much with the injured as well as those who have been temporarily evacuated from their homes and businesses."

"And the cause of the explosion, has it been determined?" she asked, cutting over his last words. Her candour struck Caslin. Many times, in previous situations, he'd have been able to keep talking without really saying anything of real note - the interviewer being happy to get anything out of him. This felt different. "Why are Major Crimes investigating a gas leak?"

"A statement will be forthcoming. Please excuse me," he said and strode away as fast as he could without appearing to be fleeing. Hunter brought the car alongside and he clambered in as more persistent questioning came in his direction. He ignored it, closing the door and Hunter accelerated away. Caslin let out a sigh of relief. He was never one who sought the limelight always preferring to defer press conferences to those who either revelled in them or were more suited to the experience.

Lowering the visor, he used the vanity mirror to observe the duo watching them drive away. He was impressed. This journalist knew her background. He very much wished she hadn't and figured it would be best to steer a path well clear of her in the future.

CHAPTER THREE

HUNTER EYED a break in the traffic and took the turn into the yard. Three men of Asian appearance were busy rubbing down a Mercedes that positively shone even on a grey morning such as this. One of them glanced over at the new arrivals and indicated for them to drive forward into the bay. Hunter shook her head and instead, reversed the car into an old parking space delineated by fading white paint put down long ago. Shrugging his shoulders, the man returned his focus to helping his colleagues finish off the car they were working on. On such a wet morning, the men operating the hand car wash would be unlikely to do a roaring trade but that mattered little in the vast scheme of things.

They were parked on an old petrol station forecourt. No longer used, all that remained to indicate the nature of the previous business was the overhead canopy. The attendant's office as well as the pumps themselves were long gone. These little enterprises were popping up all over the city, all over the country. Cheap to operate and occupying sites considered unfit for any other practical purpose, they were cash-based businesses that in themselves were becoming rarer with the advancement of the digital age. Beyond the forecourt to the rear scaffolding rose four stories and no doubt would end up even higher once the building work neared completion. A developer's sign advertised that the properties, luxury apartments close to the city centre, were available for purchase off plan.

"They are branching out, aren't they?" Hunter said, inclining her head towards the building work. Caslin pursed his lips before answering.

"Whilst not missing out on the opportunity to keep their core trade ticking over," he replied, staring at the three men as they waved off a grateful owner, leaving the forecourt in his gleaming vehicle.

Abandoned petrol stations couldn't be developed for many years due to the underground storage tanks potentially contaminating the site and the subsequent risk of explosion. Many of these sites lay to waste as speculative purchasers waited until such time as they were able to exploit the real estate. This was one such a place. The Fullers had several of these car washing facilities scattered around, wedded to other parts of their organisation consisting of fast-food outlets, minicab firms, low-end used car dealerships and dry cleaners. All businesses that handled a high turnover of cash thus making it easy to launder the wealth generated through their drug dealing, protection rackets and other illegal enterprises. Evidently, they were now channelling their funds through legitimate construction projects such as the apartment block currently springing from the wasteland of rotting premises. Built with the proceeds of crime, these apartments would undoubtedly enable them to launder even more money by way of inflated construction costs that were only ever payable on a spreadsheet.

They got out of the car. The wash attendants paid them little attention. Two were now seating themselves on camping chairs and nursing cups of coffee to warm their sodden hands in the absence of a waiting client. A third retreated into a small portacabin, reappearing moments later with a steaming mug in one hand and a mobile phone in the other. He talked into the latter, his eyes never leaving the two newcomers as they crossed the compound in search of the site office in the construction zone.

The area was cordoned off with Herras fencing and they walked along the boundary until they reached the gate. It was open, work on the site being well underway and they passed through. None of the workmen acknowledged their presence amid the sounds of a banksman directing a lorry load of supplies across the site and shouts from a foreman above to his team of bricklayers. They skirted the activity keeping to the sides and picking their way across the churned earth beneath their feet. The recent rainfall, cold weather and the heavy plant combined to turn the site into a quagmire. Scaffold boards were laid in places to make traversing the site by foot easier but even so, the going was tricky.

Noting several temporary buildings, they ended up asking where they could find the office and were directed to one on the eastern edge of the site. By the time they'd located the building word had spread of their arrival. Standing outside but leaning against the door jamb, on a ramp leading up to the door, was a young man in his thirties. He was tall, sporting close-cropped dark hair and warily watched them approach with an impassive expression.

"Good morning, Carl."

"Mr Caslin," Carl Fuller replied. "What brings you here?"

"Your brother around, is he?" Caslin countered. "The two of you are never far apart." Carl indicated inside with a brief flick of the head.

"DS Hunter," Hunter introduced herself, holding up her warrant card before Carl.

"Whatever," he said, locking eyes with her and ignoring the identification. He didn't seem inclined to break his gaze so Hunter did so, following Caslin inside.

The interior was much like any other construction site office. Wipe boards were hanging on the wall with progress charts laid out in schedules of red, blue and a black marker. Plans were laid out on one desk with a line of filing cabinets adjacent as well as opposite. Three men stood huddled around another desk at the far end, deep in discussion, with papers strewn out before them. One, in the middle with his back to them, Caslin recognised as Ashton Fuller. His giant waves of blonde hair, in stark contrast to his brother, saw him stand out without the need to see his face. Of the other two, one was heavy set and much older. Judging by his attire, Caslin figured him to be a contractor whilst the other was far younger and taking a back seat in the discussion.

Caslin cleared his throat and Ashton glanced up in their direction, unsurprised by their presence. Returning to his conversation, he looked between the two men to either side of him seeking their agreement.

"I'll take care of it," the larger man said.

"Good," Ashton confirmed. "Come back to me later, yeah?" The man nodded and turned to leave, paying the new arrivals no attention whatsoever. The younger man also left. He flicked his eyes towards Caslin as he passed in what the latter figured was a nervous action. He seemed familiar but Caslin couldn't place him. Being a part of the Fuller's crew would mean they'd probably crossed paths at some point over the years. "Detective Inspector Caslin," Ashton said warmly in a welcoming tone. "What brings you here?"

"One of your businesses going up in flames," Caslin said flatly. He noted Carl entering behind them. Glancing back over his shoulder, he saw Carl lean against the wall folding his arms across his chest in front of him. "What can you tell me about it?"

Ashton momentarily followed Caslin's glance towards his brother before addressing the question. "It is unfortunate."

"Particularly for your employees who were inside," Hunter added.

"Very," Ashton said, expressionless.

"Can you tell us who was present?" Caslin asked. Ashton nodded. Crossing the office, he retrieved a scrap of paper. Returning, he handed it to Caslin who eyed the list of names. There were four, one woman and three men.

"Sally was working the comms last night. Tom was with her and the other two were drivers," Ashton said. "Any word on how they are?"

"I thought you might be at the hospital," Caslin said. He was being disingenuous and he knew it.

"I have a business to run. Besides, I figured someone like you would be dropping by this morning," Ashton stated, pushing aside the plans atop the nearest desk and perching himself on the edge.

"Sally is dead," Caslin said. "As are two of the others but one is in surgery. They are hopeful."

"Good to know," Carl said from behind him.

"A member of the public is also in a serious but stable condition," Caslin added.

"I'm sorry to hear that," Ashton said. Caslin didn't believe him.

"You haven't asked about the cause," Caslin said, moving further into the office and turning so both brothers were in his sightline. Ashton shrugged.

"Enlighten me," he said, folding his arms.

"Gas leak," Caslin said, watching closely for a reaction. The thought occurred, Ashton must be one hell of a card player because he was unreadable.

"Should be illegal," Carl said, sniffing loudly. "Poor workmanship."

"True," Caslin said, flicking his eyes towards Carl and back to his elder brother. "How's business?"

Ashton smiled, "Booming, Mr Caslin. We're on the up."

"Any of your competition making inroads?" Hunter asked.

"What's that supposed to mean?" Carl asked. Hunter turned to him.

"In a world of finite resources when you want to grow it always comes at the expense of another, doesn't it?" she asked. "Basic market economics."

"You're a lot smarter than you look," Carl sneered. He was about to respond further but Ashton shot him a dark look ensuring he kept quiet.

"We are competitive," Ashton answered.

"How about Clinton Dade?" Caslin asked, referencing the Fullers' historical adversary. Carl scoffed, unable to contain his reaction.

"That old mincer!" he said before Ashton could speak. "He wouldn't dare."

"Dare to do what?" Caslin asked. Carl looked to his brother who, for the first time, appeared to drop the mask he so carefully maintained.

"Nothing," Carl muttered, turning his attention to the floor. Ashton took a deep breath and looked at Caslin.

"We've not come across Clinton in quite some time. There's no issue between us," Ashton argued. "Besides, I have a lot of time for the elderly. You have to look out for people, don't you?"

Caslin let the silence hang for a few moments as he assessed the brothers. They also appeared comfortable enough to allow it to continue. Caslin's gaze fell on the eldest who returned it. After a few seconds, Ashton raised his eyebrows initiating a questioning look. Caslin rolled his tongue against his cheek in the inside of his mouth. Reaching into his pocket, he withdrew one of his contact cards.

"If anything comes to you that you think I should know, do give me a call," he said, stepping forward and offering the card. Ashton glanced at it but he didn't make a move to accept it. Caslin reached past and placed it onto the desk alongside him, bringing him into close proximity with the younger man. Before stepping back, Caslin held his position and leaned in close enough that only the two of them could hear his words. "Don't do anything hasty, Ashton. And see to it no one else does either, for all our sakes," he almost whispered, casting a lingering look towards Carl who stared at him with a face like thunder. Stepping away, he added in a voice for all to hear, "We'll be in touch."

"Thanks for stopping by," Ashton replied, unmoved and glancing at his brother. Carl didn't speak as both detectives made to leave the office. They reached the threshold of the door and Ashton called after them, "Feel free to have your car washed before you go. It's on me." Caslin glanced back at him but didn't respond.

Walking down the ramp, the roar of heavy machinery and their accompanying warning alarms came to ear as the two of them set off across the site in the direction of their car. Hunter looked back to see Carl at the doorway, hands thrust into pockets and watching their departure.

"They're not giving much away," she said, raising her voice to ensure she was heard above the noise.

"You didn't expect them to, did you?" Caslin countered. Hunter agreed. "I had hoped appealing to Ashton's common sense would give us time to get it sorted."

"Do you think we managed it?"

Caslin shook his head, "To be honest, I don't know. He was expecting us and I'll bet he's already formulating a response. I know he gives over the impression of composure but he can be almost as impulsive as his little brother, albeit he's marginally more calculating."

"You think he knows where this has come from?"

"He suspects," Caslin thought aloud, "and I reckon he has in mind what they plan to do about it."

"Your instinct is Dade, right?" Hunter asked.

Caslin nodded, "Stands to reason. Despite what he says, there's no love lost between the two families and they don't go too long without stepping on each other's toes."

"Bombing one of their businesses is an escalation. A bit more than *stepping on their toes*," Hunter argued as they reached the car. She unlocked it and they got in. Caslin shut his door, instantly diminishing the ambient noise around them. He looked back towards the building site.

"They have a lot to lose if they're going to get involved in a turf war," he said.

"As would Dade," Hunter countered. "Is there anyone else? Danika Durakovic perhaps?"

"No, I don't see what she would have to gain. There isn't a great deal of overlap. The Fullers think they're big time. The family reputation is fearsome but let's be honest, the crew aren't what they once were. They haven't managed to eclipse their old man. Far from it."

"Not yet, no," Hunter stated. "But what about the possibility you floated earlier? That maybe the brothers are the aggressors here and the bombing *is* the retaliation."

"If that's the case, we had better figure it out before someone ups the ante. Otherwise this is going to get messy very quickly."

Hunter turned the key in the ignition firing the engine into life. Moving off, they negotiated the small queue waiting their turn to be valeted. Circumventing the cars, Hunter drove around the rear of the old petrol station and came to the main road. The skies were brightening as the clouds cleared bringing forth the promise of a better day ahead. Caslin's phone rang and he took it out, noting the call was from Terry Holt.

"What is it, Terry?"

"He didn't survive theatre, sir," Holt confirmed. "That's four out of the five who didn't make it."

"Okay," Caslin said, deflated. Glancing at Hunter he offered a brief shake of the head. She knew what that meant. "Head back to Fulford Road and we'll see you there. When you get back, I want…" his phone beeped to indicate there was another call incoming. Caslin checked the screen, it was Kyle Broadfoot, Assistant Chief Constable and his boss. He figured he had best take the call. "I'll get back to you, Terry," he said, hanging up and switching to the other line.

"Nathaniel," Broadfoot said by way of greeting.

"Sir," Caslin replied. "We're on our way back to Fulford Road,"

"Good, you're already out in the field. I need you to swing by somewhere and meet me," Broadfoot said. "I've got something for you to cast your eye over."

"Sir?" Caslin failed to hide his irritation. "The explosion earlier today looks very much like a targeted campaign against Pete Fuller's group."

"And you will be able to fill me in when you get here, Nathaniel."

"Where exactly are you, sir?" Caslin asked, caught off guard. For Broadfoot to be present at a crime scene so close to home before Caslin was even aware of its existence was surprising to say the least.

"East of York. Head towards Pocklington, via Kexby and you won't be able to miss us," Broadfoot said. "I'll expect you along directly." He hung up before Caslin had a chance to reply. Touching the handset to his lips, he was momentarily lost in thought before he caught sight of Hunter in the corner of his eye repeatedly glancing across at him, itching to know what was said.

"Change of plan," Caslin said, looking over towards her. "Head for Kexby."

"Why?" Hunter asked.

"Damned if I know," Caslin replied. "But ours is not to reason why…"

CHAPTER FOUR

THE ROUTE to Kexby was a much-travelled road cutting through farmland and linking various small communities between York and Market Weighton. Aside from the sparsely populated villages there was very little reason to be in the area unless working the land or attached to the small industrial estates peppering the otherwise rural landscape. Passing one such a place, Caslin eyed the liveried police car coming up on their right-hand side. Slowing down, they approached a turning into a gated area used by agricultural machinery to access the fields. Pulling up, they came to a stop alongside the police car. Looking past it, barely a stone's throw away, they could see it was one of three not including the CSI van parked nearby.

A uniformed constable stepped forward and checked their identification before allowing them access. Clearing the highway, Hunter parked beside what she recognised as Kyle Broadfoot's chauffeur-driven car. Caslin got out and looked around. Nestled into the Vale of York, the landscape was flat with trees lining the boundaries shielding the immediate area from passing traffic on the road. The access track ran off in a straight line from the road whereas adjacent to it was a patch of flooded marshland. Reeds grew in abundance nearby and beyond those he could see open water, perhaps stretching for a hundred yards. From the look of its configuration, he figured this was a man-made basin created to drain the fields of excess water.

A group were gathered near to the water's edge and Caslin could make out the lanky figure of his superior amongst the collection of high-vis jackets and white-clad forensic technicians. Both Caslin and Hunter approached as Assistant Chief Constable Kyle Broadfoot spotted their arrival, acknowledging them with a wave and beckoning them over.

"Nathaniel. Sarah. Pleased you could join us," he said in greeting, his words accompanied by a cloud of vapour. Despite the presence of the sunshine, the clearing skies belied the freezing temperature hovering barely above zero. Exposed as they were out here in the countryside, the wind chill made it feel several degrees below.

"Good morning, sir," they said in unison. He bid them to accompany him to the water's edge. The forensic team stepped aside to give them space. What they saw was no longer shocking to either of the newcomers. A body lay half into the water, much of the upper torso was submerged. It was clearly a male. Caslin figured him to be in his early thirties. However, the angle in which the body lay, face down in the water, it wasn't particularly easy to judge. There was a significant amount of damage to the rear of the skull with the hair thickly matted with blood. Caslin figured pathology wouldn't need to work too hard to determine the cause of death. The water here didn't flow and therefore it was reasonable to presume the body lay in more or less the same position in which it had entered the water.

Caslin knelt in order to get a better view. The man was dressed in jeans and a checked shirt. It was a casual shirt not an all-weather outdoor item and offered scant protection against the recent weather. Coupled with the jeans and the leather town-shoes they could rule out the man being a hiker or rambler. Looking around this seemed an odd place for a man dressed in this way to be.

"Any ID?" he asked. Broadfoot politely snapped his fingers indicating for something to be passed to him. An evidence bag was swiftly handed over and Broadfoot gave it to Caslin. Standing up, Caslin donned a pair of latex gloves and opened the bag. Withdrawing a wallet from inside, he noted it was wet, presumably having been retrieved from one of the victim's pockets. Flicking through the contents, he came across the driving licence. Even with the face being half under water, Caslin could see it was the same man. "Jody Wyer," he said aloud for Hunter's benefit as much for his own. Continuing to inspect the contents, he noted there was at least fifty pounds present, credit cards and a number of business cards. Caslin teased one out. It was damp and therefore delicate so he took great care not to damage it. The card had the business name, *Blue Line Investigations.* A registered office address in central York, along with both a land line and mobile phone number. He passed the card to Hunter. She scanned it.

"What do they investigate, does it say?" she asked.

"A private investigation agency," Broadfoot confirmed. Caslin flicked his eyes in his superior's direction and then across at Hunter.

"Any sign of the mobile?" Caslin asked. Broadfoot shook his head. "How about a car? Do we know how he got here?" he asked, looking around. Iain Robertson appeared, clad in his white suit. Caslin hadn't realised the head of forensic investigators was present when he arrived. He was caught off guard figuring Robertson would be on his way to the scene of the bombing to liaise with Mark Francis, the Fire Brigade's lead investigator.

"We have fresh tracks set down overnight just over there," Robertson indicated to where members of his team were setting up. "My guess it's an SUV of some type judging by the width of tread and the wheel base. The drop in temperature has set them quite nicely for me."

"I think we can rule out robbery as a motive based on what they left us," Caslin argued. No one disagreed. "How long would you say he's been in the water?"

Robertson looked at the body, screwing his nose up in concentration. "Bearing in mind the recent weather we've been experiencing I'd suggest a couple of days. No more than that," he said, rocking his head side to side as he offered his thoughts. "Once we get him out of the water, I'll take his temperature and then I'll be able to narrow that down a little for you. Are you happy for us to proceed?" he asked, looking to Broadfoot who nodded.

Robertson called over his technicians and the others stood aside, retreating up the shallow incline to allow them to get on with their work.

"I know you have your hands full with this bombing in the city centre, Nathaniel," Broadfoot said. "But I would like you to focus with an equal measure on this case. I've cleared it with DCI Matheson that we take the reins on the inquiry. Such is the way of things at Fulford Road at the moment I think she was only too happy for us to take it off her hands."

Caslin noted Broadfoot was staring back towards the forensics team as they retrieved the body from the water with an expression on his face that Caslin found unreadable. Usually, he found Kyle Broadfoot to be very matter-of-fact, displaying an innate pragmatism that saw his stewardship of the North Yorkshire Crime Directorate run very smoothly as well as successfully.

"Can I ask what our interest is in this case, sir?" Caslin asked. After all, as homicides went this was a fairly straightforward investigation. "I mean, why should it interest Major Crimes?" Broadfoot took a deep breath, his gaze passing over DS Hunter and falling onto Caslin.

"Jody Wyer was known to us," he said flatly.

"In what capacity?" Caslin asked, sensing reticence.

"On occasion, he would offer up information if it were mutually beneficial."

"He was an informant?"

"Not officially, no," Broadfoot clarified.

"I've never come across him," Caslin said, glancing towards Hunter who indicated the same with an almost imperceptible dip at the corners of her mouth that was missed by Broadfoot, as intended.

"Before your time here, Nathaniel."

Caslin raised his eyebrows and nodded, "Any idea what he was investigating?"

"No, I'm afraid not," Broadfoot stated. "Although, the last communication we had with him he implied he was working on something pretty big."

"When was this?" Hunter asked.

"Last month."

"Did he offer up any more detail than that?" Caslin asked. Broadfoot shook his head. Wyer's body had been photographed and was now being placed into a body bag in preparation for transportation to the morgue where an autopsy would take place. At this point, Broadfoot finally tore his gaze away from the scene.

"No, I'm afraid he didn't," he said, turning and indicating to his driver that he was ready to leave. The officer strode towards the car.

"Was he reported missing?"

"Not that I'm aware, no."

"Who found the body?" Caslin asked.

"A dog walker. That's him over there," Broadfoot said. Caslin turned to see a man talking to another officer a little way off. A Springer Spaniel sat at his feet as he offered his statement.

"Who do we contact as next of kin, sir?" Hunter asked. Broadfoot looked at her. "We'll need an official identification."

"That won't be necessary in this case, Detective," Broadfoot advised her, turning to Caslin. "Keep me posted, would you?"

"I will, sir," Caslin said. Broadfoot smiled weakly, acknowledging Hunter and set off. His hands were thrust into the pockets of his overcoat and his head bowed as he picked his way across the mud in the direction of his car. The engine was already running and his driver opened the rear door for him, swiftly closing it once Broadfoot was inside. Caslin watched the car leave, the uniformed constable opening the gate to allow them to pass.

"What do you make of that?" Hunter asked. "I've never seen him so pained."

Caslin shrugged, "Me neither. It makes it even more intriguing to find out what Mr Wyer was getting stuck into."

"You think it will be related to his work?" Hunter asked.

"Let's not rule anything in or out," Caslin said. "Maybe he criticised his better half's choice of outfit and we'll have it closed off by dinner time." Hunter laughed. It was a bitter sound.

"I guess there's a first time for everything," she said. "How do you want to play it?"

"We'll not get anything from the bomb site until later today at the earliest. Let's drop in on Wyer's office and see if we can gauge their reaction to all of this."

Caslin felt his phone vibrating in his pocket. Inclining his head in the direction of the car, Hunter nodded and set off. Taking out the phone, Caslin saw it was Karen, his ex-wife.

"Karen," he said, turning back towards Robertson and the CSI team carrying out their inspection of the deceased.

"Hi Nate," she said, coming across far more upbeat than usual. "I wanted to speak with you about the weekend."

"The weekend?" he asked, immediately concerned there was something he'd forgotten about.

"Yes. You remember, we're away in Copenhagen and we talked about you having the kids?" she said. Caslin's heart sank. He had forgotten about his ex-wife and her fiancée going away for a long weekend. Seeing two crime scene officers hoist the black body bag onto a gurney and wheel it away, struggling in their efforts to negotiate the terrain, towards the waiting transport van, he considered his position.

"Yeah, about that..."

"Nate," Karen said, her tone shifting slightly. "Don't you dare cancel on me. We've had this planned for months."

"I know," Caslin countered. "You heard about that explosion in the city this morning?"

"No, I haven't seen the news," she said. "Why? What's going on?"

"I can't say but… it's a difficult time," he began but got no further.

"Nathaniel," she said sternly, "I am going away on Friday night and you need to be with your children."

"Perhaps Sean could…"

"No, Sean is not taking responsibility for his sister! He can barely look after himself. You know that. I know your job is important to you," she said.

"It's not that it's important to me," Caslin argued. "I can't just drop everything."

"I'm not asking you to drop everything. These are your children, Nathaniel."

"I'm well aware…"

"You're having the children this weekend," Karen said, talking over him. She was emphatic.

"I… I'm sorry. I can't," Caslin replied. The line went dead. He exhaled heavily, casting his eyes skyward. The last thing he wanted to do was let his family down. In the past few months he was pleased with the progress they had made. Lizzie was developing further into the confident little girl he'd always imagined she would be and Sean was on the right track. Granted, it was a tougher climb from the darkness of his world twelve months previously but things were looking positive. The nagging irritation that Karen still appeared so quick to judge him as being willing to shirk his responsibilities flashed through his mind.

Realising there was little he could do, he pushed the negativity aside. There would be a solution and he had a couple of days to think of one. If not… well, he would cross that bridge when he reached it. Turning, he covered the short distance between himself and the car. Hunter already had the engine started. Getting in, he was grateful the heaters were on.

"Everything okay?" Hunter inquired, reading the concerned expression on his face.

"Nothing a spare me wouldn't cure," he replied. She looked at him quizzically. "So that I could be in two places at once," he explained.

"I could use one of those as well," she agreed. "Do we ever get the balance right?"

Caslin's face split a wry grin as he shook his head slightly, "Tipping the scales the opposite way every now and again would make a nice change though, wouldn't it?"

"Life could be worse," she said softly, watching Jody Wyer being loaded into the unmarked mortuary van. "Shall we go?" He nodded and Hunter pulled away. The constable manning the gate opened it and Caslin acknowledged his efforts with a brief flick of the hand as they passed through.

CHAPTER FIVE

IT WAS mid-morning by the time they arrived at Blue Line's offices. Located on the upper two floors of an imposing old Victorian terraced house, previously residential but now converted for commercial use. The ground floor was assigned to a small architect's firm and the access to the private detective's office was by way of a metal fire escape running up the side of the building. Parking was limited to the width of the building's frontage. Caslin noted the plaque on the wall, sited in the only empty bay denoting where Jody Wyer's car would be parked.

A Jaguar was in the adjacent bay, less than two years old and was designated as belonging to another employee of the company, a T. Mason. Caslin thought the name sounded familiar to him but he couldn't place it. They made their way up the stairs, their feet clattering on the metal beneath them as they went. The recent rain followed by the subsequent drop in temperature made the route up precarious as the water had frozen, but they reached the top without event. Caslin opened the outer door and ushered Hunter into the lobby. The interior had a makeshift appearance to it. The walls were painted white. The carpets were a block-blue colour and thin but hard wearing. Everything around them was functional but could have been any bland office offering any service. Nothing denoted they were in premises specialising in private investigations.

A woman appeared from a small room holding a steaming cup of tea before her and was so startled by their presence she almost jumped at the sight of them. Caslin smiled.

"I'm sorry," he said, glancing back towards the entrance and indicating it with his hand. "The door was open."

She gathered herself swiftly, also apologising. "No, please, it's not a problem. I just didn't hear the door. It was probably the kettle," she said. "How can I help?"

Caslin assessed her. She was in her late twenties, attired in business dress and fastidiously applied make up and hair. There didn't appear to be a reception of any kind, so Caslin was unsure of whether he was speaking to an employee or an investigator. He took out his warrant card and stepped forward enabling her to see it.

"I'm Detective Inspector Caslin. This is DS Hunter," he said. "And you are?"

"Donna Lafferty," she replied. "I'm Mr Wyer's personal assistant."

"Can I ask when you last saw Mr Wyer?"

"A couple of days ago," Donna said. "He's not been in much this past week or so."

"Is that unusual?" Hunter asked.

"Not really. He's been very busy recently. He's often out of the office for days on end."

"And what about speaking to him... when was that?" Caslin asked.

"The last time?" she clarified. Caslin nodded. "The same time. Two nights ago. Why? What's going on?" She said the last with a tinge of anxiety creeping into her tone as the realisation dawned on her they were there on a business call. "What's he gotten himself into now?"

"Can you tell us what Mr Wyer was working on?" Caslin asked, but Donna's reply was interrupted by the arrival of another.

"I thought I heard voices," a barrel-chested man said, stepping out from a room at the end of the narrow corridor into the interior. Caslin took his measure, late-fifties, overweight with dark brown hair swept up in a quiff that was almost certainly coloured from an over-the-counter bottle. He approached with an affable manner, a booming voice that echoed in the confined space. "How can we help?" he said, grinning. His face had reddish tones to his cheeks and he was already breathing heavily as he offered Caslin his hand in greeting.

"They're from the police, Mr Mason," Donna said.

"Detectives Hunter and Caslin," Caslin said, taking the offered hand.

"Pleasure," he replied, shaking Caslin's hand warmly. "Tony Mason. What can we do for you?"

"I'm afraid we have some bad news for you regarding Mr Wyer," Caslin said. "We haven't confirmed it officially but a member of the public found Mr Wyer early this morning."

"*Found him*?" Mason replied, a look of surprise crossing his face.

"I'm afraid, we believe Mr Wyer is dead," Caslin stated. Donna gave off an audible gasp whereas Mason appeared similarly shocked.

"I… I… don't understand… He's dead? How?"

"That's yet to be determined," Hunter offered. "Is there somewhere that we can talk? We need to gather a bit of background to help us figure this out."

"Yes… yes, of course," Mason said. "I know how it works. Please, come with me to my office."

Mason placed a reassuring hand onto Donna's shoulder before turning and leading them back along the corridor to the room he'd originally appeared from. Caslin followed with Hunter a step behind. As they made their way, the floorboards creaked and groaned under their weight and the corridor itself felt like it slanted at an angle towards the rear of the building. A sign of the building's age. As they walked, Caslin remembered why he recognised Mason's name. He was a former CID officer based out of Acomb Road Station covering the west of York. Caslin was reasonably confident Mason left the force prior to his arrival at Fulford Road, but he was certain it was him.

They entered the office and were met by another woman seated at one of the two desks present in the room. She was older than Donna, perhaps in her fifties, and a similar age to Mason.

"This is Beth, my P.A.," Mason said, the joviality in his tone no longer evident. Beth rose from her desk and greeted them with an awkward smile glancing across at her boss, aware of how his mood had changed. They introduced themselves to her. "It's Jody," Mason explained, looking to her and offering them both a seat. "He's dead."

"My God," she exclaimed, open-mouthed. "How?"

"We're working on that," Caslin said, noting Donna entering behind them. Her eyes were brimming with tears and Beth quickly crossed over and placed a supportive arm around her shoulder, offering her a tissue. "Can you tell us about Jody's caseload?"

Mason shrugged, "Nothing out of the ordinary."

"What sort of work do you take on?" Hunter asked.

"Run-of-the-mill stuff really," Mason explained. "We do insurance fraud, personal injury claims... Oh, and the usual marital affairs and such like. The former two are a bit of a money-spinner and the latter is... well... commonplace."

"What was Jody currently working on?" Caslin asked. Mason looked to Donna.

"He had three or four cases on the go," she said, her voice cracking.

"Were any of those cases threatening in nature?" Hunter asked. "Anyone taking offence at his attention?"

"Are you saying Jody's been murdered?" Mason cut in.

"What makes you ask?" Caslin countered.

"The questions you're asking," he explained. "I've been there. I know the drill. You said he was found dead. You said nothing about anything suspicious."

"Can you think of any reason someone would wish him to come to any harm?" Caslin asked. Mason sank back in his chair, shaking his head.

"No. None at all. Jody is... was... one of the good guys."

Caslin looked to the other two who both shook their heads. "Was he married?"

"Divorced. A long time ago," Mason stated. "His ex remarried and lives in New Zealand now."

"Any kids?"

Mason shook his head, "No. He never seemed too bothered about relationships either."

"How so?"

"He spent a lot of time on his own. His parents are both dead and he was an only child. All adds up to being a bit of a loner."

"What about his cases?" Caslin asked.

"We don't share caseloads," Mason explained. "We operate under the same umbrella but not in tandem, if you know what I mean?"

Caslin nodded, "How long have you known each other?"

"All his life," Mason explained. "I worked with his father in the job. We were good friends. When I was approaching my thirty, Jody suggested I join him in setting up this business. He was working as an investigator for an insurance company and there was plenty of work to go around. We set up on our own. Our combined experience gave us a decent amount of credibility in the industry, so it was a no-brainer."

"And how is business?" Hunter asked, involuntarily casting an eye around the bare office, devoid of character. Mason noticed.

"Don't let the décor fool you, Miss," he said, narrowing his eyes. "We just don't waste money on stylish furnishings. There's no point. We hardly get clients come through the door as most of our business is corporate related. Much of our time is spent out in the field. Business is punchy right now. We have three teams of investigators plus ourselves and cover a radius of one hundred miles from this very chair. You'll see from my Jag parked outside that business has never been better."

"No offence intended," Hunter said.

"None taken," Mason countered. Caslin rolled his tongue along the inside of his lower lip. Hunter was irritated by Mason's belittling reference to her but only he could see it.

"What of Jody's cases?" Caslin asked. "Which was his most pressing?"

"He had a pretty big divorce case that was coming before a court in a couple of weeks," Donna offered, regaining some measure of composure. "And he took on an embezzlement case last month. Other than that, he was working two suspected insurance scams involving personal injury claims. They were both involved in the same accident but Jody figured they were set ups."

"Can you elaborate?" Caslin asked. Donna looked to Mason who nodded.

"The divorce case is a straightforward investigation to assist a spouse improve the marital settlement from her estranged husband. He was quite abusive and played away so she is highly motivated."

"The abuse. Was it violent?" Hunter asked, making notes.

Donna nodded furiously. "Yes, absolutely. Systematic over the course of a decade. We collected medical records as well as proof of infidelity."

"Proof? In the form of what?"

"Video surveillance in the main," Donna stated.

"Was the husband aware of Mr Wyer's interest?" Donna shook her head. "And the others?"

"A firm in Leeds asked us to look into some accounting discrepancies within one of their client's accounts. They think one of their staff has been syphoning off funds."

"How much?" Caslin asked.

"We had only just begun but already we've noted twenty thousand is missing and it looks like it will rise far higher the further we go back."

"And the insurance scam?" Hunter asked, looking up from her pocket book.

"Two high value cars colliding with each other," Donna explained.

Caslin figured he knew where this one was heading. It was a popular scam. "One was a Mercedes, the other a BMW and both were written off. The total value of the car owner's claims, including personal injury, were well over a hundred thousand pounds. Plus, there are subsidiary claims from passengers totalling over five figures per claimant."

"I'll bet the accident happened on an empty street in the middle of the night?" Caslin suggested.

Donna nodded. "Don't they always?"

"And where were you with those cases?"

"Jody figured both sets of people knew each other, so he was building a case trying to link them."

"In what form?" Hunter asked. Both Donna and Beth looked towards Mason once more. He remained stoic, unflinching. "Donna?" Hunter pressed.

"He didn't say," she replied, looking to the floor.

"We'll need names, contacts… regarding everything Jody was working on," Caslin said to Mason, figuring nothing would come out of the office without his say-so. "I can obtain a warrant if you prefer?"

"That won't be necessary, Inspector," Mason said. "You'll have our full cooperation in this matter."

"Thank you," Caslin said.

"When was the last time you saw Jody?" Caslin asked Mason.

"Two nights ago. We had a bit of a knees-up in the pub under the guise of a team meeting," Mason explained. "It was a cracking night."

"And how was he? Did he seem out of sorts, distracted perhaps?"

Mason thought about it, glancing at his colleagues and frowned, "Come to think of it, he wasn't his usual self. Don't get me wrong, I couldn't put my finger on why but he wasn't really up for a night out."

"True. He left early before it all got going," Beth confirmed.

"Did he say anything that might indicate why he wasn't participating?" Hunter asked.

"He was driving and so only had a couple of drinks," Donna said. "But no, other than that, he was quite normal as far as I could tell. A bit quiet maybe but no one likes being the sober one at the party, do they?"

"I guess not. Did Jody leave his computer here by any chance?" Caslin asked.

"No. He uses a laptop and always takes it home with him," Donna confirmed.

"We'll take a look at his home address then," Caslin said, taking out two of his contact cards and giving one to both Donna and Beth. "Well, if you think of anything I might like to know, I'd appreciate it if you would give me a call."

"Be assured we will," Mason said, sitting forward. "Tell me, which CID do you operate out of?"

"We're based at Fulford Road," Caslin replied, meeting Mason's eye and ignoring Hunter's glance.

"Nice station," Mason stated.

"Yes, it is," Caslin said, stepping forward. Mason rose as Caslin offered his hand. "If we need a positive identification to take place, would you be willing?"

"Of course, yes," Mason confirmed.

"Right you are. We'll be in touch."

DESCENDING the stairs to the outside, Caslin felt eyes on their back as they reached the street. Glancing over his shoulder, he caught a glimpse of Donna and the larger-than-life figure of Tony Mason watching them from above. Looking back, he met Hunter's eye as they crossed the road in between oncoming traffic to where the car was parked.

"A penny for them?" she said.

"What's that?" he asked.

"I know that face," Hunter explained. "What is it about them that has got you thinking?"

Caslin shook his head, smiling, "You started out over at Acomb Road. What do you know about Tony Mason?"

"He left before I went into CID," Hunter stated. "But I remember him as a well-liked DI. A little too old-school perhaps for the modern era."

"Meaning?"

"Well, he'd bend the rules if he thought it would get a result. That sort of thing."

"I see," Caslin said, reaching the car and heading around to the passenger side. Hunter unlocked it and they both got in.

"Not unlike someone sitting not too far away from me now," Hunter said with a wry smile. Caslin laughed. "Tell me, why didn't you say where we worked?"

Caslin looked at her with a questioning glance. "I don't know what you mean."

Hunter turned the key and started the engine. "Yes, you do. You told him we were based at Fulford Road."

Caslin stared ahead, assessing the traffic despite the fact he wasn't driving. "That's my problem, Sarah. You see, we are based at Fulford."

Hunter smiled, "You implied we were Fulford Road CID and didn't mention we were Major Crimes..."

"Who work out of Fulford Road," Caslin countered, grinning. "He didn't ask. I just didn't correct his assumption."

"You don't trust him."

Caslin inclined his head, "Did you notice how they both looked to him for their lead."

"Beth and Donna?"

"Yeah. Every time they were asked a question, they ran it past him first."

"He is their boss," Hunter stated in mitigation.

"Yes, he is," Caslin said, returning his focus to the traffic levels before adding, almost as an afterthought, "and no... as things go, the people I have a hard time trusting, apart from ex-cons... are ex-coppers. I don't trust him. Not one little bit."

CHAPTER SIX

THE SOUND of trains clattering through the nearby station in central York carried to them, metal upon metal shrieking as the carriages came to a halt. A muffled public address system announced forthcoming arrivals and platform updates.

"Looks like nobody's home," Hunter said, peering at the darkened interior through the shuttered blinds of the bay window. They were standing outside an unassuming brick terrace. Part of a row of twenty houses separated from the road by a knee-high dwarf wall. The street was narrow and lined on the opposing side by similar properties. Parked cars were interspersed with large gaps that would be filled once residents returned from work later in the evening. The buildings traditionally housed railway workers well before the advent of the motoring age. Even with minimal outside space, on street parking and the accompanying noise of the city, they were still in a desirable location being so close to the city centre and its transport links.

"He lived alone," Caslin stated, stepping back from the front door and glancing towards the upper windows, his continued knocking remained unanswered. Two properties along, he noted a passageway to the rear of the terrace. Such was the nature of the construction rights of way were granted to the rear of neighbouring houses, allowing access to your own gardens via their boundaries. "Let's take a look around the back."

They made their way along and cut through the passage, barely a shoulder's width of space to the interior. Emerging from the darkness into a courtyard they were overlooked from the rear of the houses in the next street along. Almost all the properties had extended their living space to the rear as well as into the attic space, maximising their footprints. There would be little privacy to be had. Almost every window they looked at was shrouded in net or drawn curtains, despite it being the middle of the day, to ensure prying eyes were kept out. Gardens were fenced off or built up with imposing brick boundaries, each with a gate to allow access for your neighbours to pass through. Turning to their left, Caslin blindly reached up and over, unlocking the bolt at the top of the gate. Presumably, if you didn't know it was there, you might think the garden more secure than it actually was. Caslin doubted it would deter even the most incompetent of burglars.

Passing through the first garden they saw no one. Entering into the next, they startled a young woman standing at the window of her kitchen running herself a glass of water before the sink. She didn't recognise them and the look on her face was more one of surprise than suspicion. After all, they weren't dressed as you would expect a burglar to be. Hunter brandished her warrant card at the window, encouraging the occupant to come to the rear door for a word. She did so willingly. They exchanged names as well as greetings.

"Mrs Dempster," Hunter began.

"Natalie, please."

"Natalie. We're looking at your next-door neighbour's house," Hunter explained, leaving out the fact they had found his body. "Have you seen anyone there recently?"

"Jody?" she asked. Hunter nodded. "No, I've not seen him for a while. To be honest, he's hardly ever home. Keeps all kind of strange hours and so do I, so I often don't see or hear him for days on end."

"What is it you do?" Hunter asked, making conversation.

"I'm a nurse at the hospital," she replied. As if working out why they might be there for the very first time, she asked, "Is Jody all right?"

"No, I'm afraid Mr Wyer was found dead this morning," Hunter replied.

"Oh my God," Natalie said, glancing away and leaving her mouth wide open. "Poor Jody."

"Has there been anything unusual that you have noticed in the last few days or weeks?" Caslin asked. "It may have seemed innocuous at the time but now... perhaps not?"

Natalie shook her head, "No. Nothing out of the ordinary."

"Did you know Mr Wyer well?"

"Quite well, yes. We would share an evening every now and again," she explained. "We're not best friends or anything but I like him. Plus, he gets on with my partner which always helps."

"What kind of neighbour was he?" Hunter asked. "Did he socialise much? Have wild parties, guests at all hours, that type of thing?"

Natalie shook her head, "No, nothing like that. He was a quiet guy. Seemed to keep himself to himself, you know? Shame really."

"How so?" Caslin asked, interested.

"Well… I get the impression he was a little brow-beaten. He was that sort of guy."

"Brow beaten? By whom?"

"It's just my impression but," Natalie went on, "some people just aren't good at socialising, are they?"

"Did he have any friends? Regular visitors?" Caslin asked.

"You know what, if you'd asked me that any time in the last two years, I'd have said no but there has been a woman coming by recently. I mean, he never had a girlfriend as far as I knew and I did wonder whether he was more inclined the other way, if you know what I mean?"

Caslin affirmed that he did, "So, this was a girlfriend? Did you ever meet her?"

Natalie shook her head, "No, I only caught the odd glimpse of her coming or going. She might not have been a girlfriend. She might have been another type of lady friend, who knows?"

Caslin considered what she was implying, "A regular visitor… friend with benefits, perhaps?"

Natalie shrugged, "Maybe. He didn't strike me as particularly successful with women nor did he seem too bothered about that fact."

"What do you put it down to?"

"Certainly not a lack of character. He was a great guy to be around but I'd say he was carrying a lot of baggage. He always seemed weighed down by life."

"Right," Caslin said, nodding. "Did you get a name for this woman?"

"No, can't say I ever did. I'd know her if I saw her again though. She stands out. A redhead - flame red. Natural as well, not from a bottle. Believe me, you'd know her if you saw her."

"A bit of a knockout?" Hunter asked.

Natalie agreed. "That's why I'd be surprised if they were a couple. I mean, Jody's a lovely guy and really successful with his business and everything but… well, he's not a looker."

"You mentioned, Jody was weighed down. Can you elaborate on that? Did he ever say anything about it?"

"As I say, it's just my impression. I remember he found it tough when his dad was ill. You know, the getting to and from the hospital, arranging care and stuff? He did a lot for his old dad."

"They were close?"

Natalie frowned, "I'm not sure about that. I mean, he didn't speak highly of the man. I think it was more of an ingrained sense of duty that he carried… or had drummed into him."

"His father was overbearing?" Hunter clarified.

"I'd say so, yes. Not that Jody ever mentioned it directly but… you pick up on things, don't you?"

"Okay, thanks," Caslin said, glancing to Hunter before looking at Wyer's house next door. "Mr Wyer lived alone?"

"Yes, he did," Natalie confirmed. "Do you need to get in? I have a key."

CASLIN UNLOCKED the back door giving access to the kitchen. Stepping inside, he flicked the nearest switch bathing them in a flickering fluorescent light that eventually settled. Entering an empty property for the first time always felt a little eerie. Storm clouds were gathering and in such a built-up area very little daylight permeated the interior. Like the others in the row, Wyer's property was extended at the rear leaving the middle section of the house to cope with even less natural light. They listened for a moment but quickly decided they were indeed alone. Even so, they had to check.

Leaving Hunter to explore the ground floor, Caslin made his way upstairs. The treads creaked and groaned under his weight as he climbed them. There were two bedrooms off the landing as well as a family bathroom to the first floor with a narrow staircase curving up towards the converted attic. Casually inspecting both rooms, Caslin noted they were in a decent state of dress. The larger of the two was furnished with a king size bed and lined with contemporary wardrobes. Flicking through them, he found suits and clothing, all neatly pressed and on hangers. Jody Wyer was fastidiously neat with his attire.

Heading into the second bedroom, located to the rear, he found a spare bed that didn't appear to be in use at present. There was no sheet or bed covering. Even the associated duvet was curled up and lay at the foot of the bed. One wardrobe filled a corner to the right of the chimney breast and upon closer inspection only housed spare bedding and empty coat hangers. Clicking the double doors shut, Caslin turned and headed back onto the landing and into the bathroom. In contrast to the master bedroom this area needed a thorough clean. Scale was building up on the mixer taps and around the base of the shower mildew was leading to mould along the length of the sealant. *Nobody's perfect,* Caslin thought as he opened a mirrored cabinet set above the sink.

Careful not to disturb anything, he eyed the contents. Alongside the over-the-counter medicines commonly found in family bathrooms, Caslin spied a bottle labelled *Paroxetine*. From personal experience, he knew that to be a medication prescribed for treatment of depression. Using the end of a pen, Caslin manoeuvred the bottle so as he could fully read the label confirming that it was indeed Wyer's and also making a mental note of the dated label. They were recent. The neighbour was correct, Jody Wyer was indeed weighed down by something. Returning his attention to the surroundings, Caslin found his attention piqued by something else. Leaning into the shower cubicle he scanned the toiletries present in the rack. There was an assortment of bottles, shampoo, conditioners, organic facial-scrubs and the like. Hearing footsteps on the stairs he called out so Hunter knew where he was.

She entered the bathroom. Even with two adults present the room was still a good size. Originally, they'd have been standing in a third bedroom with the only bathroom facilities being the pre-war outside toilet.

"What do you make of that?" Caslin said, indicating the toiletries. Hunter looked in and immediately clocked what he was referring to.

"Since when do you guys care about colouring conditioner?" she asked, smiling.

"Particularly to bring out your natural red..."

"Wyer has dark hair, doesn't he?" Hunter clarified, thinking back to the body being pulled from the water.

"Second toothbrush as well," Caslin stated, pointing at the cup sitting beside the basin. Hunter looked over, curious.

"What about clothing?" she asked.

Caslin shook his head, "No. All the cupboards and drawers are full of Wyer's... unless she has a masculine style."

"That's not the impression Natalie gave us."

"No. It certainly isn't," Caslin agreed. "Did you find a mobile or laptop downstairs?"

Hunter shook her head, "No. You?"

"Still one more floor to go," Caslin said, gesturing towards the upper staircase.

They made their way up together. The attic was set out as a home office with a desk at the far end, butting up against the chimney stack. Several filing cabinets lined the adjacent wall and a large cork board was attached to the wall opposite. Hunter inclined her head to say she would check out the desk while Caslin inspected the notes pinned to the board. There were several sticky notes with single words or times scrawled upon them. They made little sense without context. What drew Caslin's eye was a map, unfolded and pinned up. This was an ordnance survey map. The area covered began just south of Middlesbrough and stretched down the east Yorkshire coast ending just past Scarborough. Inland, the map went as far west as Pickering.

Many weekends of Caslin's youth were spent walking the moorland and coastal paths of that region and therefore he also knew this wasn't a map picked up off the shelf of any tourist information office. This was a custom order, one purchased directly from the national mapping agency of Great Britain. On it, Wyer had placed pins in certain areas whereas other points were circled in red pen. The significance of these locations was unclear but Caslin found himself curious. Initially, he wondered whether this was related to the divorce case Wyer was working. Could they be locations of trysts between illicit lovers? That theory was quickly disregarded unless the couple had a fetish for old quarries, cliff-top paths or abandoned lime kilns. The random nature of the locations only served to intrigue him further.

"Any sign of his tech?" Caslin asked over his shoulder not taking his eyes from the map.

"No," Hunter confirmed. "I have a charger, hard wiring for access to his hub but no computer. I can't find a note pad, diary, mobile, or anything that tells us what his plans were. If I had to say, I reckon his office has been swept clean."

"They didn't clear all of this," Caslin said softly. Hunter came to join him just as he took out his mobile phone. Stepping back, Caslin ensured he got the board in focus and took a few shots with the camera.

"What is it?" Hunter asked, inspecting the board.

"No idea," Caslin declared. "But I'll wager this is what he's been spending time on."

"What did Donna say he was working? Divorce case, embezzlement and car insurance scams, wasn't it?" Hunter asked.

"That's what she said," Caslin agreed.

"I don't see how those cases fit in on this map, do you?"

Caslin shook his head, "No. I wonder if Wyer was doing something off the books."

"That'd make sense," Hunter agreed. "Broadfoot said he was working something big. That doesn't sound like a divorce case or an insurance scam."

"And they had only recently taken on the embezzlement case and Broadfoot said he'd been working on something for a while."

"Whatever it was, it could have been what got him killed. Do you think this redhead might have something to do with it?"

"We're going to have to track her down and ask," Caslin replied. "Even for a quiet guy, you'd think he would have mentioned her to someone."

"Mind you, do you think his colleagues know he was offering information to Kyle Broadfoot?"

Caslin raised an eyebrow, "Perhaps he's very good at keeping secrets."

Further conversation was halted by Caslin's ringing mobile. Taking it out of his pocket, he glanced at the screen and saw it was DC Terry Holt back at Fulford Road.

"Sir, uniform have located Jody Wyer's car."

"Good. What state is it in?"

"I'll text you the address."

"Any joy from the networks regarding his mobile phone?"

"I'm still waiting, sir."

"In the meantime, can you dig out as much as you can regarding Tony Mason? He's a former DI at Acomb Road as well as Jody Wyer's business partner."

"Will do, sir. What is it I'm looking for?

"Anything and everything, Terry. Thanks. I'll catch-"

"Sir?" Holt interrupted him. "Some of the guys back here are asking why we took over the Wyer case?"

"Which people?" Caslin asked.

"Oh… you know, people, people."

"When I know, you'll know, Terry," Caslin said, hanging up. Hunter looked at him with a quizzical expression. "Tongues are wagging about our interest here."

"I must admit, I'm curious too," she replied. Caslin smiled just as his phone beeped. It was a text from Holt.

"Come on. Let's take a look at Wyer's car."

CHAPTER SEVEN

JODY WYER'S Seven-Series BMW cut a solitary figure in the car park of the pub. Perhaps it was the police presence combined with the onset of rain that kept the footfall low. Only a handful of punters were propping up the bar as Caslin looked out of the window, seeing the liveried police car maintaining the integrity of the crime scene.

"How long has it been there?" he asked the landlord, a round-faced twenty-something dressed in a black tee-shirt and jeans.

"It was here two nights ago when we locked up and hasn't moved since."

"Do you know the owner? Was he a regular?" Caslin asked, glancing around the interior. It was clean, tidy and distinctly lacking in character. This was a chain pub resulting in a décor that was bland and inoffensive whilst trying to tip its hat to a bygone age. In his opinion they'd failed miserably.

"Yeah, I've seen him in here," the landlord stated, acknowledging a customer who was waving an empty pint glass in his direction. "Can I get you a drink?"

Caslin declined, "Was he here the other night, when you first noticed the car?"

"Aye, yes he was."

"What time did he leave?"

"I don't know exactly but it was early. Well before closing."

"Did he leave with anyone?"

"No idea, sorry," he replied with a shrug. "Any idea how long until I get my car park back?"

"No idea," Caslin replied with a shrug. "Sorry."

The landlord frowned and turned away and crossed to the opposing counter to serve the waiting patron.

"He was helpful," Hunter said. "Shall we take a look?" Caslin nodded and the two of them left the bar and walked out into the car park. The rain was steadily falling. Not persistent enough to drench you but hard enough to become very quickly irritating. Caslin turned his collar up and thrust his hands into his pockets as they crossed the saturated tarmac, rainwater pooling on the patchwork, uneven surface. Approaching the black car, they both donned latex gloves. Caslin eyed the interior. There was a jacket lying haphazardly across the back seat as if it were casually thrown there. Apart from that, there was nothing in view. The car was as neatly presented as Wyer's house. Caslin lifted the handle on the driver's door and found it unlocked. Casting a glance across the roof of the vehicle towards Hunter, he opened it.

Dropping to his haunches, he inspected the interior of the cabin. The side pocket of the door was empty without even a discarded fuel receipt or crisp packet. Hunter opened the opposing door and examined her side. Checking the lining of the upholstery, Caslin looked for any telltale indications of a struggle – blood stains, a scuff to the edge or a tear in the stitching – but there were none. Meeting Caslin's eye following her initial inspection, Hunter shook her head.

"Not a lot here is there?"

"He keeps things clean, doesn't he?" Caslin replied. "Glove box?" Hunter opened it, rifling through the contents. She pulled out the owner's wallet containing the service record and maintenance manual. Putting that aside, she took out an in-car charging kit for a mobile phone and what Caslin assumed was the locking wheel nut.

Shrugging her shoulders, Hunter blew out her cheeks. "That's it," she said, disappointed. Caslin popped the manual boot release and they both walked to the rear of the car. Lifting the lid, they found what they were expecting – a clean, carpeted lining with nothing present that didn't belong. Closing it again, Caslin turned and looked around them, surveying the scene.

"We'll have to confirm that this was where the office outing took place," Hunter said, thinking aloud. "But it stands to reason. He either met someone here in the car park and left with them or he decided to walk from here."

"Didn't take his coat though," Caslin said.

"Let's gather as much of the CCTV as we can from the surrounding area. We might catch a break."

"Good idea," Caslin said, pursing his lips.

"What are you thinking?"

"Just that..." he left the thought unfinished, turning his head and scanning the tree line behind them. He cast his eyes up and took in the streetlights as well as the pub's minimal exterior illumination. "Not a bad place to jump someone," Caslin said, turning to Hunter and then scanning the floor nearby. She considered the theory. Caslin stepped away from the car and dropped to his haunches, reaching out but not touching the floor. He looked to the heavens and then back at the ground.

"What is it?" Hunter asked, coming alongside.

"The tarmac is wet, so it could be a trick of the light but I think this is blood," he said, moving his hand in a circular motion indicating a patch of the car park that appeared a darker shade than that surrounding it. "It stands to reason Wyer would have taken his coat off when he reached the car and was about to get in. That's why it's unlocked with the coat on the back seat. Do you have your torch?"

"Yes," she replied, reaching into her coat pocket.

"Can you put some light on this?" he asked. Hunter set the beam to where Caslin pointed. The damp patch shone with a tinge of red. Caslin looked past the car and into the trees beyond. "There's a great place to keep an eye on things," he said, looking from there back towards the pub. "You've got a decent sightline to the exit door from the pub into the car park. Likewise, anyone entering by car. There's nothing behind the trees there to note your presence, only the gable wall of those buildings. You're totally concealed."

"You think he was ambushed?" Hunter asked.

"If it was an opportunistic robbery why didn't they take his wallet? And why didn't they just leave him where he fell?" Caslin argued, pointing to the ground at their feet.

"They went to a lot of trouble to get rid of the body but he was always likely to be found," Hunter said. "Maybe it was a robbery that got out of hand and when they realised he'd died, they panicked. Perhaps they got rid of the body because it would tie them to this area."

Caslin had to admit her logic was credible but not flawless. "The car ties it to the area though and they didn't move that. We'd better put a call into forensics and let Iain Robertson know he has another crime scene."

"He'll be happy," Hunter said, smiling.

"Ahh... he loves being miserable," Caslin countered. "It gives him something to complain about."

"TERRY, talk to me about Tony Mason," Caslin said, momentarily distracted by his mobile ringing. Picking it up off the desk, he registered the caller before quickly dismissing it and sending the call to voicemail. Putting down the handset, he turned back to DC Holt and indicated for him to continue.

"Anthony Mason, resident here in York and a former detective inspector with North Yorkshire Police. Previously a DS with Greater Manchester," Holt stated, walking over to the information board and pointing to Mason's photograph, sited alongside one of Jody Wyer. "Companies House has him registered as a director of *Blue Line Investigations*, a limited company formed five years ago as a joint enterprise between the two of them."

"What do we know about the company?" Hunter asked.

"All required filings with HMRC have been carried out on schedule. Their position is solvent with a healthy cash position," Holt said. Hunter made a note. "I checked out their website. The services they offer are much as you described - corporate investigations, insurance fraud, marital disputes."

"And Mason himself?" Caslin asked.

"The performance reviews in his personnel file were variable."

"How so?"

"He earned glowing reports throughout his early career as he climbed the ranks until hitting a downward trend in the latter years of his service. I'd interpret that as a result of a change in commanding officer alongside a shift in how we were managed."

"Is that your polite way of saying he was proper old-school in his approach to policing?" Caslin queried.

Holt nodded enthusiastically. "He received several complaints regarding his conduct in the last three years up until he hit his thirty and retired," Holt said, referring to his notes. "One of those complaints came from a fellow officer."

"Wow," Caslin said, glancing towards Hunter. "He was probably keen to get out of the door."

"Those aren't the greatest highlights on file for him though," Holt said. "He was the subject of an investigation by Complaints nearly a decade ago."

"What was their interest?" Caslin asked, finding his curiosity piqued. The Complaints Division were responsible for investigating serving police officers, covering everything from conduct to corruption.

"His financial affairs," Holt said. "He was the victim of two counts of common assault. One in 2006 and another, more recently, in 2011. The latter saw him hospitalised for over a week."

"How does that tie in with Complaints?" Hunter asked.

"There was the suggestion that this resulted from debts he had run up."

"Who with?"

Holt shook his head. "The investigations didn't go anywhere. Complaints ended theirs with a reprimand placed on his file relating to his gambling habits, recommending an ongoing process of monitoring. The thinking was that he'd left himself open to manipulation with his debts which, as you both know, is a big no-no."

"What about the assaults?"

"In 2006, the case remained unsolved. Mason claimed he had no knowledge of his assailants and there were no witnesses. In the second case, the charges were dropped when Mason himself refused to press charges. I think that was the final nail in his career. Shortly after, he was shifted across to Acomb Road to see out his thirty."

"Any suggestion as to who he owed money to?" Caslin asked. "Are we looking at loan sharks or backstreet bookies?"

Holt shrugged, "Sorry, sir. I don't have that information. I'm going to go through the archive and gather the related names and I'll run them through the database for prior convictions and known associates. I might get a steer from that. I had a thought though. If he hit the financial buffers perhaps there was a pattern in his personal life that coincided with it?"

"Go on," Caslin encouraged him.

"He moved house on several occasions in the last ten years and not only at times matching a redeployment. Now, bear in mind it's only a cursory examination but each time he was downsizing and moving to a less desirable area."

"Cashing in to fund his lifestyle?"

"Or to stem his losses," Holt countered.

"Great work, Terry," Caslin smiled, turning to Hunter. "I reckon we should pop back and have a word with Mr Mason. I think he is holding back on us a little."

"Agreed," Hunter said and they both stood up.

"Let me know what you find in the archives," Caslin said. There was a knock on the frame of the door to their office. Simon, the civilian clerk from the station's front office ducked his head around the door.

"I'm sorry to interrupt, Inspector Caslin," he said tentatively. For a man who was notoriously unaware of how mundane people generally found his presence to be, he was however, acutely aware of how Caslin felt towards him – largely disinterested.

"What can we do for you, Simon?"

"I've taken three calls for you, Mr Caslin," he said. "They are all from your father. He is trying to get you on your mobile but is not having much luck. Is there a problem with your phone?"

"No. Not at all," Caslin replied. Hunter looked away and Terry Holt turned his back stifling a grin, both well aware Caslin was being short and yet equally aware Simon wouldn't notice.

"Oh… right. Well, he's asked that you return his call when you are free."

"Thank you," Caslin said.

"He has called three times," Simon said, watching Caslin pick up his mobile and put it in his pocket.

"Thank you," Caslin repeated.

"If he calls again, what should I say?"

"Use your imagination," Caslin said, pulling on his coat and signalling for Hunter to join him. They both walked out, Hunter smiling at the bemused clerk who was trying to make sense of the exchange.

"That was mean," Hunter said playfully as they made their way along the corridor.

"I don't know what you're talking about," Caslin said with a wry grin. "Heads up," he added under his breath as DCI Matheson rounded the corner in front of them. She indicated for them to stop as they approached.

"Nathaniel," she said, also acknowledging Hunter with an expression serving to advise her that her presence was not required.

"I'll meet you downstairs," Hunter said to Caslin who nodded. Matheson waited until the detective sergeant was out of earshot before she spoke.

"As much as I appreciate your Major Crimes Unit picking up some of CID's caseload, I was wondering what your interest in the Wyer case is?" Caslin smiled. That was a popular question at present.

"Interest is ongoing, Ma'am," he replied. Caslin was confident her words of appreciation were genuine since his own recruitment to Kyle Broadfoot's crime bureau had left Fulford Road's resident investigation team shorthanded. Particularly with Caslin's insistence on taking both Terry Holt and Sarah Hunter along with him, a decision that decimated the operational effectiveness of Fulford Road's CID. Replacements were either in place on a secondment basis or in the process of being reassigned. Nonetheless, the upheaval was significant. "Besides, we have an ongoing commitment to support you until such time as Fulford Road is back to the appropriate headcount." Matheson smiled but Caslin saw past it.

"Your political nous is improving, I see," she said.

"Thank you, Ma'am."

"In the meantime, can you offer me any reassurance that this bombing will not be repeated any time soon?"

"I wasn't aware that'd been confirmed," Caslin said. Matheson frowned, her patience tested. Caslin had to concede some ground, "Early days. We don't have a motive yet but the ownership of the business is more likely to be part of the inspiration than a random act of terror. That's my instinct talking, just to be clear."

Matheson accepted the statement with good grace, "Thank you, Nathaniel. If you need my help, just let me know."

"I will Ma'am," Caslin said. "Thank you."

The DCI moved off and Caslin increased his pace, eager to hook up with Hunter and head over to see Tony Mason. Previously, he hadn't known what to expect but having met the man, Caslin didn't like him. He knew the type, bold, brash and a devil to unpick. Mason would only offer the information he knew Caslin could easily find out in other ways. Wyer wasn't talking to those around him regarding what he was working on or if he was, they weren't willing to reveal it. Either way, Caslin knew there was more information to be had and he intended to find out what that was.

CHAPTER EIGHT

Approaching Mason's office, they spied his white Jaguar pulling out into traffic and set off in the opposite direction.

"What do you want to do, call in at the office or..."

"Follow him," Caslin said. "We're already heading that way. Outside of the office he may just drop his guard and you never know, maybe he'll give us more."

Hunter kept pace with Mason's car maintaining a comfortable distance with several vehicles in between them. They passed out of the city centre heading north towards the outskirts of York before cutting east. The residential area of Rawcliffe was to their right, bordering Clifton which was the direction they were travelling. Hunter saw Mason's indicator flicker on as he took a turn onto the Clifton Moor industrial estate, the last vestige of development before they reached the countryside. The traffic was lighter here and she eased off allowing him to put a little distance between them to remain unnoticed before she also took the turn.

Mason pulled his Jaguar into a scrap metal yard, easily identifiable by the towering stacks of wrecked cars visible above the perimeter fence. Hunter pulled up a few hundred yards away. To get any closer risked their presence being revealed as the nearby businesses were set back from the highway by some distance leaving too much open ground in which to try and conceal themselves.

"Leave the car here and let's see if we can get a little closer," Caslin said, getting out of the car. Hunter did likewise having reached over and grabbed her camera from the glove box. Falling into step alongside him, she hooked her arm through his to simulate being a couple. Together, they made their way along the path on the opposite side of the road from the scrap yard, casting casual glances in that direction as they passed the entrance. Emblazoned with a bold, blue and white sign signifying *MacEwan's Metals*, Mason's car was parked before the site office but no one else was visible. They kept moving so as not to draw attention to themselves but Caslin looked to their right and the building on the opposite side of the road. It was a two-storey distribution warehouse of some kind belonging to a large logistics firm. "This way," he said to Hunter, guiding her in the direction of the entrance.

Once inside, Caslin flashed his warrant card and sought access to the upper floor. The site manager was accommodating without prying, happy their presence had nothing to do with him or his team. He showed them into his office which overlooked the frontage giving them an uninterrupted view of the scrapyard. Caslin thanked him and they were left alone. A few minutes passed and they waited. The only movement came from the operation of a large crane, bending and scooping up a mixture of tangled metal and dropping it into a hopper to await the crusher. They didn't have to wait too long before figures emerged from within the office.

Mason appeared first. Even from this distance his pink cheeks looked far flusher than they had previously. His expression was fixed and he didn't look happy. Another man followed closely behind. He was older. Caslin figured he was in his late sixties with swept back hair that appeared almost white in contrast to his tanned skin, judged most likely to be natural rather than fake. He was gesturing as he talked and it looked very much as if Mason was the target of his ire. The latter turned and replied in kind raising his arm and pointing a finger in an accusatory gesture. Seconds later another came from within the office. Clearly, this man was the calming influence who sought to reconcile the other two.

"Recognise any of these guys?" Caslin asked.

"The peacemaker is David MacEwan," Hunter said. "He's been around a bit but I don't know the other one."

"I thought I knew him," Caslin said quietly. "I didn't realise he was back from Spain though."

"Nor did I," Hunter concurred.

"What about the guy with the white hair?"

"No idea."

"Get some pictures, would you?"

Hunter took out her camera, zoomed in on the trio and began snapping away. The heat of the conversation subsided and they continued to talk but it was clear they hadn't reached a resolution. Mason clambered back into his Jaguar, slamming the door shut and rapidly firing the engine into life. The wheels spun in the gravel as he turned the car around and drove out of the yard, accelerating away at speed once the car reached the tarmac of the highway.

The remaining men continued their conversation and they were joined by another, a younger man who approached from the left and was previously shielded from view by the perimeter fence. Hunter ensured she had him in the frame as well. Moments later, he disappeared again before reappearing minutes later at the wheel of a red Mercedes. He got out leaving the engine running. They watched as MacEwan shook hands with the white-haired man and they shared a joke about something. The latter got into the car and the driver shut the door for him.

"Make sure you get that index," Caslin said, taking out his phone and putting a call into the control room.

"I've got it," Hunter confirmed as the vehicle left the yard taking a right and heading out of the industrial estate. Returning her focus to MacEwan she snapped the final picture of him and his associate as they dropped out of sight, back into the office.

"Right, thanks," Caslin said, hanging up on his call. "The Police National Computer check on that Mercedes has it registered to a hire car company based at Manchester Airport. We're going to have to get onto them directly to find out who's driving it."

"He certainly didn't get that tan in Yorkshire. Not at this time of the year," Hunter said dryly. "Should we go and have that chat with Mason now?"

Caslin shook his head looking at his watch, "No. Let's find out a bit more about the new figures before we do. Mason looked pretty pissed off with whatever the conclusion of that discussion was. Related to Wyer, do you think?"

Hunter thought on it. "MacEwan's a career criminal. We've had him a couple of times over the years but he's always managed to slip through the net when those around him end up doing serious time. It's a strange acquaintance for an ex-copper to be associating with."

"We need to know who the unidentified man is and see where he fits in," Caslin said.

"MacEwan's been sunning himself for the past few years," Hunter said. "Maybe that's one of his business partners from over there."

"Perhaps," Caslin said. "Whatever's going on, Mason is rattled."

"WE'RE NOT LOOKING at anything particularly complicated here," Iain Robertson said, addressing the group. Kyle Broadfoot was in attendance at the briefing of the initial forensic analysis of the bombing. Caslin perched on the edge of a table to the left and Terry Holt was seated with Hunter. Robertson turned and pointed to a sketch of the minicab offices owned by the Fullers. On it, Robertson had placed pins labelled with the names of the victims to denote where he believed they were standing at the moment of the device's detonation. "I think the explosion originated here," he said, indicating the back office, located in the middle of the building behind a stud wall separating the waiting area from the front lobby. "Two of the victims were present in the room, judging from the severity of their injuries."

"What was the nature of those?" Broadfoot asked.

"Massive trauma. First-degree burns and lacerations. Both of them lost limbs as a direct result of the blast," Robertson explained. "The other employees were standing in the lobby."

"We believe they were drivers," Holt added.

"One of them was most likely about to take the fare of the waiting customer," Robertson added. "The former two were standing as the blast occurred and were struck by glass from the dispatcher's sliding screen. It shattered, sending shards of razor-sharp glass directly at them. The customer was either seated or lying down on the bench and I think this was the stroke of fortune that saved his life. Although caught in the blast, being in the corner saw the shock wave strike him but most of the debris flew above and past him. Bearing in mind he was half-cut from a night out, I wouldn't be surprised if he'd fallen asleep while he waited."

"You said the device wasn't complicated?" Caslin asked.

"That's right. We're talking about an improvised explosive. No doubt, homemade but no less deadly. I'm not expecting to find a complex chemical structure to this."

"And do we have any idea yet as to how it made its way into the building?"

"We recovered the hard drive related to the internal CCTV from the rubble. It was stored upstairs and so was protected from the worst of the blast. That's the good news."

"What's the bad news?" Caslin asked.

"The cameras were switched off thirty minutes before the bomb went off," Robertson confirmed. An air of deflation swept throughout the room.

"Can we find out from the footage who was present in the building at that time?"

Robertson nodded, "I gave it to your man, there."

Holt stood up and crossed to his desk. Bringing his computer out of hibernation, he transferred the pictures to a projector before heading over and drawing the screen down so the others could see. Starting the footage rolling, Holt drew their attention to the time stamp in the bottom right-hand corner. It was forty minutes prior to the detonation. The images were split screen with nine camera angles displayed at the same time, a mixture of the interior and exterior of the building.

"We've identified five of the people we can see here and the sixth is a member of the public," Holt said, pointing them out. The customer was sitting with his feet up in the waiting area. One of the staff members, presumably a driver, came out and the two of them left the waiting area to go outside. "These four remaining are the victims along with another customer who appears in the waiting room in about eight minutes," Holt said, "whereas, this guy here," he indicated a figure approaching the rear of the building through the yard, "we are yet to identify."

They all strained to make out the details of the man's face. There was precious little light in the immediate vicinity. The figure wore a hooded jumper, pulled up over his head, and he didn't look in the direction of the cameras even once.

"He's been here before," Caslin said, watching him punch in an access code and unlock the door to the rear and pass straight through. Stepping into the dimly lit hallway behind the office and adjacent to the staff kitchen, they got their first proper view of him. Camera angles could be deceptive but he appeared to be a clean-shaven, white male, roughly six-feet in height and carrying a small backpack. The image was low quality monotone and anything more discernible about his appearance was not forthcoming. "Can you clean that up at all, Terry?"

"No, sir. Not easily at any rate but I'll give it a go."

They watched as he entered the back office to be greeted by the four occupants but again, he didn't make eye contact with the camera. The staff present appeared to pay him little attention and continued their conversation. The hooded man crossed the room and made a show of retrieving something from the corner of the room but the action was predominantly out of shot.

"Definitely familiar," Hunter observed. Moments later, he returned to the door and stepped out back into the hall. Two of the occupants glanced in his direction as he left but it was unclear if communication followed or not. The figure reappeared on the hallway camera walking back out the way he had come in only this time he moved at pace. "No backpack," Hunter said. Holt sped up the film by a factor of three. The staff went about their business with nothing of note taking place until the footage ceased.

"At least we have our bomber," Broadfoot stated.

"Although, it's going to be highly unlikely we can identify him from that. The only witnesses who could identify him would be those present and they're all dead," Hunter argued.

"No. He was well known to all of them. That's one of the Fullers' own right there," Caslin stated. "It was an inside job. He's a member of their organisation. No one batted an eyelid as he walked in and out."

"Do you think the Fullers know?" Broadfoot asked.

Caslin shook his head, "I didn't get that impression when we met with them." He looked to Hunter who shook her head to signify she agreed. "We could ask Ashton or Carl but they'd never let on. We'd just find another dead body in a couple of days."

"Or not," Hunter said. Caslin agreed. "It's a bit odd the footage going off when it did. Presumably, you reckon it was set to switch off?"

"Aye," Robertson confirmed. "Someone intentionally went into the system the day before and set it to shut the cameras off."

"You'd think that was to hide the bomber coming in but they got their times wrong."

"That's it," Robertson said. "Take another look at the time stamp. The clock was wrong on the system. They programmed it right but didn't factor in the timing was out."

"The big question for me is who put him up to it?" Caslin continued.

"Could be an internal power play," Holt suggested. "Between the Fullers themselves."

"Who stands to benefit most from the Fullers taking a hit like this?" Caslin asked.

"Clinton Dade is the obvious answer," Hunter replied. "But why now? Everything has been pretty cool between those two. It's not like the old days when Pete was knocking about."

"Gangs used to fight it out after the pubs closed back then," Caslin argued. "Business has moved on. Everyone's a bit more professional these days. Or at least that's what we've gotten used to."

"Go and pay Dade a visit, would you?" Broadfoot said to Caslin, leaning forward and resting his elbows on the table in front of him and cupping his hands beneath his chin. "Suss him out and see if he orchestrated this. If their respective organisations are reheating the old antagonisms, I want us to get ahead of the curve rather than where we are right now."

"Will do, sir," Caslin said.

The meeting was adjourned and they split up to go about their tasks. Caslin called Hunter and Holt over to him.

"Terry, can you dig around MacEwan and see what he's up to at the moment but do it quietly. If he's friendly with one local ex-copper, like Mason, then he may be friendly with more. In the meantime, Hunter and I will call in on Clinton Dade and see what he makes of all of this. Chase up the hire car company regarding the Mercedes as well, would you?"

CHAPTER NINE

THE HEAD WAS THROWN BACK with an accompanying laugh, genuine and booming, projecting across the room. He was a slightly built man, tall and rangy, and one apparently able to skip the onset of middle-age spread. The diamond studs adorning his earlobes matched the chain around his neck visible beneath the collar of a neatly pressed, pink and white striped shirt. The depth of his voice surprised Caslin based solely on his outward appearance. However, he wasn't surprised by the reaction to their visit. His eyes flicked towards Hunter who was unimpressed. The two men standing either side of Clinton Dade remained impassive, not sharing the humour.

"You find the deaths of four people amusing?" Caslin asked.

"I think your attempt to bring it to my door is," Dade countered, the smile fading. Caslin met his eye. There was a gleam of confidence carried within the gaze. If Dade was even slightly thrown by the police presence in his office, then he hid it well. He was a shrewd operator having walked the path of criminality for several decades without falling foul of the law. A handful of convictions during his rise through the criminal ranks was all that put a blot on his copybook but they were distant memories. "I should be offended by your visit," he said, tilting his head to the side and casting an eye to one of his associates who stepped forward.

"I am," the younger man said, fixing Caslin with a stare and failing to hide his animosity towards them. He was tall, powerfully built and wore his hair short, bleached a ridiculous blonde colour setting it in stark contrast to his dark eyes and skin tone.

"And you are?" Hunter asked, drawing the gaze onto her.

"Minding my own business," he replied. Dade raised a hand and placed it gently on his associate's forearm. Caslin saw it as a commanding but affectionate movement.

"Don't worry about Alli," Dade said. "He doesn't care for the attentions of the police."

"If that's the case, perhaps he should make better choices regarding the company he keeps," Caslin said.

"Perhaps," Dade agreed, a half-smile creeping across his face. "So, one of the Fullers' establishments goes up in flames and you look to me? I should expect it to be fair."

"Wouldn't be the first time you and Pete came to blows and dragged the rest of us into it," Caslin said.

"Ancient history. Besides, Pete and I haven't had cause to cross each other's paths in years."

"Largely because he's been inside for decades," Hunter argued.

"Has it been that long?" Dade said, relaxing into his chair and dropping his shoulders ever-so-slightly. "Time certainly flies. What brings you to me?"

"He was sentenced to a minimum of twenty-seven years," Caslin said, stepping forward and placing his hands on the edge of Dade's desk in a very deliberate attempt to undermine his authority by invading his personal space and signifying there was no barrier before him.

"So?"

"So, he's in the home stretch," Caslin stated. "Knowing the type of man he is, I'll bet he has plans for when he gets out. I wouldn't be surprised if you factor in some of them." Dade grinned but on this occasion the humour appeared contrived.

"And what? You think I'm getting in first?" he said. "What possible motivation would I have?"

"Destabilising Pete Fuller's power base before he can get out would be advantageous to you," Caslin said inclining his head thoughtfully. "Particularly bearing in mind the feelings he holds towards you."

"You seriously think I'll be top of his list after two decades behind bars? I wouldn't be surprised if he fancies leaving it all to the boys and putting his feet up somewhere. Maybe he'll head to Cromer. Besides, two more years is a long time in the nick. Anything can happen to an old man."

"You're the same age, aren't you? School friends, if I recall correctly?" Caslin said. Dade nodded slowly.

"A different life."

"What actually happened between the two of you, anyway? It was well before my time but I'm still curious," Caslin asked.

Dade took a deep breath. "It was all a long time ago."

"You tread on his toes? Steal one of his girlfriends?"

"Now, that would have been even further back," Dade said with a grin.

"And yet probably still relevant."

Dade sat forward bringing him ever closer to Caslin who remained leaning forward. The two were so close, Caslin could smell the other's breath.

"Bombing a rival's business is just not my style," Dade explained. "Far too volatile in nature. It would open up the prospect of similar events befalling my own. That wouldn't make a lot of sense."

"Where the two of you come into it sense goes out of the window," Caslin countered.

"Now you listen to me, Mr Caslin," Dade said pointedly, lowering his tone to one of controlled aggression. Now they were seeing a representation of Dade's formidable reputation. "Whatever befalls Pete Fuller, as well as his boys, has nothing to do with me. I'm a businessman. That is all. The past is where it is... where it belongs... and I have no intention of revisiting it."

"If not you, then who?" Caslin asked, holding the gaze for a moment longer before stepping back. Dade also relaxed if only a little.

"You should be looking closer to home," he suggested.

"The Fullers?"

"Exactly," Dade said. "You imagine this is all a result of some long-term power struggle between me and Pete? Your assertion is flawed from the outset."

"How so?"

"Pete still runs his enterprise from his cell make no mistake about that."

"Through his sons, yes," Caslin stated. "So, what's your point?"

"Maybe you're looking at the wrong struggle," Dade said softly. "By your logic, I'm not the only one to have something to lose when the big man gets out."

The door to the office opened behind them and both Caslin and Hunter turned. The arrival stopped abruptly upon catching sight of them.

"I'm sorry, Boss," he said. "I didn't realise you had company." Caslin took in his measure. He was in his early thirties and struck Caslin as familiar but he couldn't place him.

"I know you, don't I?" he asked the newcomer who appeared slightly perplexed. Sensing they were there in an official capacity, his eyes narrowed as he responded.

"I don't think we've met," he said.

"DI Caslin."

The young man shook his head and moved past him, "No. Never met."

"You must forgive Mark, Mr Caslin," Dade said, by way of an apology.

"The young men you surround yourself with are ill-mannered, Clinton," Caslin said, following Mark's passage with his eyes still trying to place him in some context within his memory. The comment made Alli bristle once more.

"I'll be sure to have a word," Dade replied. "Now, if you'll excuse me. We have a business to run."

"If I find out you have anything to do with this, Clinton. There will be no way of stopping me. If you bring a war to the streets of my city, I will tear you down one piece at a time," Caslin said in an icy tone, leaving no one present unclear on the depth of his motivation.

"Any problems with Pete Fuller are all of his own making…" Dade said, matching the tone, "and they have nothing… *nothing* to do with me."

Caslin exhaled, flicking a glance to the associates now lining up behind their boss. All of them displayed hostile expressions. He cracked a smile.

"We'll be seeing you, Clinton."

Reaching the car, Caslin waited for Hunter to unlock it and glanced back towards Clinton Dade's nightclub. The purple and blue colouring adorning the building looked strange in the gloom of the afternoon. Once night fell and the neon lit up, the place would be jumping. One of York's most popular clubs it was the jewel of Dade's organisation and where he could be found most of the time. Having been in and around the criminal fraternity for all of his adult life, it was the illegal rave scene of the early 1990s that saw him make his step up in the food chain. As legislation caught up, he was able to transfer the skills as well as the contacts he'd accumulated and adapt to a rigid presence in the club scene. Now with a string of clubs stretching across the Greater Yorkshire area providing an air of legitimacy to his business affairs, Clinton Dade was a major player. One of the key distributors of illegal drugs across the city, he used those revenues to fuel the rest of his business empire.

"Do you think he's on the level?" Hunter asked.

Caslin admitted he wasn't sure. "It's a tough call. You could make a case for his being behind it but at the same time…"

"His reasoning is just as plausible," Hunter finished for him. Caslin nodded his agreement. "Is Fuller likely to get out soon?"

Caslin shrugged. "Parole boards are unpredictable. I wouldn't like to second guess them. If it were up to me, he'd never see the light of day."

"And what Dade said about the Fullers?"

"Keep it in mind," Caslin suggested. "We'll have to pay Pete a visit."

Hunter started the car and pulled out from the side road turning left in the direction of Fulford. Caslin's phone began to ring and he saw it was Terry Holt.

"Sir," he began, "I've got a response on the red Mercedes. The hire car. It was leased to a man by the name of Brian Jack three days ago."

"Arriving at Manchester Airport?"

"Yes. I've been onto the border Force and he flew in on the 9:15 flight from Almeria."

"Spain," Caslin reiterated for Hunter's benefit glancing over to her. She smiled. "What do we know about him, Terry?"

"Nothing, sir. Brian Jack doesn't appear on any of our records. No priors, no convictions, arrests – the man is a ghost."

"Can you search through the database and see if he's a known associate of anyone we know?"

"Done it, sir," Holt said unequivocally. "Like I said, he's a ghost. I have no record of him at all anywhere in the UK… ever."

"Is he a foreign national?"

"Arrived on a British passport, sir."

"How can that be?" Caslin said, thinking aloud. "He exists. We were looking at him earlier."

"I'm going to check it out, see if I can find when the passport was issued and to which address and so on. Maybe it will become clearer."

"Good. Pass the car's index around and have everyone keep an eye out for it," Caslin said. "I don't want him pulled over. Run it through the number plate recognition database and see if we can see where he's been.

We need to know who this guy is and finding out where he's spending his time might help."

"I've got an idea on that, sir. I'm going to try and get into the car's telematics."

"Tele... what?" Caslin asked.

"Telematics, sir," Holt explained. "Modern cars are pretty much run by computers now and top end marques are selling assistance packages as part of the deal."

"Breakdown cover and so on?"

"More than that even. They can track you pretty much like we can an aeroplane. The car's internal computer sends out a ping, similar to a plane's transponder, and that gets relayed through cell towers to the manufacturer. That way, they know where you are when you need their assistance."

"Are you telling me you'll know where he is?"

"And where he's been," Holt added. "Before you get your hopes up though, let me flesh it out first."

"In case it doesn't work, Terry?" he asked playfully.

"That's about it, yes, sir."

Caslin hung up, "The world is moving forward at pace, Sarah."

"Sir?" she asked, confused.

He shook his head indicating for her not to worry about it. Turning his eye to the passing landscape, he mulled over the details of what he learned from the conversation with Dade. The CCTV from inside the minicab office was indicative of an inside job. It must have been a member of Fuller's crew who placed the bomb. No one else would have found the office so accessible. The hacking of the security system would have been possible via an external source but the suspected bomber was clearly known to the occupants. At the very least they were acquaintances and possibly even friends. Dade implied the Fullers had their own internal tug-of-war going on but for that to escalate into bombing one of their own establishments was bordering on lunacy.

"That guy, the one who came in right before we left," Caslin said. "Where do I know him from?"

"I know," Hunter agreed. "I had the same feeling but I can't place him. What was his name... Mark, was it?"

"Yes, that was it," Caslin said. "It'll come to me."

CHAPTER TEN

THERE WERE no skid marks visible on the road. The volume of rainfall overnight left a visible sheen on the surface. Caslin looked back up the road, analysing the curve of the bend as well as the adverse camber. An open stretch of highway such as this would undoubtedly see traffic moving at speed over and above the set limit for the road. They were surrounded on both sides by farmland, flat and fertile, running alongside the River Ouse. The highway was raised above the level of the land to keep the road open should the flood plain ever be required. Looking in the direction of travel, Caslin followed the route of the car. The four trenches gouged into the grass verge denoted where the vehicle left the road, doing so at a sideways angle with the driver having lost control in what must have been a four-wheel drift.

Grateful for the road closure, a police cordon was currently in effect a half-mile to the east and west, Caslin began the short walk back to the impact site. Several officers were walking the length of the road one hundred feet in each direction to try and spot any debris that may indicate the occurrence of a collision leading to the accident. Caslin reached the verge and circumvented the forensics officers, measuring and documenting where the car had left the road. Stepping up on to the bank, he looked down on the activity beneath him. Hunter saw him and offered a wave beckoning him down by way of a short path to his left. He acknowledged her but remained where he was for another moment, surveying the crash site.

The car left the road at a significant speed striking the verge at an angle with enough momentum to lift the car up and over, flipping it into the air before coming to rest on its roof at the foot of the embankment. Pieces of metal, plastic and broken glass were strewn all around them due to the car's collision with a copse of trees on its way through before coming to rest. The mangled wreckage was such that Caslin knew no one would have stepped from it alive. Checking his footing, he descended the bank to be met by Hunter as he found stable ground.

"Just the one occupant in the vehicle, sir," she said.

"Brian Jack?"

"Yes, sir," Hunter confirmed, glancing back at what used to be a prestigious make of car but was now good for nothing apart from scrap. "Early assessment suggests he would have died upon impact. We think he clipped several trees before coming to a stop where you see it now."

"Any witnesses to the car leaving the road?"

"No, sir," Hunter confirmed, looking at her notes. "Nor is there anything to indicate what caused him to lose control."

"Was he on the phone?"

"The car's bluetooth wasn't in sync with a mobile phone."

"Hire car… he might not have bothered. Have we found a handset?"

"No, not yet but we haven't finished the search. Judging by how fast we think the car was travelling, the area to cover is going to be pretty large."

"What about the victim?"

Hunter produced an evidence bag and Caslin could see a wallet within it. She passed him a set of latex gloves and he put them on while she opened the bag and removed the contents. Passing it over to him, Caslin inspected them. There were several credit cards, none of which were registered to UK banks. They appeared to be Spanish. There were business cards for a swimming pool cleaning company along with a property maintenance firm. All of them carried the name of Brian Jack.

"Pool cleaning must be quite lucrative," Caslin said, casting an eye over at the smashed Mercedes.

"We're in the wrong business, sir," Hunter said.

"Tell myself that every day," Caslin smiled. He returned the cards to the folds of the wallet and checked the remaining pockets. Apart from approximately two-hundred pounds in cash there was nothing of interest.

Passing the wallet back to Hunter, she resealed the evidence bag. Caslin walked over to inspect the car itself.

Coming to the driver's side, he found the door open. The angle, along with the severe warping of the shape, indicated a forceful impact. Iain Robertson, clad in his forensic coveralls, was knelt by the door analysing the interior. The body of Brian Jack was visible beyond him, suspended upside down and still sitting in the driver's seat. As he approached, Caslin could see the deceased man was held in position by more than merely the seatbelt. Coming to stand behind Robertson, Caslin knelt and looked up. The branch of the tree had been torn from the trunk by the force of the collision but not before punching through the windscreen and piercing the body of the driver. The branch now protruded through the body and also the rear of the seat. Easily measuring four inches in thickness, it had punctured Jack's right-hand side, travelling in a diagonal direction upwards and exiting the body just below the left shoulder blade. The windscreen itself had shattered but the glass was held in place, sprayed with blood spatter, as was the roof of the cabin.

"That had to hurt," he said aloud, drawing Robertson's attention.

"How much he would have known about it is another matter entirely," Robertson replied, greeting Caslin.

"Let's hope so," Caslin said with a frown. "It certainly made a mess of him."

"Yes, it did," Robertson sighed. "His right hand has been partially severed at the wrist. Cause of death will probably be penetrating force trauma but I'll leave that to Alison to confirm."

"Any idea how long it will take you to free him up?" Caslin asked, considering when the body could be shipped to pathology for Dr Taylor to begin her examination.

"You got somewhere you need to be?"

Caslin laughed, "Any early thoughts?"

"A few," Robertson said, standing up. "I think the car was travelling in excess of seventy miles per hour when it left the road. Judging from the impact on the verge, I'd suggest before he lost control he was going even faster. The speed would have declined as the car lost grip and the driver lost control but there was no way he would have made the bend in the road, not at that speed. I'll put a proper calculation together later."

"Have you got a cause?"

"I can rule things out rather than in at this point," Robertson explained. "Once we can get what's left of the car back to the workshop, we'll strip it down and analyse the mechanicals. It's virtually brand new though, barely ten thousand miles on the clock if I had to guess. I haven't been able to reinitialise the digital dash but the index has it as registered this year. Tyre treads show minimal wear and a cursory inspection of the brake disks hasn't thrown up anything to make me think they are faulty. I'll caveat that by saying you'll have to wait before I will go definitive on that."

"Could we be looking at something non-mechanical?"

Robertson eyed him warily, "You're expecting foul play?"

"Wouldn't rule it out," Caslin said, scanning the length of the car.

"I'll check out the obvious, brake lines, fuel lines and so on. Likewise, once I'm able to download the files from the engine management system, I'll run the diagnostics. There's always the possibility of a power steering failure. Should that happen at high speed or any speed above forty, for that matter, keeping the car on the road could become problematic. There is also this," Robertson said, pointing to the rear and indicating for Caslin to join him.

They walked to the back and then around to the nearside of the car. The ground was wet and slippery and both men took care with their footing. Caslin took in the damage to the bodywork, it was substantial. Robertson pointed out a specific section of the rear-quarter panel, just behind the wheel. The body of the car was scuffed from the edge of the arch back to and including the moulded bumper. Caslin questioned the finding with a flick of his eyes. Robertson produced a powerful Maglite and aimed the beam on the paintwork. Caslin looked closer.

"What am I looking at?" he asked.

"Red paint," Robertson said.

"The car is red, Iain."

"Look closer," Robertson pointed out, inclining his head to where he was focusing the beam. "It's a different shade of red." Caslin moved closer and at first, he couldn't make it out but as his eyes adjusted, he saw the scrape. Roughly half an inch wide with a couple of smaller scuffs running above the largest, the paint here appeared to be of a darker shade. "More of a burgundy, I would suggest."

"Agreed," Caslin said. "A collision with another vehicle?"

Robertson shrugged, "I wouldn't jump to a conclusion. You'll need to contact the hire company. There's every possibility it's historic and unrelated to the accident. This could easily be the result of poor driving in a car park somewhere."

"It could also be a PIT manoeuvre?" Caslin suggested, referring to the pursuit intervention technique where a fleeing vehicle is tagged at that specific point of the bodywork, causing the car to shift abruptly sideways and out of control. To carry out such an action at speeds in excess of seventy miles per hour on this type of road would lead to a catastrophic outcome. Casting an eye across the scene, Caslin figured that this description was certainly apt.

"The thought had occurred," Robertson said. "Have you identified any reason why he would be a target?"

"Not yet but there's quite a lot of movement around this guy and I'm yet to figure it out."

"WHAT DO we have on Brian Jack?"

"Not a lot, sir," Hunter said. "I've checked with both Europol and Interpol and he isn't on either of their radars."

"I've also made some discreet inquiries about his business interests in southern Spain, sir," Holt said. "He has a number of low-key contracts with the ex-pat communities located in and around the city of Alicante and further along the coast as far as Torrevieja."

"What kind of contracts?" Caslin said, staring at their information board and almost willing a connection to reveal itself.

"Principally in property management and maintenance," Holt confirmed. "Smaller apartment complexes rather than your large hotel chains."

"No issues with the local police?"

"None reported, sir," Holt said, tossing his pen onto the file before him. "His businesses started up from scratch three years ago. I spoke with a very helpful lady who is chair of a group representing the interests of UK citizens abroad."

"Sounds political," Caslin said, frowning.

"You would think, wouldn't you?" Holt said with a grin. "They are more of a social club from what I can gather. Organising the lawn bowls competition and barbecues."

"And she knew him?"

"Well enough. She said he was popular and had rapidly established a presence over there."

"And business was good?"

"She thought so. Although, she did voice her bewilderment at why a man of his age was so driven to launch a business at his time of life. I got the impression most of them were keen to focus on leisure time more than anything else."

"He was a bit of a workaholic?"

"That's not how I took it, sir. She raised his health as being a particular issue."

"What about it?"

Holt shook his head, "Didn't give me the specifics. I don't think she knew. Could have been gossip."

"Have any links to MacEwan surfaced or other known contacts?" Caslin said, looking to Hunter. She shook her head in the negative.

"Nothing."

"Keep digging. Brian Jack came back to the UK for a reason and we need to know what it was. The last time we saw him he was looking decidedly unhappy. Why?"

"We'll keep at it, sir," Hunter stated. Caslin stood up and reached for his coat.

"Alison Taylor has the pathology report on Jody Wyer's death ready for us and I'll see if I can draw the preliminaries out of her regarding Jack's demise while I'm there."

Caslin stepped out of the office and almost bumped into Kyle Broadfoot who was coming the other way. He stopped him in his tracks glancing over his shoulder in such a way that led Caslin to assume he didn't wish to be overheard.

"Sir," Caslin said by way of greeting.

"Where are we with the Wyer case?" he asked. Caslin was momentarily thrown. The more pressing case was surely the bombing in central York.

"Progressing, sir," Caslin said. "But at this stage we are still short of any motive although we have several lines of inquiry to follow up on. I'm just heading over to pathology to discuss the manner of his death with Alison."

"I'll walk with you, if you don't mind?" Broadfoot said, gesturing with an open hand for Caslin to come alongside. The two men set off and Caslin felt a little awkward. His superior was taking such an interest in this particular case that he sensed there was more going on than he knew. He chose to test the waters.

"What can you tell me about Jody Wyer, sir?" Caslin asked as they walked.

"A fine young man."

"You knew him well?"

"Well enough, yes."

"In what capacity?" Caslin asked. Broadfoot stopped, turning to face him. "Sir," Caslin added as an afterthought.

"Why do I get the sense that you are investigating me, Nathaniel?" Caslin raised his eyebrows and exhaled heavily.

"Probably because I am, sir," he said, seeing little sense in dressing it up. "Figuratively speaking. I wouldn't say you're not being straight with me but let's be clear, you're not telling me everything that you know."

Broadfoot drew breath, glancing along the corridor as a uniformed officer came into view before passing through a doorway and disappearing once again. "I knew Jody," he said under his breath. "I have a relationship with him beyond his use to Major Crimes."

"I see," Caslin said. That wasn't the response he'd anticipated. "What's the nature of it?"

"Personal," Broadfoot explained. "I knew Jody's father, Keith, quite well. He was my mentor when I came through the ranks."

"I didn't realise you came through the ranks, sir?" Caslin said honestly. He'd always figured Broadfoot to be what the rank and file referred to as a 'plastic' – a policeman recruited from university and advanced up the chain as swiftly as possible having never actually seen any front-line action. If Broadfoot was offended, he didn't show it.

"It was a short-lived period," he explained, "but one that shaped my views of the service. Keith Wyer was a top detective and when he asked me to be Godfather to his son, I wouldn't have dreamed of saying no." Caslin did some mental arithmetic.

"I understand that he lost his father relatively recently."

"That's right."

"Bearing in mind Jody's age…"

"I know where you're going, Nathaniel. He was a surprise to both his parents. A welcome one, I assure you. I think Keith and Sandra found it difficult… having a child so late in life. Sandra passed away some years ago. She never even got to see him graduate from school."

"Is that why you want us on this case, sir?" Caslin asked. "I'd understand. I mean… I don't need to tell you it's probably not something you should be involved in… but I understand."

Broadfoot shook his head, "I'm not using your resource to settle a personal outrage, Nathaniel. Jody contacted me a few weeks ago and said he'd come across something he thought I should know."

"And that was?"

"Genuinely, I don't know," Broadfoot said, lowering his voice. "But he wouldn't have come to me without being sure I would be interested. That's not his way."

"He must have said something."

"Only that he was gathering information and once he had it straight in his own head, he would bring it to me. I asked if I could help but he declined."

"How did he sound?"

"Looking back, I would say stressed. Agitated," Broadfoot said. "He has always been quite an anxious chap. Therefore, his mannerisms often reflected that. I didn't think too much of it at the time but now..."

Caslin glanced about them. They were very much alone in the corridor. "I'll get to the bottom of it, sir."

"Thank you, Nathaniel," Broadfoot said with gratitude before his expression clouded over in a show of apprehension. "And I know I've no right to ask this of you but-"

"It will remain between us, sir," Caslin said, understanding the fear. "Tell me, did Jody ever mention a new girlfriend to you? Perhaps, someone he may have met recently."

Broadfoot thought hard on it before shaking his head. "No. I'm sorry. He didn't mention anyone. Was he seeing somebody?"

"It would appear so, yes," Caslin replied. "I'll get on then, sir."

"By all means," Broadfoot said, giving him his blessing to leave. "Oh... and, Nathaniel?" Caslin stopped, looking back over his shoulder. "Thank you."

"Don't mention it, sir," Caslin said, acknowledging the sentiment.

CHAPTER ELEVEN

THE HINGE on the refrigerator door creaked as it opened, the handle snapping shut once released. The sounds echoed throughout Dr Taylor's pathology laboratory. Caslin shuddered, feeling the cold.

"How do you spend all day in this?" he asked, referencing the artificial light and the somewhat sterile surroundings they were standing in. Alison Taylor laughed.

"Some people surround themselves with the living," she explained, "while others, prefer the peace and quiet."

"You don't have children, do you?" Caslin asked playfully. She returned his smile.

"It's not only children that people like me choose to avoid. Some of the adults are more than irritating," she said, inclining her head in his direction.

"That's cold," he countered.

"A lot like your friend here," she said, pulling out the rack upon which Jody Wyer lay. Reaching over, she grasped the fastener and unzipped the bag drawing it down to just below his chest. Leaving Caslin to take his first look at the deceased since he was pulled from the water, she crossed to her desk and returned with her notes in hand.

"How did he die?" Caslin asked, as she ordered her paperwork.

"He suffered a low velocity impact to the back of his skull. A depressed fracture formed at the impact point leading to a severe contusion as the bone fragments ruptured the subcutaneous blood vessels. On the periphery, I found further fractures radiating out from the impact point," she explained, producing x-rays from her file. "You'll see here," she passed him one of them. "The radiating fractures stop when they meet the sutures."

"You said it was low velocity?" Caslin asked, seeking clarification.

"Yes. Human bone is relatively elastic in form, you'll probably be surprised to know. The response of the bone to the strain, or load if you will, depends on the velocity and magnitude of the force. A slow load would lead to injuries consistent with a car accident, for example, falls from height or an assault. Whereas a rapid load, or higher velocity, is attributed to ballistic injuries, discharge of firearms, munitions or explosives and so on."

"Any chance of his death resulting from a fall?"

"No, I don't believe so," Dr Taylor explained. "In general, specific types of load will produce characteristic fracture patterns. Low speed injuries involving a wide area typically produce linear fractures. When the force is applied over a wide surface such as with a fall from height it allows the kinetic energy to be absorbed and thus results in smaller injuries. Whereas a localised application of force is far more destructive. The shape and size of the object used to apply the load is highly associated with the resulting fracture pattern."

"So, he was definitely struck with an implement," Caslin said, nodding gravely.

"Without doubt. When the head is struck with or strikes an object with a broad flat surface area, the skull at the point of impact flattens out to conform to the shape of the surface against which it impacts."

"That elasticity you mentioned?" Caslin asked, she nodded. "How quickly did he die?"

"I would have thought you're looking at minutes rather than hours."

"We are working on the theory that he was assaulted in a car park in the town and then the body was later dumped in the water," Caslin explained.

"Yes, Iain Robertson was good enough to pass on his initial thoughts," Dr Taylor said. "I think you are correct."

"Any suggestion of the type of weapon used?"

"A hammer is my best guess," she explained. "The effusion of blood into the surrounding tissue is such that the weapon was rounded and evidently packing a hefty weight. Blows from a stick, bat or some kind of rod will often leave parallel linear haemorrhages. These injuries are rounded and even though the end of a stick *could* also result in a similar pattern due to the length of those types of weapon, the edges would likely be irregular and the lengths greater as they come in contact with the skin."

"A hammer," Caslin repeated almost to himself.

"There are two reasons why I think he died shortly after the attack."

"Go on," Caslin said.

"Firstly, the extent of the bruising. Usually these injuries see a blue colouring appear within the first few hours and, as I'm sure you know, these colours change as the tissue reacts to the spread of the blood giving rise to some magnificent colouration."

"It has been known on occasion," Caslin said with a wry smile.

"You'll see swelling, damage to the epithelium, extravasations and coagulation… to name but a few."

"I'll take your word for it, Alison."

"These occur within hours of the injury providing it happens ante-mortem and that's why I can be confident he died almost immediately."

"There wasn't much of that?"

"Totally absent in this case," she confirmed. "Secondly, if the victim had been alive when he was placed in the water, he would have ingested a significant level of sediment in doing so as he sought to breathe. Whether he was conscious or not is largely irrelevant. I would not necessarily expect to find indications of that in his stomach but certainly there would be large deposits within his lungs and there is no sign at all."

"He was dead when he went into the water," Caslin stated.

"Absolutely," Dr Taylor nodded. "His lungs were clear of water, so he didn't drown. Prior to death, he exhibited no signs of poor health. I would say he was above average in his general levels of diet and fitness. Toxicology reports came back as clear of any illicit substances."

"What about prescription drugs?" Caslin asked. "I came across a bottle of anti-depressants with his name on at his house."

"Yes, I picked up on that but they were low-level doses indicative of a mild approach to his treatment."

"Rather than?"

"In all likelihood, a condition that was either being managed at an early stage or one not considered to be too debilitating, rather than one needing a sterner intervention," Dr Taylor concluded. "However, his GP will be better placed to confirm his treatment."

"Great," Caslin said, looking past Alison towards her autopsy area as if he was searching for something.

"If you're wondering how I'm getting on with the RTA victim, I haven't started the procedure as yet," she said, raising her eyebrows.

"I *was* thinking about getting your initial thoughts," Caslin said doing his best to mask his impatience. Dr Taylor's face split a broad smile.

"Well, it's a good job I know you as well as I do then," she said, zipping up Jody Wyer's body bag. Caslin stepped back to allow her room to slide the tray back into the refrigerator. He closed the door ensuring the latch locked into place. "This way," she said to him as he passed back the copies of the x-rays he was still holding.

Leading him through to her office, she put Wyer's file down and picked up another, handing it Caslin. He opened the manila folder and perused the contents.

"What am I looking at?" he asked.

"He was in a bit of a state once they managed to get him out of the wreck," she said. "As I say, I've not begun the autopsy yet but when I assessed him upon arrival, I noted several surgical procedures had taken place. Nothing that looked particularly fresh but even so, clearly planned surgical procedures."

"For what?"

"You'll have to wait for confirmation of that, I'm afraid. However, I do have a working theory," she said. "Now, due to the delay in cutting him out of the vehicle, I set to work on some of the blood samples Iain's team were able to provide. He sensed you were keen to get a move on with this one, so we thought we'd get ahead."

"And?"

"Toxicological reports indicated a blood-alcohol level that proved definitively he hadn't been drinking. Nor was he under the influence of any substance as far as I can tell. However, the tox screen did come back with some interesting results."

"Interesting how?" Caslin asked.

"There are significant levels of a drug called *Pembrolizumab* in his system," she said, pointing to a chart that Caslin had before him. "This is a relatively recent addition to the arsenal used to treat cancer, one of eleven new drugs approved by the European Medicines Agency last year. It is the first cancer immunotherapy drug that has shown, in some cases, a greater efficiency than chemotherapy in first-line treatment of non-small lung cancer."

"Lung cancer," Caslin said.

"But that's not all," Dr Taylor continued. "Although considered a clinical breakthrough and widely available it is not one that we use in a large capacity here in the UK. So, that got me thinking."

"Where does he undergo his treatment?"

"Exactly," she explained. "I ran a check in our database and found no hits under his name in the UK. Your understanding is that he is resident in Spain, is that correct?"

"It is."

"Stands to reason. Spain is one of the medical tourism hotspots when it comes to cancer treatments," she said. "Their clinics have excellent ties with research institutes and their pricing structure and success rates often makes them an excellent choice in comparison to travelling to the US or Israel, for example."

"I'll bear it in mind," Caslin said. "This is all very fascinating but how does this move us along?"

"I was surprised that a UK citizen with such a condition has no medical history whatsoever in their home nation. I would have expected to be able to locate some medical history of some description."

"Good point," Caslin agreed. "We only have him appearing on the Spanish radar a few years ago. He must have lived somewhere and it doesn't appear to be here."

"I suppose he could have been living previously almost anywhere," Dr Taylor continued. "On a hunch, I explored the idea further by looking for some of the telltale signs that give away where medical treatment takes place.

"What type of signs?" Caslin asked, finding his curiosity piqued.

"Dental work is one of the most common. The amalgam fillings we use are of a different composition to that used on the continent for example."

"I would never have known," Caslin said. "Any luck?"

"Yes. His teeth showed many signs of decay and I can spot our fillings quite easily. Some of the work was done many years ago, so he was certainly treated in the UK. I took his prints and ran them through the system."

"We've already done that," Caslin said. "We didn't get a hit."

"Not through a PNC check, no," she interrupted him. "But you didn't run it through the Ministry of Defence files, did you?"

"No, we didn't," Caslin said. "Did you find a match?"

Alison Taylor nodded, "Yes. Royal Navy. He served twelve years."

"Go on," Caslin said, captivated. He knew her well enough to know when she was holding back.

"His real name is Philip Bradley. He was a Lieutenant but that's not all."

"Well?" Caslin asked, fostering his impatience.

"He was recorded as having died two years ago," she said, reaching across and leafing through a couple of pages in the file Caslin was holding and only stopping when she reached a copy of the official death certificate. Caslin scanned the document. A brief inspection revealed the dates corresponded more or less with Brian Jack's appearance in southern Spain.

"Well, I'll be damned," Caslin mumbled.

"PHILIP BRADLEY," Hunter said, approaching the noticeboard and attaching his MoD photograph next to a shot of David MacEwan, taken the day before when they observed the meeting at the scrap yard. "He served in the Royal Navy on a succession of deployments. He was present on HMS Invincible when she was sent to the Falklands."

"Any issues with his record?" Caslin asked. Hunter shook her head.

"No, his record was clean. I have his performance reviews here and he is described as both competent and diligent. However, his final appraisal back in 1983 stated he wasn't considered as having the *necessary potential for further advancement*. He left the navy eighteen months later."

"He wasn't going anywhere," Caslin said. "Where did he go next?"

"You'll not believe it, sir," Hunter said. "He came to us."

"The police?"

Hunter nodded, "Yes. He was originally from Leeds, growing up in Chapel Allerton in the north east of the city. He joined North Yorkshire Constabulary straight from his time with the navy and remained there until he transferred over to Greater Manchester in the late 1980s. He served with them reaching the level of Detective Chief Inspector until his registered time of death two years ago."

"Well, yesterday he was looking good for a guy who's been dead for two years," Caslin said, staring intently at the photograph on the board. "How was his demise reported at the time?"

"He was apparently killed aboard a yacht in an accident sailing in the North Sea," Hunter read out from her notes.

"What type of accident?" Caslin asked.

"The boat caught fire. There was an explosion," Hunter said. "The crew managed to issue a mayday call and the coastguard dispatched a helicopter along with a crew from the nearest RNLI station. When they located the ship, it was burnt out with the survivors having decamped into a lifeboat."

"And Bradley?"

"Killed in the initial explosion," Hunter said.

"At least, that's what was recorded," Caslin stated the obvious. "Witnesses?"

"Yes, sir. There were three others crewing the ship including the captain and owner of the vessel."

"If Bradley was declared dead, they must have recovered his body," Caslin said. Hunter nodded.

"Yes, the RNLI attempted to recover the vessel but it sank as they towed it back to port. What they thought was Bradley's body was fished out of the water and later identified as his."

"Well, we know that wasn't the case," Caslin said. "Who identified the body?"

Hunter returned to her notes, "Scott Tarbet. The boat's captain. He was Bradley's cousin and so was taken at his word. The other two witnesses confirmed seeing the boat go up in the explosion with Bradley aboard."

"And they were?"

"Greg Tower and Toby Ford," Hunter said.

"What do we know about them?"

"Greg Tower is deceased. Died in a car crash last year," Hunter confirmed.

"Are we sure of that?" Caslin asked with no intended sarcasm.

"I'll look into it, sir."

"And the other… what was it… Ford?"

"Toby Ford, sir," Hunter said, hesitantly. Caslin picked up on it as did Holt, lifting his head from the notes he was making. "Chief Superintendent Toby Ford is still serving with Greater Manchester Police, sir."

"Now that does make things interesting, doesn't it?" Caslin said with a smile. The other two failed to see anything amusing about it. "Terry, I want you to go through Bradley's time with GMP. See what his career highlights were. By all means take a look at his time with us as well but Manchester is more likely to be relevant. It's interesting that our friend Tony Mason also served with the same constabulary. I wonder if you'll find an overlap between the two. Did they work together or have any affiliations with each other? It's a bit of a coincidence for them to be moving in this circle without having some sort of shared past. Let's see how far it goes back but be discreet. Sarah," he said, turning to Hunter, "any idea of where the captain of the boat is now?"

Hunter returned to her notes, "Tarbet is registered at an address in Whitby."

"Good," Caslin said. "I love a trip to the coast."

CHAPTER TWELVE

PASSING out through the last remaining suburb of the north-eastern edge of Whitby, Caslin looked over his right shoulder as the water came into view. He could see the ruined remains of Whitby Abbey standing proudly on the point overlooking the town commanding as much attention now as it would have done over the previous centuries. As the coastal road descended closer to sea level, the white caps of the waves on the North Sea appeared ominous. The car was buffeted by the wind and although the skies were clear of the brooding storm clouds of recent days, there was no guarantee it would remain so.

They were heading to Sandsend, a couple of miles out of Whitby. A small village located along the route of the three-mile beach running all the way to Whitby's harbour. The approach road had a large hotel and golf course to one side with the sand and sea to the other. Along the length of the final mile of the descent were parking facilities, only a car's width but running top to tail down to the village. For most of the year space would be at a premium, however, currently in the off-season and with the weather cutting, many people were driven inland and away from the coast.

Turning his gaze out to sea, Caslin expected to see windsurfers, kayaks and the like. Today, the sea was empty beyond the cargo ships passing by in their designated lanes, hugging the coast for its safety and security. Hunter pulled off the road near to the base of the hill parking as close as she could get to the village. Caslin could see their destination. Getting out of the car, he drew his coat around him as the sanctuary of the interior was traded for the bitter easterly wind. The red flags were up along the shoreline denoting the water was off limits, deemed far too dangerous, hence the lack of activity. A few dog walkers braved the conditions, enjoying their time when the animals were permitted on the sand.

Caslin stepped over to the fence looking down at the immense concrete construction of the tiered sea wall defending the coastal cliffs from the ravages of nature. He tasted the salt on his lips as he cast an eye along the beach towards Whitby. The view was obscured by what appeared to be fog but Caslin knew better. The wind was whipping up the sand into a mist of sorts, obscuring the town in the distance.

"I bloody love this place," he said under his breath.

"What's that, sir?" Hunter called to him, returning from purchasing their ticket from the parking meter.

"Nothing," he replied, gesturing for them to head along the path. On the opposite side of the road, facing the sea, were a run of Victorian terraced houses along with a smaller group of more recent buildings. They all had signs picketed outside denoting they were for sale. For a brief moment, Caslin wondered what it would be like to live here but quickly dismissed the notion. There was no way he'd be able to afford one of those along the seafront.

At the foot of the hill they found the road narrowing as it turned inland before crossing an inlet by way of a narrow stone bridge. Cars travelling in opposing directions needed to take turns in crossing. On the seafront itself, they walked past a tourist information office, a snack bar and an outfit where you could hire kayaks or surfboards. None of them were doing a roaring trade. Beyond those buildings, they entered an area set aside for the numerous small fishing boats pulled from the water and placed behind the sea wall.

Ahead of them was the lifeboat station, its doors open with both the main boat, rigid-hulled inflatable and all-terrain track vehicle present and ready to be called upon. A few more commercial enterprises completed the run of buildings but they passed these. Calling at Scott Tarbet's address earlier, they were directed here. The neighbours advised them he spent much of his time out on the water and even on days such as this could be found pottering around the sailing club. The sailing club was little more than a shack and a launching station for the locals to set off from or lift their boats from the water.

One man could be seen sitting in the stern of an aging fishing boat. They approached him. He glanced over at them before returning his focus to what he was doing. As they came closer, Caslin could see he was either repairing or inspecting a net.

"Scott Tarbet?" he called up.

"Depends on who's asking," the man replied.

"Detective Inspector Caslin," he said, brandishing his warrant card. The man briefly looked down at them but clearly didn't pay much attention to the identification.

"In that case," he said, putting the mass of blue netting down and standing up. Coming to the port side, he leant on the edge with both hands. "What can I do for you?"

"We wanted to speak to you regarding your cousin, Philip Bradley," Caslin said. "Specifically, about the day he died."

"Why on earth do you want to drag all that up for?" Tarbet protested. "I can't see as there is anything more to say."

"Nice boat," Caslin said, casting a glance over it. Tarbet nodded.

"Yeah," he said, glancing from bow to stern. "It's seen better days but it gets me out on the water."

"A bit of a change to what you used to go out on the water in, isn't it?" Hunter asked, referencing Tarbet's former yacht. The man stared at her. She had touched a nerve, intentionally or otherwise.

"Yes, it is," he replied with no edge to his tone at all. "I'm presuming you know what happened to the last one then?" he said, looking first at Caslin and then to Hunter. They both nodded. "Ah well, it was all a long time ago. We used to love going out on the water, the wife and me. These days… it's just not the same anymore."

"This your boat?" Caslin asked. Tarbet looked at him. Then he looked away.

"Yes, this is my boat," Tarbet asked. "What of it?"

"Your last boat was more of a yacht wasn't it?"

"Things change," Tarbet said, glancing at Caslin.

"No one could blame you for losing your passion for sailing."

"I still have the passion just not the money," Tarbet stated. "My lifelong dream was to have a boat like that. I guess you should be careful what you wish for."

"Did the insurance not cover a replacement?"

"Insurance didn't pay out. The bastards."

"I read in the file that there was some sort of question mark as to how the explosion occurred," said Hunter.

"Then why are you asking?"

"Humour us," Caslin said.

"Question mark, you say? That's a euphemism. Like things weren't shit enough already," Tarbet said, his shoulders dropping as he visually deflated. "As you've most likely read, they felt there was some kind of tampering with the fuel line. I'd wanted that boat all my life and they reckon after eighteen months I would burn it just for the money? Ridiculous. The insurance money wouldn't have been enough to replace the damn boat."

"Did you fight it?" asked Caslin.

"Still am," Tarbet said. "But you didn't come all this way to talk to me about my insurance claims, did you?"

"No, we didn't," Caslin confirmed. "We wanted to ask you when was the last time you saw Philip Bradley?"

Tarbet fixed him with a stare. His expression was mixed, one of anger and mild confusion. He held the eye contact for longer than was comfortable almost as if he was trying to gauge what answer Caslin might really be after. "What?"

"You heard me right," Caslin said. "I want to know when you last saw your cousin."

"Are you taking the piss?"

Caslin shrugged, "No, I'm deadly serious."

"Well, if you are then you'll already know," Tarbet said. "I last saw him two years ago."

"The night he died?"

"Yes," Tarbet said, anger edging into his tone. "Not far from this spot," he continued, looking over his shoulder and out at the North Sea. "And I see him every night in my dreams."

"You identified his body, didn't you?" Hunter asked.

Tarbet turned his gaze on her, "Yes. What of it?"

"So, you would be very surprised to hear that Philip was alive and well until yesterday morning?"

"What?"

"It would appear your cousin Philip has been living in southern Spain for the last couple of years," Caslin said.

"Don't be daft," Tarbet dismissed the notion, his eyes narrowing slightly. "I watched him die out there… on my boat."

"So, he would like us all to believe," Caslin said. Tarbet looked at him trying to take a measure of Caslin's integrity, unsure whether Caslin was on the level.

"Are you serious?"

"We are interested to know who it was you identified as your cousin," Hunter said. "Because somebody was buried but we know for certain it wasn't Philip."

"But… but… *it was Philip*. I'm sure it was," Tarbet stammered.

"Apparently not," Caslin said. "How could you have been mistaken?"

"He was so badly burned," Tarbet said, a confused expression on his face, thinking hard. "But I recognised his wedding ring and the clothes he was wearing matched his. At least, that's what I remember. You must have made some kind of mistake."

"Quite sure we haven't," Caslin said. "What about the other two on the boat with you that night?"

"What about them? They were Phil's mates, not mine."

"Had you not met them before?"

"No, I hadn't. Phil asked me to take them out on the water as a favour. If I'd known how it was going to turn out I would have said no."

"What can you tell us about that night?" Caslin asked.

"We had had a good day. They were a decent enough bunch of guys. I wanted to head back in but they insisted on staying out. They wanted to see the coastline lit up after dark. The weather was good, so I didn't see any harm. Phil wanted to go below and put his feet up. I figured it was a mixture of alcohol and the waves. Some people really struggle once they're out on the water. To this day I still don't know what happened but there was a fire. It quickly took hold."

"The fuel line," Caslin said.

"So they say. I was bringing the sails in so that we could return to the harbour. I always did so under the motor and it was when I initiated the engine that everything went wrong. The controls didn't respond and I went to go below to check what was going on and that's when I saw the flames. I called out to Philip but he didn't answer."

"What happened then?" Hunter asked.

"The others began to panic," Tarbet stated. "I can't blame them. It was dark and we were some way off the coast. The electricity shorted out soon after and we were thrown into complete darkness. I had to rely on battery backups to put in the emergency call. It was an easy decision to make to abandon ship. At least it would have been if Phil had been with us. I had no choice."

"The three of you left together?" Caslin asked.

Tarbet nodded, "We pulled the life raft and got off as quickly as we could. We kept calling for Phil but he never answered and he never came back above deck."

"And you are sure he was still below?"

"I don't see how he could not have been," Tarbet stated. "Then there was the explosion."

"The report we have says the yacht sank as it was being towed back to port. Is that right?"

"That's right. The boat capsized. The explosion must have holed it under the water. The water put the fire out so by the time the lifeboat crew got to us they were able to retrieve Phil's body before the boat sank."

"How was his health in the time before the lead up to his death? I mean, before the accident at sea?"

"How do you mean?"

"Are you aware of any illness that he was suffering from?" Caslin asked. Tarbet thought about it for a moment before shaking his head.

"Fine as far as I know but he probably wouldn't have told me, anyway. We weren't all that close," he said. "Why do you ask?"

"It doesn't matter. I'm just trying to get a picture of the man. Have you any idea why he would fake his death?"

Tarbet shook his head, "No. It's like something out of a film."

"How often did you see each other?" Hunter asked.

"On and off... occasionally, family events and suchlike."

"Are you surprised by any of this?"

"Damn right, I am," Tarbet said with a snort of laughter. "You say he died yesterday? What happened?"

"Car accident."

"What was he doing?"

"That's exactly what we are trying to find out," Caslin said. "You identified him because you were his closest next-of-kin. You mentioned his wedding ring, was he married?"

"Divorced. He had been for a while. Marion went on some around the world trip with her sister. When she got back, she didn't fancy waiting hand and foot on Phil anymore."

"She left him?"

"Quicker than you can book a plane ticket!" Tarbet said, shaking his head. "Don't blame her, really."

"Why not?"

"Phil was a control freak, always had to be the one to make the final call on everything. I'll bet she couldn't breathe."

"You seem remarkably calm about all this," Caslin said.

"What were you expecting? Did you think I would jump up and down… scream or something? Not really my thing," Tarbet argued. "Listen, I've got several years on you son, done a few more laps of the track if you know what I mean? There's not a lot that will surprise me these days."

"I thought you might be pissed off. If a relative of mine screwed me over, I would be pretty annoyed."

"Well that's where you and me differ, isn't it?"

"I guess it is, yes," Caslin said. "Are you married?"

Tarbet nodded slowly "I was."

"Did she take off with Marion as well?"

"No, she died last year, but thanks for the memory."

Caslin looked away. He was seeking to ruffle the man's feathers but hadn't expected that answer. Now he felt pretty small and justifiably so. Hunter glanced at him. She didn't have to say anything. Her disapproval was evident in her eyes. "I'm sorry, I didn't know."

"How could you?" Tarbet said, his tone icy. "Are we done?"

"Yes, we're done," Caslin said. "For now."

"You need me to identify the body again?" Tarbet asked. Caslin wasn't sure if he was being serious or whether he was deliberately on the wind up.

"No, I think we will manage. Besides, you did such a good job last time. Enjoy the rest of the day Mr Tarbet," Caslin said, turning and walking away.

"I'm not sure he deserved that," Hunter said, catching up and falling into step alongside him.

"Maybe he did, maybe he didn't," Caslin said. "Think about it. There was a body retrieved from his yacht after the fire. If it wasn't Bradley, then who was it? Somebody died and no one seems too bothered about who that was. Unless you are going to tell me, Bradley sneaked a dead body onboard without anyone knowing then he must be in on it. If not, then I'll feel suitably bad for the next couple of hours. Fair enough?"

"Finding out that his cousin is still alive didn't throw him much, did it?"

Caslin shook his head. He was reluctant to read too much into Tarbet's response. After all, people react to events in different ways, this job taught him that. Although, it was certainly possible that Tarbet was in on this from the start. The question then became - the start of what? Passing the building that housed the lifeboat, Caslin noted a member of staff aboard the rib. Nudging Hunter with his elbow, he indicated for them to step inside. Their arrival was noted as soon as they passed through the double doors.

"Can I help you with something?" the man said, stepping out of the rib and coming to greet them. Caslin held open his wallet and displayed his warrant card.

"Detective Inspector Caslin," he said, introducing himself. The man made a cursory inspection of Caslin's identification before nodding an acceptance of who he was talking to. "Are you a crew member of the lifeboat?"

"For the last 15 years," the man said, "what can I do for you?"

"Do you remember a yacht catching fire, a couple years ago?" Caslin asked. "Four-man crew. Three were rescued and one was pulled dead from the hull."

"I remember. We get called out a lot but that one was always going to stick in the mind," he said.

"What can you tell us about it?" Hunter asked.

"Not a lot more than you will be able to read in the official reports, I should imagine."

"Nothing stood out as unusual?" Caslin asked. The man smiled.

"That was a weird one, I'll tell you that. It's not unusual for boats to catch fire but rarely do they explode. Not like that anyway."

"The insurance company thought the same," Caslin said. The man bobbed his head.

"Unsurprising," he said. "Not a lot of things made sense that night. The explosion was just one of them."

"You've got my attention," Caslin said. "Tell us about it."

"Not much to tell you, not really. Apart from the boat going up in such a manner as I've never seen before, not in thirty years at sea. No, it was more the reaction of the crew that struck me at the time."

"Reaction?" Caslin said.

"If it were me, I would have been shitting myself but they were pretty calm when we plucked them out of the water."

"We were just talking to the skipper," Caslin said. "He described the others as panicking."

"Not when we got there. You would have thought they'd hailed a taxi. It was really weird and I wasn't the only one to think so either."

"Do you know the skipper, Scott Tarbet?" Caslin asked. The man met his eye and glanced away.

"I see him around, yes. We're not friends, though. I don't think he has many friends."

"Why not?" Hunter asked. The man laughed.

"You've met him. He's a hard man to like," he explained. Checking his watch, he raised an eyebrow. "Is there anything else because I really need to be somewhere?"

"Thank you for your time," Caslin said. The man left and headed into his office, turned off the monitor on his desk and then picked up his coat which was hanging next to the door. Caslin looked at Hunter. "Do you still think I was out of order?"

Hunter shook her head. "What do you want to do now?"

"I think we should talk to the others on the boat that night, don't you?"

"Well, we know Greg Tower is dead and that leaves only one other person on the boat that we can speak to."

"What's up, Sarah?" Caslin asked playfully. "Are you worried Chief Superintendent Ford won't be pleased to see us?" Hunter shook her head. Caslin was right. They needed to speak to Ford but at the same time, the man she was walking with didn't always respect the rank.

CHAPTER THIRTEEN

THE DRIVE from the east coast of Yorkshire across the Pennines to the west of England took just shy of three hours. It was a good job they called ahead. Chief Superintendent Ford agreed to wait for them, albeit under protest. It was well after dark when they reached the station in Manchester. Hunter's satellite navigation system had struggled once inside the city limits, frequently dropping its connection but they managed to make it to their destination all the same. They were escorted up to the chief superintendent's office by a constable from Greater Manchester Police. Knocking on the door a voice from inside bid them to enter. Caslin opened it, allowing Hunter to pass through first.

Hunter was surprised to see Kyle Broadfoot sitting in a chair opposite the chief superintendent. Visually taken aback, Broadfoot smiled at her reaction.

"Pleased you could make it so quickly, sir," Caslin said from behind. Hunter looked over her shoulder at him. "Sorry, Sarah. I forgot to mention I had asked Assistant Chief Constable Broadfoot to join us."

"Detectives Caslin and Hunter," Broadfoot said, introducing them to Toby Ford.

"Caslin?" Ford asked.

"Yes, sir," Caslin said, stepping forward and offering his hand. Ford stood to meet it. "I'm sorry, have we met?" he asked, wracking his brain to try and recall if they knew each other.

Ford shook his head. "I… don't believe so, no. Now that you two are here, perhaps you could tell me what all this is about?" the chief superintendent said, his tone shifting from an unexpected display of familiarity to one of barely masked irritation.

Hunter cast a nervous glance towards Caslin. For his part, Caslin took Ford's attitude in his stride. He was tall and rangy, appearing to have the physique of a cyclist with barely an ounce of fat around his athletic frame.

"I can see you're a busy man, sir," Caslin said, noting Ford checking his watch. "We'll keep this as brief as we possibly can. I'd like to talk to you regarding your association with DCI Philip Bradley." At the mention of the name, Caslin noticed a brief flicker of something cross the chief superintendent's face. Perhaps it was surprise at the mention of a man who had been dead for two years or perhaps it was something else entirely. Either way, Caslin found his curiosity piqued.

"Bradley?" Ford said, sitting down and frowning. "What about him?"

"Specifically, sir, the night he died… for the first time."

"What on earth do you mean, *for the first time?*" Ford asked, looking directly at Kyle Broadfoot. Broadfoot didn't reply but held the gaze for a few moments before raising his eyebrows in a gesture that implied an answer should be forthcoming. "If you're here, then you know what happened to Philip. He's been dead for two years. Now, what's all this about?"

"That's exactly what we're trying to find out, sir," Caslin said. "The issue is, if he died on that boat, just as you, Scott Tarbet and Greg Tower stated, then how come he's lying in my morgue having been killed in a car crash less than two days ago?" Ford's eyes narrowed and his lips parted. "Sir?" Caslin pressed for a response.

"Nonsense," Ford said, dismissing Caslin with evident scorn. He looked again to Broadfoot, "Sir, surely this is a waste of both our time?"

Broadfoot remained impassive, "You need to listen, Toby, and then you need to provide an answer."

Ford, visibly frustrated at his superior officer's response, returned his attention to Caslin. "Philip Bradley died on that boat. I saw it happen with my own eyes," he said emphatically. "Someone has made a mistake."

"Our pathologist performed a fifteen-point fingerprint check," Caslin said, referencing the thorough examination Dr Taylor carried out. In some jurisdictions a nine-point fingerprint match, where a set of prints have that many similarities, was legally admissible in court. Alison Taylor matched Bradley's to a far greater level of accuracy making it almost a statistical impossibility that the body was anyone else's. "DCI Bradley was alive and well until his car left the road two days ago. Can I ask where you were two nights ago, sir?"

"And what the hell kind of question is that for you to ask me?" Ford said with thinly veiled aggression.

Hunter bit her bottom lip but Caslin held his ground. "It's a simple enough question, sir, and I would like an answer."

"As would I," Broadfoot said, sitting forward in his seat, breaking Ford's angry stare at Caslin and towards him instead. "If it makes you feel any better imagine it was your superior asking you the question?" Ford softened in his demeanour. Now, Hunter understood why Caslin requested Broadfoot's presence. "I'll help you. Where were you two nights ago?"

"I... I... was at home," Ford stated flatly. "I resent the need to answer the question, sir. You said Philip was killed in a car accident. Your question implies you suspect foul play?"

"The investigation is ongoing," Caslin said. "Can you think of any reason why he would have faked his own death?"

"None whatsoever."

"And yet, that was his choice," Caslin countered. "He went to great lengths to ensure he was able to vanish. Approaching the end of his service, DCI Bradley was due his retirement, associated commutation from his pension plus the pension itself..."

"And?" Ford asked.

"That's a lot to leave behind," Caslin argued. "He never re-entered his previous life as far as we could tell. No access to his bank accounts, credit cards, family members... he dropped out of sight with a snap of the fingers. Why would he do that?"

"I have not got the faintest idea."

"He executed his plan brilliantly. It's almost hard to believe he was able to manage it unassisted."

"If he had assistance, Inspector, it certainly didn't come from me," Ford countered, fixing him with a stare. "I assure you, I am as curious as you are."

"DCI Bradley. Was he a decent officer?" Caslin asked.

"Very," Ford responded immediately without needing time to consider his answer. "A man you could always rely upon."

"He didn't have any financial issues that you are aware of. Challenging relationships... troubling cases or the like?"

"No," Ford stated. "Nothing that I am aware of."

"Forgive me, sir, but this isn't making any sense. A lifetime spent in service to his country. The respect of his colleagues and yet, here we are. These aren't the actions of a man whose character everyone speaks of so highly."

"I can't answer that, Inspector. All I can do is describe the man I knew and I fail to understand why you have brought this to me."

"Your witnessing of his death gave it credibility," Caslin said. "You must know how it looks?"

"Let me be clear, Inspector Caslin… Kyle," he said, turning to Broadfoot. "I have no knowledge of these events. As far as I am aware, Philip Bradley died two years ago in a fire at sea. Now, is there anything else?"

"Not for the moment, sir, no," Caslin said. Ford stood as Kyle Broadfoot did as well. The latter offered his hand to Ford.

"Thank you for your time, Toby," Broadfoot said as they shook.

"I hope I was of some help," Ford replied. "Please do let me know the outcome of all of this."

"Oh, rest assured, sir," Caslin interjected. "Should we need to speak to you further, I'll certainly be back." Ford glanced towards him and the expression of polite familiarity slipped for a moment before being masked by a smile.

"You are welcome, Inspector Caslin. I will be only too pleased to assist you in any way I can," he said, coming from behind his desk and offering his hand to Caslin by way of a farewell. Caslin shook it, locking eyes with the senior officer.

"One more thing," Caslin said, not releasing his grip. "How did you feel that night, out on the boat?"

Ford's smile dropped. "I was terrified, Inspector. By any measurement, the scariest experience of my life."

Caslin nodded, releasing Ford from the handshake. "I can imagine. How close were you to the other officer on the boat that night, Greg Tower?"

"We were friends."

"Close friends?"

"Yes, very. I don't suppose you're going to tell me he's still alive as well, are you?" Ford replied, with a hint of sarcasm.

"I wouldn't rule it out," Caslin countered, assessing Ford's body language. It didn't tell him anything. The man looked stern, focused.

Earlier he appeared off balance, mentally at least, but now, he came across confident and rigid. "Thank you for your time, sir."

They left the office and Hunter dropped back a step as Kyle Broadfoot chose to walk alongside Caslin. The upper floors of the station were nigh on deserted. The majority of the offices were empty with the building's lighting switching to their minimal evening settings, leaving shadows all around them. Conversation could be entered into freely as concerns about being overheard were non-existent.

"You went in pretty hard on Toby," Broadfoot said, glancing over his shoulder to Hunter. She was unsure of whether she should drop back a little further and remove herself from the conversation entirely. Broadfoot didn't give her that impression, so she stayed where she was.

"I know," Caslin said. "It was intentional."

"What do you make of it?" Broadfoot asked.

"The calmest bunch of terrified men I've ever come across," Caslin said, drawing a perplexed expression from his boss.

"Meaning?"

"This is bigger than we think."

"In what way?"

"I need time," Caslin said, "and I can't promise you I won't step on more toes."

Broadfoot stopped, turning to face him. "Whatever it takes," he said directly to him before glancing to Hunter. "Whatever it takes," he repeated. Broadfoot left the two of them in the corridor, striding away.

"He's certainly motivated," Hunter said quietly.

"Personally involved," Caslin added, his gaze drifting past Hunter towards the chief superintendent's office as the door opened. Toby Ford stepped out of the room. Closing the door behind him before he noticed their presence, he met Caslin's eye but only briefly. Locking the door, he returned the keys to his pocket and turned on his heel. He set off, walking in the opposite direction to them briefcase in hand and with his coat across his forearm. "What did you make of him?"

"Defensive," Hunter said. "I think he knows more than he was letting on. You went easy on him... at least, by your usual standard anyway."

"He's not as good an actor as Scott Tarbet. I'll give you that," Caslin said, watching the departing figure make the turn at the end of the corridor and disappear from view. "He was surprised though."

"Surprised that Bradley was alive or that we'd come across him in a car crash?" Hunter sought to clarify.

"There's a question," Caslin said. "Instinct tells me he was surprised we ended up in his office."

"Maybe they've been in contact?" Hunter suggested. "Although, we're reaching when all we have is your instinct to go on."

"Philip Bradley picked those specific people to be on board the boat when he checked out," Caslin explained. "We need to know why?"

"He needed his cousin's boat," Hunter said, "and the other two were serving police officers. You could see them as a strange choice or a bold one."

"Their presence gave it an air of credibility," Caslin said, thinking aloud.

"Exactly," Hunter agreed. "And if they were co-conspirators, then their standing would deflect the focus of the investigators away. It's almost as strong as having a judge or a priest on your side in court."

"It didn't deter the claims assessor, though," Caslin countered.

"What would Ford, Tarbet and Tower have to gain from helping him?" Hunter asked. "I mean, they would need to benefit in some way, wouldn't they?"

"I wonder if when we figure out what Bradley had to gain, then that question will be answered."

"Are we any closer to understanding that?"

"No," Caslin said with a shake of the head. "We're still some way off. Bradley saw fit to hide, or the need to run, from something. We should focus on trying to find the link between all of these names. Once we do that, it will start to come together."

"What should we do with Chief Superintendent Ford?"

"I'd love to put some surveillance on him and see what he does next but we don't have the resources… nor the authority," Caslin said with regret. "So far, the only links we have are between Bradley, Mason and David MacEwan. Those on the boat are either willing participants or unwitting contributors to a cover story."

"Or both?" Hunter said, Caslin had to concede the point because all they had were theories at present.

"Let's focus on MacEwan and Mason, pull a few threads and see what unravels."

"If Iain Robertson is right, who do you think pushed Bradley's car off the road?"

Caslin shrugged, "Mason's jag is white, isn't it?"

"Yes."

"Let's run a check against everyone we've come across and see if anyone owns a red car. I doubt it will be that simple but you never know."

"You think whatever brought Bradley out of hiding also got him killed?"

"I'll put money on it."

CHAPTER FOURTEEN

"BRADLEY HAS CERTAINLY BEEN CLOCKING up the mileage on that hire car, sir," Holt said as Caslin took off his coat and pulled out a chair. Surprised to find Terry Holt was still hard at it when they eventually returned to Fulford Road, both of them were intrigued to find out what he'd uncovered. "I've downloaded the telematics data from Bradley's car and that has given us reference points for everywhere he's been in the past few days."

"Remind me. What does it tell us?" Hunter asked.

"As long as the engine is running, the system will send out a ping rather like the transponder of an aircraft. This is registered at respective cell towers along the car's route and relayed back to the manufacturer. It's kind of like low-jacking via the GPS network."

"What's he been up to?" Caslin asked, turning his focus to the board as Holt crossed to it. There were a series of coloured pins placed strategically on the map denoting Bradley's movements. A cursory analysis saw he had come to York directly from Manchester upon picking up the car at the airport.

"I've not placed every ping on the map, sir. There really isn't a need but any major route along with a deviation has been catalogued."

"Where did he spend most of his time?" Caslin asked. Holt retrieved his notes and then came back to the board.

"Like I said, he got about a bit. We have him visiting MacEwan's scrapyard on two occasions. One of which was observed by you and the other was the previous night. Now, the information relayed to us will only respect the location of the tower the car's system is communicating with. Therefore, we can't be certain as to who or where he was actually visiting. There is still a degree of supposition going on, on our part. Because you witnessed him there the following day, I'm assuming he went in the day before but equally, he may have been staking the place out from the outside. We have no way of knowing for certain."

"Understood," Caslin said. "Go on."

"Every night, he returned to this location," Holt pointed to a place on the map roughly six miles from the outer limits of the city. "There's a hotel and spa in this area so I figured he was staying there. I called them and was able to confirm he checked in on the day he arrived from Spain under his known alias. He was staying there alone and to their knowledge, he didn't receive any visitors."

"When was the last time he was there at the hotel?"

"His key card was activated on the morning of the day he died, sir. No one apart from the housekeeping staff has entered the room since. I've asked them to keep the room isolated until we can get a chance to go over and check it out."

"Good man," Caslin said, approving of his efforts. "What are the other highlights of his travels?"

"Mostly, he spent his time in and around York, sir. However, there was one notable deviation that I found very interesting."

"If you're about to tell me he drove up to Whitby, I warn you now, I'll be ecstatic," Caslin said, casting a wry grin in Hunter's direction. She smiled.

"Sorry," Holt dashed his hopes. "Although, he did head to the coast. He set off east, out of York and took the A64 in the direction of Scarborough."

"Heading for a Victorian coastal seaside resort? Maybe he was missing the lasagne and chips that he gets served up by the ex-pats back in Spain."

"Didn't make it that far, sir," Holt carried on, ignoring Caslin's tangent. "He turned off at Staxton, then continued on before re-joining the coastal road and travelling south."

Caslin thought about the route, attempting to visualise it in his head. He hadn't been that way in years. "Towards Bridlington?"

Holt nodded, "But he took the turn off at Reighton, heading down to Flamborough."

"What was he doing there?" Hunter asked.

"The telematics put him stationary out at Flamborough Head," Holt explained. "The signal was switched off for several hours. I'm presuming he parked up there. It was reactivated when he started the car that evening."

"Could have been meeting someone?" Caslin suggested.

"Could have fancied a walk along the coast and a visit to the lighthouse?" Hunter countered, before adding, "Although, I doubt it."

Caslin laughed, "I don't know. It's a stunning patch of coast. Does he have any connections in the area we are aware of?"

"None that I've come across as yet, no," Holt explained. "It is possible I will the further I go through his old case files but he was in CID for a long time."

"I know, it's a lot of data to sift through," Caslin said, reassuring him. "Has he been anywhere else?"

"He was in and around Selby for an afternoon," Holt said, glancing back at the board.

"Selby?" Caslin repeated.

"What about it, sir?" Hunter asked, perceiving Caslin's far-away look as significant.

"Nothing," Caslin explained, shaking his head. "Just reminds me that I've not called my father back."

"Wasn't that days ago?" Hunter asked, frowning.

Caslin sighed. "Yes. What are you, my ex-wife?" he retorted. She laughed. "What was he doing there?"

"He drove around the outskirts of the town in the morning before backtracking in the afternoon. He stopped around here," Holt indicated a section of the map where he'd drawn a circle to mark the range of the cell tower, "and the car was inactive for a little over two hours before he set off."

"Where did he go then?" Caslin asked.

"Back to his hotel, sir."

"All right. Keep digging. What else have you got for me?"

"I'm ploughing through his case files, sir," Holt said. "I'm looking for a crossover between the names we have but nothing has flashed up in the database as yet. I started with the most recent and I'm heading back through his career. I'm viewing these as the quick wins because pre-late 1980s, the files were not computerised. I've submitted a request for the archives to be released to me. Ours are easy to come by but I'm waiting on those from Greater Manchester."

"Any idea when they'll come over?" Hunter asked.

"Should be tomorrow," Holt confirmed. Caslin looked at his watch. It was late.

"Okay, let's call it a day and start afresh tomorrow," he said. "I'll head over to the hotel and check out his room. You two can go home and get some rest."

"I'll come with you," Hunter said. Caslin didn't object as he stood up, pulling the coat off the back of his chair and putting it on. Holt collapsed his folder before rubbing at his eyes. He'd spent hours trawling through paperwork and was obviously happy for the respite. Caslin silently approved of his attitude. When accepting the offer to head up the unit, Caslin insisted on bringing his own team with him. Hunter's inclusion was a simple decision whereas Terry Holt was a bit of a gamble. That in itself had a certain sense of irony to it, what with Holt's background of borderline gambling addiction. The young detective constable had made a concerted effort to refocus on his career, making the journey from a struggling detective to an efficient and respected member of the team. The opportunity to prove himself was something he'd grasped with both hands.

"I'll close up, sir," Holt said as Caslin and Hunter were ready to leave. They left him to shut the office down and entered the corridor. Fulford Road was deserted, their footfalls echoing on the polished floors.

"Stephen won't mind you working late again?" Caslin asked in passing. Hunter shrugged. "I know you've been pushing yourself recently."

"Don't worry about it," she replied, glancing at him and pursing her lips momentarily. He sensed there was more that she wasn't saying.

"Everything all right?"

"Stephen left last month," Hunter said, her expression remaining impassive. Caslin could have kicked himself. He had no idea.

"I'm sorry I mentioned it," Caslin said.

"It doesn't matter. Don't worry," she replied.

"Are you okay?"

"I will be," she said, looking at him and smiling. She gently elbowed him in the forearm. "Honestly, it's okay. I think it's for the best. We've been hanging on for a while now. Both of us have been kidding ourselves, and each other, that it's going to work."

"How's Stephen?"

"Relieved," she said. "I think he was putting in far more effort than I was towards the end."

"I'm sorry," Caslin said, feeling for her. "Anything I can do?"

"Not talk about it," she suggested, inclining her head.

"Understood," Caslin replied, with a smile.

A QUARTER OF AN HOUR LATER, they pulled into the car park of the Royal Hotel and Spa a few miles outside of the city. The restaurant was open to the public and judging by the number of vehicles present, the establishment was doing a roaring trade. Bradley's choice of a hotel made sense. With a two-hundred room capacity, he would be able to blend into the background rubbing shoulders with guests, diners and spa visitors. For a man not wanting to stand out it was a solid plan. He could come and go without anyone paying him much attention at all.

Caslin had called ahead and upon showing his warrant card at the reception desk was ushered towards the duty manager's office. They were greeted shortly by a young woman, Caslin assumed was in her early twenties. The thought occurred to him about how young management appeared to him these days, wondering whether it was just him getting older or the next generation developing faster.

"Has anyone entered the room since we contacted you earlier today?" he asked her.

"No," she said. "There's been no activity recorded since housekeeping did their rounds this morning."

"Did they report anything unusual after they went in?" Hunter asked.

"Nothing was noted in the file," she said. "The staff are off until the morning but I can ask them if you'd like?"

"Thank you," Caslin replied. "And he checked in under the name of Brian Jack?"

"Yes, he did," she replied, checking her register.

"Can we see the room?" Caslin asked.

The manager led them out of the office and across the lobby to the elevators. Minutes later, they stepped out onto the second floor. Approaching room 243, the manager produced a key card to grant them access. Caslin accepted it from her asking that she waited outside. Entering the card into the slot, the LED changed from red to green and the sound of the latch clicking came to ear. Caslin eased the door open. The interior was shrouded in darkness. Stepping forward, he placed the same card into another slot on the wall just beyond the entrance. As soon as he did so, the lights came on.

The room was a familiar layout for a high turnover chain hotel. The bathroom was off the entrance hall to the left. A few metres further they entered the bedroom consisting of a double bed, a small two-seater sofa and a workstation fixed to the wall with a chair underneath. A television was mounted on the wall above the desk. A suitcase lay open beside the bed with the top leaning against the wall. Caslin knelt alongside and inspected the contents indicating for Hunter to look around. The suitcase proved not to be of interest with only a few changes of clothes folded neatly and stacked atop each other. Hunter returned from the bathroom shaking her head in response to his unasked question.

"Nothing in there," she said, crossing the room to the workstation and continuing the search. "Here we go..." she said in a tone that caught Caslin's attention. He had just come across a passport in the exterior pocket of the suitcase. He brought it with him as he crossed to join Hunter, flicking through the pages as he walked. It was in the name of Brian Jack. The photo matched.

"What have you got?" he asked.

"Laptop," she said, glancing at what he held in his hands. "Is that legit?"

"It's genuine," he replied, holding up the passport. "It was issued four years ago, so it's pretty much up to date regarding the components. The anti-counterfeit foils and digital biometrics are present. This means he'd been planning his demise for a minimum of two years prior to the fire onboard the yacht."

"We'll have to get this back to the station," Hunter said, pointing at the computer. "It's locked but... this is interesting," she said, drawing Caslin's attention to a folder that she'd found alongside the laptop. Opening the flap, she withdrew the first sheet and passed it to him. Caslin scanned the document. It was a print out of a spreadsheet. There was a list of countries down the left-hand side of the sheet with the corresponding columns representing months of the year. The spreadsheet was populated with figures represented in sterling, some lodged in red, others in green. The passage of the charted figures went back for the previous twelve months. What the figures related to however, was totally lost on him. "Did you check out the source?" Caslin noted the small print at the head of the page.

"SLG Exchange," Caslin read aloud. "What's that?"

"A trading company," she explained.

"Trading what?"

"Not that kind of trading," Hunter said with a smile. "They facilitate trading on the markets. That looks like one of their market reports. You can pay them and they'll produce these for investors. For a fee, obviously."

"I didn't know you were into commodities?" Caslin asked. Hunter grinned.

"Stephen is a FOREX trader," she said. "Didn't you know?"

Caslin shook his head. "Can't say I remember. What are the figures relating to? Any idea?"

"No, sorry. It doesn't say," she said. "Perhaps his browsing history will tell us." Caslin focused on the figures seeing them in a different context. They appeared to be documenting the rise and fall of a certain commodity recorded in a dozen countries around the globe. Making a basic assumption that red denoted falls and green, rises, he noted the rough trend saw this commodity's value on the increase in the previous six months.

"On its own it may as well be written in hieroglyphics," Caslin said.

"Then there's this," Hunter said, passing him a copy of an ordnance survey map. Caslin put the copy of the spreadsheet down and took the map. It had been opened and refolded in such a way to leave certain sections of the map facing to the outside. The first location that leapt out at him was Flamborough Head. The area was circled in ink with some handwritten notes alongside but Caslin struggled to make out what they were, such was the writing style that made it almost unreadable.

"Holt said telematics put Bradley out at the Flamborough lighthouse, didn't it?"

"Yes, for several hours."

"Fancy a day out at the coast?" he asked under his breath.

CHAPTER FIFTEEN

THE SURROUNDING landscape was flat with barely a tree in sight as the sea came into view in front of them. The sky was clear and brilliant sunshine forced them to lower their visors as they drove along the appropriately titled *Lighthouse Road.* A line of single-story dwellings lay along the route, all facing out to sea. To the left of them was a golf course hugging the coastline that stretched north towards the Flamborough Cliffs. The village of Flamborough itself lay behind them a short drive inland, safe from the aggression of the sea battering the area.

They passed the original lighthouse, an octagonal structure built from chalk hundreds of years previously. The line of residences retreated inland as the road opened out into the approach to the point. A beacon stood proudly at the side of the entrance to the grounds of the lighthouse, its brazier empty and now only lit for ceremonial purposes at certain times of the year. The approach road narrowed again with open ground to either side of them, less so on their left as the land slipped down towards the water below. The popularity of the site for tourists was reinforced by the first building they came to. It was wide, squat, and two-thirds of it given over to a cafeteria whereas the remainder was occupied by a shop selling souvenirs. The lighthouse was a visitor attraction as were the coastal paths heading north up the Heritage Coast or south west, back towards the larger population centre of Bridlington.

Caslin passed the café and followed the pitted tarmac road around to the rear and the parking situated closer to the lighthouse itself. This building stood in excess of eighty-five feet towering above the attached ancillary buildings and dominating the landscape. This section of the UK coast proved treacherous for shipping with many wrecks falling foul of the combination of violent North Sea storms and the hidden dangers beneath the surface. Caslin pressed the start/stop button and the engine died. A whirring sound continued for a few seconds as the systems set themselves and then all was quiet. The sound of the bitter north-easterly wind hammering the outside of the car was all that could be heard. Hunter looked around. Clearly, she had never been here before. Caslin had, many times.

"What would Bradley be doing all the way out here?" she asked, appearing perplexed. "Not coming for a round of golf?" she half-heartedly suggested. Caslin smiled. There were some hardy souls venturing out on the course, visible to them from the approach road. The sun was shining and that was all the invitation some people needed.

"Let's go for a walk and see if we can get an idea of what he might have been here for," Caslin said, cracking the door open and being hit by a blast of cold air. Getting out of the car, Hunter joined him, wrapping her coat about her and squinting as she faced the sun, sitting low in the sky.

Caslin looked around. The residences stretched behind them in a crescent shape some distance away. There was the possibility Bradley had visited any one of these places but they'd failed to find any associations, loose or otherwise, with the registered occupants. Heading over to the lighthouse, the compound of which was encircled by a five-foot-high boundary wall fashioned from brick, Caslin noted the side road running behind it and down almost to the cliff edge. There were a handful of minor structures present on a prominent outcrop and by the look of the attached antennae, he guessed they were monitoring equipment related to the fog warning system. As for the lighthouse itself, the tower was fully automated, dispensing with the need for a traditional keeper as were almost all of those in the UK network. The wall offered them a little respite from the prevailing wind but that passed as they came around to the northern side.

A path led away from them with a signpost revealing the route of the *Way Marker Trail.* Caslin glanced about them. The business selling souvenirs was closed. A brief inspection of the sign indicated they were operating out of season opening hours. Unsurprising as footfall was light at this time of year. However, the café was open and they passed through a gate to the adjoining garden seating, an assortment of picnic benches, and entered the building. A handful of people were present. A small group of ramblers by the look of them, taking a winter hike along the coast. They approached the counter, Hunter producing a photograph of Philip Bradley. The lady staffing the counter was in her forties with dyed hair that was growing out to reveal grey shoots against the fading blonde.

"Have you seen this man around here recently?" she asked, offering up the picture. The woman looked at it closely, turning the corners of her mouth downwards and shaking her head.

"Not that I recall," she said, eyeing them curiously. "Are you police or something?"

"Yes, we are," Hunter explained with an apologetic smile producing her identification.

"Thought so," she replied. "You all walk funny."

"Is that right?" Hunter said, inclining her head. "Are you sure you haven't seen him? It would have been three days ago."

"Not me. Hang on a second," she said, stepping away and looking back into the kitchen area, standing on tiptoes as she strained to see over the coffee machine. "Geoff!" she called. Moments later a man appeared from the rear. He was short, barrel-chested and balding. He approached them warily giving Caslin the once over as he got closer.

"What is it, Mary?"

"Police," she said to him. He raised his eyebrows in response.

"What can I do for you?" he asked.

"Have you seen this man?" Hunter asked, sliding the photo across the counter towards him. "He would have been here a few days ago." The man eyed the picture but he didn't register a notable response. His gaze lingered enough for Caslin to think it was worth a nudge.

"He would have been driving a red Mercedes," Caslin said.

"Yeah, now you mention it. I think he was here."

"Are you sure?" Hunter pressed.

"He parked in front of the lighthouse, over there," Geoff said, looking out across the tables and chairs and through the large picture window. "That's restricted parking and he didn't have a permit."

"You checked?" Caslin asked.

"No, don't be silly," he explained, "if you work here long enough you get to know the cars and who owns them. It doesn't really matter this time of year but he'd be screwed in the summer. Traffic wardens love coming up here."

"Did you see him with anyone?" Caslin asked.

Geoff shook his head. "No. I mean, he may have been with someone but he was on his own when he came in here."

"Did you speak with him?"

"Only to serve him. He had a coffee and sat down over there," he said, pointing to a table by the window.

"What did he do?" Hunter asked. "Did he speak to anyone?"

"Not that I saw. He just drank his coffee, staring out of the window."

"Then what?"

"Then nothing. He left."

"That's it? You saw him drive off?"

"No. I remember seeing the car was still there when I went out for a smoke but I didn't see him again."

"Any idea where he might have gone?"

"No, sorry. He could have gone for a walk. He was dressed for it," he said. Noting both Caslin and Hunter's interest, he continued, "You know, casuals. Decent all-weather coat. I presumed he was going along the trail. Some people prefer it in the off season, fewer people to get in their way."

"Thanks for your help," Hunter said and they turned away from the counter. Crossing the café, they went to where the proprietor said Bradley had been seated. Looking out of the window all that was visible was the coastal scenery, the lighthouse and the associated car park. "Meeting someone?"

"Possibly," Caslin said, following her line of sight. "Maybe he was early or arrived to check the area out." Returning to the service counter, he drew both Geoff and Mary's attention. "Do you have any CCTV?"

"No," they replied in unison.

"What about outside, to the car park?"

"No," came the reply, only this time from Geoff alone. "Why would we need it out here? There's nothing worth stealing."

"Fair enough, thanks," Caslin said. Taking out one of his contact cards, he passed it to Mary who accepted it, scanning the details printed on the front. "Just in case anything comes to mind after we've gone," Caslin explained.

"Sure, okay," she said, nodding and then turning and walking over to a cork board mounted on the wall behind the till point. She pinned his card alongside notices put up on behalf of the locals regarding anything from lost cats to cleaning services.

The two of them left the café, Hunter acknowledging the couple's help with a wave as she passed. Stepping out, they were once again buffeted by the wind. Leaving the boundary of the café's seating behind them, they crossed the road to the top of the coastal walking path. Glancing down, Caslin could see the land slipping towards the sea. There were warning signs mounted indicating for people to stick to the marked trail and to follow the detours when they came upon them for their own safety. Noise from behind made them turn as they were approached by the same group of ramblers who were in the café when they arrived. They stepped aside to make room for the walkers who thanked them. Almost as an afterthought, Caslin caught the attention of the second to last member of the group as she came past. She was a lady in her seventies, Caslin guessed.

"Can I ask where you are heading today?"

She stopped, smiling at his interest, "We're heading up to Thornwick Bay past the Flamborough Cliffs. It's stunning on days like this. Well, on any given day to be fair."

"I'll bet," he replied, nodding and smiling warmly. "Tell me, what are the highlights along this route?"

"Many," she said. "The cliffs themselves are well worth a look as are the views on their own but all along this coastline there's so much history. There are the old smuggler's caves and with the frequent land slips the scenery changes every time you walk it. It's tremendously exciting. Are you considering heading along the path?"

"No, not today," Caslin said. "Another time. Enjoy your day." She bid them goodbye and set off to catch up with her friends who were waiting a short way off.

"This is a strange place for a meeting," Hunter said, looking back towards the car park. "I can think of any number of places in and around York that I'd rather head to. Why drive all the way out here?"

Caslin scanned the area, "Neutral ground? I mean, you'd stand out to the locals but that's about all. It's certainly a place that the rest of the world wouldn't pay attention to. There must be a particular reason. Bradley came here for something, must have done."

"What do you want to do?" Hunter asked, glancing at her watch. Caslin screwed his nose up in a mock grimace hearing the sounds of the waves crashing against the rocks as the wind dropped. They'd achieved as much as they were going to.

"We'll head over to Full Sutton."

HMP Full Sutton was a category A prison situated to the north-east of York, near Pocklington, with six hundred male inmates. A purpose-built maximum-security institution, its primary function was to house some of the most difficult, violent and dangerous prisoners currently incarcerated in the UK. Within the walls also stood the Close Supervision Centre, often referred to as the prison within a prison, housing those considered to be the greatest threats to both the public and national security. The approach road left visitors under no illusion as to where they were headed. The small village of Full Sutton was set to their left, average-size family homes, dwarfed by the facility to be found barely a stone's throw away. Signage indicated where they were, directing them towards the administration and visitors' entrance.

Caslin pulled into the car park and located one of many free spaces bringing the car to a stop. A works compound was off to the prison's right-hand side surrounded by its own security fence and razor wire. The entrance to the prison lay before them, a brick structure protruding out in stark juxtaposition to the imposing walls running the perimeter. The entire compound was illuminated by towering floodlights placed strategically every thirty feet along the perimeter ensuring the open ground around the facility could not be breached unseen.

Approaching the pedestrian entrance, Caslin eyed the security bollards, painted yellow, sited in such a way as to make ram-raiding the administration block an impossibility. Likewise, they passed through the main door with its mechanically operated security gate that would keep out even the most ambitious of attackers. Official signs were erected leaving entrants to the institution in no doubt as to what their legal requirements were, what would not be tolerated, as well as the consequences of failing to adhere to the visitation rules. All prisons were detached from the trappings of the free society but here, you really were stepping into a world alien to most.

The reception was manned. Family visitations were underway and the lobby was empty. They approached the counter, Caslin noting the glass was easily an inch thick. Feeling the need to lean towards the speaker of the intercom which wasn't necessary, he identified himself by way of his warrant card, as did Hunter. The man behind the screen asked, with a somewhat disembodied voice, for their warrant cards to be deposited within the tray before them so he could inspect them properly. They did so. The sound of sliding metal carried as they closed the lid and the prison officer opened the other side. They waited patiently as he transcribed some details and then conferred with a colleague who glanced in their direction. Their warrant cards were returned to them.

"Please approach the door to your right," the officer advised them, pointing the way. Caslin thanked him. They stepped away and heard a buzzer sound as the lock disengaged. The door came open and an officer appeared from behind it beckoning them to accompany him. Then they headed into the bowels of the prison passing through locked door after locked door. Minutes later, they emerged out into the open and were escorted across a yard towards a square building, two storeys high. Glancing around, the facility was a collection of secure compounds within the inner walls of a greater one. Every building's approach was by way of a tunnel of chain link fencing and secure access points. The hospital was visible as was what appeared to be a sports hall with an all-weather pitch attached on one side. Again, all were visible through layers of security, perhaps unsurprising seeing as this prison housed mass-murderers, terrorists and those at the top end of the criminal food chain.

Caslin saw a woman appear from inside a building they were passing, a toddler in her arms. Looking past her, he saw what looked like a soft-play area. He was momentarily taken aback. Their escort appeared to notice.

"That's the visitor's centre," he explained. "We have recreational facilities for the children. It makes it less intimidating for them and let's face it, far more appealing for families to spend time together."

"Nice," Caslin said. "Maximum security has come a long way."

"Don't let the image fool you," the officer countered with a dry laugh. "Some of them will still cut your throat as soon as look at you. Your interviewee included," he said the last, with a tilt of the head for emphasis.

"Does he cause you any trouble?" Caslin asked. The officer shook his head.

"Not really. He's an old timer. He understands how these things work."

"How do you mean?" Hunter asked.

"Lags of his generation know the boundaries. There's a mutual understanding between us and them. They know why they're here and it's our job to keep them in. It's not quite respect but that's as close a description as I can think of," he explained. "We all know where we stand."

"And the difference between them and the next generation?" Caslin asked.

"Boundaries. They'll push it to the max and don't mind taking one of us down if it comes to it. The experienced inmates keep a lid on it most of the time but if it does go off, then things go awry very quickly."

"Like a couple of years ago?" Caslin asked, referencing a riot that broke out making national news at the time.

"Just like that," the officer agreed, reaching for his keys as they came to yet another locked door. "Drugs were getting out of hand and we needed to have a crackdown, reassert the authority. You can imagine how popular it was for us to be disrupting their supply of spice?"

"Drugs are your biggest problem?" Hunter asked.

"Generally speaking, yes," the officer stated. "That and keeping the headcases from killing the paedophiles and the ex-military from topping the jihadis… and all of them from trying to give us the odd kicking."

"Sounds like fun," Caslin said with intended sarcasm.

"I'm starting to think I should have tried harder at school," the officer replied, smiling and leading them into the next building.

They found themselves in an inner lobby, standing before a security desk. Here they were reminded of the rules regarding prisoner interaction. Then they were asked to sign another form before being led into an adjoining room. Here they waited. It was only a few minutes before a second door, at the opposite end of the room from where they entered, swung open and a man was led in. Caslin took his measure. They had never met. He was in his late sixties and cut an imposing figure. Once powerful and muscular but now his frame was visibly sagging. Despite that fact, Caslin could tell if it came down to it this man would still be able to hold his own in an altercation with someone half his age. Hawkish in appearance, he carried himself with the confidence that could only be derived from the solid assurance of his position as well as a core self-belief in his own status. He eyed Hunter momentarily before turning his gaze on Caslin. There it remained, his eyes narrowing. Caslin was in no doubt he was conducting much the same assessment of his visitors as they were of him.

"Take a seat, Mr Fuller," Caslin said, polite but firm.

CHAPTER SIXTEEN

Pete Fuller pulled out a chair and seated himself placing his hands on the table before him, palms down. Rolling his tongue across the inner edge of his bottom lip, he maintained eye contact with Caslin.

"To what do I owe the pleasure, Inspector Caslin?"

"You were expecting me?" Caslin asked. It was as much a statement as it was a question.

"My boys said you would probably be paying me a visit," Fuller stated leaning back in his chair. Caslin could tell he was standing before a career criminal. Fuller had that look about him. He was not intimidated being interviewed by the law.

"You must be a little disheartened at one of your businesses being attacked in that way?"

"So, it's an attack is it?" Fuller asked in a light-hearted tone. He lifted his hands from the table and crossed his arms in front of his chest inclining his head slightly, holding Caslin's gaze. "The news said it was a gas leak."

"You and I both know that isn't true," Caslin said stepping across to the table and pulling out a chair of his own. Sitting down, he leaned forward placing his elbows on the table. "I wanted to know what your thoughts were?"

"You're the detective."

"It must be maddening for you," Caslin said. "What with you being who you are."

"How so?"

"A man of your stature being stuck in here as someone attempts to do an end run on you," Caslin said, glancing off to the left at nothing in particular. "I'll bet you're itching to find out who did it? Unless of course, you already know."

"I'm quite sure my boys can handle it," Fuller stated evenly.

"Yes, I've met your boys," Caslin said. "Ashton appears quite level headed. Carl, on the other hand, seems to be wired just like his old man. At least, the old man of his youth."

Fuller smiled at that. "They share my best qualities," he stated.

"Although, on this occasion they may well have gotten in over their heads," Caslin said drumming his fingers on the table and inclining his head. "They've acquitted themselves quite well running your enterprises. The uneasy peace between them and your competitors has been advantageous… for a decade or so, maybe more?"

"And your point is?"

"They've managed to steer clear of any major drama with your adversaries," Caslin said. "But this is different. This is a new phase and I'm not sure they're ready."

"Is that so?" Fuller asked with animosity edging into his tone. "It's a tough business."

"Particularly so where Clinton Dade is concerned," Caslin said narrowing his eyes and watching for a reaction. At the mention of Dade's name, Fuller's eyes widened in the slightest indication that Caslin might be touching a nerve. He noticed. "You and Clinton go back a long way, don't you?"

"We do."

"Is it fair to say you're not exactly on friendly terms?"

"Aye, you could say that," Fuller said raising his left hand and leaning his face against thumb and forefinger. His index finger stroked his chin as he eyed Caslin expectantly.

"Any idea why Dade would want to start up a little fracas between you? It seems rather odd timing after years of amicable relations."

"Dade is a funny old goat," Fuller said. "It must be all that time he spends with those young boys of his."

"You and he were close once, weren't you?" Hunter said from the other side of the room. Fuller glanced in her direction and smiled.

"A long time ago, lass," Fuller replied.

"What did happen between you two?" Caslin asked.

"A minor disagreement between friends."

"Friends don't go to war with each other over minor disagreements," Caslin said.

"That depends."

"Depends on what?"

"The manner of the disagreement," Fuller said sitting forward in his chair. "As well as the nature of the friendship," he added.

"There's always another way that we could view this," Caslin said. "You must be looking forward to getting out of here. Not necessarily Full Sutton but out of the system completely. How long have you got left to serve… two years, maybe three if you don't have a positive parole board but no more than that?"

"Far less than that."

"In which case, soon you will be moved to a Category C prison to prepare you for returning to society the changed man that I'm sure you are."

"So, what's your point?"

"Maybe this bombing is a response to something you've done. Are you looking to reassert your presence?" Caslin asked locking eyes with the man sitting opposite him. Fuller smiled but it wasn't genuine.

"And you think I'm that stupid?"

"You wouldn't be the first to start acting like he's already out when into the final stretch," Caslin said. "And besides, don't insult my intelligence by making out you have nothing to do with your business interests while you are in here. I'm certainly not that stupid."

"Well, you have to keep your hand in, don't you?"

"We had a chat with Clinton the other day. He was all about the business as well," Caslin said.

"There you go then."

"He thought animosity between you would be bad for both of you. Of course, he's probably drawing on previous experience, isn't he?"

"You keep on pushing that, don't you?" Fuller said fixing Caslin with a stare.

"The word on the street is that the two of you were thick as thieves on your way up. But something happened along the way. Just when the two of you were hitting the big time you had a falling out. Care to comment?" Caslin asked. There was the briefest flicker of a reaction. If they were playing poker Caslin would have known something was up.

"Water under the bridge. I don't think Clinton will be coming for me and as far as I'm concerned…" he drew a deep breath, "the past is the past and that's where it should remain. Is that clear enough for you, Mr Caslin?"

"How's the family?" Caslin asked.

"Well enough."

"Ashton and Carl will be looking forward to your return," Caslin said before sucking air through his teeth, "or maybe not." Fuller raised an eyebrow in a gesture of curiosity at Caslin's intimation but offered no comment. "After all. Despite your obvious influence, they've had their hands on the reins for years. It'll be quite a wrench to step back into your shadow, I'd imagine."

"So, they bomb their own business?" Fuller countered. "No wonder the crime rates are soaring if your level of ability is the new benchmark."

Caslin was about to respond but was interrupted by his phone ringing. Taking the handset out of his pocket he allowed his gaze to linger on Fuller as he took the call from Terry Holt.

"Sir, I've got an update for you on Bradley's case files."

"Terry, can it wait?" Caslin said barely concealing his irritation at the interruption.

"No, sir," Holt explained. "You are going to want to hear this. Believe me, it's relevant."

"Go on then, make it quick," Caslin said.

"The files from greater Manchester came over this morning and I'm going through them. The indexing is pretty good I have to say. I was looking for a crossover between Bradley and MacEwan and I found one, albeit it's a little tenuous. Do you remember the Manchester airport securities raid back in the 80s? It was headline news. I don't remember the details because I was just a kid but it rang a bell. Once I looked it up, I remembered hearing about it at the time."

"Was that the raid on the customs clearing house?" Caslin asked. Fuller was still looking at him, an impassive expression on his face.

"Yes, that's the one, sir. An armed gang hit the clearing house in the early hours escaping with an estimated haul of around £22 million worth of cash, gold and gems. As I said that was estimated with the true value never fully being revealed. And don't forget those are the values of the day, it would be a lot more now."

"How much are we talking?"

"Even a conservative estimate would put today's figure at somewhere north of £120 million," Holt stated. "And I'm not sure how much you know about the detail but there was a lot that went unrecovered."

"And how does this tie our boys together?" Caslin asked, reluctant to reveal names of an ongoing investigation in front of his present company.

"Bradley was a detective chief inspector assigned to the securities raid investigation," Holt said with obvious excitement. "MacEwan was a known associate of Fuller's and was therefore interviewed at the time."

"How was he involved?" Caslin asked.

"Nothing stuck to him, sir. It looks like he was part of the scramble to find someone responsible for such a high-profile crime. MacEwan wasn't interviewed again nor did his name appear anywhere else in the inquiry."

"Do we know who interviewed him?"

"No, sir," Holt explained. "I don't have the transcript, only a reference to the interview with the date it took place. Some of the files haven't materialised from the archive but I'm chasing them up."

"We need to know. If the DCI was in on the interview, it'd be hard to believe they wouldn't recognise each other when they met the other day," Caslin said.

"If not, there is the possibility they didn't know each other. At least, not at the time," Holt said. "But you're going to love the next bit."

"Go on."

"Who do you think we know that is currently doing time for the raid on the customs clearing house?"

"Don't tell me," Caslin said, locking eyes with the man sitting opposite him, "am I sitting in front of him?"

"Only if it's Pete Fuller," Holt said, "and there's one more thing you should be aware of. We knew Jody Wyer's father, Keith, was a serving police officer. What we didn't know was that Bradley was once Keith Wyer's DCI."

"They served together," Caslin repeated.

"At the time of the raid, yes," Holt confirmed.

Caslin hung up the phone, slowly placing the handset on the table. He looked across his shoulder behind him towards Hunter. She remained expressionless but he knew she was curious as to what information he had just received, assuming it was significant.

"Now that was very interesting," Caslin said, his lips parting and forming a smile. "You remember Detective Chief Inspector Philip Bradley?"

"Old friends," Fuller replied with a nod of the head.

"Instrumental in your incarceration, I understand?" Caslin said.

"With friends like that who needs enemies, right?"

"He's dead," Caslin said, watching intently for a similar flicker of recognition as Fuller had offered previously. On this occasion the inmate was unreadable with the only reaction being a controlled release of his breath.

"That's a shame. The good often go too early," Fuller said quietly. "My condolences to the family."

"I'm sure they are heartfelt," Caslin said. "And your old friend, David. Heard from him recently?"

"David is a common name, Inspector. I'm afraid you'll have to be more specific than that."

"MacEwan," Caslin said, his gaze narrowing. "Or have you not seen him since you were sent down?"

"Lucky Davie," Fuller said with a smile. "Last I heard, he'd emigrated."

"No, he's very much back in the game," Caslin countered, inspecting his fingernails casually. "I do wonder what he's up to though. Making friends. Influencing others. Quite the character. Nice tan."

"I'm pleased for him," Fuller said but his tone belied some buried resentment. Caslin however, was unable to interpret how deep those feelings ran. The ice cool exterior had thawed a little. They were onto something. Caslin could sense it.

THEIR DEPARTURE COINCIDED with the end of visiting times and they found themselves navigating the exit of Full Sutton along with around thirty relatives. Some of those rubbing shoulders with them were downcast, seeing loved ones under such circumstances was emotionally draining. Others, perhaps with more experience, appeared to take it in their stride. A couple even joked with the officer escorting them to the reception. Once clear of the main entrance, Caslin and Hunter picked up the pace to get clear of the pack.

"That puts a different slant on events, doesn't it?" Hunter said once Caslin had filled her in on the details of Holt's phone call. "I wasn't expecting that. Do you think both events are linked? Wyer's murder as well as the bombing?" They reached the car and Caslin leaned on the roof looking across at Hunter and fiddling with the key fob in his hands, mulling over his response.

"Possibly. The characters are interconnected to a point beyond coincidence, so to dismiss the link would be foolish but as for how, I don't know?" he said, pursing his lips. "Are they directly related or is one symptomatic of the other?"

"How do you mean?" Hunter asked. "Is the bombing a response to Wyer's murder?"

Caslin shook his head indicating he didn't know, "I'm thinking aloud. Wyer is watching MacEwan, perhaps even Bradley for some reason. These two figured in a massive case that Wyer's father worked on. The very case that saw Pete Fuller sent down for a thirty-year stretch."

"And somewhere along the line someone within Fuller's organisation sets a bomb off. Why?" Hunter asked.

"Let's not forget either that the Fullers were not targeted directly," Caslin said. "If you were trying to take them out there are any number of opportunities where you could get to Ashton or Carl but they didn't. They hit the minicab office. Are they sending a message or maybe a warning?" Caslin asked rhetorically.

"If they are then who is it aimed at, Pete… the boys?" Hunter asked. "They could have hit Pete himself in prison," she suggested. "It wouldn't be the first time."

"You're right. No one is untouchable," he said, glancing back towards the prison. "As hard as it is to get in or out, behind those walls anyone is fair game for the right price."

"Lots of questions but not many answers."

"That's what makes this job so interesting," Caslin said with a broad grin, unlocking the car.

CHAPTER SEVENTEEN

"WHERE ARE we with the raid on the clearing house, Terry?" Caslin asked, pulling out a chair and briefly scanning the noticeboard for updates he may have missed while sitting down.

"The raid took place in 1986," Holt said, referring to his notes as he spoke. "The clearing house was outsourced and run by a private contractor. The subsequent investigation was ongoing for nearly four years and resulted in twenty-six convictions. Pete Fuller was identified as one of the lieutenants on the ground largely because of his links to those with the skill set and muscle to pull off such an operation. However, it took several years to bring him in."

"How was he identified?"

"The case was quite an embarrassment for the police and the government of the day who were at that time preaching a tougher attitude towards crime. The rewards being offered for information dragged many a low-life out of their pits to throw names at us," Holt explained. "Although Fuller wasn't considered to be big-time in the 80s, he was on the rise and intel had him working on and off with several of the players in and around York. Arguably, both North Yorkshire and Greater Manchester Police underestimated just how advanced some of these guys were. Fuller's organisation was in reality already a large cog in a far greater machine."

"Who was he working with?" Caslin asked, looking at Fuller's mugshot taken upon his arrest in 1990. His features were different now.

The eyes sunken, the skin tauter. Prison life - prison food - certainly took its toll after several decades.

"The leaders of the operation were named as Harry Bates and Thomas Maguire. Both were old hands at armed robberies starting out in their youth knocking off post offices and progressing to armoured cars and the like. This was seen as their last shot at the big prize. A chance to cement their name in history… as well as a pension of sorts," Holt said, passing images of the two men across the table to both Caslin and Hunter.

"What do we know about them?" Hunter asked, checking out the photos.

"Maguire died in Pentonville Prison fifteen years ago from a heart attack. The guy was already in his seventies when he was sent down."

"And Bates?" Caslin asked.

"Still serving time. He's currently in Belmarsh," Holt said, naming one of London's toughest prisons. "But interestingly, neither of them was considered to be the orchestrator of the raid."

"Who was?" Caslin asked.

Holt shook his head, "Never identified. The file has the architect listed as a man called *Alfred* but that's only a codename used in reference to him. Despite the team's best efforts no one was either willing or able to name him. Even the offer of a reduced sentence to the convicted hadn't tempted them to reveal who he was."

"Perhaps they didn't know?" Hunter suggested.

"Or perhaps thirty years inside was preferable to grassing," Caslin said. "We all know this *honour among thieves'* line that gets bandied about is absolute rubbish. These guys would sell their own mother if they thought it worth their while. Either they were scared of him or you're right, they genuinely didn't know his name. I recall you saying not everything stolen was recovered. Is that right?"

"Correct, sir," Holt confirmed. "As I said on the phone, the estimated haul they escaped with was £22 million in a mixture of cash, gold and gems and we're talking in excess of £120 million in today's values and that's a conservative estimate. Only around £13 million has been recovered and much of that took over a decade of investigation to locate. That was achieved through tracing the flow of money between the known figures and using legislation for seizing monies derived from illegal sources rather than actually finding what was taken. That's why we can say with confidence that this Alfred character remains at large. The organisation of the raid was so meticulous that the fencing of what was stolen was so sophisticated as to render it almost invisible."

"It went somewhere," Caslin said, casting his gaze across Bradley's photograph. "What about Chief Superintendent Ford? I'll bet he slots in somewhere to all of this."

"You'd be right, sir. He was Bradley's supervising officer on the investigation. He did quite well off the back of that case," Holt said, handing over a brief listing Ford's career history. Both Caslin and Hunter began reading as he continued, "Despite not getting everyone involved, the number of those eluding arrest and the true value that went unrecovered was largely kept out of the media. The case was far from a failure but perhaps not the success it was painted as at the time."

"Which all brings us back to Bradley and his untimely demise," Caslin said, putting the document on the table before him. "Tony Mason, Wyer's business partner, was he in on this investigation?"

"No, sir," Holt said. "I checked but he did work with Bradley for a number of years. They certainly knew each other."

"Fair to assume Bradley would know of Mason's habits?"

"I would say so, sir," Holt said, as did Hunter, making her agreement visible with a nod of the head. "It still leaves us without a definite thread to bring all of this together."

"MacEwan," Caslin began, wracking his brain to try and put the pieces together, "what is he known for?"

"In the early 80s, he was considered a low-level member of the criminal fraternity," Holt said, leafing back through his notes. "A few convictions for receiving stolen goods but nothing prolific. After his death in 1985, MacEwan took over his father's scrap metal business and it was suspected he ran an outfit ringing stolen cars using the scrap yard as the legitimate front. A few months after being interviewed about the raid on the customs house, he relocated to Spain. Although he kept his business going, he doesn't resurface in the UK until the late 1990s. By which time he's a millionaire, a pretty flamboyant one by all accounts having made a fortune in time share investments and other property ventures."

"The same area of Spain as Bradley?" Hunter asked, seeking the connection.

"That, I can't say at the moment," Holt said. "I have a call into Europol and I'm waiting to hear back."

"Okay, keep digging," Caslin said, standing and crossing the room to come before the board. Raising his hand, he pointed at the picture of Jody

Wyer. "Wyer's father worked this case and now, thirty years on, his son is investigating the very same group of people only it now encompasses some of his father's former colleagues. What brought Jody into this? Was it something his father told him or that he stumbled onto? The fact his business partner is somehow linked leads me to think it was the latter for no other reason than he agreed to go into business with him in the first place. If you couldn't trust your partner, you wouldn't leave yourself open, would you? Or am I missing something?"

"Keith Wyer, Jody's father," Hunter said. "What was his career like?"

"Nondescript," Holt said. "I'd register him as a journeyman officer. There are no marks against his file. He was adequate."

"I would hope my career highlights read better when the time comes," Caslin replied.

"Seeing as MacEwan's place is the only centre point we have for these faces, I downloaded a couple of data dumps from the cell towers around the scrap yard," Holt said. "Wyer's wallet litter – the receipts and scraps of stuff inside it – had him in a nearby petrol station a few days before he died, so I ran the mobile we have registered to him against the data from the cell towers. He was in and around the area on numerous occasions recently. Sometimes for hours on end."

"Sounds like he was staking the place out," Hunter offered.

"My thoughts exactly," Holt agreed.

"Have you got anywhere with the photographs that you took the other day?" Caslin asked Hunter, referencing their time spent at the vantage point in the business opposite MacEwan's yard. She nodded opening her own file on the desk before her.

"This is the only figure we have outstanding," she said, taking out copies of the frames she had taken. Spreading them out before her on the table so everyone could see, she pointed to the young man who had retrieved Bradley's car for him that day at the yard.

"Now he looks familiar," Caslin said, tapping one of the images with his forefinger. "Where do I know him from?"

"I thought so too," Hunter said. "While we were there the other day, I took shots of as many of the cars as I could see and then ran the indexes through the system just to see who pops up. I figured we could get a list going of MacEwan's people. From that list I cross-referenced the owner's data with the DVLA as well as our own files."

"Anyone interesting?" Caslin asked.

"Your standard who's who in the thug's database..." she said with sarcasm, "and then there's this guy." Hunter took out an arrest record of the man Caslin had pointed to. Turning it ninety degrees, both Holt and Caslin leaned over to see. It was the same man, although his hair was cut shorter with none of the wavy, surfer-style locks as he carried now. The record listed arrests for drug possession, affray and common assault to name but a few. Most of the crimes were low-level, habitual lifestyle arrests rather than for organised criminality.

"Oliver Bridger," Caslin read the name aloud. "It doesn't ring any bells."

"Ollie Bridger," Hunter confirmed. "Evidently working for MacEwan and well settled into his inner circle judging from what we saw. I think the reason he looks familiar is this," she said, taking out another arrest record. Placing it on the table alongside the first, Caslin frowned. "Similar, aren't they?" Caslin eyed the new sheet. He could have been looking at the same person. Again, the hair was shorter but a darker colour and the expression of resentment in the mugshot was almost identical.

"Twins?" Caslin asked, flicking his eyes to Hunter.

"No, but they were born only ten months apart," she stated. "They were in the same school year and could easily be mistaken for twins."

"I don't know them," Holt said.

"We came across Mark," Hunter said, pointing to the second sheet, "on our visit to Clinton Dade's office which is probably why Ollie caught your eye, sir. Both have popped up on our radar on and off throughout their juvenile and adult lives but not in a senior capacity. They are bottom of the food chain, really. But their presence here is interesting."

"How so?" Caslin asked, comparing their respective records.

"Well, first off, Ollie Bridger was picked up for his participation in an assault last year along with two others. They trashed a business and put the owner in hospital."

"Why is that significant?"

"Intel has it recorded as being related to the Fullers' business interests. They were believed to be acting on Ashton's instructions."

"Pressuring a client?"

"Suspicion of debt collection or racketeering is listed on the file but nothing stuck. The victim chose not to press charges and refused to identify them. That puts Ollie as an associate of the Fullers or at least he was at the time."

"And now he's working for MacEwan."

"Where it gets really interesting is that their father was Neville

Bridger," Hunter continued. "He came through the ranks as an enforcer for a local money lender and had a criminal record as long as your arm."

"You said, *had*?" Caslin queried.

"Neville Bridger died in prison in 2004 during a riot," Hunter said. "I looked it up. His wing erupted and the inmates barricaded themselves inside taking three prison officers hostage. The standoff lasted four days until the authorities retook the wing and restored order. They found his body in the shower block. He'd been stabbed to death with a makeshift shank."

"Did they catch who did it?" Caslin asked.

"No. There wasn't any indication of who carried out the attack nor a motive for it. Most likely it was someone using the disturbance to settle a score. Let's face it, it could have been anyone."

"Sorry to ask the stupid question but is this relevant?" Holt asked. Caslin met his eye, inclining his head.

Looking to Hunter, he asked, "Is it relevant?"

"He was sentenced to eighteen years for his part in…" she held her breath, building the anticipation and watching Caslin's interest grow, "the 1986 Manchester Airport raid."

"Well, that's relevant," Caslin said smiling. "The ever-expanding circle."

"He was one of the last to be picked up hence why he received a lesser sentence than many of the others. The case had dropped from the public consciousness and I guess the judge wasn't looking to set such an example as a deterrent."

"Was Neville linked to either MacEwan, Dade or Fuller in a professional capacity prior to the customs house job?" Holt asked.

Hunter shook her head, "There isn't really enough information to make a judgement on that. Fuller and Dade were close in age and were moving in the same circles and so it would be reasonable to assume they knew each other but whether that stretched to criminal enterprise is a leap. Regarding MacEwan… the man's still a bit of an enigma. We just don't know enough about him."

"Okay, changing tack," Caslin said, returning his focus to the noticeboard. "Any lead on the mysterious redhead occupying Jody Wyer's life?"

"None at all," Hunter said. "We've been through his personal effects, the house, car… we've got nothing apart from a toothbrush, toiletries and some red hair in a brush."

Caslin sucked air through his teeth, "I can't help but think she ties in to all of this."

"Why?" Hunter asked.

"Well, for one thing because he kept her a secret from everyone else and secondly, he was working from home and keeping that a secret too. If she was spending so much time there, she might know what he was working on. It doesn't look like he was trying to hide it from her," Caslin explained, "which at most makes her a part of it or at least, a confidant. Either way, I want to find her and let's not forget, he's been murdered and she hasn't come forward. That tells me she knows something, or she's scared of someone."

"Could she also have played a part in killing him?" Holt asked.

"We certainly can't rule it out."

The sound of the doors opening behind them saw them turn. DCI Matheson entered purposefully. Caslin read the look of consternation on her face.

"Ma'am," he said in greeting.

"You've been making enquiries around Clinton Dade's operation," she said.

Caslin nodded, "Yes, we have. Why, what's up?"

"Uniform have just come across Dade," she replied, "and you're going to want to see it."

CHAPTER EIGHTEEN

THE PITCH of the engine increased noticeably as Hunter dropped a gear and pulled out from behind the slow-moving lorry. She was itching to reach the scene just as much as he was and Caslin could feel the anticipation growing inside him. The A166 towards Stamford Bridge was a busy road, east of York, the most direct route to the coast if not the fastest. They weren't going that far. Hunter slowed as the sat nav indicated an approaching left turn. Seeing the sign for the village of Holtby she eased off and left the highway.

"Through the village, wasn't it?" she asked, flicking her eyes at the screen set into the dashboard.

"Yes. Should be a right turn as we come up on Brockfield," Caslin advised her. Hunter nodded, focusing on the road ahead. Holtby came and went in a flash. One of the many tiny villages peppering the rural Yorkshire landscape, Caslin couldn't help but wonder how they came to be out here. Their route cut back to the west before turning north again, navigating the patchwork of farmland delineated by hedgerows and tree lines. Hunter turned on the indicators to signal they were turning onto Rudcarr Lane although Caslin didn't know why she bothered. There was no one out here to inform of the manoeuvre. Here, the road narrowed to such an extent that should they meet a vehicle coming in the other direction there would be the distinct possibility one or the other would need to pull off the road to give way.

Winter crops were visible in fields to either side of them and the road was interspersed with barren oak trees, their leaves shed in late autumn.

"There," Caslin said, pointing ahead to a liveried police car, its nose visible at the next turn in the road. Reaching the bend, Hunter pulled the car to the verge. They were alongside an opening to the field beyond with a small patch of flat ground between them and a gate. The gate itself was wooden and in a poor state of repair, hanging from one of the hinges. It had clearly been some time since it was opened with the hedgerow bordering the field now spreading across the posts. Alongside the gate was a stile, allowing access to the public path over the fields. This was in a far better condition. The landowner must have found a better access point for his machinery and abandoned this one years ago.

Caslin found his attention drawn to why they were there. A dark blue Mercedes was parked up, facing the highway, underneath a giant oak tree. Iain Robertson noted their arrival and beckoned them over.

"One of yours, I believe?" he said by way of greeting, approaching them and tilting his head in the direction of the car.

"Is it Dade?" Caslin asked, falling into step alongside the forensics officer.

"Identification in his wallet says so," Robertson confirmed. "But you're going to need a few tests to be sure."

"That bad?" Hunter asked.

"Aye," Robertson said under his breath, leading them down the passenger side of the car towards the rear.

The car doors were all closed. The rear passenger window was shattered with much of the glass falling inwards into the interior. The remainder was fractured in every direction but held precariously in place despite the driving wind rattling across the flat lands surrounding them. Caslin noted the drainage ditch running alongside the road, assisting to keep the farmland from flooding. Robertson noticed the glance. "We'll be dredging the ditch just in case they dumped the weapon or anyone else for that matter, in there before leaving."

"What do you think?" Caslin asked, returning his attention to the car and its passenger.

"Shotgun," Robertson said with a frown. "Most likely a sawn-off. The nature of the tissue damage is indicative of a wide directional spray from both barrel and cartridge."

Caslin peered through the window into the cabin, exhaling deeply as he registered the state of the interior. Immediately, he knew Alison Taylor would need a DNA sample to confirm the identity of the victim. Even a cursory inspection of the body slumped across the rear seat reinforced that view. In no way would a facial verification be suitable and he guessed a dental match would be equally unsuccessful. The rear window, roof, along with the upholstery were all coated in blood spatter, skin tissue and what Caslin assumed were skull and brain fragments.

"Point blank," he muttered under his breath.

"And several shots, I should imagine," Robertson stated. Caslin looked up at him. "We found two spent cartridges over there," he said, pointing to a patch of ground a few feet away. "I think the killer, or killers, put in two blasts before reloading and doing the same again. That's why you see what you see. They wanted to make absolutely certain."

Caslin shook his head, "No. That's not it."

"Then what?" Robertson asked.

"This was personal."

"Or they wanted it to appear so. Either way, I think the victim was almost certainly known to his killer," Robertson said. Caslin was intrigued.

"How do you know?"

"The window," Robertson said, pointing to the glass. Caslin looked but didn't see what he was supposed to. He raised an eyebrow in a query. "It's on its way down… or up. The victim had lowered it. The top of the glass is down four inches. If he was a smoker, then I can imagine he might want it open in this weather but there's no butt dropped either inside or out. I'd wager it's more likely he was conversing with someone, probably the killer. Liver temperature sets the time of death at around midnight."

"Who could have got Clinton Dade to come all the way out here at that time of night?" Hunter asked.

"Someone he knew," Caslin said quietly, following Robertson's hypothesis. "The end result suggests someone who held a grudge. That might be a reason why they came out here – to be on neutral ground."

"But for such a lethal threat to get this close unchallenged…" Hunter left the thought unfinished, looking to Robertson to answer the unasked question.

"No, there are no other victims as far as we can tell," Robertson confirmed. "We'll carry out a full fingertip search of the surrounding area but there are no blood trails or evidence anyone else was attacked."

"What about up front?" Caslin asked, stepping to his left and peering through the front passenger window, assessing where the driver would have been sitting. Despite a significant amount of blood in the interior, he saw nothing leading him to believe the driver was also hit.

"The spray and subsequent spatter passing from the rear to the front of the cabin is consistent with a high-velocity impact," Robertson said, bending over and following Caslin's sightlines. "Judging from where it struck," he indicated the front windscreen as well as the inside of the driver's window, "I reckon there was no one sitting there when the gun went off."

"Which gives us a further couple of questions," Caslin said, "presuming you're correct about no other victims being present. Either the driver got out of the car to speak with, challenge, or greet the gunman and then made a run for it when everything hit the fan or..." he left the thought hanging as he looked around the immediate vicinity, playing the various scenarios out in his head. "He was complicit in some way."

"He could have been the gunman?" Hunter said, clarifying the thought.

"I'm not convinced of that but it would explain how he managed to get so close," Caslin said. "And one thing's for certain, if this is Clinton Dade, he didn't drive himself out here. We need to find the person who did. If the driver's running, we'll have to find him before the killer does. Likewise, if it was the same person, Dade's crew will also be looking for him and if they get there first, he won't be telling us anything. Knowing the names of those in this circle, we're on the clock. I reckon if he survives twenty-four hours, then he'll be doing well."

"I know it's an obvious thought but you've got to put the Fullers in the frame," Hunter said. "This kind of thing is right up Carl's street, wouldn't you say?"

Caslin had to admit the thought had already occurred to him. There was every chance one or the other faction sought a meeting in order to calm the situation down, particularly as Dade was so insistent that he wasn't to blame for the bombing. A neutral location away from prying eyes was logical. Caslin looked around for the nearest sign of habitation. There were two farmhouses, each surrounded by agricultural buildings, and both were at least three hundred metres away in opposite directions across the fields. This location was nigh on perfect for carrying out such a hit. No witnesses. No cameras. No one to see either party arrive or depart. Minimal chances of being seen let alone caught. Something didn't sit right with him though. An instinctive feeling that had almost always served him well in the past.

"I can't see Ashton going for it though. Can you?" he replied to Hunter.

"Ashton got the brains of the family but Carl runs the muscle. Perhaps he didn't know," she countered. Caslin inclined his head at the suggestion.

"Any sign of other vehicles?" Caslin asked, turning his attention back to Robertson.

"The ground is frozen solid, I'm afraid," he replied. "Very little chance of pulling tyre impressions but we'll do our best."

"I'll arrange to have the local properties canvassed," Hunter said, seeking Caslin's permission with an inquiring glance. He nodded. "We might get lucky."

The sound of an approaching vehicle came to ear and Caslin turned, looking down the road in the direction of Brockfield. The car was moving at pace and it seemed to be out of the ordinary somehow. The driver eased off as he came upon the police cordon, coming to a stop in the middle of the road. Caslin watched as two men got out. Recognising the driver, he indicated for Robertson to carry on with his work and made his way towards the new arrivals. A uniformed constable was already stepping across to block their advance. A movement that was not well received. The driver of the car chose to disregard the officer's instructions and attempted to bypass him. The officer placed a firm hand on the man's shoulder and issued a direct instruction to stop but was ignored.

"It's okay," Caslin called as he approached. The uniformed officer had a firm grasp on the man's clothing and he was about to make an arrest before Caslin intervened. The second man stood a few steps behind and held his ground, watching to see what was about to happen. "Alli, isn't it?" Caslin asked. The man glared first at the constable, despite being released, and then at Caslin.

"Is it him?" Alli asked, almost spitting venom as the words passed his lips and looked beyond Caslin towards the blue Mercedes.

"We think so," Caslin confirmed. At confirmation of Dade's apparent demise, Alli visibly appeared to shrink in stature before him. He looked to the ground at his feet, drawing deep breaths and Caslin realised he was trying not to break down. "How did you know he was out here?" he asked. The bitter anger in Alli's eyes dissipated to be replaced by a somewhat lost expression. Tears welled and Caslin saw at that moment the true nature of their relationship.

"Word travels," Alli said as if that answered the question.

"Was Clinton out here to meet someone last night?" Caslin asked. All of a sudden, Alli's expression changed from grief stricken to guarded. He shrugged.

"How would I know?"

"Word travels," Caslin replied with no hint of sarcasm. "Of all people, you should know what his plans were."

"He didn't say," Alli stated. "I want to see him."

"I'm afraid that's not possible at the moment," Caslin said before adding, "and inadvisable." Alli looked past him, once again, in the direction of the car and the forensic team crawling all over it.

"They'll pay for this."

"Who will, Alli?"

"Mark my words," he reiterated.

"Remember you're talking to a police officer," Caslin warned him. "I'm not your priest." Alli met his eye. He said nothing further but the fire of revenge flared in his eyes. "Any idea who he was out here with? Who was driving?" Caslin asked, glancing first to Alli and then his associate off to his right. Again, Alli declined to answer, his gaze drifting across the scene. The second man shook his head almost imperceptibly when Caslin lifted a casual finger in his direction.

"You're going to be a busy man, Inspector Caslin," Alli stated, turning his gaze back to him.

"Leave this to us," Caslin said, as sternly as he could. For his part, Alli smiled but it was tight-lipped and cold. "The best thing you can do is tell me what Clinton was doing out here before anybody else gets killed."

The smile faded and Alli took a deep breath, drawing himself upright. In doing so he more than matched Caslin for height and his stature returned to the imposing figure of their first meeting.

"Don't worry, Inspector," he said with menacing undertones. "It'll be over soon enough."

"You'll be starting a war," Caslin warned.

"They came at us," Alli hissed.

"This is one you might not be able to win."

"We'll see about that," he said, taking a couple of steps back before turning on his heel. He snapped his fingers towards the other man who fell into step alongside him. They strode back to their car. Caslin watched and as they reached it, Alli glanced back at him while opening the driver's door. He stopped, his gaze lingering for a few moments on Caslin and then back to the crime scene beyond. Caslin remained impassive as Hunter came to stand with him. Alli got into the car, slamming the door shut. He started the engine and crunched the gears as he set the car into reverse, moving off at speed. Alli manoeuvred the vehicle into a passing area and swiftly turned the car around. With one last angry look in Caslin's direction, he accelerated away, the tyres squealing momentarily as they sought traction.

"That didn't appear to go well," Hunter said.

"No. You're quite right about that," Caslin replied. "This is going to escalate quickly."

"What do you want to do?"

"Get us a search warrant for the Fullers," he said, turning to her. "It might be best if we can take them off the streets for a while."

"Is that wise?" she asked, looking concerned. "I mean, I know they'll be targets but we don't have a lot to go on that will hold them for a second longer than it takes for their brief to turn up."

"Let's see where the warrant gets us."

"Okay, where will we search?"

"Everywhere," Caslin said. "I want every business and residential premises tied to them turned over. Oh… and I want it done today."

"That'll take some doing," Hunter stated.

"You sort out the paperwork and I'll have a word with DCI Matheson about drawing the bodies. She offered to help and this," he said, indicating over his shoulder with a flick of the hand, "should be motivation enough. If we don't put a lid on it, then Dade will just be the beginning."

CHAPTER NINETEEN

PULLING into the forecourt of the disused petrol station they found it deserted. The handful of men operating the car wash were nowhere to be seen. The cabin they operated out of was securely closed and there was no sign of recent activity. Hunter pulled their car to the side and parked up. Four liveried police vehicles pulled in behind them, fanning out and blocking both entrance and exit from the site. Getting out of the car, Caslin looked around. There were no sounds carrying from the building site to the rear either. He looked at his watch to check the time. It was a quarter after two and except for New Year's Eve, he couldn't imagine a construction site shutting down this early. Indicating to the waiting officers, they headed over to the site entrance. This too, was closed off by a length of Herras fencing. Looking beyond it and into the compound, Caslin could clearly see several vehicles parked outside the portacabin.

"Someone's here," Caslin said, grasping the padlock securing the makeshift gate in place. He shook it. The padlock was solid and held firm.

"It's almost as if they were expecting us," Hunter said.

"There's a shock," Caslin replied with a wry grin. Looking to the portacabin he could see the lights were on inside. He beckoned one of the team over. The officer approached with a set of bolt croppers in hand. "They just don't want to make it easy, that's all. Heads up everyone," Caslin said, addressing all of those present. "They'll do everything they can to get in our way. Don't let them distract you and watch your backs... and each other's."

The officer struggled for a few moments before a reassuring snap was heard and the padlock dropped away, clattering to the ground. The sound of metal on metal followed as the chain was dragged clear. Two officers lifted one end of the fence and levered it away and to the left allowing them access to the compound. The moment Caslin took a step inside the perimeter he heard a whistle, shrill and high-pitched but he didn't know where it originated from. Something seen in the corner of his eye made him turn, looking towards the rear of the site. From behind the scaffolding, roughly sixty feet away, he saw a blur of movement as several figures flashed past open sections of the building.

"What have we got here?" he heard Hunter say from behind. Everyone stopped as three dogs came into view. Caslin wasn't a fan of dogs, particularly Dobermans approaching at great speed. Instinctively, he took a step back. Looking to his left he didn't need to give the instruction as both officers who'd cleared their route were rapidly setting the barrier back into place. They managed to do so just in time as the animals arrived. They were clearly well trained as they came to a stop a few yards from them. Their ears were pricked and two of them stood their ground, eyeing the visitors intently. The third edged closer, walking the length of the fence as if assessing them. There was no growling, snarling or even a bark. They were there to deter people from entering the compound. Caslin admired their efficiency.

In the background, the door to the portacabin open and a figure emerged. It was Carl Fuller. He didn't approach them, merely folded his arms across his chest and leaned his shoulder against the building. Caslin held a fold of paper in his hands. Realising Carl had zero intention of coming over, he unfurled it. Holding it aloft against the fence, he called out.

"We are here to execute a search warrant!"

Carl shrugged, "I'm not stopping you."

"You've got twenty seconds to call your dogs off..." Caslin called, pointing at the animals. One of which was now standing before him with its head cocked.

"Or what?" Carl countered.

"Or I'll bloody shoot them," Caslin shouted. He didn't have an armed officer present and, in reality, he would never carry out such a drastic action but nonetheless, he made his point. Carl Fuller watched him for a few moments longer before stepping away from the wall. He poked his head back inside the portacabin, conversing with someone. Caslin saw him nod in response to something that was said and he turned. Putting two fingers in his mouth, he whistled and two of the three dogs visibly appeared to relax and turn away, trotting off in Carl's direction. The one staring at Caslin held its gaze for the briefest of moments before it, too, turned away and ran to join the others.

"I don't think it likes you," Hunter said dryly. Caslin smiled.

"It must be the reincarnation of my mother-in-law."

"Is she dead?" Hunter asked.

"We can but dream," Caslin replied as the fence was removed for the second time and they made to pass through. The guard dogs didn't react to their presence although every officer cast a wary eye in their direction. Hunter took care of issuing instructions to the search team while Caslin made his way towards Carl Fuller.

Walking up the short ramp to the entrance of the portacabin, he offered over the search warrant. Carl Fuller glanced at it but had no intention of taking it from him.

"Nah," he said dismissing the gesture. "I don't do paperwork."

"No, of course not," Caslin replied with a smile. "You'd need to be able to read," he added, slapping it forcefully against the younger man's chest. Carl accepted it under protest, glaring at him as he did so. Caslin brushed past him and made his way into the office. Inside, he found Ashton Fuller seated behind a desk, two associates clustered around him. He sat back in his chair, drawing a deep breath and exaggerating his exhalation as he took in Caslin's measure.

"Inspector Caslin," he said, smiling. "Back so soon?"

"You can't have heard me knocking," Caslin replied. "You two," he pointed to the men either side of Ashton, "move." The two men looked to Ashton who didn't respond. They held their position. Hunter came alongside Caslin, two uniformed constables accompanying her.

"You heard the man, *shift yersel,*" she stated firmly in her best native Yorkshire accent, indicating the search team wanted access to the filing cabinets behind them. Begrudgingly, the two men stepped aside. Hunter encouraged her officers forward before looking to Caslin. "Everything's underway."

"Good," Caslin replied with a nod of the head but his eyes never left Ashton.

"This might go better if you tell me what you're looking for?" Ashton said, sitting forward, resting his elbows on the desk before him and making a tent with his fingers. "What's all this about?"

"Terry?" Caslin asked, looking to Hunter.

"Has access to their apartments as we speak," she confirmed. Both of the Fullers lived in the city centre in adjoining apartments, prestigious addresses that saw them rub shoulders with the wealthiest residents the city of York could provide.

"I do hope you will be paying for any damage," Ashton said in an icy tone. It was the first time since their arrival that he'd exhibited anything but a smug attitude.

"Standard issue boots do tend to traipse in a lot of dirt," Caslin said. "I hope you don't have pastel carpets."

"*What is it that you want?*" Ashton reiterated, the novelty of the situation departing him as his office was systematically ransacked by the assembled officers.

"Clinton Dade is dead."

"What's that got to do with us?"

"You're not out to settle the account?" Caslin asked. Carl appeared to his left, fixing him with a stare and passing the copy of the search warrant over to his brother.

"Maybe he got depressed," Carl suggested. "Couldn't take it anymore."

"And blew his own face off with a shotgun?" Hunter asked.

"It's been done," Carl countered.

"I'd suggest it's hard to do the last three... after the first, though," Hunter said.

"Maybe he picked up the wrong boy?" Carl said, grinning.

"Where were you last night?" Caslin asked, cutting in and breaking the hostile exchange between the two. Carl glanced in his direction.

"I was at home, watching the telly."

"And you?" Caslin asked, looking to his brother. Ashton smiled, his eyes revealing what Caslin took as a glimmer of amusement.

"Watching telly," he said, flicking his eyes towards his brother. "With him."

"Anything good?" Hunter asked.

"Don't remember," Ashton replied. "Do you, Carl?"

"No, I think I fell asleep."

Caslin expected nothing more imaginative from the pair of them. They conveyed a level of confidence in their position which he found unnerving. Neither were strangers to police procedure and despite being mildly irritated by their presence, they weren't thrown by the search. That was a bad sign.

"Sir," a voice came from behind. Caslin turned to see a constable standing at the entrance trying to get his attention. He glanced back to Ashton, the smile faded but the air of confidence remained. Crossing the office, he acknowledged the officer.

"What do you have?" he asked.

"There's something you need to see," he replied, gesturing for him to step outside. Caslin beckoned Hunter over and she made to follow but Carl was in her way. She locked eyes with him, her expression one of stern authority. He didn't move.

"Carl," Ashton said from behind Hunter. The corners of Carl's mouth turned up in a slight smile and he rotated his body sideways, granting her just enough space to slip by. She did so, never removing her eyes from his. She reached Caslin as he was leaving the portacabin. Together they went outside, Hunter noting Ashton standing up and falling into step alongside his brother as both of them followed.

The constable led them down the side of the portacabin and across the building site towards the rear. In this corner of the compound they found the daily site materials were stored, ranging from concrete blocks to shrink-wrapped pallets of unopened cement sacks. Piled against the outer perimeter fence were bulk bags of sand, each easily approaching a tonne in weight, awaiting the bricklaying crew. A uniformed constable stood to the left of one of the bags, holding a rod that reached from the ground to just above his waist. He had been using it to probe the contents of the bags.

"We found something," he said in response, pointing to the first bag. Caslin looked down and saw a package jutting out from the top of the sand. Whatever was buried it was wrapped in heavy-gauge polythene and well taped up, presumably to avoid the ingress of sand to the contents. Donning a pair of latex gloves, Caslin uncovered more of the sand from around the object, sweeping it away from the edges with his hands. The package was still wedged and, in the end, he used brute strength to draw it clear from the bag.

"Well, well, well," he said, holding it before him in both hands. He turned and angled it so that Hunter could see. She smiled. The package was a little under two-foot-long and despite the multiple layers of the polythene encompassing it, the opacity was such that the shape of a sawn-off shotgun was clearly visible.

"That's a fit up!" Carl barked from behind Hunter. "You've stashed that there," he accused them aggressively. Two officers moved to stand behind him just in case he made a break for it.

"We've got better things to be doing with our time," Caslin countered, handing the gun to the constable alongside him who had made the discovery.

"You bastard," Carl said, almost spitting the words at him. Caslin looked at Ashton, who in stark contrast to his brother, remained calm and emotionless.

"Anything from you?" Caslin asked. Ashton bit his lower lip and sucked air through his teeth. His nose twitched involuntarily but he held his anger or frustration, Caslin couldn't tell which, in check.

"You'll never make this stick," he said quietly, tilting his head to one side and narrowing his eyes.

"Oh, I don't know, perhaps not," Caslin countered. "But it's going to be a lot of fun trying. DS Hunter, if you please," he said, turning to her.

"With pleasure, sir," she replied, beckoning the nearest officers forward. They took out their handcuffs as she began to read the Fuller brothers their rights.

"This is *such* bullshit," Carl stated, shaking his head and resisting the attentions of the officers who were trying to draw his arms behind his back. A brief glance in his direction from Ashton saw those efforts cease and both were taken into custody without incident.

"We'll be out before sundown," Ashton said to Caslin.

"We'll see. Separate cars for transit, please," Caslin said as they were led away. The last thing he wanted was for the two of them to concoct a story en route to the station. Turning to the officer holding the gun, Caslin eyed it. "Have that documented, photographed and then send it over to ballistics. I want to get it confirmed as the murder weapon as soon as possible."

"Will do, sir," the constable said.

Caslin turned away and headed back towards the office. Despite the find, the remaining members of the search team were still diligently going through the contents of the office. With a bit of luck, Caslin hoped they might find other incriminating evidence. He wanted to make the best use of this search as he could for if Ashton was right and they couldn't build a case that would hold up, the chances of being granted further warrants would be less likely. Magistrates didn't like to look foolish any more than anyone else did. Hunter met him halfway.

"That's a stroke of luck," she said. Caslin knew her well enough to read past the obvious.

"Meaning?"

"That the Fullers would be stupid enough to leave the murder weapon where we could find it," she said.

"Bollocks," Caslin replied with a grin. "You know as well as I do, they aren't that daft."

"Agreed."

"Someone's playing us," Caslin stated, staring into the distance and watching as Ashton and Carl were placed into the rear seats of waiting cars.

"If you think so, why did we arrest them?"

"The streets will be a little safer with them out of the way for a day or two," Caslin said. "For them as well as us."

"Someone has an interesting strategy," Hunter said, thinking aloud.

"Aye," Caslin agreed. "I'd put money on it they don't think we'll be able to pin this on the Fullers. I expect that gun is wiped clean of fingerprints and missing its serial number."

"So, what's the point?"

"At the very least it will piss them off... the Fullers, I mean," Caslin explained, "and will certainly disrupt their operations for a bit."

"There has to be more to it than that," Hunter countered.

"Without a doubt," Caslin said. "The thing is we're always one step behind. We need to get ahead of them somehow."

"If we knew who *they* were, it would help."

"We're coming at this all wrong," Caslin said. He didn't necessarily disagree with her but they had to change their approach. He was tired of another orchestrating their actions.

"I'm open to suggestions," Hunter said.

"We've been going through the old case histories and trying to link everyone together and there's only one candidate for that."

"The raid on the clearing house, back in 86."

"Exactly," Caslin agreed. "But we're no closer to knowing how this is related to the present and I don't think we're going to find the answer in the archives."

"Okay," Hunter said, following his thread. "So, what do we do?"

"Start with today and work backwards, rather than carry on with what we have been doing," Caslin explained. "There's too much information to go through from thirty years ago and Holt hasn't even been able to get hold of all the files yet. Out of the current names in the picture who do we have tying them together?"

Hunter thought on it before answering, "You've got me. Who?"

"Answer that… and I reckon we'll be getting somewhere," Caslin said, watching Hunter's irritation with him manifest itself. "I want to put some pressure on our sources and see what comes out. Rumours will be flying around and maybe one of them will be close to what's actually going on here."

"Shall we head back to Fulford Road?"

"You go," Caslin said. "I need to run an errand first. I'll see you back at the station later."

CHAPTER TWENTY

ARRIVING at the house around midday, Caslin pulled the car to the side of the road. Switching off the engine, he looked towards his father's property. Lights were visible inside and the curtains weren't drawn. Glancing at his watch, he thought that was a good sign. His father was up and about before lunchtime. No matter how often he visited his relationship with his father in his mind, he still struggled with their dynamic. Somehow, they just couldn't seem to get along for more than an hour… on a good day.

Taking a deep breath, he picked up his keys and cracked open the door. A gust of cold air hit him and he fastened his coat as soon as he was able. After constant badgering, his father now agreed to lock the rear gate and force people to the front of the house. Too often, Caslin had been able to just walk in unannounced - a situation that left his father vulnerable as he'd found out to his cost a couple of years ago, ending up with the old man fighting for his life in hospital. Although Selby was a town of some size and population where his father lived was in the established part and some way from the urban sprawl of modern development. His house was one built for the agricultural workers in the middle of the last century, one of several set apart from most of the neighbouring properties.

Approaching the door, Caslin pressed the buzzer, hearing it ring inside. There was a flicker of movement inside, a shadow passing in the hall beyond the door and Caslin waited. The noise of an engine carried to him and Caslin looked to his left, back down the road and saw an unmarked transit van pull up to the kerb on the opposite side of the street. The driver got out and walked out of sight, behind the vehicle. Caslin silently lamented the number of independent couriers he saw knocking around these days. The gig economy was roaring in Yorkshire. The sound of a chain being released from the other side of the door snapped his attention back to his father and the door opened. Caslin was surprised to find his son, Sean, standing before him in the entrance hall.

"Hey, dad," he said with a smile.

"Sean…" Caslin replied, unable to mask the surprise. "What are you…?"

"Daddy!" his question remained unfinished as another voice came from within the house. His daughter, Lizzie, came running from the living room to greet him. He knelt as she threw herself into his arms knocking him off balance. He managed not to topple over and hugged her fiercely.

"What are you two doing…"

"Karen asked if I could babysit-"

"Have us visit!" Sean said, casting a frown over his shoulder at his grandfather who held his hands up in supplication.

"Sorry, sorry," he said. "Their mother asked if they could visit for the weekend."

"Did she now?" Caslin said, exhaling through his nose.

"Apparently, her other arrangements fell through," his father said, inclining his head forward and fixing a stern gaze on his son.

"Hmm…" Caslin replied, releasing Lizzie who took off back into the living room.

"Daddy, come and see what we're watching," she said excitedly.

"Okay," he called after her, standing and stepping inside. Sean backed away to make room and Caslin went to close the door behind him. The van was still outside and Caslin thought the driver was taking his time with the delivery. "It had better not be something made on *Elm Street*," he said pointedly to his father as he walked past him placing an affectionate hand on his shoulder as he did so. The older man chuckled.

"I've never been in to anything like that," his father said, following on. "Real life is horrific enough."

"True," Caslin agreed. "You were married to mum."

"Cheeky sod," his father countered, giving him a gentle tap to the back of the head as they entered the living room. Caslin was drawn to the television, pleased to see it was an animated film of some description but not one he recognised.

"There's a singing shark," Lizzie said excitedly, glancing in his direction briefly before focusing on the screen once again.

"It's awful," Sean chipped in without looking up from his position draped across an armchair and staring at his tablet. He looked like he'd been slumped there for hours but, in reality, it was a little over two minutes. Caslin wondered if whatever held his attention was as equally stimulating as a musical shark or possibly more disturbing.

"Coffee?" his father asked.

"Please," Caslin replied. The characters on the television screen burst into song and he hurried after the departing form of his father and joined him in the kitchen. "They seem settled."

"Yes, they are good kids," his father said, taking two cups down from a shelf above the coffee machine and setting them on the work surface. "It's great to have them here, I have to say," he added, taking on a faraway look and suddenly appearing lost in thought.

"What is it, Dad?" Caslin asked. His father glanced over to him shaking his head.

"No, no, it's nothing," he stuttered as he spoke. Caslin didn't believe him but he let it go. "So, why wouldn't you have them this weekend?"

Caslin frowned, "Karen told you about that?"

"Yes, she did," his father replied, placing the filter head into the coffee grinder and running it for ten seconds, filling it and returning to the coffee machine. "She's not best pleased with you, your ex, I must say."

"Must you?" Caslin said playfully. His father smiled.

"Of all the times to drop your responsibilities this probably wasn't the best."

"*Drop?*" Caslin said. "I'm hardly dropping them."

"Work?" his father asked with an enquiring look. Caslin nodded. "I think she's past accepting that excuse."

"It was barely acceptable when we were married."

"Is it true?"

"What do you mean by that?" Caslin said, offended.

"Is it work or are you trying to mess things up between Karen and her new man?"

"Do you think I'm that petty?" Caslin asked. His father turned away from him. "And he's hardly new, is he?"

"Black?"

"What?" Caslin asked.

"Your coffee. Do you want it black?"

"Yes, thank you," Caslin replied. His father turned and passed him a cup. Caslin accepted it noting his father's stern gaze. "I really am very busy."

"What are you working on in this task force of yours?"

"It's not a task force as such," Caslin explained, not wishing to go into too much detail.

"It's major crimes, though, isn't it?"

"It should be," Caslin said, "but I've stripped Fulford Road of some of the best resources in CID and so we're still helping them out until they can re-balance the team."

"So, what is it that's keeping you away from your kids?"

"Nothing much," Caslin said. He hated discussing his work with his father. There was always a better method that things used to be done by, often now illegal, that his father would feel needed to be explained to him in great detail.

"*Nothing much* is keeping you from spending time with your kids? Karen was right then?"

Caslin sighed before sipping at his coffee, "It's complicated."

"Try me," his father said. "I like complicated."

"To start with, I've got someone fermenting a turf war between rival gangs that may or may not be instigating tit-for-tat murders," Caslin said, frowning. "Right now, we have a group of names who are all quite capable of bringing this on but nothing to explain why they would choose to do so."

"You're right. That does sound complicated," his father replied, smiling.

"Add to that a decorated policeman consorting with known criminals from beyond the grave and I have a pretty big headache right now," Caslin said. "Any ideas?" His father turned back to the machine and went to set the filter head in place to make his own cup but struggled to do so, leading to him cursing under his breath. "Having trouble?" Caslin asked.

"Bloody machine," his father said as he finally drove the head into place. He silently went about making his drink. Caslin was happy the third degree appeared to be over without him receiving the customary lecture that usually accompanied such a conversation. His father crossed to the fridge and returned with the milk, not bothering to heat it first, he added some to his freshly made coffee. "From beyond the grave, you say?"

Caslin had gotten ahead of himself, "Yeah. We all thought he was dead. Turns out we were wrong."

"I see," his father said, staring into his coffee cup and stirring a spoon in a very deliberate way. "What's that all about then?"

"If I knew, I'd be spending the weekend with my children," Caslin countered.

"What's he got to say for himself?"

"Who?"

"This policeman you're talking about. What did you say his name was?"

"I didn't say," Caslin said, drinking his coffee. "Bradley. A former DCI in Greater Manchester."

"Right," his father said, putting his cup down and crossing is arms. "And what's he got to say?"

"Not a lot... certainly without a Ouija board, anyway," Caslin said, shaking his head. "He's dead."

"Dead?" his father said, watching him intently. Caslin was slightly unnerved.

"Yeah, he died in a car crash the other day."

"I see," his father said, expressionless. Caslin was surprised at how serious the tone of the conversation was becoming.

"Relax, Dad," he said with a smile. "It's nothing for you to get into. I'll sort it out. Like I said, it's complicated."

"Of course, you will," his father said, breaking into a smile. "You always do. It's just a pity it comes at the cost of seeing your kids."

"That's a bit harsh."

"Is it?" his father countered. "You always manage to find something..."

"I don't *manage* to find anything."

"Come off it, Nathaniel. You've always been willing to pass your parental responsibilities off onto someone else. Usually it was your wife but now it's coming my way."

"You're a little out of order," Caslin said, feeling a flash of anger at the personal attack.

"I'm out of order?" his father questioned him. "Take a look at those kids in there. How long has it been since they spent more than a couple of hours with you?"

"You, of all people, should know what this job's like!"

"I knew when to call time and come home. Maybe you should take a look at yourself."

"I can't believe I'm hearing this," Caslin muttered.

"That's just it, Nathaniel. No one tells you like it is anymore. You just listen to yourself and do as you please."

Caslin finished his coffee and put the cup down on the kitchen table shaking his head, "Coming from you, that's a bit rich."

"What do you mean by that?" his father hissed.

"You set the example that I followed-"

"Are you two arguing?" a voice came from behind. Caslin turned to see both Sean and Lizzie standing at the threshold to the kitchen. Sean stood behind his sister with both hands placed reassuringly on her shoulders. He was biting his lower lip while Lizzie sought an answer to her question.

"No, we're not," Caslin explained. "Just a mild disagreement... which I'm not entirely sure how it came about."

"You and mum used to have those," Lizzie replied, taking the events in her stride as usual.

"And still do..." Sean added.

"Thank you for helping, Sean," Caslin said tilting his head and making no attempt to hide the sarcasm. "Everything's all right, nothing for either of you to worry about. Right, Dad?" he said, looking to his father.

"Of course," he replied under his breath, looking out of the window and into the garden beyond.

"You see," Caslin said, forcing a smile. It fooled no one.

"Oh right," Sean said, nudging his little sister in the back. "It's all good."

"If you say so," Lizzie replied. Stepping forward, she threw her arms around her father's legs and hugged him momentarily. He looked down and tussled her hair. Then she was gone skipping back into the living room and bumping her brother, who rolled his eyes, as she passed by him. He turned and followed. Caslin chuckled.

"Sometimes I think they're more grown up than I give them credit for," he said.

"They certainly are. More than their father, at least."

Caslin faked a smile, "And on that note I think I'll head off."

"If you like," his father grumbled, turning his back on him.

"I'll give you a call over the weekend, see how you're getting on?" Caslin said, lightening his tone and trying to appease whatever anger his father was currently fostering towards him. The only response was an almost inaudible grunt.

Caslin chose not to pursue it further and left the kitchen. He went into the living room and scooped Lizzie up in his arms. Turning her upside down, he tickled her stomach. The action was accompanied by shrieks of delight as her long blonde curls dangled down across her face. Dumping her carefully onto the sofa, he leant down and kissed her forehead. She gave him another fierce hug.

"You two have fun this weekend," he said, "and try not to give your granddad too hard a time."

"We won't," Lizzie said with a devious smile that indicated quite the opposite. Caslin crossed to Sean and was begrudgingly given a farewell hug. Soon, Caslin felt he'd be lucky to be offered a handshake as his eldest was reaching an age where any physical contact with his father would be deemed suicidal for his social credibility. Glancing over his shoulder there was no apparent movement from within the kitchen. His father was clattering around out of sight taking out his frustrations on his utensils. Somehow, they were butting heads again and not for the first time, Caslin was at a loss to explain why.

Closing the front door behind him, he stepped onto the path and headed for his car. His phone began to ring and he took it out noting it was Hunter as he answered the call. Continuing on down the path, he glanced back over his shoulder at his father's house feeling disheartened at how the visit turned out but pleased to have seen his children.

"Sarah, what do you have?" he asked.

"Hang on, sir. I'll put you on speaker. Terry's here as well," she said. Caslin waited patiently. The sound of her slightly disembodied voice came to him indicating she had opened the call to the room. "Can you hear us?" she asked.

"I can. Go ahead," Caslin replied, reaching his car. Opening the door, he saw the delivery van was still parked across the street but he gave it no more attention as he clambered into his seat. Placing the phone on the dash, he hit the engine start button and dabbed the accelerator. The car fired into life and his call was transferred to the internal speakers via the car's Bluetooth connection.

"We've been digging around in Pete Fuller's background, sir," Hunter said. "It's more than interesting."

"Go on," Caslin replied.

"Apparently, Fuller and Neville Bridger go back a long way," Hunter said.

"How so?" Caslin asked.

"They were as thick as thieves growing up well before they came onto our radar," Holt continued, reading through his notes. "They came through the system together growing up in the same care home. They were both considered problem children and, unlike Fuller's sister, neither lasted very long at foster homes. Once kids hit a certain age the odds of getting a permanent place drop rapidly. They must have been the only constant in each other's lives."

"What's the significance of the sister?" Caslin asked. Holt wouldn't have mentioned her without reason.

"Their parents were estranged with no father listed on file. The mother was an alcoholic, suffered from schizophrenia and was prone to violent outbursts hence why social services were involved. Bridger's background was pretty similar. Pete Fuller's sister, Emilia, was rehoused with a foster family and stayed with them until adulthood but their relationship remained strong despite growing up apart."

"Still waiting on the significance," Caslin said. Hunter picked up the story.

"Well, this is where it gets intriguing. Neville Bridger was married to Emilia Fuller. Which makes Ollie and Mark…"

"Pete Fuller's nephews," Caslin finished for her.

"Strange bedfellows for the two of them to be keeping under the circumstances," Holt said. "Particularly as we have Ollie still linked to the Fullers' organisation recently."

"Isn't it just," Caslin said under his breath. "If we know this, I reckon it's fair to say Dade and MacEwan know who they are as well."

"I'd be surprised if they didn't," Hunter said.

"I'd like to explore Fuller's family angle a little more," Caslin said, thinking aloud. "If Fuller and Neville Bridger were so tight how come the latter's children are working for the opposition. Which one was it?"

"Mark is a part of Dade's crew," Hunter confirmed.

"And Ollie is alongside MacEwan?" Caslin asked rhetorically. "For Mark to be welcomed into Clinton Dade's inner circle something must have gone on. Find out what it is."

"There's always another possibility," Holt added.

"What's that?" Caslin asked.

"Mark got as close as he could to enable him to make the hit," Holt suggested, "on Fuller's behalf. He's been inside a long time and I checked on the dates, he's due out in what… eighteen months to two years? Maybe he's been planning it for ages and wanted it done before his release knowing he'd be the prime suspect."

"That's a thought," Caslin said. "But where does the bombing of

Fuller's business come in to that theory? Remember, that came first. Keep it in mind, Terry, but find out if something went down between Fuller and Neville Bridger or his sons. Where are we with our own resources?"

"People have gone to ground, sir," Hunter said. "It's almost like everyone is expecting this to get worse and no one wants to get caught in the crossfire."

"Someone has to know something," Caslin stated. "Shake down every informant we have on the books. Don't worry about being polite. Do whatever you have to. This is too big for this level of silence. We're missing something… and it's really starting to piss me off."

"Will do," they both replied in unison and Caslin ended the call.

CHAPTER TWENTY-ONE

"ASHTON AND CARL'S brief is kicking off downstairs," Hunter said, ducking her head into Caslin's office. "Threatening to sue us for wrongful arrest, harassment and anything else she can come up with." Caslin glanced up from reading the folder before him with an expression that almost indicated he hadn't heard a word she'd said.

"We found the likely murder weapon in a homicide on their property," he countered with a frown which quickly transferred to a smile. "What does she expect?"

"The custody sergeant wants to know what we plan to do with them."

"In what way?"

"Are we going to interview them further?"

Caslin shook his head, "No point. They've not given us anything and I don't see that changing. Usually, I'd look to play one off against the other but that approach won't work with these two."

"They're pretty arrogant too," Hunter said.

"Much as I hate to disagree with you... because they are arrogant... but I'd argue their attitude is more to do with confidence," Caslin said. "They know we won't be able to make a case without a witness, or forensics, to tie them to the weapon. Where are we with that?"

"As you said, the shotgun was wiped clean. No serial number and although we can tie the shotgun cartridges to Dade's hit, there are no ballistics matches with any prior cases," Hunter explained.

"So, there's no previous case that can link them to ownership even circumstantially."

"That's right. All we have is their enmity towards Dade and the fact the gun was found on their building site. It's barely enough to hold them for the initial detention period let alone get an extension."

"You're right," Caslin said, sucking air through his teeth.

"Do we bail them?"

"No. Let's keep them here for the full twenty-four hours," Caslin said. "Let them sweat for a little while."

"Their brief will go mental," Hunter argued.

Caslin shrugged, "If she's on an hourly rate it will be a nice earner although she'll give the custody suite a group headache. Who's the sergeant today?"

"Steve Owen."

"Tell him I'll buy him a pint."

Looking beyond his office, Caslin saw Terry Holt enter. He took off his coat and threw it in the general direction of the coat rack but missed by some margin. He failed to notice as he made a beeline for them scooping up a folder from his desk as he passed - a determined expression on his face. Appearing alongside Hunter, he was almost breathless as he spoke.

"Sir, I've just met with an informant and I think you'll be interested to hear what he had to say." Caslin beckoned him in and Holt pulled up a chair, sitting down and catching his breath.

"About the Fullers?" Caslin asked. Holt shook his head. Evidently, he'd run through the station to get back and was feeling the effects of the exertion.

"Neville Bridger," Holt said. "The word is that someone grassed Neville up for his role in the Manchester raid. Did anyone else find it odd that in the months following the raid multiple members of the gang were picked up, often in quick bursts, but then there was nothing until Neville Bridger was collared well over a decade later?"

"Associations come to light and you only need a couple at a time for them to lead to others," Hunter argued. Holt agreed.

"Yes, but the case was cold... not even being investigated at the time of Bridger's arrest," Holt said, opening the folder in his hands and leafing through the contents. He couldn't find what he was looking for and gave up, placing the documents down on Caslin's desk. "Officially, the case was never closed but there were no active officers assigned to the investigation but then, all of a sudden, Neville gets fingered for it and goes down for a stretch soon after."

"I don't remember anything in the file relating to an informant in his arrest," Caslin said, spinning Holt's file one-hundred-and-eighty degrees and scanning the contents himself.

"You won't have, sir," Holt said. "I checked. But that's not the only thing that bothers me. I can't see where they got the information from about his involvement. If you look at the evidence, the Crown Prosecution Service had – locations, dates, times, bank accounts – it was all there."

"I didn't see any of that," Hunter said.

"You wouldn't have," Holt said. "Bridger pleaded guilty at the time so there was no trial. I imagine the evidence was so well stacked against him he realised his best option was to do so and go for the reduced sentence in return."

"So, who gave us Bridger?" Caslin asked.

"The honest answer to that is *we have no idea,*" Holt said. "However, my informant reckons it came from Fuller."

"Pete grassed on his brother-in-law?" Hunter said, sounding incredulous.

"And his childhood friend," Caslin added pointedly.

"Not buying it," Hunter clarified, shaking her head.

"My guy says that when Pete was sent down, it was Neville who laid claim to his business interests. Which is logical bearing in mind their history and family ties," Holt said. "However, his wife, Emilia, died in 1991 and then things began to change. Whether Neville liked having the power or his temporary position as head of the organisation didn't garner the respect needed to maintain control, I don't know but he started to make changes. Many of Pete's most trusted allies dropped from view. A couple of them were subject to enquiries by our colleagues but nothing ever came of the investigations."

"Neville was disposing of his competition…" Caslin said aloud.

"That was the talk of the day," Holt confirmed.

"Why wouldn't Fuller just take care of it himself?" Hunter asked. "From what I know of him, he doesn't look the sort to roll over on his associates and let's face it, he's more than capable."

"It might not be true," Caslin countered. "But people talk and the rumour mill can get a lie halfway around the world before the truth has got its pants on."

"Bridger was killed inside, wasn't he?" Hunter asked.

Holt nodded. "May have been connected, might not," he said. "It could just as easily be the settling of a score on the inside as much as being a hit orchestrated by Fuller."

"I'm with Sarah on this," Caslin said, indicating Hunter. "I don't think it's Fuller's style but if that became common knowledge, or even the spoken rumour, that might explain why the Bridger boys lined up with the opposition."

"Exactly," Holt said emphatically. "Whether Fuller had Neville killed or not is irrelevant. Both Mark and Ollie held Fuller responsible for their father's death. As a result, there's no love lost between the cousins either. Mark had a major falling out with Carl Fuller a couple of years back. He shows up amongst Dade's business interests shortly after."

"What about the other one…?" Caslin momentarily forgot the name.

"Ollie," Hunter reminded him.

"Yes, Ollie. What about his relationship with the Fullers? What do we know about it?"

Holt shook his head, "There's no intel to suggest he piled in with his brother on the Fullers. As you said, he was arrested recently when apparently still working for them. By all accounts, Ollie is the calmer one of the two and far more calculating."

"Like Ashton Fuller is to his brother, Carl," Hunter said.

"I would say so," Holt confirmed. "Looking at his history, Ollie was still popping up in relation to the Fullers long after Carl and Mark came to blows, which I found interesting. Perhaps, he didn't hear the old rumours or buy into them."

"Or there was something else going on?" Caslin argued.

"Such as?" Hunter asked. Caslin's brow furrowed in response but he didn't elaborate further. His mobile phone began to vibrate on the desk in front of him. Glancing at the screen the call originated from a number he didn't recognise. Picking it up, he answered.

"Caslin," he said flatly.

"I see you've not refrained from only bothering me," the voice said at the other end of the line. Caslin was thrown for a brief moment. He recognised the controlled aggression of the bearer and shouldn't have been surprised. The fortified walls and strict regime meant nothing if you were the right person with the requisite resources. Caslin glanced to both Hunter and Terry Holt, indicating for them to make themselves scarce. Neither of them questioned the request although both noted the change in his demeanour. Hunter closed the door behind them, glancing back in his direction through the glass. Caslin looked away and sank back in his chair.

"Well, this is unexpected," he said, flashes of what might be motivating the caller passing through his mind.

"You appear to be taking a great deal of interest in my affairs as well as those of my family," Pete Fuller said, keeping his voice low and commanding.

"There is much to see," Caslin countered.

"Why are you holding my boys?" Caslin thought about his response for a few seconds catching Hunter's eye as she looked on from a distance.

"They are suspects in a murder inquiry."

"That's bullshit…" Fuller replied, "and you know it."

"What I do know," Caslin said, drawing a deep breath, "is that a lot of people in and around your circle are very active all of a sudden. Some of whom haven't been seen in years and as soon as they surfaced, people started dying."

"Very tragic," Fuller replied.

"And somehow it all seems to be revolving around you."

"Is that a fact?"

"Now, why might that be, Pete?" Caslin asked. He then fell silent allowing a pause in the conversation and waited patiently. The sound of Fuller's breathing carried down the line. There was more to be said. Caslin knew it. "This situation is escalating rapidly, Pete. If we don't get a handle on it more people are going to be killed. You know this."

"You sound sure of yourself," Fuller said, after a few moments.

"I can't help but think Neville Bridger has something to do with it."

"You've been doing your homework, Mr Caslin."

"Staying up late, that's true."

"Neville's been a long time dead."

"And yet, his shadow casts itself some way into the future, does it not?"

"Neville Bridger didn't bomb my business," Fuller said.

"Nor did he shoot Clinton Dade in the face," Caslin added. "But someone did both."

"And someone is trying to put my boys in the frame."

"So, it would appear," Caslin concurred.

"You know this and you're still keeping them in a cell?"

"Where they belong," Caslin countered. "Either for this or for everything else they have done."

"Now, you listen to me, Inspector," Fuller said, his voice lowering and taking on a new level of malevolence, Caslin hadn't heard previously. "If you pin this on my two, you'll be fitting them up for something they haven't done. You mark my words if you take down my family for this then the gloves are off."

"That sounds like a threat."

"It is," Fuller stated. "You've come after my family and that brings yours into play."

Caslin heard the words and didn't need time for them to sink in. The intent was obvious. "Be careful with your threats, Pete. You're in the home stretch now. Six months from now you'll be moved to a D-Cat," Caslin said, referring to when a prisoner is approaching parole and not considered a flight risk, they are often moved to an open prison ahead of release. "Are you willing to jeopardise that and risk seeing out the rest of your sentence inside?"

"I'd take it twice over for the sake of my children," Fuller said. Caslin assessed his tone and didn't doubt his commitment. "You're standing in a glass house, Caslin. *Let he who is without sin cast the first stone.*"

Caslin knew Fuller hadn't found God from within the prison walls and felt somewhat baffled by the reference. "Now what are you talking about?"

"Instead of wasting time trying to hang my boys out to dry maybe you should be focusing on the real players in this game."

"And they are?" Caslin asked, noting Terry Holt attempting to catch his eye from his seat. The DC had a phone pressed to his ear and an open-mouthed expression on his face. He waved in Caslin's direction drawing Hunter to him in doing so. He said something to her and she immediately looked to Caslin. Something was wrong.

"You seem distracted, Inspector Caslin," Fuller said.

"I'm still here," he replied. "Waiting for you to give me a steer… like you did my colleagues a few years ago regarding Neville."

Fuller chuckled. "I've heard that one too. I didn't give him up no matter what you've heard to the contrary."

"Then tell me who's throwing Ashton and Carl to the wolves?"

"You're asking the wrong man the wrong questions," Fuller said. Caslin watched as Terry Holt slowly replaced the receiver of his phone down on the desk. He glanced again at Hunter who stepped aside giving him enough room to stand. Holt looked to Caslin with an expression that could only be described as one of nervous apprehension written across his face. Both of them came towards his office. Hunter cracked open the door and Holt shifted his weight nervously between his feet alongside her. Caslin frowned. "Soon enough, you'll find the right man," Fuller continued, "and only then will you get the answers you're after."

The phone line went silent and Caslin glanced at the screen to see if the call had disconnected. It hadn't. He was more than a little perplexed at the cryptic direction the call was taking. He turned his attention to the two officers before him putting his hand across the microphone. "What's up?" he mouthed, flicking his eyes between them. "One of you?" he whispered.

Holt cast a fleeting glance sideways to Hunter who bit her lower lip and looked away. It was Holt who spoke, "Uniform responded to what they thought was a domestic a little over half an hour ago. They arrived at the property to find an elderly male unconscious and blue-lighted him to hospital."

"And?"

"They also found two children at the scene." Caslin's blood ran cold. "They're okay," Holt stressed. "Your kids were unharmed but the male is in a bad way. We think… we think it's your father, sir. They've really done a job on him."

Caslin felt his body go light. A strange sensation coursed through him and he could feel his heartbeat increasing as it thudded inside his chest. Lowering the mobile, he looked at the screen whilst attempting to process the information. It was a few moments before he realised, he was holding his breath and almost had to tell himself to stop. Returning the handset to his ear, once again, he focused on Fuller and him alone disregarding the presence of his team.

"If you've hurt my family…" he said in a menacing tone borne out of the white-hot anger building inside him, "I will *dedicate my life* to destroying everything… and everyone you hold dear."

"You should be careful with *your threats,* Mr Caslin," Fuller countered, not missing a beat. "Sometimes the answers you seek are far closer to home than you can ever imagine."

"My family are innocent in all of this."

"Innocence was lost long ago, Inspector Caslin. Everyone must pay for their sins and sometimes it is our children who bear the brunt."

"I will come for you," Caslin said in a whisper.

"I don't doubt it," Fuller replied, and the phone line went dead.

CHAPTER TWENTY-TWO

THE THIRTEEN-MILE JOURNEY from Fulford Road to Caslin's father's house in Selby usually took half an hour but in a liveried police car, with the lights and sirens in action, they shaved a third off of that. The car screeched to a halt at the kerb side and Caslin was out of the passenger seat before it stopped moving. A handful of neighbours were huddled on the footpath offering a mixture of concern and ghoulish voyeurism. Caslin ignored them and was directed towards an ambulance parked a short distance away by a uniformed constable standing at the entrance to the house. The rear doors were open and rounding the corner of the vehicle to the back, he found both his children being attended to by a paramedic.

Lizzie stood up and launched herself into his arms. His daughter clung to him as if to let go would risk falling to her death such was the tightness of her grip.

"I've got you," he said reassuringly. Looking through the tangled curls of her hair, Caslin saw his son, Sean, sitting on a gurney with a red blanket around his shoulders. He was huddled beneath it, his face pale even in the darkened rear of the ambulance. He smiled in response to Caslin's unasked question to his well-being. It was weak and Caslin could see signs of bruising to the side of his cheek. Anger flared but he suppressed it. "Are you okay?" he asked.

"I'm all right, Dad," Sean replied.

"Your son's taken a blow to the side of the face," the paramedic said, glancing to Caslin but maintaining his focus on Sean. "I'm sure it's nothing serious but we want to take him in just as a precaution."

"I understand," Caslin replied, nodding appreciatively. Footsteps behind him marked the arrival of DS Hunter. She had followed on in her car. Coming alongside, she placed an affectionate hand on Lizzie's arm to show her support and smiled at Sean.

"Have you been inside?" she asked. Caslin shook his head gently.

"You have a few minutes, if you like?" the paramedic said. "We're not ready to leave yet."

Caslin used his free hand to push the bundle of blonde curls away from Lizzie's face, she leaned back and he made eye contact.

"Stay here with your brother. You're quite safe now. I'll be back in a minute and we'll go to the hospital together. Okay?"

"Okay," Lizzie replied. "How is granddad?"

Caslin looked to the paramedic who flicked his eyebrows up and returned his gaze to Sean. "I'm sure he'll be fine," he replied, smiling. "He's tough like your old dad." Placing her carefully back down, she resumed her place alongside her brother who extended his blanket and put an arm around her. "I'll be back," Caslin said to his son who nodded.

The two of them made their way up the path to the front door where they were greeted by the constable who stepped aside to allow them to pass. Caslin entered first. The usual anticipation that he experienced when entering a crime scene was tinged by anxiety on this occasion. Seldom did work crossover into his personal life but when it did, the gut-wrenching feeling and the associated guilt hit Caslin hard.

"Three men," the voice of the constable on the door came from behind them as they entered the living room. The scene was chaotic. The coffee table, with its glass top, was smashed and whatever once rested upon it lay in pieces across the floor. His father's sideboard and drinks cabinet had suffered a similar fate and the room stank of alcohol from all the broken bottles of wine and spirits. "They forced entry at the front door," the officer continued as Caslin surveyed the room, "pushing back here where… I'm sorry, sir… where they attacked your father."

"Did they say anything?" Caslin asked, ignoring the sentiment not because he was unfeeling or didn't care but because he needed to keep his emotions in check.

"No, sir. They didn't speak," the officer explained. "Your children were incredibly brave, sir."

"Thank you."

"Your eldest tried to intervene which is when he was struck, over there," the constable said, pointing to the entrance to the kitchen.

"Did they go for my kids?" Caslin asked, his voice cracking and briefly betraying his emotional state. If the officer noticed, he didn't show it.

"No, sir. It would appear they were targeting your father alone. You'll probably know better than us but it doesn't appear as if anything was taken."

Caslin scanned the room afresh passing over the bloodstains on the carpet and walls, looking for a sign of anything missing. Of course, there were none. Caslin knew why they were there and it wasn't with robbery in mind. "No. Looks clean," he said, eyeing Hunter. "Any descriptions to go on?"

"Three men. Probably white," the constable said, "but they wore ski-masks and overalls."

"Overalls?" Caslin asked.

"Yeah, like uniforms. I spoke with a couple of neighbours, the ones who called in the report of a domestic, and they said they saw the men leaving in a transit van."

Caslin cursed himself under his breath. "A delivery van?"

"Yes, that's right. It was dark brown or black. They weren't sure which."

"I saw it," he explained to Hunter. "They were outside when I bloody left earlier."

"There's no way you could have known," Hunter argued. "You can't blame yourself."

"That's funny because I'm doing exactly that," he said, running a hand through his hair pain evident in his expression. "Get onto Broadfoot, would you? I want an armed presence at the hospital just in case they want to try and finish the job."

"I will. How is your father?" Hunter asked.

"I don't know," Caslin said, feeling the guilt magnify for not having already asked that very question.

"He was unconscious when we arrived," the constable said. "The paramedics were on scene within five minutes. They took great care with him."

"Thank you," Caslin said, turning to Hunter. "I'm going to the hospital with the kids. I'll find out and let you know. Can you stay here, canvas the neighbours and find out as much as you can about what anyone saw?"

"What do you want to do about Fuller? He orchestrated this."

Caslin was silent for a moment, his anger worn visibly on his sleeve. "Nothing, yet."

"But, sir. With the phone call and all…"

"Nothing," Caslin snapped. "He's not going anywhere and we all know he's crossed a line. I'll make sure he gets what's due to him."

"Yes, but why did he do it? He has so much to lose."

"He also knows we'll struggle to link this to him directly, it's all circumstantial. We'll take him… but when I choose to and not before."

"Okay, sir. Your call," Hunter said.

Whether she agreed was irrelevant to him. Fuller was sending him a direct message and there had to be more to it than merely protecting the interests of his children. Their telephone conversation played over and over in his mind. It seemed far more significant now than he had given it credit at the time. Fuller's words were out of character somehow, his choice of phrase, his tone… something, but Caslin couldn't quite comprehend the inference. Not yet, at least. Perhaps once his anger subsided. If his anger subsided.

"We will take your brother through and once we have him settled, we'll come back for you," the nurse said to Lizzie, smiling affectionately and instantly placing the little girl in a comfortable state of mind. Caslin squeezed her shoulder gently, his arm already around her as Sean was led out of the cubicle for a precautionary examination. The initial assessment in Accident and Emergency from both the triage nurse and the doctor indicated he'd probably suffered a small concussion but they were being thorough and following up with a scan. Caslin appreciated it. For her part, Lizzie had stumbled and fallen in the melee at his father's house and was complaining of her arm being painful. She would be taken for an x-ray as soon as the department could make room to fit her in.

"Thank you," Caslin said to the departing nurse.

"No problem," she replied, offering both of them another wide smile, friendly and reassuring.

Caslin turned to his daughter. "It's nothing to worry about, I promise."

"When will Mummy be here?"

"I called her before I got to granddad's house, so any-"

"I'm here," Karen said, appearing through the closed curtain to the cubicle. Lizzie leapt up from her seat and her mother dropped to her haunches and embraced her tightly. Too tightly as it turned out with Lizzie wincing as her bruised arm was pressed. "I'm so sorry, darling," Karen said, releasing her grip and pulling back so she could look into the little girl's face. "Mummy's here now," she said, drawing the girl close to her chest again.

Karen was out of breath and sweating, clearly having rushed to get there as quickly as she could. Now her daughter couldn't see, the compassion exhibited in her expression was abandoned as she turned her gaze towards her former husband.

"Sean's been taken for a scan," Caslin advised her. The visible anger subsided and was replaced by concern. "It's purely precautionary."

"And Lizzie?" she asked, stroking her daughter's head which appeared fixed to her mother's chest.

"She'll be going for an x-ray soon. Again, just as a precaution."

"What about... your father?" Karen said, hesitating and fearful of the answer. Caslin pursed his lips and stood up.

"I have to go and see. By the time we got here, he'd already passed through A and E. He needed surgery," Caslin said. Looking to Lizzie, he indicated he didn't want to say further at the risk of scaring the child. The truth was his father was admitted unconscious and rushed to theatre for emergency surgery. The extent of the injury was unknown to him and he was agitated at the thought of the severity of his condition. "I'll let you know as soon as I do."

Karen nodded, "Please do."

Caslin knelt down and Lizzie turned her head to the side so she could see him. "Mummy's going to stay with you while I go and see your granddad, okay?" She nodded and he reached across cupping her cheek with the palm of his hand. He smiled and she returned it. Standing up, he pulled the curtain aside and stepped out looking around for a sign in order to get his bearings. For the life of him, he couldn't remember which direction he'd entered from. Thinking he'd approached from his left, he set off in that direction. Within a few steps he heard the sound of the curtain being drawn behind him and footfalls.

"Nate," Karen called after him. Caslin stopped and turned as she trotted towards him. Looking past her, he could see the curtain was closed. There was no sign of Lizzie. "Just one thing," she said catching up to him.

"Yes?" he asked as Karen slapped him across the face. The blow stung his cheek. It was the last thing he'd expected.

"You promised me you'd keep your job away from this family," she accused him, waving an extended finger in front of his face.

"You're blaming me for this?"

"After what happened to Sean... *you promised me!*" she hissed. A sudden, fresh pang of guilt stabbed at his chest upon hearing those words. They tore through him. After nearly losing Sean when he was caught up in a case along with the subsequent years of trying to repair the mental damage, Caslin swore he would never let his children come to harm again as a result of his job. Karen was right. He hadn't seen this coming. The rational response would be to deny his culpability but the emotional one was damning.

"I... I'm..." he stammered as she turned her back on him and stalked back towards the cubicle. "Sorry," he said to himself, watching as she disappeared from view and back to comfort their daughter. Taking a deep breath, he resumed his course. A handful of people were present either waiting to be seen or relocated to their respective wards. They saw the exchange and he read their shocked expressions as a further indictment of his failure.

Ten minutes later, Caslin had given up on wandering aimlessly and sought help from a passing member of the medical staff. An internal phone call followed and he was directed to a specialist diagnostic ward, a temporary placing where his father could be assessed as to his medical needs before being found a permanent place on the respective ward. Confident of his route through the maze that was York Hospital, he finally arrived.

The entrance was secured with access only granted via use of a programmed key card or by a member of staff unlocking it from within. The days of wandering onto any ward without permission were rapidly becoming a distant memory. He pressed the intercom set alongside the entrance door and glanced up at the security camera overhead. The speaker crackled and he leaned in as the voice greeted him.

"Detective Inspector Caslin," he said into the microphone. "I believe you have my father on the ward."

There was an audible click as the lock was released and Caslin entered. There were doors off the corridor to either side giving access to storage, offices and what he guessed were treatment rooms of some sort but the main hive of activity was further along. Here, he came across the nurse's station where he identified himself once again. Looking along the corridor to his right, he saw the unmistakable figure of an armed policeman standing outside a room. He realised then that his father was inside and he could have saved himself a bit of time by contacting Fulford Road and seeing where the protection had been placed rather than wandering the corridors aimlessly.

"The doctors are with your father now," the nurse said, pointing to the room.

"How is he?" Caslin asked, apprehension edging into his tone.

"I believe the surgery went well," she told him, "but the doctors will be able to tell you more."

He thanked her and headed for the room. Not recognising the protection officer, he took out his warrant card and brandished it as he approached. The officer nodded approval and Caslin rapped his knuckles lightly on the door and entered. His father was in a private room. There were two windows off it facing to the outside and a third internal one with a view to what appeared to be a staff room. Two doctors were standing at the foot of his father's bed, deep in discussion. Both acknowledged his arrival and he identified himself. Taking in his father's appearance, he was struck by how pale and gaunt he was, far more so than normal. A clear indication of the trauma he'd been through. His left arm was connected to a drip and the right-hand side of his face was red and swollen, the skin already darkening as the bruising developed. His head was heavily bandaged, wrapped around his crown and down across his left eyebrow. The eye itself was covered with a large gauze pad and taped in place. Oxygen was being fed to him via a tube to his nostrils.

"Your father has taken quite some damage, I am afraid to say," the consultant explained. "The emergency surgery was to repair tissue damage around the eye."

"Is he… will he be all right?"

"It will take some time but we are very confident about his prognosis," the doctor stated with a smile. "Mainly, he has sustained bruising and trauma that is largely superficial. It will take time to heal but it looks far worse than it is. Obviously, your father's age will determine how long it takes regarding recovery time but he is in no immediate danger. When he wakes up, we will know more about how the trauma has affected him."

"And the eye?" Caslin asked.

"We will have to wait and see," he replied, tilting his head slightly. "Once the swelling goes down, we will be able to run some tests. In the meantime, please be positive."

Caslin looked at his father. Without the medical paraphernalia and the obvious wounds, he could be forgiven for thinking he was at peace, asleep and resting comfortably. "Has he woken?"

"He came around in the ambulance on his way to the hospital and remained so until we took him into theatre. Usually, with the possibility of a concussion we don't do so, but in this case, he was given a general anaesthetic to allow for the procedure. His CAT scan didn't give us any concerns around his head injury so we pressed ahead. I should imagine he will be asleep for the next hour or so. When he comes around, he will most likely be groggy and a little disorientated."

"That sounds like good news, Doctor," Caslin said, feeling the anxiety he felt dissipate slightly.

"It is good news, Mr Caslin. Your father has come through this ordeal remarkably well for a man of his years, at least physically."

"Thank you," Caslin said, conveying his gratitude.

"You're welcome. Please excuse us," the consultant said and the two men left Caslin alone with his father.

Approaching the side of the bed, he reached out and placed his hands onto the old man's. Suddenly, his father - the fierce, embittered, aggressive man who held such sway over him - looked every bit as fragile as his seventy-plus years might dictate. The man who was always the strongest, most prominent character in his life reduced to this state was troubling to see. If he needed a reminder that everyone was mortal, then this certainly qualified. Caslin's phone began to ring.

"Sir, it's Terry Holt. How is the family?"

"They'll be okay, thanks, Terry," Caslin replied quietly, looking at his father and hoping the doctors were right. "What do you have for me?"

"I had a thought... after you left the office earlier," Holt said, and Caslin could infer from his tone the DC was somewhat pensive.

"What is it, Terry?"

"I don't think Fuller was trying to hurt you."

CHAPTER TWENTY-THREE

"I REVISITED the telematics data we took from Bradley's wrecked Mercedes and came at it from a different angle. Now, we didn't know why he was making the stops that he did but figured there had to be a reason, right?" Holt said.

"As in when he took a drive out to the lighthouse at Flamborough Head?" Caslin clarified.

"Exactly. He's resurfaced from his secret life in obscurity with a goal in mind. Therefore, it follows logically that every stop he made and every visit to a location had a purpose. I doubt he came back for the weather. At the time, I only plotted his course over the main roads he used and the places where he frequented the most," Holt said, standing and crossing to one of the several noticeboards they were utilising to display case information. "So, I went back and added everywhere he travelled to documenting where the engine was turned off, presumably where he stopped, as well as for the length of time in each location. We had him making two stops in Selby on two separate occasions."

"Selby," Caslin repeated. Holt met his eye. Hunter flicked hers between the two of them grasping the significance.

"Your father?" Hunter asked. Caslin frowned and looked to Holt encouraging him to continue.

"We can't be sure of why he was in Selby but the day after he arrived in the country and then again two days before he died, Bradley's car was stationary in the town. Not only *in the town* but on the outskirts."

Caslin sat back in his seat. "Presumably, you have more?"

"I do," Holt said, returning to the table they were seated at and picking up a folder. From this, he withdrew the copy of a map and passed it across to them. Routes were marked out, highlighted in different colours representing separate days. Caslin scanned them. "We still don't know what Jody Wyer's interest was in this case. We know from his mobile phone records that he was paying attention to MacEwan and his operations. What we didn't do was take a look at the telematics data from his car."

"And you have?" Hunter asked.

Holt nodded enthusiastically, "I cross-referenced the information I got from Wyer's BMW with that of Bradley and I got a hit."

"They crossed paths?" Caslin asked, looking up from the map he held in both hands in front of him. Holt nodded. "Where?"

"Selby," Holt stated. "The signal from both cars was relayed via the same cell tower on that first date. The day after Bradley arrived from Spain."

"Are you saying they met?" Hunter asked, trying to put the pieces together. Holt turned the corners of his mouth downwards and opened his palms in a gesture of uncertainty.

"We've no idea, really. But what we can say with certainty is they were in the same location at the same time. Wyer could have been following Bradley or they could have been setting up a meeting. We've no way of knowing."

"And why Selby?" Caslin asked before casting his mind back to the phone call at the hospital that'd brought him back to Fulford from his father's bedside. "You said on the phone you didn't think Fuller was targeting me?"

Holt pulled out his chair and sat down reaching into his folder. "I've got an answer for both," he said, looking at Caslin, "but… I don't think you're going to like it."

"That's certainly my reality today, Terry. What do you have?"

Holt took a deep breath gathering his thoughts. Holding both hands out in front of him, he presented his palms up splaying his fingers wide and raising his eyebrows, "Just hear me out. I haven't followed it all the way through yet but…"

"We're listening, Terry."

"All right. Cast your mind back to the 80s. The Customs Clearing House is hit at Manchester Airport. It's a massive job, bold, high profile, caught everyone by surprise and is an embarrassment for both the police and the government. The authorities of the day tried to keep a lid on the details by not releasing what was taken, but in today's money, we're looking at one hundred and twenty to thirty-million pounds. You can imagine the resources that were thrown at the investigation. Greater Manchester immediately put fifty officers on the case but once the scale was fully established, they knew they needed more."

"They would have sought help from surrounding forces particularly those with connections to anyone who potentially could be in the frame," Caslin said, following Holt's logic.

"That's what I thought," Holt said, raising a finger in the air and smiling. "So, I went back to the case files I brought out of the archive, those I have anyway as the remaining ones still haven't materialised despite repeated assurances…"

"Terry… focus," Caslin said, masking thinly veiled irritation. He knew Holt was going somewhere and he was eager to join him.

"I totted up the number of officers from the initial assignation right through to when the case was in full swing. Over three hundred officers in one form or another plus more on top when it came down to raiding addresses around the country. One name caught my eye," Holt said, spinning a sheet of paper on the table before him and sliding it in Caslin's direction. Both Caslin and Hunter looked at it. It was a list of names. Holt had highlighted one with a yellow marker pen.

Caslin had to read it twice before he could fully process the information. He glanced at Hunter and then back to Holt. Hunter spoke first, "Your father?"

"There must be a mistake," Caslin said, briefly shaking his head. "He was uniform all of his life. He never went into CID."

"I thought so too," Holt said. "But I checked and then I checked again. He was seconded from North Yorkshire onto the investigation team almost as soon as it was expanded. He remained there for a little over a year."

Caslin's eyes narrowed, his expression accompanied by a deep frown. "He never told me that. Are you sure?" Holt nodded. "Where does he fit in… I mean… why would he be the target? I presume that's where you're going with this?"

"If he wasn't… then, it's incredibly coincidental," Holt explained. "My initial thought, as was yours I imagine, was Fuller was retaliating against you personally for targeting Carl and Ashton. Maybe that's still the case. Perhaps Jody Wyer thought your father had some information he could use and went to see him or maybe his father knew yours. Did he ever mention Keith Wyer to you either in passing as an acquaintance or as a colleague?"

"Not that I recall," Caslin said. "This is all news to me."

"Regarding your father's participation in the Manchester investigation, I've no information on that. I tried to find out what the scope of his role in the team was if he was desk-based or in the field. Who he reported to... that kind of thing but I've not had any joy? At the moment, he's just a name on that paper in front of you."

Caslin slapped both hands down on top of the very sheet of paper, Holt was referring to. "Let's keep it like that for now. This information doesn't leave this room. Understood?" he asked, meeting eyes with both of them in turn. Holt nodded without speaking. Hunter appeared pensive. "If you have a problem with it, say so," Caslin said.

"No, sir," she replied, "but we need to get this clarified as soon as possible. Otherwise..."

"All right," Caslin said quietly, covering his mouth and nose with his hands. "All right... I know."

"How do you want to proceed?" Hunter asked.

Caslin thought on it casting an eye across the information boards erected all around them. "I want the two of you to stay here. Terry, you carry on trying to find out where my old man fits into the securities raid but... do so quietly. The key figures in this seem to be a step ahead of us at every turn, so let's not tip our hand. Sarah," he turned to Hunter, "Jody Wyer was deeper into this than we are and I'm finding it hard to believe the all-consuming passion he had for this case was kept secret from his lover. I should imagine the nameless redhead is either linked or related to someone in and around his investigation. He wouldn't be dragging an innocent person into all of this, not someone he cared about. He knew how dangerous it was. That's why he kept everyone in the dark... but not her. She's involved somehow, I'm positive, and she'll have information we can use. Find her!"

"If they were onto Wyer, then it's logical they may have been onto her as well," Hunter suggested. "That might be why we can't find her. She could be dead already."

"Then where's the body?" Caslin said. "They weren't too fussed about where they dumped Jody."

"She may have killed him," Holt said, almost apologetically. "Would have been able to get close enough and knew what he was up to."

"Find her and we'll ask," Caslin replied.

"Where will you be, sir?" Hunter asked him.

Caslin took a deep breath, his expression one of thoughtful introspection. "I'll be at the hospital."

SOMETHING CAUSED him to wake with a start. Blinking furiously, he looked around trying to get his bearings. It was dark outside but the sky was changing. The night replaced by the brooding slate-grey of an overcast morning. His vision adjusted to the surroundings. His father slept six feet away, his breathing shallow and steady. He'd had a good night. Although not waking from his surgery, the staff seemed unconcerned and that was reassuring. The time to worry was when the medical team did so. Looking to the door, Caslin saw the outline of a figure standing on the other side. Sitting forward, he stretched out feeling a twinge in his lower back. He winced. These chairs weren't designed for sleeping in. Standing up, he went to the door and cracked it open. The armed officer turned to him offering a smile and a nod in greeting. Caslin mirrored the gesture and closed the door, returning to his father's bedside.

The old man was stirring. Perhaps that was what had woken him, he didn't know. Caslin helped himself to a cup of water from the jug placed on his father's table alongside the bed. He wouldn't need it for a while. The water had an aftertaste of plastic. It had been sitting there since the previous day. Looking at his watch, he wondered whether the visitor's restaurant would be open yet. He'd kill for a cup of coffee.

"You look dreadful."

Caslin realised his father's unbandaged eye was open, watching him. For how long, he didn't know. "You don't look in great shape yourself, Dad," Caslin replied, putting the cup down beside the bed. His father smiled faintly.

"That's good because I feel awful."

"You're going to be okay," Caslin said, bestowing as much confidence in the prediction as he could.

"Then why does your face look like I've already died?"

Caslin shook his head, "It's complicated."

"There's that word again," his father whispered. "You're a terrible liar, Son."

"I'm not lying."

"Then what? *Lizzie and Sean*!" he said, trying to sit upright as the memories flooded back through his mind.

Caslin reached over and placed a firm but reassuring hand on his chest easing him back down on the bed. "They're all right. I promise. No harm done."

"I couldn't stop them..." his father said. "Damn it, I tried but..."

"It's okay. You did your best," Caslin said calmly. "No one can ask anymore of you than that. Can you tell me about them?"

His father sighed, rolling his head to the right and looking out of the window. "Three men... maybe four... I'm not too sure. It all happened so fast. They wore balaclavas. I couldn't see their faces."

"Did they say anything?"

His father shook his head. "Not that I recall. There was a knock on the door and I answered it. As soon as I cracked it open, they forced their way in. I tried to push back but... he was too strong. I shouted at the kids to run but... it all happened so fast. I'm so sorry, Son."

Caslin pressed his hand into his father's, seeing tears welling in the old man's eyes. He couldn't recollect his father ever apologising to him for anything in his entire life. "It's okay. Don't be too hard on yourself."

"What did they want? What did they take, do you know?"

Caslin loosened his grip and turned sideways allowing himself to perch on the side of the bed alongside his father. "I need to ask you a few questions, Dad. Is that okay?"

"Yes, of course."

"And I need you to be honest with me."

"That sounds ominous."

"You were seconded to a case back in the 80s. The raid on the Customs House at Manchester Airport, outsourced and run by a company called Manchester Securities. Do you remember? What can you tell me about it?"

"That was a long time ago, Nathaniel. Why on earth are you asking me about it now?"

"After I left yours yesterday, I couldn't understand why we'd argued as we did. It felt like it came out of nowhere."

"Usually does when you're involved," his father said, turning his head and facing away. If he'd been able, Caslin figured he'd have left the room by now.

"And today, that's got me thinking. The mood change happened after I mentioned DCI Phil Bradley, didn't it?"

"What are you talking about?"

"You knew him," Caslin said quietly. "More than that, you worked with him. Perhaps, even for him."

"So, what if I did?"

"People are dying, Dad," Caslin said, maintaining his composure for if he were to try and force the conversation, he knew his father would throw up the barriers and not allow him in. That was a trait they shared. "Sean and Lizzie were there." At the mention of his grandchildren, his father broke down. The façade of indignation slipping away as quickly as it had been conjured.

"I'm so sorry… so, so sorry," his father repeated as the tears fell.

"Did Bradley come to see you?" Caslin asked. His father wiped his cheek with the back of his free hand, the other was constrained by the drip. He shook his head.

"I… I can't…"

"I'm going to get to the bottom of it, Dad. Whatever this is all about it is going to come out, I assure you. You have to talk to me. The time for burying your head in the sand and hoping it will all go away has passed."

His father took a deep breath, closing his one good eye as he did so. Opening it, he fixed his gaze on his son. Suddenly, he appeared frail again, much as when Caslin first set eyes on him in the hospital bed. "Okay," he whispered softly, bobbing his head almost imperceptibly in agreement. "Bradley did come to see me but… he wasn't the first."

CHAPTER TWENTY-FOUR

"You have to realise what was going on at the time," his father said, glancing nervously towards the corridor as the shadow of his armed guard crossed the threshold under the door and momentarily broke the shaft of light.

"I'm listening," Caslin said. "Take as long as you need."

"I was having a tough time," his father explained. "A few months prior your mother had packed her bags and left taking both you and Stefan with her. No word. No discussion. You'll not remember, or not realise, but I came home after a night shift to find you were all gone. Just a letter on the table telling me it was over."

Caslin shook his head. His memories of that day were very different. He wasn't even a teenager at the time, barely into double figures. Their mother took both boys aside and told them they were going to miss school and head off on an adventure with her that day. Neither his brother Stefan nor himself had a clue that their mother never planned on them coming back. She had packed most of their clothes while they'd slept, rousing them early and ushering them out to the car where her friend waited. He was a decent man. One they grew to love in a strange sort of way despite his elevation into their mother's affections, displacing their father and themselves along the way. Eventually, they would marry and live happily. Stefan and himself found their placement in the boarding house of the independent school quite challenging. It was far from what they were used to in York but they managed.

As for his father, they'd never discussed the impact of his mother's actions nor the causes that led her to do what she did. From a distance however, it was clear how detrimental the break up had been for him. His descent into alcoholism was fuelled by it but often his mother had hinted, over the years, that the drinking came first. The truth wasn't known to him much like huge swathes of his father's life.

"I don't remember much," Caslin said, not wishing to revisit those days for they held pain he himself had never processed.

"I kept going as you do but I struggled. I'm not ashamed to admit it. Anyway, I was drinking too much. I knew it. Everyone knew it," his father said, his face contorting with the anguish of revisiting those feelings. "Until one day, I went into work… I was still hammered from the night before… and it wasn't the first time."

"What happened?"

"I was sent home on sick leave. I guess it'd be different now. I'd have been out on my ear," his father said. Caslin didn't comment. They had more in common than he'd thought for he, too, had rocked up at work in an unfit state on occasion. "Two days later, my superintendent paid me a visit at home. He suggested that I try something fresh. Get out of uniform for a while. He figured it might help bring me back. Anyway, they were assembling a task force to try and tackle the Manchester raid and some of the names being touted had associations with Yorkshire, York specifically, and that's how I got involved."

"What were you focused on?" Caslin asked.

"We knew a job like that took a lot of planning and needed a sizeable network in order to pull it off. The raid itself was carried out by a group of ten… and they were professional about it too. These weren't DIY homeowner specials, they were skilled. But that was the easy part. To be able to fence that much cash, jewellery and gold bullion in particular, they needed expertise that just weren't commonplace back then if ever."

"If you have a large organisation or businesses with a high turnover of cash, then the money can be dropped back into circulation relatively quickly," Caslin argued, "but on the scale of what they took you're right. The speed necessary to keep that number of people happy by paying them off quickly would've been challenging."

"And that's just the money. When it came to fencing the remainder there aren't too many people with the resources and know how to shift that volume. We knew they needed to call on countless others to process it and that's where we figured we'd be able to pick them off. In many cases it worked too."

"You worked for Bradley?" Caslin asked.

"I was assigned to his team and paired with another officer from Greater Manchester under the umbrella of a detective sergeant."

"Keith Wyer?" Caslin asked, putting two and two together.

"Yes. How did you know?"

"Keith's son was taking an interest in Bradley… and perhaps you as well."

"Jody," his father said quietly. "A good kid."

"A dead kid," Caslin replied. His father looked at him, nodding solemnly. "You met him?"

"I did. After Jody paid me a visit, Bradley showed up shortly after."

"Had you met him before?"

"No, not at all," his father said, shaking his head. "But he was Keith's son and apparently, his father spoke highly of me."

"Did you remain friends, you and Keith?"

"Not really. I didn't know he had died until Jody called."

"What did he want?"

"To ask questions… get answers."

"About what? Bradley?"

"Among other things. Neither of them knew what they were getting into. They thought they did. They thought they had it all figured out but they didn't realise who they were dealing with. Is the girl okay?"

"Which girl?"

"Jody's girlfriend. She is such a pretty little thing. I'd hate to think of her caught up in all of this."

"Redhead?" Caslin clarified. His father nodded. "I don't suppose you caught her name, did you?"

"Lovely young lady, very sweet. Louise, I think he introduced her as but I didn't catch her last name."

"Okay, thanks," Caslin said, making a mental note. "Can you go back a bit? Back to where you got involved in the investigation."

His father drew a breath as he sought to remember details from decades previously. "It didn't take us long before we began to focus on a second-generation scrap merchant here in York."

"MacEwan," Caslin confirmed.

"Yes. You've heard of him?" he asked. Caslin nodded that he had but didn't want to reveal everything he knew. It was an odd sensation, speaking to a relative as one would a potential suspect in a criminal investigation but these were rapidly becoming strange days. "A few of us had the long-held belief that he was part of the crew using his businesses to both store and ship the proceeds of the raid out of the country in his boats. He owned a boatyard up the coast in Whitby."

"I read in the case files that MacEwan was interviewed but released without charge and no further investigation was undertaken," Caslin stated, a little confused.

"Yeah, that sounds about right. That was Bradley. At least, I think it was."

"Go on."

"This is when things started to go a little awry, Son," his father said, eyes flitting around nervously, anywhere but meeting Caslin's. "You have to realise I was a mess… vulnerable."

"What happened, Dad?"

"I'm not sure how it came about. Genuinely, I don't," his father said. "We paid MacEwan a visit at his yard. It was just myself and Keith Wyer at this point. It wasn't a raid. We didn't have a search warrant or anything. At that moment, MacEwan wasn't considered to be a key suspect. We were on a fishing expedition, running down the names we'd come up with as possibles. Imagine our surprise when we stumbled across the smelting operation."

"The gold?" Caslin asked.

"Damn right!" his father said, sounding excited as he recalled it. "Turns out we were right in that MacEwan was fencing some of the proceeds but we had no idea he was one of those smelting down the bullion. Rendering it untraceable, he was then shipping it to his network of associates on the continent via his boats up the coast."

"None of this is in the files."

"It wouldn't be. Keith and I managed to detain those present, there weren't many, and called it in to the DCI."

"Bradley?"

"The very same," his father confirmed. "He came down to the yard to see us. I couldn't believe it. A few months into my first CID investigation and it was going to make my career. Some guys work their entire lives without a collar like that."

"I know," Caslin agreed.

"Bradley's eyes nearly popped out when he arrived. We'd rumbled the largest part of the operation pretty much by stumbling across it. A pure fluke. But he didn't react as I expected."

"I don't think I'm going to like this, am I?" Caslin said.

"I'll not insult you by asking you not to think less of me, Son. I know that'll be impossible. Not a day passes where I don't question what we did back then. *What I did.*"

"What did you do... cut a deal?" Caslin asked, failing to keep the disdain from his tone. It was far from a leap to realise the upshot of what occurred that day bearing in mind the absence of detail in the files and how MacEwan didn't see time inside for his role.

"Bradley negotiated it," his father said, staring down and refusing to meet Caslin's eye. "We hadn't made it common knowledge where we were going and so... no one knew. Bradley and Wyer went back a way and... I think they weren't strangers to helping themselves to things they came across if you know what I mean?"

"I know the type."

"Anyway, Bradley wasn't sure about me. He didn't know if I was one of them."

"Whether you'd be willing to take a cut?" Caslin clarified. His father nodded.

"I felt intimidated. Threatened. Not that I'm diminishing my role in any way. I was there and just as culpable as the others. As it turned out, Keith Wyer vouched for me and it sort of... happened."

"Dad... for the love of..." the words tailed off as Caslin's head sank into his hands.

"Like I said... I was a mess. Most of the time I could barely hold it together and... I figured I had nothing to lose. Your mother was gone. You boys..."

"I'm not letting you pin the guilt of this one on me, Dad. Not this time!" Caslin snapped. The silhouette of the armed guard, visible through the opaque glass, turned at the door at the sound of the raised voice. Seconds later he turned away again. Caslin lowered his voice. "What were you thinking?" he hissed barely above the sound of a whisper.

"That's just it, Nathaniel," his father said quietly. "I wasn't really thinking at all."

"How much?"

"Did we take?"

"Forty pieces of silver?"

"If you think I'm proud of what I did… what we did, then you are mistaken," his father said, reaching out and gripping Caslin's forearm.

"How much?" Caslin repeated.

"An even split," he explained. "An even split of everything MacEwan had in his possession."

"How the hell did you make that fly?" Caslin said, shock evident in his tone. "I mean, you're talking millions of pounds."

"Well, it wasn't all MacEwan's. Obviously, he couldn't give away the share of everyone else. These people were serious criminals. MacEwan took the arrangement further up the chain and smoothed things over. Their network was already in place and having us onboard gave them a shield from the investigation. MacEwan himself was also highly motivated to avoid some serious jail time. It was not the millions you're talking of but still a lot by anyone's standards."

"The people further up the chain, did you ever meet them… get to know their names?"

"No, not at all. We all figured that was for the best."

"But how did you manage to keep it quiet?" Caslin asked, profoundly impressed whilst disgusted in equal measure.

"That would have been impossible, so we took precautions. Each of us agreed not to touch our share for the foreseeable future. Not until we were out of the job. All of us. That way, we could move on with our lives, distancing ourselves from our past and no one would notice."

"No one would notice? You mean, you'd bypass friendships… even family so your change in circumstances would go unnoticed?"

"Exactly. Out of sight, out of mind," his father said. "How many of your friends do you still speak to since you left the Yard? Not many, I'll bet. It wouldn't take much. Move to a new location, retire abroad." Caslin could see the logic. He could count the people on one hand – two fingers if he was honest about it. "Time would pass. The money would be there. We just had to bide our time before we could lay our hands on it."

Caslin let out a deep sigh, "And MacEwan, how did he feel about this?"

"Once he was in the clear, he went to Spain. That was the last dealing I had with him. I only found out he was back on the scene recently."

"What about the others? I can't see how the rest of the gang benefitted from this little arrangement."

"They didn't," his father told him. "MacEwan handed them to us on a plate. After all, he was in the clear and the more of them who went down the greater his share became."

"I still don't see how you managed to keep this quiet. Who else was in on it?"

His father shrugged, "Besides Bradley, Keith and myself… I've no idea but there could have been others. With hindsight, there almost certainly were but remember most of the officers around the investigation were from another patch. I didn't know them and I never asked. Didn't want to know."

"For Bradley to get such a massive career break and never to rank higher than DCI, there must have been something else going on. Did anyone wonder how you guys got the breakthroughs you did?"

"None of us took the credit. We did it through a series of anonymous tip offs. It was a slow and roundabout way of going about it but eventually the information would land on the right desks and arrests were made. For us to take the credit would have drawn too much attention to us. We couldn't allow that and nor could MacEwan. If we'd hooked them all at the same time but left MacEwan out, then it would have been obvious. We all had to be invisible."

Caslin got off the edge of the bed his legs felt unsteady and he pulled over a chair. Sitting down, he rubbed at his cheeks with the palms of his hands before locking eyes with his father.

"Where's the money?"

"It's safe. I never touched it, not once and it's been a long time since I had any intention of ever doing so. I want you to believe that. It's important to me that you do," he implored his son. "If I could change what I did back then… believe me, I would."

"It's offshore?"

"In various bank accounts, yes."

"Did everyone do the same?"

"For the most part," he explained. "Despite our best efforts at removing MacEwan from the focus of the investigation, he couldn't continue the smelting operations. It's quite a slow process and there was so much to do. So, he had to put all of that on hold."

"Are you saying there's still gold bullion leftover from that raid sitting somewhere, out of circulation?"

"Maybe. I don't really know. Bradley promised to keep an eye on him - MacEwan. Once the deal was made with whoever was in charge, the remainder would be split between us, MacEwan and the lower elements of the gang. Bradley thought there was no way MacEwan could have moved what was ours on to the market without making waves. Bradley was wise to it. Besides, much of what was taken had already been shipped and without needing to pay back those who were sent down, MacEwan was sorted. He didn't need to run the risk of double crossing us. We could all wait it out."

"What did Bradley want when he came to see you?"

"He felt it was time to cash in."

"Apparently, he was suffering from cancer. From what we've found out about his secret life he was probably already living off of dodgy funds and it stands to reason he wanted to make the most of what time he may have left."

"Was it terminal?"

Caslin shook his head, "I've no idea but even if not, maybe it gave him the motivation to move things along. You said the arrangement was to wait until you were all retired."

"Yes. That was what we agreed."

"Keith Wyer's dead. You've been out of the job for years. Bradley faked his death a couple of years back so why now?"

"I don't know," his father said. "I know he was back here with MacEwan. He said as much when he came to see me. I should imagine they were hatching some kind of plan for the remainder but I wanted no part of it."

"No part of what?"

"I didn't ask. I didn't want to know and I told him as much too."

Caslin thought about it allowing the information to sink in. It was going to take time. Of all the eventualities he'd considered in this case this particular outcome would never have crossed his mind as plausible. How should he feel about it – about his father – he had no idea?

"What did Jody Wyer ask of you?"

His father fell quiet, appearing pensive. A few moments passed where the silence weighed heavily on both of them. "I think he was hoping his father would live up to the memories he still held of him."

"What did you tell him?" Caslin asked.

"Nothing. I couldn't destroy the lad's memories, so I sent them away. I thought we could bury it forever," his father said, his gaze drifting down to meet Caslin's eye. "No son should ever have to face his father's demons."

"It looks to me as if someone else has figured out what was going on,"

Caslin replied flatly, folding his arms before him. His father realised the inference of those words.

"What happens now?"

Caslin stood up and crossed the short distance to stand next to his father. Placing a reassuring hand on his arm, he smiled weakly and gently shook his head. "I honestly don't know."

"It had to come out eventually, I suppose."

"I'll figure something out," Caslin replied, and not for the first time those words sounded hollow. He had no idea how to resolve the situation.

CHAPTER TWENTY-FIVE

BACK AT FULFORD ROAD, Caslin reached the door to their investigation room but held off from entering. Looking through the inset window, he eyed both Hunter and Holt busying themselves. They were working hard, especially so since his family had come under threat. The nagging question, one he'd wrestled with from the moment his father had broken his silence right up to this point, was still churning through his mind. His duty as a police officer was clear, his duty to his family equally so. The problem was the two roles were not necessarily compatible with each other in this situation. A uniformed constable appeared at the end of the corridor catching his eye. Forced into action, he spun and walked confidently into the room. Greeted by both of them, he beckoned them to come together.

"I've got a lead on our mysterious redhead," he said, sounding upbeat. "She was introduced as Louise but I've not got a surname. Terry, can you run it through the information we have and see if that name comes up associated with, or related to, anyone we already know?"

"Will do, sir," Holt replied, setting to work.

"How did you come by the name?" Hunter asked, coming alongside Caslin.

"I met with a source," he replied, meeting her eye briefly and looking away immediately concerned she would see straight through him.

Glancing back up, he raised his eyebrows and explained, "Jody Wyer introduced them."

"That's great. It gives us something," she said.

"Better than that it would appear MacEwan is back in the frame for fencing the proceeds of the Manchester raid back in the 80s. My source fingers him as the ringleader who smelted the stolen gold and also arranged for it to be shipped out of the country. The word is there is still more to be had and that's where we need to focus."

"Your source," Hunter asked. "How credible is it?"

Caslin took a deep breath unsure of what to say. "If you'd asked me that last month, I would have said impeccable but right now I'd say it was it's worth serious consideration. Good enough?"

"Of course."

"It looks very much as if MacEwan not only ripped off his co-conspirators when it came to the laundering of what was stolen, but he is also implicated in giving them up to us over a period of time following the robbery."

"So, it wasn't Fuller who grassed on Neville Bridger?" Hunter said, open-mouthed. Caslin shook his head.

"Doesn't look like it, no."

"And Fuller himself?" Holt asked, glancing up from the paperwork he was sifting through. "Did MacEwan sell him out too?"

"I'm pretty certain, yes," Caslin confirmed. "What's more, I think Fuller might have worked it out."

"After all this time? How?" Hunter queried.

"That... I haven't figured out yet but I'm confident that's the case. He may not know it all but he's getting there."

"What makes you so sure of that?" she asked.

"MacEwan is still alive," Caslin said. "Perhaps Fuller wants his money seeing as he'll be getting out soon or he doesn't have all the facts yet. It'll only be a matter of time though. I want us to focus on how and where MacEwan would be likely to store stolen bullion for the last thirty years and how he's planning on taking it out of the country under these circumstances. He's savvy enough to know where the heat will be coming from, both us and Fuller's crew, and he'll want to move it to where he feels safe and that's not here."

"Spain?" Hunter suggested.

"My thoughts exactly," Caslin agreed. "With Fuller nipping at his heels, MacEwan will no doubt want to make the move soon so let's get on it."

"We had to release both Ashton and Carl this morning," Hunter advised him. "We had no grounds to hold them for any longer."

"That'll expedite things a little. More motivation for MacEwan," Caslin said before heading for the sanctuary of his office and breathing a sigh of relief that he'd managed the briefing without giving too much away. How long he could keep it up for, he didn't know.

"Sir," Hunter called after him as he reached the threshold of his office. He turned to face her. "All of this started with the bombing of the Fullers' premises."

"Yes."

"What sparked that?"

Caslin had already formulated a theory but would admit the details were sketchy. "I think Bradley and MacEwan were working together to launder the proceeds of the robbery. Bradley's faked death plays into it nicely. Who would look for a bent copper when he's already dead? Both of them came back here at the same time for a reason. Whether that was triggered by Fuller's forthcoming release or not, I don't know but that's what they're here for. And if you're looking to pick someone's pocket… again, it would be best if that person was looking in the other direction when you do."

"A distraction," Hunter said. "Have Fuller and his entire organisation geared up against the likes of Clinton Dade."

"Exactly. I wouldn't rule out them having put a hit out on Dade just to stoke the fires further," Caslin theorised. "If two rival gangs are looking to tear the other apart - what better smokescreen to use in order to slip out with a lot of their money?"

"It follows," Hunter said, "but it's thin."

Caslin nodded, "I know but I want us to run with it."

"And where do the Bridger boys fit in to all of this? I mean, if they thought Fuller had got their father sent down but in reality, it was MacEwan… how come one of them is working for him?"

"MacEwan's been playing one side off against another for decades giving them and us the run around. Do you reckon he would think twice about the manipulation of two young lads with an axe to grind? Think about it."

Hunter frowned, seemingly unconvinced. "If Fuller knew about Bradley, assuming your source is correct, why would he tip off MacEwan by eliminating Bradley? Surely, he would be better off following them to where they've been keeping it and taking retribution then. It would make more sense, wouldn't it?"

Caslin had to admit the logic was sound. "Maybe he wants MacEwan to make his move."

"To flush him out?"

"Makes sense too," Caslin argued.

"In which case, when we take down MacEwan we'll probably have to contend with Fuller's goons at the same time," Hunter concluded. "What makes you so sure Fuller is on to this? Your source, who is it?"

"I'd prefer not to say at the moment," Caslin replied. Hunter's eyes narrowed but she said nothing. He turned and walked into his office. With his back to them both, he let out a sigh and closed his eyes attempting to settle his breathing. The less the team knew about his father's role in this the better, for the time being at least. There would come a time when that would no longer be possible and he feared that wasn't too far away.

It was Fuller's own words that implied he knew the score. When he told Caslin to look closer to home he was referring to far more than the safety of his family. Fuller knew. Caslin was sure of it but he had chosen not to say. Nothing would have him removed from this case faster than having his father implicated right at the heart of it. The gangster was playing the game by his rules and Caslin had to work out what his next move was likely to be as well as how to counter it. He felt a sharp stab of pain in the back of his head – a well-recognised symptom that manifested when he was under times of significant stress. Pressing a thumb and forefinger into both his eyes, he sought to relieve it.

"I've got it," an excited shout carried from the other room. Caslin turned to see the animated form of Terry Holt celebrating his eureka moment. He saw Caslin looking through the window. Hunter went to him, looking over his shoulder. "I've found Louise!"

Caslin came out of his office and joined them, eager to put a face to the ghost they'd been searching for. Looking at the screen, he noticed Holt had a social media page up.

"Do I pay you for surfing this?" he asked playfully. Holt laughed.

"Quickest way to find a picture," he explained.

Caslin spied the name – Louise Bennett. "Do we know her?"

Holt shook his head. "No. She's not known to the police."

"Who is she?" Caslin asked.

"I cross checked the names of everyone involved in the case starting with the most recent - those we're investigating now or have spoken with in the past week - and it didn't take long. She's divorced but kept her married name. You'd know her better by her maiden," Holt said, opening another tab on the screen and displaying a gallery of photos she had uploaded to her page. Scrolling down, he found what he was looking for and double-clicked on it. The computer took a few seconds to process the request before enlarging the image in the middle of the screen. A picture of an attractive, redheaded woman appeared, seated on what looked like a sea wall and taken on a bright and warm day judging by their clothing. She was with an older man and woman, both standing behind her, the man with a hand on her shoulder. It was a family picture but was unlikely to be recent. Caslin recognised the man and knew his current appearance resembled someone far more aged, if not haggard, than he was depicted here.

"Scott Tarbet," Caslin confirmed, naming DCI Bradley's cousin and witness to the latter's apparent death.

"She's his daughter?" Hunter asked, looking to Holt.

"The one and only," the DC confirmed. "The only child of Scott and Margaret Tarbet."

"You thought he was holding out on us when we spoke to him, didn't you?" Hunter asked Caslin. "How did she end up with Jody Wyer?"

"I don't know," Caslin said, mulling it over. "Did Jody even know who she was?"

"I'll wager her father has something to do with it," Hunter said. "Shall we pay him another visit?"

"Hold fire on that," Caslin said, turning to Holt. "Do you know where she is?"

Holt shook his head, "No. She was an avid poster on social media, doing so daily until about a month ago and then she dropped off the site and hasn't posted since."

"She was dating Wyer by then. Any sign of him on her feed?" Hunter asked.

"Nope. Scanning through it, she was a pretty upbeat character espousing the virtues of democracy, vegetarianism and... *dancing cats...*"

"Cats?" Caslin asked. Holt shook his head.

"Never mind. The point is, pretty usual stuff until about five months ago. Then the general mood of her posts changed and I think I know why," Holt said, closing down that particular image and scrolling across to another. He opened that up. It was a shot at a cemetery. "The anniversary of her mother's death. Looks like it hit her hard."

"How did she die?" Hunter asked.

"Cancer," Holt confirmed. "But, judging from the details Louise has been sharing, she put down underfunding of the NHS alongside stress as a major contributory factor. She posted several times about how she wished she could have taken her mother abroad for treatment."

"Stress? Caused by what?" Caslin asked, intrigued.

Holt shrugged. "No idea but I'll see what else I can find. Needless to say, she's not been active recently, so I've no lead on where she is."

"Any indication of Bradley visiting Tarbet since he returned to the UK?" Caslin asked, looking up at the noticeboards and casting his mind back to the telematics data that Holt had acquired.

"He didn't go anywhere near Whitby," Holt confirmed. Caslin walked over to the boards and began tracing the routes they knew Bradley had taken revisiting them in his mind as he did so.

"He went out to Flamborough Point though. That's on the east coast but nowhere near Whitby," Caslin said, looking over his shoulder. Hunter came alongside.

"But if you're looking for a safe place to meet a dead man..." Hunter suggested. "Pretty much guaranteed to ensure there's no chance of their meeting being witnessed by anyone who knows them."

"But to what end?" Caslin said aloud. His father thought Jody was looking for confirmation that Keith Wyer wasn't involved in anything untoward but now Caslin wasn't so sure. There was another possibility opening up before him. Bearing in mind the co-conspirators' agreement, Keith died well before he would have had the opportunity to claim his share of the proceeds. Similarly, if Scott Tarbet's account were to be believed, he was substantially out of pocket when his vessel was burnt out and the insurance payment was withheld. "What if... they are all working towards the same goal?"

"Money?" Hunter queried.

"The money or the gold," Caslin confirmed. "There are those who lost out such as Tarbet and Wyer senior. Then there're those who are greedy like Bradley and MacEwan. Our next task besides figuring out when and where MacEwan will make his move is to nail down their motivations. If we can do that, then we'll know where those people," he pointed to the key individuals listed on the board, "fit with one another."

"And let's not forget those who have been robbed?" Hunter added, thinking of Fuller and the other gang members currently serving time.

"Of both wealth… and liberty," Caslin said, glancing at her with a knowing look.

"So, whose door do we lay Jody Wyer's murder at?" Holt asked.

Caslin's gaze drifted across the noticeboards, the pictures of the dead, the likely suspects and the links between them. There was a case that could be made against any number of them if the truth were known. It was frustrating.

"We're close," he said, in answer to the question. "This is all going to shake down in the coming days, I can feel it. We need to be ready to move as and when they do."

CHAPTER TWENTY-SIX

THE UNMISTAKABLE SOUND of a multitude of metal keys coming together carried to him as Caslin waited. The door creaked open on its hinges, reinforced metal and the better part of two inches thick. The prison officer appeared beckoning him to pass through. Caslin thanked his escort and joined the newcomer in the adjoining room. Following the attack on his father, Caslin left nothing to chance. Pete Fuller was placed within HMP Full Sutton's *Close Supervision Centre.* As they walked, Caslin could feel the difference within moments. Full Sutton was a maximum-security prison but here, within the centre, those procedures were elevated to another level entirely. For the majority of the day the prisoners were often kept in isolation from one another. Many of them had extreme personality disorders to go along with their criminal convictions and couldn't be trusted to interact with others and therefore when given their exercise time they did so alone.

"Any famous names in here at the moment?" Caslin asked his escort casually.

The officer glanced at him over his shoulder. "Plenty who are notorious. Don't know about famous. Did you have anyone in mind?" he asked as an inmate began shouting somewhere nearby. Caslin couldn't tell from where. A number of other voices picked up the baton and soon the jeering reverberated all around them.

"Didn't you have that guy the papers called the UK's Hannibal?"

Caslin asked, referencing a murderer sentenced to a full-life term back in the 1970s.

"Used to," the officer confirmed as they reached yet another security door. He looked up at the camera mounted above the door, itself securely fixed behind a protective screen. There was an audible buzz and the lock clicked to signal the door was unlocked. The escort pushed it open. "He was moved to the *Monster Mansion* last year and they're welcome to him."

"The Monster Mansion?" Caslin asked, following. Once they were through the door was closed and this time the securing of the locks sounded as a deadened thud. They were well into the bowels of the prison here. Metaphorically speaking, Caslin felt the sun didn't shine anymore.

"Wakefield's equivalent," the officer explained. "They get most of the big-time psychos, sociopaths and nutters who like to eat people."

"You must miss him," Caslin replied with a dry sense of humour. There was a grunt in response that Caslin took as unappreciative of his sarcasm. They came to another locked door at the end of a short corridor. The officer opened it and they entered the room. Inside was a table and two chairs. Caslin noted all three were bolted to the ground. That alone was mildly unsettling. He was ushered through.

"You know the procedure?" the officer asked. Caslin indicated he did but the rules were explained to him once more. He was advised to keep his distance, not to interact in any physical way and that they were under constant surveillance from a camera mounted in the ceiling. He had already surrendered his personal effects, mobile phone, wallet and even his belt was considered unacceptable to take with him. "Wait here and we'll bring him to you," the officer said once he was happy the protocols were fully understood. Caslin wasn't too concerned about Fuller. His request to place him inside the centre was considered reasonable under the circumstances. He sold it as a way to ensure Fuller could no longer direct his associates beyond the walls.

However, if he was honest, his motivation had been less about that and more an act of spite in retaliation for the attack on his family. Holt's revelation about his father's involvement in this case left Caslin in something of a dilemma. Was Fuller sending him a message that his family were touchable or was the attack aimed squarely at his father? Perhaps it was both. Either way, Caslin chose to respond in kind.

He didn't have long to wait. Within a few minutes, the door to the room opened and Pete Fuller shuffled in. His feet and hands were manacled between ankle and wrists, minimising the length of the steps he could take. He looked older than at their last meeting, arguably suffering from the stricter regime and lack of creature comforts the prison's black-market could provide. Within the centre such luxuries were far harder to come by even for someone as adept as Fuller. He was deposited into his chair and he sank back drawing breath as he eyed Caslin, standing on the other side of the room with his back to the wall. His lips parted in a thin smile, the eyes gleaming with satisfaction.

"Lovely to see you, Inspector Caslin," Pete Fuller said, the smile broadening. He clasped his hands together in front, interlocking the fingers. Caslin looked to the accompanying prison officer.

"You can leave us," he said. The officer cast a glance in his direction and then another at Fuller but didn't question the request.

"Behave yourself, Fuller," he said as he approached the door in an authoritative tone. The prisoner tilted his head slightly to the left but his eyes never left Caslin nor did the smile leave his face. The door slammed shut and Caslin heard the key turn in the lock.

"Alone at last," Fuller said. His eyes scanned the room drifting around the plain walls and back to the table in front of him. He attempted to look beneath it but couldn't angle his body shape to do so because the chair was fixed in place.

"Lost something?" Caslin asked.

"I don't see a recorder," Fuller stated. "And you haven't brought one of your colleagues with you."

"Your point?"

"This an unofficial visit, is it?" he asked, grinning. "How's the family?"

Caslin took a slow deliberate step forward and then launched himself across the room catching the inmate totally by surprise. He grasped Fuller's shirt firmly, first pushing him backwards before pulling him forward and slamming his face against the table. "My kids were there!" Caslin snarled, wrenching Fuller back upright and leaning in with fury written across his face. For his part, Fuller, red-faced and wide-eyed attempted to throw himself toward Caslin and land a blow with his forehead but the latter was wise to it and retreated just out of reach. Caslin sent an open-handed slap with the palm of his hand against the side of Fuller's head. The inmate wrestled with his restraints but was powerless to respond.

"You're a *big man*, aren't you, Caslin?" Fuller hissed at him, spittle dropping from his mouth as he spoke. "You think you can walk over me just as yer old man once did, huh? Is that it? Bent coppers run in the family…" Fuller's breathing was ragged, the adrenalin coursing through him.

Caslin took a step back seeking to calm himself. He hadn't known how he would approach the discussion and was shocked by his own level of aggression. He was astonished at the speed with which he lost control. The realisation struck him that such outbursts were no longer confined to his past. That unnerved him.

"They were my kids," Caslin said, placing clenched fists on the table opposite the chained prisoner. "If you so much as look at my children again, I will bury you."

Fuller glared at him still breathing heavily but the anger dissipating as the seconds passed. "Your father robbed me of nearly thirty years."

"No. He took from you what you stole from others. He's not why you're in here," Caslin countered.

"He put me here while he's out there spending *my money*."

"David MacEwan put you in here."

"*MacEwan?*" Fuller questioned, his eyes narrowing. Not for the first time, Caslin took pause. Fuller watched him intently as if he was assessing the validity of the statement. "He hasn't got the balls."

"You didn't know," Caslin said. Now it was his turn to smile. "All this time here was me thinking you were ahead of the curve and I was playing catch up and… *you had no idea*?"

"You're messing with me," Fuller said but his expression belied the assumption. The final pieces were fitting into the jigsaw puzzle in his mind and the scale of the deceit was coalescing.

"How frustrating it must be for you," Caslin said, glancing around the room, "to learn of this whilst you are stuck in here."

"How do you figure?"

"By the time you get out of the centre, let alone your jail cell, MacEwan will be in the wind. Taking all your money… and your gold… with him. He's been playing you for nearly three decades. I'm willing to wager you thought he was safeguarding your share whilst all the time he's been setting you up. You and everyone else."

Fuller kept his counsel, Caslin watching as the fury steadily built within him. Finally, he spoke, "There's always a way."

"If you can find him. He's been planning this for months if not years."

"I'll find him," Fuller replied in an icy tone.

"There is another way."

"And that is?"

"You give him to me."

"Fuck off, Caslin."

"Think about it. There's no way I'm going to let MacEwan leave the country. He's making arrangements to do so as we speak. The only way you can be sure of getting to him is to help me."

"And what would that do for me?" Fuller asked.

"You'll know where to find him."

"He'll be inside," Fuller said. Caslin nodded.

"And a man with your connections can always get to him within a prison. Where could he run to?"

"Aiding and abetting, Inspector Caslin?" Fuller asked.

Caslin shrugged, "Once he's jailed that's my job done. MacEwan becomes the responsibility of the prison service. What do I care?" Caslin argued. Fuller sat back thinking it over. "Of course, you could take your chances. Perhaps MacEwan will slip past us, get out of the country and disappear. Perhaps you're right and you will be able to find him. He'll only have an eighteen-month head start."

"I won't have to wait."

"Oh… right," Caslin said, leaning against the wall and folding his arms in front of him. "You can rely on Carl and Ashton to step up. The only problem with that plan is that I have them locked up at Fulford Road. Due to the overwhelming evidence amassed against them for Clinton Dade's murder, I was able to extend their custody to the thirty-six-hour mark and they'll be officially charged this afternoon."

"You bastard! They didn't do it. They've been fitted up and you bloody know it," Fuller challenged him.

"Yes. You're right, I do," Caslin countered. "But that's the thing about the law. It doesn't matter what I know only what I can prove and I can place your boys at the scene. It's not too big a leap for a jury to put the gun in their hands and thanks to joint enterprise it won't matter who pulled the trigger. They'll both go down for it. Maybe we can arrange a family reunion here at Full Sutton, what do you think?"

"I'll see your father in here too," Fuller bit back.

"He made his choice and he'll have to live with the consequences," Caslin stated coldly. Allowing the conversation to drop, he waited. The isolation of Fuller's incarceration played into his hands. Caslin was banking on Fuller being ignorant of his sons' release. Although confident it still remained to be seen if he could get this one over the line. After what felt like an age, Fuller sat forward. Placing his elbows on the table and bringing his hands together, he made a tent with his fingers.

"And what makes you so sure I know where MacEwan will be?"

Caslin came to the table and sat down on the free chair directly opposite him. "Because you know MacEwan and he will have found a way to let you know what he was doing with the gold. Otherwise you would have suspected him long ago. Clearly you didn't which means you trust him. Misplaced trust as it happens. The money's gone, Pete," Caslin argued. "What you can do now is ensure MacEwan gets what he deserves."

Fuller met Caslin's eye, "I can always earn more money."

"Earn is an interesting choice of words but... yes, you can."

"Know this, Caslin," Fuller said, leaning forward and lowering his voice, delivering the words with menace. "This may well allow you to get your hands MacEwan... but it sure as hell isn't going to keep me from your father."

Caslin felt his blood run cold. "I know you've got everyone who wronged you in your sights but... I'm sure there's a compromise to be had." Fuller flinched almost imperceptibly but the movement was there, nonetheless. He was curious. "There must be something we can do to... alleviate the situation."

Fuller sat back glancing up at the camera in the ceiling and then back to Caslin. "What do you have in mind?"

"My father never touched his share of the money. Everything he had is safe. None of it is traceable as far as I know and sitting in various accounts on the continent."

"Just what are you offering, Inspector Caslin?" Fuller asked, the reappearance of the thin smile crossing his lips once again.

"You know what I'm offering."

"I want to hear you say the words," Fuller said in a whisper.

Caslin took a deep breath. "The money he took... in exchange for his life."

"There... that wasn't so hard," Fuller replied, grinning. "One more thing, Inspector."

"And what's that?"

"Don't think that this settles everything and leaves us even. If you make this deal, you should know that it means more than just your father's safety."

"Yeah, and what does that *mean*?"

"After this you will be my man now," Fuller said quietly, ensuring with his expression that Caslin knew exactly what he was implying. He lowered his right hand extending it across the table, palm up. Caslin looked at it and then into the eyes of the man offering it. Tentatively, he reached out and accepted the handshake. Immediately, Fuller took a firm grip and dragged Caslin towards him. At the same time, he threw himself forward and head butted Caslin square in the face. Caslin's vision momentarily went dark as a searing pain shot upwards and into his brain, all awareness overcome by a wave of nausea that swept over him.

Caslin struggled to break free from Fuller's grip but the hold was too strong. No matter how much he tried to pull away, he couldn't. Seconds passed that felt like minutes as he strained against Fuller's iron grip. There was movement around them as the door burst open and two prison officers entered.

Grunts and raised voices came to Caslin's ear as his senses reasserted themselves. The officers were attempting to free him. Just as he thought he would never break loose - the hold was broken and Caslin's momentum carried him backwards and he almost fell, recoiling from his attacker. Throwing out his arms, he braced against the wall to stop himself from slumping to the floor. Blinking furiously, lights danced before his eyes and something wet was running across his mouth. Steadying himself with one hand against the wall, he probed the area of his face with the other. Taking his hand away, he saw the fingers were covered in blood. It was pouring from his nose and further inspection made him think it might be broken. His mouth was wet and Caslin swallowed hard.

The unmistakable taste of his own blood made him feel sick. Looking back across to the other side of the room, Fuller was grappling with the two prison officers as they unceremoniously attempted to drag him from the room.

"Wait!" Caslin yelled and both men stopped. Fuller ceased his resistance. The bottom half of his body lay on the ground with his legs behind him, his torso supported in the air. Each officer had a firm grip under Fuller's armpits. The inmate made their task harder by holding his manacled hands aloft, extending his arms fully to ensure they had as little purchase on his body as possible. His shirt was half pulled over his head. The struggle was certainly not over, not unless Fuller wanted it to be. Caslin stumbled over holding one hand against his nose in an attempt to stem the flow of blood.

Fuller stared up at him. His face was flushed with all the exertion of the moment but his eyes shone with satisfaction.

"Where will I find MacEwan?" Caslin asked, taking his hand away from his face and snorting up blood that threatened to flow. Fuller's breath came in short ragged gasps.

"White Hart Farm," Fuller whispered in between breaths. "Just south of Reighton. You'll never tie it to him... but that's where it should be."

"Reighton," Caslin repeated.

Fuller nodded. "It's a good deal, Inspector Caslin. You remember that."

"Get him out of here," Caslin said and both the officers resumed their efforts. The prisoner offered no further resistance but did nothing to assist. Fuller was dragged from the room. All the while his eyes never diverted from Caslin.

Watching on, Caslin felt a sense of shame that he had never previously experienced.

CHAPTER TWENTY-SEVEN

THE VILLAGE of Reighton sat on the cusp of the border between north Yorkshire and the East Riding, on the coast. With a population of fewer than five-hundred residents the assembling of an armed assault team would be sure to make waves amongst the locals. To that end, Caslin addressed his team in the relative obscurity of a yard owned by a small haulage firm in the nearby village of Grindale. The premises were located on the site of a former agricultural facility used for storing and processing grain. The silos were long gone and the concrete hard standing was being utilised by the current owners for trailer parking. There were no permanent offices on site and the route to the entrance along the access road took them far from the main highway. A line of trees was a bonus providing them with an extra screen to shield them from curious eyes.

Caslin walked to the head of the group, each member was busy checking and rechecking their equipment was in order. They arrived under cover of darkness several hours before sunrise and would soon decamp in order to carry out their objective. The radio crackled and Caslin brought it up. Hunter was in situ several hundred metres away from the gated entrance to White Hart Farm where Pete Fuller had told them to expect to find MacEwan. A surveillance operation on MacEwan's scrap metal business rewarded them with little information. There had been no activity there in the previous couple of days. Likewise, a check with the border force delivered no hits on his passport recording him leaving the UK. It would appear he was prepping for his departure. Either that or he was already gone.

"Go ahead," Caslin said, depressing the talk button.

"It's quiet," Hunter told him in a calm and authoritative tone. "There's been no movement since we've been here."

"Okay, keep me posted."

Caslin surveyed the men and women readying themselves to raid the farm. Twenty officers, specially trained in weapons and tactics, were preparing to advance on MacEwan's location. The anticipation was building and so was the anxiety. The officer with operational control, Chas Freeman, approached alongside Assistant Chief Constable Broadfoot. Caslin knew the former quite well, a highly skilled and competent specialist. Caslin greeted both of them.

"Any further word on the numbers we're expecting to encounter?" Freeman asked.

Caslin shook his head. "Not yet. There's no sign of movement in or out according to my people on the ground.

"So, we might encounter no resistance at all?"

"Unlikely… If our source is correct then I would expect a handful but no more than ten. MacEwan has never been seen with a massive entourage. Besides, in this case, it'll draw too much attention to them and he wants to leave unnoticed."

"Fair enough."

"You still want to take them at the farm and not wait for them to leave?" Broadfoot asked. "They would be constrained by their vehicles."

"Once they're on the move we'll be into *hard stop protocols*," Freeman explained. "Although my people can most likely control it multiple targets will add to the risk for both them and us. Not forgetting the members of the public. I'd rather strike at the farm where we can keep those risks to a minimum. Our surveillance of the site yesterday showed that the farmhouse itself is in such a state of disrepair that it's unlikely they will be using it. In all likelihood, they will be housed in one of the outbuildings. We will take them there."

"Understood," Broadfoot said.

"My team are ready to deploy," Freeman stated, adjusting his earpiece.

"Let's do it," Caslin replied, glancing to Broadfoot who nodded. Freeman called out the order and en masse they clambered into vehicles, a mixture of unmarked saloons and SUVs.

Caslin indicated in the direction of his car and Broadfoot fell into step alongside him. Caslin cast an eye skywards as they walked. Dawn was breaking and for the first time in days it promised to be a bright start. There were few clouds overhead. Today, he would have gladly embraced the darkness. The overcast mornings they'd been getting used to would have given them the added advantage of masking their approach. With a bit of luck, MacEwan would be caught completely unawares. Reaching the car and opening his door, he got in. Broadfoot went to the passenger side and joined him. The senior officer was nervous, too, Caslin could tell but his ability to hide his emotion was far superior to his own. Lifting the radio, he contacted Hunter.

"Any change?"

"None," came the reply.

"We're inbound," Caslin stated. "ETA is about five minutes."

"Roger that," Hunter confirmed.

Caslin felt his stomach churn. The last-minute doubts that always struck him whenever he rolled the dice were clear and present. If this proved to be an impulsive act based on poor intelligence, then he would be at fault. The responsibility lay with him and his assessment of Fuller's credibility. As the minutes ticked past, he couldn't help but wonder whether or not this was a gamble he should have initiated. If MacEwan evaded capture in this raid, then they would have shown their hand and alerted him to their interest. He hadn't been seen in days and the fear that he'd already left the country was also chipping away at Caslin's confidence. The only way they could tie him to any of this was to catch him in the act. There was no other material evidence. Should this day end empty handed then, in all likelihood, their shot at MacEwan would have passed. Going along with it would be Caslin's chances of protecting his father.

Starting the car, he selected first gear and accelerated away in pursuit of the strike team. They would carry out the raid and once the suspects were in custody and the scene secured, Caslin could then move in. Catching up to the rear of the convoy, he slowed the car down. They were less than two miles from the farm and the operation was expected to be over within minutes of them entering.

"How confident are you with the accuracy of Fuller's information?" Broadfoot asked for what must have been the fourth or fifth time.

"As confident as I can be," Caslin replied, following the lead of the cars in front as they were forced up onto the grass verge in order to pass a tractor they'd come upon on the narrow lane. "We searched the ownership of White Hart Farm and what Fuller told us certainly checked out. MacEwan is the proprietor. He purchased the farmhouse and all the ancillary buildings twenty-five years ago but has never run it as a going concern or listed it against any of his other businesses. The ownership is via a series of shell companies, all of which are registered outside of Europe. Without Fuller's information, we would never have come across it. It stands to reason he has kept it off the books for a purpose we're not aware of."

"If Fuller's on the level, then we're in for a big day," Broadfoot said.

"Yes, sir."

"Tell me," Broadfoot began, changing tone. "Where are we with identifying Jody's killer?"

Caslin didn't doubt his commanding officer's commitment to breaking this case but his personal angle was equally important to him if not more so. The murder of his Godson was an open wound that he wanted to close. "We are still unsure as to why he was killed, sir. By all accounts, he was following up on the inquiry his father worked in the 80s but as to why, or to what depth he reached in doing so, we still don't know. We think we've identified his girlfriend and once we've tracked her down, she may be able to provide some answers."

"Yes, Louise. Scott Tarbet's daughter. Hunter filled me in," Broadfoot said. "You've had no joy in locating her?"

"No, sir. Not so far. Because of the obvious association with her father, the lead witness in Bradley's faked death, I'm reluctant to descend on her network with all of our resources. She's disappeared from sight and is probably using friends or relatives to help keep her head down. We could pick her up at one of their addresses but equally we could miss her. If so, she might be spooked and take off. So far, she's been quite adept at staying under the radar and when we have the chance, I don't want her to slip past us."

"Hmm..." Broadfoot murmured, an indication tantamount to disagreement. Caslin glanced across at him.

"She will be my next priority after we take down MacEwan, sir. You have my word."

Broadfoot remained silent for a few moments before cracking a thin smile. "I don't doubt it. Thank you, Nathaniel."

They crossed over the main Scarborough Road bringing them to a point just south of the village of Reighton and within direct view of the sea. An orange glow spread as far as the eye could see as the sun crested the horizon.

Caslin brought his radio up to his mouth, "You should be seeing us any moment." The convoy took the next right and soon came upon Hunter sitting in her car in a layby screened from the main road by overgrown foliage. As they passed, she started the engine and pulled out behind Caslin picking up the rear. "We'll hang back and let Freeman lead the assault. Once we have the all clear, we'll go in and bring out our guy."

"Can't wait," Hunter replied.

The target area had been reconnoitred in great detail on the previous evening but no one managed to get close enough to observe any movement on the site. Vehicles were present parked under cover in one of the barns and light was visible from within another.

The convoy took the turn off the highway and onto the farm's approach road at speed. A more clandestine approach was proposed, considered, and roundly rejected due to the topography of the surrounding farmland. In every direction the terrain was flat giving rise to concerns that the assault team would be too exposed to mount a successful operation. The suspects would potentially have a three-hundred-and-sixty-degree view with which to spot their arrival. The access road to the farm was both the one way in and out. A high-speed assault along with the element of surprise was determined to yield the greatest chance of success.

They sped up the access road and into the complex of agricultural buildings, a horseshoe set up of brick barns behind the dilapidated farmhouse. The incumbents within each car were aware of their individual tasks and had their feet on the ground before any of the vehicles came to a full stop. The first team moved on the farmhouse and the remainder fanned out with the intention of sweeping the adjoining buildings. Caslin and Hunter pulled up outside of the yard parking their cars horizontally across the access road in an attempt to cut off any escape route. Hunter got out of her car and joined Caslin and Broadfoot as they took cover behind their vehicles. The three of them waited patiently, listening to the discussion of the assault team as they relayed their progress via an open communication link. Caslin looked around, showing concern.

"What is it?" Broadfoot asked.

"I don't see their cars," he replied.

"No one left last night," Hunter confirmed.

The first minute of the assault seemed to pass slowly as the team battered in doors to gain entry but with the passing of each subsequent one, Caslin felt his confidence ebb. The assault team were split into five groups of four and were proceeding to sweep the interior, shouts sporadically coming their way through the speaker to indicate another room was successfully cleared. There were no shots and no apparent sign of resistance. A quick glance towards Hunter revealed her thoughts were similar to his. Caslin rubbed at his forehead. Those who entered the farmhouse appeared outside once again, making for the ancillary buildings to support their colleagues. Despite the absence of an opposition they moved as a unit with weapons at the ready to respond at any given moment. Until they knew the scene was secure, they would proceed with caution.

"This isn't good," Caslin muttered under his breath. Broadfoot glanced at him but said nothing. The disappointment was etched into his face. Within moments their fears were realised as Chas Freeman's voice came across the radio.

"The scene is secure. Zero contact," he said quietly. "They're gone."

Caslin's heart sank and he let out a deep sigh. He was gutted. "Shit."

"How is that possible?" Broadfoot asked.

Caslin shook his head. "There must be another access to the farm that we missed. It was dark last night, a lot of cloud cover."

"There's nothing on the map," Hunter said, disappointed.

Caslin inclined his head in the direction of the yard indicating they should go in. "It might not even be on the map. These farms have been here for centuries. Who knows when the paths were last documented?"

They came out from behind the cars and headed for the yard. By the time the three of them entered, the assault team were already coming out. The built-up tension of the previous fourteen hours had now dissipated to be replaced by a deep sense of frustration. Freeman appeared from the cart entrance to one of the barns crossing the uneven cobbles to meet them.

"Well, someone's been inside," he said, looking to Broadfoot before Caslin and pointing to the building he'd just come from. "Someone's dropped a bollock though because they're definitely not here now."

"How long?" Caslin asked.

"I'd say recently. Very recent, if I had to guess."

"Thanks, Chas," Caslin said, walking past him. Freeman set about organising his team's withdrawal. "Come on. Let's take a look."

They entered the barn and looked around. There was nothing of note to set their eyes upon but in stark contrast to the attached farmhouse this section of the farm appeared to be better cared for. The floor was concrete, showing signs of cracking and breaking up in places but didn't appear prone to damp. In fact the closed shutters hid windows that were in good condition and a brief inspection of the locks to them and the doors revealed they were relatively new and in perfect working order. At one end of the barn were a couple of tables and some casual chairs. Hunter crossed to the table and examined some discarded wrapping and plastic bags.

"Interesting," she said, rummaging through one of the bags.

"What's that?" Caslin asked. He went to join her while Broadfoot walked around scanning the interior for something, anything, to assist the investigation.

"Takeaway containers," Hunter said, focusing on the contents. She brought out a slip of paper that was scrunched into a ball. As she unfurled it, Caslin could see it was a receipt. "Dated yesterday," she confirmed, passing it to him. Caslin took it and briefly read through what was listed on it.

"What do you think? Four, maybe five people?" he asked. Hunter nodded.

"That's be my guess."

"It looks like Fuller sold you a pup," Broadfoot stated, coming to stand with them.

"Not necessarily, sir," Caslin replied, passing him the receipt. Broadfoot eyed it suspiciously but having checked the date, he looked to Caslin.

"Then we've missed them."

Caslin thought on it. Turning to Hunter, he asked, "You were in position from what… four o'clock yesterday?"

"A little after, yes."

"And no one came or went after that time?"

"A car came in a little after seven but no one left."

Caslin crossed to one of the windows and opened it pushing the shutter away. He looked to the rear of the complex. There was a dirt track heading across the field to the east. "So, that receipt was time and date stamped at seven o'clock when they bought it."

"Yes."

"It's a bit late in the day to make a big move, isn't it? They wouldn't decamp across there in the dark at that time. If they were going to they would have left earlier."

"Not gone to pick up a takeaway, you mean?" Hunter queried.

"Exactly. Which means they were on the move early this morning. How was MacEwan shipping the gold out previously? Via his boatyard up the coast," Caslin said, remembering the details his father provided him with. "What if he's doing the same now?"

Hunter shook her head, "I went through his business interests with Holt. He offloaded that boatyard years ago."

Caslin's theory fell apart before he had even begun to flesh it out. He sighed. The sense of disappointment among them was palpable.

"Keep at it," Broadfoot demanded. "I'll head back with Freeman. Get back to me with your next steps by the close of play."

Their commanding officer walked away without another word. Caslin closed his eyes and grimaced. "There goes an unhappy man," Hunter said softly watching Broadfoot leave ensuring only Caslin could hear her words.

"Get on to Terry back at Fulford. Have him run down the businesses that we know MacEwan has a stake in along with any residences, land or assets within a fifty-mile radius of this location. We're due a bit of luck. We still have time. We know the area they're in which narrows down the search parameters," Caslin said, conveying confidence that Hunter didn't share.

They stepped outside into bright sunlight. The smell of the sea carried to them on the breeze. Freeman and his team were finishing the packing up of their gear into the lock boxes of their vehicles and were now preparing to leave. Caslin thrust his hands into his coat pockets. Despite the sun the day was still freezing.

"I had better move my car so they can get out," Hunter said, striding away. Caslin acknowledged Freeman's wave as he got into the passenger seat of his Range Rover. The car pulled away followed closely by the other four vehicles. Judging from the forlorn expressions on the departing faces the morning failed to match up to their expectations. Caslin's phone was vibrating in his pocket and he took it out. Glancing at the screen it showed a number he didn't recognise. His first thought was of Pete Fuller but he knew he was still being held in isolation at Full Sutton. He tapped the answer tab.

"DI Caslin," he said, watching the last of the vehicles drive out of the yard.

"Is that Inspector Caslin?" a man's voice asked. It seemed remotely familiar to him but he couldn't quite place where he recognised it from let alone assign a face or a name.

"Yes, it is. Who is this?"

"It's Geoff. Geoff Thomas."

"From…?" Caslin asked, straining to remember where they'd met.

"From Flamborough Head. I run the café, out at the…"

"Lighthouse," Caslin finished for him. "Of course. What can I do for you, Geoff?"

"I'm sorry to bother you so early but there are some strange goings on out here this morning, Inspector. Not sure what to make of it to be honest."

CHAPTER TWENTY-EIGHT

THE COASTAL ROAD was set back barely half a mile from the sea, picking its way through farmland to either side. The main road, the A165, carried you inland down to Bridlington, south of Flamborough and further around the coast. The road Caslin took was more direct and less travelled but the trade-off was the increased journey time. Easing out of his lane to get a better view, he sought to pass the slow-moving car in front only to be forced back as the oncoming vehicle flashed its lights and sounded a warning blast of its horn. Even at this speed the journey itself should only take fifteen minutes. The dashboard lit up to signal he had an incoming call. He looked to the heads-up display and saw it was Terry Holt.

"What did you find out?" Caslin asked, dispensing with the customary greetings. Leaving Hunter back at White Hart Farm to secure the scene and await the forensic search team, the call from Flamborough Head had piqued his curiosity.

"A lot of historical info about when it was built..."

"Skip the history, Terry," Caslin interrupted him.

"Sorry," Holt replied. "Trinity still own, maintain and run the lighthouse although it's a fully automated system now so they haven't needed keepers for twenty-odd years. However, what is interesting to us is that once they took the lighthouse under remote operation, they retained the tower and fog warning station whilst selling off the attached real estate."

"Who bought it?" Caslin asked.

"That's what's taken me the time. It's another case of a company within a company. Well, more like several companies within several more," Holt continued. "Long story short – I don't know... yet. What I would say is the ownership is so vague that I wouldn't be surprised if it turns out we can tie it to one of MacEwan's shells. I always get suspicious when the answers aren't obvious. I wouldn't necessarily put money on it..."

"If you were playing the percentages?"

"Seeing as MacEwan is in the area and Bradley was recently as well. I'd say pretty high," Holt replied. "Is Hunter there with you?"

"No," Caslin replied, dropping through the gears, indicating and pulling out into oncoming traffic and forcing his way through much to the annoyance of other road users. "I left her back at the farm."

"That's not good," Holt stated, concern edging into his voice. "I think we may have just found..."

"Where MacEwan is. I know but let's not get carried away," Caslin said. "Call Hunter and tell her what's going on. I'll check it out."

"What about ACC Broadfoot?" Holt asked, thinking ahead.

Caslin was reticent, worried about raising the alarm on the back of a hunch. "Our local contact advised me there were a handful of them coming and going this morning. They were there when he arrived to unlock his business. If it is MacEwan, we have to assume they are moving what they have and using the lighthouse as a way station. If it's them, I'll try and slow them down."

"If they're there what were they keeping at White Hart Farm?" Holt asked. It was a good question. "Never mind. I'll get onto them."

"Thanks, Terry," Caslin said, hanging up. He swore loudly, frustrated at his lack of forethought.

In all likelihood, Bradley wasn't out at Flamborough to meet someone or not primarily in any event. If their theory was right, then he probably knew MacEwan owned the buildings and was observing them but to what end, he couldn't say. Caslin's mind was reeling as he made yet another unadvised passing manoeuvre. This time, he was forced to apply his brakes and swerve back into his lane to avoid a certain head-on collision with an oncoming van.

Moments later, he came upon the outskirts of Flamborough town itself. The route circumvented the centre and he reached a junction. Turning left and heading directly to the coast, Caslin was acutely aware there was only one road to or from Flamborough Head and he was driving along it.

Keeping his eyes trained on the road, Caslin paid attention to the traffic passing in the opposite direction. Unsure of what MacEwan could have stashed out here, they could be using any type of vehicle. The location came to the forefront of his mind. No one would think to look out here but equally the nearby farm was just as remote and safe from prying eyes. There was a reason. There had to be. Perhaps MacEwan had several locations in which he was using to spread the risk of discovery.

There was little movement on the road and Caslin suddenly felt vulnerable as he approached the visitors' car park. The wide-open expanse in the run up to the lighthouse left him exposed. Caslin pulled in to Selwick Drive, the residential road set across from the lighthouse to the rear of the café. Should anyone be paying attention, he could be taken as visiting friends or returning home. He parked the car with his target still roughly one hundred yards distant and the café and gift shop between them. From his vantage point, he could see two cars and a van parked alongside the lighthouse's outer perimeter wall. There was another mini-van a short distance away and Caslin considered one of these must belong to the café's proprietor who had called him earlier. No one was visible and after a few moments, Caslin knew he would need to get closer. If he couldn't confirm the theory, then there was no point in his being there.

Getting out of the car, he shut the door and scanned the nearby vicinity. It was still early and there didn't appear to be many residents in and around the nearby assortment of bungalows. Those in employment had probably already left for work and the remainder were still behind drawn curtains. The wind coming in off of the North Sea was strong with frequent gusts buffeting him as he set off across the open ground towards the lighthouse. Caslin used the café as a cover for his approach. The only part of the complex where he could be seen was from within the tower of the lighthouse itself.

Coming to the white buildings, Caslin slipped between a storage block and the café approaching the rear door to the kitchen. It was closed but he saw movement on the other side. He rapped his knuckles on the glass three times. Moments later, a figure appeared on the other side distorted by the obscured glass. The door cracked open and a face peered hesitantly through the gap.

"Geoff? It's DI Caslin," he said, needlessly lowering his voice for there was no way anyone would be able to overhear their conversation. The door opened wider and the familiar face of the café's owner appeared.

"Come in," he said, stepping back.

"You're on edge," Caslin stated. The man nodded.

"It's that lot, over there," Geoff said, indicating with a flick of his head in the direction of the lighthouse. "They were here when I arrived. One of them didn't take kindly to me looking at them."

"What did he say?"

"Nah… it was more the look he gave me. I called the wife – told her he was a wrong-un. Not someone I want to meet on a dark night for sure."

"What are they up to, do you think?" Caslin asked. "How many are in there?"

"Four or five, I reckon," Geoff confirmed. "And I've no idea what they're up to. Never seen them here before either. I probably wouldn't have given it much thought except Mary remembered your visit and suggested I give you a call. What do you think is going on?"

Caslin looked past him and out of the window towards the lighthouse. All was quiet. "I don't know but…" he said, addressing him directly, "it's best if you stay in the kitchen out of the way for the time being. Is it just you here?"

Geoff nodded. "But we have staff arriving in the next half an hour. Is that all right?"

Caslin looked at the clock. It was approaching 8 a.m. and he did a quick calculation in his head. He knew Hunter would be here soon enough but how long it might take for Broadfoot to arrive with the armed support was anyone's guess and he still needed confirmation. He didn't want to put any members of the public in danger but by the same token, he couldn't risk the word getting around to the residents there was a police operation underway. "Do your staff arrive by car?"

"Usually, yes."

"Where do they park?"

"At the back, behind the café."

"And they enter the same way I did?" Caslin asked. Geoff nodded, suddenly looking concerned. "That should be fine but do me a favour, would you? I want you to let me out of the front door but then close it behind me and keep it locked. No one in that way, no one out. Understood?" Geoff nodded vigorously.

Walking to the front entrance, Caslin peered out of the window but still didn't see any indication of movement. The perimeter wall was five-foot-high and curved around the building with the access to the visitors' car park passing alongside. The wall met a double-entry gate alongside the head of the coastal walking trail, itself a similar height, and offered access to both the lighthouse complex and the monitoring station on the nearby point. Nodding to Geoff, the owner stepped forward and turned the key in the lock before sliding back the bolts, located top and bottom, and pulled the door open. Caslin took his radio from his pocket and switched it off before setting his mobile to silent. The last thing he wanted was for either of them to give away his position at an inappropriate moment.

"Thanks," Caslin said, slipping out. He heard the bolts being slammed back in place and got the impression Geoff would be on the phone to his wife within seconds. He figured it didn't matter. Turning right as he left the café, he squeezed between the outside seating and hopped over the knee-high boundary wall of the outside dining area. Hugging the exterior wall of the gift shop, Caslin reached the corner of the building and eyed the fifty feet of open space between himself and the lighthouse's boundary wall. Breaking into a run, he covered the distance as quickly as he could and dropped to his haunches alongside the first of the parked vehicles.

Popping his head up, he looked for a reaction to his approach but everything remained quiet. This close to the wall, he had no chance of seeing over it so he crept forward keeping low until he reached the brick. The gate was further around and to his left. Caslin ignored it instead choosing to move to his right. As the wall began to curve, he stopped. Level with the tower, Caslin turned and backed up a couple of steps in order to be able to get a run at the wall. Three quick steps forward and he leapt up throwing his arms over and gripping the edge of the wall on the other side. Scrambling up with confidence that the tower masked his efforts, Caslin hauled himself up onto the top. Keeping himself flat, he rolled over and dropped his legs down the other side. Carefully lowering himself to the ground, he stopped to listen. The sound of the waves crashing upon the rocks nearby was all that could be heard.

Moving quickly and with purpose, Caslin made his way around the tower keeping as close to the wall as he could. With every step the attached building revealed itself and Caslin felt his vulnerability increase. Each window was an opportunity for those inside to see him. With no way of knowing the interior layout, he had no ability to mitigate the chance of discovery. That is if they were still inside. The building attached to the lighthouse was rectangular and double storey. As Caslin came around the side, he chanced a look through a small ground-floor window. The glass was dirty and smudged to such an extent that he couldn't make out much detail. It appeared to be a storeroom of some description and barely six-feet square. Content that he wouldn't be seen at this point, he moved on, skirting the side of the building and passing to the rear.

Peering around the corner, he came upon a grassed area reasonably well maintained and encompassed entirely by the perimeter wall. From here, Caslin could see the access gates on the far side. Movement in the corner of his eye caused him to freeze in position pressing his back to the wall and attempting to become one with it. It was the form of a figure passing by the window next to him and once confident that he wouldn't be seen, Caslin slowly leaned over in order to see through it. He could make out three people standing together plus the one who'd originally caught his eye. Due to the build-up of muck and grime on the glass, he was unable to identify any of them. Scanning the interior, he sought an access point that might allow him to eavesdrop or at the very least give him a decent view of them. The interior was mostly open plan from what he could tell. The door to the storage room he had just walked past was ajar on the far side but apart from that the only other option appeared to be the main access door.

Easing himself away from the window, he made his way back around from where he had come. His confidence boosted, he made a more detailed assessment of the room. It appeared to be a large store cupboard, an offshoot from a kitchenette and probably converted at some point post construction. The window was secure appearing to have been painted shut years ago. In any event, it was probably too small for him to fit through. Caslin could see light coming into the room from above. There was a drainpipe running down the corner of the exterior where the building met the base of the tower and Caslin gave it a tug. It was cast iron and felt securely fastened to the wall. With great care, he reached up and then used the ninety-degree junction between the buildings to brace against as he began the short climb. The flat roof was only around seven feet above the ground and Caslin made the ascent with relative ease.

Once on the top, Caslin made his way to the skylight. It was single-glazed and in a poor state of repair. The frame was steel and the combination of the salt air and sea mist had corroded many of the fixings. Even a cursory attempt to prise it saw enough movement to indicate his efforts would bear fruit. Taking a firm grip with both hands, Caslin levered the frame from side to side and found he was able to lift it from its housing with minimal noise and exertion. Placing it down at his side, he looked into the room below. The sound of muffled voices came to him but they were too distorted to comprehend. The drop of seven feet wasn't going to be a problem because there was a table set almost directly beneath the skylight but the gap to squeeze through was only marginally wider than Caslin's upper body.

Lowering his feet through first, he braced both arms at either side and eased himself through the gap. Momentarily fearful he might fall, Caslin wondered whether he should retreat but realised he was already committed. Levering himself to one side, he put his left arm down, supporting himself with only his right. The strain was immense and he struggled to regulate his breathing as his chest was clamped to the sides of the opening, legs flailing as they sought to gain purchase on the table beneath. Ultimately, he reached the point where he had little choice but to have faith in his plan and make the drop.

Hitting the table with a thud saw him immediately off balance. His inability to look beneath him and therefore to properly assess the drop made his landing awkward. In trying to counter balance, Caslin overcompensated and fell backwards off the table. Despite managing to get his feet out from under him and break his fall, he still staggered into the opposing wall. Holding his breath, he waited for the shout to go up signifying his discovery but it didn't come. Breathing a silent sigh of relief, he crept to the doorway and peered into the next room through the gap between door and frame.

Three figures were in view although one, a woman, stood with her back to him. She was a brunette and her hair was cut short. She was dressed in hiking gear. Of the other two, Caslin recognised both Mark Bridger, who was similarly attired to the woman, and the man who was currently speaking, David MacEwan.

"You told me he would be here," MacEwan said accusingly. Despite being unable to see the entire room and anyone who might be out of view, Caslin guessed he was addressing the woman. A theory confirmed by her response.

"And he *will be*," she replied. MacEwan swore under his breath. "You just have to be patient. With this wind, the swell will be up..."

"We should have been out of here before sunrise," MacEwan snapped. Turning to someone out of view, he said pointedly, "It was your bloody plan. The longer we stay here the greater the chance of them finding us."

"They didn't see us leaving the farm this morning and they haven't tied this place to you in twenty years, so there's no reason they should now," a calm voice argued but Caslin couldn't see who it belonged to. He tried to improve his angle of vision but to no avail.

"He'll be here," the woman repeated.

"Well, he better be here soon," MacEwan said, looking to Mark Bridger beside him. Caslin was quite taken by how rattled he appeared to be. For all his perceived connections and criminal participation over the years, MacEwan struck him as a nervous individual quite far removed from the imposing figure of his imagination. The sound of the main entrance door opening and a burst of noise from the outside came along with it as another person entered. Caslin shifted position again and eyed the newcomer. He was athletically built and walked with the poise of a military man. Caslin assumed he was another of MacEwan's men.

"Is he here, Brad?" MacEwan asked the new arrival.

"He's here," the man confirmed. "He's dropped anchor and is bringing the boat in now."

"It's about bloody time," MacEwan complained bitterly.

"You see," Ollie Bridger said, striding into view from Caslin's right. "Nothing to worry about." He walked towards MacEwan and tapped Brad on the side of his arm in an overly friendly gesture. "Let's get things down there."

"Wait," MacEwan said. Ollie turned to face him with an inquiring look on his face. "It's too late. People might see. We should call it off today."

"No way," Ollie replied, shaking his head and coming back to stand before MacEwan. "We're too far advanced for that. I know I said they won't find us but tomorrow's another day."

"No. It's too risky now. We should have been gone under cover of darkness."

Ollie looked to his brother who met his eye. The two exchanged something unsaid between them. The significance of which only brothers as close as they were would comprehend. "Do you think?" Ollie asked.

Mark shrugged, "It was going to be later… but now is as good a time as any."

"Fair enough," Ollie said, drawing a concealed pistol from the rear of his waistband.

"What are you doing?" MacEwan barked. In one fluid motion, Ollie brought the gun to bear and shot MacEwan twice in quick succession, once in the upper thigh of each leg.

CHAPTER TWENTY-NINE

THE GANGSTER SCREAMED and collapsed as his legs gave out beneath him. Caslin jumped back in shock, overbalancing and stumbled, falling backwards. Reaching out and grasping a shelf he attempted to break his fall but it failed to support his weight, breaking away from the brackets holding it in place. Caslin hit the ground hard with the contents of the shelf coming down on top of him. A further two shots sounded coming almost on top of one another. Then silence descended for a few seconds before a final, solitary shot echoed around the building.

Caslin was momentarily frozen in place. *Had the shots and the screams masked the sound of his fall?* Listening carefully, the sound of MacEwan groaning carried through from the adjoining room.

"I can't believe the bastard shot me!" he heard Mark Bridger say. He sounded surprisingly calm. Tentatively, Caslin detached himself from the miscellaneous items in and around him, careful not to make any further noise.

"It wasn't supposed to go down like that, Ollie," the woman's voice said.

"Plans change, Babe," Ollie replied and footsteps could be heard echoing on the concrete floor.

Managing to get to his feet without drawing attention to himself, Caslin shook his head. He had no idea what his next move should be. Listening in, the woman was talking about the swell. With a boat anchored off the coast they were planning to move their haul out of the country by sea after all. Caslin looked at his watch carrying out a mental calculation in his head. Returning to his vantage point, he peered through the crack once more. Something crossed his sightline completely obscuring his view. He flinched taking a step backwards vainly hoping not to be seen. It was already too late. The door opened fully and there she stood with a gun trained on him. Her hair was far shorter and by the look of it recently dyed but she was unmistakable. Louise Bennett looked him up and down, smiling.

"Inspector Caslin," she said. "Very nice of you to join us."

She gestured for him to come towards her with the barrel of the gun, walking backwards as she did so. Caslin raised his hands slightly, palms up in a gesture of subservience. Stepping through into the room beyond, Caslin got his first look at what just happened. MacEwan lay where he had fallen with blood pooling around his legs. He was breathing heavily, ashen-faced and most likely experiencing the onset of shock. To their left the man MacEwan identified as Brad lay prostrate on the ground with what appeared to be a gunshot wound to the chest and another to the head. The latter was dead centre in his forehead, execution style. A semi-automatic pistol lay to his right as if he'd lost his grip on it as he went down.

Mark Bridger was sitting on the ground nearby cradling a pistol in his lap. Ollie had placed his own weapon on the floor next to them and was tending to his brother. Neither man paid Caslin much attention. Ollie levered his brother's arm from the sleeve of his jacket rather unceremoniously which brought a howl of derision as a fresh wave of pain struck.

"Bloody hell, man," Mark chastised him.

"Behave," Ollie replied, taking out a knife from his pocket and widening the opening in the sleeve of Mark's undershirt in order to inspect the wound. Checking both sides of the arm, Ollie gently patted his sibling's cheek. "It went clean through, little brother. You're going to be fine."

"That's easy for you to say," Mark replied. "You're not sitting here with a hole in your arm."

Ollie took the knife and cut the remainder of the sleeve off. Using it as a makeshift dressing, he tied it around the wound, tightening it which brought forward yet another complaint. Glancing to Louise, he flicked his eyes towards a window overlooking the approach road.

"Take a look," Ollie instructed her before retrieving his gun, standing and coming over to Caslin. Louise backed up a couple of steps ensuring she kept her weapon fixed on Caslin and quickly looked around outside. Ollie Bridger used both of his hands to frisk Caslin, presumably hunting for either a weapon or technology to indicate he was in communication with the outside world. He took Caslin's mobile as well as his radio.

"It looks clear out there," Louise said, coming back.

"I fear I may have underestimated you," Ollie told him.

"People often do," Caslin replied.

"I didn't think you'd piece it together this quickly. Although," Ollie said, glancing around, "this probably wasn't your most intelligent move."

"You'll get no argument from me."

There was a flash of light in Ollie's hand as the screen lit up to display an incoming call. Ollie's eyes lowered to the mobile phone in his hand. Caslin flicked his eyes to Louise as she shifted position slightly. Any doubts he may have had around her ability with firearms were dismissed as Caslin realised she was ensuring Ollie was out of her firing line if he should make a move. He had no intention of doing so.

"I'm very sorry, Inspector but you're going to miss Hunter's call," Ollie declared, dropping the mobile onto the floor. The screen smashed and then he stamped on it with the heel of his boot. Caslin winced as he heard the crunch and saw the screen go blank.

"What are we going to do with him?" Louise said, indicating MacEwan with a tilt of the head. Ollie glanced at the gangster lying on the floor and then back to Caslin. With a slight shake of the head, he left his side and crossed to MacEwan. He beckoned his brother to come over and Mark laboured to his feet. The two brothers stood over the stricken man.

"You thought you were so clever, didn't you?" Mark said accusingly.

"You want it all. Is that it?" MacEwan accused them both.

"This wasn't about money," Mark replied.

"Thought you could grass on our father and get away with it," Ollie said. "You've been around enough. You know what happens to the likes of you." The brothers brought up their guns and aimed them at MacEwan. Ollie cracked a smile whereas Mark remained stone-faced.

"Fuck you!" MacEwan hissed just before both brothers squeezed their triggers. Two shots sounded throughout the room as MacEwan's head fell backwards striking the floor. Ollie raised a hand and placed it on his brother's shoulder applying an affectionate squeeze.

"It's done," he said softly.

Mark met his brother's eye and nodded before looking at Caslin. "And him?"

"Yes, what are we going to do with Caslin Junior? You've got some balls coming in here by yourself," Ollie said.

Caslin shrugged. "I could say similar to you."

"How so?"

"You and your brother going up against Fuller, Dade..." Caslin said, glancing at MacEwan's dead body, "and him."

Ollie laughed. "Oh... that's one way of looking at it, yes."

"And now you're going up against the police as well. There's no end to the list of enemies that you're willing to rack up in pursuit of what... revenge, money?"

"It was never about the money," Mark Bridger snapped.

"You could have fooled me," Caslin argued.

"This was about justice," Mark explained.

Now it was Caslin who laughed. "Justice. Is that what Jody Wyer's death was all about? I've seen the result of your kind of justice. What a load of bullshit. People like you are all the same... take whatever you want regardless of who gets hurt and dress it up with some twisted code of honour."

"Our father did what he was supposed to do. He played by *all the rules*... loyalty... trust... and we had no better example," Ollie argued. "Look what happened to him - turned over by the very people who were supposed to be his friends."

"That's naïve," Caslin countered. "There are no friends in this business. I'm amazed you haven't learned that by now."

"You're right, Caslin. When it comes down to it, the only people you can count on is your family," Ollie said. "And we set our own rules, same as you."

"What the hell do you mean by that? The rest of us follow the law," Caslin stated.

"Is that so?" Mark countered. "Can the same be said of your father? Where was his moral compass and your precious law when he was lining his pockets?"

"My father will have to answer for what he's done."

Ollie laughed. "And you will see to that, will you? You'll take down your old man? We both know you'll do everything you can to keep him out of prison because you're not so different to us. You put your family first and morality comes second. A distant second at that. We're not altogether different, you and me Mr Caslin. I'd argue we're the same."

Caslin looked at MacEwan's dead body. "Where is it going to end?" he asked. "You planted the bomb in the minicab office. You were family. *They trusted you*. Then you lured Clinton Dade out into the middle of nowhere and killed him. For what? To start a war between his people and Pete Fuller's. Where does Dade fit into your righteous indignation?"

"An unfortunate casualty but please don't try to convince me that you'll shed any tears over the loss of Clinton Dade. He was no better than Fuller or his two sociopathic children."

"Pete Fuller's figured this out. You know he's going to come for you?"

"He knows as much as we've allowed him to. If he manages to come for us," Ollie said, with no apparent concern for that eventuality, "we will be waiting."

"Fuller didn't grass on your father," Caslin said.

"But he failed to protect him," Ollie said. Caslin looked to Mark and then back to Ollie. "Our father was one of the last to be rounded up, you know that. When he went inside, Fuller was still trying to figure out where the heat had come from. He and Dad went back so far. He was married to his sister and kept his business afloat after good old Uncle Pete was sent down. And what thanks did he get? Pete shunned him. He may not have pointed the finger directly but by doing that word got around and people talked. Events took their own course as they were always likely to."

"He threw our father to the wolves," Mark said, venom in his tone. "Pete Fuller deserves everything coming to him and one day soon he'll be out. Then, he'll be ours."

"This is never going to end," Caslin argued. "The bitterness. The hatred. It will keep growing. You'll have to take out Ashton and Carl, too, otherwise they'll come after you. Ultimately, this will consume you until at some point in the future someone will put you down. This is the reality. These are the people you have taken on with your vigilante crusade. You've done well so far but you cannot expect to get away with it forever."

"Funny," Mark said, "we're pretty good at it."

Caslin thought about their apparent confidence. They didn't strike him as fly-by-night. These two had proved quite adept at orchestrating their Machiavellian revenge mission perhaps with even more depth than he realised. If they were feeding information to Fuller, then they were arguably controlling his response in some way.

"Fuller didn't get to Bradley, did he?" Caslin asked. Mark looked to his brother and Ollie smiled.

"No. We took care of Bradley. It was too good an opportunity to miss. We might not have got a better chance. He doesn't come back to this country very often and once we realised, he was negotiating with MacEwan to be paid up then we knew he was going to disappear again. Just like he did two years ago. He had everybody fooled, even us. Not MacEwan, obviously but that was one fact he kept to himself."

"What about the police?" Caslin asked. "What about my father?"

"That wasn't us," Ollie stated. "That was all Fuller."

"Someone must have tipped him off. If not you, then who?"

"I'm not going to tell you where he got his information from," Ollie added, with a smile. There was a smug satisfaction conveyed in that expression. He was toying with him. Caslin knew it.

"You are a crafty little bastard," Caslin accused.

"Taken as a compliment," Ollie said, the smile broadening into a grin.

Caslin glanced to his left in the direction of Louise. "And where do you fit into all of this?" he asked. "Did you have any feelings for Jody Wyer or were you just manipulating him for the benefit of these two clowns?" For the first time there was a chink in Ollie's demeanour. Perhaps he had hit something of a nerve there.

"Jody was a means to an end," Louise argued.

"When he outlived his usefulness, these monkeys killed him. Is that about right?"

"You think Jody was on some personal crusade of his own?" Mark asked Caslin, the former breaking out into a fit of genuine laughter. "He was looking for his father's share... his crooked father's share... so that he could get out of a job where he was sitting up all night watching married men banging their mistresses on the side. Wyer was no better than the rest of us."

"He wasn't a killer though, was he?" Caslin argued.

Ollie shrugged. "He thought he could slip in and take a share of the money and then disappear. He fancied himself as a big-time player but he couldn't even get the better of his business partner."

"Mason dropped Jody right into your hands."

"Mason was useful for MacEwan. Gambling debts make for decent leverage. But, at the same time, he was prone to running his mouth which is most likely what put Wyer onto us in the first place."

"Wyer didn't know he'd let a fox into the hen house," Caslin said, flicking his eyes towards Louise.

"I watched my father lose everything because of what Phil Bradley did. His own blood," she argued. "The police, the insurance company investigation and all the accompanying stress from the debt. Not to mention the guilt. My mother got sick and I watched as the doctors tried to save her but couldn't. Then I watched her give up. Watched her die and my father crumble in front of me. The man he once was destroyed… Fifty years of graft to end up where he is now. A bucket load of debt and a…" her voice cracked momentarily, "and a dead wife. All of that while living with the suspicion of having killed his cousin for an insurance scam."

"Ah… I see," Caslin said. "So, you've done all of this in order to give your dad a nice retirement? I didn't understand, I'm so sorry," Caslin said with emphasised sarcasm. "That's what the rest of us call life. It's not fair and you don't always get what you deserve but you persevere and make the best of it you can."

"Thanks for the advice, Inspector but I'll go about things my way," Louise bit back.

"You do that," Caslin said, "and then watch as your lover here gets tired of you. Then you'll be the next one floating in the sea." Caslin inclined his head in Ollie's direction. "How devoted to a woman do you think a man can be if he's willing to pimp her out to get his hands on some money. Albeit a lot of money, I'll grant you, but still makes him no better than your pimp and you… well, you know what that makes you. Come to think of it that's probably giving you too much credit. Some people sell themselves as it's the only way they can get by. You didn't just sell yourself for money but you cost Jody Wyer his life."

Ollie stepped forward and struck Caslin across the face with the butt of his pistol. Caslin staggered backwards grimacing at the sharpness of the pain from the blow. Blinking tears from his eyes, he felt blood running from his nose. Reaching up, he wiped it with the back of his hand. "That's enough," Ollie said, through thinly veiled aggression.

"What are we going to do with him?" Mark asked.

"We're a little short of hands all of a sudden," Ollie said, pointing to the still forms of both dead men lying on the floor but his eyes never left Caslin. "We can always use some help to get stuff down to the boat."

"Speaking of which," Louise said, "we probably ought to get a move on. Dad will be waiting."

"So that's the plan, is it? Daddy brought his fishing boat down the coast and you're going to load it up and get across the channel."

Ollie laughed. "You're one hell of a detective."

"I expected something a little more sophisticated, I have to say. We'll be carrying it along the cliffs, will we?"

"Something like that," Ollie said, smiling. "You look like a man who could do with a workout."

Ollie gestured for Caslin to walk towards him at the point of a gun. Caslin held his hands up in supplication. Ollie shook his head.

"Put your hands down Inspector, it looks embarrassing." Caslin did so as Ollie stepped to one side, indicating for him to continue. Caslin walked towards the main entrance door. "That will do," Ollie said. He stopped where he was, Ollie pointed to his right. "Open that door."

Caslin eyed the cabinet next to the main door. It was a standalone cabinet, nondescript with two doors. He pulled open the left-hand door and inside were a number of rucksacks stacked against each other. They looked full. Heavy. Casting an eye over them, he raised an eyebrow at Ollie.

"If they're full of gold, I've no chance of lifting it."

Ollie laughed. "They are full of cash, Inspector. We've been trading the gold a little at a time. It's not as profitable an exchange rate but cash is a lot easier to spread around."

"Any particular one?"

"Whichever takes your fancy."

CHAPTER THIRTY

REACHING FOR THE NEAREST RUCKSACK, Caslin took a hold and tested the weight. It was heavier than he'd thought. Looking at the others, he knew this couldn't be all of it. There were only four. As if reading his mind, Mark Bridger answered the unasked question.

"You didn't think it would all still be here, did you?" he said, grinning. "We've been shipping it out bit by bit over the last few months."

"I thought that's why Bradley came back from the dead," Caslin said over his shoulder. He'd dropped to his haunches and was awkwardly attempting to fit the straps over his shoulders.

"No. Bradley's been receiving it at the other end on the continent," Mark explained. "He figured he'd done his bit and wanted to be finished with it all."

"That's why we had to make a move," Ollie explained. "Couldn't risk him doing another vanishing act which is exactly what I expect he was planning. Only this time, we would have had no idea where he was headed."

"Still figured you'd have more," Caslin argued.

"MacEwan cut a deal with whoever masterminded that job years ago. He probably didn't get to keep as much as you thought."

"I see," Caslin said, nodding and hefting the rucksack into the air and over his shoulders.

"While you're at it, you can help Mark to put one on."

Caslin looked at the younger of the Bridgers. Mark had managed to slide his coat back on but there was no way one of his arms could be used to bear the weight of the remaining rucksacks. Caslin looked down at them choosing a black one with yellow trim. He pointed to it.

Mark nodded. "Yeah, that's my colour."

With the weight of his own, Caslin struggled to pick up the rucksack. With a surge of effort, he managed to hoist it up just high enough for Mark to slip his arms through the straps and then onto his shoulders. The younger man grunted as he took the strain. It would certainly be an uncomfortable walk for him down to the shoreline. Ollie looked to Louise.

"I've got him," she confirmed, keeping an eye on Caslin. Putting his own gun back into his waistband, Ollie crossed over and picked up the next rucksack. Once he'd adjusted the straps, he assumed responsibility for Caslin again. Louise then picked up hers. The last one remaining.

"Let's go," Ollie said. "Mark, you take the lead, then Louise with our friend here and I'll bring up the rear."

Mark unlocked the front door. Poking his head out, he double-checked that their route was clear before leading them out into the brilliant sunshine. The sudden change in light caused Caslin to put his hand up to shield his eyes from the glare. Following the first two, he walked to the gate. There was every chance that they would bump into Hunter. He prayed that they didn't. She should have been there by now and would almost certainly have come across his car. The real question would be whether Broadfoot, Freeman and his team would make it in time. Caslin doubted it.

Louise took hold of the gate and opened it fully, allowing the others to pass through all the while scanning the approach road for signs of trouble. If it weren't for the bloodstains on the sleeve of Mark's coat as well as his own bloody nose which thankfully had stopped flowing, they could have been forgiven for being out on a day's hike. Apart from Caslin that is for he looked very much out of place, dressed in his suit but there was no one there to see them in any event.

"To the right," Ollie instructed, guiding Caslin towards the start of the walking path along the cliff top. He chanced a glance in the direction of the café, hoping to see a friendly face but he didn't. His heart sank.

The path was a well-known rambling trail that extended from Bridlington around the coast to the Flamborough Cliffs and on to North Landing. Subsequently, the going here was relatively easy with the path being well managed to accommodate the number of visitors throughout the year. After descending in single file for approximately a hundred yards the path split with the left fork marked as the continuation of the coastal trail. The right-hand fork continued downwards in a steeper descent to the water's edge of Selwick Bay. The sea was crashing against the cliffs and on another day Caslin would have been uplifted by their beauty but from his vantage point as they walked, he could see a small boat anchored some distance off the coast. He assumed that was Scott Tarbet's. The water here was too shallow for him to bring the boat closer. However, an inflatable rib was beached beneath them with one solitary figure sitting at the stern watching the small party descend towards him.

The weight of the rucksacks was significant. Along with that fact the steep incline also forced them to take their time in order to reach the pebble beach safely. They were in a natural cove, hemmed in by vertical chalk cliffs on both sides. The bay was not large and was accessible by the rib until high tide. By then the approach would be far too treacherous. Had Scott Tarbet managed to arrive before dawn, as expected, there would have been every chance they could have been well clear before anybody knew that they had ever been there. As it was now, only the café's owner had noted their arrival. Without Caslin's previous visit, he would no doubt have made very little of the presence of the small group of hikers nor even seen the rib landing below.

Crossing the beach towards the boat, Caslin saw Scott Tarbet become increasingly agitated as he realised Caslin was with them. No sooner had they come within earshot, he jumped off the rib and marched purposefully towards them.

"What the bloody hell is he doing here?"

"Calm down, Scott," Ollie said, attempting to placate the older man.

"He's a bloody policeman."

"I know exactly who he is," Ollie stated forcefully. "And I will handle it."

"Handle it!" Tarbet barked, red faced. "How exactly are you going to do that?"

"I'll do what I have to do," Ollie replied calmly before adding, "same as always."

"Is that so?" Tarbet said in a condescending tone mocking the younger man.

"Dad," Louise cut in. "If Ollie says he'll deal with it, then he will okay?" Tarbet seemed to accept his daughter's word.

Caslin laughed. "That means they plan to kill me, Scott. Are you comfortable with that? You might be many things but not a killer."

"You know nothing about me, Carson."

"Caslin," he corrected him. "Although, you did turn a blind eye to these two killing your cousin."

Tarbet looked into Caslin's eyes and then at the Bridgers in turn. He made a show of not caring but he didn't fool anybody. The news was a shock to him. He shrugged. "Phil hung me out to dry. What kind of man does that to his own family? I guess he had it coming."

"I don't know. Perhaps the same kind of man who allows his daughter to get mixed up with the likes of this scum," Caslin said pointedly, looking directly at Ollie Bridger. If the latter was offended, he didn't show it. He merely grinned at the insult. "Just one more innocent life taken for your ridiculous moral crusade."

"Ridiculous?" Mark asked.

"Ridiculous," Caslin repeated. "Those people who died in the bombing. Clinton Dade. The carnage that is likely to follow his assassination. All of that so little Mark and Ollie can settle a score on Daddy's behalf… and earn themselves a fortune while they're at it."

"Too right," Mark said. Caslin looked to him. He was sweating but it was clearly more than just the result of the short hike down from the lighthouse. The bullet may well have passed clean through his arm but he was still bleeding and the last thing you really want to do with a gunshot wound was cart a heavy rucksack down a cliff face.

"I think your little brother is going to need to see a doctor quite soon," Caslin said, turning back to Ollie.

"He will be just fine," Ollie countered. "Won't you, Mark?"

"I'll be grand. Don't worry about me," Mark said, but his tone was edged with a touch of fear belying the bravado.

"Get in the boat," Ollie said to Caslin.

"He's not coming with us," Tarbet said, remonstrating with Ollie.

"What? You suggest we just leave him standing here on the beach?"

"We don't want him with us, do we?" Tarbet argued, the pitch of his voice raising to match his anxiety level.

"I don't know," Ollie said, thinking about it. "It'd be quite poetic for a son to face the sins of his father, don't you think?"

"Another angle for your revenge?" Caslin asked. He was acutely aware that every minute he gained on the shoreline offered his colleagues a better chance of reaching them before they put to sea, but he had no way of knowing how much extra time was required.

"We weren't intending to go after the bent coppers," Ollie said. "From our point of view getting nicked is an occupational hazard even if the arresting officers are lining their own pockets at the same time. Sometimes, these types of people can prove to be quite useful.

"Yes, you found Bradley useful," Caslin said. Something in Ollie's reaction indicated that wasn't who he was referring to. If not Bradley, then who?

His mind was racing through the key elements of the case. The Bridgers managed to carry out their revenge attack on Bradley, running his car off the road, with or without MacEwan's knowledge. It was an act that Caslin had wrongly attributed to Pete Fuller. The attack on his father was initiated by Fuller no doubt as a result of the Bridger's intervention. Both Keith Wyer and Greg Tower were already dead and that left only one other, Chief Superintendent Toby Ford. A man who was at the heart of the original investigation commanding DCI Bradley, Keith Wyer and his own father. A man with the power to direct the inquiry. He was also the surviving witness to Bradley's apparent death at sea. Caslin's father implied there may well be others further up the chain, names he claimed not to know. Ford had the potential to orchestrate everything that had come to pass. The moment of their first meeting flashed through his mind, the recognition of Caslin's name when they were introduced. He picked up on it at the time but failed to realise the significance.

"I see the wheels turning, Inspector Caslin," Ollie said as he interpreted his facial expressions. "People say you need a little luck in this life. Personally though, I prefer to make my own. You're right. Mark and I couldn't have done all of this by ourselves. I mean, we're good… but we're not that good. Life becomes far easier with a benefactor, doesn't it?"

"Even the limit to your revenge has its price, eh?"

"We made our peace and we cut a deal."

"And I've figured out who with. I met him for the first time recently, you know, and I'll take great pleasure in bringing him down."

Ollie read Caslin's determination. He was unnerved. "The problem for you is if you were *somehow* able to get yourself out of your current predicament, then the only way you can take him down is to burn your own father. Are you prepared to do that, Mr Caslin? Or are you willing to trade those principles of yours to save him?"

"We do what we have to," Caslin said calmly, reiterating Ollie's own position. "But you are right about one thing?"

"What's that?"

"We do have our own choices to make." Caslin reached up and unhooked the straps of his rucksack, arching his shoulders back and allowing it to slide down his arms and on to the beach.

"Pick it up," Ollie instructed. Caslin smiled but remained as he was. "Pick... it... up!" he repeated. Caslin glanced down at the rucksack and then at the gun Ollie was waving at him, gesturing with it towards the rucksack. Caslin proceeded to fold his arms across his chest. "What do you think you're doing?"

"Making my own luck," Caslin argued. "There's no way you're getting me into that boat."

"Bloody hell!" Mark exclaimed, depositing his rucksack in the rib with Tarbet's assistance. Drawing his brother's attention, he pointed back up the path. Ollie turned and followed Mark's indication up the cliff face. A number of figures, all clad in black, were heading down the path at speed. Caslin felt a sense of relief but he knew he was far from out of danger. Knowing they were without a sharp shooter amongst them it would be minutes before they were in a position to aid him. Ollie looked back in his direction.

"Get his rucksack," he barked at no one in particular having given up on forcing Caslin into the rib but that didn't mean he wouldn't shoot him.

Louise ran past her boyfriend and came alongside Caslin. "You know, you're a massive pain in the arse," she said aggressively.

"You sound like my ex," he replied. She knelt and braced herself. Taking a hold of the rucksack, she made to lift it. As she rose, Caslin grabbed her shoulder and spun her so she was between himself and Ollie Bridger. The rucksack fell to the ground. Slipping both arms under hers, he brought his hands up behind her head interlocking his fingers at the base of her skull and clamped them in place. Louise struggled but no matter how much she attempted to wrestle herself free, Caslin held her in a vice-like grip.

Ollie stepped forward, raising his gun and aiming for Caslin's head. Ensuring Louise was in between them so Ollie couldn't get a clean shot, he leant into her making it harder still. A shout came from above. It was a warning from the armed police even though they were in no position to action an arrest. Caslin knew they were following their engagement protocols. Once a warning was given, they were legally allowed to open fire if they felt it necessary. Caslin appreciated their forethought.

"Get the bag," Ollie shouted. The police were closing in and Caslin recognised the growing panic in his voice. For all his cunning, the meticulous planning, everything was beginning to unravel.

"Just leave it," Mark shouted.

"Get it!" Ollie barked. Mark clambered back out of the rib and ran the short distance up the beach to where Caslin held Louise. Tentatively, he ducked low in order to keep out of his brother's line of fire. Grabbing the bag, he dragged it clear of Caslin. The exertion made him wince.

"What about my daughter?" Tarbet shouted from the boat. He and Mark had already turned the boat into the breakwater and Tarbet was firing up the outboard engine.

"Let her go," Ollie said.

"Not going to happen," Caslin whispered, his face pressed firmly against the back of Louise's head. Ollie looked towards his brother heaving the weighty rucksack out of the water and into the rib before clambering aboard himself. Then he spied the distance between them and the officers approaching as fast as they dared. Weapons were trained upon those below but they had to acknowledge from that range they would endanger everyone by firing. Likewise, to descend any faster could put themselves at risk. Should they receive fire, then they needed to be able to take cover. All this combined to make Caslin's wait feel like hours rather than minutes.

"Fair enough," Ollie said, squeezing the trigger twice in quick succession. The first round struck Louise in the chest and the second, her shoulder. The force of both shots struck her like hammer blows and she was punched from her feet and thrown backwards taking both her and Caslin to the ground. The air flew from his lungs as he hit the pebbles, Louise on top of him.

"No!" Tarbet screamed from the rib only a second before Mark Bridger put a round into him as well. Tarbet flipped backwards from the stern and into the shallow sea water. Caslin struggled to break free from the weight of Louise atop him in a desperate attempt to give him options. Ollie was coming to kill him, he was certain and he'd be damned if he would lie there and wait for it. His would-be assassin appeared in his peripheral vision and Caslin felt a surge of panic. Then there was a shot followed by another which caused Ollie to duck out of Caslin's view. Another round struck Louise. She didn't make a sound. Nor did she when there was a fourth.

Further shots came and Caslin angled his head to the bottom of the path where it met the beach. Chas Freeman and his team were on the beach and approaching. They were exchanging fire in the direction of the rib. Caslin felt a degree of safety and he managed to roll Louise off of him. He did so gently and once he was clear, he knelt alongside and looked at her. Her face was expressionless and her eyes wide. She was dead. A bullet fizzed past him far too close for comfort as he felt the change in the air pressure and what sounded like a crack as it went by. Throwing himself forward onto the beach, the overpowering smell of rotting seaweed filled his nostrils.

Staring towards the shoreline the rib was afloat, Mark Bridger hunkered in the stern attempting to steer them out to sea. Ollie was alongside, lying against the port side and sending volley after volley at the advancing police officers. The two were heavily out-gunned and now there were no hostages in play, Freeman's team openly returned fire. There was an audible bang as the outboard motor was struck and it gave out billowing smoke from within the housing. The rib floundered having not yet fully escaped the breakwater. With nowhere near enough momentum to carry them out to sea it was only a matter of time until the tide would return them to land.

Caslin wondered whether they would give up but he dismissed it rapidly. Mark Bridger turning his own weapon towards the beach answered that question. The Bridgers began firing in unison despite their vessel being holed in multiple places and the desperation of their situation acutely apparent. The battle was short lived. From Caslin's vantage point, he watched as Mark was struck first slumping backwards into the rib and disappearing from view. Ollie reached down, reappearing with his brother's gun and attempted to use both. He was hit in the chest a number of times and one final shot took him in the head and he fell forward dropping both weapons into the sea.

It was over.

With no one in charge of the rudder, the rib turned sideways and was carried to the beach by the swell. Caslin stood upon wobbly legs watching as the boat was first swamped by a large wave and then picked up and flipped by the next. Looking behind him, he saw the approaching forms of Hunter and Kyle Broadfoot, both bore concerned expressions. Hunter appeared relieved when she saw he was unhurt. Turning back towards the shore, Scott Tarbet's body was retrieved by two of the armed officers wading knee-deep into the water with the breakers crashing against them. Judging from their reaction, Caslin assumed he was also dead. They dragged his body further up the beach so that it wouldn't be carried back into the water and eyeing the tide as it retreated, Caslin saw it tinged red as blood flowed from the dead man.

"Are you okay?" Hunter asked, placing a hand on Caslin's forearm and noting how battered his face was.

"Yeah. It's fine," he said, with a weak smile. "I… I'm… fine."

"Is that all of them?" Broadfoot asked.

Caslin inclined his head in the direction of the lighthouse. "There are two more bodies back up there. MacEwan and one other. They're both dead. The Bridgers killed them."

"Right," Broadfoot said, glancing towards the water. Ollie's body was being carried to the beach, prostrate and face down among the breakers. Broadfoot flicked his eyes to Caslin and asked in a soft voice, "Jody?"

Caslin nodded, "Yes. I think Jody worked out what was going on and they used Scott Tarbet's daughter, Louise, to get close to him. A classic honey trap. Then they exploited Jody's connection with his business partner, Mason, and lured him into a situation where they killed him. I'm sorry."

Broadfoot's expression took on a faraway look, staring out to sea. "Thank you, Nathaniel. That's all of them then?"

Caslin felt a pang of guilt. Toby Ford was still at large. A serving police officer and a senior rank. A man supposedly held to a higher standard than most in society but how Caslin could square this circle, he didn't know. The Bridgers were right. In bringing down Ford, his own father's involvement would be revealed. Morally, there was only one course of action but loyalty to his father was pushing him in another direction.

"I believe so," Caslin said quietly. Hunter caught his eye. She knew him well. Very well. Broadfoot reached across and offered Caslin his hand. He took it. The handshake was brief and Broadfoot turned away setting off to speak with Freeman. There were tears in his eyes. Caslin felt for him. He had lost his Godson, someone he loved and cared for. Caslin chose to keep Wyer's motivations for his investigation to himself. Destroying the lad's reputation in death wasn't necessary and would serve no purpose. Whether he was looking to lay his hands on the proceeds of the robbery was largely irrelevant now. Besides, the Bridgers were hardly the most credible of witnesses.

"There's more, isn't there?" Hunter asked once their senior officer was out of earshot.

"Later," Caslin said. "I've got one more conversation to have first," he added, making it very clear he held no desire to discuss it further and walked away.

CHAPTER THIRTY-ONE

During the drive back to York, Caslin found himself ruminating on the complexity and intrigue of this case. For all the horrendous actions carried out by the Bridger brothers enacting their Machiavellian revenge plot, Ollie made one point that Caslin found undeniable as much as it was inescapable. It was this thought that kept repeating on him. Many times, throughout his career, he chose to look the other way and on those occasions the decision was always related more to his inherent sense of justice rather than a desire to circumvent the law. People often referred to such moral dilemmas as grey areas. A case could be made for acting in whichever way necessitated their desired outcome. No matter which angle of approach he took in his reasoning, this wasn't one of those times.

Arriving at the hospital, Caslin was lucky to find an empty parking bay and left the car. Every step towards the entrance felt heavy, weighed down by the decision he knew was inevitable. To keep his father from suffering, Caslin had to allow another to walk free – a murderer, a thief, a disgrace to the uniform – none other than Chief Superintendent Toby Ford. He fed the Bridgers all of the information they needed and may well have influenced their course of action. All to ensure that he would walk away without ever needing to look over his shoulder. All to fulfil one of the negative base desires of humanity – that of greed. There was no way Caslin could bring a case against Ford without, as Ollie so colourfully described it, burning his own father. There was a distinct possibility that even if he was prepared to do so, it may not lead to a successful conviction. If they could attribute any of the money to Ford or find some communication between him and the Bridgers, then maybe. However, if Ford was adept at covering his tracks as so many others in this case appeared to be, then Caslin could see his father on trial and gain nothing in return.

Taking the stairs rather than the lift, Caslin made his way up to the second floor. A memory came to mind. When he and his brother, Stefan, were children they found themselves momentarily unsupervised in the local newsagent. Their mother was searching for something, he couldn't recall what it was and as a result the member of staff was with her at the rear of the shop. The two boys, no strangers to mischief, saw an opportunity to help themselves to the sweets their mother had already denied them. Egging each other on they took as much as they dared. Leaving the shop minutes later exhilarated by their achievements, both he and Stefan shared satisfied looks with one other. The scale of their theft was completely missed by the adults. Only much later when their father stumbled across them sharing out the stash was the truth revealed.

Caslin remembered anticipating his father's wrath, expecting a beating or at the very least to be verbally abused but no, his father sat calmly with them and talked. The image of that face, one of such profound disappointment remained fresh in his mind to this day. They discussed what they had done why it was wrong as well as what the consequences should be. Following that conversation both boys made the walk back to the shop to not only return what they had taken, pay for what they couldn't but also to apologise. That walk – a very long walk at the age of seven – carried with it the strongest sense of shame that he could remember. Of all the words his father said to him that day one sentence crystallised in his mind.

"You can't hide from what you've done," his father had told them, *"and you have to accept the consequences of your actions. Only then, can you move forward."*

The message was understood, even at such a young age. The current situation he found himself in was worth far more than a handful of sweets but the path forward was clear. No matter how painful it would be to walk it.

Coming to the ward's entrance, a young couple were leaving and kindly held the door open for him and Caslin slipped through, avoiding the wait to be buzzed in by the staff. The nurses' station was unmanned as he walked past heading for his father's room. Strangely, the armed guard was no longer present which irritated him. News travelled fast but until he was certain the threat had passed, he would have expected the protection to remain in place. He tapped lightly on the door and entered.

The curtains were open with sunshine streaming in but he found the room empty. The bed was made with fresh linen. Monitoring equipment was switched off and pushed to the side of the room. Caslin noted the absence of personal effects and considered whether his father had been discharged without his knowledge. Perhaps they had switched him to an open ward. Turning on his heel he left the room and walked back to the nurses' station. At which point he was met by Karen. Caslin's face lit up as he was able to confirm the case was over and their children were safe but something struck him as odd. A subtle shift in her demeanour as she set eyes on him. Her response was fleeting and yet telling.

He approached her. "Karen? What is it?"

She opened her mouth but words didn't follow. She met his eye and tears welled. The nurse accompanying her stepped forward. Her expression was solemn.

"Mr Caslin," she began. "We've been trying to reach you for the past few hours."

"My phone..." Caslin said, moving to retrieve the mobile from his pocket before remembering Ollie Bridger smashing it at the lighthouse. "Why? What's..." the words tailed off. Karen came closer and reached out, taking his hand in hers.

"I... I'm so sorry, Nate," she said, tears falling down her cheeks. Caslin looked into her eyes and then to the nurse alongside.

"I'm afraid there were complications overnight," the nurse explained. "I'm sorry but your father passed away this morning."

"No... no, that can't be right," Caslin mumbled. Karen threw her arms around him and Caslin crumpled. His legs felt hollow, almost unable to take his weight and he felt the strangest sensation pass over him. They took a step backwards and Caslin almost stumbled but Karen guided him to a chair set against the wall in the corridor. He sat down. She knelt before him. "But... he was going to be okay..."

"I'm so sorry," Karen repeated, staring into his eyes and cupping his cheeks with the palms of her hands. She pressed gently and Caslin's head dropped into them, tears flowing. She pulled his head into her chest. "There was nothing anyone could do."

They stayed like that for the next five, maybe ten minutes. Caslin didn't know how long for sure. The moment passed and he regained his composure. Moving his head away, Karen stroked the side of his face, smiling.

"Your father loved you, Nate. I know he had a hard time showing it but he did... very much."

Caslin nodded. "I know," he replied. The statement felt inadequate under the circumstances. His father was a man who struggled to convey positive emotions. They were far more alike than either cared to admit.

"They said they can arrange for you to spend some time with him, if you would like," Karen said.

"I would like that very much," Caslin replied, standing. He approached the nurse sitting behind her workstation. "Could I borrow your telephone? I need to make a call."

"Of course."

Caslin withdrew from Karen's grasp, she was reluctant to let him go. "I can come with you," she said. He smiled. Following the nurse, she led him into an adjoining office to give him privacy.

"I'll just be a moment," Caslin said, using the back of his hand to clear his eyes. Picking up the receiver, he dialled Kyle Broadfoot's personal mobile. The call was answered within three rings.

"Nathaniel," he said. "I'm terribly sorry to hear about..."

"Thank you, sir. That's very kind," Caslin cut him off. "There's one more name we have to pick up, sir."

"There is?" Broadfoot said, surprised.

"Chief Superintendent Ford, sir."

There was a moment of silence at the other end of the line. "On what charge?"

"Start with conspiracy to commit the murder of Jody Wyer... misconduct in public office... and then we can go from there..."

"Understood, Nathaniel," Broadfoot said, his tone conveying his shock at the revelation. "Do you want to make the arrest?"

"No, sir," Caslin replied. "This one is all yours," he said and hung up. Replacing the receiver, he took a deep breath and closed his eyes. "I love you too, Dad," he said quietly to himself.

A
DARK YORKSHIRE
CRIME THRILLER

THE SIXTH PRECEP

J M Dalgliesh

"We are what we think. All that we are arises with our thoughts. With our thoughts, we make the world."

Gautama Buddha

CHAPTER ONE

THE CELLS on the spreadsheet merged as eye-strain overcame her. She pressed thumb and forefinger to the lids and gently squeezed them towards one another, meeting at the bridge of her nose. Blinking furiously, she waited until her eyes refocussed. Glancing at the mobile on her desk, she noted the missed call. The second of the evening. Checking the time, it was pushing eight o'clock.

She saved the document and resolved to pick up where she left off first thing in the morning. Closing down the applications, she switched off the monitor and detached the laptop from the hub, sliding it into her carry bag. Lastly, she turned off the desk lamp and got to her feet. Crossing the office and taking her coat from the stand, she put it on and slipped the straps of her bag over her shoulder and left, closing the door behind her.

The carpeted corridors were deserted and were now illuminated only by secondary lighting, in place to allow the contract cleaners to set about their routines. They paid her no attention as she reached the lift, accompanied by the grating sound of a vacuum cleaner. Summoning the lift to the fourth floor, she waited, checking her watch once more. Thomas would be annoyed. Another figure came into view, rounding the corner at the far end. Despite the lack of light, the sizeable frame gave away the identity of the night shift security guard. He smiled at her as he approached.

"Working late again, Miss Ryan?"

"Heading home now, Marcus."

"You work too hard."

"Isn't that the truth." A ping sounded and the doors parted before her. Entering the lift, she turned and pressed the button for the basement parking level. "Goodnight, Marcus."

"Goodnight, Miss Ryan."

The doors closed and the lift began the descent. Moments later, she stepped out into the underground basement. There were perhaps a dozen cars scattered around the parking level. Apparently, there were employees outdoing even her with their commitment to the cause. She moved to the left, her heels echoing through the parking level the only sounds that carried. Descending a ramp to the lower level, she set eyes on her BMW, parked in her designated space. Alongside was a transit van and she was irritated by the proximity of it to her own. To be fair, the spaces were narrow and not marked out with wider vehicles in mind but even so, she cursed the driver under her breath for being so thoughtless.

Approaching the car, the keyless entry system registered her presence and the car unlocked itself. Opening the boot, she placed the shoulder bag containing her laptop flat inside. Removing her coat, she lay that alongside it too. Shutting the tailgate, she was forced to turn sideways and slip down between the two vehicles. Whilst assessing how much of a gap would be needed to enable her to get into the driving seat, something in the corner of her eye caught her attention. Looking across the parking level, she tried to see what it was. For a moment she thought she'd heard something and seen a flicker of movement.

The level was well lit with only the huge concrete supporting pillars and the occasional parked car interrupting her line of sight for fifty yards in every direction. She waited, straining to see or hear what had alerted her – but nothing. Only the muted drumming from within the ventilation duct overhead could now be heard. Realising she was holding her breath, she dismissed her overactive imagination. The mobile phone in her pocket began to vibrate and she took it out. It was Thomas again. She directed the call to voicemail, putting the handset back in her pocket and grasped the door handle. The sliding door of the van opened and before she could react, something struck her in the back. Intense pain tore through her as her body went into spasm moments before her legs gave out and she collapsed, falling against the car on her way down. The fluorescent strip lights hanging from the roof appeared to swing from left to right as strong hands took a firm hold of her.

Then, there was only darkness.

SOMETHING WAS WRONG. Opening her eyes, her lids felt heavy. Gritty. The darkness of the night was all-encompassing. The smell of the outdoors; damp soil. Something was wrong... very wrong. Attempting to stand, she found herself held in place somehow, panic flared; she feared she'd been in an accident and was paralysed or worse still: dead. Her left ankle throbbed. Although unable to move her foot, any flexing of the muscles in her leg caused a sharp painful sensation. Relieved she could still feel all of her extremities, despite their apparent cold, she cast her mind back. Leaving the office, speaking to Marcus and arriving at her car... but then, nothing. Breathing was difficult. There was something restricting her mouth, taut and unforgiving. She couldn't move her lips. Trying to call out gave off a muffled sound, elevating to a scream. Only when trying to reach up with her hand to free her mouth did she realise that she couldn't move at all.

No amount of struggling or exertion, using all of the strength she could muster, could move her even the slightest. She cried out again, as loudly as she could, but her muffled screams passed into despairing tears as frustration turned to fear and then panic. A thud sounded nearby, not particularly loud but it drew her attention. Her eyes were slowly beginning to adjust to the darkness and she looked around but couldn't make out what had made the noise. Then there was another, only this time much closer. A third sounded behind her, a little way off. Then silence returned.

The wind whispered from nearby trees and then came the realisation. She was by woodland. The damp soil, the trees... the cold. Shadows moved. It was hard to judge but she thought it was a person, perhaps twenty feet away but she couldn't be sure. Craning her neck, she tried to make out any detail but moving caused her discomfort. All of a sudden, she was bathed in bright light. Screwing her eyes tightly shut, she screamed again. Slowly opening her eyes, she squinted against beams of car headlights. They illuminated everything around her.

Nearby, she saw a rock, perhaps the size of a closed fist. To the right was another. They looked somehow out of place, as if recently deposited. Another thud. Another rock, landing to the left of her head. She screamed. Something struck the top of her head sending a shooting pain across her skull. Her screaming ceased, replaced by confusion. Then another. This one struck her forehead before dropping to the ground in front of her. Liquid flowed across her eyebrow and trickled into her eye.

She was bleeding. Something else passed through her line of sight, striking her on the cheek. Horrified, she silently begged for help but none was forthcoming.

Another strike. Her vision swam… and the darkness returned.

CHAPTER TWO

CASLIN FOLLOWED the line of Garfield Terrace, picking his way along the narrow road. With cars parked on either side negotiating the small housing estate made up of Victorian semi-detached and terraced houses was not easy. Doing so on a Saturday morning, following a rather sociable Friday evening, made it even tougher. To the left was the railway yard, its lines feeding into both York Central train station and the National Railway Museum, whereas a short distance to his right they were further hemmed in by the river Ouse, winding its way through central York.

Reaching the turn at the end of the road, Caslin kept an eye out for Hunter. He had been making himself his second cup of coffee of the day when she had called. They were summoned to Stamford Street, a small cul-de-sac on the edge of the Holgate area of the city. The houses here were originally built for the railway workers but were now residential homes at the cheaper end of the scale. As cheap as houses ever got in York, anyway. A few of the buildings had been transformed into small businesses, Caslin spied a sandwich shop just behind him and he wondered whether it would be open on the weekend. The road angled to the right onto Garnett Terrace and immediately he spotted Hunter's vehicle parked half on the pavement, directly opposite the entrance to the street. As he approached, her driver's door opened and DS Sarah Hunter stepped out acknowledging him with a wave.

Pulling his car in behind hers, Caslin pulled on the handbrake and switched off the ignition. Getting out, he nodded towards her by way of greeting and he could see the effect of an early start written across her face as well. She reached back into the car and reappeared with a takeaway coffee, handing it towards him. Caslin took it gratefully.

"You took your time," Hunter said.

"I've barely been to sleep. So, what are we doing here?" Looking directly opposite into Stamford Street itself, uniform had already cordoned off the road with blue and white tape, signifying it was now a crime scene. Looking beyond the cordon, Caslin could see perhaps half a dozen houses. All were nondescript, of a uniform design and appeared largely functional in their aesthetics. Glancing at the neighbouring streets, the design was commonplace. None of the houses had driveways nor gardens to the front. Most of the houses still had their curtains drawn and of those that didn't, nets obscured the view of the interior. A handful of residents stood at the edge of the cordon speaking with the uniformed officers, present to maintain the integrity of the scene. Most likely, they were trying to find out what was going on.

"Your guess is as good as mine," Hunter said. "When ACC Broadfoot couldn't get a hold of you, he called me."

"Well, he can't have tried very hard."

"You didn't just ignore his call like normal then?"

Caslin laughed. "I'm not that bad. So, what did he say?"

"He gave me this address and said there was a situation developing here. One that might see a crossover."

"Crossover?"

"Yes. Seemingly an address that the drug squad has red flagged flashed up late last night, and the concern is that there may be greater ramifications as a result."

Caslin looked at her inquisitively. "And this concerns us how?"

Hunter shrugged. "You know as much as I do. Broadfoot told us to ask for DI Craig Templer. Do you know him?"

"No. Not someone I've ever come across. So, shall we go and see what's going on then?"

Caslin sipped his coffee as they crossed the street. The constable saw them approaching and, recognising them, lifted the tape. Both Caslin and Hunter ducked underneath and entered Stamford Street. Hunter glanced towards the constable who pointed in the direction of the crime scene. He needn't have bothered because the intensity of the police presence at the address made it quite clear where they had to go. There were three liveried police cars as well as a CSI van parked outside.

They were met at the front door by another uniformed officer. She stepped aside to give them entry. The hallway was narrow, allowing them only to pass through one at a time.

"We're looking for Templer?" Caslin asked.

"You'll find him in the living room."

"Thanks."

Reaching the door, set to the left of the hallway, they stopped and took in the scene before them. Two forensics officers dressed in their white coveralls were busy mapping the scene with a sketchpad. A third was taking photographs. To their right was another whom Caslin guessed was DI Templer. He looked too young to be a DI in Caslin's eyes. Mind you, as the years passed, he found himself saying that about his colleagues more often. Casting an eye around the room, Caslin could see what he assumed this house was; a drug den. Four people, three men and one woman were seated in the room. Two were on a sofa, one an armchair and the remaining body lay sprawled out face down upon the floor. All four were clearly dead.

Eyeing their arrival, Templer crossed the room and came to greet them. Removing his latex gloves, he extended a hand and Caslin shook it. The latter introduced himself and then DS Hunter who Templer acknowledged with a brief nod in her direction.

"What do we have here?" Caslin asked.

"That's just what we are trying to figure out," Templer replied, gesturing for them to enter. Caslin stepped forward into the middle of the room and immediately paid closer attention to the nearest bodies, sitting on the sofa. One of the males and the only female present were alongside each other. The male had a thin leather belt tied around his left bicep that, although still in place, was no longer tight. The inside of his elbow was exposed and Caslin could easily tell that this man was a habitual drug user due to the number of scars, scabs and bruising in that area. Leaning over the pair he could see a syringe on the sofa between them. It was empty but the needle was still visible. Turning his attention to the woman, Caslin cast a glance over her uncovered arms and was not surprised to see similar markings on both.

Caslin looked to Hunter and indicated for her to check out the remaining deceased. She nodded whilst putting on her own forensics gloves to avoid contaminating the scene with her own fingerprints. Stepping past the photographer, she moved to investigate the body on the far side beneath the window overlooking the street. For his part, Caslin looked at the coffee table at the centre of the room. Visible for all to see was the paraphernalia that accompanied those with an extensive drug habit. On the table were syringes, spoons, with some kind of semi-translucent substance or residue left on them, and ruffled sheets of blackened aluminium foil. Dropping to his haunches, Caslin looked at the underside of the spoons and saw carbon residue on those as well. Most likely as a result from holding a naked flame beneath them. There were also a couple of packets of cigarettes, two lighters, a mobile phone and some empty wraps that Caslin knew from his experience would once have contained drugs. There were several small bags fashioned from clingfilm, rolled up and sealed at the top, and in them was a brown substance. Caslin glanced towards Templer.

"Heroin."

Templer nodded. "I would assume so. Plus, we found some crack cocaine along with mixed amphetamines and some synthetics. Probably spice but we'll have to wait for the lab tests to confirm that. But that's not all. Come with me." Templer beckoned Caslin to join him. He followed the young DI into the adjoining room. Caslin's eyes narrowed and he exhaled slowly as he entered. On the table were several foil-wrapped bricks. One of which was open and the contents appeared to be a block of processed heroin. Alongside these blocks were bundles of cash in used tens and twenties.

"This isn't your average crack house," Caslin said.

"No, it isn't," Templer confirmed.

"Hunter says you had this address flagged. Is that right?"

"Yeah. This is a known address for one of the key players in the North Yorkshire trade. We've been tracking his movements for months, watching him expand his operation in this direction."

"Expanding from where?"

"Eastwards, out of Leeds."

"This isn't the usual area for a place like this, is it?" Caslin asked, referring to the middle-class suburb they were in.

Templer shook his head. "No. The days of your average crack den being in a squat or some other semi-derelict location are long gone. For some reason they seem to draw less attention to themselves once they become established in suburbia. Most of the houses we find that have been converted to grow cannabis are usually rentals in the heart of affluent estates. It is amazing how they manage to go under the radar, but they do."

"Even so, this isn't normal."

"No, you're right. This is definitely not normal."

"Whose house is it? One of the victims?" Caslin asked, indicating back towards the living room with a flick of his head.

"No, I don't believe so. We can't say for sure who runs this particular part of the operation, as well as who owns it. Neither would be partaking of the refreshments, if you know what I mean? Not with this much gear," he added, indicating what was on the table in front of them.

"Good point." Caslin was in agreement. "Do you think they did a runner when that lot overdosed?"

"If they overdosed?" A voice said from behind them. Caslin turned to see Iain Robertson, the head of Fulford Road's crime scene investigation team.

"Iain," Caslin said. "I didn't realise you were here."

"Aye. That's because you don't recognise me with my clothes on," Robertson said with a grin.

"Forgive the assumption," Caslin said, "but I didn't see any wounds to indicate violence. Three of them appeared to die in the chairs."

"You're right there," Robertson agreed. "And the fourth managed to get up… just about."

"If not an overdose, then what are we looking at?" Templer asked. "A poisoned supply?"

"Unfortunately, you're both going to have to wait for that answer, but my guess would be a tainted supply. Now, whether that's intentional or accidental will be for you to decide."

"Instinctively?" Caslin asked.

Robertson sucked air through his teeth. "Well, judging by what all of them are missing, I would suggest the former rather than the latter."

"Missing?" Templer asked.

"I thought you two were supposed to be detectives? Go back and have a look at their right hands."

Both Caslin and Templer left the room and made their way back to where Hunter was examining the victims. She smiled as they approached. Obviously, she had overheard the exchange and found it amusing.

"Here," she said, indicating the man lying on the floor at her feet. Caslin bent over and immediately saw what he had initially missed. The index finger of the man's right hand was missing. There was a little bit of blood but not a great deal which indicated it had been removed post-mortem. Caslin glanced over towards the sofa where the man and woman were sitting. Templer met his eye and nodded in answer to the unasked question.

"They've both been cut off too," he said. "Looks like a clean cut."

"Surgical?" Caslin asked, as Robertson appeared at the threshold of the door.

"Possibly," he replied. "Could just as easily be achieved with a gardening tool."

"And the fourth?" Caslin asked Hunter, gesturing to the final victim with his eyes.

"Same."

"And have you seen this?" Robertson asked, pointing to the table. Caslin stood up and took two steps to come alongside him.

"What do you have?"

"The only thing of beauty in the house of the dead," Robertson stated flatly. With his pocket torch, he illuminated the centre of the table. In amongst the empty wraps, crack cocaine residue, razor blades and syringes, was the head of a flower. The centre was bright yellow and surrounded by layers of white petals that morphed into a hot pink at the points.

"What is it? Magnolia?" Caslin asked.

"Perhaps, not my speciality. Could be a waterlily of some type," Hunter suggested, going to stand alongside Caslin. "I agree with Iain. It seems a little out of place."

"You said they were moving into this area?" Caslin asked Templer.

"They are, yes."

"Any chance this is a result of the locals pushing back?"

"I would think that is pretty likely, yes," Templer said. "We've seen a number of places just like this being turned over in the last few months. There will always be some kind of response when these guys start crossing imaginary lines into the other's territories. That's to be expected."

"Anything quite like this happen recently?" Hunter asked.

Templer shook his head. "More commonly they trade blows at a lower level. Street dealers will get a kicking, perhaps the odd mule will be intercepted. This however, this is an approach I've not come across before. Poisoning someone's supply, getting into their supply chain before it reaches their network of dealers is a new one on me."

"Is that why we are here?"

"I don't need you to be here," Templer stated, rather dismissively in Caslin's eyes. "But someone upstairs thinks it might be bigger than just a turf war."

"You disagree?"

"Too early to say," Templer said. "I'm more than happy to run with it as a narcotics inquiry, all the same. Feel free to pass it back upstairs that you are not required, if you aren't interested."

"I didn't say I wasn't interested," Caslin replied with a smile. "Let's see where it takes us."

CHAPTER THREE

CASLIN STEPPED out of his office and drew Terry Holt's attention. The detective constable looked up from his laptop with an inquisitive raise of the eyebrows.

"What have you got from the scene?" Caslin asked.

"Robertson has sent over the detailed inventory."

"Anything interesting?"

"Obviously, we are still waiting on the pathology reports, but Dr Taylor has promised she will pass us the preliminary findings as soon as they're ready. Likewise, the chemical analysis of the drugs you found at the scene hasn't come in yet, but what I do have are the results for the mobile phones. I've already got the serial and telephone numbers over to the respective networks, along with a warrant and I'm expected to hear back from them very soon. Once I have that I'll start cross-referencing the call history logs, text and voice calls, and I'll start piecing these people's lives together."

"Good work," Caslin said, patting him on the shoulder. "Did Iain give you anything else?"

"Off the record, he was pretty certain their stash was interfered with."

"Yeah, doesn't take a genius to figure that one out."

The conversation was interrupted by Hunter walking into the room. "ACC Broadfoot wants to see you in his office."

"Now?"

"Now."

"Terry, can you bring Hunter up to speed and I'll be back as soon as I can," Caslin said as he left the room. Assistant Chief Constable Broadfoot's office was on the third floor but it was unusual for him to summon Caslin upstairs. Usually, he was left to his own devices and only checked in with the senior officer as and when he felt the need. Caslin's shoes squeaked on the polished stairs as he made his way up to the next floor, coming across DCI Matheson on the way.

"You've got visitors," she said in passing.

Caslin stopped. Turning to look at her he raised an eyebrow. "Anyone I know?"

"I don't," she said. "They look serious, mind you. Nice suits as well."

"They're certainly not from around here then. Thanks for the heads up."

"Any time," Matheson replied, resuming her course downstairs.

Caslin continued upward, leaving the stairwell at the next landing and entering the corridor housing the senior officers of Fulford Road. Upon reaching the office, Caslin sidled up to Broadfoot's PA, placing his hands gently on hers as she reached for the telephone receiver, presumably to announce his arrival.

"Who's in there?" he whispered.

"Nathaniel, you know better than to ask that," she said.

"Am I going to like them? You can tell me that."

Unfortunately, the question went unanswered as the door to Broadfoot's office opened and the man himself appeared.

"I thought I heard voices. Come on Nathaniel, we are waiting on you." Broadfoot glanced at his PA and without another word retreated into his office. Caslin followed, raising his eyebrows as high as he could, walking around the desk and towards the office. Broadfoot's PA stifled a laugh and merely smiled as Caslin almost skipped past her. Entering the office, Caslin glanced around. Besides Broadfoot, there were three others present. He immediately recognised Templer but the other two were men unknown to him.

"DI Nathaniel Caslin, please meet DCI Sean Meadows and Detective Chief Superintendent Myles Henry. I believe you already know Craig Templer," Broadfoot said, indicating the youngest man in the room. Caslin nodded to the latter and then acknowledged the two senior officers.

Eyeing the two men, Matheson had been right. Their suits were not off-the-peg. They were possibly not tailor made but at the very least, high quality. That set these men aside from the norm. If you had to guess, then he figured they were highly influential, possibly beyond their rank. Not least because Broadfoot appeared to behave differently towards them than any other senior officers Caslin could recall, not deferential, but respectful to a greater degree than usual.

"What can I do for you sir?"

"We were just discussing the narcotics investigation, Nathaniel," Broadfoot said.

"I'm glad you brought that up sir," Caslin said, before Broadfoot could continue. "I'm not convinced that this is a narcotics investigation."

That comment caused some consternation amongst the assembled people. "We brought you in," Meadows stated.

"Because you thought there might be a crossover between narcotics and major crimes," Caslin said. "Correct?"

"That's right, yes," Meadows confirmed. "Out of common courtesy if nothing else."

"But the early indication is the drug supplies have been tampered with."

"I haven't heard that," Templer said. "I'm the senior investigating officer until it's decided otherwise. Why wasn't I informed?"

Caslin shrugged. "I've only just been made aware myself. Perhaps you need to improve your communication channels."

"Gentlemen, please," Broadfoot interrupted the exchange. "What point are you trying to make Nathaniel?"

"Well, as DI Templer rightly pointed out yesterday, at the scene, rival dealers don't usually poison each other's supply chains in order to get the upper hand. Therefore, it follows that if the drugs have been tampered with in some way that led to four deaths, then we are looking at a multiple homicide. That's definitely major crimes and not narcotics."

"That's bull shit, Caslin," Templer stated, shaking his head with an irritated smile on his face.

"It's still major crimes," Caslin argued.

"And if the dealers are cutting their heroin with something else to increase a street value and that accidentally results in users dying, then it remains a narcotics investigation," Meadows stated, locking eyes with Caslin.

"And how many dealers do you know would flee the scene of an overdose, leaving their supply on the table, not to mention a shit load of cash?" Caslin said.

"It's not as simple as that, Inspector," DCS Henry said pointedly.

"Perhaps you could fill us in?" Caslin asked. The three officers from narcotics exchanged glances, something that wasn't missed by either Broadfoot or Caslin.

"Yes, perhaps you should fill us in?" Broadfoot said evenly.

Meadows and Henry exchanged something unsaid between them and the latter nodded. Meadows exhaled heavily. "The drug house in question is owned and run by Lawrence Metcalf. Metcalf is someone we've been tracking for a long time. His market share in West Yorkshire has been steadily growing over the last five years. He started out as a loyal lieutenant in another organisation until his own ambition got ahead of him and he branched out. Metcalf isn't your typical drug dealer. He's taken efficiency to a whole new level, reaching beyond the normal level of criminality to work in his business."

"How do you mean?" Caslin asked.

"He's not using your average thug for his muscle. He's recruiting ex-military, mercenary types and, in some cases, former police officers. He likes having the latter around because he feels it gives him credibility, window dressing to the public eye, and I dare say it's to stick one in the eye to people like us."

"Fair enough. He sounds like someone you'd like to take off the streets. If you know so much about him, why haven't you done so already?"

"Metcalf has moved ahead of his competition to such an extent that he is broadening his horizons, which brings him to York. We think he has ambitions to stretch his operation from the west coast of England to the east, hoovering up anything in between. Like I said, we've been watching him, building our case and when we're ready, we will take him down. But we don't just want Metcalf. We want his entire operation, from his dealer network right through to his supplier and all the links in between."

"Where do you think these four deaths in one of his drug houses come into it?" Caslin asked.

Myles Henry picked up the narrative. "The honest answer is we don't know, but what we do know is that we have an inside man and we believe he can help us."

"This inside man," Broadfoot began, "who is he and where does he fit into this?

"He's been working in Metcalf's organisation for the past eighteen months and he's been feeding us information. Quality intelligence since day one," Meadows said.

"This is an employee of Metcalf's?" Caslin asked. "An informant?"

"No, this is an undercover officer. We spent two years developing his back story and his experience, giving him a name that will allow him to freely enter Metcalf's organisation. He is both experienced and highly skilled."

"Have you been able to make contact with him?" Broadfoot asked.

Meadows shook his head. "He was supposed to check in with us last night. When he didn't, we followed protocol, which was to give him six hours, and if there was still no further contact, we were to follow up."

"And?"

"He didn't get in touch," Templer said quietly.

"Come on guys," Caslin said failing to mask his irritation. "You may as well give us the rest."

"Fowler was running Metcalf's drug house last night. As you know, he wasn't at the scene and we've been unable to make contact through the usual channels."

"Well, that certainly puts a different slant on things, doesn't it?" Broadfoot stated. "Information we probably should have been abreast of earlier." His tone was snippy.

"This doesn't change anything," Caslin said. "This is still a major crime's case."

"How the hell do you figure that out?" Templer argued.

"If you've got an undercover officer who was at this scene and has gone missing, then I would argue there is even more reason for narcotics to stay well away."

"And you can get to fuck!" Templer snapped, momentarily forgetting himself and then holding a hand up in apology towards the senior ranks.

"I think everybody can appreciate the sentiment that DI Templer is exhibiting, if perhaps a little overzealously," Henry stated. "Perhaps there is some accommodation that we can come to?" He looked to Broadfoot, seeking a compromise.

Broadfoot nodded. "I think major crimes should take the lead in this investigation, albeit with narcotics represented in the team." Caslin was about to interrupt and lodge an objection but one stern look from his superior nipped the protest in the bud. "Until such time as it becomes clear whose case this should be. As and when that is established, we can discuss it further. I suggest that Caslin here takes the lead and you assign a liaison to work alongside him, presumably DI Templer would suffice?"

Templer also looked ready to protest but any opportunity to voice his objection was immediately curtailed by Henry's agreement. "I think that is a workable solution, Kyle."

"That's settled then," Broadfoot said. "Perhaps, Nathaniel, you could take Templer aside and bring him up to speed with what you've already uncovered while we finish up here."

It was quite clear that the decision had been taken and the two junior officers were being politely pushed aside, whilst the high-level protocol was discussed between themselves. Caslin didn't mind. That was the element of his former position that he missed the least – the politics – and why he loved his new role so much. He said his goodbyes and went to the door, grasping the handle firmly. Opening it, he gestured for Templer to pass through before him. The younger man didn't seem as pleased to be leaving as Caslin did and it took another glance from his DCI before he reluctantly left the room. Caslin closed the door and smiled at Broadfoot's PA as they passed her desk.

"Thanks for that," Templer said.

"You're welcome." Caslin ignored the sarcasm.

"This was my case."

"It still is your case," Caslin countered. "At least, you're still on it, aren't you?"

"Anyone ever tell you you're an arsehole, Caslin?"

Caslin smiled. "Frequently."

Leading them downstairs and along the corridor, back to the ops room, the two men spoke little. If Hunter and Holt were surprised at Caslin reappearing with the detective inspector from the Drugs Squad, they hid it well. Hunter dealt with the introductions and Templer pulled up a chair, apparently burying his frustration at losing the lead role in the investigation.

"What can you tell us about your man on the inside? Has he ever done anything similar?" Hunter asked.

"You mean, like going off script?"

"Yes, exactly. Can you think of any reason why he would ditch protocol like this?"

Templer shook his head. "No, I've known him and worked alongside him for a long time, and I've been his handler since we brought him on board. He would have to have a very good reason to go to ground like this, and I'm at a loss to think what that would be."

"You said you don't think this will be a rival gang?" Caslin asked. "Not an act of retribution."

"That's right. I don't believe so."

"Is there a possibility he may have been abducted by a rival gang in order to make some kind of point?"

"The only friction we've seen between the groups has been at street level. You know, new dealers moving into areas, streets, that they haven't been in before but even that's been at a minimum."

"How so?" Caslin asked.

"Metcalf has been. He's been unsettling his rivals by disrupting their supply chains, which makes their street level dealer network more susceptible to switching. That way he isn't putting his guys up against theirs."

"He's just been recruiting their own dealers to sell his supply rather than that of his rivals," Holt clarified.

"Exactly. That way, his rivals are looking down the chain rather than up at him. So far, it's proved to be quite a successful strategy. Fowler has been in at the ground level since Metcalf has expanded eastwards. We've got names. We have places and we've been tracking his links back up through the distribution network to where his merchandise is entering the country. With some help from abroad, we are looking at bringing down his entire operation. We're so deep into his network that I'm very surprised at this turn of events. I mean, it's not the first time we've lost an asset."

"You had other people in his network?" Hunter asked. Templer nodded. His expression was grave. "And they've disappeared too?"

"Anyone that we managed to embed before has been uncovered in one way or another. Fowler was the first undercover officer we've successfully integrated. Previously, informants or employees we managed to flip have all been dealt with."

"When you say dealt with, you mean killed?" Caslin clarified.

"Some have disappeared, certainly. However, we've always had an inkling that something wasn't right and they've never caught us completely cold. They were managed gambles."

"With people's lives," Hunter said accusingly.

"Don't hate the player. It's the game."

"But this time it's different?" Caslin asked. The question broke Hunter's disgust at Templer's perceived intransigence.

"It would appear so."

"Did Fowler wear a wire?" Caslin asked.

Templar nodded. "Sometimes, but not always. Only when he figured he was safe to do so. Metcalf is no fool."

"Last night?"

Templar shook his head. "I don't know."

"Okay, Terry, where did you get to with these mobiles?"

"None of them are burners, sir. Therefore, it's fair to assume that the four phones recovered from the scene belong to the four victims. Any low-level dealer that I've ever come across uses a burner for obvious reasons. Now if you look at the board," Holt pointed up at a sketch of the crime scene, mounted on a notice board, "you'll see I've marked victims one to four, with three and four being the man and woman on the sofa. These two have exchanged many texts and phone calls in the past few months, so I think it is reasonable to assume that they are a couple. The other two victims, numbered one and two, along with this couple, only have one other number that seems to crossover between all four call logs."

"Presumably that number will be their dealer," Caslin suggested.

Holt nodded his agreement. "That would make sense. Particularly, as that specific number is registered to a burner phone and we have no record of who owns it."

"Is there any sign of that phone at the scene?" Hunter asked.

"Not so far," Holt confirmed.

"Can I see the number?" Templer asked.

"Sure." Holt passed a sheet of paper across the table to him. Templer scanned it.

"That's a number used by Fowler."

"You sure?" Caslin asked.

"Absolutely," Templer confirmed.

"Then let's get that number flagged. If it comes up on the mobile phone network, pings off of a cell tower, whatever, then I want us to know about it. I want to have you," Caslin indicated Hunter and Holt, "to chase up scenes of crime with as much detail as you can. In the meantime, Templer and I will head over to pathology and see what we can find out from Alison Taylor."

Terry Holt's phone rang and the DC answered the call. "You've got to be kidding me?" His response ensured all subsequent conversation ceased as his tone was picked up by the others. His conversation continued for another minute and then he hung up without saying another word.

Turning to his laptop, he brought it out of hibernation and connected to the Internet. The others were curious, recognising his enthusiasm was born of something significant. Holt hit return and the screen before him changed and he sat back in his chair, scanning the faces of those around him. "You are not going to believe this."

CHAPTER FOUR

THE FOUR OFFICERS huddled around Terry Holt's laptop. The window he opened on the screen was small and the three of them, peering over Holt's shoulder, struggled to make out the detail of the footage.

"Can you brighten that up and enlarge it a little?" Caslin asked.

"Hold on, I'll throw it up on the projector if someone can pull down the screen," Holt said. Hunter crossed to the other side of the room and lowered the projector screen into position. Holt linked his laptop via the office Wi-Fi and moments later, the video footage was displayed for all of them to see.

"What are we looking at?" Templer asked.

"That's the house, Metcalf's place, isn't it?" Hunter asked. That became clear as the person wielding the camera panned around the room. It was night-time and there were only a few lamps on in the room, but it was quite clearly the house in Stamford Street they were present at the day before. The four victims were unconscious, perhaps already dead, and were in the same positions as they were discovered in. The camera zoomed in on each of them, although their features were obscured by selective blurring of the image before the shot panned back out and around the room.

"Any sign of Fowler?" Caslin asked Templer. The latter shook his head.

"No, not yet."

"Do you think he's holding the camera?"

"Can't say."

There didn't appear to be any audio accompanying the footage, or if there was then it was inaudible. The camera hovered over the man lying face down on the floor. A left hand came into shot. It was gloved and reached down, picking up the man's right arm at the wrist. The right hand came into view alongside the left and this hand brandished a pair of secateurs.

"Well, I guess that answers that question," Caslin said as the figure placed the victim's index finger in between the blades. At this point the graphic detail was smudged, as if a blob of Vaseline had been smeared over the screen, but an active imagination was not required to realise he had sliced through flesh and connective tissue with ease. Holt sucked air through his teeth, grimacing. He was the only one viewing the footage who was yet to see the reality of the scene. "How do you think he's filming this?"

"Looks like a head cam, to me," Holt replied. "There's no way someone is standing with the camera over this guy's shoulder filming that. He must be wearing a head cam."

The camera moved out as the man who they all assumed was the likely killer moved to the next victim, removing their index finger in the same way. There was no reaction, no grunt of pain, no response, so either the victim was already dead or, at the very least, effectively in a drug-induced coma to such an extent that they felt little or no pain.

"Where are you getting this from, Terry?" Caslin asked.

"A friend of mine works in media relations and she picked this up on the net, just now."

"Who's streaming it?" Hunter asked.

"It's on *The Post's* website," Holt stated, glancing up at her and then back to the footage. "From the timeframe, they've only just uploaded that themselves."

"Irresponsible bastards," Templer said.

"I think we found something we can agree on, at last," Caslin said. Holt split the screen and brought up the website homepage of the city's premier local newspaper. Alongside the usual headlines and links to stories was the headline story of the day. The title read *Vigilante killer strikes crack house*.

"That's a bit of a shift from their usual journalistic approach," Holt said.

"Yes, that's got tabloid written all over it," Hunter added. "Do you think Jimmy had something to do with it?"

"Let's go and find out once this has played out," Caslin said. He was hopeful that Jimmy Sullivan was not involved in the editorial decision making. His background with the London red-tops implied he had form but that was years ago.

The small group continued to watch the footage in silence as the two remaining victims, the couple seated on the sofa, had their index fingers removed as well. As the cut was made on the woman's hand, she appeared to flinch momentarily and her head lolled from one side to the other, but other than that, there was no reaction. The figure stepped back and, once again, allowed the camera to pan around the room, taking in the scene.

"Can you pause that, Terry?" Caslin asked. Holt did as he was requested and stopped the playback.

"Look at the table," Caslin said to no one in particular.

"What are we looking for?" Templer asked.

"Wait a second. Terry, press play." Holt did so, and the playback resumed, only this time everyone was focused on the coffee table in the middle of the room. The video footage blurred as the wearer of the camera appeared to look down towards a bag at their feet before kneeling and reaching inside. Drawing out their hands, they were cupping a pink and white flower, which was carefully and gently placed at the centre of the table. The person then stood up, stared down at it, focusing the camera footage directly on the flower. The cameraman's head tilted forward and they got a brief shot of his boots. They appeared to be workmen's footwear, wide, with heavy treads as the soles projected beyond the leather to either side. They were treated to one more panoramic shot of the scene before the video footage faded out into darkness. The bar creeping along the bottom of the footage indicated there was more to play out and they waited in silence, patiently. A few seconds passed before the number five faded into view. This was held in place for a few seconds more before it once again passed back to black.

"What's the significance of the five, do you think?" Hunter asked.

"How many victims were there? Four, wasn't it?" Holt asked.

"That we know of," Caslin said. He was conscious of Templer's relationship with the undercover detective. Everyone in the room was experienced enough to know that if the officer was present, then there was every likelihood that he could well be a fifth victim. "Terry, you and

Hunter go back over this footage as many times as it takes and detail everything that you see. Then chase up Iain Robertson for his crime scene analysis and compare the two. I want to know if there are any differences, any inconsistencies, anything at all that stands out, no matter how large or small. Understood?"

"Will do, sir," they both said in unison.

"Templer and I will head over to *The Post* and see what we can find out."

"Ask them for all the data they have regarding the video that was sent to them," Holt said. "With a bit of luck, we might be able to track the video back to the sender. At the very least, we could see where it was uploaded from. Their tech guys will know what I'm looking for." Caslin was grateful for the latter clarification as despite his coming a long way regarding new technology in the last few years, his knowledge barely scratched the surface of the detective constable's.

THE OFFICES of where the newspaper was based were in central York. The journey from Fulford Road into the city centre took less than five minutes, largely because at this time on a Sunday morning the city was at its quietest. Pulling into the car park, at the rear of the building, there were plenty of available parking spaces. With only a handful of staff on shift this day, eighty percent of the bays were empty.

"So, who is this Jimmy that DC Holt was talking about?"

"Jimmy Sullivan. He's a journalist. Formerly, quite an established name in the national tabloids but following a few, how should we put it, high-profile errors of judgement found his way back home to Yorkshire."

"Looking to make a name for himself again, do you think?" Templer asked.

Caslin shook his head. "No longer Jimmy's style, if I had to say."

"You know him well?"

"Jimmy's a friend of mine. Believe me, if he was looking to regain his old status, then he would have had plenty of opportunities in the last few years to do so but he didn't. There will be an explanation for this."

"Career motivations can change, you know?" Caslin couldn't disagree but somehow, he didn't view Jimmy in that way, not any more, at least.

They returned to the front of the building and found the entrance door locked. Pressing the intercom button, Caslin stepped back and the two men waited. A minute passed and there was no response from within the building, so Caslin pressed the buzzer again, only this time adding two or three extra bursts for good measure. Still there was no response. Caslin cursed under his breath. A figure appeared to his left, rounding the corner and mounting steps to the front door. He eyed both the officers warily as he approached. Caslin took out his warrant card and brandished it to the young man as he moved past them, reaching for the number panel and preparing to enter his code.

"Detectives Caslin and Templer," he said, identifying them. "We need to speak to the duty editor."

The newspaper employee gave Caslin's identification only a cursory inspection and nodded briefly. "I'll let him know."

Punching in his access code, he opened the door and passed through, pulling it closed behind him and making it clear he had no intention of conversing with them any further. The detectives exchanged glances, irritation evident on both their faces. Another couple of minutes passed and there was still no movement from within the building.

"Do you think they're doing this just to annoy us?" Templer asked.

"I wouldn't be surprised." Caslin reached forward and entered five digits onto the control panel followed by the sound of the lock clicking free.

"You were paying attention."

"I always do," Caslin replied, pulling open the door and entering the building. Templer followed. They barely reached the reception desk when someone appeared from a corridor to their left. It was a familiar face. Sullivan split a broad grin as he clapped eyes on Caslin. Quickening his pace, he offered Caslin his hand and they shook warmly.

"I figured someone would be calling," Sullivan said, maintaining the grin. "I should have known it would be you."

"What are you playing at, Jimmy?" Caslin asked. "You shouldn't have run that recording without speaking to us first."

"Oh, come on, Nate," Sullivan protested. "You couldn't expect us to sit on that, could you?"

"Jimmy, we've got no idea what we're dealing with yet. It's pretty irresponsible for you to run footage of an active crime scene such as that. What were you thinking?"

Sullivan looked around him nervously, as if worried he might be overheard. "Look, we've got a new editor on board. Things are changing around here a little bit. They're not as straitlaced as they used to be. It's a pretty common story in the print industry these days. Falling advertising revenues, readership, online competition. If we're going to survive, we have to get the clicks up. That's the nature of the beast, these days."

"Well, your editor has just broadcast the scene of a multiple homicide to the world. Any chance I'll be able to get him to take the footage down?"

"You'll have to ask *her* yourself, Nate. But I have to tell you, I don't rate your chances. They gave her predecessor the boot despite his best efforts at… lowering the tone."

Sullivan led them into the interior of the building and to the elevators. He pressed the button and summoned one of them to the ground floor. They didn't have long to wait before the doors slid open and the three men stepped in. The doors closed and Sullivan directed the lift to head up to the fourth floor. Once here, he guided them off to the right and across the open plan office space that Caslin knew would be populated by the team of journalists. Being a Sunday, however, there were only a couple of people present in an office in the north-western corner of the floor.

Sullivan rapped his knuckles on the door, more out of courtesy than to announce their presence. Their approach had already been noted by the incumbents through the wall of glass that sectioned the office off from the remainder of the floor. Opening the door, Sullivan led them in.

"Claire Markham, meet Detective Inspector Caslin and…" Suddenly Sullivan realised he had not been introduced to the accompanying detective alongside Caslin and with a somewhat embarrassed flick of his eyebrows, he indicated that one of the newcomers should do the honours.

"DI Craig Templer," he announced himself.

"Pleased to meet both of you," she replied, acknowledging them in turn. Caslin took her in. She was in her fifties. Professionally attired and immaculately presented with her hair and make-up. The fact it was a Sunday with only a skeleton staff present didn't incline her towards dressing down. "What can I do for you today?"

"I want to know who sent you the video you uploaded this morning?" Caslin said flatly.

"I'm afraid I don't have the answer to that question, Inspector," she replied, smiling. "But I'll be happy to provide you with whatever we do have. Good enough?"

"We would appreciate that. Now, where did you get off putting that kind of footage online without running it past us first?"

"Since when do I need your permission?" she countered.

"This isn't social media," Caslin argued. "*The Post* has a decent reputation to uphold, a tradition that I thought even a new editor, looking to make a name for themselves, would adhere to."

"There's a reason I'm here, Inspector, and that's to make a success of this publication. The way I choose to do that is no concern of yours."

"You are aware that revealing evidence of an active crime scene could lead to a future mistrial?"

"If you can make a case for that, Inspector, then I'll be more than happy to listen to your point of view, but at this time, I would argue your point is largely one based on supposition. Now, would you like to go on the record and give us a comment as to what the motivations of the cameraman are or the significance of the number five?"

"The case is ongoing. I'm certain there will be a press release given out at some point later today. In the meantime, I'd be grateful if you would take down the footage from your website."

"Why would I do that, Inspector?"

"I don't know. Human decency. Respect for the families. Either or both."

"I think it's a little late for that."

"Why would you say that?" Templer asked. Markham looked to her associate standing next to her, a young assistant, keen and polished, indicating for him to answer.

"The clip has already gone viral," he said, glancing at the tablet in his hand. With a few swipes of his finger, he looked up. "We have thousands of views already on our website and the clip has been downloaded and shared dozens of times. The count is going up every second. I'm afraid that even if we wanted to take down the footage, the impact will be negligible."

"It's already out there, Inspector," Markham stated. "That horse has already bolted."

"What can you tell us about the sender?" Caslin asked. Markham's associate picked up the narrative, once again.

"The clip was sent into us two hours ago. It was attached to an anonymous email which I traced back to a Google account, and before you ask, yes, I did try to trace the source. The DNS appears to be shrouded by a VPN."

Caslin rolled his eyes. Sullivan smiled. "What he's saying, Nathaniel, is the sender masked his location so we would have no idea where he was."

"He used a virtual private network," Templer confirmed for Caslin's benefit, sensing he knew more about technology than his colleague.

Markham nodded. "Apparently, the email originated in South Africa but, unless he managed to travel back in time, there's no way the sender actually filmed it, which we are assuming he did."

"Is there anything you can tell us?" Caslin asked. "Anything useful, I mean."

"Todd here, will give you everything that we have, Inspector," Markham said, indicating her assistant, who Caslin assumed was their in-house technician.

"In the future, I would appreciate you contacting us before you run the risk of compromising our investigation."

Markham smiled. It was a knowing smile. "Are you expecting another, Inspector?"

"Just call us if a similar situation arises, okay?" Caslin was haughty, irritated by her dismissal of their concerns.

"We can do that," Markham said. "Doesn't mean I won't run the footage though."

"I'd expect nothing less," Caslin said, indicating for them to leave. Sullivan held the door open and the two detectives, along with the technician, passed through it and he fell into step behind them. Caslin dropped back, placing a gentle hand on Sullivan's forearm to indicate they should hang back a little. Once confident they would not be overheard, having put a little bit of distance between themselves and the other two, Caslin addressed his friend.

"I don't expect Markham will keep her word, unless it suits her, obviously."

"Yeah, I think that's pretty astute of you," Sullivan agreed.

"If *anything* else comes in, can I count on you to bring it to me?"

Sullivan hesitated. "Aye, will do, but try and leave me out of it, would you?"

"Of course. Thanks, Jimmy."

They reached the lifts, with the plan being to take them downstairs to Todd's office, where he would put together the files containing the video footage and everything else they gathered regarding the video's origin. The doors parted and the first three walked in but Sullivan held back, remaining on the fourth floor.

"Meet for a drink later?" Sullivan asked.

Caslin nodded. "If I have time, no problem."

The doors closed and the elevator descended.

CHAPTER FIVE

"I THOUGHT Fulford Road was south of here?"

"It is," Caslin replied. "I think it would be worth stopping by pathology on the way back."

"You reckon they'll be done by now?"

"No chance of that, but we'll be able to get the steer as to whether our theory is correct regarding the contaminated supply."

"Your pathologist must be a lot more amenable than mine," Templer stated. Caslin chuckled. "The last time I tried to hurry a pathologist, I took a right kicking. Verbally speaking."

"Didn't you know, we're a lot friendlier in the north?" Caslin mocked his counterpart's southern origins.

Templer laughed. "So everyone keeps telling me."

Caslin slowed the car and flicked on his indicator, turning across the oncoming traffic in between two vehicles and accelerated into the car park. Coming to a halt, he turned off the engine and got out. Together, they approached the pathology building. Before they reached the front door, which was locked, Caslin was already on his mobile phone. The call he made was answered swiftly.

"Yeah, I'm here."

An almost inaudible buzz sounded and Caslin opened the outer door giving them access to the building. Templer followed, closing the door behind them and ensuring the lock clicked into place. He quickened his pace to catch up with Caslin, who knew his route through the building as if he were a permanent resident. Entering a stairwell, they descended to a lower floor. Templer assumed they were heading into a basement but, in reality, due to the slope of the surrounding terrain, they were merely descending to a lower level at the rear of the complex.

They arrived at Dr Taylor's pathology lab shortly after. Caslin pushed open the door and entered. Alison Taylor, York's senior pathologist, was on the far side of the room and they had to walk past two autopsy tables to join her. One of which had a cadaver covered over with a sheet whereas the second, the one closest to her desk, had the body of a deceased male. She looked up from the paperwork she was reading, smiling to Caslin before her eyes passed to the newcomer.

"Good morning, Nate." Her smile broadened. "And it's always a pleasure to see a new face."

"Alison, this is DI Craig Templer."

"Pleased to meet you," Templer said.

"Likewise."

"How far have you got, Alison?"

"Somehow, Nathaniel, I knew you would want an answer as quickly as I could get one. I've completed two of the autopsies, the male and female found side-by-side, at the scene. Plus, I rushed through the toxicological tests on all four victims and there are no prizes for guessing the results are similar for all four."

"Are we looking at poison?" Caslin asked.

"Not quite the right terminology, but the end result is the same," she confirmed. "All four had high concentrations of heroin in their blood streams, two others had traces of cocaine. The two autopsies I have concluded revealed they died of toxic shock, for want of a better phrase. You are familiar with how dealers are looking to increase the street value of their merchandise, often by cutting it with something else?"

"Back in the old days they'd cut their heroin with baking powder in order to increase the supply and therefore the profit margins, yes."

"You're right, that was old school," Dr Taylor agreed.

"These days, I think you'll find they are a little bit more advanced with what they are using," Templer said, drawing her attention towards him.

"Care to enlighten us, Craig?" she asked, interested to test his knowledge. Caslin was mildly amused.

"Suppliers are using synthetic opioids to massively increase their profit margins," Templer explained. "These synthetic drugs can be anything from fifty to one hundred times the strength of morphine, so cutting it with their heroin no longer results in an inferior product and therefore doesn't drive away the client base."

"Very good, Detective Inspector," Dr Taylor said with no hint of sarcasm. "You should keep this one around, Nate."

Caslin smiled. "You were saying, about the supply."

"Having run the blood tests and evaluated the toxicological results, I took a look at the samples that Iain Robertson supplied me with, from the scene, and I tested those alongside the blood samples. The heroin came back with two such synthetic opioids, as Craig here described, those being *Fentanyl* and *Carfentanyl*. Thousands of people each year are currently dying of overdoses related to these drugs, tens of thousands per year across the Atlantic, in the US."

"What's unusual in this scenario, is the level of synthetic opioids in this supply of heroin. Suppliers and dealers are well aware of the potency of these drugs and, I think we can all agree, they wouldn't consider it in their interests to kill off their customers. So, I would suggest that this is a case of intentional overdosing rather than accidental mixing of too much of the synthetics. Unless the person mixing got the ratio drastically wrong."

"You sound quite sure of this," Caslin said.

"Once these guys shot up with this particular batch, there was only going to be one outcome."

"What can you tell us about the effects?"

"Fentanyl overdoses can be deadly. Even at low levels the result can lead to a weakening of the muscles, dizziness, confusion, and can often leave the person suffering from extreme sleepiness. With a slightly higher dose, they can quite easily lose consciousness. Those however, are the external symptoms that we can all see."

"A video surfaced online this morning, apparently footage of these four dying, or in several cases perhaps already dead. Three of the four seem to be completely comatose but the fourth, the woman, still appeared responsive as her index finger was cut off," Caslin said.

"I'll get to the finger in a minute," Dr Taylor replied. "I'm not surprised to hear you describe that. As I said, those are the external signs. Internally is where the real damage takes place. A high dose of something such as Fentanyl lowers the body's blood pressure and leads to a profound slowing of the heartbeat. Now, when a dangerous dose is ingested, in whichever manner of choice, the heart may slow to such a pace that it almost stops beating and also, you may find the patient stops breathing altogether. Such respiratory depression can quite easily lead to hypoxia, which can cause permanent brain damage in the individual should they survive."

"In which case, how can dealers get away with cutting their heroin with the synthetic opioids?" Caslin asked.

Templer answered before the pathologist could. "Those who abuse Fentanyl regularly can build up a tolerance to it just the same as they can with any other drug."

"He's right," Dr Taylor agreed. "What the user doesn't realise though is that this tolerance may build up against the effects of pain relief or euphoria. The tolerance develops non-uniformly, leaving them at a heightened risk of experiencing overdose effects that are less impacted by their tolerance, such as respiratory depression. So, for example, any period of abstinence will see their tolerance level diminish, meaning that what was considered a tolerable dose nearly a fortnight previously could now become utterly lethal."

"So, what you're saying is, if someone is used to a supply cut with something such as Fentanyl, then as long as they continue to use, the dealer would expect them to have no ill effects but any break in that supply, or mixing of dealers, could lead to the events you're describing? Caslin said.

"That's a reasonable hypothesis, yes. And needless to say, if the user is also taking other stimulants or alcohol, benzodiazepines, in combination with heroin and Fentanyl, they can have compounding and or contradictory effects. It's a risky pastime to say the least."

"And you don't think the mix could have been accidental?"

Dr Taylor shook her head emphatically. "The levels contained within this heroin, there's no way anyone, with a healthy tolerance level or not, could have survived without an emergency medical intervention. Of that, I am absolutely certain."

"These synthetic opioids, how accessible are they?"

"Well, you can't walk into your local pharmacist and buy them over the counter, they are controlled substances. But, like any other synthetic drug, once the chemical structure is known then it can easily be replicated."

"You said easily?" Caslin asked.

"By someone with chemical knowledge, yes, but even that isn't necessarily a requirement in this day and age."

"They are readily available on the dark web." Templer advised Caslin. "Hell, I'm pretty sure you can import them from China without even accessing the dark web. You run the risk of them being picked up as they pass through customs in the UK, but things get through all the time."

"What did you find in the autopsies?" Caslin asked. Dr Taylor stepped down from the stool she was sitting on and crossed the room to the first of the autopsy tables. Both Caslin and Templer joined her and she passed him a file containing the notes made during the examination. Caslin recognised the male who was seated on the sofa.

"The first thing to note is there are no signs of a struggle, or any indication of violence whatsoever on this man's body. Therefore, I think it's safe to conclude that he was a willing participant and injected himself with the heroin. Similarly, with the woman, who I'm led to believe is probably his partner," she said glancing to Caslin, he nodded, "also exhibits no signs of forced coercion."

"They had no idea what they were taking," Templer said quietly.

"That is my conclusion," Dr Taylor said.

"What about the fingers? We've seen from the footage that they were cut off with a set of secateurs," Caslin said.

"That doesn't surprise me. If you flick through to page four, that was my guess. The damage to the remaining skin tissue, where the finger was detached, indicates a sharp blade but not of surgical grade, and also the level of pressure exerted implied a tool that magnified the force the user was able to apply."

"If you'll indulge me, please could you apply your psycho analysis skills to the removal of the fingers?"

"I'd be lying if I said I hadn't given it some thought already," Dr Taylor said.

"Would I be hopelessly simplistic to suggest the removal of the fingers is merely trophy hunting?"

"Not... hopelessly... simplistic, no," Dr Taylor replied. "However, I think we should be careful about hypothesising too much regarding this particular killer's motivations. Without more data to go on, it might steer you in the wrong direction."

"Fair enough, I promise not to make what you say the focal point of the investigation. What you think?"

"Many killers who carry out detailed schemes need to objectify their victims. This separates any level of empathy the killer may have for their victims or their associated friends and family. Mutilation goes hand in glove with objectification and allows for an unchallenged possession of the victim."

Caslin thought about the level of planning necessary to contaminate a supply and also ensure the users, in this case four people, willingly ingested the drugs and died as a result.

"You'll probably be aware of many serial killers who will often have had sex with the bodies of the victims, commonly after death, which is the ultimate form of intimacy."

Caslin nodded. "The likes of Bundy, Dahmer, they did that."

"Now, that isn't the case in this scenario but each victim has been mutilated. The act of mutilation or the act of copulation with the dead body are not in themselves acts that you would necessarily associate with someone's desire to achieve sexual satisfaction, which many believe is paramount with these killers, but they are more about control. You mentioned a video of this particular crime scene being uploaded on the Internet."

"Yes, it was sent to a local paper."

"I'm not surprised to hear that in the least. That in itself is an extension of control. Capturing the victim on video either before, during, or after the murder is a form of exerting unmitigated, absolute, and irreversible control over that person. The killer is aspiring to 'freeze time' in the still perfection that he has choreographed. The victim is motionless and defenceless. The killer is attaining their long-sought object permanence where the victim is unable to leave them."

Caslin pondered on the last point for a moment. If Alison was correct, then there was every possibility the killer suffered some past trauma from an abandonment or humiliation. That gave them an insight that could prove helpful in identifying him. At this point he was unsure of how they would do that unless he made a mistake.

As if reading his mind, she elaborated. "People who commit multiple homicides are often desperately trying to avoid a painful relationship. They may be terrified of society seeing what they are and then fear being discarded. This is most likely subconscious, resulting from an abusive upbringing or a lack of a stable parental figure in their life. This scene may lack the blood and gore that you often find with a serial killer but make no mistake, you are dealing with a very twisted individual and a very dangerous one at that."

"What are the chances that this is the result of a rival drug gang trying to take out a supplier who has overstepped the mark in their territory? Although again, I accept this is pure conjecture on our part." Caslin flicked a brief glance in Templer's direction. He knew the question was for his benefit.

"It's okay, Dr Taylor, you don't need to answer the question. I've never known a turf war to be played out in this manner," Templer said, meeting Caslin's eye and conceding ground.

"Just to be clear," Dr Taylor said, "it will be the strangest act of gang retaliation I've ever heard of."

"Do you have anything else for us?" Caslin asked.

"Only to say that both of the victims that I have studied so far were habitual drug users. Both of them frequently injected themselves, most likely with heroin, and I also found traces of methadone in their system."

That meant to Caslin that both victims must be registered in a drug counselling programme, perhaps making it easier to identify them.

"I will continue with my examination of the remaining two victims today and I'll ensure you have the headlines of all four autopsies by first thing tomorrow. The detailed write-ups will be with you by the end of day."

Caslin's phone rang in his pocket and he excused himself, stepping away from the other two. He saw Hunter's name flash up on the screen as he answered the call.

"Go ahead, Sarah."

"Sir, Terry Holt has double-checked the origin of the video sent to the newspaper offices. They were telling the truth. The email account is being bounced off a VPN and we've got no chance of working out the source. However, he not only sent it to the newspaper but he subsequently uploaded it to the Internet himself. Holt's doing his best to track its route back to the source but again, we suspect he is using the same software to mask his location."

"He's looking for attention."

"I agree. That's never a good sign." Hunter sounded pensive. "It usually indicates that this is just the beginning."

"There is one good thing about attention seekers though, Sarah."

"Yeah, what's that?"

"They want to be talked about. They want us to see them. Eventually, they must speak to us and that's when they come out of the shadows."

"I hear that. There's another reason I'm calling, sir. We red-flagged Fowler's mobile number. Once we loaded it into the system, we immediately got a notification that a call was made from that number to the emergency services overnight."

"A 999 call?"

"Yes. The call-handler didn't hear a voice on the other end of the line but followed standard procedure. She gave the caller time to communicate and tried to attract attention but nothing was forthcoming. Ninety-nine times out of a hundred these turn out to be accidental, or prank, calls. Made by kids, that type of thing. As per procedure, the call was passed to a colleague who initiated a call back once the line was terminated. No one answered but the location of the cell tower was logged."

"Have we tried calling the number again?"

"Yes, rings out, but the handset is still connected to the same tower east of the city."

"Do we have a location?"

"It's rural, so we can't pinpoint it but we've narrowed it down. We have a helicopter inbound and a uniform presence searching the vicinity. I'll text you the centre point. Shall we meet you there?"

"We're on our way." Turning, he caught Templer's eye. "We're on the move."

CHAPTER SIX

THEIR ROUTE TOOK them eastwards out of the city, via Heslington, before turning north and passing Dunnington and Stamford Bridge on the way to Westow, a village on the cusp of the Howardian Hills. The journey took them nearly three quarters of an hour. A few spots of rain graced the windscreen as they left pathology but now, approaching their destination, the rain was steadily falling as they circumvented the village and cut west along the line of the River Derwent.

They were on a back road linking the village to Kirkham and its ruined abbey only a couple of miles distant. The line of the road curved following the route of the river, but as they made the turn, they came across a liveried police car parked on the verge. The uniformed officer present stood out in his all-weather high visibility jacket. He flagged them down. Stooping low, the officer peered through the passenger window as Templer lowered it, identifying them. Pointing off to the left, he indicated an unmade track that headed south, parallel to the flow of the river. Shielded from the road by woodland, if you didn't know it was there then in all likelihood you would have driven past and paid it no attention whatsoever.

Caslin took the car down the track and as soon as the road disappeared from view behind them, they reached a gated entrance to what presumably used to be a working farm. Here, they were met by another officer who pulled back the gate and ushered them through. As they passed through more police vehicles came into sight. Recognising Hunter's car, Caslin pulled up alongside. Both men got out and looked around them. The immediate vicinity saw little activity but a short distance away was a clearing surrounded on three sides by dense woodland. They could see uniformed activity through the trees. Caslin turned the collar of his coat up against the rain as it intensified. Looking to Templer, he glanced down at the younger man's footwear.

"Nice shoes."

"Thanks," Templer replied, confused.

"The woods are going to love those," Caslin said, breaking into a smile.

"Yeah," Templer agreed ruefully, eyeing the terrain around them. "Thanks again."

They set off and once they breached the tree line, the scene before them took on a macabre appearance. A blue BMW was parked in the centre of the clearing with the headlights on, illuminating everything before it. The oppressive cloud cover and ensuing rainfall, aided by the mature trees all around them, left the clearing shrouded in relative darkness despite the hour of the day. Forensics officers were endeavouring to set up a tent with which to cover the target area, but before they could do so the surrounding scene needed to be photographed and catalogued. This process couldn't be rushed but the elements were applying pressure for them to do so.

Hunter spied their arrival and crossed to greet them.

"Not seen one like this before."

Her grim expression told Caslin to brace himself. "How did you find it?"

"The aerial unit took up a grid-by-grid search pattern, extending out from the cell tower. They spotted the car from above. The lights on made it stand out. I don't think there's any doubt our guy wanted us to find it."

"What makes you say that?" Templer asked.

"You'll see." Gesturing for them to walk with her, she turned and headed towards the car.

Rounding the car, a nearly new BMW, Caslin immediately saw what Hunter was talking about. Less than fifteen feet from the front of the vehicle, he could see a human head on the floor. As they moved closer, he noted the level of damage to the face as well as the top of the skull. He thought it was a woman's head but the injuries were so severe, it was tough to tell. On the ground in front of her was a mobile phone. Caslin dropped to his haunches to inspect both it and the victim.

"That's Ben Fowler's phone," Templer said.

"You're sure?" Caslin asked over his shoulder.

"It's the model I issued him with." Caslin turned his attention to the woman. Her face was battered, with much of her features disfigured by multiple blows, lacerations and swelling. Her hair, which he presumed would be shoulder length, if he could see her shoulders, was matted with dried blood. Leaning in closer, he could see extensive damage to the skin of the scalp and was left in no doubt that she died in the most brutal and painful manner.

"I don't see any cuts to the neckline," Caslin said aloud to nobody in particular. "Presumably there's more of a body beneath?"

"That was my thought too," Iain Robertson said in his thick Glaswegian, approaching from behind. "We put a probe down and met resistance. My thinking is she's buried up to her neck."

Caslin moved aside and Robertson came past him, rustling in his white coveralls. Kneeling down, he took a small trowel in one hand, something akin to a decorator's paintbrush in the other, and gently began to loosen the soil around the neck and brush it aside. Ensuring not to taint any of the forensic evidence, within a few minutes, he was confident enough to confirm his initial suspicions. Looking up to Caslin, he nodded.

"Aye, it looks like she's all here."

"You think she was beaten before burial?" Caslin asked.

"That's possible. If you cast your eyes around at the assorted stones and rocks nearby, you'll note they don't really belong where they've fallen."

Caslin did as he was bid and checked the assorted stones. Some were larger than a tennis ball whilst others were smaller, pieces of jagged flint the size of a walnut. In some cases, they rested on fresh grass flattened beneath them and others lay atop damp moss. They were recent additions to the area. Caslin cast his eyes skyward.

"Nasty way to go, isn't it?" Robertson said flatly.

"Man, that's cold," Templer said softly.

"The mobile?" Caslin asked Robertson, with a flick of his eyes in the direction of the phone.

"Yes," Robertson said, "it's been catalogued and printed."

Caslin donned a pair of latex gloves and Hunter took out an evidence bag, bringing it over to him. Carefully, Caslin picked up the phone and placed it inside the transparent plastic bag. Sealing it, he passed it to Hunter.

"Let's get this back to Fulford Road as quickly as possible," Caslin began, "and have Terry confirm that it's Fowler's phone. Then, see if he can find where it's been and who has been in contact with it in the last forty-eight hours."

Turning his attention to the BMW, Caslin was joined by Templer. Both of them walked around the car looking for any signs of damage on both the interior as well as the exterior, looking for any indication as to how the vehicle ended up there. Even a cursory inspection revealed the car was in near perfect condition.

"Who's the car registered to?" Caslin asked, opening the driver's door.

"The DVLA has the owner recorded as a Kelly Ryan. She is a forty-two-year-old resident of York, sir, and the only recorded keeper since its first registration," Hunter said.

Caslin glanced back at the victim who was slowly and painstakingly being released from her early grave. "Does her description match the victim?"

"I believe so, sir."

"Do you think she was here meeting someone?" Templer asked, looking around and squinting against the rain.

"Iain, any sign of another vehicle?" Caslin called out. Robertson looked up, briefly pausing what he was doing. He passed the trowel and brush to a colleague and rose. Walking over to join them, he shook his head.

"We haven't found any indication of another vehicle. No tyre impressions nor evidence of a turning circle in the grass."

With the changeable weather recently, Caslin judged the ground underfoot was soft and damp. Any other vehicle would have left some kind of sign, so the vehicle was possibly left on the highway. "Have someone walk the lane just to be sure. What do we think, Craig?"

"It's out of the way. You're safe from prying eyes here. It wouldn't be a bad place for a tryst."

"Are you talking from experience?" Hunter asked, with a wry grin. That brought some much-needed lightness to the scene and all those nearby smiled, if only briefly.

"It's also a cracking place to bring someone to if you want to torture them to death," Caslin said, returning his attention to the car. Leaning into the interior he looked around. The upholstery was leather and in immaculate condition. In fact, the cabin in its entirety was a damn site cleaner than any vehicle or house he had ever owned. Templer opened the passenger door and dropped to his haunches, casting a wary eye around the interior.

"Clean. No sign of any struggle."

"Agreed."

Caslin popped the boot and both men retreated from the interior and walked to the rear. The boot space was empty. It was lined with carpet, matching the interior of the cabin, and as they rooted around, they found what they would expect the manufacturer to provide with nothing else that seemed out of place.

Caslin looked along the length of the car and caught Hunter's attention. "What else do we know about Miss Ryan?"

"She was reported missing two nights ago."

"Reported missing? By whom?"

"Her husband, Thomas," Hunter said. "He called the police a little after midnight, two days ago, stating he was concerned that his wife had failed to return home from work and wasn't answering his calls."

"Did anyone follow up?"

"Uniform called by the residence within an hour and had a word with him, but it was a little early to ring the alarm bells," Hunter said.

"Within an hour?" Templer said. "It must have been a quiet night."

"True," Caslin said, smiling. "Why was he so concerned, did he say?"

"The officers who attended reported that he felt her actions were out of character. Her husband had already contacted friends and relatives but to no avail. After visiting her place of work and finding her car missing, he rang around the local hospitals to see if she had been involved in an accident. Needless to say, she hadn't been admitted."

"We'll have to pay him a visit," Caslin said. "Once we have her out then he will need to carry out a formal identification. We'll also have to find out where she works and call in on them as well to see if she was in work yesterday. I want to start building a timeline of the hours since she was last seen alive. Start from the point of the 999 call we received last night, from this location, and work backwards from there. Do we have the recording from the call?"

"Terry Holt was looking to get that just as I was leaving to head out here," Hunter said.

"Well, this is interesting," Robertson said from within the blue tent, lifted into place to protect the crime scene from the elements while they were talking. Raising his voice so they could hear him, Robertson called the three detectives back to where the victim was buried. Moving the entrance flap aside, they came to stand behind the CSI officers, looking over his shoulder. "It looks like she's not been buried here long. The soil hasn't had a chance to compact around her and is fairly loose against the body."

The team were making fast work of clearing the surrounding soil away from the body of the victim, albeit working to ensure they maintained the integrity of the crime scene. The right-hand side of the body had been partially revealed. The loose soil assisted in the speed of their work. The shoulder, down to the waistline, was visible as the soil had been carefully removed and cleared away. The earth behind the body was still in place, keeping her upright. Presently, she had the look of a living statue being excavated by a team of archaeologists.

"What's interesting?" Caslin asked.

"Just give me a second," Robertson said under his breath. He was kneeling in front of the victim and reaching down, extending his arm and appeared to be brushing something away with smooth strokes. "Yep, I was half expecting this."

"What have you got?" Caslin was impatient.

Robertson brought himself upright and looked back over his shoulder. "Come and take a look." Caslin stepped forward and crouched down, peering into the hole. Although the left arm of the victim was still encased in soil, her left hand was now revealed as it was clasped against the right. Her wrists were bound together by a cable tie, pulled tight enough for the plastic to have broken through the skin. "I'll bet she was struggling to free herself so much that the binders cut into her. Do you see what I see?"

"The index finger?" Caslin said quietly.

"Just like back at Stamford Street. For some reason, I was expecting it," Robertson said with grim satisfaction.

"Something tells me he didn't bury her, stone her to death, then go back and dig her out in order to cut off a finger."

Robertson shook his head, "No, I doubt that very much. More likely, he cut it off before she was buried."

"And before he killed her." Caslin ran a hand across his eye and left cheek before shaking his head gently. "It might also explain why there's no sign of a struggle."

"You think he brought her here in her own car?" Robertson asked.

Caslin nodded. "If she wasn't meeting someone, I figure it's likely."

"If I can't find a trace of another vehicle present, then I'd have to agree. Once we get her out and back into the city, we'll run her clothes for carpet fibres and see if he transported her in the boot of the car. Do you see this here?" Robertson asked, directing Caslin to a point on the victim's face, near to her mouth. Caslin couldn't see what he was talking about and leaned in closer, meeting the forensic officer's eye with an unspoken query. "There, around the mouth." Robertson indicated the corner of her mouth with a sweeping arc movement of his index finger from one side to the other and back again. "You see the redness there, extending from one side of the mouth to the other and taking in the chin as well as the upper lip, below the nose? That's skin irritation, most likely caused by gaffer tape or some other restraint stuck to her mouth."

"She was gagged?"

"Yes, and then he removed it."

"To hear her scream?"

Robertson frowned and shrugged at the same time. "Perhaps the tape spoiled his presentation?"

"For us, do you mean?"

"Your guess is as good as mine, lad. Your guess is as good as mine."

CHAPTER SEVEN

Darkness had well and truly fallen by the time Caslin and Hunter returned to York. Bypassing the centre, they arrived in the suburbs on the south-western edge of the city. Taking a right turn off the Tadcaster Road and onto Mount Parade, Caslin found the first available parking space at the side of the road and pulled over. Eyeing the street scene, Caslin scanned the Georgian terraces. This was one of the most prestigious postcodes in York, with even a two-bedroom apartment costing significantly above the national average house price.

"She was doing well," Hunter offered, following Caslin's gaze.

"It's not a bad place to be living, certainly."

"Tell me, what do you make of Craig?"

"Templer?" Hunter nodded. He thought on it for a moment before responding. "I'll hold fire on passing judgement, if you don't mind? He's not going anywhere, that's for sure."

Caslin got out of the car and Hunter followed. Stepping up onto the pavement, he looked to her.

"Which one is it?" he asked. She pointed to the house three doors along from where they parked. The two of them walked the short distance and mounted the steep steps to the front door. Caslin reached up and took hold of the door knocker, before drawing attention to anyone inside, he glanced at her. "This never gets any easier, does it?"

"No, it doesn't."

Caslin rapped the knocker a couple of times and then released his grip, standing back to await a response. There were lights on in the interior and they didn't have to wait long before the sound of a chain being released on the inside could be heard. The panelled door swung inwards and a man stood before them. He was in his early forties, Caslin assumed, wearing suit trousers and a shirt, open at the neck with the sleeves rolled part way up along his forearms. He was slim, clean shaven and he figured this man would normally be very well presented but today his eyes appeared sunken and hollow. His stubble was perhaps a day or so old, mostly black, matching his hair, but with flecks of grey visible.

"Mr Ryan?" Caslin asked, withdrawing his warrant card from within his wallet and displaying it before him. "Detective Inspector Caslin and Detective Sergeant Hunter, based out of Fulford Road. May we come in?"

"Of course, Inspector." Thomas Ryan stepped back and gestured for them to enter. The hall was an expansive area that gave them enough room to pass by him, standing casually until he pushed the door closed. He addressed them pointedly. "Do you have news of Kelly?" The expressions on their faces conveyed the worst fears that he must have had playing through his mind. "What is it, what happened?"

"Perhaps we should sit down somewhere and have a chat," Caslin said.

"What's happened to her?" Ryan pressed, fear edging into his tone. "Have you found her?"

"We believe so, Mr Ryan," Hunter said.

"Is she… is she okay?" The change in expression on his face, as well as the shift in his body language, suggested he already knew the answer to the question. His eyes were fearful, dreading the answer.

"We are very sorry, Mr Ryan, but we believe we have found your wife. We still have to carry out more checks in order to be certain, but the person we have found matches your wife's description and was found alongside her car. At this time, we do believe it is Kelly."

"Dear God." He took a step back, bracing himself against the wall of the hallway as his legs appeared unsteady beneath him. Caslin reached out just in case the man was about to collapse, but Thomas Ryan held up a hand to indicate that wasn't necessary. Caslin retreated.

"Perhaps, we should take a seat, Mr Ryan," Hunter reiterated. He nodded and beckoned for them to follow him deeper into the house, along the hallway. The first doorway they reached was the entrance to the sitting room, located in front of the house, with a large fifteen-pane window overlooking the street outside. Ryan offered them a seat on the sofa, a large three-seater in keeping with the decor of the rest of the room. A fire was set in the hearth with logs burning, crackling away, flickering shadows cast around them as the flames danced.

"What happened to Kelly?" Ryan asked, as he seated himself facing them in a Chesterfield club chair.

"We're still trying to figure that out," Caslin said. "I'm afraid I have to inform you that it is strongly apparent that your wife was murdered." He broke down at the news, his head bowing and he wept unashamedly. Both detectives let the moment carry, reluctant to put any extra pressure on to someone so visibly upset. Often, in this type of scenario, Caslin would give the immediate relative some space in order to process such information. He could always ask his questions at a later time, however, in this situation, they needed to get the inquiry up to speed as fast as possible and he didn't feel he had the leeway on this occasion. After a few minutes, Ryan managed to compose himself and raised his head, wiping streaks of tears from his cheeks with the palm of his hand.

"What is it you would like to know?"

"When you reported your wife missing two nights ago, had you any reason to expect her not to return home after work?"

Ryan shook his head. "No, we had a dinner reservation for nine o'clock. She often works late but when I thought she was cutting it fine, I called her mobile but she didn't answer."

"What time was that?" Hunter asked, taking out a notebook and pen.

"About eight o'clock, I think. Perhaps, a little earlier. Then I called again, a little after half past. To be honest, I'm angry at myself."

"Why?" Caslin asked, intrigued.

Ryan chuckled but without any genuine humour. "I thought she was just wrapped up at work, as usual. I thought maybe she was… trying to make me angry. How self-centred is that?"

"Was that normal behaviour, by your wife, I mean?" Caslin asked in a non-accusational manner.

"Sometimes." He met Caslin's gaze. "She could be quite single-minded, could Kelly. Something that I think I taught her in our marriage."

"So, she never answered your calls… either of them, or got back to you with a text or email?" Hunter asked.

Ryan shook his head. "No."

"What did you do then?"

"I waited. At first, I just assumed she had forgotten about our plans and lost herself in her work. Once it was past ten-thirty, that's when I got really concerned and I phoned a couple of friends to see if she had dropped by with any of them, but they hadn't seen or heard from her either."

"What work does she do?" Caslin asked.

"She works for one of the national banks, here in the city."

Caslin nodded. "Doing what for them?"

"Debt management."

"And how was her work, did she talk about it much?" Caslin asked.

"Not with me, no."

"And after you phoned your friends?" Hunter asked, returning their focus to the night in question.

"I got in the car and drove to her office. It's just on the edge of the city centre. I know where she parks, although it's in an underground car park, beneath the offices, I thought I might be able to meet her in her office or something."

"And?" Hunter pressed.

"And nothing," Ryan said, shaking his head. "The entrance to the parking lot was gated and I couldn't get in. So, I went around to the entrance, buzzed the intercom and waited for a few minutes but no one came out. I figured the security guard would be there and I could ask them whether she was still at her desk."

"But no one came to speak to you?"

"No. I waited... It must have been ten minutes or so but no one came."

"What did you do then?"

"I headed home. I thought maybe we had passed each other on the road, and I half expected her to be waiting for me at the house, annoyed that I wasn't there when she got in. Obviously, she wasn't here and then I got really worried and I phoned the hospital. To see if she had been admitted in some kind of accident or something, but they had no one matching her description. Then I called you."

"Have you spoken to anybody at her place of work since that night?" Caslin asked.

"Yes, I have. At least, I tried to find out as much as I could but they weren't very helpful."

"Who wasn't?" Caslin asked.

"Her boss, colleagues." He was visibly annoyed. "I just wanted to know whether she'd been there or not."

"They wouldn't tell you?" Caslin asked, mildly surprised.

"No. They gave me some guff about data protection and whatnot." He was dismissive, irritated. "Honestly, sometimes I think this country's gone mad."

"Can you give us the address of her office?" Hunter asked and Ryan nodded that he would.

"Do you live here alone, besides you and Kelly, I mean?" Caslin asked.

"Yes, it's just the two of us."

"Is there anyone that we can call for you, Mr Ryan?" Caslin asked, worried about leaving him alone at this time.

Ryan shook his head. "No, thank you. I have people to call on, if I need to. My sister, Miche, lives nearby."

"If you are sure?" Hunter said. "It's no trouble."

"Thank you for the offer, you are very kind," he replied, "but I'll be fine. When can I see her?"

"I'm afraid we're still processing the scene," Caslin explained. "As soon as we can return her to York, we'll look to bring you down and you can see her then. It will be some time tomorrow, I imagine."

"Thank you, Inspector," Ryan said softly, his head dropping as he spoke.

Caslin took out one of his contact cards and handed it to him. Ryan accepted it gratefully and scanned the name and telephone number. "You can reach me on that mobile number at any time, Mr Ryan."

"Thank you."

"We'll see ourselves out," Caslin said, indicating for Hunter to come with him. She stood up and crossed the room to the door. As Caslin joined her, he paused and turned back. "Can you think of any reason why your wife would have driven out towards Kirkham two nights ago?"

Ryan sat back, appearing thoughtful. "I don't believe either of us know anyone who lives out that way. No, sorry. Is that where you found her?"

Caslin nodded slowly. "Yes, it is. She was in a wooded area a little way off the beaten track. It is possible that she drove out there to meet someone. At least, that's one line of inquiry. Is there anyone that she may have been meeting out there. Perhaps it is someone you might suspect she could have been meeting but were unaware of?"

Ryan met his eye. "Is that your diplomatic way of asking me if my wife was having an affair, Inspector?"

"Yes, Mr Ryan. It is."

Thomas Ryan's expression remained impassive and he didn't blink. "The honest answer to that question, Inspector, is that I really don't know what my wife might have been doing out there. Could she have been having an affair?" he said, shaking his head and breaking the eye contact. "I genuinely don't know what Kelly might have been capable of, these days."

"I appreciate your candour," Caslin said. "I have another question that you might find slightly… unpalatable at this time, but I'd appreciate an answer, nonetheless."

"If it helps you catch her killer, ask me whatever you want."

"Did your wife… did Kelly have a drug habit that you are aware of?"

"What kind of a bloody question is that, Inspector?" Ryan said, his tone turning hostile.

"A pertinent one, Mr Ryan. One that I'm afraid I have to ask."

"Why on earth would you think Kelly had a drug habit?"

"We have reason to believe that your wife's murder may be linked to another case that we are working on."

"One that involves… what… drugs?" Ryan asked.

"Yes, that's the case," Caslin replied, waiting for the answer to his question.

Ryan appeared agitated, shaking his head. He looked up at Caslin. "No, Inspector. To my knowledge, Kelly does not take drugs nor has she ever done so. Any other questions?"

"Not at this time, Mr Ryan, but thank you. I appreciate that these questions would be difficult at the best of times and truly awful at the worst. We'll be in touch tomorrow and in the meantime should you need anything, please do give me a call on that number," he said, indicating the contact card that Ryan was fiddling with his hands. "As I said, we'll see ourselves out. I'm very sorry for your loss."

The two of them left Thomas Ryan sitting in his living room and walked back into the hallway and then out into the street without further conversation. Once onto the pavement, Hunter glanced in Caslin's direction before casting her eyes back towards the house and caught sight of Ryan, standing at the window overlooking the street, watching them depart. They reached the car and Caslin hugged the side of the vehicle as oncoming traffic passed by, before opening the driver's door and getting in.

"What did you make of all that?" she asked, staring up at the now empty window. Ryan was gone.

Caslin exhaled, following her gaze. "Marriage is seldom easy."

"I'll take your word for that," Hunter said, smiling.

"One day you'll know exactly what I'm talking about, I'm sure. Interesting though. He couldn't bring himself to say it, could he?"

"He thinks she might well be having an affair."

"Or, he knows damn well that she is."

"And the office… with the whole data protection thing when he called?"

"There's definitely more going on here than he just gave us," Caslin said. "We'll stop by her office first thing in the morning and find out whether she was in work two nights ago as Ryan thought. It will certainly narrow down the timeframe from when she was last seen to when we believe she was killed."

"Or blow it wide open if she never turned up for work," Hunter added.

"It's all very interesting though, isn't it?" Caslin was thinking aloud. "Then again, most murder cases are."

CHAPTER EIGHT

THE RECEPTION FOYER was furnished with designer seating. At least, the *Le Corbusier* style they were trying to achieve was close, and may well have fooled the untrained eye, but anyone who knew how to spot the real thing would recognise these as cheaper imitations. They didn't have long to wait before a door opened on the far side of the room and a man stepped through. He was in his late 50s, balding, and bore a frown that Caslin figured was quite likely a permanent feature. The man glanced to a member of staff, seated at a desk to his left, and she indicated towards Caslin and Hunter. He crossed the foyer and smiled in greeting, the frown dispersing before their eyes.

"Mr Alexander?" Caslin asked. He nodded in reply. "I'm Detective Inspector Caslin. We spoke on the phone."

"Yes, I remember. Pleased to meet you."

"This is DS Hunter," Caslin introduced her. Hunter took the offered hand in greeting.

"Please, do come with me," Alexander said, gesturing for them to accompany him back the way he had just come. Swiping an access card against a small panel next to the door, the lock clicked and he pulled it open, allowing both of them to pass through before him.

"You are Kelly Ryan's line manager, is that right?" Caslin asked.

"Yes, I was. I still can't believe this has happened to Kelly. Such a damn shame."

"Was she popular?" Hunter asked.

"Very." Alexander was talking over his shoulder as they approached another door. He opened it and passed through, leading them into his office. Offering them both a seat in front of his desk, he closed the door, glancing somewhat nervously along the corridor as he did so, in Caslin's mind. "Although this is a large company, we have a very close-knit team. I don't wish it to sound clichéd but we are something of a family here. Kelly was integral to that."

"I understand she worked in debt management," Caslin said.

Alexander nodded. "Mortgage debt specifically, yes. Kelly managed a small team who process mortgage arrears and repossession orders."

"Busy times?"

"Always busy times, I'm afraid to say. Not quite what we faced during the last financial crash, and we manage our risk in a much more cautious way than we used to, but nonetheless, people's circumstances change or they've overreached... It's the nature of the beast that some will fall by the wayside, sadly."

"How would you describe Kelly Ryan? In terms of her ability, work ethic, standing among her colleagues," Caslin asked.

"As I said, she was very popular within the team. She has... had... a lot of friends here. Regarding her work I have absolutely no complaints. Her work ethic and performance were second to none. More often than not she was the first person through the door and the last to leave at night."

"And two nights ago, the night she went missing, her husband stated she was working late. Can you confirm this?" Hunter asked, taking notes. Caslin watched the man intently, appearing almost casual but in reality, he was weighing up every word he uttered.

"Yes," Alexander said firmly. "I understand she was one of the last to finish for the day and even spoke to one of our night shift security guards as she left the building. After your call earlier, I double checked and he confirmed that she left shortly after 8 PM."

"We would like to speak to the security guard, if you can arrange it?" Caslin said.

"Of course. Marcus was on shift last night and I spoke to him this morning and he offered to wait in case you wanted a word with him. He's ex-military. A top man."

"What about Kelly's work? Has she had any problems that you are aware of recently? Perhaps a disgruntled customer, any threats?"

Alexander shook his head emphatically. "No, nothing like that. Kelly's team is very much admin focussed. The only contact she has with people facing repossession orders or debt restructuring is done through paperwork. Her position at the bank isn't a customer facing role."

"How well do you know her?" Hunter asked. "You said your team was like a family, so, unless that's a soundbite, I'm presuming you are close to one another. Was there anything going on in her life that might appear unusual, particularly in light of what's just happened?"

Alexander drew breath, appearing uncomfortable at the question. "I'm not entirely sure what you're asking me," he said, his eyes flicking between the two of them.

"How was she within herself?" Caslin asked. "Did she say anything to you regarding her personal life or whether she was experiencing marital issues?"

"I'm not really sure that's for me to say."

"How well do you know Thomas, Kelly's husband?" Caslin asked.

"I've met him a handful of times," Alexander said. "At the occasional work do… Christmas. He's attended the staff summer barbecue once or twice. That type of event but I can't say I know him well."

"Being Kelly's line manager, presumably you fielded his call the other day, when he was trying to find out about Kelly's whereabouts."

"Yes, I did." He lowered his gaze to the desk in front of him momentarily but it was enough to pique Caslin's interest.

"He described you as not forthcoming with helpful information."

"Is that how he put it?" Alexander asked, his micro-expression giving away far more than he perhaps realised. Caslin fixed him with a stare, one that he clearly found uncomfortable. "To be honest, I don't have a lot of time for the man and at that point, I had no reason to believe that anything untoward had befallen Kelly. For all I knew, she may have…"

"May have what, Mr Alexander?" Caslin pressed.

"May have left him." The man appeared to feel awkward commenting on Kelly's personal life. "It was no secret amongst the team that Kelly had a somewhat trying marriage."

"Please could you define *a trying marriage?*"

"They were not without their problems and, quite often, Kelly was unable to leave them at the door when she pitched up to work, Inspector. God knows, anyone who's faced a marital breakup would understand how difficult that can be. Particularly when the spouse follows your member of staff into the office."

"Thomas Ryan would come here?" Hunter asked, surprised.

"Not quite, no. But he would often be chasing her, trying to pursue their… confrontations over the phone rather than allowing her the space to breathe."

"Was this behaviour recent?" Caslin asked.

"On and off for the past couple of years," Alexander explained, the forlorn expression returning. "I get the impression he's a man used to getting his own way and Kelly was no pushover, I assure you."

"I noticed you had a swipe card to get through into the back offices," Caslin said. Alexander nodded. "Do all members of staff have access cards?"

"Yes, they do."

"So, can you tell us the exact time when Kelly left the building?"

"I can do better than that, Inspector. I can tell you which door she went out of, whether she went on foot or in the car. Each access door has its own data point in our security system and the software logs not only date and time but also which point of entry or exit is used. Similarly, the underground car park has the same software and you need to swipe your access card to pass through the barrier."

"Her husband said he knew where Kelly parked and he tried to see if her car was still here on the night she disappeared."

"Well, we have extensive CCTV in the underground car park so I'm sure we will be able to tell you as much as we can. Marcus can walk you through the footage when you speak with him."

"Do you think we could do that now?" Caslin asked.

"Certainly. Please, come with me."

They stepped out of the office and turned right. Alexander led them down the corridor and into a stairwell, taking them up one floor. Entering a staff room, there was only one person present and it was obvious from his uniform that he was a member of security. He stood up as they approached, taking one last mouthful of coffee before placing the cup on the table in front of him and stepping forward.

"Mr Alexander," he said.

"Marcus, these are detectives Caslin and Hunter," Alexander said. "They want to speak to you about your conversation with Kelly two nights ago. I would be grateful if you could also walk them through our security system and give them any and all access to the camera footage that they require."

"I'd be happy to," Marcus replied, nodding a greeting to both of them and smiling, although Caslin felt it was slightly forced. Caslin and Hunter exchanged glances.

"We'll be in touch, if we need anything further from you, Mr Alexander. Feel free to carry on with your business," Caslin replied. He lingered, almost as if he was reticent to leave. Caslin judged him as curious, bordering on nosey. Turning back to the security guard, he said, "Maybe we can do this in your security office?"

"Yes, of course."

A short walk and two minutes later, Marcus unlocked the door to the security room. The space was cramped for the three of them. Marcus was a big man, easily over six feet tall and heavy set. During his time in the military, there was every possibility that much of his body mass would have been muscle. Now though, he was more flab. A number of monitors displayed split-screen footage from various points inside the building, as well as from those cameras mounted on the exterior. The footage appeared to be rotating through the predesignated routine and Caslin watched for a few seconds, taking into account the movements of staff and customers along with pedestrians passing by outside. From what he could make out there were four angles covering the underground car park.

"Tell me," Caslin began, "the car park, how do you get in and out?"

Marcus turned his attention to the footage. "There's only one entrance and exit and you have to swipe your card to raise the barrier to get in or out. It's a staff only car park."

"Did Kelly Ryan use the car park two nights ago?"

"Yes, she did. I spoke to her that evening as she was leaving work. She was just getting into the lift to take her down. When I came on shift, there were only a handful of cars parked downstairs and I recognised hers as being one of them."

"She definitely left in her car?" Hunter asked.

"I assume so," Marcus said. "But we can have a look. Just give me a second to bring up the footage." He sat down at his desk and started thundering away at the keyboard, searching for the relevant files.

"How did she seem the other night, when she left work?" Caslin asked.

Marcus glanced up, over his shoulder. "Quite normal, I must say. We didn't speak for long but she was the same as usual. Always friendly, willing to take the time and effort to speak to you. A lovely lady. Here it is."

They turned their attention to the monitor directly in front of Marcus's keyboard as he brought up the black and white footage from the night in question. Focussing on the cameras recording events in the underground car park, the screen was split four ways. They waited patiently as Marcus fast-forwarded through the footage until the time stamp hit 8 o'clock and then he pressed play. He pointed to the top right quarter of the screen, indicating that that was where they should focus. The camera was aimed at the elevators and when the time stamp read four minutes past the hour, the doors to the lift opened and a woman stepped out.

"That's Kelly," Marcus stated. They watched as she walked towards, and then beneath, the camera, disappearing from view. The security guard then pointed to the top left quadrant footage and she could be seen walking into view. She was alone in the parking level. Looking at the footage from the other three cameras, no one else appeared to be present in the car park.

"Which car is hers?" Caslin asked.

"That one there." He pointed to a BMW that was visible in the bottom left of the screen, on the lower level. Caslin now recognised the same car they'd seen in the clearing of the woods the day before. However, only the rear quarter panel of the car could be seen as a van was parked alongside, obscuring the view. They watched as she approached the vehicle. She appeared to pause as she reached the back of her car, staring at something not in the view of the camera due to the presence of the van.

"Is she talking to someone?" Hunter asked.

Caslin narrowed his eyes, trying to decipher as much as he could from the grainy footage. "It doesn't look like it." After a brief moment, she turned sideways and moved between the car and the van, disappearing from sight.

"I think the van's parked too close," Hunter suggested. "Wind that back, would you?"

"Sure," Marcus said, reaching forward and rewinding the footage. Pressing play once again, they watched and Hunter pointed out her thinking.

"You see, she turns sideways in order to squeeze down the gap between them. And look at the wheels of the van, how close they are to the edge of the bay."

"The van could be trying to avoid the support pillar on the offside," Marcus suggested, indicating the giant concrete pillar, one of many supporting the floors above.

"Whose van is that?" Caslin asked. Marcus shook his head to indicate he didn't know. "Do you have all employee vehicles on record?"

"Absolutely." The security guard paused the footage, then accessed another file and executed a search for the van's registration details. "What is that, a Transit?" he asked, trying to ascertain the make and model in order to narrow down the search. Caslin agreed. Moments later, Marcus turned to them and shook his head with a frown. "There's nothing registered to any employee."

"What about a visitor, maintenance perhaps?" Caslin asked.

"Give me a sec," Marcus said, resuming his search of the database. "No, nothing recorded that day."

"Okay, go back to the footage and roll it forward," Caslin said. They resumed playback. A couple of minutes after Kelly disappeared from view, the car reversed out of its parking bay with the rear of the BMW at the forefront of the camera footage. It then set off away from the current camera with the focus shifting to the last of the four displays, the one mounted alongside the exit. This camera was mounted on the exterior of the building and faced the nearside of the cars departing the underground car park. The BMW came into view, stopped at the barrier and an arm reached out in order to swipe the access card against the panel and the barrier was raised. The car then turned right onto the street outside and disappeared from view.

"Can you take that back a bit?" Caslin asked. "Back to where she reversed the car out of its bay." Marcus did so and once again, they watched the car's reversing lights come on as the BMW came into view. "Pause it there," Caslin said and Marcus did so. They peered at the footage.

"What are you looking for?" Hunter asked him.

"Can't see who's driving," Caslin said. "Go forward to when she leaves the car park." Marcus fast-forwarded to the point where the car came into view at the barrier and froze the frame.

"You still can't see," Hunter said. The positioning of the camera, as well as its viewing angle, made it impossible to get a shot of the face of the driver. The security guard edged the footage forward a few frames at a time but Kelly Ryan's face did not come into view. When she reached out with a pass card, Caslin tapped Marcus on the shoulder and he paused the playback.

"When she came out of the elevator, she was wearing her overcoat, wasn't she? What colour was it, grey?" Caslin asked.

"Not sure – but certainly light," Hunter agreed.

Caslin pointed at the footage frozen at the point of exit. "Unless she changed coats, she's not driving that car."

The arm extending from the driver's window was wearing a dark coloured coat and gloves. "You're right," Hunter said quietly.

Caslin placed a hand on Marcus's shoulder. "We're going to need to know the names of every single person who came in and out of the garage that day, and I want to know who was driving that van parked alongside Kelly Ryan's car."

CHAPTER NINE

CASLIN PUSHED OPEN the door to Dr Taylor's pathology lab and walked in. He held the door open as he looked across the room and realised the pathologist was still in the middle of her examination. Glancing across in his direction, she raised a hand and beckoned him to enter.

"You couldn't have timed your arrival any better, Nate," she said, as he approached. Alison Taylor lifted the splash visor that both protected her face from any bodily fluids and at the same time preserved the integrity of the body from any potential contamination. Taking a step back from the autopsy table, she smiled a greeting.

"I'm sorry," Caslin said. "I would have left my visit until later if I'd known you weren't done yet."

"I'm just finishing up, to be fair. You won't be surprised by the cause of death."

Caslin shook his head slowly, eyeing the damage to Kelly Ryan's face and head. Often, once a body was removed from the crime scene and processed through pathology, it would appear somewhat cleaner than it had done upon initial discovery. In this case, however, there was little improvement to be seen. The level of damage to her head was such that even a seasoned detective such as Caslin felt his stomach turn. "It was certainly a brutal way to go," he stated.

"You'll get no argument from me," Dr Taylor replied, removing her gloves by rolling them off over her hands and depositing them in a waste bin to await incineration. Picking up her notes from her desk she returned to where Kelly Ryan's naked body lay. Standing opposite Caslin, on the other side of the table, she flicked through her paperwork. "She suffered multiple blows to the head and face from heavy objects, with each being a different shape and size. It's quite clear to me that these injuries were sustained from a prolonged assault. The rocks and stones catalogued at the scene are your weapons."

"A medieval stoning," Caslin said, under his breath.

"So, it would seem. The victim suffered several sub-cranial haematomas, multiple lacerations and contusions, resulting in a dozen skull fractures, breaks to her jaw, nose and a dislocation of her right eye from its socket. Her right cheek also suffered several fractures that transferred almost from her ear to the nose."

Caslin let out a deep sigh. "Are there any other injuries besides having her right index finger removed?"

"You were there when Iain revealed that?"

Caslin nodded. "We're still to determine how she reached the scene, whether she was abducted and forced there or whether she went there of her own free will. We have CCTV footage of someone else driving her car away from her work place, which was also the last time she was seen alive. She's not visible in the car, so I'm leaning towards the former."

Dr Taylor scanned through her notes as she spoke. "There are two small marks, two inches apart, on the back of her neck where her head meets the shoulders. I'm inclined to think they're the result of a close contact Taser strike. That might answer part of your question."

"What about the removal of the finger?"

"That was done prior to burial. There is evidence of significant blood flow from the base of the finger that wouldn't be there had it been removed post-mortem. Her hands were clasped together and bound with a cable tie in such a way that the blood flowed over the other hand. That wouldn't have been the case were she already dead."

"Any evidence of resistance?"

"No. There are no defensive wounds or bruising that could imply she fought off an attacker at any point. The cable ties were used both on her wrists and ankles, and although there does appear to have been some damage to the skin tissue in those areas, most likely caused by her struggling to free herself, it would appear that didn't happen as much as you might think."

"What you mean by that?"

"If she spent a great deal of time struggling, I would expect there to be greater tissue degradation." She took her pen and leaned over, pointing out the areas she was referring to. "The ties have cut into her skin, most notably at the wrist but not so much at the ankles. This suggests that her legs were immobilised to a greater extent, and judging by the way she was buried in the ground, I think it suggestive that she was unconscious and awoke to find herself there. She wasn't buried standing up, her knees were bent and brought up almost to her waist."

"The killer didn't dig the hole deep enough," Caslin said. "He may not have had time or the inclination to do so."

"It's customary practice when carrying out the sentence of stoning for the victim to be buried before the act takes place. A man is buried up to his waist, whereas a woman is buried up to her shoulders," Dr Taylor explained.

"Why is that?"

"To protect her modesty, I believe," Dr Taylor said with a frown.

Caslin shook his head at the apparent irony of a desire to protect somebody's modesty alongside the barbaric brutalisation of the same body to the point of death.

"And yet it still goes on," Dr Taylor said. "But even the most religious of states tend to lean towards making the practice illegal even when turning a blind eye to its use in some regions."

"Iain Robertson said he would ask you to look further for any trace evidence. He was hopeful that you might find something for us to go on."

"Yes, indeed. I've sent her clothing to the CSI team for further analysis but I did find fibres underneath her fingernails. Iain is going to try and match those fibres either to the carpet of the floor of the car or the lining of the boot. Even a cursory check under the microscope shows me they're unlikely to be clothing fibres and more likely to come from the car."

"Is there any evidence of drug use either recreational or habitual?"

"As you asked, I did thoroughly inspect the body for any indication of needle marks and found none. I even looked for the hidden entry points for needles such as you find when someone is attempting to hide their abuse."

"Such as in between the toes, that type of thing?"

Dr Taylor nodded confirmation. "But as I said, there was nothing. I also carried out a full toxicology analysis on her system and that returned trace levels of alcohol but nothing significant. I think it's quite likely that she'd had a glass of wine at lunchtime. Or perhaps, she had ingested a smaller volume of alcohol at some point during the evening, based on the time it would have taken her body to process the alcoholic content and still be present in her system at the time of death."

"We have her leaving work shortly after eight, so what time do you judge she died?"

"Ian's liver test, taken at the scene, suggested a time between 11 o'clock and 1 AM. From my analysis, I think that's a pretty accurate timeframe and I don't think I can narrow it down any further."

Caslin did some mental arithmetic. If Kelly was abducted shortly after eight and died between eleven and one, that gave the killer a minimum of three hours to take her from the car park to where she was buried in the woods and then killed.

"Can I throw something else into your timeline to confuse things a little?"

"Sounds intriguing," Caslin said.

"Kelly Ryan had sex on the day of her death," Dr Taylor said, referring to her notes. "But I can't tell you when."

"Any indication of sexual assault?"

Alison shook her head. "There was certainly no damage in or around the vagina to imply the sex was not consensual. Likewise, there was no damage to her underwear or other clothing indicative of a forced removal. Therefore, I would conclude that it wasn't a result of a sexual assault but that doesn't mean that her killer wasn't the person who had sex with her. The method of her death, or should I say, her execution, because that's what it was, does imply a level of intimacy with the killer."

"It's a close-up crime, very brutal," Caslin agreed. "It does suggest a personal level of complexity, certainly."

"We spoke the other day about objectification and the killer's desire to have an ongoing intimate relationship with their victim."

"About them having unresolved trauma surrounding relationships?"

"That's right. The killer transfers those subconscious emotional frustrations onto their victims. In a case like this, I wouldn't be surprised for the killer to have had sex with the victim. Quite often that is post-mortem."

"That would explain no evidence of force being exerted on her," Caslin said flatly. "But then he got her dressed afterwards? That would be unusual. Did you retrieve any trace evidence that might point to who the sexual partner was?"

"Yes, I did. With the vaginal swab I've collected a strong semen sample and I anticipate a decent DNA profile will result from that. Also, I've been able to collect pubic hair that doesn't match the victim, being of a completely different hair colour, but I'll confirm that with the proper analysis. Either way, we will be able to run the profile through the database. If there isn't a match in the system, should you locate a suspect, I'm sure we will be able to rule them in or out."

Caslin was puzzled. In the two crime scenes, the killer appeared to be extremely methodical in his approach, leaving very little behind to enable him to be tracked or identified. There was every chance this was a mistake, Caslin expected him to make them but he sensed this killer was different to those he had met before.

"Do you think he won't make an error?" Dr Taylor asked, almost able to read his thoughts. "Even the most prolific of serial killers make mistakes somewhere along the line, even the most intelligent. Although, I agree, having unprotected sex with the victim would be quite an error in this day and age for one as meticulous as he seems."

"Well, let's hope it's the mistake that brings us to his door. You said you were just finishing up. Is there anything else I should know ahead of you producing your final report?"

"Oh, that's right, I almost forgot." She turned away and walked back to her desk. Plucking a fresh pair of gloves from a box on the desk, she returned to the autopsy table, dropping the visor back into place and putting on the gloves. "There was one more thing I was about to do when you arrived."

Caslin was intrigued. "Is it interesting?"

Dr Taylor met his eye as she bent over and picked up two of her instruments from a tray at the side of the body. "It looks as if there's something obstructing her airway and I was just going to remove it." With the tools of her trade in hand, Dr Taylor prised open Kelly Ryan's mouth until her jaw was slightly over an inch separated from the roof of the mouth. Caslin strained to see what might be inside but couldn't, resigning himself to watching as Alison Taylor reached into the mouth cavity with a pair of tweezers and deftly removed something from within. "Now that is certainly interesting," she said quietly.

"What is it?"

She brought the tweezers away from the mouth and placed the object in a stainless-steel bowl on the table. Caslin moved closer and inspected it. It was yellow vegetation, now tinged brown, and had the appearance of the ovule of a plant or flower. Returning to the mouth, moments later she produced several further pieces of detritus. Although degraded and decomposing, each one was a combination of pink and white, with the former most prominent on the outer edges but all were easily discernible as petals from a flower. Two minutes later, satisfied that everything present had been removed, she took off her gloves, discarded them to one side and removed her visor.

"Have you ever seen anything like that?"

Caslin flicked his eyes from the bowl to the pathologist and back again, examining the contents. "No, I can't say I ever have." Using the camera on his phone, he took a couple of shots of the petals.

Any further comment was cut off by Caslin's phone ringing.

"Sir, it's Hunter. There's been another video uploaded to the net."

"Not the bloody *Post* again?" Caslin asked, frustration creeping into his tone.

"No, not this time. This time, it's on social media and is already going viral. It's being shared like wildfire."

"What does it show?"

"Kelly Ryan's murder, sir. In graphic detail," Hunter explained. "I think this killer is definitely looking for attention."

"Well," Caslin said, casting a lingering look across the still form of Kelly Ryan, "he's certainly got mine."

CHAPTER TEN

THEY WATCHED in silence as the footage played out in front of them. ACC Broadfoot had joined the briefing at Caslin's request, so that he could see how the case was developing. The video was recorded on a mobile phone and therefore the footage was of relatively low quality. The footage was jumbled and bounced around a lot as the holder of the camera walked the scene in darkness. Only when the mobile was placed in one location and the car headlights turned on, were they able to see exactly what was going on.

In the beam of the headlights, they could make out Kelly Ryan, buried up to her neck a short distance away from the camera. Gaffer tape was visible across her mouth and it was obvious that she was conscious, if disorientated, as the first of the stones were thrown in her direction. Several missed their target but the fourth struck her. Several members of the team looked away at that point. In truth, no one wanted to be watching this footage but they all knew that even the slightest detail could provide the lead that could take them directly to her murderer. The five of them watched the grisly scene develop and listened to the gut-wrenching, terrifying sounds that were picked up through the microphone.

The video continued for what felt like an age but the time code denoted it was a little over seven minutes long. At the end, the battered, mutilated figure of Kelly Ryan slumped forward. The killer retrieved the mobile phone from its vantage point and crossed the clearing, keeping the victim firmly in shot. Standing before her, he zoomed in on Kelly's face drawing audible gasps from those watching back at Fulford Road. Then the footage faded out to be replaced by a black screen and the number two appeared. The numeral remained, dominating the screen, until it slowly faded back to black and the playback ceased.

"I've issued a press release," Broadfoot said, breaking the heavy silence. "Requesting that all media outlets do not replay this footage or use stills in their publications, on the grounds that this twisted individual is seeking media attention. The last thing we want to do is fuel his fetish any further."

"Do you think they'll listen?" Caslin asked.

Broadfoot inclined his head to one side, appearing thoughtful. "The reputable ones will but I fear the traditional media isn't going to be our problem."

"There's no chance of taking it down from the Internet, is there," DI Templer said. It was rhetorical. He was right. The video was across multiple social media platforms and had already been widely shared, with footage gaining traction in the prominent news stories of several countries abroad. Somewhere along the line, he had been entitled *The Night Stalker*. Such an emotive name would no doubt feed the imagination and potentially provide fuel to the fire of the media interest.

"What's the significance of the numbering?" Broadfoot asked, his eyes scanning the team in front of him.

"We've not got an answer for that yet, sir," Caslin replied. Their initial thoughts were disproved by the appearance of the second video release. "The number five was displayed on the first video, at the drug house. We considered that the four victims present plus the dealer who we now know is undercover officer, Ben Fowler, would total five, but it would appear it is not as simple as that."

"You mentioned something about the flower." Broadfoot's expression was focussed, displaying no emotion as he moved to the next point he wanted to address.

"Yes, sir," Caslin replied, standing up and crossing to a whiteboard mounted on the wall. "We managed to identify the bud of the flower that was deposited in the mouth of the second victim, Kelly Ryan. It's been identified as *Nelumbo nucifera*, the *Lotus Flower*. This is significant because one of these was left at the centre of the crime scene at Stamford Street, with the four deceased victims around it. Alison Taylor found similar lodged in the mouth of Kelly Ryan."

"And the significance is?" Broadfoot asked.

Caslin indicated for Terry Holt to pick up the narrative. "This particular species of lotus is sacred to both Hindus and Buddhists. Hindus revere it, with the divinities Vishnu and Lakshmi often portrayed sitting on a pink lotus in their religious iconography. The lotus is seen as the symbol of what is divine, or immortal, as well as inhumanity and is also a symbol of divine perfection. In *Tantric* and *Yogic* traditions, the lotus symbolises the potential of an individual to harness the flow of energy moving through the *chakras*. Whereas, in Buddhism, the lotus represents purity of the body, speech and the mind. It's a representation of purity floating above the dirty waters of material attachment and physical desire."

"Are we looking at some kind of religious fundamentalist here?" Broadfoot's expression remained unchanged but his tone was edged with concern.

"It's too early to reach for any conclusion like that, sir," Caslin argued. "We are still trying to make sense of this but the flower is somehow symbolic." He indicated for Holt to continue.

"The lotus flower has references in several religions of Southeast Asia, India, China and right the way through even to Christianity. All parts of the flower are edible and the seeds have often been used in Chinese herbal medicine. They still are today and the by-products of the production process are widely consumed in Asia, throughout the Americas and Oceania. That's largely due to the high content of physiologically active substances. The use of the plant and its seeds dates back 3000 years."

"We can't say for sure how this ties in but somewhere along the line, one or more of these belief systems must come into play," Caslin said.

"Right, I need to make a statement to the press." Broadfoot stood up, he was tense, Caslin could tell. "This has suddenly become far higher profile than the deaths of a handful of junkies. I will need some answers on this, and I'm going to need them soon."

"We'll keep at it, sir," Caslin replied.

Broadfoot excused himself and as he passed out of the room, a uniformed sergeant poked his head around the door frame, immediately taken aback by the senior officer stepping in front of him. He addressed Broadfoot politely, who nodded in acknowledgement but continued on his way without another word.

"Caslin," the sergeant said, grabbing his attention. "You have a visitor downstairs."

"Who is it?"

"Michelle Cates."

Caslin flicked his eyebrows in Hunter's direction to signify the name meant nothing to him. "See if you can figure out where that video was uploaded from and also, if we can get anything from the footage that might indicate who this guy is." In response to a question that he knew was about to be asked, he added, "I know it's a long shot. I reckon he's covered his tracks again but you never know."

Leaving the team to get on with their tasks, Caslin made his way downstairs to the front office. Passing through the secure door into the foyer, he looked around. There were two people standing at the counter speaking to the civilian clerk, Simon, and they paid him no attention whatsoever. An elderly man was seated in the corner. His eyes were drawn to a woman who noted his arrival. Catching him scanning the people present, she stood up and tentatively approached him.

"Inspector Caslin?" she asked, raising her eyebrows in a way that belied her uncertainty.

"Yes, I am," he replied. She smiled and something about her demeanour lightened the darkness that this case found him wading through. Although certain they had never met, he felt a warmth towards her, a familiarity, but where that stemmed from, he had no idea. She was attractive to him, instantly he brought himself upright and almost as quickly he realised the impact of her impact on him. A flush of red crossed over him. That was unsettling. "I don't believe we've met." He was hopeful that he was right, the fear of embarrassment leapt into his mind.

She shook her head, broadening her smile. For a moment, he was lost as he took in her appearance and then remembered where he was. "I was hoping I could speak with you, Inspector," she said. "I'm Michelle Cates. My brother is Thomas Ryan."

Caslin felt a slight stab in his chest as he was brought back to reality with a bump. "Oh… I see. Of course, please come this way." He led her to the family room on the edge of the reception. Knocking on the door just in case it was occupied, he waited until there was no response and then opened it. As expected, there was no one inside and he held the door open for her.

Pulling out a chair, he offered it to her and she sat down. Caslin went to the other side of the table and took a seat opposite.

"What can I do for you, Mrs Cates?"

"Miss Cates." She corrected him before waving away his apology just as he started to utter it. "I'm worried about Thomas," she said. "About his state of mind. He told me about your conversation with him and, although I don't doubt he misconstrued some of the narrative. I'm concerned about the impression he may have left you with."

"Concerned? In what way?" Caslin was confused.

"Thomas and Kelly had their problems." She lowered her voice as if she was betraying a confidence. "Neither of them is without fault but... Thomas would never harm Kelly. He loves her. Probably too much for either of them, if the truth be known."

"What do you mean by that?"

"I don't wish to... I'm in an awkward position here, Inspector." Her head dropped as she spoke. "I wouldn't like to betray a confidence and if I do, it will leave me in something of a predicament in the relationship with my brother."

"Your sister-in-law is dead, Miss Cates. She's been murdered and if there's anything you think I should know, then you ought to tell me."

She raised her head and met Caslin's gaze. "The confidence isn't the issue, really," she replied. Caslin sensed her reticence. "You see, Kelly and I were close. She was immensely supportive during the breakup of my marriage and I've tried my hardest to reciprocate in the last year or two."

Caslin nodded in a manner designed to put her at ease. At the same time, he observed her wringing her hands across the table, noting the absence of a wedding ring. "Please, go on."

"I think there's a possibility that Kelly was having an affair." She glanced up and away from Caslin, flicking her eyes nervously around the room as if to merely voice the suggestion was tantamount to betrayal. "In fact, I'm almost certain of it."

"Did Kelly talk about this with you?"

After a moment, she nodded slowly. "Yes, she mentioned it."

Caslin understood her situation. If Thomas was unaware, although clearly, he had his suspicions, then his sister knowing but not telling him would damage the trust in their relationship. "Did she tell you who the affair was with?"

Michelle Cates shook her head. "No, she never gave me any details. I don't even know how serious it was. It may have just been a casual thing and could have ended by now. I don't know."

"What did she tell you about him?"

"Nothing much. Just that it was a lot of fun and she hadn't felt so alive in years."

"Did your brother know?"

She shook her head. "Probably sounds strange, doesn't it? That I knew my sister-in-law was cheating on my brother but I didn't tell him."

"A little." Caslin was honest.

"I love my brother, Inspector. I also accept that he can be… difficult to live with."

"Difficult, how?"

"They are both… strong characters. They each like to have their own way and there was always an undercurrent of a power struggle within their relationship from day one." She shook her head slowly. "They're both career minded people and to get as far as they both have, you need to have a degree of single-mindedness, to be fair."

"You said they had problems?"

"Thomas has always been fixated on two things in his life. First, he wanted to have a successful career, which he has certainly achieved. Secondly, he wanted a family. Unfortunately, he sees that as something of a failure in his life."

"They couldn't have children or Kelly didn't want them?"

"No, not at all. She wanted a family just as much as he did but you're right, she couldn't have children. It was a source of intense friction between them. Almost constant. They tried IVF but that failed and then they discussed adoption but neither of them could agree on a path forward. As much as I hate to say it, Thomas was… perhaps too hard on Kelly and that's why I have so much sympathy for her… as I did for her."

Caslin could understand how much pressure that situation could place a couple under. The years of trying for a baby, followed by the medical tests, experimentation, all ending up with nothing for their efforts aside from the mental anguish of accepting what they desired was not achievable. A sense of hollow loss, all that remained. "Forgive me for asking this, Miss Cates."

"Please, call me Michelle."

"Forgive me. Was your brother ever violent towards Kelly?"

"No, never!" She was emphatic and apparently unfazed about him asking the question. "Thomas is an awkward bugger but he is not violent, never has been."

"I'm sorry, I had to ask."

"That's okay, Inspector. I understand."

"As far as you're aware, was Kelly ever a recreational drug user or in and around people who moved in those circles?"

Michelle Cates laughed. He liked the sound of it. "Kelly worked in the banking sector. I should imagine that recreational drug use was rife among many of her colleagues, but as for Kelly, no. Not as far as I'm aware and believe me, I would be aware."

"Did she have any hobbies that you are aware of? I'm thinking that with a highly pressurised job, if she were to be having extramarital relations then it would most likely be either with someone sharing a mutual interest or a colleague."

"No, Kelly didn't really have hobbies. She wasn't sporty and didn't really mix with people outside of those she worked with. So, I would expect you to have the most joy looking there."

Caslin took out one of his contact cards and passed it across the table to her. She took it willingly and read the details. "If you need anything, my contact numbers are on there and even if I'm not available when you call, I will call you back. Likewise, if you think of anything else that you feel I ought to know, then I'd appreciate you being just as candid with me as you've been today."

"I will, thank you," she replied, smiling and standing up. Caslin followed suit. Moving across to the door, he grasped the handle to open it and see her out. Assessing her body language as she put on her coat and picked up her handbag, Caslin thought it looked as if a great weight had been lifted by her revelations.

"At some point, your brother might need to know this information," Caslin said almost apologetically.

She nodded. "I'll be the one who tells him. I'm very much afraid that he will hate me for it, and some might argue that would be justifiably so."

"Perhaps," Caslin said. "But he will need people around him who care in the coming months. He'll come around."

"Thank you for taking the time to see me, Inspector," Michelle replied, placing an affectionate hand on his forearm. "I appreciate it."

"I meant what I said. Please call me if you need to."

She smiled again and Caslin opened the door. Leaving without another word, Caslin watched as Michelle Cates crossed the reception foyer and stepped out into the steady rainfall outside. She glanced back over her shoulder. If she noticed his attention, then she didn't offer a reaction, merely fastening her coat and descending the steps towards the car park.

Caslin watched her for a moment longer before heading back upstairs, all the while considering how in this job, he met people he liked in the most random of circumstances.

CHAPTER ELEVEN

ENTERING THE OPS ROOM, Caslin summoned the team together for a briefing. They were diligently gathering and filtering all the relevant data from the previous twenty-four hours in an attempt to build a timeline, not only for the movements of Kelly Ryan but also trying to find a crossover with the deaths at Stamford Street.

"Terry, talk to me about Kelly Ryan's place of work," Caslin instructed him.

"Security has been very helpful. They've sent us all of the CCTV footage from Kelly's last day at work, recording everything in the underground car park along with the footage from the cameras showing who entered and left the building on foot."

"Did you go over the abduction again?" Caslin asked.

"We did. Craig and I reviewed it together," Holt referred to DI Templer.

"However, we came to the same conclusion as you did," Templer said. "You can't make out the actual abduction because the van parked alongside her car obscures the camera footage. My guess would be he was waiting inside the van, parked it so close to her car in order for it to be a distraction. When she squeezes down between the two vehicles, he slides open the side door grabs her, pulls her into the van and immobilises her in some way."

"Alison Taylor believes she was stunned with a Taser," Caslin said.

"That figures." Templer nodded his agreement. "For him to have incapacitated her, bundled her into the car and out of sight before reversing out as quickly as he did in the footage, she must have been rendered unconscious in pretty quick time."

"It's quite a brazen attack," Hunter stated. "I mean, it's one thing to hit someone in a public car park with multiple entrance and exit points, but to do so in a controlled space on private property is risky."

"I'd hazard a guess, he had already worked out where the security camera was but that covers the abduction," Caslin said. "You're right, it is a risky move on his part. He still needed to enter the car park in the van. Have you made any headway with that?"

Holt nodded. "The transit van enters the car park at half past seven, driving around slowly before pulling in alongside Ryan's car." Templer tapped away at his keyboard and then gestured towards the projector screen. Seconds later, footage from the camera mounted at the entrance appeared.

"Here it is arriving," Templer stated. The van turned off of the main road and pulled up at the barriers. Despite the camera mounted above and giving a direct shot of the interior cabin, the driver inside was still masked in shadow. The driver was dressed all in black with not only a heavy overcoat and gloves but his face and head were covered with a balaclava.

"Damn it," Caslin muttered under his breath.

"Yeah, he certainly knew about the cameras," Templer agreed with Caslin's sentiment.

"What about the index?"

"No joy there. He switched the plates. These belong to a Vauxhall Corsa, registered in Plymouth. Forensics have been through it. The interior is wiped clean, so no use to us there." Caslin was disappointed but that would be an obvious error for the abductor to make. "But this is where it does get interesting." Templer pointed back to the footage as the driver lowered his window and reached out to press something against the security panel. Withdrawing it, the barrier lifted and he was able to drive forward, down the ramp and into the car park.

"He had an access card," Caslin said.

"It gets better than that," Holt said excitedly. "You will note the time stamp on the camera when the van entered, 7:31 PM. We were able to balance that timeframe with the recorded entries of people entering and exiting the building and we know whose access card was used."

"Excellent," Caslin said. "Who was it?"

"That's where the puzzle gets more complicated," Templer said. "The driver of the van used Kelly Ryan's access card."

That information threw Caslin for a moment. "Have you checked whether she reported hers lost or stolen?"

Holt shook his head. "I spoke with her boss, Simon Alexander, and he said there was no record of her reporting the loss of her card. He went so far as to check with security as well as the department who issue new or replacement cards, and they confirmed that nothing had been reported missing."

"What's more," Templer continued, "we checked whether Kelly used her own card that day and she did, entering the building just after 8 o'clock in the morning. In this scenario, if Kelly's card wasn't stolen or lost, then we must be looking at someone who has cloned her card in the days, weeks, or months leading up to her abduction."

"Then we have another line of inquiry," Caslin said. The killer must either be known to her or else she had some kind of contact with her abductor recently. They couldn't rule out the possibility that she may have been having a sexual relationship with someone, possibly even her killer. Alison Taylor told him Kelly Ryan had sexual intercourse with somebody on the day of her death and the revelation of an extramarital relationship in the recent past, confirmed by Michelle Cates, tempted him to think they were one and the same person. "We need to get into this woman's life and find out where she's been going as well as who she's been seeing. Did you have any luck tracing the second upload?"

"No. He used the same virtual private network to hide his location," Holt said. "This guy is pretty good at covering his tracks."

"It's easier to do when you're faceless and hiding behind technological barriers," Caslin stated, "but once you start factoring in building relationships with people or coming into contact with them it becomes a damn sight harder to maintain your anonymity. Somehow, if the bank's data is correct, he got close enough to Kelly Ryan to not only get access to her card but also to clone it and put it back without her being any the wiser as far as we know."

"Unless of course, the killer also works at the bank," Hunter suggested. "A bank insider could possibly get hold of her access card or necessary details in order to produce a copy, and there's every possibility no one would realise."

Caslin thought on it. There was a logic to that theory but how that factored into the murders at the drug house in Stamford Street, he couldn't figure. "Let's keep an open mind on that. Go back to Simon Alexander and produce a list of employees with as much information as we can get from him. Then, start working through the names and try and see how they interact with Kelly, her personal and professional life. Make sure we expand the list beyond just her team but include anyone who would have the capability or access to the data required. This includes our helpful security guard."

"I'll get on it," Hunter said.

"Terry," Caslin turned to the DC. "I want you to go through Kelly Ryan's personal digital footprint. Mobile phones, emails, financials and see if anything stands out."

"Are we looking for anything specific, sir?"

"Look for anything abnormal but bear in mind she's been having something of a casual fling somewhere along the line. That may still be ongoing or it may have fizzled out, we don't really know. But if we're looking for someone who had close enough access to her possessions to bypass the security at the bank, it's fair to assume that someone participating in an adulterous affair would fit the bill. She's managed to keep this from a husband for quite some time despite his obvious suspicions. The links may not be obvious but they will be there. Don't underestimate her ability to conceal what she's been up to."

"Our killer's decided that these junkies and Kelly Ryan's death should be tied together," Templer said as Hunter and Holt set about their new tasks, leaving the two senior detectives alone. "By making a call to the emergency services from the scene of Kelly Ryan's murder, on Fowler's phone, he guaranteed that we would not only find her pretty quickly but also there would be a direct link between the two crime scenes."

"How did you find out about the house in Stamford Street?" Caslin asked. "Did you have someone with eyes on Fowler?"

Templer shook his head. "No, Fowler was pretty much a kite. You know, we didn't have any string attached to him. It was far too risky, hence why he had to be so careful about when he recorded anyone covertly. To have a permanent watch on him… now, there's no way that would have flown."

"Did he miss a check in?"

"No, we hadn't been out of contact that long. The call came in to North Yorkshire's tip line and obviously we have the address flagged, so it came straight down the network to us."

"Who called in the tip?"

"It was anonymous. If I recall correctly, they said they thought a burglary was in progress and that the residents were home with young children."

"Clever boy," Caslin said quietly. "That would ensure an immediate response with regard to the safety of the family. He's no doubt disguised his voice but let's get a hold of the recording and run it through some analysis just in case it reveals anything."

"Will do. He wanted them to be found," Templer said quietly. "This guy is crazy."

"I don't doubt that but I think there's more to it," Caslin said sitting forward and forming a tent with his fingers beneath his chin. "Tell me, how many serial killers have you investigated? It's not a trick question, I'm curious."

"None. This is my first."

"In my experience, most serial killers kill because they can't control their urge to do so but in every case I've come across, it was the urge to kill that either gave them the thrill or at the very least satisfied their desire, if only for a short while. This guy is different in that he wants us to see what he's doing. He wants us to know what he's getting away with and is trying to send us a message."

"How do you know?"

"The flower. The Lotus," Caslin said pulling the file towards him containing the crime scene photographs. He leafed through the folder and took out the relevant shots depicting the lotus flower on the coffee table at the drug house, in Stamford Street, and also the pictures from Alison Taylor's pathology lab that he photographed before leaving that morning. "He's placed these at both scenes which is another way of tying the two together. This, plus the numbering and the videos, is telling us something."

"It tells us this guy's a crazy son of a bitch," Templer stated, scanning the pictures in front of them.

"Calculating, dangerous son of a bitch," Caslin added. "And I'm telling you now there will be more to come. This guy is two or three moves ahead of us and unless we catch up fast, the body count is only going to increase."

"Presume, just for a moment, that he doesn't know Kelly Ryan. For instance, he's not her lover," Templer argued. "How we can get to him if there is no direct link. Don't get me wrong, I think every line of inquiry we're pursuing is legitimate but if this guy's as calculating as we think then we need to draw him out."

"I'm open to suggestions as to how we do that."

"He wants our attention?" Templer asked. Caslin nodded his agreement. "Well, if he wants our attention, then maybe we should give it to him. He sent the first video to the press to get the story out. The second, he uploaded himself because he knew everybody was going to be looking for it. Now he's got the eyes of the country, if not the world, focussed on him but he's achieved it on his terms. How about we put the spotlight on him through our lens rather than his?"

"Yeah, what are you talking about?"

"He's probably revelling in this *Night Stalker* name the press has saddled him with, it's kind of catchy. How about we get something out in the media that he might not like? Perhaps you could have a word with your friend, the one who works at *The Post*?"

Caslin sat back in his chair allowing Templer's suggestion to filter through his mind. "You mean play to his narcissism?"

"Exactly," Templer said, grinning. "But just imagine how he'll react if we don't talk about his genius and creativity and merely point out what a sad loser he is? We have to make him angry. It may well poke a reaction. I'll wager he won't be able to resist pushing back."

"Risky strategy. The reaction is unpredictable. It could be strong and escalate matters."

"He's already killed five people with an undercover officer unaccounted for. How much worse can it get?" Templer countered. "Besides, the reaction might lead to a mistake."

"An interesting idea," Caslin said, mulling it over. "You have experience of this sort of approach?"

"I read criminology for my Masters Degree," Templer explained. "Believe me, it's a sound strategy."

"Who do you think we should use to bait him? After all, that's what you're suggesting we do."

"I think you should do it."

"You're probably better qualified," Caslin argued, willing to defer to his colleague's wider knowledge and experience of psychology.

"We're looking to rile him. I hardly know you, Caslin, but I've not met anyone more naturally gifted at getting up someone's nose than you." Caslin was about to object but noted Hunter stifling a grin in the background, whereas Terry Holt erupted into laughter.

"Thanks very much… team," Caslin replied, shaking his head and splitting a grin of his own.

"You've got to admit, he has nailed you in two days," Hunter said, returning her eyes to the computer screen in front of her.

"Comments like that will not get you a pay rise, Sergeant," he replied. "I meant to ask, where did we get to in running down the victims from Stamford Street? Anyone revealing connections to either Ryan or your investigation and Detective Fowler?"

"No, as far as we've been able to ascertain, they were all customers. None of them are known elements of the network Fowler infiltrated. They all have criminal records in one form or another. Petty crimes – shoplifting, theft, burglary and a couple of convictions for fraud. Nothing high level. We're still running down known associates but we'll need to draw some manpower as it's a lot of ground to cover."

"I'll have a word with Broadfoot, extra resources won't be an issue," Caslin replied.

"Are you going to run it by him?" Templer asked.

"Our plan to flush him out?" Caslin clarified. Templer nodded. He shook his head. "Broadfoot's far too cautious to approve that. Better that we do it and I justify it afterwards."

"Yeah, somehow I figured you'd say something like that."

CHAPTER TWELVE

THE TWO CAMERAS were making him feel self-conscious. Despite the recording having already taken almost half an hour, Caslin hadn't settled in to the process at all. That didn't surprise him. Many years ago, he had had his brush with fame among the media circles. Initially, the attention had massaged his already exaggerated ego but when the attention spiralled into notoriety, as the case went bad, what had once left him with a sense of achievement, now tasted bitter. Since that day, Caslin chose to defer the spotlight, allowing it to pass on to colleagues whilst he took a backseat and got on with his job. Attention was neither sought nor desired. However, on this occasion, he had to put himself back at the centre of the media scrum, but at least it wasn't for anything so trivial as vanity or kudos. This time, he was trying to entrap a dangerous and brutal killer.

"What type of person are you dealing with here?" Jimmy Sullivan asked. This was the portion of the interview that the entire event was engineered to bring them to. Previously, they skirted around the investigation, the set up regarding the number of officers involved as well as the details of each crime scene, the most gruesome of which were not up for discussion. The format was well agreed in advance between the investigative team and the editorial team of the paper. The subject matter, the line of questioning, down to the very detail of the tone of the interview, had been well choreographed to reach this point, ensuring as much as possible that the interview didn't appear a total concoction. After all, the exchange had to be realistic for two reasons, not least to guarantee the newspaper's willingness to take part but also, perhaps more importantly, in order to fulfil the entire object of the exercise and draw their killer out of the shadows.

"This person wants to be seen as something special," Caslin said flatly, turning his head and speaking directly to camera. "He has the nagging desire to be recognised, to be seen as some kind of macabre genius. Perhaps even to be revered at the same time as being feared."

"Is this how you see him?"

"No," Caslin stated emphatically, shaking his head, his lips parting into a half-smile. "This man is none of these things. My experience, along with the psychological assessment of several experts that I've discussed the case with, leads me to the certainty that what we are dealing with is a very warped individual indeed. Now, we are not sure what life events would have led him to become so twisted but it's most likely we're looking for an inadequate person who is of below-average or limited intelligence."

"And where do you think he fits into society?" Sullivan asked.

"I should imagine he's one of two types of people. Either he's drifted from one job to the next and never managed to stick at anything past the point where he was found wanting by those around him," Caslin suggested. "Or he's one of these guys, we've all met them, who spend a lifetime in one role, barely ever managing to be promoted but at the same time irritating all of their work colleagues by suggesting everything would run a lot better if only he was put in charge, fostering a grievance against all those who move up the chain."

"Yes, we all know those," Sullivan said with a chuckle. "So, you see in this quite a weak character?"

"Weak? I would say so, yes. Regarding his character, he may well be someone his friends, if he has any, and neighbours think they can trust but scratch the surface and you will almost certainly find an individual who you wouldn't want to spend more than ten minutes in the company of, standing alongside the staff room coffee machine."

"What about his personality?"

Caslin shook his head. "A distinct lack of charisma, would be my guess and believe me, I've been in this job long enough to know the type of person I'm looking for."

"I know you won't be able to give us exact details regarding an active case, Inspector Caslin," Sullivan said, following the script. "But how close are you to putting a name to this killer?"

Caslin shifted his gaze towards the camera off to his right, once again, staring straight at the lens. "I can assure you and everyone watching that we have active lines of inquiry and we are not far off. The net is tightening and this killer will be off the streets soon enough, I give you my word."

"That almost sounds like a promise, Inspector."

Caslin held his line of sight in the direction of the camera. "We're closer than he thinks. He is arrogant, narcissistic and thinks he's got the better of us. The truth is, he couldn't be more wrong."

Sullivan wrapped up the interview there and then, and the cameras stopped recording. Unhooking the microphone clipped to his shirt, Caslin drew the cable out and passed the equipment to the sound engineer who accepted gratefully. Having made the decision to try and draw a reaction from the killer, at the suggestion of Sullivan's editor, they went for more than just an interview to be published in the following day's paper. By recording the exchange on camera, they would be able to put it up almost immediately on the paper's website giving maximum opportunity for it to be widely distributed.

"I think that went well," Sullivan said smiling. Despite the interview being something of a ruse, it was still a fact that the paper was obtaining a significant scoop. Once the case played out, their role in catching the killer would give them another angle for them to write about in the copy, not to mention the attention and focus that would be brought the paper's way by airing the interview in the first place. A raising of the publication's profile would have the knock-on effect of higher advertising revenues, so from a purely economic point of view, the paper couldn't lose.

"Let's hope it has the desired effect," Caslin said, watching the dismantling of the equipment and it being packed away. "You missed your calling, Jimmy. I could see you hosting *Question Time* or perhaps some regional news programme on an obscure cable channel, in the early hours of the morning."

"High praise indeed," Sullivan replied broadening his smile into a grin. "You never made that pint the other day. How about later?"

Caslin shook his head. "I'll see how it goes with all this." He waved his hand in a circular motion, indicating the cameras. "But I doubt it."

"Okay but you know where I'll be if you change your mind."

Opening the door to the media room of Fulford Road Station, usually set aside for large press conferences, Caslin was met by Craig Templer. He was present during the interview but upon receipt of a phone call stepped out of the room.

"That was going well as I left," he said to Caslin, falling into step alongside him.

"I thought so."

"Broadfoot got wind of it," Templer said. "He wants a word with you upstairs."

"Is he putting the brakes on it?"

"Not sure. I imagine if he had already made up his mind, he would have shut it down immediately," Templer argued. "The fact that he wants to see you… got to be a good sign."

Minutes later, Caslin approached Broadfoot's office. His personal assistant smiled as he approached, picking up the receiver on the desk before her. Presumably she was calling through to announce his anticipated arrival and by the time he reached the desk she was already ushering him through. Entering the office, ACC Broadfoot was standing behind his desk with his back to the door and looking out of the window. From his vantage point on the top floor, the view across the centre of York was striking. The overcast skies of the previous days had cleared that afternoon and now the sun was setting, bathing the city in soft yellow light. Caslin reached the centre of the room, coming before his superior's desk. He waited.

Broadfoot took a deep breath but remained where he stood, transfixed on the view. "This is a very dangerous approach you are taking, Nathaniel."

"It's a calculated risk, I'll grant you."

"An approach that could well blow up in our face," Broadfoot said, turning to face him. His expression was controlled and his tone measured, but the underlying concern was clear to see.

"I know this isn't standard procedure, sir," Caslin said. Broadfoot inclined his head in agreement. "But this case is different. This killer is different. If we going to end this before it gets bloodier, then we need to get ahead of him rather than be where we are."

"We've been here before though, Nathaniel," Broadfoot countered. "This is not the first serial killer you've investigated."

"No, sir, you're right but the others have always lived in the shadows. They didn't seek the limelight, they didn't want to be known. They satisfied their urges and then moved on. This guy wants the opposite. He wants everyone talking about him and he wants us to be fearful of him… and I believe, he craves our respect. This interview is all about drawing him out."

"You're goading him," Broadfoot said. Caslin didn't disagree.

"Yes, I am. Absolutely," he replied. "This is someone who is randomly picking his victims off the street as and when the opportunity arises. He's planning this, meticulously. No matter how intelligent they are, these types of killers will always make a mistake at some point, but I don't want us to pick up his mistake in two, three… four years' time and catch him then. I want to force him into making a mistake now."

Broadfoot crossed his arms in front of him and brought his left hand up to his chin, stroking it whilst thinking through Caslin's logic. "In that case, I'll make a call and let's see if we can broaden your message."

Caslin left the office as Broadfoot reached out to his own high profile media contacts. Any prospect of meeting Jimmy Sullivan for a pint at Lendal's was forgotten as an interview for the evening television news was hastily arranged.

LEAVING THE TELEVISION STUDIO, Caslin had lost all track of the time. The completely unfamiliar environment of visiting the make-up department, the green room as well as discussions with various producers and other members of the studio team, whose roles Caslin could only guess at, had taken their toll. Entering the building in the fading sunlight of the late afternoon, he now emerged into the artificially lit city centre, under the cover of darkness. He considered going for a late-night drink but in all honesty, fatigue was catching up with him. Deciding to skip the nightcap, he set off for his apartment in Kleiser's Court.

Feeling his phone vibrating in his pocket, his first thought was that the traffic noise was drowning out the ringing but then he remembered the production team had asked him to silence his phone just in case it rang whilst he was on air. Reaching into his pocket, he drew it out and glanced at the screen. The number was displayed but was not one he recognised.

"DI Caslin," he announced.

"Hello, Inspector," a female voice said. It was one that sounded familiar to him but he couldn't place it. "It's Michelle Cates."

"Miss Cates," Caslin acknowledged her, surprised to find her calling him. "What can I do for you?"

"I'm sorry to trouble you, Inspector, particularly so late," she said, sounding genuinely apologetic. "But you did say to call if I needed to."

"And I meant it. How can I help?"

"You're probably going to think I'm mad," she said. "But I saw you on the television and what you were saying about… the man who… killed Kelly and I'm… frightened."

"I appreciate why you would be but—"

"No, you don't understand, Inspector." She interrupted him. Whereas her tone initially was contrite, now it switched to assertive. It was as if she had something burning inside of her that she wanted to get out. "Earlier, I thought there was someone outside my house. In the garden. It's a secure space. The boundary wall is five feet high and for someone to be there, they would… they can't just walk in. It wasn't just me, my daughter saw him too. What if it's him?"

"Did you call the police?" Caslin asked, concerned. He had no reason to doubt what she had seen and under the circumstances, her anxiety levels were justifiably high.

"I did, yes and the operator advised me they would send a patrol car through the area as soon as they could but in the meantime, we should stay in the house and keep the doors and windows locked."

Caslin checked the time. Responding to a possible prowler wouldn't be considered a high priority if there were more pressing incidents, particularly if the threat was considered vague. "Okay, Miss Cates," Caslin said reassuringly, "I'm going to make a call and have a uniformed car come to your address as soon as possible. I want you to follow the operator's advice and stay in the house. Can you give me the address please?" She told him where she lived with her daughter and he realised he was only a short walk away. The address was only a minor detour from his route home. He looked at his watch. "I'm actually nearby. So, I could also stop by myself, if that's okay?"

"Thank you, Inspector. That's very kind. If it's not too much trouble?" Her reply sounded genuine, both surprised and relieved in equal measure.

"I'll be with you in about ten minutes," he said, reassuring her, "and please, try not to worry."

CHAPTER THIRTEEN

It was probably closer to fifteen minutes by the time Caslin mounted the steps to the home of Michelle Cates. Taking hold of the door knocker he rapped it twice and waited. Looking over his shoulder behind him, the river Ouse flowed past only a stone's throw away. The residence was one of the Georgian townhouses, built on the quayside, and directly opposite the old merchant warehouses on the river bank opposite. These had long since been converted into prestigious residential apartments but the exteriors still tipped their hat to their industrial heritage.

He didn't have long to wait before the door opened and he was met by a rather agitated Michelle Cates. "Thank you for coming so quickly." She opened the door wider and invited him in. "I'm starting to think my paranoia got the better of me and I'm wasting your time."

"It's no trouble, honestly," Caslin said, smiling. "The old saying of better to be safe than sorry still applies."

She led him further into the house and through into an open-plan kitchen and dining area. The original building was tall and narrow, being made up of four storeys including the basement area, which was at the level of the quay. The residential floors were elevated in order to mitigate the damage in the event of the river bursting its banks which did happen from time-to-time, flooding parts of the city centre. The room they were in now was a modern addition of contemporary glass and aluminium construction in stark juxtaposition to the traditional building materials.

"I was sure I saw someone out there," Michelle said, indicating the garden beyond the curtain wall of glass. Caslin moved past her and approached the door. Much of the garden was shrouded in darkness due to the established foliage and the presence of centuries-old trees. The interior lighting also made it difficult to make out the details outside. The property was an end terrace. Beyond the gable end were the *Tower Gardens*, named after the nearby *Clifford Tower*, a medieval tourist attraction. The light pollution from the city centre did help a little. The orange glow of the street lighting penetrated part of the garden. He eyed the locking mechanism and glanced back to her. "Yes, it's locked," she said in response to the look he gave her.

"I'll have a look around." Caslin opened the door. Immediately, the sounds of the city at night could be heard, the traffic passing by and the occasional shout. "Lock the door behind me, just in case." She nodded and approached as he stepped out into the darkness. The door closed behind him, the sound of the lock engaging as Michelle did as he requested. Looking around, there was nothing that jumped out at him that was untoward. The boundary wall was brick, solid and well maintained as far as he could see. Walking forward, his eyes began to adjust to their surroundings and he listened acutely in order to try to distinguish between the night-time sounds of the city and anything that might be close by.

Aware that the mind could play tricks in the darkness, Caslin tried to tune out the natural response of seeing danger in every shadow and the rustle of the wind through every branch. Locating the gated access to the garden at the rear of the property, Caslin found it secured with a slide bolt. There was no evidence that it had been open recently but when he tested it, he found it moved with ease. Located at the top, it was conceivable that if someone lifted themselves up onto the wall alongside it, they could have reached over and unlocked the gate from the outside. Similarly, although the wall was solid it was topped with curved brick, an attractive detail but hardly a deterrent or barrier to someone seeking entry.

The cultivated borders were a mixture of small and large plants. Moving some of the larger ones aside with his arm, Caslin found he could step through and place himself between the boundary wall and the bushes. Moving around the garden, he found several vantage points where he could stand quite comfortably, giving him an unobstructed view towards the house, confident that he wouldn't be seen by those within. The third of these locations, he thought would be the most likely place that a would-be prowler, or burglar, might observe from. Caslin's torch was in the boot of his car, so he took out his phone and activated the torch, illuminating the surrounding area.

Searching for footprints left in the mud or signs of recently broken branches in the surrounding plants, Caslin spied three cigarette butts at his feet. Dropping to his haunches, he eyed them more closely. Having been a heavy smoker for many years previously, he thought they looked as if they'd been thrown there recently. Discarded cigarette butts, exposed to the elements for a significant period of time, took on a different appearance. Taking a tissue out of his pocket, Caslin picked one up, examining it in the palm of his hand. Bringing his light to bear, he thought it could have been recently smoked. Discarding the butt to the floor, he put the tissue back in his coat pocket.

With one last glance towards the house, he watched Michelle inside her kitchen busying herself tidying up. Although he found nothing to indicate she was in immediate danger, he was perturbed by his own thoughts and feelings. Had she imagined it? Despite the acknowledgement of the tricks his senses might be playing, his instinct suggested he shouldn't dismiss her concerns. Brushing aside the bushes in front of him, he stepped back out onto the lawn and returned to the house. Upon reaching the door, Michelle noticed and crossed over to unlock it, allowing him to come inside.

"Did you find anything?" Something in her tone told him she was fearful of the answer.

"No, there was nothing for you to be worried about," he said, smiling. Her shoulders dropped as relief washed over her. "Tell me, do you smoke?"

She shook her head, momentarily thrown by such a random question. "No, I don't. Never have done. Why?"

"Do you have a gardener? Someone who takes care of the landscaping?"

"My mother used to. This was her house. After my marriage broke up, we moved here. Partly out of necessity but also to help take care of my mother. I have to admit, since she passed away, I've been less inclined to do things with the garden. Plus, it's expensive and... well... I don't have the same income that she did, if you know what I mean?"

"I'm sorry to hear that. I lost my father quite recently too."

"I'm sorry, had he been ill?"

"No, it came about quite quickly." Caslin immediately sought to change the direction of the conversation.

"My mother was ill for a very long time," Michelle said, her expression one of profound sadness. "She suffered with Alzheimer's and developed a host of other illnesses that wore her down over a number of years. She was tough, though. Never one to give in and she never let anything get on top of her. Sometimes I wish I was much more like her."

"It must have been hard."

"It was, particularly after the divorce. My mother was very much of the opinion that marriage was for life, no matter what. Despite… I'm sorry, Inspector, I'm sure you don't want to hear all this."

If the truth were known, Caslin found her company enjoyable, even though the two occasions he had spent with her were professionally related. He felt like he had known her for years. Forcing his mind back to the matter in hand, he asked, "I was just wondering if the gardener smoked or whether anybody else has been in the garden recently who does?"

Michelle shook her head. "No, not that I'm aware of."

"It's okay," Caslin said. "Probably somebody walking past in the street and throwing their butts over the wall."

"Mummy." A child's voice came from behind them. Both of them turned and Caslin saw a young girl, perhaps no older than ten years of age, roughly the same as his own daughter, Lizzie, standing in the doorway. She was dressed in her pyjamas and rubbed furiously at her eyes, indicative of having recently woken. Michelle crossed the kitchen and knelt down before the girl, placing both hands on her upper arms reassuringly.

"Did you wake up, darling?" she asked softly, smiling. The girl nodded.

"Who's that man?" She pointed at Caslin.

"That's a friend of Mummy's." Michelle glanced in Caslin's direction.

"What's his name?"

Michelle flicked her eyes from Caslin to her daughter and back again. Caslin came a little nearer and also knelt, so they met at her eye level. "My name is Nathaniel. My friends call me Nate," he said smiling.

The little girl eyed him warily, as if assessing his trustworthiness. "I'm Carly," she said. Seemingly, he had passed her initial test.

"Well, I'm very pleased to meet you, Carly," he replied, holding out his hand. She glanced at it and then back at him before reaching out and they briefly shook hands.

"And I think we should get you back to bed, shouldn't we, young lady," Michelle said. The child put up no resistance and with her mother's reassuring hand on her shoulder, she turned and happily set off back towards her bedroom. Michelle looked over his shoulder at Caslin and smiled, silently mouthing the words *thank you.*

Walking back across the kitchen, Caslin returned his gaze to the garden. There was every possibility Michelle Cates and her daughter had seen tricks of light and shadow, their minds filling the gaps in detail with the worst possible scenario. With what happened to Kelly so fresh in their thoughts, it would be completely understandable. However, equally there was every possibility that it wasn't paranoia and someone was there, watching. Glancing at the counter alongside him, Caslin noticed his contact card lying next to a mobile phone. Picking it up, he noticed some hand-written words on the reverse and he flipped it in his hand. On the back someone had added – *a decent man* – in blue ink. He considered what a strange twist of fate had brought him here, not that he believed much in the hand of fate.

The silence was broken by a knock on the front door. Caslin walked into the hallway with the knowledge that Michelle would most likely not be down for a few minutes yet. Opening the door, two uniformed officers were surprised to find him standing in front of them.

"It's okay," Caslin said. "I've walked the perimeter and there's no sign of an intruder. At least, not now. Are you two on shift or are you clocking off at midnight?"

"We're on six-to-two," the first officer advised him, glancing to his colleague. Caslin thought his name was Atkinson but he couldn't be sure.

"In that case, I want you to swing by here as much as you can during the remainder of your shift. Can you do that?"

"Yes, sir. We can. Is something going on we should know about?"

"The residents are relatives of a recent murder victim, this so-called *Night Stalker.*" He hated using the media name attributed to the case but it was how the killer was referred to by almost everyone outside of his team. "There is a woman and young child living here alone, so a reassuring uniformed presence would be appreciated."

"Of course."

"And if there is anything out of the ordinary, I want you to contact me directly and I don't care what time of night it is."

"What about when we finish?"

"I'll make a call and have someone put it out on the wire," Caslin said, advising them that he would ensure a uniformed presence periodically throughout the night.

He bid them good night and closed the door. Turning around, Michelle descended the stairs towards him. "Thank you, Inspector."

"That's okay. I have a daughter of a similar age and I know it can be a little unsettling to find a stranger in the house unexpectedly."

"For that too, but also for what you just did with those officers." Caslin didn't realise she had overheard the conversation.

"It's just as a precaution. I wouldn't want you to be unduly alarmed."

"No, I'm not. Not now anyway." She came to stand next to him. "You're a good man, Inspector."

"Please, Miss Cates, you can call me Nathaniel… or Nate, if you prefer?"

"Are we friends now, Nate?" She smiled, playfully.

Caslin's cheeks flushed and suddenly he felt incredibly self-conscious. In a desperate act to recover his composure, he checked the time on his watch. "I should probably be off, Miss Cates," he said despite wanting to do anything but. Michelle appeared disappointed at the suggestion.

"You should call me Michelle. I remember my teachers always called me *miss*, and I didn't care for it much then, either."

"You prefer Michelle, or Miche?" he asked. Her eyes narrowed and he thought perhaps he was over familiar, misjudging the situation. She appeared to notice.

"My ex-husband always called me *Miche*. Not a fan." She shook her head and Caslin thought he needed to recover.

"I'm sorry. Your brother, Thomas, also—"

"That figures. He cottoned on to how much I hate it and does it for fun. I guess it kinda stuck with him. Thank you for coming out."

"Happy to do so, and you have my number." Caslin words felt hollow and sorely inadequate. Not for the first time when he figured he had a good thing going with a woman, he'd found a way to douse water on the flames. "Just in case."

"Just in case," she replied, the smile broadening. Caslin turned and unlocked the front door. Stepping out into the night, he looked over his shoulder as Michelle placed a hand on the door ready to close it once he had left. He shot her an awkward half-smile, worried that she would see through the brittle mask that shrouded his attraction to her. Without another word, he descended the steps and upon reaching the quayside, looked back up and saw her still standing in the doorway watching him walk away. The briefest flicker of excitement passed through him as he considered the prospect that the attraction might not be one-sided after all. The door closed.

Taking the next right, he walked uphill towards the city centre in the direction of his apartment. His mobile rang and such was his preoccupation with his thoughts regarding Michelle Cates, he didn't bother to look at the screen as he answered the call.

"You've been doing the rounds in the news rooms, I see." Caslin didn't recognise the voice but something about the tone made him stop, feeling the need to focus his attention fully on the call.

"Who is this?"

"You don't rate me at all, do you?"

"Should I?"

"You think you've got me all figured out." The caller was irritated, his tone hostile. "But the truth is you have no idea what I'm trying to achieve… but you will, I promise you."

Caslin briefly considered whether this was a crank but something told him this caller was genuine. "Why don't you enlighten me? If you're so sure I don't understand you."

"You're the same as everybody else, Inspector Caslin. You want all the answers to every question handed to you, spoon fed, but the reality is the answers will only come if you work for them."

"And what exactly should I do in order for that to happen?"

"Don't worry. I'm here as your guide, to educate. Soon enough, you will come to understand."

The accent was broad Yorkshire. He was local. "How about we meet and you can tell me all about it?"

"You genuinely believe I am stupid." The caller's tone was turning aggressive, his anger rising despite the controlled manner in which he spoke.

"I think you have real problems that you need help with. You're going to get caught."

"I believe I have options, Inspector."

"You do. Several," Caslin agreed. "Your best is to come to me. If you have a message to get out, then I can help with that. There's no need for anyone else to die."

"I disagree. The path to the light must be cleansed prior to the journey. We are all the same when it boils down to it, Inspector."

"You've lost me."

"Death is the way of the world and killing is a part of that, whether it's animals for food, insects at bedtime or the *worst kind* of people. At least I'm honest about it."

"You're murdering people. That's not the same," Caslin countered.

"It's exactly the same! If able to or given the chance, you'd all do it too. The real difference is I'm willing to embrace my desires so I can show you the path. Whereas the rest of you live in denial." His tone switched to contemptuous. Caslin's stance was getting under his skin.

"I think you went wrong somewhere along the line," Caslin said. "Lost your way."

"Like I said, Inspector," he countered, his tone now exuding the calm, measured delivery of earlier in the call. "You will understand. I assure you."

"I understand you're a whacko," Caslin said coldly. There was a sound at the other end of the line, in the background, Caslin strained to work out what it might be but it wasn't distinctive enough.

"Please don't fall back on cheap insults. You do yourself and your intelligence a disservice." His voice sounded somewhat laboured, as if he was doing something physical whilst speaking on the phone. The conversation seemed to have become a distraction to the caller. "I've left you something, Inspector Caslin. Please don't wait too long to find it because things go off when you leave them out."

The voice chuckled and the line went dead.

Immediately, Caslin double checked the call had disconnected. Then he hit the speed dial connecting him straight to the control room. Identifying himself, he instructed the operator. "I received a call on this number and I want you to run an immediate trace. Forward the ticket to my investigation team. Flag it as a high priority, please."

Hanging up on the call, he touched the mobile to his lips, striking a thoughtful pose. As desired, they had instigated a response but what that meant, he was still unsure.

CHAPTER FOURTEEN

THE FISHERGATE AREA lay beyond the city walls to the south-east of York. Taking the turn onto Cemetery Road, Caslin kept an eye out for the entrance. It was a short stretch of road and the old stone Gatehouse appeared on the right-hand side. A police car was parked at the entrance and the uniformed officer, recognising Caslin, waved him through and indicated for him to follow the road bearing off to his right, disappearing through the trees.

"It seems somehow fitting in a poetic kind of way, don't you think?" DI Templer spoke quietly, sitting in the passenger seat. Caslin glanced across at his colleague but didn't respond. Templer had fallen quiet since they received the call first thing in the morning, with the report reaching them shortly after seven o'clock. It was obvious what was going through the young man's mind. There were no words of comfort that Caslin could offer him despite having personal, very painful experience of losing colleagues during an investigation.

The gravel lined road opened out before the chapel. There was enough room for multiple vehicles to park. Caslin pulled up alongside Hunter's car. Getting out, he looked back at the imposing neo-classical inspired chapel, constructed by the Victorians well over a century earlier. Templer joined him and both men looked around trying to locate the crime scene. York Cemetery was spread over twenty-four acres of land and consisted of well-maintained paths, terraces and gardens amidst mature tree-lined surroundings. It was easy, surrounded by such greenery, to forget how close to the city they were.

An officer appeared on the path running directly from the centre of the chapel, stretching for several hundred yards with various branches off it. The two detectives headed that way and were greeted by the constable as they passed. Having checked with him, they took the next right turn and the crime scene appeared almost immediately. The path ran in a straight line but soon split, moving off to the left and the right, forming a circular walk. To each side of the path were headstones, many of them from a bygone era with names and dates largely unreadable due to the erosion of the stone. They took neither branch, continuing on.

The sounds of conversation carried to them now as they approached their destination. The path split once again to form yet another circular walk, only smaller and set within the larger. However, at the centre of this inner circle, they found the team already hard at work. The threat of rain was absent this morning with the clear skies of the previous afternoon carrying through the night. This brought dense fog to the Vale of York and the low sun was yet to make any headway in burning it off. The air felt damp, cold and the body hanging from the tree at the centre of the circle capped the scene off as dark and foreboding.

Caslin stepped forward but Templer hesitated. Caslin noticed and turned, placing a reassuring hand on the younger man's shoulder.

"Come on, let's see if it's him." Caslin addressed Templer's worst fears for the first time since they left Fulford Road. The two of them moved closer. They came to within ten feet of the body and Caslin watched as Craig Templer visibly deflated, exhaling deeply.

"It's not him." The sense of relief was obvious in his expression, let alone his tone. "It's not Fowler."

"We've not found an ID yet," Hunter said, rising from her kneeling position a short distance away. "We started searching from here and have people fanning out just to see if anything has been discarded."

Caslin looked up at the victim. He was a middle-aged white man, perhaps in his early to mid-forties. He was dressed for the weather in jeans, trainers and a thick overcoat. Looking at his face, despite the swelling and purple complexion, expected in a hanging, Caslin couldn't see any indicators to suggest he had been involved in an altercation.

"Any idea how he got here, to the cemetery, I mean?" Caslin asked.

"There were no cars left overnight or present this morning," Hunter confirmed. "There's a funeral here at ten, and the staff were coming in to make the preparations. They found him."

Caslin moved around the body, maintaining his distance so as not to risk contamination of the ground beneath, just in case there was any trace evidence that may be disturbed. Narrowing his focus, he paid close attention to the victim's hands looking for any cuts, scrapes or bruising that might indicate he had fought with an attacker. Again, he was surprised to find nothing other than what had become a signature – the apparent ritual removal of the victim's right index finger.

"No sign of a struggle," Caslin said aloud.

"Not even around the neck," Iain Robertson said, coming to join them. Caslin hadn't noticed he was there yet.

"Good morning, Iain. Say that again, please."

"Look around the neck. Although, I know you don't have the best view or the aid of a stepladder, like I did. I don't doubt Alison Taylor will be better placed to confirm it but I reckon there wasn't much of a struggle to get him into the noose," Robertson explained. "Further to that, the abrasion around the neck is almost exactly where the rope is now, which means there was very little movement from the ligature during suspension."

"Meaning?" Templer asked.

"That's indicative of the noose being securely tightened prior to suspension," Robertson said.

"Suggesting there was no struggle?" Caslin asked. "Any possibility of this being a post-mortem hanging?"

Robertson dismissed the notion. "I don't believe so, no. We've detailed the surrounding area thoroughly and there is no evidence of a body being dragged here. Judging from the victim's height and estimated weight, I would expect to see some if he were. I agree that would explain how the noose could have been fixed in place so securely, but if you look where the rope is situated." He pointed to where the rope looped over the branch of the tree above. "In a post-mortem hanging, the noose is secured and the rope thrown over and then the victim is pulled into the air before tying it off. That leaves a very obvious sign of wear, particularly with this thick, fibrous rope. Whereas, in a suicidal hanging, the wear pattern runs the opposite way as the weight of the victim stretches the rope in a downward motion." With a closed fist, he drew his hand down in a sharp motion, enacting the passage of the rope. "There's no doubt in my mind."

"No signs of a fight?" Caslin asked, seeking confirmation.

"As you rightly pointed out, no scratches or abrasions on his knuckles or extremities. The fingernails are intact and don't appear to have anything beneath them, skin, blood or suchlike. Nothing to indicate there was any form of conflict. Likewise, his clothing has no mud visible on it nor any signs of scuffs, scratches or tears."

"You're describing it as if this man went voluntarily to his death," Templer said, sounding surprised.

"I'll give you the science, you can figure out the psychology," Robertson said with a wry smile. "You may find what's on the ground before him very interesting."

In front of the hanging body lay a smart phone alongside a carrier bag. The latter appeared empty and it was weighed down with a forensic number marker, presumably to stop it from blowing away in the wind. Alongside the bag were bundles of cash, stacked neatly alongside one other. Next to these, and in front of the phone, was a blooming lotus flower, the diameter of which was approximately an adult hand-span.

"Once Iain's CSI team had photographed everything in situ, we took the money from the bag and placed it there," Hunter said.

"How were they found?" Caslin asked.

"The phone and flower were as you see them now, with the money inside the bag alongside."

Caslin knelt and focussed his attention on the mobile phone. The handset appeared to be connected to a social media page, although without picking it up and scrolling through it, he was unsure of the significance. Hunter appeared to anticipate his next question and she crossed to where the CSI officers had deposited the majority of their kit, returning with a tablet in hand. Caslin stood and she activated the screen before passing it to him.

Caslin's first thought had been correct and it was indeed a social media page. Hunter had searched for the page, looking it up online with her device.

"The account is open to the public," she advised him. "Everyone can view it."

Glancing up at the victim's face and then back at the screen, Caslin judged it to be logged into the victim's profile page, or at least a profile page using this man's photograph. "Andrew Connelly," Caslin read aloud, largely for Templer's benefit, angling the screen in his direction.

Scrolling down the page, he saw multiple comments posted from the account on the previous day. Looking at roughly when they were posted, he did a quick bit of mental arithmetic and figured the entries ceased around the same time as he had visited Michelle Cates's house on the previous night. Each of the posts from the account were shocking and repulsive. In fact, they would be deemed inappropriate and offensive to any right-minded person. Some were provocative whilst others were downright graphic and vulgar in their content. Every single one of them were photographs, or stills from video footage, featuring what were quite clearly underage children alongside a man who he recognised as the victim, Andrew Connelly.

Continuing to work through each of the posts, there were too many for him to keep count. Caslin judged there were multiple victims. Even when the faces of the children were distorted, presumably to hamper their identification, he was still able to spot racial backgrounds, genders and rough age groups. Similarly, there appeared to be shots of Connelly appearing far more youthful. He had been an active child abuser for many years. Caslin took his eyes off the images and passed the tablet back to Hunter, meeting her eye and casting a glance skyward. His stomach turned, as it always did when forced to face this subject matter. A few moments passed before anyone chose to speak.

"Is it his phone, do we know?" Templer asked.

"No, it's the same phone he called you from last night," Hunter said. "What's more, it's Kelly Ryan's."

Caslin released a controlled exhale, returning his attention to the evidence before him. Dropping to his haunches, he cast his eye across the bundles of cash. They were a mixture of mostly ten and twenty-pound notes, along with three bundles of fifties. They were freshly issued and came sealed with a band of wraparound paper. Upon closer inspection each band was initialled.

"These were drawn across the counter of a bank and recently too, I should imagine," Caslin said. "Has anyone counted it yet?"

"£2860," Hunter confirmed.

"That's a random figure." Caslin was surprised.

"We counted it three times just to be sure," Hunter replied. "But you're right, it is an odd sum."

"Does it look like any has been removed?" Templer asked.

Hunter shook her head. "The amount has been noted and initialled, by the cashier, I should imagine. The odd total is recorded on a transactional slip that was in the bag along with the money. You're right, it was withdrawn yesterday from a bank here in the town."

"Right, as soon as the doors open, I want you in there finding out who withdrew it, when and why, as well as any other details you can come by. CCTV footage, the lot," Caslin instructed. Hunter nodded.

"Was the transaction slip time stamped?"

"It was printed at two-thirty-five, yesterday afternoon," Hunter confirmed.

"We found a wallet," Terry Holt said, appearing from an adjoining path. He approached brandishing a transparent evidence bag containing a black leather wallet.

Coming over to them, he opened the bag and took out the wallet. Hunter passed Caslin a pair of forensic gloves. He donned them before taking the offered wallet. Opening it up, the first thing he found was a photocard driving licence bearing the name of Andrew Connelly. The residential address was within York's city walls. Opening up the sections revealed no further cash, only debit and credit cards in the same name. There was a small dogeared photograph of a woman and a young girl. The picture didn't seem particularly old, merely ragged as a result of being kept in a wallet. Caslin flashed the image to Hunter, whose gaze lowered to the ground and she gave an almost unnoticeable shake of the head.

"Wife and daughter?" Caslin suggested.

"Most likely," Templer agreed.

"This gets better." Caslin pulled a business card from among the credit cards. Reading the information on the front, he slowly shook his head.

"What is it?" Hunter asked.

"He works for a community trust," Caslin said flatly. "Aimed at providing access to extracurricular activities for underprivileged children."

Murmurings of outrage and disgust emanated from everyone present as they processed the magnitude of that revelation.

"There's your suicidal motivation, right there," Robertson stated.

"What about the money?" Holt asked. "Why did he have it and why was it left?"

"Let's not jump to any conclusions until we've had a chance to process the scene," Caslin said. "Terry, once you're not needed here, I want you to have a sweep of the area and pull any footage that you can from traffic cams, private CCTV, dash cam footage from taxis, buses, anything you can think of. I want to try and catch Connelly's arrival here last night as well as anyone who he could have been meeting. In the meantime, Hunter and I will go to the registered address on his driving licence. Maybe his wife can help us with his movements yesterday."

"What can I do?" Templer asked.

"I'm presuming we haven't found Connelly's phone?" Iain Robertson glanced in his direction and shook his head. "The number is on his business card. I want you to get hold of the records to find out who he's been speaking to and get it flagged on the network. If I'm right, then the killer has it and is no doubt planning his next move. In all likelihood, the next time the phone is active will be when there's another victim to be found. However, if it pops up before that, we need to be ready to move on the location."

"I should imagine he'll be uploading another video soon as well," Templer said, "so I'll follow that through at the same time."

"Can you also contact Child Protection and bring someone in to follow up on the footage that's been posted on his social media account? We will need to start identifying these kids. They might still be vulnerable and need to be brought into safety or… let's just find out who they are." Caslin paused, taking a moment to collect his thoughts. Everyone felt revulsion but his own children came to mind. "I doubt any of us is going to shed a tear over Andrew Connelly's death, but let's do our jobs and try to put it to the back of our minds what he may have been up to. Some of these kids might still be in danger and I dare say, they all need us focussed right now. And what's more, remember who we are dealing with. Put aside whether you think Connelly had this coming or not. Our killer is acting on his own motivations. We have judges and juries to decide on punishment. This man doesn't get to choose, no matter how abhorrent his target."

CHAPTER FIFTEEN

PULLING UP AT THE ADDRESS, a rather unassuming 1960s semi-detached property in the Foxwoods suburb to the south-west of York, Caslin looked around as Hunter turned the key in the ignition. This wasn't an area he was familiar with, being one covered by officers based at the Acomb Road station. However, it was a leafy residential suburb with wide streets and a variety of green areas suitable for young and growing families.

"I think it's that one over there." Hunter indicated a house with a small driveway, neatly manicured garden and white weather boarding lining the exterior of the upper floor. Getting out of the car, Caslin pushed the door closed and scanned the driveway. A dark green hatchback was parked there and beyond that, at the entrance to the garage, a children's bicycle was propped against the wall. Walking up the path they both noticed movement as a figure passed the front door, a blur of motion through the obscured glass panel to the left.

Caslin reached up and pressed the button to the doorbell, hearing it chime in the interior. They only had to wait a few moments before someone came to answer the call. They were met by a woman in her thirties. She smiled warmly, assessing the callers, appearing almost ready to dismiss whatever it was they were about to say. That was until Caslin identified himself and showed her his warrant card.

She was genuinely taken aback at their presence, as most people were when the police came calling. "I'm so sorry. We get a lot of cold callers… They are usually nice enough people but it does become tiresome."

"Mrs Connelly?" Caslin asked. She nodded. "Do you think we could speak inside?"

"Yes, of course." She stepped back, beckoning for them to come inside but at the same time her expression changed from welcoming to fearful. "Has something happened to Rebecca?"

"Rebecca is your daughter?" Hunter asked. The woman nodded and Hunter responded quickly. "I'm sure she's fine. We're not here about your daughter."

Hunter closed the door and they were led from the hall into the living room. The Connolly's home was immaculately presented, aside from what appeared to be the remnants of breakfast still present on the dining table.

"I'm sorry, you have to forgive the mess. I wasn't expecting company. I figured I'd have everything put away by the time my husband gets home from work."

Caslin dismissed her concerns with a wave of the hand as she gestured for them to sit down. "That's okay, Mrs Connelly. I'm afraid we have some rather distressing news for you."

"It's Andy, isn't it?"

"Andrew Connolly is your husband, is that right?"

"Yes, he is," she confirmed. "Has he got himself into some kind of trouble with speeding again? I told him you'd throw the book at him if he didn't slow down."

"I'm very sorry to have to tell you this, Mrs Connolly," Caslin interrupted, "but we believe your husband has passed away." He delivered the news as gently as he could in a matter-of-fact tone. In his experience, that was the best way. She looked at him with an expression that questioned the validity of his statement.

"I… I don't understand."

"Your husband's body was found this morning, here in York," Caslin explained.

She shook her head emphatically. "No, there must be some kind of mistake. Andy travelled to Leeds yesterday, for work."

"We will have to carry out an identification in order to be sure but I am in no doubt that this is your husband." At that moment, her head sank into her hands, the realisation hitting home.

"How?" She uttered the word almost inaudibly.

"We are only at the early stages of the investigation but it would appear that your husband committed suicide." She broke down at that point and Caslin glanced across the room, meeting Hunter's eye and he could tell she didn't necessarily agree with his casting her husband's death purely as a suicide. There would be a time to share the complexities of how her husband died but there was a logic to Caslin's approach. Until he knew otherwise, he would consider Andrew Connolly's widow as both a potential witness and a suspect in his deviant behaviour. Whether she was a willing participant or turned a blind eye to her husband's activities, Caslin intended to find out. Equally, there was the possibility she was totally unaware and, in that case, he sought to spare her the graphic details.

They allowed her a few minutes more for the news to sink in and then, when she had regained her composure, she lifted her head to meet Caslin's gaze. Tears lined her cheeks.

"When was the last time you saw or spoke with your husband?"

"Yesterday," she said glancing up and to the left. "Shortly after lunchtime, I think. He called me from work."

"Did he seem out of sorts?"

She appeared thoughtful. "He wasn't his usual self, I must say. He was distracted but nothing he said… made me think anything was wrong."

"What did he say?"

"That something had come up and he had to travel to Leeds to sort it out. He told me not to worry and that he didn't know when he'd be back, but I shouldn't wait up. If it got too late and he was too tired, he would just stay over and drive back today." She flicked her eyes between the two detectives. "I wasn't expecting him back until after work this evening."

"What kind of work did your husband do, Mrs Connelly?" Hunter asked.

"He works for a charitable trust," she explained. "They work within the community providing extracurricular activities and developmental opportunities for underprivileged and vulnerable children. That can be anything from confidence building weekends away to daily after-school clubs. Not all working parents can provide wraparound care. He is very passionate about it."

Caslin shot Hunter a look. One that didn't go unnoticed. He turned back to Mrs Connolly. "Has your husband ever suffered from any form of mental illness or struggled with depression in the past?"

"No, not at all," she said. "I don't understand how he could have done this. Are you sure there hasn't been a mistake?"

Caslin shook his head. "I don't believe so, Mrs Connelly. Tell me, your husband was found with a rather large sum of money on his person. Does this ring any bells with you?"

She seemed rather confused at that suggestion. "How large?"

"Somewhere in the region of three thousand pounds."

"Where on earth did he find that kind of money?" She was visibly stunned at the amount.

"It seems it was withdrawn from the bank yesterday afternoon," Caslin stated. "Did your husband have access to the bank account of the business he worked with, or is it possible he withdrew it from a personal account?"

"I know for certain he doesn't have any involvement with the finances at the trust," she said, frowning. "And we have a joint account for the house but we don't have any savings or anything like that."

"Do you think we could have a look at your most recent bank statement, if you have it to hand? That way, we can check whether it's from your bank or from somebody else's account."

"Yes, of course. I keep the statements over here." She stood up on unsteady feet. Caslin went to offer her physical support but she waved him away, walking across the room to the nearby bookcase. Taking down a lever arch folder, she returned and placed it on the coffee table in front of her.

Opening the folder, she flicked through the dividing sections separating credit cards and utility statements. Reaching the section where they kept the bank statements, she passed the folder over to Caslin. Hunter got up from her seat by the front window and came to join him, peering over his shoulder.

"That's the same bank as recorded on the withdrawal slip," Hunter confirmed.

"Mrs Connelly," Caslin said, looking over to her whilst tracing his finger across the bank statement in front of him, the previous month to the current one, "there appears to be several cash withdrawals this month and last. Here, on the first, and again on the fifteenth of each month to the value of £700. Can you tell me what these were for?"

She leaned over and he pointed out the transactions and from the look on her face it was quite obvious she was unaware of the withdrawals. "I… I don't understand," she said, flustered. Flicking back to the previous month's statement, they found the same withdrawals were made at similar intervals. The woman was becoming increasingly agitated, the pace in which she was turning the pages threatened to tear the statements such was her aggression.

Caslin placed his hand over hers. It shook as she withdrew it. "Do you have any knowledge of these withdrawals?" he asked.

She shook her head slowly. "No, we don't have... things have been tight for a while. Andy told me not to worry and that he was working on something and that things would get better."

"Did your husband have any expensive habits?" Hunter asked.

Mrs Connelly looked across with an inquisitive expression on her face. "I don't understand what you mean."

"Was he a regular gambler? Did he frequent the bookies?"

She shook her head. "No, nothing like that. Andy is a very conservative man. He likes things to be as they should be. Besides, how could he show his face in front of the congregation every Sunday if he held such vices?"

"What do you think he was taking the money for?" Caslin asked.

"I've no idea." She shook her head.

"Has your husband made reference to anything unusual recently?" Caslin asked. "Either something happening at work or someone new coming into his life that may have caused him concern."

"Not that he's mentioned." She looked away, thinking hard. "Come to think of it, he has been distant recently but, what with the finances, I thought he was just suffering from a bit of stress."

"Do you work, Mrs Connolly?" Caslin was curious. With money tight and a child in school, there was always the possibility for a second income.

"No! I used to before we were married but afterwards, Andy didn't want me to. I suggested I could go back to work but he wouldn't hear of it." Suddenly, her mouth fell open, tears welling. "Whatever will I tell my daughter? Inspector, I must go to the school and pick her up."

"I know this is difficult, Mrs Connelly, but we need to speak with you about another matter first. We will contact the school on your behalf and have them take Rebecca out of class, just in case word gets out before we can bring her home," Caslin said. She nodded and Caslin indicated for Hunter to step out of the room and make the call.

"What else is it, Inspector?"

"Was your husband active on social media?"

"A little, yes. Personally, I find it all nonsense and an incredible waste of time but Andy said it was important he had an account so that he could stay in touch with Rebecca."

"How much time did he spend on social media then?"

She smiled as she thought about the answer to the question. "Well, that was his argument but secretly I think he really enjoyed it. He was always sharing jokes with Rebecca and her friends, as well as the kids from the centre. I didn't think it did any harm. Why do you ask?"

Hunter returned from the kitchen. She smiled as she sat down. "I've spoken to the Head at your daughter's school and she's going to take Rebecca to her office and wait there."

"Thank you," Mrs Connolly said, breathing a sigh of relief.

"Would you say that Andy spent rather a lot of time interacting with the kids by social media then?" Caslin flicked a glance in Hunter's direction, thereby bringing her up to speed with what they were discussing.

"Sometimes I did tell him that he should let them get on with their own lives without an old man jumping in all the time," Mrs Connelly said, chuckling. "That said, the kids seem to like having him around. That might be because he was always bringing them things."

"What type of things?"

"Magazines, sweets, chocolates. Nothing too extravagant," she explained. "What's this got to do with anything?"

The detectives both held impassive expressions. She appeared to find them unnerving. "Mrs Connelly, we have an active social media account that appears to show your husband in… compromising situations with children," Caslin said flatly.

"Compromising?" Her eyes narrowed as she spoke. "In what way?"

"I'm afraid there's no easy way to tell you this but your husband was abusing them."

Mrs Connelly's mouth fell open, eyes wide. She shook her head emphatically. "No! That can't be right. You've made a mistake!"

"There are pictures… many, many pictures," Caslin said, meeting her eye. "There is no doubt."

She broke down as those words sank in. Her entire body shaking as she wept uncontrollably. Eyes closed tightly, her lips curled in such a fashion as to indicate a person wrought with suffering and pain. After a few moments the sobbing subsided and she regained a measure of composure, mumbling almost inaudibly, "My Rebecca."

"We don't know." It was an honest reply. Caslin couldn't sugar coat the facts but nor did he want to speculate. "Did you ever have any inclination about your husband's behaviour around or towards the children?" It was a harsh but a necessary question. At this point, they did not know whether

Connelly's widow could somehow be complicit in the apparent systematic abuse of the children. Until they did, either way, they would tread carefully as no one could be given an easy ride.

She shook her head again, staring into Caslin's eyes, hers shot through with red and brimming with tears. "Never. How could I as a mother?"

"I appreciate this is very difficult for you," Caslin said, adopting a conciliatory tone, "but it is very important for us to ask. Looking back, was there anything unusual in his behaviour? Not necessarily recently."

"I find this all fanciful. Andy has never... he wasn't particularly interested in... the physical aspects of a relationship. If you know what I mean?" She said the last quietly, almost wishing the words not to be heard. Caslin encouraged her to continue. "Once we had Rebecca, he lost interest in that type of thing. For a long time, I thought it must have been me." She reached for a box of tissues, wiping the tears from her cheeks and blowing her nose. "I guess it wasn't me, after all."

Caslin glanced toward Hunter and drew her attention. "Perhaps, I should make us all a cup of tea. If that's okay with you?" He looked to their host, not wanting to take liberties but he had an ulterior motive. She said that was okay and he got up. Hunter's eyes followed. Once he was sure he wouldn't be seen, he pointed two fingers towards his eyes and then angled them away, signifying he intended to have a look around. Hunter acknowledged with the briefest incline of her head, a movement that would mean nothing to anyone who didn't witness the exchange.

Caslin entered the kitchen, pulling the door to. Looking around, he found the kettle and filled it to its maximum with water, setting it to boil. Knowing that would give him a few minutes' grace, he entered the hallway through another door so as not to be seen from those in the living room. Risking a glance into the living room, he saw that Hunter had moved into his seat and Mrs Connelly was now looking in the opposite direction to where he stood. Quickly crossing the gap, he crept up the stairs treading as lightly as he could.

There were three bedrooms and a bathroom off the landing. One bedroom, to the front of the house, was very small and little more than a box room. This was utilised as something of a home office or study and Caslin quickly leafed through some of the paperwork, but nothing particularly caught his eye. Everything was neatly arranged, ordered. The sign of a controlling personality. There was a laptop and as soon as the warrant came through, he would ensure that got back to Holt. Framed photographs adorned the walls. The majority of them were shots of

Connolly alongside various children, boys and girls, of different ages. Some appear to have been taken on camping trips, hill walking or on sporting occasions. With each face that Caslin examined, that same familiar churning of his stomach returned.

The next bedroom he entered was Rebecca's. It was much the same as his daughter, Lizzie's, was at home. The two girls must have been a similar age and a flash of anger rose inside Caslin as he considered the prospect of someone like Connolly targeting his own daughter. The anger subsided as he thought about the man's widow. If she was as innocent as she seemed, he considered what she would be feeling at this moment. Leaving the room largely untouched, he briefly cast an eye over the master bedroom. Everything was tidy, clean and well presented. He wondered whether Andrew Connelly's desire for everything to be just right extended to controlling his entire family's movements and behaviours?

Returning downstairs, he entered the living room, not bothering with making the tea. He figured she was so shocked by their news that his ruse to snoop around wouldn't be discovered. "Mrs Connelly." She looked up at him. Although her face was tear-stained, she appeared calmer now. "We're going to have a few officers come by and go through your husband's possessions. In the meantime, we will arrange for a couple of plain clothes officers to take you to the school and pick up your daughter. Perhaps, it might be best for the two of you to stay away from the house for a while. Is there anyone you know that you can visit with for a couple of days? I'm afraid once the press get a hold of this, they will come calling. And they will be persistent."

"Yes, I have family nearby. We could probably stay with them. Should I call them?"

"Please do. We will also need to take a formal statement from you in due course."

Caslin beckoned Hunter to step out into the hall with him as Mrs Connolly reached for the telephone. "There's a home office upstairs devoted to Connelly's favoured pastime of mixing with the children. There's also a computer and I imagine we'll find an awful lot more on the hard drive. Get Terry on it quickly as possible."

"Where are you going to be, sir?"

"I don't doubt the video will be uploaded within the next couple of hours, so I'm going to go over to his workplace and find out as much as I can before everything hits the fan."

CHAPTER SIXTEEN

Caslin pulled open the left hand door and entered. He was in a short, squat rectangular building fashioned from a mixture of prefabricated concrete panels and an old corrugated roof that was most likely full of asbestos. He judged it was once a commercial unit, thrown up at some point in the sixties and approaching the end of its useful life. Nobody was present at the reception desk, little more than a table with a signing-in book and a scattering of information leaflets, home printed by the look of them. Sound carried from beyond another set of double doors in front of him and he migrated towards it.

Pushing open the door, Caslin found himself in one large room that stretched almost to the rear boundary but signs at the far end indicated there were toilets and changing facilities through the doors. In one corner there was a boxing ring with what appeared to be netting hanging around the exterior. Off to his right were various pieces of gym apparatus and on the walls behind these were photographs of gymnasts in action. Moving closer, Caslin noted that many of the shots were taken in this very building.

"Can I help you?" A voice came from behind. Caslin was startled having not heard anyone approach. There was another door to his left and they must have come from there. He smiled and took out his identification.

The man paid it a cursory inspection as Caslin identified himself. "Is this your place?"

"Aye, I'm Tommy Banner," he said, smiling warmly. He was a stocky individual, tattooed and balding. "At least, I look after the day-to-day running of the centre."

"You provide services for disadvantaged kids, is that right?"

"Yes, we do. We're not limited to those from less well-off backgrounds, you understand. We also help where we can with vulnerable children, providing somewhere for the kids to go if the parents are working. Not many have a steady nine-to-five these days."

"You say working with vulnerable children. The local authority must be involved somewhere along the line."

"Oh, yes," Banner agreed. "This centre is part funded by the local council. We would need them on board to be able to do what we do."

"Where does the rest of the funding come from then?"

"Much of it comes from a local church group, whereas the remainder comes from donations or fundraising activities we take on ourselves. The children are often a large part of that; we try to arrange as many family days as we can. Doing so really brings the community together."

"I see. How long have you been going?"

"These past four years." The man exuded pride, obviously pleased with their accomplishment. "Funding is becoming an issue, though. Between you and me, I'm not entirely sure how much longer we can keep going."

"I'm sorry to hear that." Caslin couldn't help but think the revelations surrounding Connolly's activities would kill off any future source of local authority funding, let alone the black mark in the eyes of the general public.

"It's not the first time we've been in this situation. We'll work something out," Banner said with confidence. "I'm sure you're not here at this time of the morning to ask me about charitable funding. How can I help you, Inspector?"

"I'm afraid I have some bad news about one of your colleagues; Andrew Connolly."

"Andy? What's he been up to?"

"I'm sorry to have to tell you that Mr Connolly was found dead this morning."

Banner appeared visibly shocked. "When, how?"

"He was found early this morning," Caslin informed him, deliberately withholding any further detail. "The circumstances surrounding his death are still under investigation. What can you tell me about him? He worked here full time, is that correct?"

"Yes, he was one of three paid members of staff," Banner said, still trying to take in the news.

"There are only three of you?"

"Three paid staff, yes. The remainder are made up of part-time volunteers who agree to help out for a set time period, perhaps two months at a time. In reality, it tends not to work that way as people stay on or provide more hours as and when they are available. People are very generous. You only have to spend a little time here with the children to see the positive impact that you can have in their lives," Banner replied, a measure of the pride returning amid the sadness. "Forgive me, I think I need to sit down."

"That's okay." Caslin indicated towards a handful of circular tables behind them. They walked over and both men pulled out a chair. Caslin noticed the door that Banner had walked out of led to a kitchen.

"I can't believe Andy's gone." Banner shook his head.

"Has he been with you long?"

"He was one of the first to volunteer when I opened this place. He quickly made his presence known and I saw the value in having him around and so, when things really got going and I needed full-time staff, it was a no-brainer to take him on."

"And what do you know of him, personally?"

"I didn't really socialise with him outside of work." His tone was very matter-of-fact, genuine. Banner took on a thoughtful expression. "To be honest, this place is everything to me and I don't really do much else. It's come to dominate my life. My wife keeps the books and ensures everything ticks over financially. That leaves me to do what I do best, keeping the children out of mischief."

"Tell me, did Andy ever have access to the finances here?"

Banner appeared surprised at the question and scratched the stubble of his face, shaking his head. "No, not at all. Why do you ask?"

"I spoke with his wife this morning and there's some odd activity in their account. She was at a loss to explain what was going on. We're just trying to build a picture."

"Oh, I see. I only ever met his wife on two occasions… I think that's right, yes. June, isn't it? Or Jane. You know, I'm not sure now." Banner looked to the ceiling, struggling to remember. "He brought his wife and daughter, Becky, I remember her, lovely girl, to a couple of our family days over the summer last year. They seemed like a nice family. They must be devastated."

"How close was Andy to the children?"

"Oh, he was marvellous with them," Banner said, expressing true delight with one of his team. "To see how Andy could take some of those children under his wing and really look out for them was something to behold. He was great with the group as a whole, but he was truly gifted at spotting those that needed something more, you know? Andy was always willing to go the extra yard. Sometimes I wonder where he got his passion and motivation from."

Caslin nodded but didn't say what was going through his mind. "*Jane Connelly* was under the impression that her husband was required to travel to Leeds yesterday, for work."

"No. That's not the case at all. I don't understand where she got that idea." Banner was genuinely baffled. "I mean, we do have an affiliation with a similar project in Leeds and we often carry out joint trips and events. It allows for a sharing of the costs, but there was no reason for Andy to travel there yesterday. Not anything that I'm aware of."

"And you would know?"

"Yes! Of course, I would know."

"Were you here yesterday?" Caslin asked. Banner nodded that he was. "What about Andrew?"

"Yes, he was here too. Until lunchtime anyway."

"He left?"

Banner nodded. "He was supposed to be working a full shift and I was going to take the afternoon off but all of a sudden, Andy said something had come up and he had to go."

"Did he say what?" Caslin took out his pocketbook and a pen.

"No, he didn't. He said he had to shoot off for a little bit and then he'd come back but he never showed." The recollection triggered a display of irritation but it soon passed. "I assumed it was something to do with *Jane*, or maybe Becky, so I didn't get too upset about it."

"What made you think that?"

"Well, he was fine in the morning but then around midday he took a phone call. After that he was somewhat agitated and left shortly after. That's why I figured he'd had a call from home or the school and had to rush off."

"Anything like that ever happen before?" Banner thought about it and then shook his head. "Presumably, you keep records on all the children who attend here or pass through?"

"Of course, yes. We would anyway but the local authority demand it and we have good links with the local social workers."

"I'm going to send some officers down here at some point today, Mr Banner, and I would appreciate it if you could help them gather that information as soon as possible, along with a list of the other paid staff and your volunteers."

Banner appeared taken aback and it dawned on him that there was something going on he was unaware of. "This is unusual. Is there a problem?"

"I've no doubt this will be hitting the media in due course, but there are aspects to Andrew Connolly's life that you are going to find unpalatable, to say the least." Caslin watched the man for a reaction, however small. "Everyone who works here or has volunteered, either in the past or the present, will need to be interviewed by my team and I dare say you'll be spending more time with child services in the coming days and weeks. All the children who passed through your centre will need to be assessed."

"Are you saying… Andy…" The penny dropped. "That can't be?"

"This is your worst fear coming to pass, I assure you," Caslin said flatly, "and I take no pleasure in telling you."

"THE LATEST VIDEO IS UP." Holt called to Caslin as he entered the ops room. Taking off his coat, he hung it on the back of his chair before sitting down.

"Can you put it up for me?" Caslin pointed at the projection screen. Holt tapped away on his keyboard and moments later the projector fired up and the footage started to roll. Both Hunter and Templer turned away from what they were doing, all eyes on the screen. Details were difficult to make out as the footage was shot at night and there was very little external light to help. The previous night was overcast and despite the cemetery being on the edge of a populated suburb, the sheer scale of the site, as well as the mature trees, protected the area from the encroaching light pollution. To the east, past the cemetery's boundary, there lay an equally large area devoted to allotments.

The video was filmed on Connelly's mobile phone and was evidently hand held. The footage was unstable, adding to their difficulty in making out the detail. The picture dropped in and out of focus frequently as the holder moved around.

"There doesn't appear to be any confrontation between the two of them," Templer said. The camera angle zoomed out, widening the picture. The only sounds that could be identified came from traffic in the distance and the occasional snap or rustle of booted feet treading on the vegetation beneath their feet or the wind whistling through the branches overhead.

A momentary break in the clouds allowed shafts of silver moonlight to illuminate the scene. At that point, the person operating the camera zoomed in on the recognisable figure of Andrew Connolly placing his head through a noose. The image blurred as the cameraman approached, the mobile angled to the ground. They had to conclude he was tightening the rope at the nape of Connolly's neck. Stepping away, the camera came back up focussing on Connelly as he mounted a stepladder. Turning gingerly at the top, he looked directly at the camera. He was sobbing, his bottom lip quivered. Again, the cameraman moved around to the rear and the picture went black but sounds still emanated, sounds they struggled to interpret but the footage was still recording.

"What do you think he's doing now?" Hunter asked.

"He's taking up the slack of the rope," Caslin replied. The mobile was retrieved and the holder panned back to Connelly, sweeping back around to the front, viewing the victim's face. There were a few more seconds where both men stared at each other. Connelly mouthed the words *I'm sorry*. He seemed paralysed with fear. The watching detectives waited patiently for Connolly to step off but he remained where he was. The footage wobbled. Caslin could imagine the holder either encouraging him to step off or growing frustrated at the delay. Seconds later, there was movement as the camera surged forward, losing all focus. There was a panicked scream and the sound of a thud accompanied by the rattle of metal. The team looked at one another.

"Did he just kick the stepladder over?" Holt asked. No one replied.

The footage came back into focus, held once again by a steady hand. Heavy breathing could be heard. Connolly was swinging from left to right. Caslin was transfixed whereas the other three looked away. The footage held steady as Connelly struggled for breath, his face contorted in a mixture of pain and sheer terror. Caslin was grateful for the darkness that masked the final moments of the man's life.

Minutes passed before the camera panned down from the body to the ground, moving closer in order to film the carrier bag as well as its contents. Even in this light, the cash was visible. The angle of the camera changed to reveal the lotus flower held in the palm of a gloved hand. This was then placed on the ground, next to the bag before the footage returned to the form of Andrew Connolly, suspended from the tree. No longer was he gasping for breath, no struggling, no clawing at the rope or fighting for life. The footage paused and then faded to black. The number three appeared for the remainder of the video before playback ceased.

"What is it with the money?" Holt asked.

Caslin exhaled deeply. "Hunter and I saw repeated withdrawals from Connelly's bank account over the past few months. Always the same dates, always the same sum. Jane, Connolly's wife, was unaware of any reason for this cash to be withdrawn. My theory is that somehow our killer found out what Connelly has been getting up to and was bleeding him dry."

"Blackmail?"

"I think so, yes." Caslin looked back at the screen, the number three still visible. "He is meticulous. We know he plans these events in great detail. They aren't random or opportunistic attacks. For him to know what Connelly has been getting up to, he must have been around him for some time. If we go back through the Connelly's accounts and see when Andrew started making these withdrawals it might give us an idea how long the killer has been targeting him."

"But if he's been blackmailing him, why did he leave the money? There's nearly three grand there," Holt argued. "Do you think Connelly didn't turn up with enough?"

"He doesn't care about the money," Caslin countered. "He may have needed it before but for some reason, he doesn't need it now. Last night wasn't about money." Caslin played through the scenario in his mind. The killer arranged to meet Connelly, either demanding a larger payoff or perhaps he suggested this would be the final one. Regardless, he drew him to the cemetery to carry out his ruthless power play. "This was all about control. It was a pre-planned exercise in manipulation designed to torment his victim and drive him to suicide. Who knows what was said to Connelly in the build-up to last night but when he got there, he was presented with the reality of his darkest secrets going public. Then, he offered him a way out."

"Suicide." Templer rubbed at his face. "And when Connolly didn't look like he was going to take it, the killer booted him off the ladder and stood there watching him die."

"And not forgetting he also filmed it so the rest of us wouldn't miss out," Caslin added.

"Why didn't he film the removal of the finger this time?" Templer made a valid point.

"Although he does it to every victim, and has done in the past, I don't think that's part of his message to us."

"Then why does he do it?" Templer asked.

"That's an act for him," Caslin replied, "and him alone."

CHAPTER SEVENTEEN

"I PULLED every bit of CCTV from any camera surrounding the entrance to the cemetery or covering the approach road," Holt said. "There's only one vehicular access as well as the pedestrian gate. There isn't a lot to go on but I did find this footage produced by a security camera located on the exterior of a building opposite. The system is high quality, so I'm pleased with the clarity of the picture."

"That's good news, Terry." Caslin placed an approving hand on his shoulder.

"Yeah, don't get carried away though," Holt replied. "It doesn't give us much to run with." Holt brought up footage and Caslin's eyes narrowed as he concentrated. The picture was black and white, predominantly covering the foreground in the immediate vicinity of the building the camera was mounted on. However, at the top of the shot could clearly be seen the imposing wrought-iron gates of the entrance to the Victorian cemetery.

After a few moments, a car passed by and Holt dismissed it with a casual wave of the hand to imply it was nonsignificant. Instead, he pointed to a pedestrian. Appearing from out of shot to the left, they watched as a man approached the cemetery's gate, stopping and glancing around him in every direction before entering.

"I know it's hard to tell from this distance but he looks nervous to me," Caslin said aloud.

"And that was before he realised he was walking to his death," Holt added. They knew it was Andrew Connolly, it was obvious, not only because the clothing matched but he looked in the camera's direction. The resolution was such that they could identify him.

"Is that time stamp correct?" Caslin asked.

"I'll check but if it's out then I don't think it's by much, judging from the volume of traffic passing by in the footage I've seen," Holt stated.

"This puts him arriving at around 8:30," Caslin said. "I received a call from his tormentor around an hour later. Whether Connolly was alive at that point, I don't know but during the call he appeared distracted. While he was talking to me, I reckon he was at this particular crime scene. Any sign of our mysterious suspect?"

Holt shook his head. "I've been through the footage for an hour and a half prior to Connolly's arrival and through to two hours after the estimated time of death, and there's no sign of him."

"I didn't see Connolly carrying his own stepladder. Did the killer fly it in with a drone?"

"Yeah, along with himself." Holt was despondent.

The adjoining allotments offered the perfect opportunity to both arrive and depart unobserved. The CSI team, assisted by a large uniformed contingent, carried out a fingertip search in the immediate vicinity of the scene. A stepladder was found inside the groundskeepers' lock-up.

"I don't suppose there's any chance that they've been able to lift any prints?" Caslin asked.

"They picked up multiples from the lock-up as well as documenting the equipment stored within just in case he was careless. However, he was wearing gloves in the video, so I don't think we should get our hopes up," Hunter said.

"He's going to slip up somewhere along the line, they always do," Caslin replied. "What about the bank footage? Any joy there?"

"We went through it, sir," Hunter said. "Connolly is seen on an exterior camera approaching the bank in broad daylight, alone. He enters and fills out a withdrawal slip and takes it to the teller. They have a brief discussion and she counts out the money for him, putting it into an envelope, and he leaves."

"What about the member of staff, did you speak with them?"

"We did, yes," Holt said. "With that sum of money, it's borderline as to whether they fall back on their protocols or not. However, she did ask what he wanted the money for?" When a customer withdraws a large sum of cash, standard procedure is to look for signs they may be acting under duress. "Nothing in his demeanour, or what he said, indicated that Connolly was under any pressure. Therefore, she allowed the withdrawal to take place. Admittedly, both the teller and her line manager said they tend to pay closer attention to pensioners than they do to customers like him. He didn't exhibit any of the signs to trigger their concerns."

Caslin sighed. With the payments always being in cash, there was no electronic path between Connolly and his presumed blackmailer. However, it did leave them with an avenue to investigate. If he was right, then Connolly had a relationship with the killer. That wasn't to suggest they knew each other, although they couldn't dismiss the possibility. "They've had conversations and unless Connolly was leaving envelopes stuffed with cash in agreed random places, then there is every possibility they physically met on more than one occasion. This means that their paths have crossed and if we can pinpoint Connolly's movements, either through his phone, places he frequented or his ritual habits, then maybe we can determine where these meetings took place. I know that's a long shot, before anyone says it."

"How did he know what Connolly was up to?" Hunter asked.

"The same way he got your phone number, I expect, sir. I mean, he's tech savvy. He's been able to mask his domain every time he's been online to upload a video, and he got hold of your number in order to call you the other night. Perhaps he's also hacked Connolly's social media."

"I don't doubt his tech skills," Caslin agreed but they were missing something. "He still needed to get on to Connolly in the first place before moving on to hacking his account. Paedophiles like Connolly don't tend to operate in isolation. They may carry out systematic abuse alone but often they have the urge to share that experience with others, whether in online chat rooms or across the dark web for instance."

"You think they met in an online chat room?" Hunter asked, inclining her head in such a way to indicate she saw it as a possibility.

"It's not beyond the realm of possibility that he went looking online for someone like Connolly, then narrowed it down locally once he integrated himself deeper into the community," Caslin suggested. "Again, that suits his style to spend time methodically researching his targets."

"Or it could be simpler than that." Templer spoke up from the other side of the room. The three of them turned to look at him inquisitively. "It could just as easily be a relative of one of his victims who found out and decided to set themselves up as judge, jury and executioner. Let's not forget we are also considering the same scenario as a possibility with the victims of the poisoning in Stamford Street. This could all be some disaffected member of their own community."

"Where would Kelly Ryan fit into that?" Caslin asked. "Not that your logic isn't sound."

Templer shook his head. "I don't have an answer for that. We need to know more about her life."

Caslin's mobile rang and he glanced at the screen. Although he hadn't saved the number, he recognised it was Michelle Cates. A brief flicker of excitement tugged at his chest and he excused himself from the group, answering the call on the way into his office.

"Michelle." Closing the door behind him, he faced away from those in the room in a primitive attempt to avoid anyone picking up on his pleasure at receiving the call.

"Nate, I'm sorry to call you," she said hastily, flustered.

"That's okay." Fearful for a moment there had been another unwanted visitor at her home, he tried to reassure her. "Is something wrong?"

"I know this probably has nothing to do with you but what with everything that's been going on recently…" Her voice cracked as she spoke.

"It's okay, Michelle. What's on your mind?"

"Carly is home from school. She's quite upset. One of her friends… she was pulled out of class today and left early. It turns out her father killed himself."

"Yes, I'm aware of the case and the circumstances are under investigation."

Michelle's voice raised in pitch and she started to ramble almost incoherently. "They're saying on the news… and all over social media, that he was abusing kids… Carly is… she's been to this place where he works. She knows Becky. She's been to this girl's home! Nathaniel, I bloody sent her there. Do you know what I've… what if…?"

"Michelle, I need you to take a breath," Caslin said. "I know this is difficult. I have children myself and the thoughts running through your head must be awful, but I'll tell you this, I was at the centre earlier today speaking with the management. Now, I shouldn't really be speaking about it but we are investigating."

"My little girl," Michelle said, bursting into tears at the prospect of every parent's worst nightmare coming true.

"I know this is hard," Caslin repeated, trying his best to be upbeat. "There are hundreds of children who have passed through the centre at different times. The probability of your daughter being a… one of those affected is very slim. Try to hold on to that."

"I know you've no reason to, Nathaniel," she said, "but could you come around… later… if you have time?"

Caslin knew he shouldn't because that could compromise his objectivity in the case but, at the same time, he was confident he could navigate a safe path and besides, he wanted to. "I'll stop by this evening on my way home." He looked over his shoulder, worried he would be overheard despite standing alone in his office. Hunter caught his eye but looked away as soon as he clocked her observing him.

"Thank you." Michelle sounded relieved. "I'll see you then."

Caslin hung up on the call, touched the handset to his lips and smiled. He could certainly have reassured her over the phone but the prospect of seeing her again was too appealing. The excitement of the anticipation of their next meeting rose within him.

Leaving his office, Templer beckoned him over.

"I've been putting some thought into this numbering sequence that appears at the end of each video," he explained.

"What have you come up with?"

"The motivation cannot simply be focussed on his craving for attention. Were that the case, then he wouldn't be going to such great detail in staging each scene."

"You're talking about leaving the lotus flowers as well as the numbering, aren't you?"

Templer nodded. "He's sending us a message. Not only us, but the wider world in general. If your primary objective is to have all eyes on you, then his actions have succeeded but, in that scenario, you wouldn't be leaving the money behind at Stamford Street nor the carrier bag stuffed with cash, let alone staging the flowers. He has a greater purpose."

"Terry looked into the flowers earlier," Caslin said.

"Yes, he did," Templer agreed, "but he was looking specifically at the lotus flower, which is widely used across the world in the iconography and belief systems of multiple religions. Focussing on the numbers and tying them to a religious belief narrows the focus significantly."

Caslin thought on it for a few moments. "You're going down the line of *The Ten Commandments* or *The Five Pillars* of Islam, right?"

Templer nodded to indicate they were thinking along the same path. "Right. Although, every religion seems to have a list of rules, guidelines that practitioners should live their life by. In fact, many of the regions have multiple lists. From *The Ten Commandments* to the *Seven Deadly Sins* through to Judaism's *613 Commandments*, whoever has the time to memorise all of those, I don't know. Anyway, specifically cross-referencing the numbering with the added emphasis of the lotus flower I've tied it to Buddhism."

"Isn't Buddhism considered to be the most peaceful of the dominant faiths?" Caslin countered.

"Don't all religions classify themselves as religions of peace?" Templer argued. From the disdain with which he made the comment, Caslin figured he was far from a religious man. "The reason I focussed on Buddhist practice is because of how prominently the lotus flower is connected with it in western society. If you had asked me before Terry did his research, then I would have thought of this one first because I didn't know it had any significance in other religions."

"Okay, you've got my attention," Caslin said, indicating for him to continue and pulling up a chair.

"Well, the first thing I came to was *The Four Noble Truths*. They focus specifically on suffering, the truth of suffering, the causes, the end of suffering as well as the path that leads to the end. These are described as the essence of the Buddha's teachings."

"I can already see a flaw in this," Caslin said. "The video recording at Stamford Street…"

"Finished with the displaying of the number five. Yes, I know," Templer interrupted him. "However, as I said previously, religions often have several numbered lists in which to adhere to during your life. Buddhism is no different. Beyond *The Four Noble truths* there are *The Five Precepts*."

"Precepts?" Caslin asked. "Like rules?"

"Not so much rules. More like guidelines. Buddhism doesn't set out rules or commandments. They are commitments that all followers of the Buddha's teachings try to adhere to. In their simplest interpretations they could fit with our three crime scenes so far."

"I'm not so keen on the *so far* part of what you just said," Caslin replied, indicating for him to continue. He waved to Hunter and beckoned her to join them. She did so, bringing Terry Holt with her. Caslin had a sense that DI Templer was onto something.

"As I said, we have to look at these very loosely because, as I understand it, the precepts are actually very detailed and go far deeper than the first few lines of a headline search on the Internet. However, go with me on this," Templer said, as the others sat down. "The murders at the drug den on Stamford Street were documented with the number five. The Fifth Precept, simplistically, asks for people to refrain from the taking of intoxicating substances because they cloud the mind. That ranges from alcohol through to recreational drugs, even gambling if it's a habitual action, so I think it's quite easy to see how that ties in."

"The precepts are a moral code, as I recall," Hunter said. "I remember seeing a documentary about them a while back."

"The third precept focuses on refraining from sexual misconduct," Templer continued. "As I say, it does go far deeper but I think we can all agree that Andrew Connelly's behaviour certainly ticks that box. My understanding is that the teachings reflect sexual relations within marriage as the acceptable moral path. Molesting children would certainly fall foul of that guideline."

"What about Kelly Ryan?" Caslin asked. "There's some indication that she was having a relationship beyond the confines of her marriage."

"But the number two was assigned to her, wasn't it?" Holt asked.

"That's right, it was," Templer confirmed. "The second is often thought to be referring to stealing but I've done a little bit of reading around it and a better interpretation would be to define it as *taking what is not freely given*. That's not exactly the same thing."

"What was it her line manager said her team did?" Caslin asked.

"They worked on debt management." Templer was growing in stature as the outline of his theory developed. "The administration of repossession orders when clients couldn't meet their mortgage repayments was part of their role. Very few people willingly want to be evicted from their homes."

Caslin considered their next step. "Terry, I want you to go back to Kelly's line manager, at the bank, and pull up a list of all the repossession cases she's been working on recently. Add to that list any she has underway where the clients haven't been evicted yet."

"Yes, sir," Holt said, making a note. "How far back do you want me to go?"

"Six to twelve months. Perhaps further if there are a significant number," Caslin said. "He may have been planning this for some time, so we have no idea when he first conceived of the idea. While you're there, I want you to revisit her colleagues. Apparently, Kelly Ryan didn't have many interests outside of her work. Therefore, it stands to reason if she mentioned who she was sleeping with on the quiet, they will be the ones who she spoke to about it."

"We've already interviewed them, sir," Hunter stated, with a shake of the head. "They didn't offer us anything."

"If Kelly was involved with a senior member of the staff, they may have felt threatened. Give them a further nudge and apply a bit of pressure. You might get a favourable response."

"Will do, sir," Holt said.

"I'll come with you," Hunter said.

Caslin then exchanged glances with Templer. His logic was sound. "You said there are five in total? That leaves us two more."

"There are Five Precepts, sure. If I'm right, then we still have the first and the fourth to come."

"And they are?" Caslin asked.

"The *precept of truthfulness* and then there's the big one, the first. The one considered more important than any other, covering *the harming of living things.*"

"There's no irony there then," Caslin countered with intended sarcasm.

CHAPTER EIGHTEEN

CASLIN LOOKED AT THE CLOCK. It was late afternoon and a thought occurred to him. Standing up and moving away from the table, he left the others still discussing Templar's theory. Retrieving his coat, he slipped it on and headed for the door. Catching Hunter's eye as he passed her, he replied to the unasked question.

"I'm just popping out for a bit."

"Okay, what shall I say if anyone asks for you?"

"Tell them I've gone out," Caslin replied, not looking back. Making his way along the corridor, he carried out a brief Internet search and was pleased to find his idea bearing fruit. The address was on the edge of the centre, just beyond the city walls, although he had no recollection of this particular building despite driving past on countless occasions.

Leaving the station and setting off for his car, Caslin was pleased that the threat of rainfall appeared to have passed. There was a strong breeze and despite clear skies and warm sunshine, it still felt colder than perhaps it should have been at this time of year. Starting the car, he turned right out of the car park and onto the Fulford Road leading into York. The traffic on the ring road was building as he drove the short distance to his destination. Not quite sure which building he was looking for, Caslin scanned the street scene as he approached. There was a large intersection where several routes converged, either passing in or out of the city itself or continuing to circumvent it. Waiting at these traffic lights, Caslin saw what he was looking for.

The sequence of the lights went from red through to green and Caslin imposed his lane change on an unsuspecting motorist, drawing an angry blast of a car horn. York was one of those cities where people unfamiliar with the location often fell afoul of incorrect lane choice as the route was not always clear. On this occasion, Caslin's destination was a building much the same as any other on the street, nothing stood out to differentiate it from the surrounding ones apart from signage that, unsurprisingly, was low key. Pulling across the traffic, he mounted the pavement and parked the car at the front of the building. There was limited space but he left it there, nonetheless. Another driver sounded a blast of their car horn and Caslin pretended not to notice, despite it being undoubtedly aimed at him.

The building was a detached residential address, the likes of which were, these days, more often than not converted into commercial premises rather than occupied as domestic homes. Such properties were large, expensive to own and run, and because of their proximity to the city usually came with very little outside space. The combination of these factors made them unviable, as well as undesirable, as family homes in the modern era.

Caslin rang the bell but then realised the door was unlocked, with the latch open, and he entered. The interior was clean and well presented, white painted walls with the original pattern tiles laid out on the floor before him. There was a small table to the left with an abundance of leaflets set in holders. He cast an eye over them. The sound of creaking treads announced someone coming down the stairs. Caslin turned to see the approach of a short man, probably in his mid-sixties. He was bald from forehead to crown and unlike many with the same growth pattern, he chose not to keep the sides and back of his head close cropped. White hair bulged out in a horseshoe around his head. Aside from that, he wore jeans and an ivory knitted jumper, one that his late father would have described as a cricketer's offering. Caslin was surprised. The approaching man noticed the reaction, drawing a wide and genuine smile.

"What were you expecting?" He spoke in a broad Yorkshire accent.

"Is it that obvious?" Caslin returned the smile.

"You can always tell the newcomers who are here for the first time. I think many people expect to find us all shaven headed, walking around in orange robes, chanting and tapping cymbals."

Caslin laughed. "I have to admit the thought did occur."

"I'm Chen Tao, one of the teachers here at the centre." He introduced himself, offering Caslin his hand.

"Detective Inspector Caslin."

"Now it's my turn to look surprised." Chen Tao raised his eyebrows. "What can I do for you, Inspector, is this a professional call?"

"I'm afraid so, yes. I'm not very aware of your traditions and I was hoping you could fill in some gaps to my knowledge regarding Buddhism, as well as the motivations of those people who follow it."

The smile returned. "Now there's a challenge. I'm certainly willing to try. Please, do come through."

Chen Tao led them further into the building. They bypassed the original drawing room and through to what would have been the dining room but had now been substantially increased in size with a large extension to the rear. The room was now a meeting hall with perhaps two-dozen chairs stacked along one side. Collapsed trestle tables were neatly ordered against the opposite wall.

"How many people attend here?" Caslin was impressed by the scale. With no idea of the group's popularity, he was impressed by the potential numbers they could accommodate.

"We have a diverse group. We run evening classes for those who are exploring the *Dharma* - the teachings of the Buddha – along with meditation classes, yoga sessions and various other community-focussed evenings. We can have anything up to thirty people present for those but when we have a guest speaker, then that number can swell into the hundreds. In those case we often have to book somewhere else. The centre is too small."

"That's impressive," Caslin said, not intending to sound as surprised as he appeared.

"We also run weekend retreats here."

"Places for people to come to… recharge?"

"That is dependent on the nature of the retreat," Chen Tao explained. "There is a different focus for each but all are beneficial either for spiritual development or reinforcement."

"Presumably you've seen an uptake in numbers with mindfulness so much in the public consciousness these days?"

Chen Tao laughed. "It has certainly become fashionable, hasn't it? Mindfulness is a part of what we do but I would argue it has been practised for thousands of years, not only in the last decade."

Caslin was apologetic. "I'm sorry, I didn't mean to offend you."

"No offence is taken, I assure you. Secular mindfulness is useful but, and I don't wish to appear dismissive, it will only take you so far. Nevertheless, it would be fair to say the centre has grown in the last few years which we are all very pleased with."

"You refer to it as a centre rather than a temple?"

"A temple has certain connotations, particularly in western society. We welcome people from all faiths and backgrounds, no matter whether they are Christian, Muslim, or of any other denomination. Even committed atheists attend here. We are here to help guide people along their spiritual path and their progression is largely by their own will. Practising from a centre is far more appropriate. Is there anything specific that you are interested in because your enquiry is rather broad?"

"I'm very interested in the *Five Precepts*."

"Ahh… the ethics. Fascinating subject, even for those who have studied them for years."

"Ethics?" Caslin asked.

"The precepts form the basis of Buddhist doctrine for both lay and monastic followers," Chen Tao explained. "In their most basic form they are principles that we aspire to live by that will aid us along our path to enlightenment. The ultimate goal of any Buddhist."

"I'm led to believe they are guidelines, things that we should refrain from doing. Bad things, for want of a better phrase," Caslin said.

Chen Tao shook his head indicating that he disagreed. "They are a set of guidelines but are often misconstrued in the way you describe, Inspector. I think that's a hangover from western society where previous generations have been raised along religious paths and their… dogma… has transposed itself."

"I don't understand."

"For instance, if you talk about *The Ten Commandments*, then they are rigid and are not open to any form of interpretation. *Thou shalt not kill,* for example, is quite explicit but the precepts are not solely focussed on the negative because everything in our existence is about balance. Let me explain with an example." He lifted a chair from a stack, offering it to Caslin before retrieving one for himself. "The fourth precept covers the *principle of truthfulness*. In its negative form, we are expected to refrain from *false speech* which can obviously be interpreted as lying, but also extends to gossiping. However, there is also a positive form of this principle. That being we should work towards a more truthful communication. In doing so, we *purify our speech* which also purifies our mind."

"I see." Caslin thought about it. "So, there is a positive and negative aspect to each of the precepts?"

"Absolutely. In this case we could define truthfulness as *a courageous respect for reality*, even when acknowledging and facing up to the truth goes against what we see as our self-centred goals, or when it might cause us our greatest discomfort."

"That's interesting. Most of us don't really get past the headlines."

"Many don't. The precepts are not simple guidelines, they are not soundbites used to adjust your frame of reference or perception of the world around you. They are guidelines set out in order to help you develop the qualities that you will need on your path. They are about straightforwardness, integrity and challenging yourself to understand how your views and reactions are shaped by not only your own actions but also how your perception of the world around you forms what you are and see."

"They are about developing you, helping you to..."

"Without wishing to confuse you, Inspector." Chen Tao politely held up a hand, interrupting him. "I think you would find that the Buddha would most likely point out that there is no *you* to speak of, for we are all linked within this universe, but I understand that may be one step too far in the confines of this conversation." He smiled. It was clear he wasn't being dismissive but genuinely attempting to help Caslin to understand.

"And this is all geared towards achieving enlightenment?"

"We all hope to achieve enlightenment, but to do so in one lifetime I believe is unlikely. It is quite possible that before a person can obtain enlightenment, they may well pass through several lifetimes beforehand."

"Can I deduce from what you're saying that there is no punishment within Buddhism for failure to follow these guidelines?"

"As Buddhists, we must adhere to the laws of the land in which we live. There can be no opt out from society's rule of law but you are correct, punishment is not part of our tradition. I'm sure you'll be aware of the concept of karma?" He inclined his head in Caslin's direction. Caslin nodded that he was. "I should imagine, not wishing to leap to judgement, that your knowledge of the concept of karma is also slightly skewed."

"Karma is a case of what goes around comes around, isn't it?"

"In essence, in its simplest form, that has become a commonly held view. However, karma is upheld as the consequence of your behaviour, be it positive or negative. Karma is the action that we do and it is the *vipaka* that is the ripening of that karmic action, or the consequence that we then experience. And again, people tend to view this blend of action and consequence in isolation whereas, in reality, what we are all doing is gathering karma throughout this life, the previous one, as well as our future lives and it will ripen at different times along the path."

"So, forgive the colourful language, but if someone is a total bastard in this life then there is every possibility that the consequence may only strike them in the next?"

Chen Tao shrugged. "That is possible, yes."

"In which case, what is there to deter someone in this lifetime from carrying out horrendous acts of violence?"

"Eventually, if a person follows the Dharma, they will come to realise the pain and suffering they inflict on others will revisit them at some point. But, in a direct answer to your question, I think there is nothing within Buddhism, or outside of it for that matter, that can ensure someone will think along the lines you describe. Tell me, does the threat of capital punishment deter a man from taking another's life?"

"No, I don't believe it does."

"Therefore, the concept of punishment as a deterrent is a fallacy."

"For the most part, I would have to agree," Caslin said, nodding. "I'm sure many others wouldn't."

"I don't doubt that, Inspector."

"But the law is clear. Prison sentences are both a deterrent and an opportunity for rehabilitation," Caslin argued.

"To my knowledge, the rehabilitation programmes that exist within the prison reform structure have mixed success rates," Chen Tao responded. Caslin didn't disagree. "However, the only thing that will truly rescue these people from their negative path is the Dharma."

"Only if they are prepared to learn," Caslin countered.

Chen Tao smiled. "For that, we all need an open mind as a starting point. May I ask, what is the nature of the case that you are investigating?"

"You'll understand that I can't openly discuss an ongoing investigation, but we have a working theory that someone is using the precepts as a moral justification for carrying out awful attacks on people," Caslin said, choosing his words carefully.

"Are you talking about this *Night Stalker*, who is all over the news?"

"And here's me thinking I was being cryptic." Caslin smiled, drawing one from the man next to him. "There is the distinct possibility that he is mentally unstable or is something of an extreme radical when it comes to his belief system. Somehow, I can't see a true practitioner of Buddhism allowing himself to persecute others in such a violent and grotesque way."

Chen Tao waved the index finger of his right hand from side to side dismissing Caslin's comment. "Only if that were true, Inspector. Unfortunately, not all followers of Buddhism walk the same path. Just as there are offshoots of other religious orders who follow their own doctrine, there are those who interpret the Buddhist canon in ways that many of us do not find agreeable."

Caslin was intrigued as he had always considered Buddhism to be the one religion devoted purely to spiritual development. Sitting forward in his chair, he encouraged the teacher to elaborate. "Please, go on."

"There is an ethno-nationalist branch of the *Theravada* sect, the most conservative of the traditions and commonly practised in Thailand, Laos and Cambodia as well as in Sri Lanka. They believe a peaceful and calm state of mind cannot exist until all practitioners of the Muslim faith have been eradicated."

Caslin's mouth dropped open. "To the extent of acts of violence?"

"*Extreme* acts of violence." He took on a melancholy look. "This is how we come to see the persecution of the *Rohingya* in Myanmar for example. Sri Lanka, in response to the changes brought under the British colonial rule of the late nineteenth and early twentieth centuries, saw the rise of modern *Sinhalese Buddhist Nationalism*, fuelling an incredible level of violence and hatred in its name. They targeted any who were perceived as antagonistic towards Buddhism. By the way, that included fellow Buddhists of Tamil descent."

"So how did they square that circle with their Buddhist teachings?" Caslin was genuinely surprised. The conversation highlighted his own ignorance of world events. Until this point, he always thought his knowledge was extensive but he knew little of this. He felt a degree of embarrassment.

"Sinhalese nationalism was rooted in local myths denoting them as a religiously chosen people, racially pure, and of special progeny. The *Dravidian Tamils* were regarded as inferior. Any minority unwilling to support the newly created ethnocentric system was an open target. Sadly, it doesn't take much for those who are creative and possess destructive beliefs to commit terrible acts in their name."

"Have you ever come across anyone espousing such beliefs here in the UK, or York, for that matter?" Caslin asked.

Chen Tao shook his head. "Many come to the centre who are perhaps not ready to walk the path or demonstrate what we refer to as *unskilled behaviour*, but no one with attitudes that come even close to those I've described."

Caslin glanced at the clock on the wall and then double checked by looking at his watch. It was late in the day. "Thank you for your time." He stood, offering his hand.

Chen Tao took it. "I hope I was of some help, Inspector. We have a meeting in around half an hour. You'd be more than welcome to join us and participate in the discussion. You may even find it eye opening."

"Perhaps another time but I am afraid I have a prior engagement."

"You're welcome any time."

Caslin turned and began to walk away before pausing and looking back over his shoulder. "This may seem like an odd question…" Chen Tao was open to another question. "Is there anything you've ever come across within Buddhism regarding the mutilation of a person's body?"

Chen Tao was perplexed but he thought it for a moment. "There are stories, myths, one might say." He indicated for Caslin to wait as he crossed the room, kneeling before a cupboard and opening the door. Inside were several shelves crammed with books, some old and some new. Scanning along the spines, Caslin watched as he sought the one he was looking for. Plucking it from the second shelf from the top, he pushed the door to. Returning to Caslin, he handed him the book.

Caslin scanned the cover. It was heavy and well worn, with the pages taking on a dark brown colour such was the book's age. "This is… meaty," he said, not wishing to sound ungrateful.

Chen Tao laughed. "That is a brief history of the past 2000 years and the development of Buddhism within that timeframe. There are many tales documented within it that have been recanted in one form or another. Feel free to borrow it and read it at your leisure. You never know, you may find what you're looking for in there."

"Thank you. I'll get this back to you." Caslin held the book up, nodding appreciatively. "Tell me, what comes after the *Fifth Precept*?"

"For those who pass on to become *Mitras*, or who go on to be fully ordained, there are further precepts to study but they are more monastic undertakings for those post-ordination. More related to religious ceremony and spiritual retreats than daily life. For example, a vow of celibacy or abstaining from food on certain religious days. In terms of living guidelines, we have *The Noble Eight-fold Path* but these are unrelated to the precepts. There truly is much scope for further development."

"Are most people aware of this? The way the precepts change, I mean."

Chen Tao smiled. "Lay persons… probably not. There is little call for lay Buddhists to adhere to these stricter precepts."

"Thank you again." Caslin silently pondered the last as he set off for the exit. *Where would their killer go when he reached the fifth?*

CHAPTER NINETEEN

MOUNTING the steps to the Cates's residence, Caslin reached for the door knocker and suddenly felt self-conscious. Logically, there was no reason for him to be nervous but nevertheless, he considered his outward appearance momentarily before dismissing the doubts. A warm flush passed up the back of his neck. He rapped the door three times and stepped back to wait. Soon after, the door opened and he was greeted with Michelle's broad smile although she too, appeared slightly bashful as their eyes met. She wore her hair down, adorned in minimal make-up and jewellery and cut an attractive and classy figure in a two-piece red trouser suit and cream blouse.

"Please, Nathaniel, come in." Standing to one side, she welcomed him in. "I hope you didn't mind me calling you?"

Caslin shook his head enthusiastically. "No, not at all. You can call me Nate, if you prefer."

Michelle Cates appeared taken aback. "Sorry, I meant earlier this afternoon, when I phoned."

Caslin felt his cheeks flush red with embarrassment. "Sorry, my mistake." He flicked his eyes away from hers.

"No, I'm sorry… I am addressing you personally, aren't I? I shouldn't presume—"

"No, no, it's not an issue, I'm quite happy with it," Caslin replied, attempting to stave off the growing awkwardness of their exchange but only seeming to add to it further. He stopped talking and looked down at the floor. Taking a deep breath, he brought his head up and met her eye once again. She smiled again whilst closing the door. It was a relief for him to see and he returned it. Michelle visibly relaxed and he thought she might be experiencing similar feelings to his own. At least he hoped so.

"Shall we start again?"

"Perhaps that would be a good idea," Caslin replied, broadening his smile into a grin.

"Have you brought some light reading?"

Momentarily confused, Caslin stood open-mouthed before realising he was holding the book given him by Chen Tao. "Oh, this." He laughed. "Someone lent it to me and I've not been home yet."

Inclining her head in order to read the spine, Caslin offered the book up to make it easier. "Interesting choice of subject matter. I get the impression you're a man of many surprises. I was just about to have something to eat." She gestured for him to follow her towards the kitchen. He glanced at his watch. "Yes, I know it's late. Carly had netball training earlier this evening and it always sets us back."

Glancing around, looking for somewhere to place the book, he chose an occasional table adjacent to a coat stand. The last thing he wanted was to have this tome next to them while they ate. The history of Buddhism wasn't likely to sell him as an exciting date. "Is Carly around?"

"What with the events at school today and then training, on top of everything else we are dealing with at the moment, she's absolutely shattered. She's already in bed. I checked on her earlier and she's out for the count."

"How is your brother, Thomas?" Caslin asked as they entered the kitchen.

Michelle glanced over her shoulder towards him, offering him a stool at the breakfast bar. "Are you asking out of courtesy or in a professional capacity?"

Caslin was unsure how to interpret her response. If he were more familiar with her personality, he would no doubt be able to judge the seriousness in her tone. "I'm off duty." The reply was ambivalent.

Michelle's ability to read him was finer tuned than his regarding her. "I'm just kidding, Nate. Relax. To be honest, I'm not sure how Thomas is coping. I think it's always a struggle when you lose someone close to you but to do so under these circumstances, I've no idea how he's feeling. I try to at least speak with him daily since... but he's not a man who likes anyone to make a fuss. I don't really know what to do for the best."

"As long as he knows you're there for him if he asks."

"I floated the possibility of him moving in with us for a while. The house is big enough, after all." She raised her eyes heavenward, angling her head in a reflective pose. "But I'm not sure he's even come to terms with our mother's passing yet, and this place is so full of memories," she said, her eyes tracking around the room before settling on Caslin.

"He didn't go for it then?"

Michelle shook her head. "Are you hungry? You never said." Caslin had to admit his mouth was watering at the smell of the food simmering on the stove. "It's nothing exciting, just a puttanesca that I threw together. There's plenty to go around."

"Thank you. That would be lovely. Is there anything I can do," he asked, looking past her and across to a casual dining table at the end of the contemporary glass addition.

"You could set two places at the table." She pointed in the direction he was looking. Taking off her jacket and hanging it up alongside the doorway to the hall, she gestured to a cabinet behind him. "You'll find cutlery and everything else you need in those drawers to your right."

Ten minutes later, Caslin pulled out a chair for himself along with another for his host, as she came to the table with two bowls of steaming pasta. Michelle encouraged him to sit down while she walked to the fridge and returned with a block of Parmesan cheese, picking up a bottle of red wine along the way. She brandished both, one in each hand, and smiled. Caslin nodded appreciatively and looked around for a bottle opener.

"You did say you were off duty," she said, indicating a dark hardwood sideboard behind him. "In the top drawer." Caslin searched where instructed, turning back with a bottle opener in hand and set about cracking the seal and removing the cork. Michelle retrieved two large glasses from a nearby shelf, setting them down alongside each other on the table. The bottle was opened and Caslin lifted it, angling it slightly towards the light in order to read the label. He was impressed at the quality of her taste. "Is it to your satisfaction?" Her tone was playful.

"You can't go far wrong with a *Grand Vin*."

"You like your wine?" she asked, finely grating the cheese over their food without asking him if he wanted any. He didn't mind. The more the better.

There was once a time when he was laughably picky when it came to decisions on which wine best accompanied a given meal but these days, he would judge his younger self to be pretentious. However, he chose not to share the self-deprecating thought. "I appreciate the finer things in life," he said, glancing from the label towards his company. The comment sounded much like something his younger self would have said and he regretted saying it. She didn't appear to notice. "Should I let it breathe?"

"It hasn't breathed in twelve years, so let's not worry about that now," Michelle replied with a half-smile. Caslin laughed and poured each of them half a glass.

"You said earlier you were worried about Carly," Caslin said, re-taking his seat and picking up both a fork and a spoon before setting about his meal. She nodded. "Have you noticed any change in her behaviour recently?"

Michelle thought on it for a moment, picking up her glass and tasting the wine once she'd finished her mouthful of food. Placing the glass back down on the table, she kept a hold of the stem between thumb and forefinger gently turning the glass where it sat. "Nothing that I've found unusual. She has been a little quiet since Kelly..."

"What about your relationship with her? Do you get on well?"

Michelle bobbed her head. "Yes, we are very open with each other, always have been."

"You said Carly knows Andrew Connolly's daughter?"

"They share classes at school. Not to mention they play in some of the same sports teams which is how she wound up at the centre he works at. It's not easy being a single mum, working and trying to open the door to as many experiences for your daughter as you can," she said, taking on a reflective expression.

"Yes, I know where you're coming from."

"You have children, don't you?" Caslin nodded. Usually, he would try to keep conversation regarding his children to a minimum, not wishing to expose his disjointed personal life. "Do they live with you?"

"No, they live with their mother but I understand the restrictions children place on your time, particularly when you're doing everything alone."

"I wasn't suggesting you were humouring me." She reached across the table and gently touched the back of his hand. "You just have the look, you know?"

Caslin inclined his head to one side, frowning. "*The look?*"

"Yes. The look of a man who probably throws everything he has into his work in order to mask his loneliness."

Caslin was taken aback at both her assessment of him as well as her candid nature. "You are… direct."

Michelle was immediately apologetic. "I'm sorry, I didn't mean to offend you, I just… I often find I'm good at reading people. If I'm way off the mark—"

Caslin smiled and shook his head. "To be honest, I think you're right on the money." A strange emotion passed through him. On the one hand, her critique could be taken as a slight but truthfully, she had read him very well indeed. He raised his glass, tilting it in her direction and raised it to his lips.

"I'm also experienced in relationship failure. Carly wasn't exactly an immaculate conception."

Caslin laughed. "Divorced?"

"Separated." She raised her own glass to her lips, taking on a faraway look. "For now, at least…"

"Having a difficult time?" Caslin asked before seeing the change in Michelle's expression and quickly adding, "Sorry, not really any of my business."

"No, don't worry. We had our problems. We married young… that seems like such a long time ago now." She shook her head, smiling ruefully. "My Mother fell ill and Daniel lost his job with the council and couldn't find work. Then his mother died suddenly. It was a shocking time for all of us. I had to return to work to try and make ends meet. It was one thing after another. Eventually something had to give." She took another drink, almost finishing her glass. Caslin thought she was hitting it pretty hard. He'd been there. "Now we have all of this… and Carly…"

"Hey, if you're half as good at reading your own daughter as you are me, then I should imagine you've got nothing to worry about."

"It would be easier if I knew what I was watching out for."

Caslin sipped his wine before answering, savouring the aftertaste on his tongue. He approved of her choice. "Any frequent bouts of aggression. Withdrawing into herself and wanting to be alone or making excuses as to why she can't take part in physical activity because she doesn't want to get undressed in front of others." Caslin was thinking aloud. "Has she become obsessive or suffered from anxiety at all?"

Michelle shook her head. "No, nothing like that. Carly's very confident and outward looking. She can't wait to try new things, a lot like her mother in that respect."

Caslin felt there was more behind her expression, her smile. He hoped so. "How has she been in general, regarding her eating and sleeping patterns? Does she skip school or experiment with alcohol, hang out with friends who take drugs? That kind of thing."

"No, certainly not." Her response implied the very notion was laughable.

"Then, in that case, I should imagine you have very little to worry about."

"But she's been around that man," Michelle replied. The warm smile switched to be replaced by a stern look. "I can't know for sure, can I?"

"Paedophiles like Connelly are clever," Caslin explained. "They will put themselves in positions of responsibility and trust around children. They gravitate to those roles. It's almost as if they are drawn to certain professions. They systematically work out, for want of a better word, who their best targets are. They may have access to a hundred children and from that group they will know which ones to target. These will be the most vulnerable or the most damaged… the ones they think will be the easiest to manipulate and therefore ensure it remains secret. That might be a very small percentage of those who they are in contact with overall. From what you've told me, Carly doesn't fit the profile. I think you can be very confident."

"What about the unlucky ones?"

Caslin took a deep breath and sipped his wine. "We are working to identify them and get them into safety if we can."

"Those poor children."

"I know."

"It's almost hard to judge someone for killing him, isn't it?" Michelle said, catching Caslin off guard. She noticed his reaction. "Not that I'm condoning it."

"I know what you mean," Caslin said, choosing his words carefully, "but let's not forget why we have the rule of law in the first place, precisely to stop people exercising their own forms of vigilante justice. Connelly may very well be beneath our contempt or our sympathy, but not every case is likely to be as cut and dried." Immediately, Caslin regretted his last comment, remembering Kelly Ryan's death at the hands of the same murderer. "Forgive me, that was insensitive."

Michelle reached across the table again and took a firm grip on Caslin's hand this time, meeting his eye. "That's okay, honestly. You're right of course."

Conversation moved onto lighter subjects as they enjoyed the remainder of their meal. For a short time, both of them slipped into a level of comfort neither would claim to have recent experience of. For Caslin, it was a snapshot of what life used to be like before a succession of terrible personal life-choices steered his path in an entirely different direction. An hour passed that felt like mere moments. The sound of a little girl calling out from upstairs carried to them, breaking through their laughter.

"That's Carly," Michelle said, placing her glass on the table and rising. "I'll just go and check on her." Caslin watched her leave the room. The sway of her hips caught his imagination and when she glanced back over her shoulder, she realised it too. Michelle smiled and he felt his face reddening for the second time that evening.

Caslin took his wine and came to stand before the bi-fold doors overlooking the garden. Casting his thoughts back to the last time he was there, investigating the potential prowler, he was pleased there was no reoccurrence of the intruder. The stepping up of patrols in the area returned no further sightings and he was left to wonder whether Michelle had been right that evening – her paranoia placing figures in the shadows where there were none to be seen. If not for the cigarette butts, he'd found, he would think so too. Staring out into the darkness, unable to see anything because of the interior light, he felt the hair on the back of his neck standing, the sense that someone was watching him.

Unlocking the first of the doors, he opened it and stepped out onto the patio. The sounds of the city at night came to him. The evening was cool with a gentle breeze. His eyes slowly adjusted to the light and he scanned the perimeter, watching the branches of the trees swaying gently to and fro. His mobile rang and Caslin withdrew it from his pocket, answering without looking at the caller.

"Sir," Hunter said, "I'm sorry to call you so late but we have another victim."

Caslin was deflated. "So soon? Are you sure it's one for us?"

"I'm afraid so but this one's different," she replied. "We're on *Bishophill Senior*. Are you at home?"

Caslin glanced back into the kitchen to see Michelle returning from upstairs. She saw he was on the phone and set about clearing away the dishes. "No, I'm somewhere else. I'm in the city though. I'll meet you there shortly."

With one last look around, the feeling of being watched had left him. Returning inside, he closed the door behind him, securing the lock. Slipping the mobile back into his pocket, he smiled as Michelle came over to him. She poured herself more wine from the bottle and offered him a top up.

Pursing his lips, he shook his head. "I'd love to but something has come up," he said, regret edging into his tone. "I have to go."

"Always on duty after all?" she replied, raising her glass in his direction.

"I'm sorry."

"That's okay." She was smiling as she spoke but without conviction. "It's not like we're on a date, is it?"

"Perhaps another time?"

"A date?" she countered. This time, he was unfazed, confident even.

"I would like that."

Putting her glass on the counter, she walked with him to the front door. Releasing the latch, she opened the door, leaning against it, cradling the edge against her shoulder where her arm met her chest. Caslin paused at the threshold, turning to her, unsure of how he should behave. Michelle read his indecision and moved in his direction. He mirrored her movement and they met. Her lips felt smooth, soft to the touch, and he felt a wave of excitement that matched his anticipation as they kissed. Withdrawing, she followed and he responded, reaching around her waist and drawing her to him. Michelle arched her back and pressed into him. The embrace lasted for a few moments longer before he released his grip and she lowered herself, moving away from his lips but remaining close.

"I'll be seeing you, Nate Caslin," she said in a sultry whisper, one final flirtation for him to take with him into the night.

"You will," Caslin replied, fumbling his response. She touched his forearm as he moved off, her eyes directing him to his left and the book he'd placed there earlier. "Thanks."

Bidding her goodnight, he descended the steps to the street below. Glancing back up, he saw her watching him walk away. Turning, he walked backwards for a few steps, smiling and offering her a wave, indicating she should go inside. Michelle returned it, closing the door, and Caslin resumed his course, walking tall, his smile widening with every step.

Bishophill Senior was on the opposite bank of the river Ouse, barely a ten-minute walk from his current location if he crossed the Skeldergate Bridge. For the first time in years, Caslin felt a motivation for something beyond his immediate family's needs and the requirement of his caseload. He was already looking forward to seeing her again.

CHAPTER TWENTY

By the time Caslin reached the scene, a uniformed presence had already taped off both ends of the road, securing it from passers-by as well as traffic. A constable lifted the tape allowing Caslin to slip underneath. Eyeing Hunter's car, he opened the passenger door and dropped the book on the passenger seat before approaching the small group gathered nearby. Both DS Hunter and Craig Templer were present. Templer greeted him.

"Caslin, this is an interesting turn of events," he said, indicating over his shoulder at the body of a young man lying at Hunter's feet where the road met the pavement. She left her inspection of the deceased and came to join them. Local residents were coming together at the edge of the cordon in an attempt to make sense of the commotion as well as, no doubt, feeding their growing morbid curiosity.

"Apparently, he ran out into the middle of the road without looking and was clocked by that car," Hunter informed Caslin, pointing at a white hatchback. The car had subsequently mounted the pavement and struck a lamppost but, by the look of the damage, Caslin presumed the impact had happened at a relatively low speed.

"We have the driver?" Caslin asked.

Hunter nodded. "She's over there." Caslin looked to his right, seeing a female figure sitting in a liveried police car. "We've had a word, breathalysed her, but not taken her statement yet. She's negative on the blood alcohol content."

Caslin turned his attention to the body and the other detectives parted to make room for him to approach. The man lay in an unnatural position. Caslin assumed at least one of his legs and an arm were broken, judging by the angle in which they lay. Whether that was a result of the impact of the car or of hitting the tarmac or the kerb, he couldn't be sure. The man's eyes were open and his face bore a look of shock, an expression frozen in time. Had he been fully clothed, then Caslin would have described the victim as slim but naked as he was, his frame was skeletal and emaciated rather than slender.

Leaning in closer, Caslin took in his features. The eyes appeared hollow, sunken, his skin tone was pale with dark rings hanging under the eyes. The skin across his cheekbones and jaw was depressed and scanning the length of his body, Caslin noted the lack of muscle definition from head to foot. Shifting slightly to his left and stooping, he angled his head to get a better look at the underside of the man's arms. There were multiple needle points, scars and scabs that were indicative of a heavy drug user. Hunter saw him make the observation and dropped to her haunches alongside him.

"The other arm is the same." She pointed to the left arm.

"Do you think he was high?"

DI Templer answered the question. "The car that hit him had a dash cam mounted."

"Have you reviewed the footage?" Caslin asked, over his shoulder.

"Yes, but only on the camera itself so detail is a little hard to make out bearing in mind the view is only illuminated by the street lighting. He comes into the picture running from the left, from Fairfax Street. As I say, it's hard to tell but his run looked erratic to me. He charges out into the street and to be fair to the driver, there wasn't a lot she could do."

Caslin looked up the road, towards the car embedded in the lamppost. "She swerved but clipped him on the way through before being forcibly stopped over there." Hunter concurred. Turning his attention back to the dead man, Caslin found it hard to judge how old he was but figured him to be in his late thirties or early forties, but the physical shape he was in made him appear a lot older. "No chance of any ID then."

"He looks familiar though," Hunter said, flicking her eyes from Caslin to the body. "I know him from somewhere but I just can't place him."

Caslin also returned his gaze to the deceased. "Do you think you've nicked him before? Can't say I recognise him at all. Could he be a junkie that you've come across in another case?"

Hunter shook her head. "Not sure but it'll come to me."

"Take his prints."

"Now?"

Caslin focussed on the missing index finger of the right hand. "Yes, do it. I know we'll get cleaner prints when Alison carries out the autopsy but our killer is ramping things up at an alarming rate. If we can get ahead on the identification, then all the better."

"It's strange for it to go down this way," Templer said, looking in both directions up and down the street. Caslin glanced at him with a querying look. "I mean, the other killings have all been methodically planned and controlled whereas this," Templer indicated the surrounding area with a swirl of his left hand, "is about as uncontrolled as it could be."

"I know what you mean," Caslin agreed. Every previous crime scene was well-managed. This was in stark contrast. "The index finger has already been removed, but at previous scenes it's looked like he did it near to or shortly after death."

"Maybe this one escaped?" Templer suggested, re-evaluating the scene. They were standing in an established residential location on the edge of the city centre. Lines of terraced houses were present on both sides of the street as well as those in the adjacent roads. It was a pleasant and unassuming area.

"If so," Caslin began, following Templer's lead in scanning the nearby properties, "then he can't have come far dressed like this. He must have been close."

"I'll round up some bodies and start going door-to-door," Templer said. Caslin agreed. If the dead man fled his captor at the point of his planned murder, then the killer may still be in a nearby property. Templer took out his radio and contacted the control room to request as many bodies as he could to assist them. Caslin returned to where Hunter was, still standing alongside the dead man. She glanced in his direction and held her gaze. He noticed. Something about her expression troubled him.

"Been anywhere nice this evening?" she asked.

"How do you mean? I had dinner."

"Looks like she was good company." Hunter's face split into a half-smile and she tapped her lower lip. Caslin got the message and wiped across his mouth with the back of his hand. Even with only the benefit of the street lighting, he recognised the lipstick residue.

"Thanks," he said, running his tongue around his lips in an involuntary motion.

"Is she nice?"

Caslin smiled, looking away and feeling sheepish. "Another time, Sarah. Another time."

"Sorry to have disturbed you," Hunter said, smiling playfully with a flick of her eyebrows.

Caslin ignored her amusement at his obvious discomfort and turned the attention back to the body.

"If you know him, then his prints will most likely be in the system."

"Give me a sec, I might have it," she said, taking out her mobile phone and connecting to the Internet. Waiting patiently, Caslin scanned the watching members of the public. The thought occurred to him that if the killer were nearby, he might not be able to deny himself the thrill of mingling with the faceless crowd and observing his handiwork. It wouldn't be the first time. "Take a look at this, sir."

Caslin tore himself away from observing the watchers and came alongside her. She angled the screen of the phone in his direction and he cocked his head, taking in the picture. "That looks like him."

"I'd say so," Hunter agreed, looking from the deceased to the photograph on her mobile and back again. "He was in much better shape when this was taken though."

"Probably why you didn't recognise him. I still don't know him. Should I?"

"I never met him but I remember the case," Hunter explained. "You'll have heard of it."

"Remind me."

"Alex Moretti, or Alessandro, if I remember right," Hunter said. "He was the GP accused of assisting a number of his patients in their suicides."

"Ah… yes. Now I remember," Caslin said excitedly, narrowing his eyes as he sought to recall the detail of the case. "No charges were ever brought though."

Hunter shook her head. "No, the *General Medical Council* investigated and ruled there was not enough evidence against him for him to face being struck off."

Caslin nodded. "And the police inquiry found similar, so the CPS ditched it. When was this?"

"Beginning of last year, or the end of the year before," Hunter suggested with uncertainty. "Give me a second and I'll read the article here."

"Yeah, you can always believe what you read on the Internet," Caslin said with intended sarcasm. "Any sign of a lotus flower yet?"

"No, nothing, which feeds into Craig's theory that he escaped his captor."

"Do I need to run a PNC check for his home address or are your journalistic talents able to find them on the net?"

"Lower Priory Street," Hunter said, glancing up from her phone. Pointing towards nearby Fairfax Street. "Barely a hundred yards away." Caslin looked in that direction and called for Templer to join them. Instructing a uniformed officer to ensure nobody went near the victim, the three detectives set off.

Breaking into a trot, Templer put in a request for confirmation of Moretti's home address with the control room. The media article reported the street where he was known to live but not the house number. Reaching the end of the road, directly opposite was the grass bank running the length of the city walls, encircling their location. Lower Priory Street ran off both to the left and the right of them and they pulled up just as Templer's radio crackled into life.

Looking to the nearby houses, Templer directed them to their left.

"This way," he said, taking the lead. They ran the short distance to Moretti's house, a Victorian end of terrace with an alleyway to one side, giving access to the rear of the adjacent houses on Fairfax Street. There was a larger property attached on the other side. The only entrance to the latter was around the next corner. Unusually, Moretti's house was effectively a standalone building with no other property overlooking it.

The front door opened straight onto the street. Caslin eyed the above windows. The interior was shrouded by closed curtains and no light emanated from within.

"There must be a back door or window," Caslin said, indicating for DI Templer to head down the alley and the detective turned. Seconds later, he disappeared from sight, running into the darkness. "We'll go through the front."

"Should we wait for assistance?" Hunter asked.

For all they knew, the killer could still be inside with an undercover detective held captive. The last thing Caslin wanted was for a drawn-out hostage situation to develop. "No, if he still here let's take him by surprise."

"Let's do it," Hunter replied confidently.

Caslin hammered his fist on the door. Hunter kept her eye on the curtains for a signal that someone was inside. Meeting Caslin's look, she inclined her head towards the door. Caslin took three steps back, inhaled a deep breath, and launched himself forward raising a booted foot and applying as much force as he could against the door, aiming as close to the latch plate as he could. The first attempt was a failure but he stepped back and redoubled his efforts. The second kick saw the wood of the door jamb splinter and he forced the lock to detach. With one final surge, he struck the door and it flew inwards at pace, swiftly followed by the two detectives, Caslin in the vanguard.

"Police!" he shouted without response. They were in a narrow, unlit hallway. One door was set to their right. The stairs to the upper floor were in front of them and along the corridor lay the kitchen. The sound of breaking glass came from the rear of the building. Reaching the first door, Caslin pushed it open with his left hand and chanced a look inside. The sitting room was empty apart from a sofa and a few pieces of standalone furniture. DI Templer appeared at the threshold to the kitchen. He stopped there and waited.

Caslin pointed to the dining room and Templer nodded, kicking the door open, the two of them piled in. This room was also empty. Templer crossed to the far side, drawing back the curtain and looking out into a paved courtyard to the rear. The nearby street lighting barely stretched to cover the area but the glow of the orange light illuminated a small pond in one corner. The remainder of the courtyard was paved in concrete slabs. Caslin flicked the nearest light switch but nothing happened. They remained in the dark. The two men returned to the hall and joined Hunter as she slowly climbed the stairs to the first floor.

Activating the torch on her mobile phone, she cast an eerie blue light up the stairwell. All three tuned their senses, preparing for anything that might come at them from the darkness. The air was stale. The smell stung their noses. There were three doors off the landing and the first was open, leading to a bathroom above the kitchen. This had a pitched roof with a small skylight set into it, providing the only source of natural light. The bathroom was cramped and empty. The two remaining doors were to separate bedrooms, one at the front overlooking the street and another to the rear. The landing doubled back from the stairs, almost to the front of the house. Anyone in the front facing room would need to get past them to escape.

Mouthing a silent three count, Hunter shoved open the first door to the rear bedroom and both she and Templer entered. Caslin waited on the landing with one eye on the remaining bedroom. Seconds later, they reappeared with a shake of the head. Together, they approached the last room and repeated the procedure. This time Hunter opened the door and Caslin passed through first.

As they found with the previous rooms, this one was also empty. Caslin leaned against one of the walls while Hunter located the light switch, flicking it on had the same effect as downstairs.

"Maybe they've tripped?" she said, scanning the room by the light of her mobile.

Templer stood at the doorway and glanced around. "I'll have a look for the fuse box downstairs."

Caslin turned his attention to the room he was in. There was a double bed set against the far wall. The mattress was covered with a sheet but there were no pillows or duvet. There was the overbearing smell of urine and excrement. The sheet was heavily soiled and apparently lay unchanged for quite some time. The headboard, as well as the foot of the bed, was crafted from wood and lined with upright slats. Attached by chains at all four corners were manacles you might expect to find in the bedroom of a BDSM enthusiast. At the centre of the mattress lay a blooming lotus flower, white petals fading to pink on their exterior.

"He left us his calling card," Caslin said.

"Whether Moretti escaped or was released, the killer can't have been gone long," Hunter concluded.

Caslin stood, glancing in the direction of the bedroom window, overlooking the front. His eye line carried to the stone walls of the city and the often-trod tourist path along it. Barely fifty yards away was a gated exit leading beyond the medieval walls. "Once out of the centre, he'll be in the wind."

"We should pull the CCTV in the area and see if we get lucky," Hunter said. Caslin nodded.

Returning his focus to the bed, he moved closer and inspected the restraints. These were hard-core, not the playful fur-lined variety couples might use to experiment with. These were manufactured from cold hard metal. Although difficult to judge in the available light, Caslin observed a dark smudge on the rim to one of them. He frowned, an expression that didn't go unnoticed. "Blood," he said quietly, answering Hunter's unasked question.

"Probably straining to get free."

"Judging by the state of the sheet and the smell, I'd say he was chained here for weeks."

"Or even months," Hunter added, drawing his attention towards the corner of the room where she was standing. Caslin crossed over, looking past her to see. There was a wicker waste bin. Piled to the point of overflow were transparent pouches. Caslin knelt alongside, separating them with a pen that he took from his pocket. "Drip bags by the look of them."

Caslin looked up at her over his shoulder, noting the IV stand in the far corner of the room. He had missed it before. "That will explain some of the needle marks then."

Hunter opened a freestanding wardrobe, nestled into the alcove to the right of the chimney breast. "And that's not all." She tapped Caslin on the shoulder. Cardboard boxes were stacked atop one another inside. On the shelves above these were intravenous bags, still full of liquid. The shipping labels stuck to the exterior of the boxes were marked with logogram writing, suggesting they had been imported from East Asia.

"I'll be interested to see what's in these," Caslin said. "Something tells me it's not only nutrients."

"If I had to guess, I'd argue Moretti was a junkie, wouldn't you?"

"Yes, but somehow I doubt that was a decision of his own making. Let's get CSI in here."

"Caslin!" A shout came from below. Leaving the bedroom, Caslin made his way downstairs. He found Templer at the entrance to the dining room.

"What is it?"

"You need to see this." He beckoned him to follow.

Templer led them out of the set of French doors of the dining room and into the courtyard. Caslin was drawn to the pond. Clearly not well tended, the vegetation spread across the surface in a haphazard and aggressive manner. Kneeling, Caslin spotted what he would have thought were water lilies but now he knew better. They were lotus flowers. Standing up, he joined Templer at a timber door to an outbuilding, aged, rotten and with flaking green paint. The brick structure doubled as a coal shed and the outside toilet. Mounted on the exterior was a plastic box housing the electricity meter. It was heavily damaged, as if it had been violently forced open. The door hung on its hinges and Caslin eased it open.

An enforcement notice was taped to the interior indicating it had been replaced with a prepayment meter. Such action was only ever done for non-payment of outstanding bills. The date on the notice was only a fortnight ago. Templer gestured for Caslin to enter. Inside, he was acutely aware of the smell of damp along with another, intense and recognisable smell that he would never forget. A chest freezer dominated the space and, glancing to his colleague with an inquisitive look, Caslin approached warily. Using the edge of his hand to lift the lid, Caslin jumped back, startled.

"Strewth!" He threw a hand across his mouth and nose. Meeting Templer's eye, he misread the younger detective's expression. "Fowler?"

"No, it's not him. I've no idea who this is."

Caslin peered into the freezer. The capacity was barely enough to contain the body of a grown man. By the way he lay inside, it was reasonable to presume several of his limbs were broken in order to cram him into the available space. For what purpose, he couldn't begin to imagine. The urge to return to fresh air was overwhelming and, using his elbow to close the lid, the slapping sound of the seal engaging carried through the silence.

CHAPTER TWENTY-ONE

"DI Caslin, North Yorkshire Police." He held up his warrant card.

"What can I do for you, Inspector?" Caslin took in his measure. He was an ascetic-looking man in his late fifties, stiff, immaculately presented and unfazed by their presence.

"We need to speak to you regarding Alessandro Moretti." At mention of the name, colour drained momentarily from his features and he ushered both Caslin and Hunter away from waiting patients and through a security door towards the consultation rooms.

"I thought the investigation was concluded." The man was irritated by their presence without having heard why. Opening the door to an office with a sign matching his name, William Logan, the practice manager, held the door for them. Upon their arrival, he'd been summoned as soon as they mentioned to the receptionist why they were there. His frustration at the recurrence of an inquiry he thought long buried appeared to frustrate him.

"Does it bother you to discuss it?" Caslin sensed the reluctance.

Logan pulled out his chair and sat down, offering them a seat opposite at the same time. "It is not that it bothers me, Inspector. There has just been so much upheaval since the inquiry. Patients were unsettled, as were the staff… the practice also changed hands as a result. Despite assurances to the contrary, there existed a perceived failure in the leadership."

"Failure?" Hunter asked.

"Unjustly, in my opinion." Logan's reply was somewhat haughty.

"The criminal investigation found insufficient evidence for the CPS to bring a prosecution," Caslin said.

Logan scoffed. "Nor did the *General Medical Council* but that is nowhere near the same as a proclamation of innocence. The inquiries took months and we all had to work under a very dark cloud indeed."

"And the families were left to wonder as to how their loved ones died," Caslin replied, irritated by the man's attitude.

"Yes… of course." Logan dropped much of the attitude, meeting Caslin's eye with a flicker of regret in his own. "I was speaking from a purely professional… operational, point of view."

"Moretti?"

"What is it you want to know that hasn't already been investigated? You're not opening up more cases are you? I thought—"

"No, this is another associated inquiry. Alessandro Moretti died late last night."

Logan was visibly shocked. "That's awful. May I ask what happened?"

"He was hit by a car," Hunter said.

"Awful," Logan repeated. "Here, in York?"

"Yes," Caslin confirmed. "You seem shocked by that."

"I am. I thought he had returned to Italy months ago."

"Is that what he told you his plans were?"

Logan shook his head. "No, not at all. We were never friends, not really. I… we… all thought that's what he would do. What with taking the suspension so badly."

"Did he? Take it badly?" Caslin asked.

Logan nodded. "To be expected. No one likes to be accused of professional misconduct."

"He was investigated for far more than that. Three counts of murder were on the cards at the beginning."

"And none were proven," Logan reminded them. Caslin felt he was still endeavouring to protect the reputation of the practice. "I know Alex… Alessandro… felt aggrieved but there was little option under the circumstances. We were advised not to communicate with him until the GMC, as well as yourselves, were finished with the inquiries."

"When was the last time you spoke with him?" Caslin asked.

Logan thought hard. "Early last year, I should imagine. I'm not sure exactly."

"Around the time of his suspension?"

"Yes. Like I said, we were asked to keep away. Once the case was settled, there was the opportunity that he would return but none of us really thought he would come back."

"Why not? You thought him guilty?"

"Certainly not." He was indignant. "But mud sticks, Inspector. Patients were already requesting to not be seen by him if he returned. The contract of trust had broken down. His position would have been untenable."

"You expected him to move on then?" Hunter asked.

"Why, yes. It's not like he was a partner in the practice. He was a junior GP, recently settled in the UK and we thought he would go home... well, back to Italy anyway."

"And no one followed up with him... even after he was cleared in the investigation? Not particularly caring, was it?" Caslin pressed.

"You must understand the internal workings of the practice, Inspector," Logan said, taking on a conciliatory tone. "The suspicions were first raised by fellow practitioners. Alex's own colleagues brought it to the attention of management and the GMC. Many bridges were burned in the exchanges. There was little love lost between Alex and the staff."

"Who accused him of murdering his patients?" Caslin said the fact aloud that Logan was dancing around.

"Assisting their suicides would be more accurate," Logan said, lowering his voice despite no one else being present to overhear their conversation.

"Nonetheless, Dr Moretti was investigated for potentially murdering three elderly patients in his care. Your colleagues, those who raised the alarm, felt that some of these deaths were somewhat surprising as well as untimely. Other cases were also investigated, we understand."

"That is true," Logan agreed but raised a finger, wagging it like a parent does to an unruly child. "No further cases were brought before the GMC or prosecuted as well you know."

"The doctors who put up the flag," Caslin asked, "are they available to speak with us?"

Logan shook his head. "I'm afraid neither of them is still with us. It was a trying time, as I'm sure you can understand, but I can give you their contact details."

"Thank you," Caslin said. "Before this whole mess developed, what was your impression of Dr Moretti?"

"A diligent practitioner. Very capable with a bright future."

"Were there any threats made against Dr Moretti either before the investigation or during it?"

"Not that I am aware of. Many of his patients expressed quite the opposite. He was a popular young man, particularly among the elderly. Alex would often go the extra that many others wouldn't."

"In what way?"

"After hours home visits. If a patient couldn't make it in or if there was no availability within the appointment schedule."

"Sounds like the type of GP everyone needs," Hunter said. Logan did not disagree.

"Thank you for your time," Caslin said as he rose. "If we need anything further, we'll be in touch."

Logan accepted Caslin's offer of a handshake, appearing confused. "I don't understand why you are asking these questions. I thought you said Alex was struck by a car."

"He was, Mr Logan. He was."

"CAUSE OF DEATH was certainly the result of being struck by the car," Dr Taylor explained to Caslin whilst Hunter was scanning the initial autopsy report. "Aside from a fractured skull that led to a bleed on the brain, he suffered massive internal injuries to the abdomen, several ribs punctured his left lung and his spleen ruptured. Even had he been in decent physical shape, which he wasn't by the way, I'm not sure he would have made it."

"Nasty." Caslin looked the body up and down. In the artificial light of the pathology lab, Moretti appeared far older than his thirty-two years, an emaciated, skeletal figure with the skin drawn tightly around his frame.

"If it's any consolation, I doubt he would have known much about it," Dr Taylor said, turning and crossing to her workstation. Returning with a print out, she passed it to him. Caslin cast an eye over the detail – a list of drugs as far as he could tell.

"I recognise the heroin," he said, glancing up at her.

"To name but one of the opioids in his system," she explained. "This man was under the influence."

"And when you say *under the influence*?"

"High as a kite, is probably more apt. Not only from heroin but his blood toxicology results revealed high levels of both *Fentanyl* as well as

Carfentanyl. They are synthetic opioids that I presume you remember from—"

"The house at Stamford Street, yes, I remember," Caslin confirmed. "The dealers often cut them with the heroin to increase the street value of their product."

"Right," Dr Taylor said. "You don't need a pathology qualification to realise this man had a history of drug use, you can see it with your own eyes."

"Not according to his medical records," Caslin said. "His performance evaluations were exceptional and nothing in his background leads us to believe he was a recreational drug user let alone an addict."

"I can see that. If you look at his wrists and ankles." She indicated the specific areas with a pen. "You will note abrasions and bruising consistent with the application of repeated pressure. Presumably some kind of restraints."

"We found those at his house."

"He was a heavy drug user," Dr Taylor continued, "but whether he was voluntarily doing so is for you to investigate."

"You don't believe so?" Caslin asked.

"I deal in facts, Nate. I leave the speculation to you… most of the time." She glanced in his direction through the corner of her eye. "The drugs in his bloodstream would prove fatal to many, so there is the likelihood he built up quite a resistance to them. Helped by the fourth drug on that list you have."

Caslin read further down. "*Naloxone*. What's that?"

"It's an opioid antagonist medication, specifically designed to block or reverse their effects. It has a high affinity for opioid receptors, where it has an inverse reaction, causing the rapid removal of any other drugs bound to these particular receptors. As you know, if heroin reaches the level of an overdose it can lead to respiratory depression, absent pulse rate and a reduced heart rate to name but a few symptoms."

"Ultimately leading to death," Caslin said quietly.

"Exactly. *Naloxone* causes a rapid reversal of the depression of the central nervous system. It saves lives."

"Somehow, I don't see Dr Moretti administering this to himself," Caslin theorised. "Rather, he was being forcibly addicted to the heroin but at the same time monitored so as he didn't overdose."

"I think you're right," Dr Taylor agreed. "Whoever was… I don't want to say *caring for him*… administering to him is probably a better description, took great care to ensure he didn't die during the process."

Caslin thought on the information. Something didn't make sense to him but it was Hunter, apparently thinking along the same lines, who responded first. "We saw dash camera footage of his last moments before he was run over and his movements were erratic. Hardly in keeping with cognisant thought."

"That's not surprising," Dr Taylor said. "He could well have been entering a state of severe psychosis."

"He may have overdosed, even if he hadn't run out into traffic?" Hunter asked.

"That would be quite possible, judging from the state of his heart as well as his circulation. Quite frankly, I'm amazed he was still alive last night."

"In your opinion, Alison, how likely is it that a man with these levels of intoxication could escape from restraints and run from a would-be killer?" Caslin asked, seeking clarity.

Dr Taylor considered the question. "I doubt he was thinking clearly at all. We cannot underestimate the basic human survival instinct but I would be reaching if I suggested that as a reason for his escape."

Caslin exhaled deeply, passing back the paper in his hand. "Thanks, Alison."

"I'll get my final analysis on Moretti over to you as soon as I can," she replied. "In the meantime, I'll move onto the victim you found in the deep freeze."

Hunter's phone rang and she answered it, stepping away. "Where are you with that?" Caslin asked, looking around.

"It took Iain Robertson and his team hours to get him out of the chest freezer. Other than the fact he didn't have a digit missing, I'm afraid you'll have a few hours to wait before I can tell you more than you know already. He was severely bloated, indicative of having thawed out days before."

"Yeah. It looks like the power company had cut him off. Probably would have been worse in the height of summer. Thanks, Alison. We'll speak soon."

Hunter fell into step alongside him with both of them leaving pathology together, Caslin holding the door open for her. She hung up on the call as they walked, their footfalls echoing on the polished floor.

"That was Terry," she said. "The killer has uploaded his latest video."

"Footage of Moretti being run over in the street," Caslin replied without looking at her.

"Yeah," she said, surprised. "How did you know?"

"He let him go and then followed." Caslin sounded bitter. He was. "I'll bet the car was a bonus. You heard what Alison said, if not the car then the drugs would have taken him. He'd already removed the finger and staged the house for us to find. We're the mouse to his cat. The bastard's toying with us."

"We've managed to ID the body in the freezer too. His prints were on file from a decade ago when he was pulled over for driving under the influence."

"Who is he?" Caslin asked, stopping and turning to face her.

"Christopher Maitland. Aside from the twelve-month driving ban and a nominal fine, he has no other prior arrests or convictions."

"What else do we know about him?"

Hunter consulted the brief notes she'd taken during Holt's telephone call. "He was fifty-two. Divorced. He is listed on the electoral register in Sheffield and until recently held a position at *The Post*."

"What position?"

"News Editor," Hunter confirmed.

"Jimmy said the previous editor was sacked because of the paper's poor performance."

"Where could he fit in to this?"

"Let's get a bit of background." Caslin took out his mobile. He scrolled through his contacts and selected Sullivan's number. Moments later, he hung up, frustrated. "Straight to voicemail." Caslin checked the time on his watch. Choosing another entry, he dialled again, only this time calling the journalist's desk extension. The phone rang without reply and he was about to give up when the call was answered. "Jimmy—"

"No, sorry, it's Katie. Jimmy's not at his desk. Can I help… or take a message?"

Caslin remembered her from an earlier meeting, although they'd never spoken directly. "Katie, it's Nathaniel Caslin from Fulford Road. Is Jimmy around? I need to speak to him about something."

"No. I've not seen him at all today and he hasn't called in. If you do get a hold of him." She lowered her voice to not be overheard. "Can you let him know he's in the shit with the boss?"

Caslin laughed. "Not for the first time, I'm sure. Likewise, if he surfaces can you let him know I need a word?"

"Will do, bye."

Caslin put his mobile away, looking back down the corridor as if something occurred to him.

"What is it?" Hunter asked.

He shook his head. "Did Holt say what number came up at the end of Moretti's video?"

"The number one. Why?"

"That's *do no harm to living things*."

"If he judged the doctor guilty, then Moretti certainly failed that one."

"Which leaves us what?" Caslin asked out loud.

"The fourth?" Hunter said, trying to remember. "But what happens after that?"

Caslin let the question hang. One thing he could be reasonably sure about was this killer was too controlling and manipulative to have not considered his next move. Whatever was planned, they needed to stop him before he reached that point.

CHAPTER TWENTY-TWO

Pressing the buzzer once more, only this time holding it for three or four seconds before releasing it, Caslin stepped back and looked to the first floor. Still there was no sign of movement from within the apartment. The curtains remained drawn and no one responded on the intercom. Glancing at his watch, he pursed his lips as the gnawing sensation he was missing something reasserted itself with a vengeance. Taking out his mobile, he called Sullivan's number again, only this time, straining to hear if it rang inside. The call rang out, passing to voicemail as it had done with each attempt.

A woman appeared in the communal hall beyond the security door. Approaching the entrance, she eyed him warily as he put his phone away and waited expectantly for her to open the door. She was elderly and her movement was frustratingly slow. Assessing him with a watchful eye, standing outside in his suit, she must have judged him non-threatening, disregarding his obvious impatience, and addressed him directly.

"Can I help you?"

Caslin took out his warrant card. "Police, madam. Do you live here?"

"I do, yes. In apartment two."

"Have you by any chance seen Mr Sullivan today?"

"James?" She thought about it for a moment. "Can't say I have seen him for a while. You're more than welcome to go in and try yourself."

Caslin thanked her, holding the door open to allow her to pass before entering the building. Taking the stairs two at a time, he reached the door to Sullivan's apartment. Hammering on it with a closed fist, he waited. When there was still no reply, he looked around. It was mid-afternoon. Most residents were still at work and a glance through the window of the communal landing to the outside revealed few cars parked below. Sullivan's SUV was visible, parked in his allocated space. Reaching into his pocket, Caslin took out a small leather pouch. With one last furtive look around, he opened it, withdrawing two slender metal instruments. They were slim, to the untrained eye they would look like dental tools. The first had a thin paddle at one end while the other, a small hook.

Kneeling, Caslin slipped them into the lock, one atop the other. It took a few minutes of patient exploration for he was out of practice, but soon the reassuring sense of the mechanism moving as each point fell into place, came to him and he smiled. Seconds later, the lock disengaged and he stood. Slipping the picks back into his pocket, he grasped the handle. With one last furtive glance over his shoulder, he opened the door and entered Sullivan's apartment, closing the door behind him.

The interior was dark. Every curtain in the small apartment was drawn. The air was stuffy and in desperate need of an open window. Making his way along the corridor, every room within the apartment sprang off it and his senses were heightened. Listening out for anything untoward, Caslin heard nothing but the ticking of a clock hanging on the wall a few feet away. Despite not having anything to justify the sensation, something felt wrong. Reaching the first doorway, the entrance to the kitchen, he poked his head in and scanned the interior. Alongside the sink, stacked on the countertop, were some dirty crockery appearing to contain the remnants of what was an evening meal. Upon closer inspection, it was probably the previous night's.

Moving on, he pushed open the door to the bathroom. It too was empty. A dirty towel was cast over the side of the bath and the air still smelt damp. The next room was the solitary bedroom of the apartment. Sullivan was divorced, never one who seemed bothered about relationships, and Caslin knew he saw nothing of his children despite the occasional text or phone call. One bedroom was more than adequate for his lifestyle. The bed was unmade with the duvet thrown back. A few items of clothing were scattered around. Retreating, Caslin turned right as he re-entered the hall, heading for the living room.

Entering, he found the room to be much as it was on the occasion of his last visit. Jimmy Sullivan was the middle-aged bachelor of stereotype. If anything, the place was tidier than Caslin had come to expect. Crossing to the nearest window, the first of two, he pulled back the curtains. The grey light of an overcast sky filled the room and he surveyed the scene. There was nothing out of place. The furniture was undisturbed. The remote controls for the television and satellite television sat on the coffee table alongside a tea-stained mug. Nothing present should concern him and yet… the unsettled feeling would not subside.

The silence broke with the sound of a ringing mobile. Reaching into his pocket, Caslin eyed the screen and breathed a sigh of relief, answering the call.

"Jimmy, where have you been?" His sense of relief dissipated as quickly as it had arrived. No voice came down the line but a muffled sound, similar to someone struggling in the background was all that he could make out. Listening acutely, Caslin felt his stomach tighten as a knot of fear took hold. There was movement but unsure of whether it was someone walking or background noise, Caslin frowned. The sounds became starker, the muffled noises louder but were now accompanied by ragged breathing and what he thought was a gurgling noise. He couldn't discern what it was. Silence followed and Caslin listened, wondering for a moment if the call may have disconnected but checking the screen, it hadn't.

A high-pitched scraping sound shot through the earpiece and Caslin winced, pulling the mobile away from his ear momentarily. Someone picked up the handset. Now, he heard measured breathing, controlled, and yet clearly the result of the expenditure of significant energy. Moving to the window, Caslin scanned the outside. Unsure of what he was looking for, he waited, his heart pounding in his chest.

"Jimmy?" he asked quietly. The response was sneering. A dismissive gesture that struck fear into Caslin's heart.

"He's not available. Come to the chapel." The voice was condescending, cold and firm. The line went dead.

Caslin stood staring out into the empty car park, a sense of dread seizing him. An all-encompassing paralysis, even the inability to draw breath lasted until the mobile, still cupped in his palm, rang once more. The sound brought him out of his mental state, the paralysis replaced by a flash of searing anger.

"Now, you listen to me–" he snarled.

"Sir? It's Terry Holt."

Caslin was thrown, his confusion offsetting his rage. *"Terry…"*

"He's online again, sir."

"Uploading?" Caslin turned, picking up his pace, he set off for the front door.

"Not this time, sir. He's streaming – *live*," Holt explained with obvious excitement. "We've got him. We know where he is."

"York Cemetery Chapel," Caslin stated, leaving the apartment and running down the stairs as fast he dared. His voice echoed in the stairwell.

"Yeah..." Holt replied, stunned. "How did—"

"Never mind, Terry. Get as many bodies as you can and flood that area immediately. Approach with caution and be advised there is a possible hostage situation in progress." Caslin thundered through the communal entrance, sending the door bouncing against the jamb as he charged it.

The cemetery was barely a four-minute drive from Fulford Road Police Station but Caslin was closer. Sullivan's apartment block was south of the city, along the Barbican Road. Clambering into his car, he fired the engine into life and put his foot down. The wheels spun and the tyres shrieked in protest as the car accelerated away. An oncoming vehicle swerved to avoid a collision as Caslin turned across the oncoming traffic. The driver of the vehicle responded with a blast of the horn by which time, Caslin was long gone. Swerving in and out of traffic, he sought to cover the distance in the shortest available time.

Through gritted teeth, he took the turn into the cemetery following a risky overtaking manoeuvre that saw him mount the kerb, collecting part of a hedge and almost clipping the stone archway of the entrance as he passed through. Flooring the accelerator, Caslin flew down the access road, coming from beneath the canopy of trees and into the parking expanse in front of the old chapel. The car skidded to a halt on the gravel and Caslin was out of his seat without applying the handbrake. The sound of approaching sirens met him as a police car tore along the road behind him, also sliding to a halt.

The two uniformed officers within leapt out, running to the rear and lifting the boot. Caslin set off for the entrance, an imposing double door, dwarfed by the massive stone columns to the frontage supporting the pediment above.

"Sir, wait!" one of the officers shouted as he strapped on his body armour. The second was already preparing his semi-automatic rifle. The armed response unit was the first deployed vehicle in attendance and they intended to take the lead but Caslin ignored them, running for the entrance.

Slowing as he came before the doors, he approached with caution. The right-hand door was cracked open and he tentatively peered through into the interior. He had been here before for a colleague's funeral and now, he wracked his brains to remember the layout. The thought came to him that the building was recently renovated, although he recalled there was only one way in or out and he was standing before it. Despite the neo-classical construction, imposing in both height and grandeur, the chapel only consisted of one room with large sash windows set high in the walls to every aspect, bar the frontage. If the killer remained then Caslin stood between him and escape. *If* escaping was his plan.

Reaching for the door, Caslin felt a firm hand on his shoulder. Glancing back, the armed officers joined him and the first indicated for him to step aside with a silent two-finger gesture, pointing towards his right. Allowing them to lead, Caslin watched as the door was pushed open and the two men entered. Their movements were precise and controlled. Caslin slotted in behind them. Their stealth was wasted. Inside, the black and white polished marble floor and stone walls reverberated even the slightest sound, magnifying the sound of their presence as it echoed throughout the interior.

The room was one large expanse, open to the apex of the roof. The huge windows, three per aspect, allowed any light penetrating through the trees outside to pass into the interior, casting shadows and eerie reflections across the surfaces. The building appeared empty, aside from a solitary figure seated with its back to them away to their left, at the far end. The uniformed officers altered their angle of approach, putting a little space between them, as the three men ventured farther. They kept watchful eyes in every direction, as well as above, as they made their way. Caslin felt the adrenalin building. His heart was thudding within his chest and his mind saw danger in the flicker of every shadow cast from the surrounding trees.

Moving closer, they could see the figure was male, sitting upright, arms dangling by his side. His head hung to the left, unsupported. The pool of crimson spreading out around him in an ever-increasing circle across the smooth marble was indicative of near death if not already passed. The sheer volume of blood lost, Caslin judged, was enough to almost guarantee death. The uniformed officers indicated to each other for one to provide cover whilst Caslin and he inspected the body.

Coming around to face the man, Caslin slipped as he inadvertently stepped in the growing pool of blood despite his best efforts, his attention consumed by the horror before him. Jimmy Sullivan's lifeless eyes stared at him. Although the flow had apparently ceased, the journalist's beard was matted with blood. The flow passed down across his chin and his upper body. Caslin fought to tear his eyes away but he couldn't. He was transfixed. Sullivan's lips were parted and a rag of cloth had been stuffed into his partially open mouth. This too, was soaked in crimson. His throat had been slashed almost from ear to ear and the subsequent blood loss had soaked into his clothing, almost from head to foot, now pooling on the floor below.

Caslin reached forward and tried to find a pulse despite knowing it to be a futile gesture. Glancing to the floor, next to Sullivan's right foot and floating in his life blood, lay a blooming lotus flower. The petals were streaked with blood. The index finger of his right hand was missing and the blood dripped onto the flower below. Scattered randomly around it, or possibly strategically placed for it was impossible to tell for sure, Caslin noted a number of coins. Dropping to his haunches to inspect them, they were silver and of varying denominations. Caslin's catholic school upbringing flashed the connection in his mind. *Thirty pieces of silver*. The symbolism was strong; a reference to the selling of principles. Standing, tears welled in his eyes and he clenched his teeth as he shuddered involuntarily.

"Bastard!" Caslin shouted. The sound carried all around them, echoing, bouncing off ceiling and walls. The two officers accompanying him exchanged concerned glances before continuing their sweep of the room. Caslin remained where he was, staring into the eyes of his dead friend. "I'm so sorry, Jimmy," he whispered. His mobile rang. At first, he chose to ignore it but eventually rewarded the caller's persistence and answered.

"Sir."

"For fuck's sake, Terry, what is it?" Caslin snapped.

"He's still streaming, sir." His tone was apologetic, almost embarrassed.

"What do you mean?"

"The feed... it's still up. You're... *you're live on the internet*, sir," Holt said awkwardly.

Caslin hung up. Putting his phone away he sought to quell the rising fury within. Looking around for the source of the feed, he wanted to kill it immediately. There were few places to hide a camera with so little furniture present. It didn't take long. Caslin caught sight of something against the wall in the corner, barely eight feet away. Crossing to it, he found a mobile phone strapped to the wall with gaffer tape. The screen was covered but following the camera's line of sight, it was positioned to have a perfect view of both the entrance as well as their approach to Sullivan.

Caslin took a tissue from his pocket. Leaning in closer to the phone, he stared into the camera.

"I will find you. I promise you that." His words were cold, measured, belying the unchecked rage building inside him. He spoke with assured certainty. Using a finger, covered by the tissue, to press and hold the standby button, he powered down the device. More sirens could be heard approaching. Given the all-clear to approach by the armed response team, they were now bringing their presence closer and securing the scene. Looking back to his friend, Caslin took a deep breath and whispered, "I will find him."

CHAPTER TWENTY-THREE

THE BARMAN SET the glasses down in front of him. Caslin passed a ten-pound note across the bar and picked up the chaser. Seeing it off in one swallow, he placed the glass down just as his change arrived.

"Same again." The barman nodded, albeit with an awkward accompanying smile as his gaze lingered on him. Caslin watched as he poured out another double measure of *Edradour*. He returned and Caslin scooped up the scotch along with his pint, left coins on the counter and set off back to his booth in the lower bar. Descending the steps on unsteady feet, his wayward movement saw him spill the top of his beer. The foam ran down the glass and across the back of his hand. He was relieved to slip back onto the safety of his seat. Shaking off the excess, he wiped his hand on his jacket before picking up the beer and taking a mouthful.

Opening the book on the table before him, he caught sight of the bar staff looking in his direction. They were hardly subtle regarding their discussion. There was no doubt in his mind that they were talking about him. Whether it was the lack of his usual affability or they had seen the viral clip of Jimmy Sullivan's murder, where he'd played a starring role, he wasn't sure and if the truth be known, he didn't care. Seeking out the bookmark, a fragment of a torn receipt, Caslin located his place.

The tome Chen Tao lent him was proving fascinating but somewhat gruelling to get through. More of an encyclopaedic collection than a narrative, Caslin was finding it difficult to find what he was looking for.

Therein lay the problem, *he didn't really know what he was looking for.* The basics were fairly clear. The study of the teachings of the Buddha alongside their application in a person's life would guide them along a developmental path, improving them spiritually and leading towards a state of enlightenment. Provided that is, if they could devote themselves to the path and be prepared for the process to take a lifetime, if not several. Caslin felt somewhat impressed by those who walked the path. The modern world, particularly western society, gravitated towards immediate gratification.

Chen Tao's insight on the violent beliefs held by practitioners of certain traditions was eye opening, if not disturbing. Until that point, Caslin was unaware such extremes existed within Buddhism. Turning his thoughts to their target, he considered that at some point he had chosen a path steeped in the harmonisation of the body, speech and mind, only for it to warp into a twisted reality that sought to justify acts of barbarity that made sane people retch. The truly frightening prospect was that he was not insane at all, but cool and calculating, in full control of his actions and beliefs. Caslin was banking all along on him making a mistake for they usually did. *How many more would die before the window of opportunity presented itself? Could he have acted differently?*

Picking up the scotch, Caslin tilted his head back and drained the glass. Closing his eyes, he savoured the taste alongside the fleeting burning sensation spreading across his chest. Returning the empty glass to the table, he realised someone was standing next to him. He hadn't seen her arrive. Blowing out his cheeks, he forced a smile in greeting.

"Hi Nate," Alison Taylor said. "I figured I would find you here."

"Hey, Alison."

"I'd say I'll get you another but by the looks of it, you're doing okay already." She took off her coat, threw it across the back of the seating and slipped into the booth opposite him.

"I'm doing all right," he whispered, picking up his pint, avoiding her gaze.

"Are you?"

He inclined his head to one side and eventually was compelled to meet her eye. "I've had better days."

A member of staff appeared alongside them, smiling at Alison but glancing nervously at Caslin. "A dry white wine for me, please."

"And a—"

"Just a dry white wine." Alison cut Caslin off before he could order another scotch. The waitress left and neither spoke until she was out of earshot.

"I think the management will be concerned that the staff are spending a lot of time on social media," Caslin said, looking out of the corner of his eye towards the bar.

"Or they are simply observant." Alison casually pointed to his left hand.

Caslin glanced down and saw nothing. Lifting his forearm, he looked on the underside. Blood had soaked into the cuff of his shirt. "Scotch would fix that."

"Don't you dare, Nathaniel."

The hostility in her tone caught him off guard. "Dare what?"

"Sit here drowning in scotch and your own self-pity, that's what." She snapped at him, reminiscent of how she once did when they were together. Alison was never one to pull her punches with him. He needed that. He respected it. "What happened to Jimmy *is not your fault*. Do you hear me?"

"That's funny," Caslin replied, picking up his pint and sipping at it, frowning. "Because I sort of see that it is, really."

"He's to blame. The sick bastard who did it. Not you."

Caslin sat forward in his seat. She appeared startled by the aggression in his eyes. Putting his pint aside, he leaned forward and focussed his attention on the book, leafing through the pages to another bookmarked spot. Spinning the book to face her on the table, he gently pushed it towards her. Alison looked down and scanned the page. "See?" he said. "*My fault*."

"No, I don't see," she countered.

"The Fourth Precept," Caslin stated emphatically. "Or, as they refer to it in there." He indicated the book. "The principle of truthfulness. With every single one of the Five Precepts there are both positive and negative forms."

"Go on." Her drink arrived and she thanked the waitress, drawing the glass towards her and cradling the stem, looking for Caslin to continue.

"In the negative form practitioners must undertake the training to refrain from false speech."

"I see where you're going," Alison said, sipping at her wine.

"It's not a case of where I'm going," he argued. "I put Jimmy up to that interview. I put him front and centre, spinning a yarn about how this guy is some pathetic weirdo. I stoked the fire and therefore, it's on me."

"Jimmy knew what he was doing."

"That doesn't matter," Caslin snapped. "I put him in that predicament."

"So, by your logic, you had Jimmy put out a pack of lies or suppositions to instigate a response," Alison said, raising her eyebrows, "in order to rattle this guy's cage."

"Exactly."

"And it brought Jimmy into the firing line."

"The body in the deep freeze was Jimmy's former boss."

"I know," Alison said.

"I reckon he was the intended victim for the fourth precept, the archetypal news editor who spreads rumour and gossip, but then..." Caslin said, his voice tailing off as he broke eye contact. "Then I brought him Jimmy."

"No. *You brought him you*," she countered.

That got his attention. "What the hell are you talking about?"

"You wanted to provoke a response and you got one. You were hoping it would push him into making an error and it has. You just haven't managed to exploit it yet."

"You've lost me," Caslin said, returning to his pint.

"This wasn't about Jimmy. This was about you. You presented yourself as the authority figure. The man with the moral superiority and that goes against everything in his make up."

Caslin sat forward, intrigued. "How so?"

Alison sat back, nursing her drink. "Serial killers represent a dual failure, both of their own development as fully fledged, well-rounded and productive individuals, as well as a failure of the culture and society they develop in. In a materially focussed society, such as we have, social anomies proliferate."

"Meaning?"

"The usual ethical and moral standards within a group can go missing. Studies have shown that in this scenario, psychologists see a pattern of what they call malignant objectifiers growing in numbers – people devoid of empathy."

"Narcissists?"

"Exactly. The killer's megalomania manifests against your challenge to his moral framework, which he sees as far superior to yours. It's no surprise that he is using the teachings of wisdom set out over thousands of years as a cloak to justify his actions. He believes he is more knowledgeable, ethically pure and morally on a different level to you. To all of us. The fact no one else can see this will only enrage him further."

"Why focus on me?"

"You challenged him. You judged him and that's antagonised him. Perhaps it has driven him on in order to prove you wrong."

Caslin nursed his drink. "This doesn't alleviate my guilt."

"The point is, it doesn't matter whether it was Jimmy," she said, holding up her hand to dampen his protest. "It could have been any of us, anyone important *to you*. You're the counterpoint to his quest, his mission. You are the authority figure. That's why he keeps coming back at you. That's why he's taunting you."

"He's emboldened. The stunt today with the live streaming shows his confidence is growing."

"As is his recklessness," Alison replied. "He's building up to something. Up until now, he's been methodical and calculating. Every step has been planned in great detail, weeks if not months, in advance. Now, he's starting to make it up on the fly." She sipped at her wine while Caslin worked through her logic. "The change of plan regarding the victim. How long did he have the editor locked up?"

"He hadn't been seen by his neighbours for over a month. Everyone thought he was taking an extended holiday after the events last year when he was sacked." Sullivan had been right. The paper had been in a spiral of decline for some time. Dwindling circulation saw failing advertising revenues and a demand from the ownership to stem the flow. The editorial staff shifted focus, looking for headline grabbing material. They believed they'd stumbled across a real scoop involving private enterprise and local government corruption, running the story without fully verifying the facts. The subsequent lawsuit almost put the paper into bankruptcy.

"So, no one who knew him missed him?" Alison asked.

"That's right. He was never reported missing because no one knew he was. Unmarried, single and not particularly sociable – a perfect candidate."

"And yet the killer changed his plan at the last moment, substituting him for Jimmy. Once he was no longer needed, he killed him and stuffed him in the deep freeze without a second thought."

"Where is he taking it now?" Caslin wasn't expecting her to know, he was thinking aloud.

"My theory is that the plan he's been working to has changed. Most likely due to more than merely your interference. The repeated acts of escalating violence, alongside the culmination of his well-made plans are failing to alleviate an almost overwhelming anxiety and depression. This is a very damaged individual."

"He's approaching his end game."

Alison drank her wine, sitting forward and placing her elbows on the table. She took a deep breath, meeting his gaze with a stern expression. "Whatever he is working towards… and it will be something… you will be at the centre of it. You have to be careful, Nate."

Caslin held the eye contact. He sensed there was more she wanted to say, to communicate to him but the moment passed and she placed her drink down on the table before standing up. Picking up her coat, she put it on. Leaning down, she kissed him on the cheek and left without another word. Watching her mounting the steps, Caslin mulled her theory over in his head. Thoughts passed to his family, considering their safety if he was indeed a target but he dismissed the notion. If Alison was right, the killer wanted his attention, not to punish him. There were no indications that Caslin himself was facing a moral judgement. She could be right in that as the principle lead in the investigation, the killer wanted Caslin to understand the motivation, to agree with him, or at least respect the man's actions.

Pushing his drink aside, Caslin returned his focus to the book. Revisiting the chapters relating to Buddhist ethics, he flicked ahead of where he'd last read, passing the precepts themselves in search of references to justice. His working theory was one of a maligned individual, meting out punishment on the morally corrupt. In which case he wanted to see what punishments were considered by followers. Skim reading, he found a section describing the purpose of punishment was *only a requirement when it came to reforming character* which Caslin found wholly unfulfilling as an answer. Glancing at his watch, he considered picking Chen Tao's brains but it was far too late in the day.

Continuing on, he came across a character by the name of *Angulimala,* a revered figure spanning multiple Buddhist traditions in relation to childbirth and fertility. However, it wasn't those associations that drew Caslin's interest. Nor was it the fact he was widely regarded as an example of a complete transformation, the power and influence of the Buddha's teachings. The literal translation of his name pulled Caslin from the drunken malaise he was sinking towards. It was the name, *Angulimala – he who wears a finger necklace.*

His phone rang. Reluctantly, he tore his attention away from the pages to answer it.

"Nathaniel, are you okay?" a female voice asked. It was Michelle. His heart leapt at the recognition before a wave of guilt washed over him, the fleeting joy in stark contrast to the cloak of shame he insisted on carrying since Sullivan's murder. "I saw you… on the television news, just now. I mean, I recognised you in the background."

"This guy's making me famous," Caslin replied, ignoring her initial question.

"You looked so upset. I'm not surprised," she added swiftly. "Anyone would be but… did you know him? The man who died."

Caslin bit his lower lip and he found himself fighting back tears, not for the first time that day. "Yes. He was a friend of mine. A good friend."

"Oh, Nate. I'm so sorry. Is there anything I can do?"

"No!" Caslin responded, realising immediately that he was unintentionally curt. "I'm sorry, I didn't mean to sound dismissive."

"That's okay. Would you like to come over? Carly is sound asleep. We could talk." Caslin said nothing. The silence carried. "Or, we could say nothing and just sit," Michelle added, lightening her tone.

"No. I would like to but I have work to do."

"You sound like you're in a bar."

"And… you sound like my ex-wife," Caslin replied without hostile intent.

Michelle laughed. "Duly noted. I'll be up for another couple of hours if you change your mind. Otherwise, I'll speak with you soon?" Her tone was born of optimism rather than a statement of fact.

"Yes, of course," Caslin replied. "Goodnight."

"Take care, Nate."

He hung up, placing the mobile down on the table. Pulling the book into his lap, he sat back and retraced his finger to the beginning of the story.

The parallels were stark. The story dated back over two thousand years. *Angulimala,* born in the ancient Indian city of *Sāvatthī,* into the priestly caste to a father who served as a king's chaplain. Sent to study as a young man at the hands of a famous teacher in the Brahman priestly traditions, he excelled, rapidly earning both favour and extended privileges from the teacher, much to the jealousy of his fellow students.

Such was his favoured status, his peers schemed to curtail his progress, alleging an affair between the latter and their teacher's wife. Caslin found himself wondering at the accuracy of events, whether they could be after such passage of time. Returning to the story, he read how the teacher was unwilling to confront the younger man, either for fear of *Angulimala's* status or personal strength, the book didn't say. The teacher fabricated a conclusion to his student's *Brahman* training, telling him his studies were nearly at an end. In order to complete them, *Angulimala* must provide the traditional offering… the gift of a thousand fingers. Only then would his training be complete.

Caslin reached for his pint, momentarily distracted by a couple taking their place in the booth adjacent to his own. Returning to the story, he sipped at his drink while he read. *Angulimala* protested the request, claiming to be from a peaceful family but his teacher insisted, finally persuading him. The young student then set out on his mission leaving his teacher comfortable in the belief the younger man would eventually be killed in the process. He preyed on travellers, becoming ever more successful, and brutal, as he honed his skills. The story told how people avoided the roads only for the killer to enter villages and drag victims from their homes, murdering them in the street.

Carefully bookmarking his place, Caslin stood, putting on his coat. Every direction in which he looked there were people enjoying the end of their evening. His thoughts passed to the many occasions he and Jimmy had propped up this very bar, staggered between the levels and helped one another home. Lifting his glass, Caslin tilted it in a silent toast to his friend and drained the remainder in one motion. Tucking the book under his arm, he climbed the steps to the lower bar and headed for the exit and his apartment in Kleiser's Court. The story about the ideological young man reinforcing his beliefs through murder, turning over and over in his mind as he walked.

CHAPTER TWENTY-FOUR

PLEASED to find the team already at their desks when he arrived, Caslin clapped his hands together and grabbed their attention. Despite the fog clouding his thoughts, an aftereffect of the previous night, he was drawn to revisit their suspect with renewed vigour.

"So far our suspect is still a ghost to us. Pull your case notes together because we are going back to the beginning. We know he's meticulous in his planning, leaving nothing to chance. Locations are scouted, he knows where to expect the security cameras to be, how we can trace people through his vehicles or contacts but—" Caslin raised a finger for emphasis. "He spends a great deal of time either with his victims or researching them prior to killing them. That suggests they are not random targets or at least, they aren't by the time he kills them."

"So, he's either a friend or colleague?" Hunter asked.

"Correct," Caslin replied. "Perhaps not long term though. Maybe he was a temporary employee or a delivery driver. Someone who could potentially have had minimal contact with the victim but their paths have almost certainly crossed. Our suspect is somewhere in these files." Caslin slapped a hand down on a folder on the table in front of him.

"What makes you so sure of that?" A voice came from the other side of the room. All heads turned to see the arrival of Kyle Broadfoot. They were all so focussed on Caslin, no one heard him enter.

"It stands to reason, sir," Caslin argued. "To get as close as he needed to, to find out their darkest, most intimate secrets requires time and personal contact. Either with the victim or with someone within their inner circle. We may not have the suspect's true name on file but he's in there. I'm absolutely certain."

Broadfoot inclined his head. Leaning his back against the wall, he folded his arms in front of him and gestured for Caslin to continue. "Carry on. Don't let me interrupt."

"I want us to revisit the statements you've all taken from family, friends and work colleagues. Similarly, workplaces, hobbies, any opportunity for them to have either met new people or been introduced to friends of friends," Caslin stated, watching them for a reaction. Not one of them appeared angry at being asked to return to square one. Each and every member of the team was focussed on getting a result. "Hunter, revisit Kelly Ryan's life, both professional and personal. Find the link."

"Do we look again at Thomas Ryan, sir?" she asked.

"We look at everyone again."

"I'm on it," Hunter said, reaching for the corresponding paperwork.

"Terry, I want you on Andrew Connolly. You've got his computer and we all know what he was up to. Perhaps he's the one victim where there is a digital fingerprint linking him to the killer."

"I didn't find anyth—"

"Look again." Caslin cut him off. He was adamant they'd missed something, not necessarily through incompetence but perhaps it appeared insignificant at the time. They needed to revisit the case with a fresh approach, disregarding any conclusions they'd already reached. "Likewise, see how *Child Protection* are getting on with identifying Connolly's victims. Are there aggrieved family members or even grown up victims who might fancy some retribution?" Holt raised his eyebrows but didn't protest. "Maybe it's a long shot, Terry, but do it anyway."

"What about me?" Templer asked, sitting forward in his chair. Caslin lowered his gaze to his fellow DI. Of all of them, perhaps besides Caslin himself, it was Craig Templer who appeared to have found the case the most draining. Unsurprisingly. He was still missing a colleague and they were no closer to finding out his fate, let alone knowing if he was dead or alive.

"Revisit the Moretti inquiry. If I'm correct, then he's close to it."

"That was a very public investigation," Templer argued. "High profile. He could just have easily read about it in the papers."

"True." Caslin tilted his head to one side. "But everything else we know about him suggests an intimate knowledge, a close connection. He killed Jimmy Sullivan to draw me further into his world. He's making it personal. To me, that says this entire mission of his is personal."

"That means family members," Templer said, thinking aloud. "Those who feel the police or General Medical Council didn't do what they were supposed to."

"Not only," Caslin added. "Put Moretti's colleagues on the list. It was them who blew the whistle in the first place. Subsequently, the case was not proven and the whistle blowers were hauled over the coals, professionally destroyed, even when they made the correct moral call. On this occasion, Moretti was ruled innocent. The practice manager of Moretti's surgery said the colleagues who pointed the finger moved on due to the stress of it all. What's the betting they weren't given a great deal of choice in the matter. They could have an axe to grind."

"Got you," Templer said, his body language demonstrating he was up for the challenge.

"Regarding Kelly Ryan, sir," Hunter said. "I got the impression from one of her colleagues that she knew more than she was letting on. I'll give her another squeeze."

"Good. Push her hard. We only need to crack the link with one victim and then the others will follow. I'm certain. Then, once we've done all of this, we're going to do what we didn't do and should have done so already – and that's catch this man before anybody else gets killed. Understood?"

The team replied positively, in unison, and Caslin stepped away. Broadfoot lifted himself off the wall and crossed the room. Signalling for them to move into Caslin's office for a private word. Caslin caught Hunter eyeing them with a sly sideways glance as they entered his office. Closing the door behind them, Caslin offered his superior a seat but Broadfoot chose to stand.

"I am sorry for what happened to your friend." Broadfoot's tone was heartfelt and genuine.

"Thank you, sir." Caslin appreciated the sentiment but didn't want his focus clouded by grief. Mourning the dead would have to wait. He glanced out of the window. Rain was steadily falling.

"I have been speaking with the chief constable." Turning his back to Caslin, Broadfoot observed the team through the internal glass divide. Glancing at him sideways, he continued, "He has raised concerns over the handling of this case."

"My handling?" Caslin clarified, biting his lower lip and flicking his superior a contemptuous look.

"Yours specifically, yes. But don't imagine that his focus on you deflects any disproval away from me," Broadfoot countered, turning his gaze inwardly to the room. "When things start to go bad, there is always a tendency for some to look at shifting the chairs around."

"Shifting the blame more like."

"To be candid, yes. That's true."

"Are you here to replace me, sir?"

"Don't be such a child, Nathaniel," Broadfoot said, "you have my backing as much as at any time previously."

"But..."

"Your set up here is rather unorthodox in that you don't have the respective layers of command that you should."

"I'm well aware of the latitude, sir."

"Then you will appreciate how easy this is to maintain when things are going well. Should that not continue... well, you know how political things become around here."

"In your world."

"You need to bring closure to this case soon," Broadfoot said, turning to face him and bordering on losing patience. "Otherwise, it will be taken out of my hands and neither of us want that. The knock-on effect will be damaging to both of us."

"Understood, sir." Eyeing Iain Robertson entering from the corridor, Caslin checked whether their impromptu meeting was at an end and Broadfoot indicated it was. Caslin left his office, acknowledging Robertson's greeting.

"I've got the preliminaries from the chapel. Would you like to go through it now or I could leave it with you?"

"No, let's run through it now while everyone is here," Caslin replied.

Broadfoot came alongside him. "Keep me in the loop, Nathaniel."

They waited until he left the room before Robertson passed out copies of a two-page document to all those present. It was a summary of his initial findings. The last person to receive a copy was Caslin himself. As he took a hold of it, Robertson held his grip. "Are you sure you want to do this now? The rest of the team and I can..."

Caslin cut a half-smile, one of resignation. "I need to do this, Iain, but thanks."

Robertson nodded and released his grip on the paper. Turning, he pulled out a chair and sat down. Caslin scanned the summary. The details were graphic, hard for him to read but he meant what he said. This was something he needed to hear.

"The victim," Robertson began, choosing not to mention Sullivan by name deliberately, thereby maintaining objectivity, "suffered a sustained and brutal attack. Dr Taylor will confirm, I'm sure, but we've documented defensive wounds to both hands and forearms. There is evidence of one heck of a struggle, but it didn't take place at the chapel. Rubber streaks were found on the marble flooring." Robertson reached into a folder and withdrew a set of crime scene photographs, placing them on the table for others to see. "Near to the entrance. I should imagine he was dragged into place in the chapel."

"If he was unconscious, could he have been killed elsewhere?" Hunter asked.

Caslin cut in. "No. Too much blood. He died in the chapel."

"Correct," Robertson agreed. "The victim sustained a beating but we do believe he was unconscious or unable to resist. That sets the killer as quite a large man or at least, very strong. The victim weighs over seventy-eight kilos and that's a lot of dead weight…" Caslin drew a sharp intake of breath. "Sorry, Nathaniel. The victim was a large man. Moving someone of that size is damn difficult unless you have a lot of upper body strength. Not to mention technique."

"Cause of death was blood loss, I'm presuming?" Caslin flipped to the end of the report.

"You'll have to wait for Alison, I'm afraid," Robertson said, glancing awkwardly across at him. "I've spoken with her this morning and it is possible he was asphyxiated. The killer…" Robertson hesitated.

"What is it?" Caslin pressed.

"The killer removed his tongue… and forced him to swallow it."

Caslin missed the wave of revulsion expressed by his team, such was the depth of his own reaction. Moments later, he recovered his composure. "Then his throat was cut."

"Aye, it was," Robertson said. "Judging from the passage of the blade and the… smooth nature of the wound, Alison and I believe the victim most likely lost consciousness prior to it happening."

"He did it for the presentation value," Caslin said aloud.

"That was all for the cameras," Robertson said.

"As well as for me," Caslin replied. "Any DNA, trace evidence?"

"No. I'm convinced your suspect knows what we look for."

Caslin resisted the temptation to focus on that last point. Grasping for leads could have led them towards someone with forensic know-how or law enforcement experience but Caslin knew better. Their processes were detailed on multiple websites, and modern dramas did a half decent job of recreating police procedures these days. He saw fit not to read too much into the comment.

"What about Sullivan's apartment? We don't know how or where he was abducted. His car was still outside his apartment. Have you been through his place?" Caslin asked.

"We have, yes. Pulled a number of prints, some of which are unidentifiable. However, we got a partial I'm convinced belongs to the killer."

"How can you be so sure?" Caslin asked.

"There was a match with another smudged partial taken from Alessandro Moretti's residence. It's the only plausible explanation. It looks like a thumb print." Robertson fished out the copies, handing them to Hunter. "We ran them through the system but there were no hits."

"One partial thumb print?" Caslin asked. Robertson nodded. "That guy must have been either living at Moretti's house or at least visiting it frequently for months and you've only found one print."

"Partial," Robertson said, wishing to be clear.

"I went through Moretti's financials," Templer interjected. "How long did Dr Taylor reckon he was incapacitated for, while he was being pumped full of heroin and Fentanyl?"

"Months," Caslin said.

"His bank account and credit cards have been active in that time. Repeated withdrawals of cash at various times every week. Not to mention regular payments to supermarkets and other online retailers. If Moretti hasn't been capable, then who's been using his money?"

"That's how he's living under the radar," Caslin said. "No one's been shielding him, no one has a friend who has been acting weird. He is effectively off the grid, living somebody else's life and money. Get onto the bank—"

"Find out which ATMs he's been withdrawing the cash from." Templer finished for him. "Maybe the security camera on the cashpoint got a decent snapshot. The supermarket purchases are also on a regular fortnightly pattern. That suggests to me they're home deliveries. He wouldn't be stupid enough to walk into a building with a sophisticated CCTV system and use Moretti's credit card for his groceries. Utilising home delivery means he gets one delivery driver, probably different each time, who is making multiple drops and unlikely to remember him if asked months later."

"Possibly at night too," Hunter added.

"We should ask the drivers, anyway. It's worth a shot," Templer stated.

"Good thinking." Caslin turned back to Iain Robertson, raising his eyebrows. "One print?" he repeated, incredulous. "He couldn't live with gloves on all the time, surely?"

"I'm at a loss," Robertson replied. "I can only tell you what I found. Why just the one and from a thumb… I don't understand how he managed it. He can't have been sweeping the prints away because we have multiple other sets."

Caslin thought on it but in the end, he was merely going around in circles, so he chose to move on. "Craig, while you're looking at financials. Pull everything for the man in the deep freeze as well. Perhaps he's been making a habit of living like this."

Templer made a note. "If the money was running out, that would explain why the power was cut off and why he was bleeding money from Andrew Connolly. He needed funds to live off but, in that case, why would he leave the final pay off behind? And why not take the money from the dealers at Stamford Street? I don't understand."

Caslin was equally confused. Templer had a point. "Before, he was playing the long game. Maybe something has changed. Find out if Moretti had a car. I don't see Jimmy going anywhere quietly, so he must have had transport. If there's a print in his apartment, there was no altercation inside because I've been there and seen it for myself. It stands to reason he's using some kind of vehicle. Maybe it's Moretti's. If so, he might still be driving it."

"Give me half an hour," Templer said.

"There's something else, Craig," Caslin said. The edge to his tone made Templer stop as he was about to crack on. He sat down again, looking inquisitively towards Caslin. "It's tough but I have to ask. Your man, Ben Fowler. How well do you know him?"

Templer looked confused. "Well enough. Why do you ask?"

Caslin glanced away and then back again. "We are yet to find him… or any evidence of what has happened to him… if anything."

"Don't go there, Caslin."

"We have to consider the possibility."

"I've worked with him for over a year as his handler," Templer argued. "I have no doubt that he's not gone rogue."

"He's been under a long time," Caslin countered. "Living that way. A high-pressure double life will exert a lot of stress."

"You said it yourself, Caslin. This is personal," Templer stated. "There is nothing personal to Ben about these other victims. Let it go."

Caslin had to admit it, he had a point. Despite allowing the matter to drop, the question regarding where Fowler was couldn't be so easily put aside.

CHAPTER TWENTY-FIVE

"I don't understand what I'm doing here? I answered all of your questions and gave you everything you asked for."

Caslin sat forward in his seat. The interview room had no natural light. The room was purposefully cold. Caslin turned the heating off with the deliberate intention in mind to make the conversation as unpleasant as he possibly could.

"I don't understand what I am doing here, I really don't."

Simon Alexander, Kelly Ryan's line manager, shifted nervously in his seat.

"And yet you failed to mention how you and Kelly were involved," Caslin said, folding his arms across his chest.

"Involved? We were—"

"You were lovers, Mr Alexander."

He stammered. "I... I... don't know where you heard that."

"It's common knowledge among your staff," Caslin said.

"Gossip..."

"Don't lie to me," Caslin barked, slamming a flat palm against the table. Alexander jumped in his seat, startled. "People are dead! Stop lying to me."

Alexander took a deep breath, holding his hands up in supplication. His nervous mannerisms appeared to magnify. "All right... all right." He looked across at Caslin, hunching his shoulders conspiratorially and gently shifting his head from left to right, as if frightened someone might overhear.

"You were in a relationship," Caslin told him. It wasn't a question. "Why did you keep it from us?"

"I didn't think it was relevant. It isn't relevant."

"I'll be the judge of what is and isn't relevant. How long were you seeing each other?"

Alexander shrugged, demonstrating a degree of petulance. "The past year on and off. No big deal."

"Your staff seem to think it is."

"People love to talk," Alexander said. "They'd do so whether it was true or not."

"Who knew?"

"About the relationship?"

"Yes, obviously."

"I don't know… maybe Kelly told someone else as well."

"As well as who?"

Alexander looked momentarily confused, his eyes moving to the ceiling. "I… erm…"

"You said she may have told *someone else*. The time for secrecy has passed. You need to talk to me."

"He came to visit me, at the office," Alexander said quietly, resigned to revealing the nature of the tryst. "A few months back. Her husband. Kelly's husband."

"Thomas Ryan?" Caslin asked, genuinely surprised. Alexander nodded. "Specifically, about the affair?" Alexander nodded but said nothing. "How did he know?"

He shook his head, turning the corners of his mouth down in an exaggerated manner. "Kelly must have told him. I never called her at home or after hours, and it's not like we met all that often for someone to… catch us. There's no other way. She must have done."

"What did he want when he came to see you?"

"To tell me to stay away from his bloody wife! Like it was all my fault."

"Are you devoid of blame?" Caslin asked, raising his eyebrows.

Alexander responded with further childish petulance. "She *pursued* me. I was a married man."

"You could have said no," Caslin countered, masking his incredulity.

"Kelly wasn't a woman who took no for an answer." His response a mixture of denial tinged with a dose of excitement at the memory.

"Did he threaten you?" Caslin asked.

"Not as such… He was angry… sure, but…" Alexander paused, as if a realisation was dawning on him. "Do you think he did it?"

"The visit he paid you, did that put a stop to the relationship?"

Alexander shook his head. "No, of course not. If anything, Kelly upped things a little. I think… she enjoyed it… the thrill was everything for her. It needn't have been me. If not me, then it would have been someone else."

"Where did you used to meet?" Caslin asked.

Alexander appeared irritated at having to discuss the subject. Caslin sensed animosity. "Various places. Sometimes we would get a hotel, others… well, wherever. You know how it is."

Caslin didn't reply but he remembered his own days of infidelity well. Creeping around, experiencing the thrilling sensation of the forbidden fruit, feeling that curious mixture of achievement and shame in almost equal measure. *Almost.*

"Did you ever meet in the countryside?" Caslin asked, watching closely for a reaction.

Alexander averted his eyes from Caslin's gaze. "Occasionally."

"Where?"

"We found a little place where we could be alone." His reply came with obvious reticence and an associated nervous cough. "Near to the Derwent, on the outskirts of a village."

"Westow?"

Alexander snapped to attention, tilting his head to the side. "Yes. How… how did you know?"

"That's where we found Kelly. In a small clearing alongside the river."

"Oh…" Alexander said, his head sinking into his hands.

"Sound familiar?"

"Yes." Alexander nodded solemnly. His expression switched from guarded embarrassment to animated shock. "Listen. You don't think he's going to come for me, do you? I mean, the things this man has done are terrible. What if he comes after me? You need to protect me."

"I should think if he was looking to punish you, then you and I wouldn't be having this conversation right now, Mr Alexander. Kelly is dead. She suffered, perhaps, so you didn't have to."

"Oh, right. Yes, of course. Dreadful business," Alexander said, shaking his head. "I… I don't suppose we could keep all of this out of your investigation, could we? Like I said, it's largely irrelevant."

"And you wouldn't want your wife to find out, would you?"

"No, certainly not."

"I'll see what I can do, Mr Alexander," Caslin said, standing. "You hang on here for a bit and we'll get you home later."

Caslin glanced sideways at the man and then up towards the camera, mounted in the corner where two walls met the ceiling, as he left the room. Although far from a shrinking violet and guilty of his own extramarital affair in the past, Caslin still found this particular individual worthy of his contempt. Even now, he was still seeking to protect his own marriage and reputation at the expense of a murder investigation. The murder of his lover no less, and offering no thought to anything but his own desires. Caslin was met in the corridor by DS Hunter who was watching via a monitor in a separate room. She fell into step alongside him.

"What do you want us to do?" she asked.

"Get Thomas Ryan in here. He's another one who's been lying to us and I wouldn't mind knowing why. You never know, there may be a few other details his mind has let slip recently."

"What about him? I don't think he's involved, do you?" Hunter indicated towards the interview room where Simon Alexander waited.

"No. He's certainly not involved. An utter waste of oxygen. Have Terry Holt take his statement again. I want all of what he just told me on the record. His wife will no doubt find it an interesting read when it's read out in court."

"Right you are," Hunter said, smiling.

"We'll leave him to stew on things for a bit. Have uniform put someone in there with him but make sure they don't talk. That'll make him feel uncomfortable."

"You're cruel."

"How did you get on with revisiting Kelly's caseload?" Caslin asked as they made their way to the stairs.

"Repossessions are far from the peak levels experienced a few years ago but her team were busy. No one they came into contact with was happy about the process but aside from the verbal abuse the staff have come to expect, there didn't appear to be anyone who ticks the boxes."

"No threats?"

"None specifically aimed in her direction, no, and none that were given anything but passing credence."

Holt met them when they were halfway up the stairs.

"Sir, I've just heard back from *Child Protection*. I asked for an update on their identification of the victims in the Connolly investigation."

"How are they getting on?" Caslin asked.

"Slow progress, sir. They've positively identified six of the children thus far. Four of whom are currently attending the centre where Connolly worked. They've started with the most recent and are working backwards but as I said, it's slow progress."

"Background checks on the victims' family members?" Caslin asked as they re-entered their investigation room. Templer acknowledged their arrival.

"I've run the names through the *PNC* and none have returned any hits regarding violent history or criminal records," Holt explained. "We'll have to go out to them and take fingerprints in order to compare them with those Robertson lifted from Moretti's house."

"What about the addicts at Stamford Street?" Caslin asked.

Holt returned to his desk, retrieving a sheet of paper. "You'll not be surprised to find each and every one of them has a place in our rogues' gallery. However, none can be judged as anything other than petty criminals. I went back over every name but turned up nothing new. We have arrests and convictions for robbery, theft and assault. All of which arguably stem from the need to service their addiction."

Caslin took the offered paper, glancing over at the whiteboards mounted on the ops room wall. "Any crossover with other victims or known associates?"

Holt shook his head. "No, sir. None that we can see. Maybe they're not related in any way and he's selecting them at random. He's methodical, willing to take his time. These religious fundamentalists can harbour things for years before they crack."

"Let's hope you're wrong, Terry," Caslin said, shooting him a sideways glance. "Besides, I don't think we have a fundamentalist on our hands. At least, not a devout one anyway."

"What makes you think that?" Templer asked. "He's throwing the imagery at us each time he orchestrates something."

"He's throwing us part of it," Caslin countered. "None of what he does has a place in the devotion to Buddhist traditions. This man isn't a zealot. At best, I believe he's acting out his twisted world vision using the religion as a shroud to either justify it, or to try and demonstrate a moral superiority."

"A lot like a religious zealot, then," Templer stated.

Caslin couldn't disagree. "I still think despite the obvious planning and the creative vision he employs we are dealing with a lay believer, and that is why he will have an association with one of the victims that will take us to him. Craig, what can you tell me about the Moretti investigation?"

Momentarily distracted by some shouting from the street outside, Caslin turned back to Templer as he crossed to a board where he'd already detailed the associations of the key names in the investigation.

"Moretti's colleagues, two of them, raised concerns regarding a number of cases in which patients of the good doctor appeared to have died relatively unexpectedly."

"Relatively?" Caslin queried.

"They were all elderly patients suffering from various ailments associated with old age," Templer explained. "Most had multiple conditions, either being treated on an outpatient basis in conjunction with the local hospital, or directly by staff at the medical centre Moretti worked at. The problems were that none of those who died were thought to be at risk."

"The *CPS* focussed on three cases, I believe?" Caslin asked.

Templer nodded. "That's correct. However, they considered up to six more. Four of those were cremations, so there was little or no forensic evidence to work with. The investigation team, working out of your sister station at Acomb Road, applied to investigate further back to his time in Italy where he originated from."

"What happened with that?"

"Judged unnecessary. I imagine the cost implications were considered too high. There may have been a different outcome if the case had gone to trial and delivered a guilty verdict," Templer said. "As it stands, the details were passed to the Italian authorities and they were left to do their own investigation. No idea whether they acted on it though."

Caslin glanced to the window again as more shouting carried to them. The disturbance seemed to be growing but he pushed his curiosity aside. "What of the three cases?"

"They were burials, so the team applied for exhumations with the approval of the families, although the decision was not uniformly welcomed by all according to the case notes. Further autopsies were carried out. Higher levels of painkiller medication were found than expected in all three, whereas in one case, a medication used in the treatment of acute schizophrenia was found in a patient who had never been prescribed the drug."

Templer picked up a marker. Underlining the first name, he turned to face them. "Iris Baker," he said, tapping the name for effect. "Suffering from arthritis, a thyroid complaint and dementia, died within three hours of a home visit from Moretti. He administered a dose of steroids, according to her medical notes. At the time, her age, frail nature and long medical history didn't cause an alarm to ring."

"Who signed the death certificate? Moretti?"

Templer nodded. "Correct. The family called the surgery when Iris took a turn for the worse and Moretti paid them a second visit, by which time she had already passed. There were no suspicious circumstances noted."

"What about the next?" Caslin asked.

"Peter Scarrow. An eighty-four-year-old man diagnosed with *COPD*, a chronic lung condition that left him in almost permanent need of extra oxygen. He was pronounced dead following his arrival at Accident and Emergency." Templer shrugged, picking up a summary document and passing it to Caslin. "Been in and out of hospital on several occasions in the prior months due to his condition."

Caslin speed read the sheet. The cause of death was noted as a cardiac arrest, brought on by continual stresses placed on the heart by his condition. He couldn't help but wonder if the conclusion may have been reached too hastily.

"Don't tell me, Moretti paid him a visit as well?" Caslin asked, flipping to the photographs of the deceased. All three images depicted smiling faces. Despite their age and varying levels of infirmity, all appeared content in life and were surrounded by loving family members. That was part of what made the suggestion of murder even more unpalatable for the doctor would need to have the trust of not only the patient, but their relatives as well in order to get close enough to kill them.

"Right, yeah. You're seeing the pattern. Moretti saw him that afternoon. Going downhill shortly after, he needed to be admitted to hospital and the family called for an ambulance."

"And the last one they investigated?" Caslin stood, feeling the onset of cramp. He had the urge to stretch his legs. The growing commotion outside drew him to the window overlooking the exit from the station out onto Fulford Road, and he observed a number of uniformed officers fanning out at the edge of his field of vision, but as to why, he had no idea.

"Eleanor C—" Templer was cut off by a ringing phone. It was the landline to Holt's desk and he apologised, rushing to answer it. Seconds later, Hunter's kicked in followed by Caslin's mobile. The team exchanged glances. Standing at the window, the setting sun dropped below the cloud line causing Caslin to raise a hand to shield his eyes from the glare.

"Caslin," he said in greeting, lifting his mobile to his ear, watching as more officers ran past from left to right below, disappearing from view.

"You're going to need to get down here." The familiar voice of a colleague came to him. The tone was strange, strained somehow with an intonation of stress. There was something of a ruckus going on in the background with several raised voices audible but Caslin couldn't make out what was being said.

"What is it?"

"It's one of yours... down here, out front." A scream carried through the mouthpiece. Caslin hung up, turning to his colleagues.

"Something's going on. We'd better get outside." Realising from the expressions on the faces of the team, their calls conveyed the same information as his.

CHAPTER TWENTY-SIX

By the time they descended the steps at the front of the building, at least a dozen uniformed officers were present. They were drawn to the commotion away to their right and ran in that direction. Rounding the corner, a startling scene lay before them. The officers were surrounding a lone man who was clearly in an agitated state. The image struck Caslin as similar to a wounded animal, cornered and afraid, unable or unwilling to recognise the help on offer. The man, stripped to the waist, spun in eternal circles in an attempt to find an escape route. Every avenue was closed off. Officers adopted nonconfrontational gestures, offering soothing voices, attempting to talk the man down from his apparent mania.

"He's off his face," Holt said aloud, drawing a glance from Caslin.

"That a technical term is it?" he replied wryly. Holt wasn't far off with his assessment as Caslin quickly reached the same conclusion. The man was pale, his face drawn, sweating profusely despite the cool breeze of the afternoon and his minimal clothing. Heavily tattooed, Caslin didn't recognise him and the man was distinctive enough that if they'd met, Caslin would be sure to remember. The reason his team were summoned downstairs was obvious with only a cursory assessment.

The man crouched or was about to topple over, Caslin couldn't say which but he threw his arms about wildly in an attempt to ward off the surrounding ring of blue. Two officers jumped away, attempting to avoid the arc of blood flowing from a flailing arm. Even from this distance, the missing index finger of the right hand was clear. Streaks of blood ran from wounds to his upper body but such was his animated state, it was very difficult to see the true nature of the injuries. The nearest officers had donned blue latex gloves, standard procedure to avoid contact with bodily fluids.

"Dear God," Templer muttered under his breath. Caslin looked at him, seeing the mask of abject horror in his colleagues face as the wild-eyed man lunged at the nearest officer. A guttural scream of anger emanated from his mouth, lips curled, reminiscent of a rabid dog. Templer was transfixed, rooted to the spot. *"Ben…"*

Caslin returned his attention to Ben Fowler, the undercover detective missing from the house at Stamford Street. He was struggling. The exertion of his efforts to avoid capture were such that his strength was failing. He staggered and then lurched sideways to avoid two sets of hands seeking to grasp hold of him. Stumbling backwards, he fell against the exterior wall of the police station. His legs gave out from under him and he slumped downwards, eyes rolling as he sank down.

There was a moment that followed where time appeared to stand still. The sheer electricity present in the air mere seconds earlier now replaced by an eerie silence. The passing traffic on the Fulford Road all that could be heard as normality continued around them. The officers exchanged glances and one made to step forward but it was Templer who intervened, forcing his way past and standing between them and their stricken colleague.

Kneeling alongside him, he gently reached out. Fowler's eye followed the path of the approaching hand but didn't react in any other way. "It's me, Ben. It's Craig." He placed the palm of his hand affectionately on the man's shoulder. Attempting to make eye contact and seeking a sign of recognition, Templer forced a smile. "You remember?"

Fowler's gaze fell upon him but if he recognised his handler, he didn't let on. His eyes glazed over, as if staring off at some random point in the distance. Caslin came near, dropping to one knee.

"Ambulance is on the way," he said. Casting an eye over Fowler, Caslin noted the ragged breathing and rapid heart rate. The heart was beating visibly under the skin at a rate of knots far in excess of what could be considered regular. Now better able to assess Fowler's injuries. They looked fresh, crude, as if someone had taken a sharp blade to the man but intentionally refrained from going too deep with each wound. There was a noticeable level of bruising affecting both of Fowler's arms at the crook of each elbow. Scabbing was present alongside fresh needle marks. Fowler suffered a similar experience to Alessandro Moretti. Searching for a positive, Caslin concluded that at least he was still alive.

"What is it, Caslin?" Templer read his curious expression.

"Caslin!" Fowler barked, surging upright for a brief moment before falling back against the wall, accompanied by the press of a reassuring hand on the chest from Templer. "*Caslin…*" he repeated, mumbling.

"What is it, Ben?" Templer asked.

"I… I… a message," Fowler whispered, almost inaudibly. Straining to hear, Caslin looked to his colleague with an inquisitive expression.

Templer shrugged with a shake of the head. "You have a message?" he asked.

Fowler fought for breath, his eyes rolling until they eventually came to focus on Caslin. "*Message,*" he said, his head lolling to one side. Caslin reached up and placed a restraining hand gently against the side of his head, keeping him upright.

"What's the message, Ben?" Caslin repeated the question.

Fowler shook his head ever so slightly. "I'm… the message…"

Caslin exchanged glances with Templer. The shared fear that Fowler was slipping into unconsciousness struck them. Templer pressed for more detail. "What's the message, Ben? What do you have to tell him?"

Fowler's eyes closed and he passed out. Templer reached to his neck, searching for a pulse. Smiling, he announced he had one but it was erratic. The sound of an approaching ambulance could be heard, the sirens reverberating off of the buildings as it negotiated the rush hour traffic. Seconds later, the yellow vehicle appeared at the entrance to the car park. A uniformed officer directed them to the nearby group.

"That was incoherent," Templer said. "We need to know what the message was."

"He said *he was* the message," Caslin replied, frowning. The two men made room for the first of the two paramedics to reach them. A colleague joined her and Caslin stepped away, leaving Templer to fill them in on what they thought had befallen Fowler.

"Anyone see who dropped him off?" Caslin asked the assembled officers. There were blank expressions all round. Turning, he looked for Hunter. "Review the CCTV, maybe we can get a make of car and a direction of travel."

"Caslin! You need to see this."

He returned to where Templer stood. Fowler was laid out with the medics preparing to lift him onto a gurney for transport to hospital.

"Be quick," the first paramedic said to them.

Drawing back the blanket from beneath Fowler's chin to reveal his chest, Caslin was shocked. The blood across his upper body seeped from multiple injuries but the cuts were shallow. There was minimal blood flow. They were administered with a sharp blade, only stripping away the layer of skin and leaving much of the flesh beneath intact. Inclining his head sideways, Caslin could now see the cuts were, in reality, crudely shaped letters. The edges were ragged, more like barely controlled slashes than the result of focussed concentration. Perhaps Fowler didn't cooperate in the process.

"M.I.C…" he read aloud, struggling with the final letters.

"That's an *H*," Templer suggested, trying hard to read Caslin's expression. "And the last looks like an *E*… I would say. Wouldn't you? Is that the message?"

"He said the message was for me."

"Yeah. What does it mean?"

"Upstairs," Caslin began, the semblance of a thought forming in his mind along with a knot of fear in his stomach. "What were the names you had, particularly the one you were going to say before all this kicked off?"

Templer thought back to his notes on the three suspicious deaths in the Moretti investigation. "Err… Baker, Scarrow and… Eleanor something… Carter, perhaps. Sorry, not sure. Why?"

"Just a spark in the back of my mind," Caslin replied, trying to organise the jumble of thoughts flooding his mind.

"Come to think of it, it wasn't Carter. It was Cates, *Eleanor Cates*. She couldn't be related to…?"

Caslin met his eye, the links starting to come together.

"Do they… and that makes this *Miche*… what… who?" Templer asked.

"Michelle Cates. *Thomas Ryan's sister*," Caslin said quietly, "and he's telling me his next target."

Taking out his mobile, Caslin scrolled through his contact list and dialled Michelle's number. Pacing nervously as he waited for her to pick up, his anxiety growing as the call rang but without response, eventually passing to voicemail. He hung up and redialled.

"What is it?" Hunter asked, coming to join them and sensing something was wrong.

"Get the car," Caslin said, abandoning the call and putting his mobile away. "Get it now."

Something in his manner or tone hit home and Hunter turned on her heel, setting off to the rear yard where her car was parked. Caslin turned to Templer.

"If I'm right, put out a *Bolo* for Thomas Ryan. Send some units to his home address. He should be approached with caution but I think I know where we'll find him."

"In that case we need to seal off the area—"

"He's on the edge of the centre." Caslin checked his watch. "At this time in the evening we'll have no chance of doing that quietly. There will be chaos if we try. We'll be tipping our hand."

"What are you suggesting?" Templer asked as the medics hoisted Fowler up onto the gurney and ushered them out of the way.

"I'm working on it," Caslin replied, spotting Hunter pulling up at the kerbside. He set off without another word, leaving the frustrated Templer behind.

"You've not even told me where you're going!"

Caslin ignored him, opening the passenger door and clambering in. Hunter pulled away. The last thing Caslin wanted was the entire station emptying and descending on the Cates' residence. Alison Taylor was right. He was at the centre of this and the killer *wanted* him there for the finale and Caslin intended not to disappoint. A flicker of panic rose within and he sought to quell it. *Would Thomas Ryan really kill his sister … his niece?* Without doubt, the man was certainly capable.

Hunter, sensing Caslin's requirement for urgency floored the accelerator, pulling out into oncoming traffic and forcing a path through. The evening rush hour was in full swing and the routes in and out of the city were approaching gridlock as usual. For once, Caslin didn't comment on her driving skills. The whites of his knuckles on show, he gripped the door handle and braced himself while Hunter carried out her particular brand of enthusiastic driving.

The blaring horns of terrified motorists sounded in front and behind them as they progressed. Despite Hunter's best efforts, the sheer weight of traffic on the approach to the centre eventually brought them to a standstill on *Fishergate*. Caslin shifted in his seat. They were a few hundred yards short of *Tower Street*. With a clear run, Michelle's house was a two-minute drive away or a five-minute walk.

Hunter swore. Viewing the road ahead, there was something blocking the nearside lane. A broken-down vehicle by the look of it. Caslin could wait no longer. He cracked open his door and was out before Hunter could object.

"Cas…" she shouted but let the call tail off. Reaching for her radio, she depressed the talk button. The radio crackled into life and she announced her location. Despite Caslin's fears regarding tipping their hand, she couldn't allow him to go alone. Knowing how rash he could be, a strength at times but incredibly risky at others, Caslin would be more than willing to go up against Thomas Ryan alone.

Breaking into a run, Caslin cut between two stationary vehicles and mounted the pavement. Passers-by stepped aside, some clearly startled by a grown man charging towards them. Heading left and over the bridge, Caslin sprinted across the road, narrowly avoiding those cars accelerating away from the traffic lights, seeking to gain an advantage on the other drivers around them. Descending the stone steps into the Tower Gardens, located alongside the river Ouse, Caslin was breathing hard. Stopping when he reached the ground level, the sound of traffic thundering over the bridge above him, Caslin caught his breath whilst eyeing Michelle's house on the far side of the gardens.

From his vantage point, he could see the glow from the light of the rear extension, visible above the perimeter wall. He knew time was limited. There was no way the panic button wouldn't be pushed, either by Hunter or Templer. They would be right to do so. That gave him a limited window in which to act. Resuming his route across the open space, Caslin ignored those on their way home from work, fleetingly jealous of their evening routine as the reality of his own situation fixed itself in the forefront of his mind. The notion he was walking… no, *running* into a trap was obvious.

Reaching the perimeter wall, far too high for him to climb over, he skirted along its length until he came to the rear access gate. Trying the handle, he found it bolted from the inside. He could hear the sound of sirens in the distance. Looking down to his left, he noted a chunk of brick missing from the wall alongside the gate. Using it as a foothold, he threw his arms over the top of the gate and levered himself up. Peering through the foliage he looked towards the house. His view was obscured. Night had descended and, confident he wouldn't be seen from anyone inside, he hoisted himself up and rotated his body over the gate, dropping to the path below.

Inching forward, he hugged the perimeter, using the bushes to mask his approach. The rear of the house came into view, all contemporary glass and aluminium. Caslin saw three figures sitting around the dining table where he'd shared a meal with Michelle only a few days earlier. She was sitting alongside her daughter, Carly, with another figure directly opposite her with his back to him. He wore a dark, heavy overcoat and sat hunched over. From his vantage point, he was unsure whether this was Thomas Ryan. His hair colour matched but the coat made his physical frame hard to determine and therefore confirm it was him.

Narrowing his eyes, Caslin assessed what was going on. He could see little or no conversation taking place. The three of them appeared to be waiting. Edging forward, Caslin took out his mobile phone, setting it to silent mode for fear of a random call giving away his presence. A few steps further and he was as close as he could get without risking revealing himself. The sounds of the city carried on the breeze. A light in an upstairs room flickered into life in the adjoining house. Caslin watched the curtains drawn as the inhabitants went about their routine, ignorant of the unfolding drama next door.

The sirens grew ever louder and Caslin knew he was at a crossroads. Either he backed away and awaited a trained negotiator, as would be the expectation, or he could enter the house. The latter filled him with a sense of dread. Observing those inside, the stronger he felt the likelihood was that they were waiting. Waiting for him. From where he knelt, Caslin couldn't see a weapon on the table. Nor could he see any immediate threat to Michelle or her daughter. Of course, that didn't mean they were in any less danger. Still unable to see or identify the man, Caslin looked at the remaining windows. All the rear facing rooms were in darkness. *Was he another hostage? Could Thomas Ryan be elsewhere, lying in wait perhaps?*

By entering the situation, as per the killer's intention, there was every possibility Caslin would set in motion the final stages of his scheme. Potentially disastrous for everyone present. Then again, were he to refuse to participate, an equal or even a worse outcome could materialise. His eyes fell on Michelle. Even from this distance, he could see she was crying.

Taking a deep breath, he rose from his position, stepping out and revealing himself. Advancing slowly towards the house, he was ten feet from the door when Michelle saw him. Her lower lip dropped slightly in an involuntary movement but it was enough. The man turned. Caslin stopped, standing still as their eyes met. Caslin had seen similar expressions before. He could never shake the memory of the piercing stare of a killer and it made his blood run cold. This was another of those times. He beckoned Caslin forward. All the while, his cold gaze never left him.

Approaching, Caslin remained alert looking for a weapon and trying to work out what he was up against, different scenarios playing out in his head. There was no immediate threat. The man had his hands on the table in front of him, one atop the other. He seemed unfazed by Caslin's presence, returning his gaze to Michelle and Carly.

Reaching the patio, Caslin internally acknowledged his surprise. Somewhere along the line his logic had fallen down for whoever this man was, *he was not Thomas Ryan.*

CHAPTER TWENTY-SEVEN

THE FIRST OF the bi-fold doors was ajar. A distinctive smell drifted in his direction, carried by a through draft from within. Walking forward to the threshold, he paused. The overwhelming smell of petrol was intense. Caslin glanced at the floor. The tiles shimmered, reflecting the light from the fittings overhead. Inclining his head slightly, his eyes met Michelle's and she appeared to shake. Whether borne of a desire for him to keep away or an involuntary reaction to her predicament, he couldn't tell.

Michelle, aside from their first meeting, was a vivacious character, confident and a joy to be around. Here, now, her expression was unlike any he had seen before. A picture of focused control and yet fearful to the point that Caslin thought she may crack at any moment. Her complexion was pale, her make-up, usually classy and understated failed to mask how she must have been crying. Her mascara smudged around her eyes and tears welled, brimming to the point of flowing but Caslin recognised the iron will of her inner strength, a steadfast refusal to buckle.

Perhaps her motivation was her daughter. Carly sat alongside her mother. They clasped hands, her right held encapsulated by her mother's left. The grip so tight that Caslin wondered if the little girl might be in pain. For her part, she had also been crying. Tears streaked the girl's cheeks and she tentatively glanced up at Caslin before looking away, back down towards the table as if frightened to make eye contact with him. She was still dressed in her school uniform.

Casting a look around, Caslin saw signs of a limited struggle. Broken glass lay near the entrance to the kitchen from the hall, alongside an overturned plant. He swallowed hard. The fumes were overpowering and he blinked, his eyes stung.

"Are you going to stand there all night, Caslin?" The man spoke in a calm, measured tone, sounding as if he was addressing a friend.

Stepping inside set off an expanding ripple outward in the pool of petrol. Only then did he notice multiple jerry cans, the metal type used by the military, two-foot-high and stacked against the far wall. One lay on its side but each can was missing the seal. They were empty, the contents poured all around them. The worktops glistened. The build-up of pressure saw droplets run from the surface down the face of the cabinets, falling to the floor below.

Very deliberately, Caslin walked forward but careful to appear non-threatening. On the table lay a packet of cigarettes. The brand matched that of the discarded butts found in the garden all those nights ago. Atop the packet lay a wind-proof lighter. As if realising Caslin's thought process, the man smiled, reaching over and picking it up. The ends to his fingers were wrapped in fabric plasters, heavily stained and tattered.

"It's a funny thing… fire," he said, turning the lighter over and over in the palm of his hand. "So important to life. Warming. Welcoming. And yet, as much a method of intense destruction as it is renewal."

Carly burst into tears and her mother squeezed her hand tighter still, which Caslin didn't think possible. Michelle's lower lip quivered, clenching her eyes shut. The man looked at the girl. Reaching across with his free hand, he made to stroke her cheek.

"Don't you touch her," Michelle hissed at him through gritted teeth. Caslin admired her courage.

"We haven't met, have we?" Caslin asked, attempting to hijack their exchange and put himself into the centre of the dynamic.

"No, we haven't. Are you going to introduce your husband to your new lover, Miche?"

"You're… not my husband…" Michelle responded in a whisper. "He would never…"

"Don't lie!" He slammed his hand against the table in an instantaneous flash of rage. "I am your husband." Michelle jumped, startled.

Silence descended. Caslin felt the draught coming from the hallway. He could see the front door was ajar. Michelle and Carly must have been surprised as they entered the house.

"Despite my best efforts, you have me at a disadvantage." The couple shared an emotional connection and Caslin needed to assert some influence over the situation and deescalate the tension. He looked to Michelle, encouraging her with his eyes. She was silently pleading with him, her despair evident in her expression.

"This is Daniel, my ex… my husband," Michelle said, correcting herself. Flashing red and blue lights signified the arrival of the police units at both the front and the rear.

"Your friends have arrived in time," Daniel said.

"In time for what?" Caslin asked, fearful of the answer. Daniel smiled but it was one without genuine humour. No answer was forthcoming. "You've gone to great lengths to… educate… to demonstrate… your belief in the Five Precepts. You've been on quite a journey."

"The path is lit for those willing to see."

"You're not quite the scholar of Buddhist practice that people believe, though, are you?" Caslin sought to focus the conversation on what was driving his behaviour. An attempt to engage with Daniel Cates's warped world. He glanced towards Caslin but said nothing. "I came across your inspiration. Is that the right word?"

Cates fixed him with a lingering stare, a narrowing of the eyes but still offered no response. Daniel returned his gaze to Michelle. She looked to her daughter.

"Your reading of *Angulimala* is far from accurate."

"How so?" Cates asked, finally interacting. If he was surprised by Caslin's knowledge then he didn't show it externally, but there was a spark of interest in the eyes, Caslin was certain. Michelle flitted between the two of them, trying in vain to keep track but clearly lost by the reference.

"His brutal mission was brought to an end upon his meeting with the Buddha. *Angulimala's* path to enlightenment followed his conversion away from *Brahmanism* and his rejection of violence, *not* as a result of his passion for it."

Cates locked eyes with Caslin. He placed the lighter on the table before him. Caslin calculated his potential for success if he made a move for the lighter. Without weapons, neither held a distinct advantage over the other but Cates was a physically imposing man, easily taller and of greater stature than himself. Going toe-to-toe with this man would be a major risk. Reaching up, Cates grasped the zipper of his coat and slowly drew it in a downwards motion. A crudely fashioned leather cord looped around his neck, hanging almost to his waist. Threaded through were severed fingers in a macabre, ghoulish presentation. Several were blackened, a result of decomposition, while to the ends of others strings of withered flesh protruded. Michelle gasped.

"Don't look, Carly." Her tone was sharp. The words harsh. Carly turned away screwing her eyes shut, on the verge of tears once more.

"He reached his goal, as I shall mine," Cates said, defiant.

"Why stop now? *Angulimala* was tasked to collect a thousand. He had a lifetime of indoctrination in dogmatic religious belief and the pressure of royal duty to spur him on. *What do you have?* A failed marriage? Forgive me but that doesn't make you special—"

"I *show* people the way!" Cates retorted. A flash of the deadly personality contained within showed through his controlled exterior. "You dare to judge me? Those people lack the purity of their *body, speech and mind*. The *doctor* who took lives having sworn an oath to heal and care for them. Harming those who relied upon him… the frail and the weak."

"He took your mother." Caslin's tone was nonconfrontational, seeking to connect on an emotional level. Cates met his gaze and for the first time, Caslin saw what he thought was a spark of humanity. A depth of genuine pain as opposed to twisted rage. "Doctor Moretti took her from you before her time. The others… were they all worthy of such wrath? Those dealing with addictions—"

"Intoxicants cloud their minds, harming their spiritual development. Their slavish commitment to their craving is their weakness."

"Addicts fight battles every day," Caslin countered thinking of his own struggles.

Cates shot him a dark look. Rising, he unhooked the last section of zipper and slid the coat off, tossing it aside. Defiantly, he turned his left hand, palm showing, dragging his sleeve up with his right, revealing the crook of his elbow. The action revealed scarring, long since healed but indicative of a former habit.

"Their failure shows a lack of spirit… of conviction." Cates was cold, unsympathetic.

"No one is perfect. Everyone in this world is in a state of suffering. If not, we would all be enlightened."

"And there are those who require a forced renewal." Caslin saw a marked shift in his demeanour. The spark of defiance passing to anger and then finally to reflection. "A man devoting his life to caring for the most vulnerable children in our society, only to use it as a cover to satisfy his own perverted desires. A man willing to starve his family of every penny in order to hide his darkest secrets."

"Not everyone is as deserving of your anger," Caslin argued. It was certainly true that very few people, if any, would spare much sympathy for the plight of Andrew Connolly. A man who committed such vile actions against innocent children.

"You are cowed into submission by your conditions. They manifest in your hypocrisy."

Caslin shook his head in disagreement. "Not so. I've spent my adult life hunting down people like him—"

"I am honest and open about my desires!" Cates barked at him. "At the very least, Connolly knew who he was... *what he was*. If he'd had the courage of his beliefs, then he wouldn't have felt the need to hide."

Caslin saw the expression of belief in his moral superiority. The perception of a higher knowledge and understanding. Not only did Cates see himself as possessing a transparency to be admired but he found Caslin's apparent disdain to be somehow irritating. Almost interpreting it as a display of ingratitude of his efforts.

"Your protests are so predictable." Cates was dismissive, shaking his head.

"What about Kelly? Did she deserve her fate?" Caslin asked, taking a risk. Of all the victims, she was family. A close relationship ended in the most brutal of fashions. Aware of Carly's presence, he glanced sideways at Michelle who understood, reaching across and drawing her daughter into her arms. Cates looked but didn't raise an objection. Caslin took it as a sign he was making inroads into the man's psyche, deflecting his focus away from his family.

"A woman with such low morality? Profiting from those who fall below the unachievable standards set by supposedly faceless corporations. People talk about corporate greed but there is no such thing." Cates fixed Caslin with a stare. "Corporations are abstract concepts. They are run by people. Policies are set by people. *Corporate greed* is interchangeable with *personal greed*. That's what Kelly was."

"She was doing her job!" Michelle whispered, her daughter buried her head into her mother's chest. "Daniel, how could you?"

Cates appeared hurt. Stung by his former partner's criticism. "The likes of her took our home! That woman made your brother's life a misery. She couldn't keep her clothes on for—"

"That's not for you to judge," Michelle countered.

A flicker of movement caught Caslin's attention. With Cates distracted by Michelle's challenge, he chanced a sideways glance. Craig Templer stood in the hall, hugging the wall as he inched forward out of sight from those seated at the table. Upon seeing Caslin, he stopped, inclining his head and indicating pointedly in Caslin's direction with two fingers. There were officers taking position along the perimeter wall. No doubt, sharp shooters. That filled Caslin with a sense of dread. The amount of petrol in the room, coupled with the intensity of the fumes, meant the slightest spark would see the house explode with extreme ferocity.

All Caslin could do was hope Templer would realise and get the word back to the officer commanding.

"The journalist. What about him?" Caslin asked.

Cates maintained his gaze on Michelle for a few seconds longer before he turned. "The principle of true speech is far more powerful than many believe. Above all else, the spoken word must be beneficial to those who hear, if not to those who speak. The motivation for journalism is to speak the truth to power. *Your friend did not uphold that tradition.*"

"I placed him in that position."

"And by doing so, *you*, and you alone, charted his course," Cates told him.

"He was a decent man."

"And not my intended target," Cates replied, grinning maniacally. "I chose his former boss. The man who destroyed my career with unfounded lies. *Can you imagine that?* Spending your life in a profession, working hard, only to have it ruined by one man and his pursuit of a readership. They took my pride, my self-respect…" He looked to Michelle. "As well as my wife and family. And then you brought Jimmy Sullivan to me, an equally suitable candidate who came with added motivation."

Caslin felt a flash of anger surge within. Once again, he considered launching himself at the man and pounding him into the ground. As if he was able to read his thoughts, Cates lost his grin. He stared at Caslin, almost willing him to make the move. Reaching for the lighter, he scooped it up. Gripping it between thumb and forefinger, top and bottom, he squeezed. The cap of the lighter pinged open. Caslin had seen it before, a deft little party trick. Cates placed a thumb on the wheel, a moment away from sparking the flint.

"I understand the craving," Caslin said, thinking on his feet. Cates held their eye contact but his thumb remained poised to strike the flint. "Didn't the Buddha say that we live in an imperfect world? In the second of his

Four Noble Truths, he recognised the world will always be unsatisfactory. There will always be pain and suffering. We cannot escape this reality."

"You speak of *tanhā*," Daniel said and Caslin nodded. "The thirst for sensual pleasure, to both exist and to not. The principal cause of *dukkha*."

"Yes. There will always be suffering," Caslin agreed. "We live in an imperfect world. No matter what we do or how many of us try to walk the path to enlightenment, we will always see chaos and suffering all around us. I understand the craving, the longing for it to end. Believe me."

"The craving grows harder to manage," Cates said, staring off at some imaginary point in the distance. "The world is ever changing… and is innately unsatisfactory."

"Bringing more pain by way of arguments and conflict between individuals." Caslin tried to remember all that he'd read. This was his way in to the conflicted mind of this killer.

"Which is why we must renew, liberate ourselves from this material existence and continue on the spiritual path," Cates said quietly.

Caslin could tell Cates had slipped into an understanding of the *Dharma* warped by the successful spread of the teachings. By the time Buddhism reached Tibet, it had been heavily influenced by Hinduism. The concept of rebirth, the passing of a soul from one life to the next had taken root. The understanding of reincarnation interpreted in another light. Caslin understood his endgame. The Five Precepts were marked and his mission complete. Now, he sought to journey to the next life, to continue on towards enlightenment only this time, he would take his estranged family with him. They had all wondered what the Sixth Precept would be. Daniel Cates intended to mark his passing in spectacular fashion.

"But they won't see a rebirth, will they, Daniel?" Caslin said, adopting a conciliatory tone. "The Buddha spoke not of a rebirth but more of a *re-becoming*. As one candle burns to the base, the flame is used to ignite the next but what remains of the first? The passage into the next life is assured but the only way to develop spiritually is to walk the path of life, earning karma that will ripen either in this life or the next. There is no shortcut. Our spiritual path is for us and us alone. You cannot make this decision for anyone but yourself."

"Did not the *Bodhisattva* sacrifice himself as a supreme offering to the Buddha? His body flamed for a thousand years before he was reincarnated and burned again for thousands more, allowing many to reach enlightenment before he was restored."

"Your desire for self-immolation, the craving of total annihilation is admirable…" Caslin began, drawing a fearful look from Michelle. She was staring at the lighter. "But this is not for your daughter to see. She must learn from her teachers. You, her father is one of those. You must allow her the chance to walk the path."

Cates's head sank. Caslin could see his grip on the lighter tighten, the whites of his knuckles showing. His hand shook. It was a few seconds before Caslin realised the man was crying. Not openly sobbing, but tears streamed unrestrained down his face. His one weakness revealed in an otherwise impenetrable armour.

"Let her walk her own path," Caslin repeated.

Cates mumbled, the words almost inaudible and Caslin wondered if it was even coherent, let alone meant for him to hear. The words grew louder with each repetition. The same phrases over and over again.

"The world is impermanent, insubstantial, incapable of fulfilment."

Caslin had heard them before, he must have read about them but the reference was lost to him. Glancing to his left, Templer stood at the entrance to the kitchen, as close as he dared to be without revealing himself. The man's bravery was to be admired. He signalled to Caslin that everything was under control with a thumbs up gesture. Drawing Michelle's attention, Caslin silently gestured for her to stand. The legs of her chair scraped on the tiles as she did as he requested. She froze. Carly, her arms and legs wrapped around her mother, instinctively clamped herself even tighter. Cates didn't react.

Caslin sensed this was their one window of opportunity.

CHAPTER TWENTY-EIGHT

Michelle inched towards Caslin. He stepped between them and Daniel Cates. The latter dropped the lighter and it clattered against the surface of the table. Placing his head in his hands, he began to weep uncontrollably. Encouraging her in the direction of the hall, Caslin pointed to the waiting Templer. The desire to run screamed to make itself known in his mind, but he was concerned that a sudden change in atmosphere might trigger an irrational move from their captor. Templer stepped forward, taking Carly from her mother's arms and smiling in order to reassure the girl everything would be okay.

Michelle looked over her shoulder, realising Caslin was not following. He still stood between them and her husband. She mouthed to her daughter, allowing her grip of her hand to slip as Templer set off for the front door. She reached out and touched Caslin's arm.

"Don't!" she whispered, imploring him with her eyes. "Please… he was a good man once but let him go if that's what he wants. It is his choice…"

"Go now," he replied. Moving away from her grasp, he pulled the chair out that she had vacated. Michelle hesitated for a second and with a slight shake of the head, she moved away. Caslin didn't see the pained expression on her face.

Despite Daniel Cates being what he was, Caslin could see the broken man on the inside. A man who couldn't cope with what life threw at him.

If not for a freak set of circumstances bringing Caslin himself back from the brink, only a few short years ago, maybe it would have been his mind that seemed irrecoverably broken. Sympathy was non-existent, empathy… possible but what was strong in Caslin was the need for this man to face justice for his crimes. He should spend the rest of his natural life in a cell and Caslin intended to ensure it would happen.

Sitting down opposite Cates, the man lifted his head. His face contorted in pain, eyes bloodshot and swollen. Something was lost in his expression, his mind seemingly on the verge of collapse.

"You should leave too," he said quietly, reaching for the lighter. He clasped it in his palm and closed his hand into a fist.

"*Angulimala* is revered by Buddhists the world over… an example of how even the most damaged minds can be transformed."

"Not this time… not by you," he replied.

"What is it that you are looking to achieve? Everyone has a purpose in life, a career, a family, or a goal they are seeking. Tell me yours? You haven't done any of this on a whim."

Daniel Cates looked into his eyes. The stare was hard and unforgiving. "There is great evil in this world. All that we are arises with our thoughts and with our thoughts we shape the world."

"And you feel your journey towards enlightenment is somehow benefitted by highlighting the precepts and the lack of adherence to them by society?" Caslin asked, genuinely trying to understand, to build some kind of a bridgehead into this man's troubled mind. "The Precepts are but guidelines, are they not? You choose to ignore the positive aspects and focus on the negatives, ignoring the presence of the *Worldly Winds*."

"I see you have been studying the *Dharma*, Inspector." Cates smiled at the reference. Caslin found it unnerving. "Pleasure versus pain. Praise and blame. Fame and dishonour."

"*Gain and loss.*" Caslin completed the list.

Cates inclined his head. "But have you only memorised the words or can you apply an interpretation?"

Caslin saw the challenge. Cates wanted to know if he was debating an equal or someone attempting to deceive. "For me, the truth, and make no mistake for it is a truth, is that you are correct. There is a tremendous amount of evil in this world. But evil in of itself is an abstract construct. There is no entity, being or force in which this label applies. All we have is the sum of the acts carried out throughout history and around the globe. The choice we have as an individual is whether we will choose to add to that or to walk a different path. *Angulimala* realised this truth. He chose to revere life over death."

"*And accepted responsibility* for his past actions and how he would be treated. The people beat him with sticks, punished him for his past transgressions *despite* his transformation to follow the *dharma.*"

"The Buddha always said practitioners must live within the constructs of society. The same rules apply to them as everyone else."

Cates appeared to be thinking hard. Caslin was making inroads, he could sense it.

"Which is why you need to leave," he said, locking eyes with Caslin. Something changed in his expression, a veil of darkness appearing to sweep over him as he spoke. *"While you still can!"* He hissed the last comment, almost through gritted teeth.

Caslin stood slowly. "There is still time for you… what lies ahead will only cause you more pain. Either in this life or the next, unless you walk out with me now." Cates was unmoved. Caslin backed away, watching for any sign from him, any indication of what he planned to do but there was none. He remained, staring at the table in front of him.

Turning as he reached the hall, he trotted to the open front door. Reaching the threshold, he sucked in a deep breath of fresh air. It tasted sweet. The petrol fumes were still present and he felt nauseous. Caslin looked towards the assembled emergency services within the nearby cordon. An ambulance, two fire brigade appliances and multiple police cars lined the quayside. Hunter was visible, beckoning him to descend the steps to safety. The quay was taped off at both ends, no doubt the neighbouring properties had already been evacuated. People were gathering nearby. The pub on the corner had emptied to watch the spectacle unfold.

Perhaps it was because of a perceived affinity or a sign of the sheer stubborn, bloody-mindedness he was famous for, but Caslin thought that bringing Cates back from the brink would somehow lay the ghosts of his own past to rest, a sense of closure maybe. Regretting his inability to do so, he stepped forward.

There was a rush of air from behind him, similar to a fan starting up on a hot day. The warm breeze reeked of fuel. Caslin heard no sound, nor did he see the fireball surge in his direction. The pressure wave struck and he felt momentarily weightless as air escaped his lungs. His vision swam, becoming a blur of coloured lights only to be replaced shortly after by darkness. The warm breeze on his skin was now as cold as stone. The embrace of the silence was a comfort, an all-encompassing sense of belonging. Then he felt nothing. Nothing at all.

A PERSISTENT RINGING echoed in his ears. Opening his eyes, Caslin could see movement above him. Seconds passed and details emerged as shadows coalesced into shapes. Attempting to move released an intense burst of pain. It rippled along his arm before cascading down his spine. Caslin cursed although he didn't hear the words. Hunter was knelt by his side, placing a restraining hand gently on his chest. Her lips moved but it was another minute before his senses righted themselves and he could understand what was being spoken to him.

"Don't try to move," she told him, repeating herself for the second or maybe third time, he wasn't sure.

Disregarding her advice, he rolled on to one side. The pain was less intense on this occasion and he levered himself up onto his elbow. Strewn around him were assorted pieces of debris. Some were still flaming, and almost all were unrecognisable in relation to their origin. Glancing back at the house, flames licked at the exterior from the open doorway and shattered sash windows. The crews from the fire brigade were advancing on the house, attempting to suppress the fire before it could take hold and spread to the adjoining terrace.

Closing his eyes, Caslin fought a wave of nausea that washed over him. His head throbbed and something cool was running down the inside of his shirt at the base of his neck. Moving to touch it released another wave of pain and he gave up, cursing under his breath.

"You should listen to me once in a while, you know?" Hunter chastised him.

"Michelle and Carly?" Caslin asked, looking past Hunter in the direction of the nearby melee, a hive of uniformed activity.

"They're fine."

Caslin spotted the two of them, seated in the back of a parked ambulance. They were draped in a blanket, Michelle with a comforting arm around her daughter, stroking her hair and kissing the top of her head.

"Daniel Cates?" In all honesty, he already knew the answer to that particular question. Hunter shook her head. "Released from his suffering after all."

The reference was lost on Hunter, who smiled, relieved to see he was not as badly injured as first feared. Caslin looked around. He was twenty feet away from the base of the steps to the Cates house, and barely five from the river.

"That must have been some explosion." Caslin felt thankful not to have ended up in the water. A police boat approached the nearby jetty, picking its way through the debris being carried away by the current of the Ouse.

A paramedic arrived but Caslin shrugged him off, choosing to stand against the advice of those around him. He braced against Hunter, who helped him to his feet. His legs felt wobbly and every movement was painful. There was no arguing. He would need to attend the hospital. Catching sight of Michelle, he thought she was staring in his direction. Whether she recognised him or it was merely coincidence, he couldn't tell. Raising a hand, he waved, forcing an accompanying smile. She remained impassive, still staring straight ahead as the doors to the ambulance were closed and she disappeared from view.

His smile faded. Hunter noticed.

"Give her some time, Nate," she said reassuringly. He glanced at her, nodding. She knew. How she knew, Caslin could only guess. Maybe it was how they left the house together. Maybe Hunter knew him better than he realised.

"I can do that."

"She was distraught when the house went up."

"Not surprising, it was her home." Caslin looked back at the house. A ruin of its former grandeur.

"No, Nathaniel. She thought you were dead," Hunter replied, placing a warm hand on his shoulder. "And she's not the only one." She patted him gently. "Just give her some time."

Caslin watched as the ambulance moved off, carving a path through the voyeurs. For the first time in a long time, his thoughts were for anything but the job.

FREE BOOK GIVEAWAY

Visit the author's website at **www.jmdalgliesh.com** and sign up to the VIP Club and be first to receive news and previews of forthcoming works.

Here you can download a FREE eBook novella exclusive to club members;

Life & Death - A Hidden Norfolk novella

Never miss a new release.

No spam, ever, guaranteed. You can unsubscribe at any time.

ARE YOU ABLE TO HELP?

Enjoy this book? You could make a real difference.

Because reviews are critical to the success of an author's career, if you have enjoyed this novel, please do me a massive favour by entering one onto Amazon.

Type the following link into your internet search bar to go to the Amazon page and leave a review;

http://mybook.to/DY_Boxset2

If you prefer not to follow the link please visit the Amazon sales page where you purchased the title in order to leave a review.

ONE LOST SOUL - PREVIEW

HIDDEN NORFOLK - BOOK 1

HOLLY WAS GRATEFUL FOR the shelter of the dunes. The wind had a habit of rattling along the coastline, sweeping across the flatlands and cutting through even the hardiest of winter clothing. Where they were sitting, beyond the thick pine forests of the Holkham estate, there was shelter of sorts. She watched the others building a fire on the beach below, gathering driftwood and any fallen branches scavenged from the nearby woods. In the summertime, the estate routinely sent groundskeepers out to ensure open fires were not set but not at this time of year. Early spring could be lovely on the Norfolk coast, bright sunshine, warming on the skin. As long as the prevailing wind wasn't whipping in off the North Sea, at least. The sun had long since set and the chill of the evening was beginning to bite.

In a month or so, the tourist season would begin. All the local businesses running skeleton opening hours over the winter would be up and running once more. The seasonal workers would soon return, maybe. There was a lot of talk amongst the locals that this year would be different. Applications for job vacancies were down on last year and her father commented that even agencies were struggling to fulfil the roles.

It must be amazing to be one of those people with the freedom to travel beyond the confines of where they grew up, able to go to another country and experience different lifestyles and culture. The prospect of learning a new language, trying strange food or simply watching the sun set over an alien landscape was exciting, exotic. One day that would be her. Not that she could tell anyone, nor would she when the time came. She would vanish on the breeze, carried away by an unstoppable force. Maddie came to mind, watching her as she danced with her friends a short distance away. What will become of her when I leave? That last thought dampened her enthusiasm, tempering the future vision.

The fire was lit now. They were singing, the others. It wasn't a song she cared for, not one she even knew the words to but it was popular. Their shadows danced on the sand around the fire as they moved, linking arms and singing louder as more voices joined in the chorus. Holly felt a hand on her shoulder. The touch was gentle. She didn't look round. Mark slipped his arm across her shoulder, coming to sit alongside her on the blanket he'd laid out for them. Part of her wanted him to suggest they move closer to the flames. He didn't and she knew why. He would no doubt try to slip his tongue into her mouth soon. To be fair, it was to be expected. The location, the fire, and their being alone, away from the others and sitting in the darkness made for quite a romantic setting. She would probably oblige.

Mark was a nice guy. Most of their year group steered clear of him but that was less to do with his outbursts and more to do with the family reputation. If she knew of anyone less deserving of such scorn, then it would be news to her. Releasing his grip on her shoulder, Mark retrieved a bottle from a plastic bag at his side and unscrewed the cap. He offered it to her first. She could smell the alcohol and it made her stomach churn. The waves of nausea were getting more frequent but she kept quiet. The last thing she needed was another lecture on visiting the doctor. How could she? The thought of drinking made her feel worse and she declined the offer. He said nothing, sipping from the bottle and pulling an odd face as the liquid burned his mouth. That was the issue with Mark. Immature.

The bonfire was well underway. The colours, the crackling of the wood and the spiralling wisps of smoke and flame dancing into the night sky with the waves crashing on the beach was somewhat hypnotic. Holly imagined her fears being consumed by the heat, with the glow at its heart a depiction of her dreams and fantasies. One day soon she would leave this place and everyone in it behind, travel somewhere where no one knew her and become an artist, make things… jewellery perhaps. All of this would be but a memory.

She felt Mark's hand stroke the small of her back. Looking to him, he smiled. She said nothing, returning her gaze towards the bonfire and spying the whites of the breakers beyond as they approached the shoreline. Mark was a nice guy. Even so, he still couldn't come with her. There was no place for him. There was no place for any of them.

Order the first in the NEW crime series introducing DI Tom Janssen;
One Lost Soul - Hidden Norfolk Book 1

ALSO BY J M DALGLIESH

The Dark Yorkshire Series

Divided House

Blacklight

The Dogs in the Street

Blood Money

Fear the Past

The Sixth Precept

Box Sets

Dark Yorkshire Books 1-3

The Hidden Norfolk Series

One Lost Soul

Bury Your Past

Kill Our Sins

Tell No Tales

Hear No Evil

Life and Death*

*FREE eBook - A Hidden Norfolk novella - visit jmdalgliesh.com

Audiobooks

The entire Dark Yorkshire series is available in audio format, read by the award-winning Greg Patmore.

Divided House

Blacklight

The Dogs in the street

Blood Money

Fear the Past

The Sixth Precept

Audiobook Box Sets

Dark Yorkshire Books 1-3

Dark Yorkshire Books 4-6

*Hidden Norfolk audiobooks arriving 2020